The Editor

RESTORATION AND EIGHTEENTH-CENTURY COMEDY

AUTHORITATIVE TEXTS OF THE PLAYS
CONTEXTS
CRITICISM

SECOND EDITION

A NORTON CRITICAL EDITION

RESTORATION AND EIGHTEENTH-CENTURY COMEDY

Authoritative Texts of
THE COUNTRY WIFE · THE MAN OF MODE
THE ROVER
THE WAY OF THE WORLD
THE CONSCIOUS LOVERS
THE SCHOOL FOR SCANDAL

Contexts

Criticism

SECOND EDITION

Edited by

SCOTT McMILLIN
CORNELL UNIVERSITY

W · W · NORTON & COMPANY · *New York* · *London*

Printed in the United States of America

The text of this book is composed in Electra
with the display set in Bernhard Modern
Composition by Maple-Vail Composition Services
Manufacturing by The Maple-Vail Book Manufacturing Group
Cover illustration: The "screen scene" from *The School for Scandal*,
reproduced by permission of the Victoria and Albert Museum.

Library of Congress Cataloging-in-Publication Data

Restoration and eighteenth-century comedy / edited by Scott McMillin.
—2nd ed.
p.   cm.—(A Norton critical edition)
"Authoritative texts of: The country wife, The man of mode, The
rover, The way of the world, The conscious lovers, The school for
scandal; contexts, criticism."
Includes bibliographical references.
1. English drama (Comedy)   2. English drama—Restoration,
1660–1700—History and criticism.   3. English drama—18th century—
History and criticism.   4. English drama (Comedy)—History and
criticism.   5. English drama—Restoration, 1660–1700.   6. English
drama—18th century.   7. Comidies. gsafd.   I. McMillin, Scott.
PR1248.M3   1996
822'.0523—dc20   95-44942
ISBN 0-393-96334-9 (pbk.)

W. W. Norton & Company, Inc., 500 Fifth Avenue, New York, N.Y. 10110
http://web.wwnorton.com
W. W. Norton & Company Ltd., 10 Coptic Street, London WC1A 1PU

1 2 3 4 5 6 7 8 9 0

Contents

Preface to the First Edition

The plays in this volume are comedies about men and women who live in London, care for sex and money, and make fools of one another if not of themselves. There is nothing strange about that combination of activities, as anyone who has lived in London or cared for sex and money will know; and since more than a thousand comedies in English concern the same matters, the reader may wonder why these few should be drawn together for special attention. The answer is not that these few are classics which anyone interested in drama should read; and the obvious point that they belong, more or less, to one period in the chronology of English literature, while a better answer, is only a beginning. The reason for drawing together plays from one period is that in reading them, in attending to their relationships to one another and to the age from which they come, we can learn to imagine the theater at the same time as we learn to imagine history.

Take the theater first. Readers of a play are in a difficult position, because they are reading something that was not primarily meant to be read. Plays are performances, and they need actors, a stage, an audience before they fully exist. Hence, reading plays ought to make one feel a bit silly—like wearing sunglasses to see how the flower grows—until one develops an imagination to witness a printed drama as a performed event, an enactment occurring within a particular set of theatrical circumstances. The London theater from 1660 through most of the eighteenth century was a place of unusual excitement and innovation, and it deserves to be imagined. It was not a "transitional" stage, standing a bit uncertainly (as some have thought) between the Shakespearean playhouse and the theater of realism, but a coherent stage where established traditions were enlivened with new intentions, and where a sense of risk and venture could be based upon trusted conventions. Modern scholarship, particularly in the magnificent eleven-volume *The London Stage*, has finally brought this theater into focus, an achievement I have tried to represent under the heading "Stages, Actors, and Audiences." The reader will find the basic theatrical information there.

The historical imagination reaches beyond the playhouse to the city, and to the range of social and intellectual attitudes from which comedy was observed in London between 1660 and 1800. This period presents the first example in England of a transaction between the theater and an articulate body of social criticism. The drama has always been *related* to society, of course, and in earlier periods the theater was often interrupted or sustained by specific social influences. But by "transaction," I mean a continuing relationship between the theater and its observers, both sides giving a literary statement of their interests and making a record of social and dramatic change as it occurred. The first time this transaction can be witnessed in England is the period of Dryden, John Dennis, Congreve, Jeremy Collier, Addison, anonymous writers for the weekly papers, unknown essayists from the coffeehouses, and gentlemanly letter-writers from country homes. Comedy held a special position in the transaction, not only because the plays usually represented phases of contemporary London life and thus touched upon immediate social interests, but also because performances depending upon laughter, wit, and mockery pose a social criticism which some perceive as a benefit and others as a threat. Much of the background material in this volume is intended to represent the prevalent attitudes of the age about comedy, beginning with general statements about the nature of comic experience and narrowing down to the specific cases of the plays included here.

The general discussions of comedy are grouped under "Wit, Humour, and Laughter." The selections begin with Hobbes's statement about laughter as an expression of personal superiority, continue through Dryden's and Congreve's more formal approach to literary wit and humour, and pass on to various reactions of eighteenth-century writers, who tended to speak for the gentler and more benevolent qualities of comedy. The change of attitude reflected here corresponds to the emergence in drama of "sentimental" or "weeping" comedy near the turn of the century, in reaction to the raillery and licentiousness of the Restoration mode. In the final selection, Goldsmith denigrates the drama of sentiment and appeals for a return to something like the Restoration style—although his own "laughing comedies," and those of his contemporary Sheridan, surely retain some elements of sentimentality themselves.

Then follow two sections on specific critical quarrels of the age. The first concerns Jeremy Collier's notorious attack on the theater, *A Short View of the Immorality and Profaneness of the English Stage* (1698). This is an extraordinary book, for its long-winded complaining against the immorality of plays serves as the rhetorical surface of a deeply conservative reaction against what Collier regarded as the licentiousness of English social life after the abdication of James II and the political settlement of 1689. This reactionary intention, always implied but never declared, made the book both provocative and elusive—provocative because it touched political nerves, elusive because it refrained from political statement. The resulting controversy lasted for thirty years and, whatever its impact on English politics, changed the course of English comedy. I have tried to represent the first stage of the argument ("The Collier Controversy: 1698") by including a portion of the *Short View* along with the early replies of a dramatist (Congreve), a professional critic (Dennis), and one of the anonymous essayists who got into the fray (*A Vindication of the Stage*). Then, to show how the controversy later came to bear upon the theory and practice of comedy, I have reprinted selections from the prominent literary feud between Sir Richard Steele and John Dennis, which occurred early in the eighteenth century and centered on two of the plays in this volume, Etherege's *The Man of Mode* and Steele's own *The Conscious Lovers*.

Finally—and this should always be the goal of the theatrical and historical imagination—matters come home to our own time and our own language. Modern criticism of Restoration and eighteenth-century drama remains an uncertain and interesting enterprise, for the best work has not yet formed into broadly shared opinions about the meanings of these plays. Some of the possibilities of meaning, however, have been shrewdly set forth, with the result that the examples collected under "Criticism: From Lamb to the Present" are notable more for their diversity of opinion than for their consolidation of dogma. I have tried to suggest some of the earlier shifts of opinion by beginning with Charles Lamb's famous essay from 1822 (still a focal point for critics) and then supplying, in the selections from Palmer, Dobree, and Knights, three influential and divergent views from the first half of the twentieth century. The rest of the selections represent criticism since 1950 and are not meant to fall into any pattern at all. I have chosen them because they are serious efforts to discuss plays that are too often treated casually, and because they have been found helpful by some of the students I have known.

I am grateful to Professors M. H. Abrams, Cecil Price, and Robert D. Hume for their advice on the arrangement and contents of this volume. In preparing the manuscript, I am glad to have had the assistance of Michael Nash and Nancy Wallack. And on all matters, large and small, John Benedict and his staff at Norton have been expert and kind.

Scott McMillin

Preface to the Second Edition

The general arrangement of this collection remains as it was, but I have taken the opportunity to add the one play that students and colleagues have most often urged me to include, Behn's *The Rover*. I have also redesigned the Criticism section in order to provide some of the best examples of the kinds of analysis that have become prominent in the past two decades.

I am grateful for all of the suggestions I have received over the years since the first edition. I would especially mention advice received from Walter Cohen, Albert Furtwangler, and Robert T. Levine. Reports from the two anonymous consultants for Norton were very helpful in reviewing the overall design of the first edition and suggesting the best spots for revision and updating. And I am grateful to Carol Bemis and her staff at Norton for countless acts of kindness and expertise.

S.M.

A Note on the Texts

In editing the Restoration and eighteenth-century texts, I have modernized spelling and punctuation throughout, although "humour" has been retained in order to distinguish its original meaning from our casual use of the word today. The text of *The School for Scandal* calls for special comment. I have followed the text of the Georgetown Crewe manuscript, which has been accepted as authoritative since George H. Nettleton published it in *British Dramatists from Dryden to Sheridan* (1939). I have also included several stage directions from corrections in Sheridan's hand in the so-called "Second Crewe Manuscript."[1] The other plays present no major textual difficulties, and with only the most obvious emendations I have followed the text of the first edition in each case, expanding contracted forms of characters' names in speech prefixes and stage directions, and making a few necessary additions to the stage directions.

The Country Wife: quarto of 1675.

The Man of Mode: quarto of 1676. (Sir Fopling's attempts at French have not been corrected when he is obviously mispronouncing, but otherwise I have regularized these forms.)

The Rover: quarto of 1677.

The Way of the World: quarto of 1700.

The Conscious Lovers: quarto of 1722 (dated 1723).

---

1. See Cecil Price, "The Second Crewe Ms. of *The School for Scandal*," *Papers of the Bibliographical Society of America* 61 (1967): 351–56, and the textual introduction to Price's edition of Sheridan's plays (Oxford: The Clarendon Press, 1973) 1.324–50.

THE TEXTS OF THE PLAYS

The Country Wife, National Theatre, London, 1977. Susan Littler as Mrs. Pinchwife (in disguise) and Albert Finney as Horner. By permission of Zoe Dominick.

WILLIAM WYCHERLEY

The Country Wife

Indignor quicquam reprehendi, non quia crasse
Compositum illepideve putetur, sed quia nuper:
Nec veniam antiquis, sed honorem et praemia posci.[1]

Prologue

Spoken by Mr. Hart[2]

Poets, like cudgel'd bullies, never do
At first or second blow submit to you;
But will provoke you still, and ne'er have done,
Till you are weary first with laying on.
The late so baffled scribbler of this day,
Though he stands trembling, bids me boldly say,
What we before most plays are us'd to do,
For poets out of fear first draw on you;
In a fierce prologue the still pit defy,
And ere you speak, like Castril[3] give the lie.
But though our Bayes's[4] battles oft I've fought,
And with bruis'd knuckles their dear conquests bought;
Nay, never yet fear'd odds upon the stage,
In prologue dare not hector with the age,
But would take quarter from your saving hands,
Though Bayes within all yielding countermands,
Says you confed'rate wits no quarter give,
Therefore his play shan't ask your leave to live.
Well, let the vain rash fop, by huffing so,
Think to obtain the better terms of you;
But we, the actors, humbly will submit,

---

† First performed in 1675, at Drury Lane, and published in the same year.
1. Horace, *Epistles* II.i.76–78: "I hate to see something censured not because it is deemed coarse or inelegant in style, but because it is modern; when for the ancients not only indulgence but honor and rewards are demanded."
2. Who acted Horner's role.
3. A quarreler in Ben Jonson's *The Alchemist.*
4. Poet's. Bayes is the poet in the Duke of Buckingham's *The Rehearsal;* the role lampoons John Dryden.

Now, and at any time, to a full pit;
Nay, often we anticipate your rage,
And murder poets for you on our stage.
We set no guards upon our tiring-room,[5]
But when with flying colors there you come,
We patiently, you see, give up to you
Our poets, virgins, nay, our matrons too.

The Persons

MR. HORNER	*Mr. Hart*
MR. HARCOURT	*Mr. Kynaston*
MR. DORILANT	*Mr. Lydal*
MR. PINCHWIFE	*Mr. Mohun*
MR. SPARKISH	*Mr. Haines*
SIR JASPER FIDGET	*Mr. Cartwright*
MRS. MARGERY PINCHWIFE	*Mrs. Boutell*
MRS. ALITHEA	*Mrs. James*
MY LADY FIDGET	*Mrs. Knep*
MRS. DAINTY FIDGET	*Mrs. Corbet*
MRS. SQUEAMISH	*Mrs. Wyatt*
OLD LADY SQUEAMISH	*Mrs. Rutter*
WAITERS, SERVANTS, AND ATTENDANTS	
A BOY	
A QUACK	*Mr. Shatterel*
LUCY, ALITHEA'S MAID	*Mrs. Cory*

The Scene: *London*

The Country Wife

Act I. *Scene i.* Horner's *lodging*

Enter HORNER, *and* QUACK *following him at a distance.*

HORNER [*aside*] A quack is as fit for a pimp as a midwife for a bawd; they are still but in their way both helpers of nature.—Well, my dear doctor, hast thou done what I desired?

QUACK I have undone you forever with the women, and reported you throughout the whole town as bad as a eunuch, with as much trouble as if I had made you one in earnest.

HORNER But have you told all the midwives you know, the orange-wenches at the playhouses, the city husbands, and old fumbling keepers of this end of the town? for they'll be the readiest to report it.

QUACK I have told all the chambermaids, waiting-women, tire-women,

---

5. Dressing room in the theater.

and old women of my acquaintance; nay, and whispered it as a secret to 'em, and to the whisperers of Whitehall; so that you need not doubt 'twill spread, and you will be as odious to the handsome young women as—

HORNER   As the smallpox. Well—

QUACK   And to the married women of this end of the town as—

HORNER   As the great ones; nay, as their own husbands.

QUACK   And to the city dames as aniseed Robin[6] of filthy and contemptible memory; and they will frighten their children with your name, especially their females.

HORNER   And cry, "Horner's coming to carry you away." I am only afraid 'twill not be believed. You told 'em 'twas by an English-French disaster,[7] and an English-French surgeon, who has given me at once not only a cure but an antidote for the future against that damned malady, and that worse distemper, love, and all other women's evils?

QUACK   Your late journey into France has made it the more credible, and your being here a fortnight before you appeared in public looks as if you apprehended the shame, which I wonder you do not. Well, I have been hired by young gallants to belie 'em t'other way; but you are the first would be thought a man unfit for women.

HORNER   Dear Mr. Doctor, let vain rogues be contented only to be thought abler men than they are, generally 'tis all the pleasure they have; but mine lies another way.

QUACK   You take, methinks, a very preposterous way to it, and as ridiculous as if we operators in physic should put forth bills to disparage our medicaments, with hopes to gain customers.

HORNER   Doctor, there are quacks in love as well as physic, who get but the fewer and worse patients for their boasting; a good name is seldom got by giving it oneself, and women no more than honor are compassed by bragging. Come, come, doctor, the wisest lawyer never discovers[8] the merits of his cause till the trial; the wealthiest man conceals his riches, and the cunning gamester his play. Shy husbands and keepers, like old rooks,[9] are not to be cheated but by a new unpracticed trick; false friendship will pass now no more than false dice upon 'em; no, not in the city.

Enter BOY.

BOY   There are two ladies and a gentleman coming up.

Exit.

HORNER   A pox! some unbelieving sisters of my former acquaintance, who, I am afraid, expect their sense should be satisfied of the falsity of the report. No—this formal fool and women!

6. A notorious hermaphrodite.
7. Venereal disease.
8. Reveals.
9. Swindlers, cheats.

Enter SIR JASPER FIDGET, LADY FIDGET, *and* MRS. DAINTY FIDGET.

QUACK   His wife and sister.

SIR JASPER FIDGET   My coach breaking just now before your door, sir, I look upon as an occasional[1] reprimand to me, sir, for not kissing your hands, sir, since your coming out of France, sir; and so my disaster, sir, has been my good fortune, sir; and this is my wife and sister, sir.

HORNER   What then, sir?

SIR JASPER FIDGET   My lady, and sister, sir.—Wife, this is Master Horner.

LADY FIDGET   Master Horner, husband!

SIR JASPER FIDGET   My lady, my Lady Fidget, sir.

HORNER   So, sir.

SIR JASPER FIDGET   Won't you be acquainted with her sir?—[*Aside*.] So, the report is true, I find, by his coldness or aversion to the sex; but I'll play the wag with him.—Pray salute my wife, my lady, sir.

HORNER   I will kiss no man's wife, sir, for him, sir; I have taken my eternal leave, sir, of the sex already, sir.

SIR JASPER FIDGET [*aside*]   Ha, ha, ha! I'll plague him yet.—Not know my wife, sir?

HORNER   I do know your wife, sir; she's a woman, sir, and consequently a monster, sir, a greater monster than a husband, sir.

SIR JASPER FIDGET   A husband! how, sir?

HORNER   So, sir; but I make no more cuckolds, sir.

Makes horns.[2]

SIR JASPER FIDGET   Ha, ha, ha! Mercury, Mercury![3]

LADY FIDGET   Pray, Sir Jasper, let us be gone from this rude fellow.

MRS. DAINTY FIDGET   Who, by his breeding, would think he had ever been in France?

LADY FIDGET   Foh! he's but too much a French fellow, such as hate women of quality and virtue for their love to their husbands, Sir Jasper; a woman is hated by 'em as much for loving her husband as for loving their money. But pray let's be gone.

HORNER   You do well, madam, for I have nothing that you came for. I have brought over not so much as a bawdy picture, new postures, nor the second part of the *École des Filles*, nor—[4]

QUACK [*apart to* HORNER]   Hold, for shame, sir! What d'ye mean? You'll ruin yourself forever with the sex—

SIR JASPER FIDGET   Ha, ha, ha! He hates women perfectly, I find.

MRS. DAINTY FIDGET   What pity 'tis he should.

---

1. Timely.
2. Sign of the cuckold.
3. Used in treating venereal disease.
4. Horner refers to pornographic items: "postures" (obscene engravings) had long been associated with the *Sonetti lussuriosi* of Aretino (c. 1524); *École des filles*, by one Mililot, was available in London at least by 1668.

LADY FIDGET   Ay, he's a base, rude fellow for't; but affectation makes not a woman more odious to them than virtue.

HORNER   Because your virtue is your greatest affectation, madam.

LADY FIDGET   How, you saucy fellow! Would you wrong my honor?

HORNER   If I could.

LADY FIDGET   How d'ye mean, sir?

SIR JASPER FIDGET   Ha, ha, ha! No, he can't wrong your ladyship's honor, upon my honor; he, poor man—hark you in your ear—a mere eunuch.

LADY FIDGET   O filthy French beast! foh, foh! Why do we stay? Let's be gone; I can't endure the sight of him.

SIR JASPER FIDGET   Stay but till the chairs come; they'll be here presently.

LADY FIDGET   No, no.

SIR JASPER FIDGET   Nor can I stay longer. 'Tis—let me see, a quarter and a half quarter of a minute past eleven; the council will be sat, I must away. Business must be preferred always before love and ceremony with the wise, Mr. Horner.

HORNER   And the impotent, Sir Jasper.

SIR JASPER FIDGET   Ay, ay, the impotent, Master Horner, ha, ha, ha!

LADY FIDGET   What, leave us with a filthy man alone in his lodgings?

SIR JASPER FIDGET   He's an innocent man now, you know. Pray stay, I'll hasten the chairs to you.—Mr. Horner, your servant; I should be glad to see you at my house. Pray come and dine with me, and play at cards with my wife after dinner; you are fit for women at that game yet, ha, ha!—[*Aside.*] 'Tis as much a husband's prudence to provide innocent diversion for a wife as to hinder her unlawful pleasures, and he had better employ her than let her employ herself.—Farewell.

HORNER   Your servant, Sir Jasper.

Exit SIR JASPER.

LADY FIDGET   I will not stay with him, foh!

HORNER   Nay, madam, I beseech you stay, if it be but to see I can be as civil to ladies yet as they would desire.

LADY FIDGET   No, no, foh! You cannot be civil to ladies.

MRS. DAINTY FIDGET   You as civil as ladies would desire?

LADY FIDGET   No, no, no! foh, foh, foh!

Exeunt LADY FIDGET *and* MRS. DAINTY.

QUACK   Now, I think, I, or you yourself rather, have done your business with the women.

HORNER   Thou art an ass. Don't you see already, upon the report and my carriage, this grave man of business leaves his wife in my lodgings, invites me to his house and wife, who before would not be acquainted with me out of jealousy?

QUACK   Nay, by this means you may be the more acquainted with the husbands, but the less with the wives.

HORNER   Let me alone; if I can but abuse the husbands, I'll soon disabuse the wives. Stay—I'll reckon you up the advantages I am like to have by my stratagem: First, I shall be rid of all my old acquaintances, the most insatiable sorts of duns, that invade our lodgings in a morning. And next to the pleasure of making a new mistress is that of being rid of an old one, and of all old debts; love, when it comes to be so, is paid the most unwillingly.

QUACK   Well, you may be so rid of your old acquaintances; but now will you get any new ones?

HORNER   Doctor, thou wilt never make a good chemist, thou art so incredulous and impatient. Ask but all the young fellows of the town if they do not lose more time, like huntsmen, in starting the game than in running it down; one knows not where to find 'em, who will or will not. Women of quality are so civil you can hardly distinguish love from good breeding, and a man is often mistaken; but now I can be sure she that shows an aversion to me loves the sport, as those women that are gone, whom I warrant to be right.[5] And then the next thing is, your women of honor, as you call 'em, are only chary of their reputations, not their persons, and 'tis scandal they would avoid, not men. Now may I have, by the reputation of a eunuch, the privileges of one; and be seen in a lady's chamber in a morning as early as her husband; kiss virgins before their parents or lovers; and may be, in short, the *passe partout*[6] of the town. Now, doctor.

QUACK   Nay, now you shall be the doctor; and your process is so new that we do not know but it may succeed.

HORNER   Not so new neither; *probatum est,*[7] doctor.

QUACK   Well, I wish you luck and many patients whilst I go to mine.

Exit QUACK.

Enter HARCOURT *and* DORILANT *to* HORNER.

HARCOURT   Come, your appearance at the play yesterday has, I hope, hardened you for the future against the women's contempt and the men's raillery; and now you'll abroad as you were wont.

HORNER   Did I not bear it bravely?

DORILANT   With a most theatrical impudence; nay, more than the orange-wenches show there, or a drunken vizard-mask,[8] or a great-bellied actress; nay, or the most impudent of creatures, an ill poet; or what is yet more impudent, a secondhand critic.

HORNER   But what say the ladies? Have they no pity?

HARCOURT   What ladies? The vizard-masks, you know, never pity a man when all's gone, though in their service.

DORILANT   And for the women in the boxes, you'd never pity them when 'twas in your power.

5. Morally loose.
6. Pass-key.
7. It has been proved.
8. Whore.

HARCOURT   They say, 'tis pity but all that deal with common women should be served so.

DORILANT   Nay, I dare swear, they won't admit you to play at cards with them, go to plays with 'em, or do the little duties which other shadows of men are wont to do for 'em.

HORNER   Who do you call shadows of men?

DORILANT   Half-men.

HORNER   What, boys?

DORILANT   Ay, your old boys, old *beaux garçons*,[9] who, like superannuated stallions, are suffered to run, feed, and whinny with the mares as long as they live, though they can do nothing else.

HORNER   Well, a pox on love and wenching! Women serve but to keep a man from better company; though I can't enjoy them, I shall you the more. Good fellowship and friendship are lasting, rational, and manly pleasures.

HARCOURT   For all that, give me some of those pleasures you call effeminate too; they help to relish one another.

HORNER   They disturb one another.

HARCOURT   No, mistresses are like books. If you pore upon them too much, they doze you and make you unfit for company; but if used discreetly, you are the fitter for conversation by 'em.

DORILANT   A mistress should be like a little country retreat near the town, not to dwell in constantly, but only for a night and away, to taste the town the better when a man returns.

HORNER   I tell you, 'tis as hard to be a good fellow, a good friend, and a lover of women, as 'tis to be a good fellow, a good friend, and a lover of money. You cannot follow both, then choose your side. Wine gives you liberty, love takes it away.

DORILANT   Gad, he's in the right on't.

HORNER   Wine gives you joy; love, grief and tortures, besides the surgeon's. Wine makes us witty; love, only sots. Wine makes us sleep; love breaks it.

DORILANT   By the world, he has reason, Harcourt.

HORNER   Wine makes—

DORILANT   Ay, wine makes us—makes us princes; love makes us beggars, poor rogues, egad—and wine—

HORNER   So, there's one converted.—No, no, love and wine, oil and vinegar.

HARCOURT   I grant it; love will still be uppermost.

HORNER   Come, for my part I will have only those glorious, manly pleasures of being very drunk and very slovenly.

Enter BOY.

BOY   Mr. Sparkish is below, sir.

Exit.

9. Harmless or sexless escorts.

HARCOURT   What, my dear friend! a rogue that is fond of me only, I think, for abusing him.

DORILANT   No, he can no more think the men laugh at him than that women jilt him, his opinion of himself is so good.

HORNER   Well, there's another pleasure by drinking I thought not of; I shall lose his acquaintance, because he cannot drink; and you know 'tis a very hard thing to be rid of him, for he's one of those nauseous offerers at wit, who, like the worst fiddlers, run themselves into all companies.

HARCOURT   One that, by being in the company of men of sense, would pass for one.

HORNER   And may so to the shortsighted world, as a false jewel amongst true ones is not discerned at a distance. His company is as troublesome to us as a cuckold's when you have a mind to his wife's.

HARCOURT   No, the rogue will not let us enjoy one another, but ravishes our conversation, though he signifies no more to't than Sir Martin Mar-all's gaping, and awkward thrumming upon the lute, does to his man's voice and music.[1]

DORILANT   And to pass for a wit in town shows himself a fool every night to us, that are guilty of the plot.

HORNER   Such wits as he are, to a company of reasonable men, like rooks to the gamesters, who only fill a room at the table, but are so far from contributing to the play that they only serve to spoil the fancy of those that do.

DORILANT   Nay, they are used like rooks too, snubbed, checked, and abused; yet the rogues will hang on.

HORNER   A pox on 'em, and all that force nature, and would be still what she forbids 'em! Affectation is her greatest monster.

HARCOURT   Most men are the contraries to that they would seem. Your bully, you see, is a coward with a long sword; the little, humbly fawning physician, with his ebony cane, is he that destroys men.

DORILANT   The usurer, a poor rogue possessed of moldy bonds and mortgages; and we they call spendthrifts are only wealthy who lay out his money upon daily new purchases of pleasure.

HORNER   Ay, your arrantest cheat is your trustee, or executor; your jealous man, the greatest cuckold; your churchman, the greatest atheist; and your noisy, pert rogue of a wit, the greatest fop, dullest ass, and worst company, as you shall see. For here he comes.

Enter SPARKISH *to them.*

SPARKISH   How is't, sparks, how is't? Well, faith, Harry, I must rally thee a little, ha, ha, ha! upon the report in town of thee, ha, ha, ha! I can't hold i' faith; shall I speak?

HORNER   Yes, but you'll be so bitter then.

---

1. In Dryden's *Sir Martin Mar-all* (1667), the title character pretends to serenade his mistress while his concealed servant sings and plays the lute.

SPARKISH   Honest Dick and Frank here shall answer for me, I will not be extreme bitter, by the universe.

HARCOURT   We will be bound in ten thousand pound bond, he shall not be bitter at all.

DORILANT   Nor sharp, nor sweet.

HORNER   What, not downright insipid?

SPARKISH   Nay then, since you are so brisk and provoke me, take what follows. You must know, I was discoursing and rallying with some ladies yesterday, and they happened to talk of the fine new signs in town.

HORNER   Very fine ladies, I believe.

SPARKISH   Said I, "I know where the best new sign is." "Where?" says one of the ladies. "In Covent Garden," I replied. Said another, "In what street?" "In Russell Street," answered I."[2] "Lord," says another, "I'm sure there was ne'er a fine new sign there yesterday." "Yes, but there was," said I again, "and it came out of France, and has been there a fortnight."

DORILANT   A pox! I can hear no more, prithee.

HORNER   No, hear him out; let him tune his crowd[3] a while.

HARCOURT   The worst music, the greatest preparation.

SPARKISH   Nay, faith, I'll make you laugh. "It cannot be," says a third lady. "Yes, yes," quoth I again. Says a fourth lady—

HORNER   Look to't, we'll have no more ladies.

SPARKISH   No—then mark, mark, now. Said I to the fourth, "Did you never see Mr. Horner? He lodges in Russell Street, and he's a sign of a man, you know, since he came out of France." He, ha, he!

HORNER   But the devil take me, if thine be the sign of a jest.

SPARKISH   With that they all fell a-laughing, till they bepissed themselves! What, but it does not move you, methinks? Well, I see one had as good go to law without a witness, as break a jest without a laugher on one's side. Come, come, sparks, but where do we dine? I have left at Whitehall an earl to dine with you.

DORILANT   Why, I thought thou hadst loved a man with a title better than a suit with a French trimming to't.

HARCOURT   Go to him again.

SPARKISH   No, sir, a wit to me is the greatest title in the world.

HORNER   But go dine with your earl, sir; he may be exceptious.[4] We are your friends, and will not take it ill to be left, I do assure you.

HARCOURT   Nay, faith, he shall go to him.

SPARKISH   Nay, pray, gentlemen.

DORILANT   We'll thrust you out, if you wo'not. What, disappoint anybody for us?

SPARKISH   Nay, dear gentlemen, hear me.

2. Covent Garden and Russell Street were fashionable areas.
3. Fiddle.
4. Vexed.

HORNER   No, no, sir, by no means; pray go, sir.

SPARKISH   Why, dear rogues—

DORILANT   No, no.

They all thrust him out of the room.

ALL   Ha, ha, ha!

SPARKISH *returns.*

SPARKISH   But, sparks, pray hear me. What, d'ye think I'll eat then with gay, shallow fops and silent coxcombs? I think wit as necessary at dinner as a glass of good wine, and that's the reason I never have any stomach when I eat alone.—Come, but where do we dine?

HORNER   Even where you will.

SPARKISH   At Chateline's?

DORILANT   Yes, if you will.

SPARKISH   Or at the Cock?

DORILANT   Yes, if you please.

SPARKISH   Or at the Dog and Partridge?[5]

HORNER   Ay, if you have mind to't, for we shall dine at neither.

SPARKISH   Pshaw! with your fooling we shall lose the new play; and I would no more miss seeing a new play the first day than I would miss sitting in the wits' row. Therefore I'll go fetch my mistress and away.

Exit SPARKISH.

Manent HORNER, HARCOURT, DORILANT. *Enter to them* MR. PINCHWIFE.

HORNER   Who have we here? Pinchwife?

PINCHWIFE   Gentlemen, your humble servant.

HORNER   Well, Jack, by thy long absence from the town, the grumness of thy countenance, and the slovenliness of thy habit, I should give thee joy, should I not, of marriage?

PINCHWIFE   [*aside*]   Death! does he know I'm married too? I thought to have concealed it from him at least.—My long stay in the country will excuse my dress, and I have a suit of law, that brings me up to town, that puts me out of humour; besides, I must give Sparkish tomorrow five thousand pound to lie with my sister.

HORNER   Nay, you country gentlemen, rather than not purchase, will buy anything; and he is a cracked title, if we may quibble. Well, but am I to give thee joy? I heard thou wert married.

PINCHWIFE   What then?

HORNER   Why, the next thing that is to be heard is, thou'rt a cuckold.

PINCHWIFE   [*aside*]   Insupportable name!

HORNER   But I did not expect marriage from such a whoremaster as you, one that knew the town so much, and women so well.

---

5. Sparkish, keen on fashion, names well-known restaurants near Covent Garden.

PINCHWIFE   Why, I have married no London wife.

HORNER   Pshaw! that's all one; that grave circumspection in marrying a country wife is like refusing a deceitful, pampered Smithfield jade to go and be cheated by a friend in the country.

PINCHWIFE [*aside*]   A pox on him and his simile!—At least we are a little surer of the breed there, know what her keeping has been, whether foiled[6] or unsound.

HORNER   Come, come, I have known a clap gotten in Wales; and there are cousins, justices' clerks, and chaplains in the country, I won't say coachmen. But she's handsome and young?

PINCHWIFE [*aside*]   I'll answer as I should do.—No, no, she has no beauty but her youth; no attraction but her modesty; wholesome, homely, and housewifely; that's all.

DORILANT   He talks as like a grazier[7] as he looks.

PINCHWIFE   She's too awkward, ill-favored, and silly to bring to town.

HARCOURT   Then methinks you should bring her, to be taught breeding.

PINCHWIFE   To be taught! no, sir, I thank you. Good wives and private soldiers should be ignorant.—[*Aside.*] I'll keep her from your instructions, I warrant you.

HARCOURT [*aside*]   The rogue is as jealous as if his wife were not ignorant.

HORNER   Why, if she be ill-favored, there will be less danger here for you than by leaving her in the country; we have such variety of danties that we are seldom hungry.

DORILANT   But they have always coarse, constant, swingeing[8] stomachs in the country.

HARCOURT   Foul feeders indeed.

DORILANT   And your hospitality is great there.

HARCOURT   Open house, every man's welcome.

PINCHWIFE   So, so, gentlemen.

HORNER   But, prithee, why wouldst thou marry her? If she be ugly, ill-bred, and silly, she must be rich then.

PINCHWIFE   As rich as if she brought me twenty thousand pound out of this town; for she'll be as sure not to spend her moderate portion as a London baggage would be to spend hers, let it be what it would; so 'tis all one. Then, because she's ugly, she's the likelier to be my own; and being ill-bred, she'll hate conversation; and since silly and innocent, will not know the difference betwixt a man of one-and-twenty and one of forty.

HORNER   Nine—to my knowledge; but if she be silly, she'll expect as much from a man of forty-nine as from him of one-and-twenty. But methinks wit is more necessary than beauty, and I think no young

6. Injured—i.e., a deflowered or diseased woman. *Jade:* worn-out horse; also, a loose woman.
7. Cattle-breeder.
8. Huge.

woman ugly that has it, and no handsome woman agreeable without it.

PINCHWIFE 'Tis my maxim, he's a fool that marries, but he's a greater that does not marry a fool. What is wit in a wife good for, but to make a man cuckold?

HORNER Yes, to keep it from his knowledge.

PINCHWIFE A fool cannot contrive to make her husband a cuckold.

HORNER No, but she'll club with a man that can; and what is worse, if she cannot make her husband a cuckold, she'll make him jealous, and pass for one, and then 'tis all one.

PINCHWIFE Well, well, I'll take care for one, my wife shall make me no cuckold, though she had your help, Mr. Horner; I understand the town, sir.

DORILANT [aside] His help!

HARCOURT [aside] He's come newly to town, it seems, and has not heard how things are with him.

HORNER But tell me, has marriage cured thee of whoring, which it seldom does?

HARCOURT 'Tis more than age can do.

HORNER No, the word is, I'll marry and live honest[9]; but a marriage vow is like a penitent gamester's oath, and entering into bonds and penalties to stint himself to such a particular small sum at play for the future, which makes him but the more eager, and not being able to hold out, loses his money again, and his forfeit to boot.

DORILANT Ay, ay, a gamester will be a gamester whilst his money lasts, and a whoremaster whilst his vigor.

HARCOURT Nay, I have known 'em, when they are broke and can lose no more, keep a-fumbling with the box[1] in their hands to fool with only, and hinder other gamesters.

DORILANT That had wherewithal to make lusty stakes.

PINCHWIFE Well, gentlemen, you may laugh at me, but you shall never lie with my wife; I know the town.

HORNER But prithee, was not the way you were in better? Is not keeping better than marriage?

PINCHWIFE A pox on't! The jades would jilt me; I could never keep a whore to myself.

HORNER So, then you only married to keep a whore to yourself. Well, but let me tell you, women, as you say, are like soldiers, made constant and loyal by good pay rather than by oaths and covenants. Therefore I'd advise my friends to keep rather than marry, since too I find, by your example, it does not serve one's turn; for I saw you yesterday in the eighteen-penny place[2] with a pretty country wench.

PINCHWIFE [aside] How the devil! Did he see my wife then? I sat there that she might not be seen. But she shall never go to a play again.

9. Chaste.
1. Dice-box, obscenely intended.
2. Seat in the middle gallery of the theater, notorious for whores.

HORNER   What, dost thou blush at nine-and-forty, for having been seen with a wench?

DORILANT   No, faith, I warrant 'twas his wife, which he seated there out of sight, for he's a cunning rogue and understands the town.

HARCOURT   He blushes. Then 'twas his wife, for men are now more ashamed to be seen with them in public than with a wench.

PINCHWIFE [*aside*]   Hell and damnation! I'm undone, since Horner has seen her, and they know 'twas she.

HORNER   But prithee, was it thy wife? She was exceedingly pretty; I was in love with her at that distance.

PINCHWIFE   You are like never to be nearer to her. Your servant, gentlemen.

> *Offers to go.*

HORNER   Nay, prithee stay.

PINCHWIFE   I cannot, I will not.

HORNER   Come, you shall dine with us.

PINCHWIFE   I have dined already.

HORNER   Come, I know thou hast not. I'll treat thee, dear rogue; thou shalt spend none of thy Hampshire[3] money today.

PINCHWIFE [*aside*]   Treat me! So, he uses me already like his cuckold.

HORNER   Nay, you shall not go.

PINCHWIFE   I must, I have business at home.

> *Exit* PINCHWIFE.

HARCOURT   To beat his wife; he's as jealous of her as a Cheapside husband of a Covent Garden wife.[4]

HORNER   Why, 'tis as hard to find an old whoremaster without jealousy and the gout, as a young one without fear or the pox.

> As gout in age from pox in youth proceeds,
> So wenching past, then jealousy succeeds,
> The worst disease that love and wenching breeds.

> [*Exeunt.*]

Act II. Scene i. Pinchwife's *house*

MRS. MARGERY PINCHWIFE *and* ALITHEA.
MR. PINCHWIFE *peeping behind at the door.*

MRS. PINCHWIFE   Pray, sister, where are the best fields and woods to walk in, in London?

ALITHEA   A pretty question! Why, sister, Mulberry Garden and St. James's Park; and for close walks, the New Exchange.[5]

---

3. Common term for the country.
4. As a merchant husband of a fashionable (or pretentious) wife.
5. Popular gathering places. The New Exchange, a fashionable shopping arcade, is the setting for III.ii.

MRS. PINCHWIFE   Pray, sister, tell me why my husband looks so grum here in town, and keeps me up so close, and will not let me go a-walking, nor let me wear my best gown yesterday.

ALITHEA   Oh, he's jealous, sister.

MRS. PINCHWIFE   Jealous? What's that?

ALITHEA   He's afraid you should love another man.

MRS. PINCHWIFE   How should he be afraid of my loving another man, when he will not let me see any but himself?

ALITHEA   Did he not carry you yesterday to a play?

MRS. PINCHWIFE   Ay, but we sat amongst ugly people; he would not let me come near the gentry, who sat under us, so that I could not see 'em. He told me none but naughty women sat there, whom they toused and moused.[6] But I would have ventured for all that.

ALITHEA   But how did you like the play?

MRS. PINCHWIFE   Indeed, I was a-weary of the play, but I liked hugeously the actors; they are the goodliest, properest men, sister!

ALITHEA   Oh, but you must not like the actors, sister.

MRS. PINCHWIFE   Ay, how should I help it, sister? Pray, sister, when my husband comes in, will you ask leave for me to go a-walking?

ALITHEA [*aside*]   A-walking! Ha, ha! Lord, a country gentlewoman's leisure is the drudgery of a foot-post; and she requires as much airing as her husband's horses.

Enter MR. PINCHWIFE *to them.*

But here comes your husband; I'll ask, though I'm sure he'll not grant it.

MRS. PINCHWIFE   He says he won't let me go abroad for fear of catching the pox.

ALITHEA   Fie! the smallpox you should say.

MRS. PINCHWIFE   O my dear, dear bud, welcome home! Why dost thou look so fropish? Who has nangered thee?

PINCHWIFE   You're a fool.

MRS. PINCHWIFE *goes aside and cries.*

ALITHEA   Faith, so she is, for crying for no fault, poor tender creature!

PINCHWIFE   What, you would have her as impudent as yourself, as arrant a jill-flirt, a gadder, a magpie, and to say all, a mere, notorious town-woman?

ALITHEA   Brother, you are my only censurer; and the honor of your family shall sooner suffer in your wife there than in me, though I take the innocent liberty of the town.

PINCHWIFE   Hark you, mistress, do not talk so before my wife. The innocent liberty of the town!

ALITHEA   Why, pray, who boasts of any intrigue with me? What lampoon has made my name notorious? What ill women frequent my

6. Handled and fondled.

lodgings? I keep no company with any women of scandalous reputations.

PINCHWIFE   No, you keep the men of scandalous reputations company.

ALITHEA   Where? Would you not have me civil? answer 'em in a box
at the plays, in the drawing room at Whitehall, in St. James's Park,
Mulberry Garden, or—

PINCHWIFE   Hold, hold! Do not teach my wife where the men are to
be found! I believe she's the worse for your town documents already.
I bid you keep her in ignorance, as I do.

MRS. PINCHWIFE   Indeed, be not angry with her, bud; she will tell me
nothing of the town, though I ask her a thousand times a day.

PINCHWIFE   Then you are very inquisitive to know, I find!

MRS. PINCHWIFE   Not I, indeed, dear; I hate London. Our place-house
in the country is worth a thousand of't; would I were there again!

PINCHWIFE   So you shall, I warrant. But were you not talking of plays
and players when I came in?—[To ALITHEA.] You are her encourager
in such discourses.

MRS. PINCHWIFE   No, indeed, dear; she chid me just now for liking the
playermen.

PINCHWIFE [aside]   Nay, if she be so innocent as to own to me her
liking them, there is no hurt in't.—Come, my poor rogue, but thou
lik'st none better than me?

MRS. PINCHWIFE   Yes, indeed, but I do; the playermen are finer folks.

PINCHWIFE   But you love none better than me?

MRS. PINCHWIFE   You are mine own dear bud, and I know you; I hate
a stranger.

PINCHWIFE   Ay, my dear, you must love me only, and not be like the
naughty town-women, who only hate their husbands and love every
man else, love plays, visits, fine coaches, fine clothes, fiddles, balls,
treats, and so lead a wicked town-life.

MRS. PINCHWIFE   Nay, if to enjoy all these things be a town-life, London is not so bad a place, dear.

PINCHWIFE   How! If you love me, you must hate London.

ALITHEA [aside]   The fool has forbid me discovering to her the pleasures of the town, and he is now setting her agog upon them himself.

MRS. PINCHWIFE   But, husband, do the town-women love the playermen too?

PINCHWIFE   Yes, I warrant you.

MRS. PINCHWIFE   Ay, I warrant you.

PINCHWIFE   Why, you do not, I hope?

MRS. PINCHWIFE   No, no, bud; but why have we no playermen in the
country?

PINCHWIFE   Ha!—Mrs. Minx, ask me no more to go to a play.

MRS. PINCHWIFE   Nay, why, love? I did not care for going; but when
you forbid me, you make me, as 'twere, desire it.

ALITHEA [aside]   So t'will be in other things, I warrant.

MRS. PINCHWIFE   Pray let me go to a play, dear.

PINCHWIFE   Hold your peace, I wo'not.

MRS. PINCHWIFE   Why, love?

PINCHWIFE   Why, I'll tell you.

ALITHEA [*aside*]   Nay, if he tell her, she'll give him more cause to forbid her that place.

MRS. PINCHWIFE   Pray, why, dear?

PINCHWIFE   First, you like the actors, and the gallants may like you.

MRS. PINCHWIFE   What, a homely country girl? No, bud, nobody will
like me.

PINCHWIFE   I tell you, yes, they may.

MRS. PINCHWIFE   No, no, you jest—I won't believe you, I will go.

PINCHWIFE   I tell you then that one of the lewdest fellows in town, who
saw you there, told me he was in love with you.

MRS. PINCHWIFE   Indeed! Who, who, pray who was't?

PINCHWIFE [*aside*]   I've gone too far, and slipped before I was aware.
How overjoyed she is!

MRS. PINCHWIFE   Was it any Hampshire gallant, any of our neighbors?
I promise you, I am beholding to him.

PINCHWIFE   I promise you, you lie; for he would but ruin you, as he
has done hundreds. He has no other love for women but that; such
as he look upon women, like basilisks,[7] but to destroy 'em.

MRS. PINCHWIFE   Ay, but if he loves me, why should he ruin me?
Answer me to that. Methinks he should not; I would do him no harm.

ALITHEA   Ha, ha, ha!

PINCHWIFE   'Tis very well; but I'll keep him from doing you any harm,
or me either.

>   *Enter* SPARKISH *and* HARCOURT.

But here comes company; get you in, get you in.

MRS. PINCHWIFE   But pray, husband, is he a pretty gentleman that loves
me?

PINCHWIFE   In, baggage, in. [*Thrusts her in; shuts the door.*]—[*Aside.*]
What, all the lewd libertines of the town brought to my lodging by
this easy coxcomb! 'Sdeath, I'll not suffer it.

SPARKISH   Here, Harcourt, do you approve my choice?—[*To* ALITHEA.]
Dear little rogue, I told you I'd bring you acquainted with all my
friends, the wits, and—

>   HARCOURT *salutes her.*

PINCHWIFE [*aside*]   Ay, they shall know her, as well as you yourself will,
I warrant you.

SPARKISH   This is one of those, my pretty rogue, that are to dance at
your wedding tomorrow; and him you must bid welcome ever to what
you and I have.

PINCHWIFE [*aside*]   Monstrous!

---

7. Fabled serpents whose glance meant death.

SPARKISH Harcourt, how dost thou like her, faith?—Nay, dear, do not look down; I should hate to have a wife of mine out of countenance at anything.

PINCHWIFE [*aside*] Wonderful!

SPARKISH Tell me, I say, Harcourt, how dost thou like her? Thou hast stared upon her enough to resolve me.

HARCOURT So infinitely well that I could wish I had a mistress too, that might differ from her in nothing but her love and engagement to you.

ALITHEA Sir, Master Sparkish has often told me that his acquaintance were all wits and railleurs, and now I find it.

SPARKISH No, by the universe, madam, he does not rally now; you may believe him. I do assure you, he is the honestest, worthiest, true-hearted gentleman—a man of such perfect honor, he would say nothing to a lady he does not mean.

PINCHWIFE [*aside*] Praising another man to his mistress!

HARCOURT Sir, you are so beyond expectation obliging that—

SPARKISH Nay, egad, I am sure you do admire her extremely; I see't in your eyes.—He does admire you, madam.—By the world, don't you?

HARCOURT Yes, above the world, or the most glorious part of it, her whole sex; and till now I never thought I should have envied you, or any man about to marry, but you have the best excuse for marriage I ever knew.

ALITHEA Nay, now, sir, I'm satisfied you are of the society of the wits and railleurs, since you cannot spare your friend, even when he is but too civil to you; but the surest sign is, since you are an enemy to marriage, for that, I hear, you hate as much as business or bad wine.

HARCOURT Truly, madam, I never was an enemy to marriage till now, because marriage was never an enemy to me before.

ALITHEA But why, sir, is marriage an enemy to you now? Because it robs you of your friend here? For you look upon a friend married as one gone into a monastery, that is, dead to the world.

HARCOURT 'Tis indeed because you marry him; I see, madam, you can guess my meaning. I do confess heartily and openly, I wish it were in my power to break the match; by heavens I would.

SPARKISH Poor Frank!

ALITHEA Would you be so unkind to me?

HARCOURT No, no, 'tis not because I would be unkind to you.

SPARKISH Poor Frank! No, gad, 'tis only his kindness to me.

PINCHWIFE [*aside*] Great kindness to you indeed! Insensible fop, let a man make love to his wife to his face!

SPARKISH Come, dear Frank, for all my wife there that shall be, thou shalt enjoy me sometimes, dear rogue. By my honor, we men of wit condole for our deceased brother in marriage as much as for one dead in earnest. I think that was prettily said of me, ha, Harcourt? But come, Frank, be not melancholy for me.

HARCOURT No, I assure you I am not melancholy for you.

SPARKISH   Prithee, Frank, dost think my wife that shall be there a fine person?

HARCOURT   I could gaze upon her till I became as blind as you are.

SPARKISH   How, as I am? How?

HARCOURT   Because you are a lover, and true lovers are blind, stock blind.

SPARKISH   True, true; but by the world, she has wit too, as well as beauty. Go, go with her into a corner, and try if she has wit; talk to her anything; she's bashful before me.

HARCOURT   Indeed, if a woman wants wit in a corner, she has it nowhere.

ALITHEA [*aside to* SPARKISH]   Sir, you dispose of me a little before your time—

SPARKISH   Nay, nay, madam, let me have an earnest of your obedience, or—go, go, madam—

> HARCOURT *courts* ALITHEA *aside.*

PINCHWIFE   How, sir! If you are not concerned for the honor of a wife, I am for that of a sister; he shall not debauch her. Be a pander to your own wife, bring men to her, let 'em make love before your face, thrust 'em into a corner together, then leave 'em in private! Is this your own town wit and conduct?

SPARKISH   Ha, ha, ha! A silly wise rogue would make one laugh more than a stark fool, ha, ha! I shall burst. Nay, you shall not disturb 'em; I'll vex thee, by the world.

> *Struggles with* PINCHWIFE *to keep him from* HARCOURT *and* ALITHEA.

ALITHEA   The writings are drawn, sir, settlements made; 'tis too late, sir, and past all revocation.

HARCOURT   Then so is my death.

ALITHEA   I would not be unjust to him.

HARCOURT   Then why to me so?

ALITHEA   I have no obligation to you.

HARCOURT   My love.

ALITHEA   I had his before.

HARCOURT   You never had it; he wants, you see, jealousy, the only infallible sign of it.

ALITHEA   Love proceeds from esteem; he cannot distrust my virtue; besides, he loves me, or he would not marry me.

HARCOURT   Marrying you is no more sign of his love than bribing your woman, that he may marry you, is a sign of his generosity. Marriage is rather a sign of interest than love; and he that marries a fortune covets a mistress, not loves her. But if you take marriage for a sign of love, take it from me immediately.

ALITHEA   No, now you have put a scruple in my head; but, in short, sir, to end our dispute, I must marry him, my reputation would suffer in the world else.

HARCOURT   No, if you do marry him, with your pardon, madam, your reputation suffers in the world, and you would be thought in necessity for a cloak.[8]

ALITHEA   Nay, now you are rude, sir.—Mr. Sparkish, pray come hither, your friend here is very troublesome, and very loving.

HARCOURT [aside to ALITHEA]   Hold, hold!—

PINCHWIFE   D'ye hear that?

SPARKISH   Why, d'ye think I'll seem to be jealous, like a country bumpkin?

PINCHWIFE   No, rather be a cuckold, like a credulous cit.[9]

HARCOURT   Madam, you would not have been so little generous as to have told him.

ALITHEA   Yes, since you could be so little generous as to wrong him.

HARCOURT   Wrong him! No man can do't, he's beneath an injury; a bubble, a coward, a senseless idiot, a wretch so contemptible to all the world but you that—

ALITHEA   Hold, do not rail at him, for since he is like to be my husband, I am resolved to like him. Nay, I think I am obliged to tell him you are not his friend.—Master Sparkish, Master Sparkish!

SPARKISH   What, what?—Now, dear rogue, has not she wit?

HARCOURT [speaks surlily]   Not so much as I thought, and hoped she had.

ALITHEA   Mr. Sparkish, do you bring people to rail at you?

HARCOURT   Madam—

SPARKISH   How! No, but if he does rail at me, 'tis but in jest, I warrant; what we wits do for one another, and never take any notice of it.

ALITHEA   He spoke so scurrilously of you, I had no patience to hear him; besides, he has been making love to me.

HARCOURT [aside]   True, damned, telltale woman!

SPARKISH   Pshaw! to show his parts—we wits rail and make love often but to show our parts; as we have no affections, so we have no malice; we—

ALITHEA   He said you were a wretch, below an injury.

SPARKISH   Pshaw!

HARCOURT [aside]   Damned, senseless, impudent, virtuous jade! well, since she won't let me have her, she'll do as good, she'll make me hate her.

ALITHEA   A common bubble.

SPARKISH   Pshaw!

ALITHEA   A coward.

SPARKISH   Pshaw, pshaw!

ALITHEA   A senseless, driveling idiot.

8. In need of a disguise.
9. Contemptuous term for citizen.

SPARKISH   How! Did he disparage my parts? Nay, then my honor's concerned; I can't put up that, sir, by the world. Brother, help me to kill him.—[*Aside.*] I may draw now, since we have the odds of him. 'Tis a good occasion, too, before my mistress—

Offers to draw.

ALITHEA   Hold, hold!

SPARKISH   What, what?

ALITHEA [*aside*]   I must not let 'em kill the gentleman neither, for his kindness to me; I am so far from hating him that I wish my gallant had his person and understanding. Nay, if my honor—

SPARKISH   I'll be thy death.

ALITHEA   Hold, hold! Indeed, to tell the truth, the gentleman said after all that what he spoke was but out of friendship to you.

SPARKISH   How! say I am—I am a fool, that is, no wit, out of friendship to me?

ALITHEA   Yes, to try whether I was concerned enough for you, and made love to me only to be satisfied of my virtue, for your sake.

HARCOURT [*aside*]   Kind, however—

SPARKISH   Nay, if it were so, my dear rogue, I ask thee pardon; but why would not you tell me so, faith?

HARCOURT   Because I did not think on't, faith.

SPARKISH   Come, Horner does not come; Harcourt, let's be gone to the new play.—Come, madam.

ALITHEA   I will not go if you intend to leave me alone in the box and run into the pit, as you use to do.

SPARKISH   Pshaw! I'll leave Harcourt with you in the box to entertain you, and that's as good; if I sat in the box, I should be thought no judge, but of trimmings.—Come, away, Harcourt, lead her down.

Exeunt SPARKISH, HARCOURT, *and* ALITHEA.

PINCHWIFE   Well, go thy ways, for the flower of the true town fops, such as spend their estates before they come to 'em, and are cuckolds before they're married. But let me go look to my own freehold.—How!—

Enter MY LADY FIDGET, MRS. DAINTY FIDGET, *and* MRS. SQUEAMISH.

LADY FIDGET   Your servant, sir; where is your lady? We are come to wait upon her to the new play.

PINCHWIFE   New play!

LADY FIDGET   And my husband will wait upon you presently.

PINCHWIFE [*aside*]   Damn your civility.—Madam, by no means; I will not see Sir Jasper here till I have waited upon him at home; nor shall my wife see you till she has waited upon your ladyship at your lodgings.

LADY FIDGET   Now we are here, sir—

PINCHWIFE   No, madam.

MRS. DAINTY FIDGET   Pray, let us see her.

MRS. SQUEAMISH   We will not stir till we see her.

PINCHWIFE [*aside*]   A pox on you all! [*Goes to the door, and returns.*]—
She has locked the door, and is gone abroad.

LADY FIDGET   No, you have locked the door, and she's within.

MRS. DAINTY FIDGET   They told us below she was here.

PINCHWIFE [*aside*]   Will nothing do?—Well, it must out then. To tell
you the truth, ladies, which I was afraid to let you know before, lest it
might endanger your lives, my wife has just now the smallpox come
out upon her. Do not be frightened; but pray, be gone, ladies; you
shall not stay here in danger of your lives; pray get you gone, ladies.

LADY FIDGET   No, no, we have all had 'em.

MRS. SQUEAMISH   Alack, alack!

MRS. DAINTY FIDGET   Come, come, we must see how it goes with her;
I understand the disease.

LADY FIDGET   Come.

PINCHWIFE [*aside*]   Well, there is no being too hard for women at their
own weapon, lying; therefore I'll quit the field.

Exit PINCHWIFE.

MRS. SQUEAMISH   Here's an example of jealousy.

LADY FIDGET   Indeed, as the world goes, I wonder there are no more
jealous, since wives are so neglected.

MRS. DAINTY FIDGET   Pshaw! as the world goes, to what end should they
be jealous?

LADY FIDGET   Foh! 'tis a nasty world.

MRS. SQUEAMISH   That men of parts, great acquaintance, and quality
should take up with and spend themselves and fortunes in keeping
little playhouse creatures, foh!

LADY FIDGET   Nay, that women of understanding, great aquaintance,
and good quality should fall a-keeping too of little creatures, foh!

MRS. SQUEAMISH   Why, 'tis the men of quality's fault; they never visit
women of honor and reputation, as they used to do; and have not so
much as common civility for ladies of our rank, but use us with the
same indifferency and ill-breeding as if we were all married to 'em.

LADY FIDGET   She says true; 'tis an arrant shame women of quality
should be so slighted. Methinks birth—birth should go for something; I have known men admired, courted, and followed for their
titles only.

MRS. SQUEAMISH   Ay, one would think men of honor should not love,
no more than marry, out of their own rank.

MRS. DAINTY FIDGET   Fie, fie upon 'em! They are come to think cross-
breeding for themselves best, as well as for their dogs and horses.

LADY FIDGET   They are dogs and horses for't.

MRS. SQUEAMISH   One would think, if not for love, for vanity a little.

MRS. DAINTY FIDGET   Nay, they do satisfy their vanity upon us sometimes; and are kind to us in their report, tell all the world they lie with us.

LADY FIDGET   Damned rascals! That we should be only wronged by 'em; to report a man has had a person, when he has not had a person, is the greatest wrong in the whole world that can be done to a person.

MRS. SQUEAMISH   Well, 'tis an arrant shame noble persons should be so wronged and neglected.

LADY FIDGET   But still 'tis an arranter shame for a noble person to neglect her own honor, and defame her own noble person with little inconsiderable fellows, foh!

MRS. DAINTY FIDGET   I suppose the crime against our honor is the same with a man of quality as with another.

LADY FIDGET   How! No, sure, the man of quality is likest one's husband, and therefore the fault should be the less.

MRS. DAINTY FIDGET   But then the pleasure should be the less.

LADY FIDGET   Fie, fie, fie, for shame, sister! Whither shall we ramble? Be continent in your discourse, or I shall hate you.

MRS. DAINTY FIDGET   Besides, an intrigue is so much the more notorious for the man's quality.

MRS. SQUEAMISH   'Tis true, nobody takes notice of a private man, and therefore with him 'tis more secret, and the crime's the less when 'tis not known.

LADY FIDGET   You say true; i'faith, I think you are in the right on't. 'Tis not an injury to a husband till it be an injury to our honors; so that a woman of honor loses no honor with a private person; and to say truth—

MRS. DAINTY FIDGET   [apart to MRS. SQUEAMISH]   So, the little fellow is grown a private person—with her—

LADY FIDGET   But still my dear, dear honor.

Enter SIR JASPER, HORNER, DORILANT.

SIR JASPER FIDGET   Ay, my dear, dear of honor, thou hast still so much honor in thy mouth—

HORNER   [aside]   That she has none elsewhere.

LADY FIDGET   Oh, what d'ye mean to bring in these upon us?

MRS. DAINTY FIDGET   Foh! these are as bad as wits.

MRS. SQUEAMISH   Foh!

LADY FIDGET   Let us leave the room.

SIR JASPER FIDGET   Stay, stay, faith, to tell you the naked truth—

LADY FIDGET   Fie, Sir Jasper! Do not use that word "naked."

SIR JASPER FIDGET   Well, well, in short, I have business at Whitehall, and cannot go to the play with you, therefore would have you go—

LADY FIDGET   With those two to a play?

SIR JASPER FIDGET   No, not with t'other, but with Mr. Horner; there

can be no more scandal to go with him than with Mr. Tattle, or
Master Limberham.[1]

LADY FIDGET   With that nasty fellow! No—no!

SIR JASPER FIDGET   Nay, prithee, dear, hear me.

Whispers to LADY FIDGET.

HORNER   Ladies—

HORNER, DORILANT *drawing near* MRS. SQUEAMISH *and* MRS.
DAINTY.

MRS. DAINTY FIDGET   Stand off.

MRS. SQUEAMISH   Do not approach us.

MRS. DAINTY FIDGET   You herd with the wits, you are obscenity all over.

MRS. SQUEAMISH   And I would as soon look upon a picture of Adam
and Eve, without fig leaves, as any of you, if I could help it; therefore
keep off, and do not make us sick.

DORILANT   What a devil are these?

HORNER   Why, these are pretenders to honor, as critics to wit, only by
censuring others; and as every raw, peevish, out-of-humored, affected,
dull, tea-drinking, arithmetical fop sets up for a wit by railing at men
of sense, so these for honor by railing at the Court, and ladies of as
great honor as quality.

SIR JASPER FIDGET   Come, Mr. Horner, I must desire you to go with
these ladies to the play, sir.

HORNER   I, sir!

SIR JASPER FIDGET   Ay, ay, come, sir.

HORNER   I must beg your pardon, sir, and theirs; I will not be seen in
women's company in public again for the world.

SIR JASPER FIDGET   Ha, ha! strange aversion!

MRS. SQUEAMISH   No, he's for women's company in private.

SIR JASPER FIDGET   He—poor man—he! Ha, ha, ha!

MRS. DAINTY FIDGET   'Tis a greater shame amongst lewd fellows to be
seen in virtuous women's company than for the women to be seen
with them.

HORNER   Indeed, madam, the time was I only hated virtuous women,
but now I hate the other too; I beg your pardon, ladies.

LADY FIDGET   You are very obliging, sir, because we would not be troubled with you.

SIR JASPER FIDGET   In sober sadness, he shall go.

DORILANT   Nay, if he wo'not, I am ready to wait upon the ladies; and I
think I am the fitter man.

SIR JASPER FIDGET   You, sir, no, I thank you for that—Master Horner is
a privileged man amongst the virtuous ladies; 'twill be a great while

---

1. Common names for fops. Limberham would later appear in Dryden's *The Kind Keeper* (1678),
and Tattle in Congreve's *Love for Love* (1695).

before you are so, he, he, he! He's my wife's gallant, he, he, he! No, pray withdraw, sir, for as I take it, the virtuous ladies have no business with you.

DORILANT   And I am sure he can have none with them. 'Tis strange a man can't come amongst virtuous women now but upon the same terms as men are admitted into the Great Turk's seraglio; but heavens keep me from being an ombre[2] player with 'em! But where is Pinchwife?

Exit DORILANT.

SIR JASPER FIDGET   Come, come, man; what, avoid the sweet society of womankind? that sweet, soft, gentle, tame, noble creature, woman, made for man's companion—

HORNER   So is that soft, gentle, tame and more noble creature a spaniel, and has all their tricks—can fawn, lie down, suffer beating, and fawn the more; barks at your friends when they come to see you; makes your bed hard; gives you fleas, and the mange sometimes. And all the difference is, the spaniel's the more faithful animal, and fawns but upon one master.

SIR JASPER FIDGET   He, he, he!

MRS. SQUEAMISH   Oh, the rude beast!

MRS. DAINTY FIDGET   Insolent brute!

LADY FIDGET   Brute! Stinking, mortified, rotten French wether,[3] to dare—

SIR JASPER FIDGET   Hold, an't please your ladyship.—For shame, Master Horner, your mother was a woman.—[*Aside.*] Now shall I never reconcile 'em.—[*Aside to* LADY FIDGET.] Hark you, madam, take my advice in your anger. You know you often want one to make up your drolling pack of ombre players; and you may cheat him easily, for he's an ill gamester, and consequently loves play. Besides, you know, you have but two old civil gentlemen, with stinking breaths too, to wait upon you abroad; take in the third into your service. The other are but crazy[4]; and a lady should have a supernumerary gentleman-usher, as a supernumerary coach-horse, lest sometimes you should be forced to stay at home.

LADY FIDGET   But are you sure he loves play, and has money?

SIR JASPER FIDGET   He loves play as much as you, and has money as much as I.

LADY FIDGET   Then I am contented to make him pay for his scurrility; money makes up in a measure all other wants in men.—[*Aside.*] Those whom we cannot make hold for gallants, we make fine.[5]

2. Fashionable card game, with a pun on *hombre* (Spanish for *man*).
3. Castrated ram.
4. Infirm.
5. Pay the penalty.

SIR JASPER FIDGET [*aside*] So, so; now to mollify, to wheedle him.—
Master Horner, will you never keep civil company? Methinks 'tis time
now, since you are only fit for them. Come, come, man, you must
e'en fall to visiting our wives, eating at our tables, drinking tea with
our virtuous relations after dinner, dealing cards to 'em, reading plays
and gazettes to 'em, picking fleas out of their shocks[6] for 'em, collecting receipts, new songs, women, pages and footmen for 'em.

HORNER I hope they'll afford me better employment, sir.

SIR JASPER FIDGET He, he, he! 'Tis fit you know your work before
you come into your place; and since you are unprovided of a lady to
flatter and a good house to eat at, pray frequent mine, and call
my wife mistress, and she shall call you gallant, according to the
custom.

HORNER Who, I?

SIR JASPER FIDGET Faith, thou shalt for my sake; come, for my sake
only.

HORNER For your sake—

SIR JASPER FIDGET [*to* LADY FIDGET] Come, come here's a gamester
for you; let him be a little familiar sometimes; nay, what if a little
rude? Gamesters may be rude with ladies, you know.

LADY FIDGET Yes, losing gamesters have a privilege with women.

HORNER I always thought the contrary, that the winning gamester had
most privilege with women; for when you have lost your money to a
man, you'll lose anything you have, all you have, they say, and he
may use you as he pleases.

SIR JASPER FIDGET He, he, he! Well, win or lose, you shall have your
liberty with her.

LADY FIDGET As he behaves himself; and for your sake I'll give him
admittance and freedom.

HORNER All sorts of freedom, madam?

SIR JASPER FIDGET Ay, ay, ay, all sorts of freedom thou canst take and
so go to her, begin thy new employment; wheedle her, jest with her,
and be better acquainted one with another.

HORNER [*aside*] I think I know her already, therefore may venture with
her, my secret for hers.

> HORNER *and* LADY FIDGET *whisper.*

SIR JASPER FIDGET Sister, cuz, I have provided an innocent playfellow
for you there.

MRS. DAINTY FIDGET Who, he!

MRS. SQUEAMISH There's a playfellow indeed!

SIR JASPER FIDGET Yes, sure; what, he is good enough to play at cards,
blindman's buff, or the fool with sometimes.

MRS. SQUEAMISH Foh! we'll have no such playfellows.

6. Poodles.

MRS. DAINTY FIDGET   No, sir, you shan't choose playfellows for us, we thank you.

SIR JASPER FIDGET   Nay, pray hear me.

Whispering to them.

LADY FIDGET [*aside to* HORNER]   But, poor gentleman, could you be so generous, so truly a man of honor, as for the sakes of us women of honor, to cause yourself to be reported no man? No man! And to suffer yourself the greatest shame that could fall upon a man, that none might fall upon us women by your conversation? But indeed, sir, as perfectly, perfectly, the same man as before your going into France, sir? as perfectly, perfectly, sir?

HORNER   As perfectly, perfectly, madam. Nay, I scorn you should take my word; I desire to be tried only, madam.

LADY FIDGET   Well, that's spoken again like a man of honor; all men of honor desire to come to the test. But, indeed, generally you men report such things of yourselves, one does not know how or whom to believe; and it is come to that pass we dare not take your words, no more than your tailor's, without some staid servant of yours be bound with you. But I have so strong a faith in your honor, dear, dear, noble sir, that I'd forfeit mine for yours at any time, dear sir.

HORNER   No, madam, you should not need to forfeit it for me; I have given you security already to save you harmless, my late reputation being so well known in the world, madam.

LADY FIDGET   But if upon any future falling out, or upon a suspicion of my taking the trust out of your hands, to employ some other, you yourself should betray your trust, dear sir? I mean, if you'll give me leave to speak obscenely, you might tell, dear sir.

HORNER   If I did, nobody would believe me; the reputation of impotency is as hardly recovered again in the world as that of cowardice, dear madam.

LADY FIDGET   Nay then, as one may say, you may do your worst, dear, dear sir.

SIR JASPER FIDGET   Come, is your ladyship reconciled to him yet? Have you agreed on matters? For I must be gone to Whitehall.

LADY FIDGET   Why, indeed, Sir Jasper, Master Horner is a thousand, thousand times a better man than I thought him. Cousin Squeamish, Sister Dainty, I can name him now; truly, not long ago, you know, I thought his very name obscenity, and I would as soon have lain with him as have named him.

SIR JASPER FIDGET   Very likely, poor madam.

MRS. DAINTY FIDGET   I believe it.

MRS. SQUEAMISH   No doubt on't.

SIR JASPER FIDGET   Well, well—that your ladyship is as virtuous as any she, I know, and him all the town knows—he, he, he! Therefore, now you like him, get you gone to your business together; go, go to your business, I say, pleasure, whilst I go to my pleasure, business.

LADY FIDGET   Come, then, dear gallant.
HORNER   Come away, my dearest mistress.
SIR JASPER FIDGET   So, so; why, 'tis as I'd have it.

Exit SIR JASPER.

HORNER   And as I'd have it.
LADY FIDGET

> Who for his business from his wife will run,
> Takes the best care to have her business done.

Exeunt omnes.

Act III. Scene i. Pinchwife's *house.*

ALITHEA *and* MRS. PINCHWIFE.

ALITHEA   Sister, what ails you? You are grown melancholy.
MRS. PINCHWIFE   Would it not make anyone melancholy, to see you go
every day fluttering about abroad, whilst I must stay at home like a
poor, lonely, sullen bird in a cage?
ALITHEA   Ay, sister, but you came young and just from the nest to your
cage, so that I thought you liked it, and could be as cheerful in't as
others that took their flight themselves early, and are hopping abroad
in the open air.
MRS. PINCHWIFE   Nay, I confess I was quiet enough till my husband
told me what pure[7] lives the London ladies live abroad, with their
dancing, meetings, and junketings, and dressed every day in their best
gowns; and I warrant you, play at ninepins every day of the week, so
they do.

Enter MR. PINCHWIFE.

PINCHWIFE   Come, what's here to do? You are putting the town pleasures in her head, and setting her a-longing.
ALITHEA   Yes, after ninepins; you suffer none to give her those longings,
you mean, but yourself.
PINCHWIFE   I tell her of the vanities of the town like a confessor.
ALITHEA   A confessor! Just such a confessor as he that, by forbidding a
silly ostler to grease the horse's teeth,[8] taught him to do't.
PINCHWIFE   Come, Mistress Flippant, good precepts are lost when bad
examples are still before us; the liberty you take abroad makes her
hanker after it, and out of humour at home. Poor wretch! she desired
not to come to London; I would bring her.
ALITHEA   Very well.
PINCHWIFE   She has been this week in town, and never desired, till this
afternoon, to go abroad.

---

7. Fine.
8. A trick of innkeepers to prevent horses from eating.

ALITHEA   Was she not at a play yesterday?

PINCHWIFE   Yes, but she ne'er asked me; I was myself the cause of her going.

ALITHEA   Then, if she ask you again, you are the cause of her asking, and not my example.

PINCHWIFE   Well, tomorrow night I shall be rid of you; and the next day, before 'tis light, she and I'll be rid of the town, and my dreadful apprehensions. —[To MRS. PINCHWIFE.] Come, be not melancholy, for thou shalt go into the country after tomorrow, dearest.

ALITHEA   Great comfort!

MRS. PINCHWIFE   Pish! what d'ye tell me of the country for?

PINCHWIFE   How's this! What, pish at the country?

MRS. PINCHWIFE   Let me alone, I am not well.

PINCHWIFE   Oh, if that be all—what ails my dearest?

MRS. PINCHWIFE   Truly I don't know; but I have not been well since you told me there was a gallant at the play in love with me.

PINCHWIFE   Ha!—

ALITHEA   That's by my example too!

PINCHWIFE   Nay, if you are not well, but are so concerned because a lewd fellow chanced to lie, and say he liked you, you'll make me sick too.

MRS. PINCHWIFE   Of what sickness?

PINCHWIFE   Oh, of that which is worse than the plague, jealousy.

MRS. PINCHWIFE   Pish, you jeer! I'm sure there's no such disease in our receipt-book at home.

PINCHWIFE   No, thou never met'st with it, poor innocent. — [Aside.] Well, if thou cuckold me, 'twill be my own fault—for cuckolds and bastards are generally makers of their own fortune.

MRS. PINCHWIFE   Well, but pray, bud, let's go to a play tonight.

PINCHWIFE   'Tis just done, she comes from it. But why are you so eager to see a play?

MRS. PINCHWIFE   Faith, dear, not that I care one pin for their talk there; but I like to look upon the playermen, and would see, if I could, the gallant you say loves me; that's all, dear bud.

PINCHWIFE   Is that all, dear bud?

ALITHEA   This proceeds from my example.

MRS. PINCHWIFE   But if the play be done, let's go abroad, however dear bud.

PINCHWIFE   Come, have a little patience, and thou shalt go into the country on Friday.

MRS. PINCHWIFE   Therefore I would see first some sights, to tell me neighbors of. Nay, I will go abroad, that's once.

ALITHEA   I'm the cause of this desire too.

PINCHWIFE   But now I think on't, who was the cause of Horner's coming to my lodging today? That was you.

ALITHEA   No, you, because you would not let him see your handsome wife out of your lodging.

MRS. PINCHWIFE   Why, O Lord! did the gentleman come hither to see me indeed?

PINCHWIFE   No, no. —You are not cause of that damned question too, Mistress Alithea? —[*Aside.*] Well, she's in the right in it. He is in love with my wife—and comes after her—'tis so—but I'll nip his love in the bud; lest he should follow us into the country, and break his chariot-wheel near our house on purpose for an excuse to come to't. But I think I know the town.

MRS. PINCHWIFE   Come, pray, bud, let's go abroad before 'tis late; for I will go, that's flat and plain.

PINCHWIFE [*aside*]   So! the obstinacy already of a town-wife, and I must, whilst she's here, humour her like one. —Sister, how shall we do, that she may not be seen or known?

ALITHEA   Let her put on her mask.

PINCHWIFE   Pshaw! A mask makes people but the more inquisitive, and is as ridiculous a disguise as a stage-beard; her shape, stature, habit will be known. And if we should meet with Horner, he would be sure to take acquaintance with us, must wish her joy, kiss her, talk to her, leer upon her, and the devil and all. No, I'll not use her to a mask, 'tis dangerous; for masks have made more cuckolds than the best faces that ever were known.

ALITHEA   How will you do then?

MRS. PINCHWIFE   Nay, shall we go? The Exchange will be shut, and I have a mind to see that.

PINCHWIFE   So—I have it—I'll dress her up in the suit we are to carry down to her brother, little sir James; nay, I understand the town tricks. Come, let's go dress her. A mask! No—a woman masked, like a covered dish, gives a man curiosity and appetite, when, it may be, uncovered, 'twould turn his stomach; no, no.

ALITHEA   Indeed your comparison is something a greasy one. But I had a gentle gallant used to say, "A beauty masked, like the sun in eclipse, gathers together more gazers than if it shined out."

Exeunt.

Act III. Scene ii. The scene changes to the New Exchange.

Enter HORNER, HARCOURT, DORILANT.

DORILANT   Engaged to women, and not sup with us?

HORNER   Ay, a pox on 'em all!

HARCOURT   You were much a more reasonable man in the morning, and had as noble resolutions against 'em as a widower of a week's liberty.

DORILANT   Did I ever think to see you keep company with women in vain?

HORNER   In vain! No—'tis, since I can't love 'em, to be revenged on 'em.

HARCOURT   Now your sting is gone, you looked in the box, amongst all
those women, like a drone in the hive, all upon you; shoved and ill-
used by 'em all, and thrust from one side to t'other.

DORILANT   Yet he must be buzzing amongst 'em still, like other old
beetle-headed, liquorish drones. Avoid 'em, and hate 'em as they hate
you.

HORNER   Because I do hate 'em, and would hate 'em yet more, I'll
frequent 'em; you may see by marriage, nothing makes a man hate a
woman more than her constant conversation. In short, I converse
with 'em, as you do with rich fools, to laugh at 'em and use 'em ill.

DORILANT   But I would no more sup with women, unless I could lie
with 'em, than sup with a rich coxcomb, unless I could cheat him.

HORNER   Yes, I have known thee sup with a fool for his drinking; if he
could set out your hand that way only, you were satisfied, and if he
were a wine-swallowing mouth 'twas enough.

HARCOURT   Yes, a man drinks often with a fool, as he tosses with a
marker, only to keep his hand in ure.[9] But do the ladies drink?

HORNER   Yes, sir, and I shall have the pleasure at least of laying 'em flat
with a bottle, and bring as much scandal that way upon 'em as formerly t'other.

HARCOURT   Perhaps you may prove as weak a brother amongst 'em that
way as t'other.

DORILANT   Foh! drinking with women is as unnatural as scolding with
'em; but 'tis a pleasure of decayed fornicators, and the basest way of
quenching love.

HARCOURT   Nay, 'tis drowning love instead of quenching it. But leave
us for civil women too!

DORILANT   Ay, when he can't be the better for 'em. We hardly pardon
a man that leaves his friend for a wench, and that's a pretty lawful
call.

HORNER   Faith, I would not leave you for 'em, if they would not drink.

DORILANT   Who would disappoint his company at Lewis's for a gos-
siping?

HARCOURT   Foh! Wine and women, good apart, together as nauseous
as sack[1] and sugar. But hark you, sir, before you go, a little of your
advice; an old maimed general, when unfit for action, is fittest for
counsel. I have other designs upon women than eating and drinking
with them. I am in love with Sparkish's mistress, whom he is to marry
tomorrow. Now how shall I get her?

Enter SPARKISH, *looking about.*

HORNER   Why, here comes one will help you to her.

HARCOURT   He! He, I tell you, is my rival, and will hinder my love.

HORNER   No, a foolish rival and a jealous husband assist their rival's

---

9. Keeps in practice (*ure*) by playing with the scorekeeper (*marker*).
1. White wine from Spain or the Canary Isles; often drunk with sugar, although not by Harcourt.

designs; for they are sure to make their women hate them, which is the first step to their love for another man.

HARCOURT   But I cannot come near his mistress but in his company.

HORNER   Still the better for you, for fools are most easily cheated when they themselves are accessories; and he is to be bubbled[2] of his mistress, as of his money, the common mistress, by keeping him company.

SPARKISH   Who is that, that is to be bubbled? Faith, let me snack, I han't met with a bubble since Christmas. Gad, I think bubbles are like their brother woodcocks,[3] go out with cold weather.

HARCOURT   [*apart to* HORNER]   A pox! he did not hear all, I hope.

SPARKISH   Come, you bubbling rogues you, where do we sup?—Oh, Harcourt, my mistress tells me you have been making fierce love to her all the play long, ha, ha! But I—

HARCOURT   I make love to her?

SPARKISH   Nay, I forgive thee; for I think I know thee, and I know her, but I am sure I know myself.

HARCOURT   Did she tell you so? I see all women are like these of the Exchange, who, to enhance the price of their commodities, report to their fond customers offers which were never made 'em.

HORNER   Ay, women are as apt to tell before the intrigue as men after it, and so show themselves the vainer sex. But hast thou a mistress, Sparkish? 'Tis as hard for me to believe it as that thou ever hadst a bubble, as you bragged just now.

SPARKISH   Oh, your servant, sir; are you at your raillery, sir? But we were some of us beforehand with you today at the play. The wits were something bold with you, sir; did you not hear us laugh?

HORNER   Yes, but I thought you had gone to plays to laugh at the poet's wit, not at your own.

SPARKISH   Your servant, sir; no, I thank you. Gad, I go to a play as to a country treat; I carry my own wine to one, and my own wit to t'other, or else I'm sure I should not be merry at either. And the reason why we are so often louder than the players is because we think we speak more wit, and so become the poet's rivals in his audience. For to tell you the truth, we hate the silly rogues; nay, so much that we find fault even with their bawdy upon the stage, whilst we talk nothing else in the pit as loud.

HORNER   But why shouldst thou hate the silly poets? Thou hast too much wit to be one, and they, like whores, are only hated by each other; and thou dost scorn writing, I'm sure.

SPARKISH   Yes, I'd have you to know I scorn writing; but women, women, that make men do all foolish things, make 'em write songs too; everybody does it. 'Tis even as common with lovers as playing with fans; and you can no more help rhyming to your Phyllis than drinking to your Phyllis.

2. Duped.
3. Simpletons. *Snack*: share.

HARCOURT   Nay, poetry in love is no more to be avoided than jealousy.

DORILANT   But the poets damned your songs, did they?

SPARKISH   Damn the poets! They turned 'em into burlesque, as they call it. That burlesque is a hocus-pocus trick they have got, which, by the virtue of *hictius doctius, topsy-turvy*, they make a wise and witty man in the world a fool upon the stage, you know not how; and 'tis therefore I hate 'em too, for I know not but it may be my own case; for they'll put a man into a play for looking asquint. Their predecessors were contented to make serving-men only their stage-fools, but these rogues must have gentlemen, with a pox to 'em, nay, knights. And, indeed, you shall hardly see a fool upon the stage but he's a knight; and to tell you the truth, they have kept me these six years from being a knight in earnest, for fear of being knighted in a play, and dubbed a fool.

DORILANT   Blame 'em not; they must follow their copy, the age.

HARCOURT   But why shouldst thou be afraid of being in a play, who expose yourself every day in the playhouses, and at public places?

HORNER   'Tis but being on the stage, instead of standing on a bench in the pit.

DORILANT   Don't you give money to painters to draw you like? And are you afraid of your pictures at length in a playhouse, where all your mistresses may see you?

SPARKISH   A pox! Painters don't draw the smallpox or pimples in one's face. Come, damn all your silly authors whatever, all books and booksellers, by the world, and all readers, courteous or uncourteous.

HARCOURT   But who comes here, Sparkish?

Enter MR. PINCHWIFE, *and his wife in man's clothes,* ALITHEA, LUCY *her maid.*

SPARKISH   Oh, hide me! There's my mistress too.

SPARKISH *hides himself behind* HARCOURT.

HARCOURT   She sees you.

SPARKISH   But I will not see her. 'Tis time to go to Whitehall, and I must not fail the drawing room.

HARCOURT   Pray, first carry me, and reconcile me to her.

SPARKISH   Another time; faith, the King will have supped.

HARCOURT   Not with the worse stomach for thy absence; thou art one of those fools that think their attendance at the King's meals as necessary as his physicians', when you are more troublesome to him than his doctors, or his dogs.

SPARKISH   Pshaw! I know my interest, sir; prithee, hide me.

HORNER   Your servant, Pinchwife.—What, he knows us not!

PINCHWIFE [*to his wife aside*]   Come along.

MRS. PINCHWIFE   Pray, have you any ballads? Give me sixpenny worth.

CLASP[4]   We have no ballads.

MRS. PINCHWIFE   Then give me *Covent Garden Drollery*, and a play or two—Oh, here's *Tarugo's Wiles*, and *The Slighted Maiden*,[5] I'll have them.

PINCHWIFE [*apart to her*]   No, plays are not for your reading. Come along; will you discover yourself?

HORNER   Who is that pretty youth with him, Sparkish?

SPARKISH   I believe his wife's brother, because he's something like her; but I never saw her but once.

HORNER   Extremely handsome; I have seen a face like it too. Let us follow 'em.

> *Exeunt* PINCHWIFE, MRS. PINCHWIFE, ALITHEA, LUCY, HORNER, DORILANT *following them.*

HARCOURT   Come, sparkish, your mistress saw you, and will be angry you go not to her. Besides, I would fain be reconciled to her, which none but you can do, dear friend.

SPARKISH   Well, that's a better reason, dear friend. I would not go near her now, for hers or my own sake, but I can deny you nothing; for though I have known thee a great while, never go, if I do not love thee as well as a new acquaintance.

HARCOURT   I am obliged to you indeed, dear friend. I would be well with her, only to be well with thee still; for these ties to wives usually dissolve all ties to friends. I would be contented she should enjoy you a-night, but I would have you to myself a-days, as I have had, dear friend.

SPARKISH   And thou shalt enjoy me a-days, dear, dear friend, never stir; and I'll be divorced from her sooner than from thee. Come along.

HARCOURT [*aside*]   So, we are hard put to't when we make our rival our procurer; but neither she nor her brother would let me come near her now. When all's done, a rival is the best cloak to steal to a mistress under, without suspicion; and when we have once got to her as we desire, we throw him off like other cloaks.

> *Exit* SPARKISH, *and* HARCOURT *following him.*

> *Re-enter* MR. PINCHWIFE, MRS. PINCHWIFE *in man's clothes.*

PINCHWIFE [*to* ALITHEA][6]   Sister, if you will not go, we must leave you.—[*Aside.*] The fool her gallant and she will muster up all the young saunterers of this place, and they will leave their dear seamstress to follow us. What a swarm of cuckolds, and cuckold-makers, are here!—Come, let's be gone, Mistress Margery.

---

4. A bookseller. His stall is part of the scenery.
5. The *Drollery* (1672) contained songs and other selections from plays. The other titles are comedies by (respectively) Thomas St. Serfe and Robert Stapylton, performed during the 1660s.
6. She is off-stage.

MRS. PINCHWIFE   Don't you believe that, I han't half my bellyfull of sights yet.

PINCHWIFE   Then walk this way.

MRS. PINCHWIFE   Lord, what a power of brave signs are here! Stay— the Bull's-Head, the Ram's Head, and the Stag's-Head, dear—

PINCHWIFE   Nay, if every husband's proper sign[7] here were visible, they would be all alike.

MRS. PINCHWIFE   What d'ye mean by that, bud?

PINCHWIFE   'Tis no matter—no matter, bud.

MRS. PINCHWIFE   Pray tell me; nay, I will know.

PINCHWIFE   They would be all bulls', stags', and rams' heads.

Exeunt MR. PINCHWIFE, MRS. PINCHWIFE.

RE-ENTER SPARKISH, HARCOURT, ALITHEA, LUCY, *at t'other door.*

SPARKISH   Come, dear madam, for my sake you shall be reconciled to him.

ALITHEA   For your sake I hate him.

HARCOURT   That's something too cruel, madam, to hate me for his sake.

SPARKISH   Ay indeed, madam, too, too cruel to me, to hate my friend for my sake.

ALITHEA   I hate him because he is your enemy; and you ought to hate him too, for making love to me, if you love me.

SPARKISH   That's a good one; I hate a man for loving you! If he did love you, 'tis but what he can't help; and 'tis your fault, not his, if he admires you. I hate a man for being of my opinion! I'll ne'er do't, by the world.

ALITHEA   Is it for your honor or mine, to suffer a man to make love to me, who am to marry you tomorrow?

SPARKISH   It is for your honor or mine, to have me jealous? That he makes love to you is a sign you are handsome; and that I am not jealous is a sign you are virtuous. That, I think, is for your honor.

ALITHEA   But 'tis your honor too I am concerned for.

HARCOURT   But why, dearest madam, will you be more concerned for his honor than he is himself? Let his honor alone, for my sake and his. He, he has no honor—

SPARKISH   How's that?

HARCOURT   But what my dear friend can guard himself.

SPARKISH   O ho—that's right again.

HARCOURT   Your care of his honor argues his neglect of it, which is no honor to my dear friend here; therefore once more, let his honor go which way it will, dear madam.

SPARKISH   Ay, ay, were it for my honor to marry a woman whose virtue I suspected, and could not trust her in a friend's hands?

7. Cuckold's horns.

ALITHEA   Are you not afraid to lose me?

HARCOURT   He afraid to lose you, madam! No, no—you may see how the most estimable and most glorious creature in the world is valued by him. Will you not see it?

SPARKISH   Right, honest Frank, I have that noble value for her that I cannot be jealous of her.

ALITHEA   You mistake him, he means you care not for me, nor who has me.

SPARKISH   Lord, madam, I see you are jealous.[8] Will you wrest a poor man's meaning from his words?

ALITHEA   You astonish me, sir, with your want of jealousy.

SPARKISH   And you make me giddy, madam, with your jealousy and fears, and virtue and honor. Gad, I see virtue makes a woman as troublesome as a little reading or learning.

ALITHEA   Monstrous!

LUCY [behind]   Well, to see what easy husbands these women of quality can meet with; a poor chambermaid can never have such lady-like luck. Besides, he's thrown away upon her; she'll make no use of her fortune, her blessing; none to a gentleman for a pure cuckold, for it requires good breeding to be a cuckold.

ALITHEA   I tell you then plainly, he pursues me to marry me.

SPARKISH   Pshaw!

HARCOURT   Come, madam, you see you strive in vain to make him jealous of me; my dear friend is the kindest creature in the world to me.

SPARKISH   Poor fellow.

HARCOURT   But his kindness only is not enough for me, without your favor; your good opinion, dear madam, 'tis that must perfect my happiness. Good gentleman, he believes all I say; would you would do so. Jealous of me! I would not wrong him nor you for the world.

SPARKISH   Look you there; hear him, hear him, and do not walk away so.

ALITHEA *walks carelessly to and fro.*

HARCOURT   I love you, madam, so—

SPARKISH   How's that! Nay—now you begin to go too far indeed.

HARCOURT   So much, I confess, I say I love you, that I would not have you miserable, and cast yourself away upon so unworthy and inconsiderable a thing as what you see here.

Clapping his hand on his breast, points at SPARKISH.

SPARKISH   No, faith, I believe thou wouldst not; now his meaning is plain. But I knew before thou wouldst not wrong me nor her.

HARCOURT   No, no, heavens forbid the glory of her sex should fall so

8. Vehement in feeling.

low as into the embraces of such a contemptible wretch, the last of mankind—my dear friend here—I injure him!

Embracing SPARKISH.

ALITHEA   Very well.

SPARKISH   No, no, dear friend, I knew it.—Madam, you see he will rather wrong himself than me, in giving himself such names.

ALITHEA   Do not you understand him yet?

SPARKISH   Yes, how modestly he speaks of himself, poor fellow.

ALITHEA   Methinks he speaks imprudently of yourself, since—before yourself too; insomuch that I can no longer suffer his scurrilous abusiveness to you, no more than his love to me.

Offers to go.

SPARKISH   Nay, nay, madam, pray stay—his love to you! Lord, madam, has he not spoke yet plain enough?

ALITHEA   Yes, indeed, I should think so.

SPARKISH   Well then, by the world, a man can't speak civilly to a woman now but presently[9] she says he makes love to her. Nay, madam, you shall stay, with your pardon, since you have not yet understood him, till he has made an *éclaircissement* of his love to you, that is, what kind of love it is.—[*To* HARCOURT.] Answer to thy catechism. Friend, do you love my mistress here?

HARCOURT   Yes, I wish she would not doubt it.

SPARKISH   But how do you love her?

HARCOURT   With all my soul.

ALITHEA   I thank him; methinks he speaks plain enough now.

SPARKISH [*to* ALITHEA]   You are out still.—But with what kind of love, Harcourt?

HARCOURT   With the best and truest love in the world.

SPARKISH   Look you there then, that is with no matrimonial love, I'm sure.

ALITHEA   How's that? Do you say matrimonial love is not best?

SPARKISH   Gad, I went too far ere I was aware. But speak for thyself, Harcourt; you said you would not wrong me nor her.

HARCOURT   No, no, madam, e'en take him for heaven's sake—

SPARKISH   Look you there, madam.

HARCOURT   Who should in all justice be yours, he that loves you most.

Claps his hand on his breast.

ALITHEA   Look you there, Mr. Sparkish, who's that?

SPARKISH   Who should it be?—Go on, Harcourt.

HARCOURT   Who loves you more than women titles, or fortune fools.

Points at SPARKISH.

9. Immediately.

SPARKISH   Look you there, he means me still, for he points at me.

ALITHEA   Ridiculous!

HARCOURT   Who can only match your faith and constancy in love.

SPARKISH   Ay.

HARCOURT   Who knows, if it be possible, how to value so much beauty and virtue.

SPARKISH   Ay.

HARCOURT   Whose love can no more be equaled in the world than that heavenly form of yours.

SPARKISH   No.

HARCOURT   Who could no more suffer a rival than your absence, and yet could no more suspect your virtue than his own constancy in his love to you.

SPARKISH   No.

HARCOURT   Who, in fine, loves you better than his eyes, that first made him love you.

SPARKISH   Ay—nay, madam, faith, you shan't go till—

ALITHEA   Have a care, lest you make me stay too long—

SPARKISH   But till he has saluted you; that I may be assured you are friends, after his honest advice and declaration. Come, pray, madam, be friends with him.

Enter MR. PINCHWIFE, MRS. PINCHWIFE.

ALITHEA   You must pardon me, sir, that I am not yet so obedient to you.

PINCHWIFE   What, invite your wife to kiss men? Monstrous! Are you not ashamed? I will never forgive you.

SPARKISH   Are you not ashamed that I should have more confidence in the chastity of your family than you have? You must not teach me; I am a man of honor, sir, though I am frank[1] and free; I am frank, sir—

PINCHWIFE   Very frank, sir, to share your wife with your friends.

SPARKISH   He is an humble, menial friend, such as reconciles the differences of the marriage bed. You know man and wife do not always agree; I design him for that use, therefore would have him well with my wife.

PINCHWIFE   A menial friend! you will get a great many menial friends by showing your wife as you do.

SPARKISH   What then? It may be I have a pleasure in't, as I have to show fine clothes at a playhouse the first day, and count money before poor rogues.

PINCHWIFE   He that shows his wife or money will be in danger of having them borrowed sometimes.

SPARKISH   I love to be envied, and would not marry a wife that I alone could love; loving alone is as dull as eating alone. Is it not a frank age? and I am a frank person. And to tell you the truth, it may be I

1. Generous.

love to have rivals in a wife, they make her seem to a man still but as a kept mistress; and so good night, for I must to Whitehall. —Madam, I hope you are now reconciled to my friend; and so I wish you a good night, madam, and sleep if you can, for tomorrow you know I must visit you early with a canonical gentleman. Good night, dear Harcourt.

Exit SPARKISH.

HARCOURT   Madam, I hope you will not refuse my visit tomorrow, if it should be earlier, with a canonical gentleman, than Mr. Sparkish's.

PINCHWIFE   This gentlewoman is yet under my care; therefore you must yet forbear your freedom with her, sir.

Coming between ALITHEA *and* HARCOURT.

HARCOURT   Must, sir!—

PINCHWIFE   Yes, sir, she is my sister.

HARCOURT   'Tis well she is, sir—for I must be her servant, sir.— Madam—

PINCHWIFE   Come away, sister; we had been gone, if it had not been for you, and so avoided these lewd rakehells, who seem to haunt us.

Enter HORNER, DORILANT *to them.*

HORNER   How now, Pinchwife!

PINCHWIFE   Your servant.

HORNER   What! I see a little time in the country makes a man turn wild and unsociable, and only fit to converse with his horses, dogs, and his herds.

PINCHWIFE   I have business, sir, and must mind it; your business is pleasure; therefore you and I must go different ways.

HORNER   Well, you may go on, but this pretty young gentleman—

Takes hold of MRS. PINCHWIFE.

HARCOURT   The lady—

DORILANT   And the maid—

HORNER   Shall stay with us, for I suppose their business is the same with ours, pleasure.

PINCHWIFE [*aside*]   'Sdeath, he know her, she carries it so sillily! Yet if he does not, I should be more silly to discover it first.

ALITHEA   Pray, let us go, sir.

PINCHWIFE   Come, come—

HORNER [*to* MRS. PINCHWIFE]   Had you not rather stay with us? — Prithee, Pinchwife, who is this pretty young gentleman?

PINCHWIFE   One to whom I'm a guardian. —[*Aside.*] I wish I could keep her out of your hands.

HORNER   Who is he? I never saw anything so pretty in all my life.

PINCHWIFE   Pshaw! do not look upon him so much; he's a poor bashful youth, you'll put him out of countenance. —Come away, brother.

Offers to take her away.

HORNER   Oh, your brother.

PINCHWIFE   Yes, my wife's brother. —Come, come, she'll stay supper for us.

HORNER   I thought so, for he is very like her I saw you at the play with, whom I told you I was in love with.

MRS. PINCHWIFE   [*aside*]   O jeminy! Is this he that was in love with me? I am glad on it, I vow, for he's a curious² fine gentleman, and I love him already too. —[*To* MR. PINCHWIFE.] Is this he, bud?

PINCHWIFE   [*to his wife*]   Come away, come away.

HORNER   Why, what haste are you in? Why won't you let me talk with him?

PINCHWIFE   Because you'll debauch him; he's yet young and innocent, and I would not have him debauched for anything in the world. — [*Aside.*] How she gazes on him! the devil!

HORNER   Harcourt, Dorilant, look you here; this is the likeness of that dowdy he told us of, his wife. Did you ever see a lovelier creature? The rogue has reason to be jealous of his wife, since she is like him, for she would make all that see her in love with her.

HARCOURT   And as I remember now, she is as like him here as can be.

DORILANT   She is indeed very pretty, if she be like him.

HORNER   Very pretty? A very pretty commendation! —She is a glorious creature, beautiful beyond all things I ever beheld.

PINCHWIFE   So, so.

HARCOURT   More beautiful than a poet's first mistress of imagination.

HORNER   Or another man's last mistress of flesh and blood.

MRS. PINCHWIFE   Nay, now you jeer, sir; pray don't jeer me.

PINCHWIFE   Come, come. —[*Aside.*] By heavens, she'll discover herself!

HORNER   I speak of your sister, sir.

PINCHWIFE   Ay, but saying she was handsome, if like him, made him blush. —[*Aside.*] I am upon a rack!

HORNER   Methinks he is so handsome he should not be a man.

PINCHWIFE   [*aside*]   Oh, there 'tis out! He has discovered her! I am not able to suffer any longer. —[*To his wife.*] Come, come away, I say.

HORNER   Nay, by your leave, sir, he shall not go yet. —[*To them.*] Harcourt, Dorilant, let us torment this jealous rogue a little.

HARCOURT, DORILANT   How?

HORNER   I'll show you.

PINCHWIFE   Come, pray let him go, I cannot stay fooling any longer; I tell you his sister stays supper for us.

2. Exquisite.

HORNER Does she? Come then, we'll all go sup with her and thee.

PINCHWIFE No, now I think on't, having stayed so long for us, I warrant she's gone to bed. —[*Aside.*] I wish she and I were well out of their hands. —Come, I must rise early tomorrow, come.

HORNER Well, then, if she be gone to bed, I wish her and you a good night. But pray, young gentlemen, present my humble service to her.

MRS. PINCHWIFE Thank you heartily, sir.

PINCHWIFE [*aside*] 'Sdeath! she will discover herself yet in spite of me. —He is something more civil to you, for your kindness to his sister, than I am, it seems.

HORNER Tell her, dear sweet little gentleman, for all your brother there, that you revived the love I had for her at first sight in the playhouse.

MRS. PINCHWIFE But did you love her indeed, and indeed?

PINCHWIFE [*aside*] So, so. —Away, I say.

HORNER Nay, stay. Yes, indeed, and indeed, pray do you tell her so, and give her this kiss from me.

Kisses her.

PINCHWIFE [*aside*] O heavens! what do I suffer! Now 'tis too plain he knows her, and yet—

HORNER And this, and this—

Kisses her again.

MRS. PINCHWIFE What do you kiss me for? I am no woman.

PINCHWIFE [*aside*] So—there, 'tis out. —Come, I cannot, nor will stay any longer.

HORNER Nay, they shall send your lady a kiss too. Here, Harcourt, Dorilant, will you not?

They kiss her.

PINCHWIFE [*aside*] How! do I suffer this? Was I not accusing another just now for this rascally patience, in permitting his wife to be kissed before his face? Ten thousand ulcers gnaw away their lips! —Come, come.

HORNER Good night, dear little gentleman; madam, good night; farewell, Pinchwife. —[*Apart to* HARCOURT *and* DORILANT.] Did not I tell you I would raise his jealous gall?

Exeunt HORNER, HARCOURT, *and* DORILANT.

PINCHWIFE So, they are gone at last; stay, let me see first if the coach be at this door.

Exit.

HORNER, HARCOURT, DORILANT *return.*

HORNER What, not gone yet? Will you be sure to do as I desired you, sweet sir?

MRS. PINCHWIFE   Sweet sir, but what will you give me then?

HORNER   Anything. Come away into the next walk.

Exit HORNER, *haling away* MRS. PINCHWIFE.

ALITHEA   Hold, hold! What d'ye do?

LUCY   Stay, stay, hold—

HARCOURT   Hold, madam, hold! let him present him, he'll come presently; nay, I will never let you go till you answer my question.

LUCY   For God's sake, sir, I must follow 'em.

DORILANT   No, I have something to present you with too; you shan't follow them.

ALITHEA, LUCY *struggling with* HARCOURT *and* DORILANT. PINCHWIFE *returns*.

PINCHWIFE   Where?—how?—what's become of—gone!—whither?

LUCY   He's only gone with the gentleman, who will give him something, an't please your worship.

PINCHWIFE   Something—give him something, with a pox!—where are they?

ALITHEA   In the next walk only, brother.

PINCHWIFE   Only, only! Where, where?

Exit PINCHWIFE, *and returns presently, then goes out again.*

HARCOURT   What's the matter with him? Why so much concerned? But dearest madam—

ALITHEA   Pray let me go, sir; I have said and suffered enough already.

HARCOURT   Then you will not look upon, nor pity, my sufferings?

ALITHEA   To look upon 'em, when I cannot help 'em, were cruelty, not pity; therefore I will never see you more.

HARCOURT   Let me then, madam, have my privilege of a banished lover, complaining or railing, and giving you but a farewell reason why, if you cannot condescend to marry me, you should not take that wretch, my rival.

ALITHEA   He only, not you, since my honor is engaged so far to him, can give me a reason why I should not marry him; but if he be true, and what I think him to me, I must be so to him. Your servant, sir.

HARCOURT   Have women only constancy when 'tis a vice, and, like fortune, only true to fools?

DORILANT   [*to* LUCY, *who struggles to get from him*]   Thou shalt not stir, thou robust creature; you see I can deal with you, therefore you should stay the rather, and be kind.

Enter PINCHWIFE.

PINCHWIFE   Gone, gone, not to be found! quite gone! Ten thousand plagues go with 'em! Which way went they?

ALITHEA   But into t'other walk, brother.

LUCY   Their business will be done presently sure, an't please your worship; it can't be long in doing, I'm sure on't.

ALITHEA   Are they not there?

PINCHWIFE   No; you know where they are, you infamous wretch, eternal shame of your family, which you do not dishonor enough yourself, you think, but you must help her to do it too, thou legion of bawds!

ALITHEA   Good brother—

PINCHWIFE   Damned, damned sister!

ALITHEA   Look you here, she's coming.

> *Enter* MRS. PINCHWIFE *in man's clothes, running, with her hat under her arm, full of oranges and dried fruit;* HORNER *following.*

MRS. PINCHWIFE   O dear bud, look you here what I have got, see!

PINCHWIFE   [*aside, rubbing his forehead*]   And what I have got here too, which you can't see.

MRS. PINCHWIFE   The fine gentleman has given me better things yet.

PINCHWIFE   Has he so? —[*Aside*].   Out of breath and colored! I must hold yet.

HORNER   I have only given your little brother an orange, sir.

PINCHWIFE   [*to* Horner]   Thank you, sir. —[*Aside.*]   You have only squeezed my orange, I suppose, and given it me again; yet I must have a city patience.[3]—[*To his wife.*]   Come, come away.

MRS. PINCHWIFE   Stay, till I have put up my fine things, bud.

> *Enter* SIR JASPER FIDGET.

SIR JASPER FIDGET   Master Horner, come, come, the ladies stay for you; your mistress, my wife, wonders you make not more haste to her.

HORNER   I have stayed this half hour for you here, and 'tis your fault I am not now with your wife.

SIR JASPER FIDGET   But pray, don't let her know so much; the truth on't is, I was advancing a certain project to his Majesty about—I'll tell you.

HORNER   No, let's go, and hear it at your house. —Good night, sweet little gentleman. One kiss more; you'll remember me now, I hope.

> *Kisses her.*

DORILANT   What, Sir Jasper, will you separate friends? He promised to sup with us; and if you take him to your house, you'll be in danger of our company too.

SIR JASPER FIDGET   Alas, gentlemen, my house is not fit for you; there are none but civil women there, which are not for your turn. He, you know, can bear with the society of civil women now, ha, ha, ha! Besides, he's one of my family—he's—he, he, he!

---

3. Patience of an outclassed cuckold.

DORILANT What is he?

SIR JASPER FIDGET Faith, my eunuch, since you'll have it, he, he, he!

Exeunt SIR JASPER FIDGET, *and* HORNER.

DORILANT I rather wish thou wert his, or my cuckold. Harcourt, what a good cuckold is lost there for want of a man to make him one! Thee and I cannot have Horner's privilege, who can make use of it.

HARCOURT Ay, to poor Horner 'tis like coming to an estate at three-score, when a man can't be the better for't.

PINCHWIFE Come.

MRS. PINCHWIFE Presently, bud.

DORILANT Come, let us go too. —[*To* ALITHEA.] Madam, your servant.—[*To* LUCY.] Good night, strapper.

HARCOURT Madam, though you will not let me have a good day or night, I wish you one; but dare not name the other half of my wish.

ALITHEA Good night, sir, forever.

MRS. PINCHWIFE I don't know where to put this here, dear bud, you shall eat it; nay, you shall have part of the fine gentleman's good things, or treat as you call it, when we come home.

PINCHWIFE Indeed, I deserve it, since I furnished the best part of it.

Strikes away the orange.

The gallant treats, presents, and gives the ball;
But 'tis the absent cuckold pays for all.

[*Exeunt.*]

Act IV. Scene i.

In PINCHWIFE's *house in the morning.*
LUCY, ALITHEA *dressed in new clothes.*

LUCY Well—madam, now have I dressed you, and set you out with so many ornaments, and spent upon you ounces of essence and pulvilio[4]; and all this for no other purpose but as people adorn and perfume a corpse for a stinking secondhand grave; such or as bad I think Master Sparkish's bed.

ALITHEA Hold your peace.

LUCY Nay, madam, I will ask you the reason why you would banish poor Master Harcourt forever from your sight. How could you be so hardhearted?

ALITHEA 'Twas because I was not hardhearted.

LUCY No, no; 'twas stark love and kindness, I warrant.

ALITHEA It was so; I would see him no more because I love him.

LUCY Hey-day, a very pretty reason!

ALITHEA You do not understand me.

---

4. Perfumed powder.

LUCY   I wish you may yourself.

ALITHEA   I was engaged to marry, you see, another man, whom my justice will not suffer me to deceive or injure.

LUCY   Can there be a greater cheat or wrong done to a man than to give him your person without your heart? I should make a conscience of it.

ALITHEA   I'll retrieve it for him after I am married a while.

LUCY   The woman that marries to love better will be as much mistaken as the wencher that marries to live better. No, madam, marrying to increase love is like gaming to become rich; alas, you only lose what little stock you had before.

ALITHEA   I find by your rhetoric you have been bribed to betray me.

LUCY   Only by his merit, that has bribed your heart, you see, against your word and rigid honor. But what a devil is this honor! 'Tis sure a disease in the head, like the megrim, or falling sickness, that always hurries people away to do themselves mischief. Men lose their lives by it; women what's dearer to 'em, their love, the life of life.

ALITHEA   Come, pray talk you no more of honor, nor Master Harcourt. I wish the other would come to secure my fidelity to him and his right in me.

LUCY   You will marry him then?

ALITHEA   Certainly; I have given him already my word, and will my hand too, to make it good when he comes.

LUCY   Well, I wish I may never stick pin more if he be not an arrant natural[5] to t'other fine gentleman.

ALITHEA   I own he wants the wit of Harcourt, which I will dispense withal for another want he has, which is want of jealousy, which men of wit seldom want.

LUCY   Lord, madam, what should you do with a fool to your husband? You intend to be honest, don't you? Then that husbandly virtue, credulity, is thrown away upon you.

ALITHEA   He only that could suspect my virtue should have cause to do it; 'tis Sparkish's confidence in my truth that obliges me to be so faithful to him.

LUCY   You are not sure his opinion may last.

ALITHEA   I am satisfied 'tis impossible for him to be jealous after the proofs I have had of him. Jealousy in a husband—Heaven defend me from it! It begets a thousand plagues to a poor woman, the loss of her honor, her quiet, and her—

LUCY   And her pleasure.

ALITHEA   What d'ye mean, impertinent?

LUCY   Liberty is a great pleasure, madam.

ALITHEA   I say, loss of her honor, her quiet, nay, her life sometimes; and what's as bad almost, the loss of this town; that is, she is sent into the country, which is the last ill usage of a husband to a wife, I think.

5. Simpleton.

LUCY [*aside*]   Oh, does the wind lie there? —Then, of necessity, madam, you think a man must carry his wife into the country, if he be wise. The country is as terrible, I find, to our young English ladies as a monastery to those abroad; and on my virginity, I think they would rather marry a London jailer than a high sheriff of a county, since neither can stir from his employment. Formerly women of wit married fools for a great estate, a fine seat, or the like; but now 'tis for a pretty seat only in Lincoln's Inn Fields, St. James's Fields, or the Pall Mall.[6]

Enter to them SPARKISH, *and* HARCOURT *dressed like a parson.*

SPARKISH   Madam, your humble servant, a happy day to you, and to us all.

HARCOURT   Amen.

ALITHEA   Who have we here?

SPARKISH   My chaplain, faith. O madam, poor Harcourt remembers his humble service to you; and in obedience to your last commands, refrains coming into your sight.

ALITHEA   Is not that he?

SPARKISH   No, fie, no; but to show that he ne'er intended to hinder our match, has sent his brother here to join our hands. When I get me a wife, I must get her a chaplain, according to the custom; this is his brother, and my chaplain.

ALITHEA   His brother?

LUCY [*aside*]   And your chaplain, to preach in your pulpit then.

ALITHEA   His brother!

SPARKISH   Nay, I knew you would not believe it. —I told you, sir, she would take you for your brother Frank.

ALITHEA   Believe it!

LUCY [*aside*]   His brother! ha, ha, he! He has a trick left still, it seems.

SPARKISH   Come, my dearest, pray let us go to church before the canonical hour[7] is past.

ALITHEA   For shame, you are abused still.

SPARKISH   By the world, 'tis strange now you are so incredulous.

ALITHEA   'Tis strange you are so credulous.

SPARKISH   Dearest of my life, hear me. I tell you this is Ned Harcourt of Cambridge, by the world; you see he has a sneaking college look. 'Tis true he's something like his brother Frank, and they differ from each other no more than in their age, for they were twins.

LUCY   Ha, ha, he!

ALITHEA   Your servant, sir; I cannot be so deceived, though you are. But come, let's hear, how do you know what you affirm so confidently?

SPARKISH   Why, I'll tell you all. Frank Harcourt coming to me this

6. Fashionable districts in London.
7. Time proper for marriage ceremonies.

morning, to wish me joy and present his service to you, I asked him if he could help me to a parson; whereupon he told me he had a brother in town who was in orders, and he went straight away and sent him you see there to me.

ALITHEA   Yes, Frank goes and puts on a black coat, then tells you he is Ned; that's all you have for't.

SPARKISH   Pshaw, pshaw! I tell you by the same token, the midwife put her garter about Frank's neck to know 'em asunder, they were so like.

ALITHEA   Frank tells you this too.

SPARKISH   Ay, and Ned there too; nay, they are both in a story.

ALITHEA   So, so; very foolish!

SPARKISH   Lord, if you won't believe one, you had best try him by your chambermaid there; for chambermaids must needs know chaplains from other men, they are so used to 'em.

LUCY   Let's see; nay, I'll be sworn he has the canonical smirk, and the filthy, clammy palm of a chaplain.

ALITHEA   Well, most reverend doctor, pray let us make an end of this fooling.

HARCOURT   With all my soul, divine, heavenly creature, when you please.

ALITHEA   He speaks like a chaplain indeed.

SPARKISH   Why, was there not "soul," "divine," "heavenly," in what he said?

ALITHEA   Once more, most impertinent black coat, cease your persecution, and let us have a conclusion of this ridiculous love.

HARCOURT [*aside*]   I had forgot; I must suit my style to my coat, or I wear it in vain.

ALITHEA   I have no more patience left; let us make once an end of this troublesome love, I say.

HARCOURT   So be it, seraphic lady, when your honor shall think it meet and convenient so to do.

SPARKISH   Gad, I'm sure none but a chaplain could speak so, I think.

ALITHEA   Let me tell you, sir, this dull trick will not serve your turn; though you delay our marriage, you shall not hinder it.

HARCOURT   Far be it from me, munificent patroness, to delay your marriage. I desire nothing more than to marry you presently, which I might do, if you yourself would; for my noble, good-natured, and thrice generous patron here would not hinder it.

SPARKISH   No, poor man, not I, faith.

HARCOURT   And now, madam, let me tell you plainly, nobody else shall marry you; by heavens, I'll die first, for I'm sure I should die after it.[8]

LUCY [*aside*]   How his love has made him forget his function, as I have seen it in real parsons!

ALITHEA   That was spoken like a chaplain too! Now you understand him, I hope.

---

8. A pun. "To die" refers to orgasm.

SPARKISH Poor man, he takes it heinously to be refused; I can't blame him, 'tis putting an indignity upon him not to be suffered. But you'll pardon me, madam, it shan't be, he shall marry us; come away, pray, madam.

LUCY Ha, ha, he! More ado! 'Tis late.

ALITHEA Invincible stupidity! I tell you he would marry me as your rival, not as your chaplain.

SPARKISH Come, come, madam.

Pulling her away.

LUCY I pray, madam, do not refuse this reverend divine the honor and satisfaction of marrying you; for I dare say he has set his heart upon't, good doctor.

ALITHEA What can you hope, or design by this?

HARCOURT [*aside*] I could answer her, a reprieve for a day only often revokes a hasty doom; at worst, if she will not take mercy on me and let me marry her, I have at least the lover's second pleasure, hindering my rival's enjoyment, though but for a time.

SPARKISH Come, madam, 'tis e'en twelve o'clock, and my mother charged me never to be married out of the canonical hours. Come, come; Lord, here's such a deal of modesty, I warrant, the first day.

LUCY Yes, an't please your worship, married women show all their modesty the first day, because married men show all their love the first day.

Exeunt SPARKISH, ALITHEA, HARCOURT, *and* LUCY.

Act IV. Scene ii.

The scene changes to a bedchamber, where appear PINCHWIFE, MRS. PINCHWIFE.

PINCHWIFE Come, tell me, I say.

MRS. PINCHWIFE Lord! han't I told it an hundred times over?

PINCHWIFE [*aside*] I would try if, in the repetition of the ungrateful tale, I could find her altering it in the least circumstance; for if her story be false, she is so too. —Come, how was't, baggage?

MRS. PINCHWIFE Lord, what pleasure you take to hear it, sure!

PINCHWIFE No, you take more in telling it, I find; but speak, how was't?

MRS. PINCHWIFE He carried me up into the house next to the Exchange.

PINCHWIFE So; and you two were only in the room.

MRS. PINCHWIFE Yes, for he sent away a youth that was there, for some dried fruit and China oranges.

PINCHWIFE Did he so? Damn him for it—and for—

MRS. PINCHWIFE But presently came up the gentlewoman of the house.

PINCHWIFE   Oh, 'twas well she did; but what did he do whilst the fruit
came?

MRS. PINCHWIFE   He kissed me an hundred times, and told me he fancied he kissed my fine sister, meaning me, you know, whom he said
he loved with all his soul, and bid me be sure to tell her so, and to
desire her to be at her window by eleven of the clock this morning,
and he would walk under it at that time.

PINCHWIFE [*aside*]   And he was as good as his word, very punctual; a
pox reward him for't.

MRS. PINCHWIFE   Well, and he said if you were not within, he would
come up to her, meaning me, you know, bud, still.

PINCHWIFE [*aside*]   So—he knew her certainly; but for this confession,
I am obliged to her simplicity. —But what, you stood very still when
he kissed you?

MRS. PINCHWIFE   Yes, I warrant you; would you have had me discovered myself?

PINCHWIFE   But you told me he did some beastliness to you, as you
called it; what was't?

MRS. PINCHWIFE   Why, he put—

PINCHWIFE   What?

MRS. PINCHWIFE   Why, he put the tip of his tongue between my lips,
and so mousled me—and I said, I'd bite it.

PINCHWIFE   An eternal canker seize it, for a dog!

MRS. PINCHWIFE   Nay, you need not be so angry with him neither, for
to say truth, he has the sweetest breath I ever knew.

PINCHWIFE   The devil!—you were satisfied with it then, and would do
it again.

MRS. PINCHWIFE   Not unless he should force me.

PINCHWIFE   Force you, changeling! I tell you no woman can be forced.

MRS. PINCHWIFE   Yes, but she may sure by such as he, for he's a proper,
goodly strong man; 'tis hard, let me tell you, to resist him.

PINCHWIFE [*aside*]   So, 'tis plain she loves him, yet she has not love
enough to make her conceal it from me; but the sight of him will
increase her aversion for me and love for him, and that love instruct
her how to deceive me and satisfy him, all idiot as she is. Love! 'Twas
he gave women first their craft, their art of deluding; out of nature's
hands they came plain, open, silly, and fit for slaves, as she and
Heaven intended 'em; but damned love—well—I must strangle that
little monster whilst I can deal with him. —Go fetch pen, ink, and
paper out of the next room.

MRS. PINCHWIFE   Yes, bud.

Exit MRS. PINCHWIFE.

PINCHWIFE [*aside*]   Why should women have more invention in love
than men? It can only be because they have more desires, more soliciting passions, more lust, and more of the devil.

MRS. PINCHWIFE *returns.*

Come, minx, sit down and write.

MRS. PINCHWIFE   Ay, dear bud, but I can't do't very well.

PINCHWIFE   I wish you could not at all.

MRS. PINCHWIFE   But what should I write for?

PINCHWIFE   I'll have you write a letter to your lover.

MRS. PINCHWIFE   O Lord, to the fine gentleman a letter!

PINCHWIFE   Yes, to the fine gentleman.

MRS. PINCHWIFE   Lord, you do but jeer; sure you jest.

PINCHWIFE   I am not so merry; come, write as I bid you.

MRS. PINCHWIFE   What, do you think I am a fool?

PINCHWIFE [*aside*]   She's afraid I would not dictate any love to him, therefore she's unwilling. —But you had best begin.

MRS. PINCHWIFE   Indeed, and indeed, but I won't, so I won't!

PINCHWIFE   Why?

MRS. PINCHWIFE   Because he's in town; you may send for him if you will.

PINCHWIFE   Very well, you would have him brought to you; is it come to this? I say, take the pen and write, or you'll provoke me.

MRS. PINCHWIFE   Lord, what d'ye make a fool of me for? Don't I know that letters are never writ but from the country to London, and from London into the country? Now he's in town, and I am in town too; therefore I can't write to him, you know.

PINCHWIFE [*aside*]   So, I am glad it is no worse; she is innocent enough yet. —Yes, you may, when your husband bids you, write letters to people that are in town.

MRS. PINCHWIFE   Oh, may I so? Then I'm satisfied.

PINCHWIFE   Come, begin. —[*Dictates.*] "Sir"—

MRS. PINCHWIFE   Shan't I say, "Dear Sir"? You know one says always something more than bare "Sir."

PINCHWIFE   Write as I bid you, or I will write "whore" with this penknife in your face.

MRS. PINCHWIFE   Nay, good bud—[*She writes.*] "Sir"—

PINCHWIFE   "Though I suffered last night your nauseous, loathed kisses and embraces"—Write.

MRS. PINCHWIFE   Nay, why should I say so? You know I told you he had a sweet breath.

PINCHWIFE   Write!

MRS. PINCHWIFE   Let me but put out "loathed."

PINCHWIFE   Write, I say!

MRS. PINCHWIFE   Well then.

Writes.

PINCHWIFE   Let's see, what have you writ?—[*Takes the paper, and reads.*] "Though I suffered last night your kisses and embraces"— Thou impudent creature! Where is "nauseous" and "loathed"?

MRS. PINCHWIFE   I can't abide to write such filthy words.

PINCHWIFE   Once more write as I'd have you, and question it not, or I will spoil thy writing with this. [*Holds up the penknife.*] I will stab out those eyes that cause my mischief.

MRS. PINCHWIFE   O Lord, I will!

PINCHWIFE   So—so—let's see now! —[*Reads.*] "Though I suffered last night your nauseous, loathed kisses and embraces" —go on—"Yet I would not have you presume that you shall ever repeat them."—So.

She writes.

MRS. PINCHWIFE   I have writ it.

PINCHWIFE   On then. —"I then concealed myself from your knowledge, to avoid your insolencies"—

She writes.

MRS. PINCHWIFE   So—

PINCHWIFE   "The same reason, now I am out of your hands"—

She writes.

MRS. PINCHWIFE   So—

PINCHWIFE   "Makes me own to you my unfortunate, though innocent frolic, of being in man's clothes"—

She writes.

MRS. PINCHWIFE   So—

PINCHWIFE   "That you may forevermore cease to pursue her, who hates and detests you"—

She writes on.

MRS. PINCHWIFE   So-h—

Sighs.

PINCHWIFE   What, do you sigh? —"detests you—as much as she loves her husband and her honor."

MRS. PINCHWIFE   I vow, husband, he'll ne'er believe I should write such a letter.

PINCHWIFE   What, he'd expect a kinder from you? Come, now your name only.

MRS. PINCHWIFE   What, shan't I say, "Your most faithful, humble servant till death"?

PINCHWIFE   No, tormenting fiend! —[*Aside.*] Her style, I find, would be very soft. —Come, wrap it up now, whilst I go fetch wax and a candle; and write on the backside, "For Mr. Horner."

Exit PINCHWIFE.

MRS. PINCHWIFE   "For Mr. Horner." —So, I am glad he has told me his name. Dear Mr. Horner! But why should I send thee such a letter that will vex thee, and make thee angry with me?—Well, I will not send it—Ay, but then my husband will kill me—for I see plainly he won't let me love Mr. Horner—but what care I for my husband? —I won't, so I won't send poor Mr. Horner such a letter—But then my husband—But oh, what if I writ at bottom, my husband made me write it?—Ay, but then my husband would see't—Can one have no shift? Ah, a London woman would have had a hundred presently. Stay—what if I should write a letter, and wrap it up like this, and write upon't too? Ay, but then my husband would see't—I don't know what to do—But yet y'vads[9] I'll try, so I will—for I will not send this letter to poor Mr. Horner, come what will on't.

She writes, and repeats what she hath writ.

"Dear, sweet Mr. Horner"—so—"my husband would have me send you a base, rude, unmannerly letter—but I won't"—so—"and would have me forbid you loving me—but I won't"—so—"and would have me say to you, I hate you, poor Mr. Horner—but I won't tell a lie for him"—there—"for I'm sure if you and I were in the country at cards together"—so—"I could not help treading on your toe under the table"—so—"or rubbing knees with you, and staring in your face till you saw me"—very well—"and then looking down, and blushing for an hour together"—so—"but I must make haste before my husband come; and now he has taught me to write letters, you shall have longer ones from me, who am, dear, dear, poor, dear Mr. Horner, your most humble friend, and servant to command till death, Margery Pinchwife."

Stay, I must give him a hint at bottom—so—now wrap it up just like t'other—so—now write, "For Mr. Horner"—But, oh now, what shall I do with it? for here comes my husband.

Enter PINCHWIFE.

PINCHWIFE [*aside*]   I have been detained by a sparkish coxcomb, who pretended a visit to me; but I fear 'twas to my wife.—What, have you done?

MRS. PINCHWIFE   Ay, ay, bud, just now.

PINCHWIFE   Let's see't; what d'ye tremble for? What, you would not have it go?

MRS. PINCHWIFE   Here. —[*Aside.*] No, I must not give him that; so I had been served if I had given him this.

PINCHWIFE [*he opens, and reads the first letter*]   Come, where's the wax and seal?

MRS. PINCHWIFE [*aside*]   Lord, what shall I do now? Nay, then, I have it. —Pray let me see't. Lord, you think me so arrant a fool I cannot seal a letter; I will do't, so I will.

9. In faith.

Snatches the letter from him, changes it for the other, seals it, and delivers it to him.

PINCHWIFE   Nay, I believe you will learn that, and other things too, which I would not have you.

MRS. PINCHWIFE   So, han't I done it curiously?[1] —[*Aside.*] I think I have; there's my letter going to Mr. Horner, since he'll needs have me send letters to folks.

PINCHWIFE   'Tis very well; but I warrant you would not have it go now?

MRS. PINCHWIFE   Yes, indeed, but I would, bud, now.

PINCHWIFE   Well, you are a good girl then. Come, let me lock you up in your chamber till I come back; and be sure you come not within three strides of the window when I am gone, for I have a spy in the street.

Exit MRS. PINCHWIFE.

[PINCHWIFE *locks the door.*] At least, 'tis fit she think so. If we do not cheat women, they'll cheat us; and fraud may be justly used with secret enemies, of which a wife is the most dangerous; and he that has a handsome one to keep, and a frontier town, must provide against treachery rather than open force. Now I have secured all within, I'll deal with the foe without with false intelligence.

Holds up the letter.

Exit PINCHWIFE.

Act IV. Scene iii.

The scene changes to HORNER's *lodging.* QUACK *and* HORNER.

QUACK   Well, sir, how fadges[2] the new design? Have you not the luck of all your brother projectors, to deceive only yourself at last?

HORNER   No, good domine[3] doctor, I deceive you, it seems, and others too; for the grave matrons and old, rigid husbands think me as unfit for love as they are; but their wives, sisters, and daughters know some of 'em better things already.

QUACK   Already!

HORNER   Already, I say. Last night I was drunk with half a dozen of your civil persons, as you call 'em, and people of honor, and so was made free of their society and dressing rooms forever hereafter; and am already come to the privileges of sleeping upon their pallets, warming smocks, tying shoes and garters, and the like, doctor, already, already, doctor.

QUACK   You have made use of your time, sir.

1. Cleverly.
2. Succeeds.
3. Master.

HORNER   I tell thee, I am now no more interruption to 'em when they
sing, or talk, bawdy than a little squab[4] French page who speaks no
English.

QUACK   But do civil persons and women of honor drink, and sing
bawdy songs?

HORNER   Oh, amongst friends, amongst friends. For your bigots in
honor are just like those in religion; they fear the eye of the world
more than the eye of Heaven, and think there is no virtue but railing
at vice, and no sin but giving scandal. They rail at a poor, little, kept
player, and keep themselves some young, modest pulpit comedian to
be privy to their sins in their closets,[5] not to tell 'em of them in their
chapels.

QUACK   Nay, the truth on't is, priests amongst the women now have
quite got the better of us lay confessors, physicians.

HORNER   And they are rather their patients, but—

Enter MY LADY FIDGET, *looking about her.*

Now we talk of women of honor, here comes one. Step behind the
screen there, and but observe if I have not particular privileges with
the women of reputation already, doctor, already.

QUACK *steps behind screen.*

LADY FIDGET   Well, Horner, am not I a woman of honor? You see I'm
as good as my word.

HORNER   And you shall see, madam, I'll not be behindhand with you
in honor; and I'll be as good as my word too, if you please but to
withdraw into the next room.

LADY FIDGET   But first, my dear sir, you must promise to have a care of
my dear honor.

HORNER   If you talk a word of your honor, you'll make me incapable
to wrong it. To talk of honor in the mysteries of love is like talking of
Heaven or the Deity in an operation of witchcraft, just when you are
employing the devil; it makes the charm impotent.

LADY FIDGET   Nay, fie! let us not be smutty. But you talk of mysteries
and bewitching to me; I don't understand you.

HORNER   I tell you, madam, the word "money" in a mistress's mouth,
at such a nick of time, is not a more disheartening sound to a younger
brother than that of "honor" to an eager lover like myself.

LADY FIDGET   But you can't blame a lady of my reputation to be chary.

HORNER   Chary! I have been chary of it already, by the report I have
caused of myself.

LADY FIDGET   Ay, but if you should ever let other women know that
dear secret, it would come out. Nay, you must have a great care of
your conduct; for my acquaintance are so censorious (oh, 'tis a

4. Dumpy.
5. Private rooms.

wicked, censorious world, Mr. Horner!), I say, are so censorious and
detracting that perhaps they'll talk, to the prejudice of my honor,
though you should not let them know the dear secret.

HORNER   Nay, madam, rather than they shall prejudice your honor, I'll
prejudice theirs; and to serve you, I'll lie with 'em all, make the secret
their own, and then they'll keep it. I am a Machiavel[6] in love,
madam.

LADY FIDGET   Oh, no, sir, not that way.

HORNER   Nay, the devil take me if censorious women are to be silenced
any other way.

LADY FIDGET   A secret is better kept, I hope, by a single person than a
multitude; therefore pray do not trust anybody else with it, dear, dear
Mr. Horner.

> *Embracing him.*
> *Enter* SIR JASPER FIDGET.

SIR JASPER FIDGET   How now!

LADY FIDGET [*aside*]   Oh, my husband!—prevented—and what's
almost as bad, found with my arms about another man—that will
appear too much—what shall I say?
    Sir Jasper, come hither. I am trying if Mr. Horner were ticklish,
and he's as ticklish as can be; I love to torment the confounded toad;
let you and I tickle him.

SIR JASPER FIDGET   No, your ladyship will tickle him better without
me, I suppose. But is this your buying china? I thought you had been
at the china house.

HORNER [*aside*]   China house! That's my cue, I must take it.—A pox!
can't you keep your impertinent wives at home? Some men are troubled with the husbands, but I with the wives. But I'd have you to
know, since I cannot be your journeyman by night, I will not be your
drudge by day, to squire your wife about and be your man of straw,
or scarecrow, only to pies and jays, that would be nibbling at your
forbidden fruit; I shall be shortly the hackney[7] gentleman-usher of
the town.

SIR JASPER FIDGET [*aside*]   He, he, he! Poor fellow, he's in the right
on't, faith; to squire women about for other folks is as ungrateful an
employment as to tell money for other folks.—He, he, he! Ben't
angry, Horner.

LADY FIDGET   No, 'tis I have more reason to be angry, who am left by
you to go abroad indecently alone; or, what is more indecent to pin
myself upon such ill-bred people of your acquaintance as this is.

SIR JASPER FIDGET   Nay, prithee what has he done?

LADY FIDGET   Nay, he has done nothing.

SIR JASPER FIDGET   But what d'ye take ill, if he has done nothing?

6. Shrewd plotter.
7. Hired.

LADY FIDGET   Ha, ha, ha! Faith, I can't but laugh, however; why, d'ye think the unmannerly toad would come down to me to the coach? I was fain to come up to fetch him, or go without him, which I was resolved not to do; for he knows china very well, and has himself very good, but will not let me see it lest I should beg some. But I will find it out, and have what I came for yet.

Exit LADY FIDGET, *and locks the door, followed by* HORNER *to the door.*

HORNER [*apart to* LADY FIDGET]   Lock the door, madam. — So, she has got into my chamber, and locked me out. Oh, the impertinency of womankind! Well, Sir Jasper, plain dealing is a jewel; if ever you suffer your wife to trouble me again here, she shall carry you home a pair of horns, by my Lord Mayor she shall; though I cannot furnish you myself, you are sure, yet I'll find a way.

SIR JASPER FIDGET [*aside*]   Ha, ha, he! At my first coming in and finding her arms about him, tickling him it seems, I was half jealous, but now I see my folly. — He, he, he! Poor Horner.

HORNER   Nay, though you laugh now, 'twill be my turn ere long. Oh, women, more impertinent, more cunning, and more mischievous than their monkeys, and to me almost as ugly! Now is she throwing my things about and rifling all I have, but I'll get in to her the back way, and so rifle her for it.

SIR JASPER FIDGET   Ha, ha, ha! Poor angry Horner.

HORNER   Stay here a little; I'll ferret her out to you presently, I warrant.

Exit HORNER *at t'other door.*

SIR JASPER FIDGET   Wife! My Lady Fidget! Wife! He is coming in to you the back way.

> SIR JASPER *calls through the door to his wife; she answers from within.*

LADY FIDGET   Let him come, and welcome, which way he will.

SIR JASPER FIDGET   He'll catch you, and use you roughly, and be too strong for you.

LADY FIDGET   Don't you trouble yourself, let him if he can.

QUACK [*behind*]   This indeed I could not have believed from him, nor any but my own eyes.

Enter MRS. SQUEAMISH.

MRS. SQUEAMISH   Where's this woman-hater, this toad, this ugly, greasy, dirty sloven?

SIR JASPER FIDGET [*aside*]   So, the women all will have him ugly; methinks he is a comely person, but his wants make his form contemptible to 'em; and 'tis e'en as my wife said yesterday, talking of him, that a proper handsome eunuch was as ridiculous a thing as a gigantic coward.

MRS. SQUEAMISH   Sir Jasper, your servant. Where is the odious beast?

SIR JASPER FIDGET   He's within in his chamber, with my wife; she's playing the wag with him.

MRS. SQUEAMISH   Is she so? And he's a clownish beast, he'll give her no quarter, he'll play the wag with her again, let me tell you. Come, let's go help her. — What, the door's locked?

SIR JASPER FIDGET   Ay, my wife locked it.

MRS. SQUEAMISH   Did she so? Let us break it open then.

SIR JASPER FIDGET   No, no, he'll do her no hurt.

MRS. SQUEAMISH   No. [*Aside.*] But is there no other way to get in to 'em? Whither goes this? I will disturb 'em.

> *Exit* MRS. SQUEAMISH *at another door.*

> *Enter* OLD LADY SQUEAMISH.

OLD LADY SQUEAMISH   Where is this harlotry, this impudent baggage, this rambling tomrig?[8] O Sir Jasper, I'm glad to see you here, did you not see my vile grandchild come in hither just now?

SIR JASPER FIDGET   Yes.

OLD LADY SQUEAMISH   Ay, but where is she then? where is she? Lord, Sir Jasper, I have e'en rattled myself to pieces in pursuit of her. But can you tell what she makes here? They say below, no woman lodges here.

SIR JASPER FIDGET   No.

OLD LADY SQUEAMISH   No! What does she here then? Say, if it be not a woman's lodging, what makes she here? But are you sure no woman lodges here?

SIR JASPER FIDGET   No, nor no man neither; this is Mr. Horner's lodging.

OLD LADY SQUEAMISH   Is it so, are you sure?

SIR JASPER FIDGET   Yes, yes.

OLD LADY SQUEAMISH   So; then there's no hurt in't, I hope. But where is he?

SIR JASPER FIDGET   He's in the next room with my wife.

OLD LADY SQUEAMISH   Nay, if you trust him with your wife, I may with my Biddy. They say he's a merry harmless man now, e'en as harmless a man as ever came out of Italy with a good voice,[9] and as pretty harmless company for a lady as a snake without his teeth.

SIR JASPER FIDGET   Ay, ay, poor man.

> *Enter* MRS. SQUEAMISH.

MRS. SQUEAMISH   I can't find 'em. — Oh, are you here, Grandmother? I followed, you must know, my Lady Fidget hither; 'tis the prettiest lodging, and I have been staring on the prettiest pictures.

---

8. Tomboy or strumpet.
9. A castrated singer. Italian male sopranos and altos were popular in the period.

Enter LADY FIDGET *with a piece of china in her hand, and* HORNER *following.*

LADY FIDGET   And I have been toiling and moiling for the prettiest piece of china, my dear.

HORNER   Nay, she has been too hard for me, do what I could.

MRS. SQUEAMISH   O Lord, I'll have some china too. Good Mr. Horner, don't think to give other people china, and me none; come in with me too.

HORNER   Upon my honor, I have none left now.

MRS. SQUEAMISH   Nay, Nay, I have known you deny your china before now, but you shan't put me off so. Come.

HORNER   This lady had the last there.

LADY FIDGET   Yes, indeed, madam, to my certain knowledge he has no more left.

MRS. SQUEAMISH   Oh, but it may be he may have some you could not find.

LADY FIDGET   What, d'ye think if he had had any left, I would not have had it too? For we women of quality never think we have china enough.

HORNER   Do not take it ill, I cannot make china for you all, but I will have a rol-waggon[1] for you too, another time.

MRS. SQUEAMISH   Thank you, dear toad.

LADY FIDGET [*to* HORNER, *aside*]   What do you mean by that promise?

HORNER [*apart to* LADY FIDGET]   Alas, she has an innocent, literal understanding.

OLD LADY SQUEAMISH   Poor Mr. Horner! He has enough to do to please you all, I see.

HORNER   Ay, madam, you see how they use me.

OLD LADY SQUEAMISH   Poor gentleman, I pity you.

HORNER   I thank you, madam. I could never find pity but from such reverend ladies as you are; the young ones will never spare a man.

MRS. SQUEAMISH   Come, come, beast, and go dine with us, for we shall want a man at ombre after dinner.

HORNER   That's all their use of me, madam, you see.

MRS. SQUEAMISH   Come, sloven, I'll lead you, to be sure of you.

Pulls him by the cravat.

OLD LADY SQUEAMISH   Alas, poor man, how she tugs him! Kiss, kiss her; that's the way to make such nice women quiet.

HORNER   No, madam, that remedy is worse than the torment; they know I dare suffer anything rather than do it.

OLD LADY FIDGET   Prithee kiss her, and I'll give you her picture in little, that you admired so last night; prithee do.

HORNER   Well, nothing but that could bribe me; I love a woman only

1. China vase, cylindrically shaped.

in effigy and good painting, as much as I hate them. I'll do't, for I could adore the devil well painted.

Kisses MRS. SQUEAMISH.

MRS. SQUEAMISH   Foh, you filthy toad! Nay, now I've done jesting.
OLD LADY SQUEAMISH   Ha, ha, ha! I told you so.
MRS. SQUEAMISH   Foh! a kiss of his—
SIR JASPER FIDGET   Has no more hurt in't than one of my spaniel's.
MRS. SQUEAMISH   Nor no more good neither.
QUACK [*behind*]   I will now believe anything he tells me.

Enter MR. PINCHWIFE.

LADY FIDGET   O Lord, here's a man! Sir Jasper, my mask, my mask! I would not be seen here for the world.
SIR JASPER FIDGET   What, not when I am with you?
LADY FIDGET   No, no, my honor—let's be gone.
MRS. SQUEAMISH   Oh, grandmother, let us be gone; make haste, make haste, I know not how he may censure us.
LADY FIDGET   Be found in the lodging of anything like a man! Away!

Exeunt SIR JASPER, LADY FIDGET, OLD LADY SQUEAMISH,
MRS. SQUEAMISH.

QUACK [*behind*]   What's here? another cuckold? He looks like one, and none else sure have any business with him.
HORNER   Well, what brings my dear friend hither?
PINCHWIFE   Your impertinency.
HORNER   My impertinency! —Why, you gentlemen that have got handsome wives think you have a privilege of saying anything to your friends, and are as brutish as if you were our creditors.
PINCHWIFE   No, sir, I'll ne'er trust you any way.
HORNER   But why not, dear Jack? Why diffide[2] in me thou know'st so well?
PINCHWIFE   Because I do know you so well.
HORNER   Han't I been always thy friend, honest Jack, always ready to serve thee, in love or battle, before thou wert married, and am so still?
PINCHWIFE   I believe so; you would be my second now indeed.
HORNER   Well then, dear Jack, why so unkind, so grum, so strange to me? Come, prithee kiss me, dear rogue. Gad, I was always, I say, and am still as much thy servant as—
PINCHWIFE   As I am yours, sir. What, you send a kiss to my wife, is that it?
HORNER   So, there 'tis—a man can't show his friendship to a married man, but presently he talks of his wife to you. Prithee, let thy wife alone, and let thee and I be all one, as we were wont. What, thou art

2. Distrust.

as shy of my kindness as a Lombard Street alderman of a courtier's civility at Locket's.[3]

PINCHWIFE   But you are overkind to me, as kind as if I were your cuckold already; yet I must confess you ought to be kind and civil to me, since I am so kind, so civil to you, as to bring you this. Look you there sir.

Delivers him a letter.

HORNER   What is't?

PINCHWIFE   Only a love letter, sir.

HORNER   From whom?—how! this is from your wife!—hum—and hum—

PINCHWIFE   Even from my wife, sir. Am I not wondrous kind and civil to you now too? —[*Aside.*] But you'll not think her so.

HORNER [*aside*]   Ha! Is this a trick of his or hers?

PINCHWIFE   The gentleman's surprised, I find. What, you expected a kinder letter?

HORNER   No, faith, not I, how could I?

PINCHWIFE   Yes, yes, I'm sure you did; a man so well made as you are must needs be disappointed if the women declare not their passion at first sight or opportunity.

HORNER [*aside*]   But what should this mean? Stay, the postscript. — [*Reads aside.*] "Be sure you love me whatsoever my husband says to the contrary, and let him not see this, lest he should come home and pinch me, or kill my squirrel." —[*Aside.*] It seems he knows not what the letter contains.

PINCHWIFE   Come, ne'er wonder at it so much.

HORNER   Faith, I can't help it.

PINCHWIFE   Now, I think, I have deserved your infinite friendship and kindness, and have showed myself sufficiently an obliging kind friend and husband; am I not so, to bring a letter from my wife to her gallant?

HORNER   Ay, the devil take me, art thou the most obliging, kind friend and husband in the world, ha, ha!

PINCHWIFE   Well, you may be merry, sir; but in short I must tell you, sir, my honor will suffer no jesting.

HORNER   What dost thou mean?

PINCHWIFE   Does the letter want a comment? Then know, sir, though I have been so civil a husband as to bring you a letter from my wife, to let you kiss and court her to my face, I will not be a cuckold, sir, I will not.

HORNER   Thou art mad with jealousy. I never saw thy wife in my life but at the play yesterday, and I know not if it were she or no. I court her, kiss her!

3. Lombard Street was in the financial district; Locket's was a fashionable tavern. The sense is that Pinchwife suspects Horner's friendliness as a financier would suspect a courtier's politeness in seeking a loan.

PINCHWIFE   I will not be a cuckold, I say; there will be danger in making me a cuckold.

HORNER   Why, wert thou not well cured of thy last clap?

PINCHWIFE   I wear a sword.

HORNER   It should be taken from thee lest thou shouldst do thyself a mischief with it; thou art mad, man.

PINCHWIFE   As mad as I am, and as merry as you are, I must have more reason from you ere we part. I say again, though you kissed and courted last night my wife in man's clothes, as she confesses in her letter —

HORNER [*aside*]   Ha!

PINCHWIFE   Both she and I say, you must not design it again, for you have mistaken your woman, as you have done your man.

HORNER [*aside*]   Oh — I understand something now. — Was that thy wife? Why wouldst thou not tell me 'twas she? Faith, my freedom with her was your fault, not mine.

PINCHWIFE [*aside*]   Faith, so 'twas.

HORNER   Fie! I'd never do't to a woman before her husband's face, sure.

PINCHWIFE   But I had rather you should do't to my wife before my face than behind my back, and that you shall never do.

HORNER   No — you will hinder me.

PINCHWIFE   If I would not hinder you, you see by her letter, she would.

HORNER   Well, I must e'en acquiesce then, and be contented with what she writes.

PINCHWIFE   I'll assure you 'twas voluntarily writ; I had no hand in't, you may believe me.

HORNER   I do believe thee, faith.

PINCHWIFE   And believe her too, for she's an innocent creature, has no dissembling in her; and so fare you well, sir.

HORNER   Pray, however, present my humble service to her, and tell her I will obey her letter to a tittle, and fulfill her desires, be what they will, or with what difficulty soever I do't, and you shall be no more jealous of me, I warrant her and you.

PINCHWIFE   Well, then, fare you well, and play with any man's honor but mine, kiss any man's wife but mine, and welcome.

Exit MR. PINCHWIFE.

HORNER   Ha, ha, ha! doctor.

QUACK   It seems he has not heard the report of you, or does not believe it.

HORNER   Ha, ha! Now, doctor, what think you?

QUACK   Pray let's see the letter — hum — [*Reads the letter.*] "for — dear — love you" —

HORNER   I wonder how she could contrive it! What say's thou to't? 'Tis an original.

QUACK   So are your cuckolds, too, originals, for they are like no other common cuckolds, and I will henceforth believe it not impossible for you to cuckold the Grand Signior amidst his guards of eunuchs, that I say.

HORNER   And I say for the letter, 'tis the first love letter that ever was without flames, darts, fates, destinies, lying and dissembling in't.

Enter SPARKISH, *pulling in* MR. PINCHWIFE.

SPARKISH   Come back, you are a pretty brother-in-law, neither go to church, nor to dinner with your sister bride!

PINCHWIFE   My sister denies her marriage, and you see is gone away from you dissatisfied.

SPARKISH   Pshaw! upon a foolish scruple, that our parson was not in lawful orders, and did not say all the Common Prayer; but 'tis her modesty only, I believe. But let women be never so modest the first day, they'll be sure to come to themselves by night, and I shall have enough of her then. In the meantime, Harry Horner, you must dine with me; I keep my wedding at my aunt's in the Piazza.[4]

HORNER   Thy wedding! What stale maid has lived to despair of a husband, or what young one of a gallant?

SPARKISH   Oh, your servant, sir—this gentleman's sister then—no stale maid.

HORNER   I'm sorry for't.

PINCHWIFE   [*aside*]   How comes he so concerned for her?

SPARKISH   You sorry for't? Why, do you know any ill by her?

HORNER   No, I know none but by thee; 'tis for her sake, not yours, and another man's sake that might have hoped, I thought.

SPARKISH   Another man! another man! What is his name?

HORNER   Nay, since 'tis past he shall be nameless. —[*Aside.*] Poor Harcourt! I am sorry thou hast missed her.

PINCHWIFE   [*aside*]   He seems to be much troubled at the match.

SPARKISH   Prithee tell me—nay, you shan't go, brother.

PINCHWIFE   I must of necessity, but I'll come to you to dinner.

Exit PINCHWIFE.

SPARKISH   But, Harry, what, have I a rival in my wife already? But with all my heart, for he may be of use to me hereafter; for though my hunger is now my sauce, and I can fall on heartily without, but the time will come when a rival will be as good sauce for a married man to a wife as an orange to veal.

HORNER   O thou damned rogue! Thou has set my teeth on edge with thy orange.

SPARKISH   Then let's to dinner—there I was with you again. Come.

HORNER   But who dines with thee?

SPARKISH   My friends and relations, my brother Pinchwife, you see, of your acquaintance.

4. An open arcade in Covent Garden. V.iii. occurs there.

HORNER   And his wife?

SPARKISH   No, gad, he'll ne'er let her come amongst us good fellows. Your stingy country coxcomb keeps his wife from his friends, as he does his little firkin[5] of ale for his own drinking, and a gentleman can't get a smack[6] on't; but his servants, when his back is turned, broach it at their pleasures, and dust it away, ha, ha, ha! Gad, I am witty, I think, considering I was married today, by the world; but come—

HORNER   No, I will not dine with you, unless you can fetch her too.

SPARKISH   Pshaw! what pleasure canst thou have with women now, Harry?

HORNER   My eyes are not gone; I love a good prospect yet, and will not dine with you unless she does too. Go fetch her, therefore, but do not tell her husband 'tis for my sake.

SPARKISH   Well, I'll go try what I can do; in the meantime come away to my aunt's lodging, 'tis in the way to Pinchwife's.

HORNER   The poor woman has called for aid, and stretched forth her hand, doctor; I cannot but help her over the pale out of the briars.

Exeunt SPARKISH, HORNER, QUACK.

Act IV. Scene iv. The scene changes to PINCHWIFE's *house.*

> MRS. PINCHWIFE *alone, leaning on her elbow. A table, pen, ink, and paper.*

MRS. PINCHWIFE   Well, 'tis e'en so, I have got the London disease they call love; I am sick of my husband, and for my gallant. I have heard this distemper called a fever, but methinks 'tis liker an ague, for when I think of my husband, I tremble and am in a cold sweat and have inclinations to vomit; but when I think of my gallant, dear Mr. Horner, my hot fit comes and I am all in a fever, indeed, and as in other fevers my own chamber is tedious to me, and I would fain be removed to his, and then methinks I should be well. Ah, poor Mr. Horner! Well, I cannot, will not stay here; therefore I'll make an end of my letter to him, which shall be a finer letter than my last, because I have studied it like anything. Oh, sick, sick!

> *Takes the pen and writes.*
> *Enter* MR. PINCHWIFE, *who seeing her writing steals softly behind her, and looking over her shoulder, snatches the paper from her.*

PINCHWIFE   What, writing more letters?

MRS. PINCHWIFE   O Lord, bud! why d'ye fright me so?

> *She offers to run out; he stops her, and reads.*

PINCHWIFE   How's this! Nay, you shall not stir, madam. "Dear, dear,

5. Cask.
6. Taste.

dear Mr. Horner"—very well—I have taught you to write letters to good purpose—but let's see't.

"First, I am to beg your pardon for my boldness in writing to you, which I'd have you to know I would not have done had not you said first you loved me so extremely, which if you do, you will never suffer me to lie in the arms of another man, whom I loathe, nauseate, and detest."—Now you can write these filthy words. But what follows? — "Therefore I hope you will speedily find some way to free me from this unfortunate match, which was never, I assure you, of my choice, but I'm afraid 'tis already too far gone. However, if you love me, as I do you, you will try what you can do, but you must help me away before tomorrow, or else, alas, I shall be forever out of your reach, for I can defer no longer our—our" [The letter concludes.]—What is to follow "our"?—Speak, what? Our journey into the country, I suppose—Oh, woman, damned woman! and love, damned love, their old tempter! for this is one of his miracles; in a moment he can make those blind that could see, and those see that were blind, those dumb that could speak, and those prattle who were dumb before; nay, what is more than all, make these dough-baked, senseless, indocile animals, women, too hard for us, their politic lords and rulers, in a moment. But make an end of your letter, and then I'll make an end of you thus, and all my plagues together.

    Draws his sword.

MRS. PINCHWIFE   O Lord, O Lord, you are such a passionate man, bud!

    Enter SPARKISH.

SPARKISH   How now, what's here to do?

PINCHWIFE   This fool here now!

SPARKISH   What, drawn upon your wife? You should never do that but at night in the dark, when you can't hurt her. This is my sister-in-law, is it not? [*Pulls aside her handkerchief.*] Ay, faith, e'en our country Margery; one may know her. Come, she and you must go dine with me; dinner's ready, come. But where's my wife? Is she not come home yet? Where is she?

PINCHWIFE   Making you a cuckold; 'tis that they all do, as soon as they can.

SPARKISH   What, the wedding day? No, a wife that designs to make a cully[7] of her husband will be sure to let him win the first stake of love, by the world. But come, they stay dinner for us; come, I'll lead down our Margery.

MRS. PINCHWIFE   No—so, go, we'll follow you.

SPARKISH   I will not wag without you.

---

7. Fool.

PINCHWIFE [*aside*]   This coxcomb is a sensible[8] torment to me amidst the greatest in the world.

SPARKISH   Come, come, Madam Margery.

PINCHWIFE   No, I'll lead her my own way. What, would you treat your friends with mine, for want of your own wife? [*Leads her to t'other door, and locks her in, and returns.*] —[*Aside.*] I am contented my rage should take breath.

SPARKISH [*aside*]   I told Horner this.

PINCHWIFE   Come now.

SPARKISH   Lord, how shy you are of your wife! But let me tell you, brother, we men of wit have amongst us a saying that cuckolding, like the smallpox, comes with a fear, and you may keep your wife as much as you will out of danger of infection, but if her constitution incline her to't, she'll have it sooner or later, by the world, say they.

PINCHWIFE [*aside*]   What a thing is a cuckold, that every fool can make him ridiculous!—Well, sir—but let me advise you, now you are come to be concerned, because you suspect the danger, not to neglect the means to prevent it, especially when the greatest share of the malady will light upon your own head, for

> Hows'e'er the kind wife's belly comes to swell,
> The husband breeds[9] for her, and first is ill.

[*Exeunt* PINCHWIFE *and* SPARKISH.]

Act V. Scene i. MR. PINCHWIFE's *house.*

Enter MR. PINCHWIFE *and* MRS. PINCHWIFE. *A table and candle.*

PINCHWIFE   Come, take the pen and make an end of the letter, just as you intended; if you are false in a tittle, I shall soon perceive it, and punish you with this as you deserve. [*Lays his hand on his sword.*] Write what was to follow—let's see—"You must make haste and help me away before tomorrow, or else I shall be forever out of your reach, for I can defer no longer our"—What follows "our"?

MRS. PINCHWIFE   Must all out then, bud? [MRS. PINCHWIFE *takes the pen and writes.*] Look you there then.

PINCHWIFE   Let's see—"For I can defer no longer our—wedding—Your slighted Alithea."—What's the meaning of this? My sister's name to't. Speak, unriddle!

MRS. PINCHWIFE   Yes, indeed, bud.

PINCHWIFE   But why her name to't? Speak—speak, I say!

MRS. PINCHWIFE   Ay, but you'll tell her then again; if you would not tell her again—

PINCHWIFE   I will not—I am stunned, my head turns around. Speak.

MRS. PINCHWIFE   Won't you tell her indeed, and indeed?

---

8. Acutely felt.
9. Sprouts horns.

PINCHWIFE   No, speak, I say.

MRS. PINCHWIFE   She'll be angry with me, but I had rather she should
be angry with me than you, bud; and to tell you the truth, 'twas she
made me write the letter, and taught me what I should write.

PINCHWIFE [*aside*]   Ha! I thought the style was somewhat better than
her own. —But how could she come to you to teach you, since I had
locked you up alone?

MRS. PINCHWIFE   Oh, through the keyhole, bud.

PINCHWIFE   But why should she make you write a letter for her to him,
since she can write herself?

MRS. PINCHWIFE   Why, she said because—for I was unwilling to do it.

PINCHWIFE   Because what—because?

MRS. PINCHWIFE   Because, lest Mr. Horner should be cruel, and refuse
her; or vain afterwards, and show the letter, she might disown it, the
hand not being hers.

PINCHWIFE [*aside*]   How's this? Ha! —then I think I shall come to
myself again. This changeling could not invent this lie; but if she
could, why should she? She might think I should soon discover it—
stay—now I think on't too, Horner said he was sorry she had married
Sparkish, and her disowning her marriage to me makes me think she
has evaded it for Horner's sake. Yet why should she take this course?
But men in love are fools; women may well be so. —But hark you,
madam, your sister went out in the morning, and I have not seen her
within since.

MRS. PINCHWIFE   Alackaday, she has been crying all day above, it
seems, in a corner.

PINCHWIFE   Where is she? Let me speak with her.

MRS. PINCHWIFE [*aside*]   O Lord, then he'll discover all! —Pray hold,
bud; what, d'ye mean to discover me? She'll know I have told you
then. Pray, bud, let me talk with her first.

PINCHWIFE   I must speak with her, to know whether Horner ever made
her any promise, and whether she be married to Sparkish or no.

MRS. PINCHWIFE   Pray, dear bud, don't, till I have spoken with her and
told her that I have told you all, for she'll kill me else.

PINCHWIFE   Go then, and bid her come out to me.

MRS. PINCHWIFE   Yes, yes, bud.

PINCHWIFE   Let me see—

MRS. PINCHWIFE [*aside*]   I'll go, but she is not within to come to him.
I have just got time to know of Lucy her maid, who first set me on
work, what lie I shall tell next, for I am e'en at my wit's end.

Exit MRS. PINCHWIFE.

PINCHWIFE   Well, I resolve it; Horner shall have her. I'd rather give him
my sister than lend him my wife, and such an alliance will prevent his
pretensions to my wife, sure. I'll make him of kin to her, and then he
won't care for her.

MRS. PINCHWIFE *returns.*

MRS. PINCHWIFE   O Lord, bud! I told you what anger you would make me with my sister.

PINCHWIFE   Won't she come hither?

MRS. PINCHWIFE   No, no, alackaday, she's ashamed to look you in the face, and she says, if you go in to her, she'll run away downstairs, and shamefully go herself to Mr. Horner, who has promised her marriage, she says, and she will have no other, so she won't.

PINCHWIFE   Did he so—promise her marriage?—then she shall have no other. Go tell her so, and if she will come and discourse with me a little concerning the means, I will about it immediately. Go.

Exit MRS. PINCHWIFE.

His estate is equal to Sparkish's, and his extraction as much better than his as his parts are; but my chief reason is, I'd rather be of kin to him by the name of brother-in-law than that of cuckold.

Enter MRS. PINCHWIFE.

Well, what says she now?

MRS. PINCHWIFE   Why, she says she would only have you lead her to Horner's lodging—with whom she first will discourse the matter before she talk with you, which yet she cannot do; for alack, poor creature, she says she can't so much as look you in the face, therefore she'll come to you in a mask; and you must excuse her if she make you no answer to any question of yours, till you have brought her to Mr. Horner; and if you will not chide her, nor question her, she'll come out to you immediately.

PINCHWIFE   Let her come; I will not speak a word to her, nor require a word from her.

MRS. PINCHWIFE   Oh, I forgot; besides, she says she cannot look you in the face though through a mask, therefore would desire you to put out the candle.

PINCHWIFE   I agree to all; let her make haste—there, 'tis out.

Puts out the candle.

Exit MRS. PINCHWIFE.

—My case is something better. I'd rather fight with Horner for not lying with my sister than for lying with my wife, and of the two I had rather find my sister too forward than my wife; I expected no other from her free education, as she calls it, and her passion for the town. Well—wife and sister are names which make us expect love and duty, pleasure and comfort, but we find 'em plagues and torments, and are equally, though differently, troublesome to their keeper; for we have as much ado to get people to lie with our sisters as to keep 'em from lying with our wives.

Enter MRS. PINCHWIFE *masked, and in hoods and scarves and a nightgown*[1] *and petticoat of* ALITHEA's, *in the dark.*

What, are you come, sister? Let us go then—but first let me lock up my wife. —Mrs. Margery, where are you?

MRS. PINCHWIFE   Here, bud.

PINCHWIFE   Come hither, that I may lock you up; get you in. [*Locks the door.*]—Come, sister, where are you now?

MRS. PINCHWIFE *gives him her hand, but when he lets her go, she steals softly on t'other side of him, and is led away by him for his sister* ALITHEA.

Act V. Scene ii. The scene changes to HORNER's *lodging.*

QUACK, HORNER.

QUACK   What, all alone? Not so much as one of your cuckolds here, nor one of their wives! They use to take their turns with you, as if they were to watch you.

HORNER   Yes, it often happens that a cuckold is but his wife's spy, and is more upon family duty when he is with her gallant abroad, hindering his pleasure, than when he is at home with her, playing the gallant. But the hardest duty a married woman imposes upon a lover is keeping her husband company always.

QUACK   And his fondness wearies you almost as soon as hers.

HORNER   A pox! keeping a cuckold company, after you have had his wife, is as tiresome as the company of a country squire to a witty fellow of the town, when he has got all his money.

QUACK   And as at first a man makes a friend of the husband to get the wife, so at last you are fain to fall out with the wife to be rid of the husband.

HORNER   Ay, most cuckold-makers are true courtiers; when once a poor man has cracked his credit for 'em, they can't abide to come near him.

QUACK   But at first, to draw him in, are so sweet, so kind, so dear, just you are to Pinchwife. But what becomes of that intrigue with his wife?

HORNER   A pox! he's as surly as an alderman that has been bit, and since he's so coy, his wife's kindness is in vain, for she's a silly innocent.

QUACK   Did she not send you a letter by him?

HORNER   Yes, but that's a riddle I have not yet solved. Allow the poor creature to be willing, she is silly too, and he keeps her up so close—

QUACK   Yes, so close that he makes her but the more willing, and adds but revenge to her love, which two, when met, seldom fail of satisfying each other one way or other.

1. Dressing gown.

HORNER   What! here's the man we are talking of, I think.

> *Enter* MR. PINCHWIFE, *leading in his wife masked, muffled, and in her sister's gown.*

Pshaw!

QUACK   Bringing his wife to you is the next thing to bringing a love letter from her.

HORNER   What means this?

PINCHWIFE   The last time, you know, sir, I brought you a love letter; now, you see, a mistress. I think you'll say I am a civil man to you.

HORNER   Ay, the devil take me, will I say thou art the civilest man I ever met with, and I have known some. I fancy I understand thee now better than I did the letter; but hark thee, in thy ear—

PINCHWIFE   What?

HORNER   Nothing but the usual question, man: is she sound, on thy word?

PINCHWIFE   What, you take her for a wench, and me for a pimp?

HORNER   Pshaw! wench and pimp, paw[2] words. I know thou art an honest fellow, and hast a great acquaintance among the ladies, and perhaps hast made love for me rather than let me make love to thy wife.

PINCHWIFE   Come, sir, in short, I am for no fooling.

HORNER   Nor I neither; therefore prithee let's see her face presently. Make her show, man; art thou sure I don't know her?

PINCHWIFE   I am sure you do know her.

HORNER   A pox! why dost thou bring her to me then?

PINCHWIFE   Because she's a relation of mine—

HORNER   Is she, faith, man? Then thou are still more civil and obliging, dear rogue.

PINCHWIFE   Who desired me to bring her to you.

HORNER   Then she is obliging, dear rogue.

PINCHWIFE   You'll make her welcome for my sake, I hope.

HORNER   I hope she is handsome enough to make herself welcome. Prithee, let her unmask.

PINCHWIFE   Do you speak to her; she would never be ruled by me.

HORNER   Madam—[MRS. PINCHWIFE *whispers to* HORNER.] —She says she must speak with me in private. Withdraw, prithee.

PINCHWIFE [*aside*]   She's unwilling, it seems, I should know all her undecent conduct in this business. —Well then, I'll leave you together, and hope when I am gone you'll agree; if not, you and I shan't agree, sir.

HORNER [*aside*]   What means the fool? —If she and I agree, 'tis no matter what you and I do.

> *Whispers to* MRS. PINCHWIFE, *who makes signs with her hand for* PINCHWIFE *to be gone.*

2. Naughty.

PINCHWIFE   In the meantime, I'll fetch a parson, and find out Sparkish and disabuse him. You would have me fetch a parson, would you not? Well then—now I think I am rid of her, and shall have no more trouble with her. Our sisters and daughters, like usurers' money, are safest when put out; but our wives, like their writings,[3] never safe but in our closets under lock and key.

Exit MR. PINCHWIFE.

Enter BOY.

BOY   Sir Jasper Fidget, sir, is coming up.

Exit.

HORNER   Here's the trouble of a cuckold, now, we are talking of. A pox on him! Has he not enough to do to hinder his wife's sport, but he must other women's too? —Step in here, madam.

Exit MRS. PINCHWIFE.

Enter SIR JASPER.

SIR JASPER FIDGET   My best and dearest friend.
HORNER   [*aside to* QUACK]   The old style, doctor. —Well, be short, for I am busy. What would your impertinent wife have now?
SIR JASPER FIDGET   Well guessed, i'faith, for I do come from her.
HORNER   To invite me to supper. Tell her I can't come; go.
SIR JASPER FIDGET   Nay, now you are out, faith; for my lady and the whole knot of the virtuous gang, as they call themselves, are resolved upon a frolic of coming to you tonight in a masquerade, and are all dressed already.
HORNER   I shan't be at home.
SIR JASPER FIDGET   [*aside*]   Lord, how churlish he is to women! —Nay, prithee don't disappoint 'em; they'll think 'tis my fault; prithee don't. I'll send in the banquet and the fiddles. But make no noise on't, for the poor virtuous rogues would not have it known for the world that they go a-masquerading, and they would come to no man's ball but yours.
HORNER   Well, well—get you gone, and tell 'em, if they come, 'twill be at the peril of their honor and yours.
SIR JASPER FIDGET   He, he, he!—we'll trust you for that; farewell.

Exit SIR JASPER.

HORNER

Doctor, anon you too shall be my guest,
But now I'm going to a private feast.

Exeunt.

3. Legal documents.

Act V. Scene iii. The scene changes to the Piazza of Covent
Garden.

SPARKISH, PINCHWIFE

SPARKISH [*with the letter in his hand*]   But who would have thought a
woman could have been false to me? By the world, I could not have
thought it.

PINCHWIFE   You were for giving and taking liberty; she has taken it
only, sir, now you find in that letter. You are a frank person, and so is
she, you see there.

SPARKISH   Nay, if this be her hand—for I never saw it.

PINCHWIFE   'Tis no matter whether that be her hand or no; I am sure
this hand, at her desire, led her to Mr. Horner, with whom I left her
just now, to go fetch a parson to 'em, at their desire too, to deprive
you of her forever, for it seems yours was but a mock marriage.

SPARKISH   Indeed, she would needs have it that 'twas Harcourt himself
in a parson's habit that married us, but I'm sure he told me 'twas his
brother Ned.

PINCHWIFE   Oh, there 'tis out, and you were deceived, not she, for you
are such a frank person—but I must be gone. You'll find her at Mr.
Horner's; go and believe your eyes.

Exit MR. PINCHWIFE.

SPARKISH   Nay, I'll to her, and call her as many crocodiles, sirens, har-
pies, and other heathenish names as a poet would do a mistress who
had refused to hear his suit, nay more, his verses on her. —But stay,
is not that she following a torch at t'other end of the Piazza? And
from Horner's certainly—'tis so.

Enter ALITHEA, *following a torch, and* LUCY *behind.*

You are well met, madam, though you don't think so. What, you have
made a short visit to Mr. Horner, but I suppose you'll return to him
presently; by that time the parson can be with him.

ALITHEA   Mr. Horner, and the parson, sir!

SPARKISH   Come, madam, no more dissembling, no more jilting, for I
am no more a frank person.

ALITHEA   How's this?

LUCY [*aside*]   So, 'twill work, I see.

SPARKISH   Could you find out no easy country fool to abuse? none but
me, a gentleman of wit and pleasure about the town? But it was your
pride to be too hard for a man of parts, unworthy false woman! false
as a friend that lends a man money to lose; false as dice, who undo
those that trust all they have to 'em.

LUCY [*aside*]   He has been a great bubble by his similes, as they say.

ALITHEA   You have been too merry, sir, at your wedding dinner, sure.

SPARKISH   What, d'ye mock me too?

ALITHEA   Or you have been deluded.

SPARKISH   By you.

ALITHEA   Let me understand you.

SPARKISH   Have you the confidence—I should call it something else, since you know your guilt—to stand my just reproaches? You did not write an impudent letter to Mr. Horner! who I find now has clubbed with you in deluding me with his aversion for women, that I might not, forsooth, suspect him for my rival.

LUCY [aside]   D'ye think the gentleman can be jealous now, madam?

ALITHEA   I write a letter to Mr. Horner!

SPARKISH   Nay, madam, do not deny it; your brother showed it me just now, and told me likewise he left you at Horner's lodging to fetch a parson to marry you to him, and I wish you joy, madam, joy, joy! and to him, too, much joy, and to myself more joy for not marrying you.

ALITHEA [aside]   So, I find my brother would break off the match, and I can consent to't, since I see this gentleman can be made jealous. — O Lucy, by his rude usage and jealousy, he makes me almost afraid I am married to him. Art thou sure 'twas Harcourt himself and no parson that married us?

SPARKISH   No, madam, I thank you. I suppose that was a contrivance too of Mr. Horner's and yours, to make Harcourt play the parson; but I would as little as you have him one now, no, not for the world, for shall I tell you another truth? I never had any passion for you till now, for now I hate you. 'Tis true I might have married your portion, as other men of parts of the town do sometimes, and so your servant; and to show my unconcernedness, I'll come to your wedding, and resign you with as much joy as I would a stale wench to a new cully; nay, with as much joy as I would after the first night, if I had been married to you. There's for you, and so your servant, servant.

Exit SPARKISH.

ALITHEA   How was I deceived in a man!

LUCY   You'll believe, then, a fool may be made jealous now? For that easiness in him that suffers him to be led by a wife will likewise permit him to be persuaded against her by others.

ALITHEA   But marry Mr. Horner! My brother does not intend it, sure; if I thought he did, I would take thy advice, and Mr. Harcourt for my husband. And now I wish that if there be any overwise woman of the town, who, like me, would marry a fool for fortune, liberty, or title, first, that her husband may love play, and be a cully to all the town but her, and suffer none but fortune to be mistress of his purse; then, if for liberty, that he may send her into the country under the conduct of some housewifely mother-in-law; and if for title, may the world give 'em none but that of cuckold.

LUCY   And for her greater curse, madam, may he not deserve it.

ALITHEA   Away, impertinent! —Is not this my old Lady Lanterlu's?[4]

LUCY   Yes, madam. —[*Aside.*] And here I hope we shall find Mr. Harcourt.

Exeunt ALITHEA, LUCY.

Act V. Scene iv.

The scene changes again to HORNER's *lodging.* HORNER, LADY FIDGET, MRS. DAINTY FIDGET, MRS. SQUEAMISH. *A table, banquet, and bottles.*

HORNER [*aside*]   A pox! they are come too soon—before I have sent back my new mistress. All I have now to do is to lock her in, that they may not see her.

LADY FIDGET   That we may be sure of our welcome, we have brought our entertainment with us, and are resolved to treat thee, dear toad.

MRS. DAINTY FIDGET   And that we may be merry to purpose, have left Sir Jasper and my old Lady Squeamish quarreling at home at backgammon.

MRS. SQUEAMISH   Therefore let us make use of our time, lest they should chance to interrupt us.

LADY FIDGET   Let us sit then.

HORNER   First, that you may be private, let me lock this door and that, and I'll wait upon you presently.

LADY FIDGET   No, sir, shut 'em only and your lips forever, for we must trust you as much as our women.

HORNER   You know all vanity's killed in me; I have no occasion for talking.

LADY FIDGET   Now, ladies, supposing we had drank each of us our two bottles, let us speak the truth of our hearts.

MRS. DAINTY FIDGET AND MRS. SQUEAMISH   Agreed.

LADY FIDGET   By this brimmer, for truth is nowhere else to be found. —[*Aside to* HORNER.] Not in thy heart, false man!

HORNER   [*aside to* LADY FIDGET]   You have found me a true man, I'm sure.

LADY FIDGET   [*aside to* HORNER]   Not every way. —But let us sit and be merry.

LADY FIDGET *sings.*

1

Why should our damn'd tyrants oblige us to live
On the pittance of pleasure which they only give?
    We must not rejoice,
    With wine and with noise.

4. Lanterloo was a card game; also called "loo."

In vain we must wake in a dull bed alone,
Whilst to our warm rival, the bottle, they're gone.
    Then lay aside charms,
    And take up these arms.[5]

2

'Tis wine only gives 'em their courage and wit;
Because we live sober, to men we submit.
    If for beauties you'd pass,
    Take a lick of the glass,
'Twill mend your complexions, and when they are gone,
The best red we have is the red of the grape.
    Then, sisters, lay't on,
    And damn a good shape.

MRS. DAINTY FIDGET   Dear brimmer![6] Well, in token of our openness and plain-dealing, let us throw our masks over our heads.

HORNER   So, 'twill come to the glasses anon.

MRS. SQUEAMISH   Lovely brimmer! Let me enjoy him first.

LADY FIDGET   No, I never part with a gallant till I've tried him. Dear brimmer, that mak'st our husbands shortsighted.

MRS. DAINTY FIDGET   And our bashfull gallants bold.

MRS. SQUEAMISH   And for want of a gallant, the butler lovely in our eyes. —Drink, eunuch.

LADY FIDGET   Drink, thou representative of a husband. Damn a husband!

MRS. DAINTY FIDGET   And, as it were a husband, an old keeper.

MRS. SQUEAMISH   And an old grandmother.

HORNER   And an English bawd, and a French surgeon.[7]

LADY FIDGET   Ay, we have all reason to curse 'em.

HORNER   For my sake, ladies?

LADY FIDGET   No, for our own, for the first spoils all young gallants' industry.

MRS. DAINTY FIDGET   And the other's art makes 'em bold only with common women.

MRS. SQUEAMISH   And rather run the hazard of the vile distemper amongst them than of a denial amongst us.

MRS. DAINTY FIDGET   The filthy toads choose mistresses now as they do stuffs, for having been fancied and worn by others.

MRS. SQUEAMISH   For being common and cheap.

LADY FIDGET   Whilst women of quality, like the richest stuffs, lie untumbled and unasked for.

HORNER   Ay, neat, and cheap, and new, often they think best.

---

5. The glasses.
6. Full glass.
7. Doctor for the "French pox" (venereal disease).

MRS. DAINTY FIDGET No, sir, the beasts will be known by a mistress longer than by a suit.

MRS. SQUEAMISH And 'tis not for cheapness neither.

LADY FIDGET No, for the vain fops will take up druggets[8] and embroider 'em. But I wonder at the depraved appetites of witty men; they use to be out of the common road, and hate imitation. Pray tell me, beast, when you were a man, why you rather chose to club with a multitude in a common house for an entertainment than to be the only guest at a good table.

HORNER Why, faith, ceremony and expectation are unsufferable to those that are sharp bent; people always eat with the best stomach at an ordinary, where every man is snatching for the best bit.

LADY FIDGET Though he get a cut over the fingers. —But I have heard people eat most heartily of another man's meat, that is, what they do not pay for.

HORNER When they are sure of their welcome and freedom, for ceremony in love and eating is as ridiculous as in fighting; falling on briskly is all should be done in those occasions.

LADY FIDGET Well, then, let me tell you, sir, there is nowhere more freedom than in our houses, and we take freedom from a young person as a sign of good breeding, and a person may be as free as he pleases with us, as frolic, as gamesome, as wild as he will.

HORNER Han't I heard you all declaim against wild men?

LADY FIDGET Yes, but for all that, we think wildness in a man as desirable a quality as in a duck or rabbit; a tame man, foh!

HORNER I know not, but your reputations frightened me, as much as your faces invited me.

LADY FIDGET Our reputation! Lord, why should you not think that we women make use of our reputation, as you men of yours, only to deceive the world with less suspicion? Our virtue is like the statesman's religion, the Quaker's word, the gamester's oath, and the great man's honor—but to cheat those that trust us.

MRS. SQUEAMISH And that demureness, coyness, and modesty that you see in our faces in the boxes at plays, is as much a sign of a kind woman as a vizard-mask in the pit.

MRS. DAINTY FIDGET For, I assure you, women are least masked when they have the velvet vizard on.

LADY FIDGET You would have found us modest women in our denials only.

MRS. SQUEAMISH Our bashfulness is only the reflection of the men's.

MRS. DAINTY FIDGET We blush when they are shamefaced.

HORNER I beg your pardon, ladies; I was deceived in you devilishly. But why that mighty pretense to honor?

LADY FIDGET We have told you. But sometimes 'twas for the same rea-

---

8. Cheap woolen material.

son you men pretend business often, to avoid ill company, to enjoy the better and more privately those you love.

HORNER But why would you ne'er give a friend a wink then?

LADY FIDGET Faith, your reputation frightened us as much as ours did you, you were so notoriously lewd.

HORNER And you so seemingly honest.[9]

LADY FIDGET Was that all that deterred you?

HORNER And so expensive—you allow freedom, you say—

LADY FIDGET Ay, ay.

HORNER That I was afraid of losing my little money, as well as my little time, both which my other pleasures required.

LADY FIDGET Money, foh! You talk like a little fellow now; do such as we expect money?

HORNER I beg your pardon, madam; I must confess, I have heard that great ladies, like great merchants, set but the higher prices upon what they have, because they are not in necessity of taking the first offer.

MRS. DAINTY FIDGET Such as we make sale of our hearts?

MRS. SQUEAMISH We bribed for our love? Foh!

HORNER With your pardon, ladies, I know, like great men in offices, you seem to exact flattery and attendance only from your followers; but you have receivers about you, and such fees to pay, a man is afraid to pass your grants.[1] Besides, we must let you win at cards, or we lose your hearts; and if you make an assignation, 'tis at a goldsmith's, jeweler's, or china house, where, for your honor you deposit to him, he must pawn his to the punctual cit, and so paying for what you take up, pays for what he takes up.

MRS. DAINTY FIDGET Would you not have us assured of our gallant's love?

MRS. SQUEAMISH For love is better known by liberality than by jealousy.

LADY FIDGET For one may be dissembled, the other not. —[*Aside.*] But my jealously can be no longer dissembled, and they are telling ripe. —Come, here's to our gallants in waiting, whom we must name, and I'll begin. This is my false rogue.

Claps him on the back.

MRS. SQUEAMISH How!

HORNER [*aside*] So, all will out now.

MRS. SQUEAMISH [*aside to* HORNER] Did you not tell me, 'twas for my sake only you reported yourself no man?

MRS. DAINTY FIDGET [*aside to* HORNER] Oh, wretch! Did you not swear to me, 'twas for my love and honor you passed for that thing you do?

HORNER So, so.

LADY FIDGET Come, speak, ladies; this is my false villain.

9. Chaste.
1. Accept your gifts.

MRS. SQUEAMISH   And mine too.

MRS. DAINTY FIDGET   And mine.

HORNER   Well then, you are all three my false rogues too, and there's an end on't.

LADY FIDGET   Well then, there's no remedy; sister sharers, let us not fall out, but have a care of our honor. Though we get no presents, no jewels of him, we are savers of our honor, the jewel of most value and use, which shines yet to the world unsuspected, though it be counterfeit.

HORNER   Nay, and is e'en as good as if it were true, provided the world think so; for honor, like beauty now, only depends on the opinion of others.

LADY FIDGET   Well, Harry Common, I hope you can be true to three. Swear—but 'tis no purpose to require your oath, for you are as often forsworn as you swear to new women.

HORNER   Come, faith, madam, let us e'en pardon one another, for all the difference I find betwixt we men and you women, we forswear ourselves at the beginning of an amour, you as long as it lasts.

Enter SIR JASPER FIDGET, *and* OLD LADY SQUEAMISH.

SIR JASPER FIDGET   Oh, my Lady Fidget, was this your cunning, to come to Mr. Horner without me? But you have been nowhere else, I hope.

LADY FIDGET   No, Sir Jasper.

OLD LADY SQUEAMISH   And you came straight hither, Biddy?

MRS. SQUEAMISH   Yes, indeed, Lady Grandmother.

SIR JASPER FIDGET   'Tis well, 'tis well; I knew when once they were thoroughly acquainted with poor Horner, they'd ne'er be from him. You may let her masquerade it with my wife and Horner, and I warrant her reputation safe.

Enter BOY.

BOY   Oh, sir, here's the gentleman come whom you bid me not suffer to come up without giving you notice, with a lady too, and other gentlemen.

HORNER   Do you all go in there, whilst I send 'em away, and, boy, do you desire 'em to stay below till I come, which shall be immediately.

Exeunt SIR JASPER, LADY SQUEAMISH, LADY FIDGET,
MRS. DAINTY, MRS. SQUEAMISH.

BOY   Yes, sir.

Exit.
Exit HORNER *at t'other door, and returns with* MRS. PINCHWIFE.

HORNER   You would not take my advice to be gone home before your husband came back; he'll now discover all. Yet pray, my dearest, be persuaded to go home, and leave the rest to my management; I'll let you down the back way.

MRS. PINCHWIFE   I don't know the way home, so I don't.

HORNER   My man shall wait upon you.

MRS. PINCHWIFE   No, don't you believe that I'll go at all; what, are you weary of me already?

HORNER   No, my life, 'tis that I may love you long, 'tis to secure my love, and your reputation with your husband; he'll never receive you again else.

MRS. PINCHWIFE   What care I? D'ye think to frighten me with that? I don't intend to go to him again; you shall be my husband now.

HORNER   I cannot be your husband, dearest, since you are married to him.

MRS. PINCHWIFE   Oh, would you make me believe that? Don't I see every day, at London here, women leave their first husbands, and go and live with other men as their wives? Pish, pshaw! you'd make me angry, but that I love you so mainly.

HORNER   So, they are coming up—in again, in, I hear 'em.

Exit MRS. PINCHWIFE.

Well, a silly mistress is like a weak place, soon got, soon lost, a man has scarce time for plunder; she betrays her husband first to her gallant, and then her gallant to her husband.

Enter PINCHWIFE, ALITHEA, HARCOURT, SPARKISH, LUCY, *and a* PARSON.

PINCHWIFE   Come, madam, 'tis not the sudden change of your dress, the confidence of your asseverations, and your false witness there, shall persuade me I did not bring you hither just now; here's my witness, who cannot deny it, since you must be confronted. —Mr. Horner, did not I bring this lady to you just now?

HORNER [*aside*]   Now must I wrong one woman for another's sake, but that's no new thing with me; for in these cases I am still on the criminal's side, against the innocent.

ALITHEA   Pray, speak, sir.

HORNER [*aside*]   It must be so—I must be impudent, and try my luck; impudence uses to be too hard for truth.

PINCHWIFE   What, you are studying an evasion or excuse for her. Speak, sir.

HORNER   No, faith, I am something backward only to speak in women's affairs or disputes.

PINCHWIFE   She bids you speak.

ALITHEA   Ay, pray, sir, do; pray satisfy him.

HORNER   Then truly, you did bring that lady to me just now.

PINCHWIFE   O ho!

ALITHEA   How, sir!

HARCOURT   How, Horner!

ALITHEA   What mean you, sir? I always took you for a man of honor.

HORNER [*aside*]   Ay, so much a man of honor that I must save my mistress, I thank you, come what will on't.

SPARKISH   So, if I had had her, she'd have made me believe the moon had been made of a Christmas pie.

LUCY [*aside*]   Now could I speak, if I durst, and solve the riddle, who am the author of it.

ALITHEA   O unfortunate woman! A combination against my honor, which most concerns me now, because you share in my disgrace, sir, and it is your censure, which I must now suffer, that troubles me, not theirs.

HARCOURT   Madam, then have no trouble, you shall now see 'tis possible for me to love too, without being jealous; I will not only believe your innocence myself, but make all the world believe it. — [*Apart to* HORNER]. Horner, I must now be concerned for this lady's honor.

HORNER   And I must be concerned for a lady's honor too.

HARCOURT   This lady has her honor, and I will protect it.

HORNER   My lady has not her honor, but has given it me to keep, and I will preserve it.

HARCOURT   I understand you not.

HORNER   I would not have you.

MRS. PINCHWIFE [*peeping in behind*]   What's the matter with 'em all?

PINCHWIFE   Come, come, Mr. Horner, no more disputing; here's the parson. I brought him not in vain.

HARCOURT   No, sir, I'll employ him, if this lady please.

PINCHWIFE   How! what d'ye mean?

SPARKISH   Ay, what does he mean?

HORNER   Why, I have resigned your sister to him; he has my consent.

PINCHWIFE   But he has not mine, sir; a woman's injured honor, no more than a man's, can be repaired or satisfied by any but him that first wronged it; and you shall marry her presently, or —

> *Lays his hand on his sword.*
> *Enter to them* MRS. PINCHWIFE.

MRS. PINCHWIFE [*aside*]   O Lord, they'll kill poor Mr. Horner! Besides, he shan't marry her whilst I stand by and look on; I'll not lose my second husband so.

PINCHWIFE   What do I see?

ALITHEA   My sister in my clothes!

SPARKISH   Ha!

MRS. PINCHWIFE [*to* MR. PINCHWIFE]   Nay, pray now don't quarrel about finding work for the parson; he shall marry me to Mr. Horner; for now, I believe, you have enough of me.

HORNER [*aside*]   Damned, damned, loving changeling!

MRS. PINCHWIFE   Pray, sister, pardon me for telling so many lies of you.

HARCOURT   I suppose the riddle is plain now.

LUCY   No, that must be my work. Good sir, hear me.

Kneels to MR. PINCHWIFE, *who stands doggedly, with his hat over his eyes.*

PINCHWIFE   I will never hear woman again, but make 'em all silent, thus—

Offers to draw upon his wife.

HORNER   No, that must not be.
PINCHWIFE   You then shall go first, 'tis all one to me.

Offers to draw on HORNER; *stopped by* HARCOURT.

HARCOURT   Hold!

Enter SIR JASPER FIDGET, LADY FIDGET, LADY SQUEAMISH, MRS. DAINTY FIDGET, MRS. SQUEAMISH.

SIR JASPER FIDGET   What's the matter? what's the matter? pray, what's the matter, sir? I beseech you communicate, sir.
PINCHWIFE   Why, my wife has communicated, sir, as your wife may have done too, sir, if she knows him, sir.
SIR JASPER FIDGET   Pshaw! with him! Ha, ha, he!
PINCHWIFE   D'ye mock me, sir? A cuckold is a kind of a wild beast; have a care, sir.
SIR JASPER FIDGET   No, sure, you mock me, sir—he cuckold you! It can't be, ha, ha, he! Why, I'll tell you, sir—

Offers to whisper.

PINCHWIFE   I tell you again, he has whored my wife, and yours too, if he knows her, and all the women he comes near; 'tis not his dissembling, his hypocrisy, can wheedle me.
SIR JASPER FIDGET   How! does he dissemble? Is he a hypocrite? Nay, then—how—wife—sister, is he an hypocrite?
OLD LADY SQUEAMISH   An hypocrite! a dissembler! Speak, young harlotry, speak, how?
SIR JASPER FIDGET   Nay, then—oh, my head too!—O thou libidinous lady!
OLD LADY SQUEAMISH   O thou harloting harlotry! Hast thou done't then?
SIR JASPER FIDGET   Speak, good Horner, art thou a dissembler, a rogue? Hast thou—
HORNER   Soh!
LUCY [*apart to* HORNER]   I'll fetch you off, and her too, if she will but hold her tongue.
HORNER [*apart to* LUCY]   Canst thou? I'll give thee—
LUCY [*to* MR. PINCHWIFE]   Pray have but patience to hear me, sir, who am the unfortunate cause of all this confusion. Your wife is innocent, I only culpable; for I put her upon telling you all these lies concern-

ing my mistress, in order to the breaking off the match between Mr.
Sparkish and her, to make way for Mr. Harcourt.

SPARKISH   Did you so, eternal rotten tooth? Then, it seems, my mistress
was not false to me, I was only deceived by you.—Brother that should
have been, now, man of conduct, who is a frank person now? to bring
your wife to her lover—ha!

LUCY   I assure you, sir, she came not to Mr. Horner out of love, for she
loves him no more—

MRS. PINCHWIFE   Hold, I told lies for you, but you shall tell none for
me, for I do love Mr. Horner with all my soul, and nobody shall say
me nay; pray, don't you go to make poor Mr. Horner believe to the
contrary, 'tis spitefully done of you, I'm sure.

HORNER [aside to MRS. PINCHWIFE]   Peace, dear idiot.

MRS. PINCHWIFE   Nay, I will not peace.

PINCHWIFE   Not till I make you.

>   Enter DORILANT, QUACK.

DORILANT   Horner, your servant; I am the doctor's guest, he must
excuse our intrusion.

QUACK   But what's the matter, gentlemen? For heaven's sake, what's the
matter?

HORNER   Oh, 'tis well you are come. 'Tis a censorious world we live in;
you may have brought me a reprieve, or else I had died for a crime I
never committed, and these innocent ladies had suffered with me;
therefore pray satisfy these worthy, honorable, jealous gentlemen—
that—

>   Whispers.

QUACK   Oh, I understand you; is that all? —[Whispers to SIR JASPER.]
Sir Jasper, by heavens and upon the word of a physician, sir—

SIR JASPER FIDGET   Nay, I do believe you truly. —Pardon me, my virtuous lady, and dear of honor.

OLD LADY SQUEAMISH   What, then all's right again?

SIR JASPER FIDGET   Ay, ay, and now let us satisfy him too.

>   They whisper with MR. PINCHWIFE.

PINCHWIFE   An eunuch! Pray, no fooling with me.

QUACK   I'll bring half the surgeons in town to swear it.

PINCHWIFE   They!—they'll swear a man bled to death through his
wounds died of an apoplexy.

QUACK   Pray hear me, sir—why, all the town has heard the report of
him.

PINCHWIFE   But does all the town believe it?

QUACK   Pray inquire a little, and first of all these.

PINCHWIFE   I'm sure when I left the town he was the lewdest fellow
in't.

QUACK I tell you, sir, he has been in France since; pray ask but these ladies and gentlemen, your friend Mr. Dorilant. —Gentlemen and ladies han't you all heard the late sad report of poor Mr. Horner?

ALL THE LADIES Ay, ay, ay.

DORILANT Why, thou jealous fool, dost thou doubt it? He's an arrant French capon.[2]

MRS. PINCHWIFE 'Tis false, sir, you shall not disparage poor Mr. Horner, for to my certain knowledge—

LUCY Oh, hold!

MRS. SQUEAMISH [aside to LUCY] Stop her mouth!

LADY FIDGET [to PINCHWIFE] Upon my honor, sir, 'tis as true—

MRS. DAINTY FIDGET D'ye think we would have been seen in his company?

MRS. SQUEAMISH Trust our unspotted reputations with him!

LADY FIDGET [aside to HORNER] This you get, and we too, by trusting your secret to a fool.

HORNER Peace, madam. —[Aside to QUACK.] Well, doctor, is not this a good design, that carries a man on unsuspected, and brings him off safe?

PINCHWIFE [aside] Well, if this were true, but my wife—

DORILANT whispers with MRS. PINCHWIFE.

ALITHEA Come, brother, your wife is yet innocent, you see; but have a care of too strong an imagination, lest like an overconcerned, timorous gamester, by fancying an unlucky cast, it should come. Women and fortune are truest still to those that trust 'em.

LUCY And any wild thing grows but the more fierce and hungry for being kept up, and more dangerous to the keeper.

ALITHEA There's doctrine for all husbands, Mr. Harcourt.

HARCOURT I edify, madam, so much that I am impatient till I am one.

DORILANT And I edify so much by example I will never be one.

SPARKISH And because I will not disparage my parts I'll ne'er be one.

HORNER And I, alas, can't be one.

PINCHWIFE But I must be one—against my will, to a country wife, with a country murrain[3] to me.

MRS. PINCHWIFE [aside] And I must be a country wife still too, I find, for I can't, like a city one, be rid of my musty husband and do what I list.

HORNER Now, sir, I must pronounce your wife innocent, though I blush whilst I do it, and I am the only man by her now exposed to shame, which I will straight drown in wine, as you shall your suspicion, and the ladies' troubles we'll divert with a ballet.—Doctor, where are your maskers?

2. Impotent man.
3. Plague.

LUCY   Indeed, she's innocent, sir, I am her witness; and her end of
coming out was but to see her sister's wedding, and what she has said
to your face of her love to Mr. Horner was but the usual innocent
revenge on a husband's jealousy—was it not, madam? Speak.

MRS. PINCHWIFE [*aside to* LUCY *and* HORNER]   Since you'll have me
tell more lies—Yes, indeed, bud.

PINCHWIFE

> For my own sake fain I would all believe;
> Cuckolds, like lovers, should themselves deceive.
> But—[*Sighs.*]
> His honor is least safe, too late I find,
> Who trusts it with a foolish wife or friend.

A dance of cuckolds.

HORNER

> Vain fops but court, and dress, and keep a pother,
> To pass for women's men with one another;
> But he who aims by women to be priz'd,
> First by the men, you see, must be despis'd.

FINIS

Epilogue

Spoken by Mrs. Knep.[4]

> Now, you the vigorous, who daily here ⎫
> O'er vizard-mask in public domineer, ⎬
> And what you'd do to her if in place where; ⎭
> Nay, have the confidence to cry, "Come out!"
> Yet when she says, "Lead on," you are not stout;
> But to your well-dress'd brother straight turn round
> And cry, "Pox on her, Ned, she can't be sound!"
> Then slink away, a fresh one to engage, ⎫
> With so much seeming heat and loving rage, ⎬
> You'd frighten listening actress on the stage; ⎭
> Till she at last has seen you huffing come, ⎫
> And talk of keeping in the tiring-room, ⎬
> Yet cannot be provok'd to lead her home. ⎭
> Next, you Falstaffs of fifty, who beset
> Your buckram maidenheads,[5] which your friends get;
> And whilst to them you of achievements boast,
> They share the booty, and laugh at your cost.

4. Who played Lady Fidget.
5. Buckram is stiff, and hence troublesome to "Falstaffs of fifty." But the line also alludes to
Shakespeare's *1 Henry IV* II.iv., in which Falstaff, having been robbed (by his friends, as it
turns out), lies about the number of "rogues in buckram" he killed in the fray.

In fine, you essenc'd boys, both old and young, ⎫
Who would be thought so eager, brisk, and strong, ⎬
Yet do the ladies, not their husbands, wrong; ⎭
Whose purses for your manhood make excuse,
And keep your Flanders mares[6] for show, not use;
Encourag'd by our woman's man today,
A Horner's part may vainly think to play;
And may intrigues so bashfully disown
That they may doubted be by few or none;
May kiss the cards at picquet, ombre, loo, ⎫
And so be thought to kiss the lady too; ⎬
But, gallants, have a care, faith, what you do. ⎭
The world, which to no man his due will give,
You by experience know you can deceive,
And men may still believe you vigorous,
But then we women—there's no coz'ning us.

FINIS.

---

6. Mistresses.

GEORGE ETHEREGE

The Man of Mode

or

Sir Fopling Flutter

To Her Royal Highness
The Duchess[1]

MADAM,

Poets, however they may be modest otherwise, have always too good
an opinion of what they write. The world, when it sees this play dedicated to your Royal Highness, will conclude I have more than my share
of that vanity. But I hope the honor I have of belonging to you will
excuse my presumption. 'Tis the first thing I have produced in your
service, and my duty obliges me to what my choice durst not else have
aspired.

I am very sensible, madam, how much it is beholding to your indulgence for the success it had in the acting, and your protection will be
no less fortunate to it in the printing; for all are so ambitious of making
their court to you that none can be severe to what you are pleased to
favor.

This universal submission and respect is due to the greatness of your
rank and birth; but you have other illustrious qualities which are much
more engaging. Those would but dazzle, did not these really charm the
eyes and understandings of all who have the happiness to approach you.

Authors on these occasions are never wanting to publish a particular
of their patron's virtues and perfections; but your Royal Highness's are
so eminently known that, did I follow their examples, I should but paint
those wonders here of which everyone already has the idea in his mind.
Besides, I do not think it proper to aim at that in prose which is so
glorious a subject for verse, in which here-after if I show more zeal than

---

† First performed in 1676, at Dorset Garden, and published in the same year.
1. Mary of Modena, Duchess of York.

skill, it will not grieve me much, since I less passionately desire to be esteemed a poet than to be thought,

>Madam,

>>Your Royal Highness's
>>>most humble, most obedient,
>>>>and most faithful servant,

>>>>>GEORGE ETHEREGE

Prologue

By Sir Car Scroope, Baronet[2]

Like dancers on the ropes poor poets fare:
Most perish young, the rest in danger are.
This, one would think, should make our authors wary,
But, gamester-like, the giddy fools miscarry;
A lucky hand or two so tempts 'em on,
They cannot leave off play till they're undone.
With modest fears a muse does first begin,
Like a young wench newly enticed to sin;
But tickled once with praise, by her good will,
The wanton fool would never more lie still.
'Tis an old mistress you'll meet here tonight,
Whose charms you once have looked on with delight.
But now, of late, such dirty drabs have known ye,
A muse o'th' better sort's ashamed to own ye.
Nature well-drawn and wit must now give place
To gaudy nonsense and to dull grimace;
Nor is it strange that you should like so much
That kind of wit, for most of yours is such.
But I'm afraid that while to France we go, ⎫
To bring you home fine dresses, dance, and show, ⎬
The stage, like you, will but more foppish grow. ⎭
Of foreign wares why should we fetch the scum,
When we can be so richly served at home?
For, heav'n be thanked, 'tis not so wise an age
But your own follies may supply the stage.
Though often plowed, there's no great fear the soil
Should barren grow by the too-frequent toil,
While at your doors are to be daily found
Such loads of dunghill to manure the ground.
'Tis by your follies that we players thrive,
As the physicians by diseases live;
And as each year some new distemper reigns,

2. Poet and courtier.

Whose friendly poison helps to increase their gains,
So, among you, there starts up every day
Some new, unheard-of fool for us to play.
Then, for your own sakes, be not too severe,
Nor what you all admire at home, damn here.
Since each is fond of his own ugly face,
Why should you, when we hold it, break the glass?

Dramatis Personae[3]

MR. DORIMANT	
MR. MEDLEY	
OLD BELLAIR	} Gentleman
YOUNG BELLAIR, [in love with Emilia]	
SIR FOPLING FLUTTER	
LADY TOWNLEY, [sister of Old Bellair]	
EMILIA	
MRS. LOVEIT, [in love with Dorimant]	} Gentlewomen
BELLINDA, [in love with Dorimant]	
LADY WOODVILL, and	
HARRIET, her daughter	
PERT	
and	} Waiting women
BUSY	
A SHOEMAKER	
AN ORANGE-WOMAN	
THREE SLOVENLY BULLIES	
TWO CHAIRMEN	
MR. SMIRK, a parson	
HANDY, a valet de chambre	
PAGES. FOOTMEN, etc.	

The Man of Mode

Act I. Scene i.

*A dressing room. A table covered with a toilet; clothes laid ready.
Enter DORIMANT in his gown and slippers, with a note in his hand
made up, repeating verses.*

---

3. No list of actors was published in the original edition, but other sources indicate that the great actor Thomas Betterton played Dorimant and that Elizabeth Barry, beginning a brilliant career, took over the role of Mrs. Loveit in an early revival. In the following year, Barry played Hellena and Betterton played Belvile in *The Rover*. Mary Betterton played Bellinda in *The Man of Mode* and Florinda in *The Rover*. Elinor Leigh, Lady Woodvill in *The Man of Mode*, went on to Moretta in *The Rover*.

DORIMANT

> "Now, for some ages, had the pride of Spain
> Made the sun shine on half the world in vain."[4]

Then looking on the note.

"For Mrs. Loveit." What a dull, insipid thing is a billet-doux written in cold blood, after the heat of the business is over! It is a tax upon good nature which I have here been laboring to pay, and have done it, but with as much regret as ever fanatic[5] paid the Royal Aid or church duties. 'Twill have the same fate, I know, that all my notes to her have had of late; 'twill not be thought kind enough. Faith, women are i' the right when they jealously examine our letters, for in them we always first discover our decay of passion.—Hey! Who waits?

Enter HANDY.

HANDY   Sir—

DORIMANT   Call a footman.

HANDY   None of 'em are come yet.

DORIMANT   Dogs! Will they ever lie snoring abed till noon?

HANDY   'Tis all one, sir: if they're up, you indulge 'em so, they're ever poaching after whores all the morning.

DORIMANT   Take notice henceforward who's wanting in his duty; the next clap he gets, he shall rot for an example. What vermin are those chattering without?

HANDY   Foggy Nan, the orange-woman, and swearing Tom, the shoemaker.

DORIMANT   Go, call in that overgrown jade with the flasket of guts before her. Fruit is refreshing in a morning.

Exit HANDY.

> "It is not that I love you less,
> Than when before your feet I lay—"[6]

Enter ORANGE-WOMAN *and* HANDY.

How now, double-tripe, what news do you bring?

ORANGE-WOMAN   News! Here's the best fruit has come to town t'year. Gad, I was up before four o'clock this morning and bought all the choice i' the market.

DORIMANT   The nasty refuse of your shop.

ORANGE-WOMAN   You need not make mouths at it. I assure you, 'tis all culled ware.

DORIMANT   The citizens buy better on a holiday in their walk to Totnam.[7]

---

4. The opening lines of Edmund Waller's "Of a War with Spain, and a Fight at Sea."
5. Dissenter. The Royal Aid and church duties were taxes.
6. Waller again. The opening lines of "The Self Banished."
7. Tottenham, a lower-middle-class district.

ORANGE-WOMAN   Good or bad, 'tis all one; I never knew you commend anything. Lord, would the ladies had heard you talk of 'em as I have done.

Sets down the fruit.

Here, bid your man give me an angel.[8]

DORIMANT [*to* HANDY]   Give the bawd her fruit again.

ORANGE-WOMAN   Well, on my conscience, there never was the like of you.—God's my life, I had almost forgot to tell you, there is a young gentlewoman, lately come to town with her mother, that is so taken with you.

DORIMANT   Is she handsome?

ORANGE-WOMAN   Nay, gad, there are few finer women, I tell you but so, and a hugeous fortune, they say. Here, eat this peach, it comes from the stone; 'tis better than any Newington y' have tasted.

DORIMANT [*taking the peach*]   This fine woman, I'll lay my life, is some awkward, ill-fashioned country toad, who, not having above four dozen of black hairs on her head, has adorned her baldness with a large white fruz,[9] that she may look sparkishly in the forefront of the King's box at an old play.

ORANGE-WOMAN   Gad, you'd change your note quickly if you did but see her!

DORIMANT   How came she to know me?

ORANGE-WOMAN   She saw you yesterday at the Change.[1] She told me you came and fooled with the woman at the next shop.

DORIMANT   I remember, there was a mask[2] observed me, indeed. Fooled, did she say?

ORANGE-WOMAN   Ay; I vow she told me twenty things you said too, and acted with head and with her body so like you—

Enter MEDLEY.

MEDLEY   Dorimant, my life, my joy, my darling sin! How dost thou?

Embraces him.

ORANGE-WOMAN   Lord, what a filthy trick these men have got of kissing one another!

She spits.

MEDLEY   Why do you suffer this cartload of scandal to come near you and make your neighbors think you so improvident to need a bawd?

ORANGE-WOMAN [*to* DORIMANT]   Good, now, we shall have it, you did but want him to help you. Come, pay me for my fruit.

8. Gold coin, worth about ten shillings.
9. Short, curled wig.
1. The New Exchange, a fashionable arcade of shops.
2. A masked woman.

MEDLEY   Make us thankful for it, huswife, bawds are as much out of fashion as gentlemen-ushers: none but old formal ladies use the one, and none but foppish old stagers employ the other. Go, you are an insignificant brandy bottle.

DORIMANT   Nay, there you wrong her. Three quarts of canary[3] is her business.

ORANGE-WOMAN   What you please, gentlemen.

DORIMANT   To him! Give him as good as he brings.

ORANGE-WOMAN   Hang him, there is not such another heathen in the town again, except it be the shoemaker without.

MEDLEY   I shall see you hold up your hand at the bar next sessions for murder, huswife. That shoemaker can take his oath you are in fee with the doctors to sell green fruit to the gentry, that the crudities may breed diseases.

ORANGE-WOMAN   Pray give me my money.

DORIMANT   Not a penny! When you bring the gentlewoman hither you spoke of, you shall be paid.

ORANGE-WOMAN   The gentlewoman! The gentlewoman may be as honest[4] as your sisters, for aught as I know. Pray pay me, Mr. Dorimant, and do not abuse me so. I have an honester way of living; you know it.

MEDLEY   Was there ever such a resty[5] bawd?

DORIMANT   Some jade's tricks she has, but she makes amends when she's in good humour.—Come, tell me the lady's name, and Handy shall pay you.

ORANGE-WOMAN   I must not; she forbid me.

DORIMANT   That's a sure sign she would have you.

MEDLEY   Where does she live?

ORANGE-WOMAN   They lodge at my house.

MEDLEY   Nay, then she's in a hopeful way.

ORANGE-WOMAN   Good Mr. Medley, say your pleasure of me, but take heed how you affront my house. God's my life, in a hopeful way!

DORIMANT   Prithee, peace. What kind of woman's the mother?

ORANGE-WOMAN   A goodly, grave gentlewoman. Lord, how she talks against the wild young men o' the town! As for your part, she thinks you an arrant devil: should she see you, on my conscience she would look if you had not a cloven foot.

DORIMANT   Does she know me?

ORANGE-WOMAN   Only by hearsay. A thousand horrid stories have been told her of you, and she believes 'em all.

MEDLEY   By the character, this should be the famous Lady Woodvill and her daughter Harriet.

ORANGE-WOMAN [aside]   The devil's in him for guessing, I think.

---

3. Wine from the Canary Islands; *canary-bird* was also slang for *whore*.
4. Chaste.
5. Restive.

DORIMANT Do you know 'em?

MEDLEY Both very well. The mother's a great admirer of the forms and civility of the last age.

DORIMANT An antiquated beauty may be allowed to be out of humour at the freedoms of the present. This is a good account of the mother. Pray, what is the daughter?

MEDLEY Why, first, she's an heiress, vastly rich.

DORIMANT And handsome?

MEDLEY What alteration a twelvemonth may have bred in her, I know not, but a year ago she was the beautifulest creature I ever saw: a fine, easy, clean shape; light brown hair in abundance; her features regular; her complexion clear and lively; large, wanton eyes; but above all, a mouth that has made me kiss it a thousand times in imagination—teeth white and even, and pretty, pouting lips, with a little moisture ever hanging on them, that look like the Provins rose fresh on the bush, ere the morning sun has quite drawn up the dew.

DORIMANT Rapture, mere[6] rapture!

ORANGE-WOMAN Nay, gad he tells you true. She's a delicate creature.

DORIMANT Has she wit?

MEDLEY More than is usual in her sex, and as much malice. Then, she's as wild as you would wish her, and has a demureness in her looks that makes it so surprising.

DORIMANT Flesh and blood cannot hear this and not long to know her.

MEDLEY I wonder what makes her mother bring her up to town? An old, doting keeper cannot be more jealous of his mistress.

ORANGE-WOMAN She made me laugh yesterday. There was a judge came to visit 'em, and the old man (she told me) did so stare upon her and, when he saluted her, smacked so heartily—who would think it of 'em?

MEDLEY God-a-mercy, Judge!

DORIMANT Do 'em right, the gentlemen of the long robe[7] have not been wanting by their good examples to countenance the crying sin o' the nation.

MEDLEY Come, on with your trappings; 'tis later than you imagine.

DORIMANT Call in the shoemaker, Handy!

ORANGE-WOMAN Good Mr. Dorimant, pay me. Gad, I had rather give you my fruit than stay to be abused by that foul-mouthed rogue. What you gentlemen say, it matters not much; but such a dirty fellow does one more disgrace.

DORIMANT [to HANDY] Give her ten shillings. [To ORANGE-WOMAN.] And be sure you tell the young gentlewoman I must be acquainted with her.

6. Absolute.
7. Lawyers.

ORANGE-WOMAN   Now do you long to be tempting this pretty creature. Well, heavens mend you!

MEDLEY   Farewell, bog!

Exeunt ORANGE-WOMAN *and* HANDY.

Dorimant, when did you see your *pis aller*,[8] as you call her, Mrs. Loveit?

DORIMANT   Not these two days.

MEDLEY   And how stand affairs between you?

DORIMANT   There has been great patching of late, much ado; we make a shift to hang together.

MEDLEY   I wonder how her mighty spirit bears it?

DORIMANT   Ill enough, on all conscience. I never knew so violent a creature.

MEDLEY   She's the most passionate in her love and the most extravagant in her jealousy of any women I ever heard of. What note is that?

DORIMANT   An excuse I am going to send her for the neglect I am guilty of.

MEDLEY   Prithee, read it.

DORIMANT   No, but if you will take the pains, you may.

MEDLEY [*reads*]   "I never was a lover of business, but now I have a just reason to hate it, since it has kept me these two days from seeing you. I intend to wait upon you in the afternoon, and in the pleasure of your conversation forget all I have suffered during this tedious absence."—This business of yours, Dorimant, has been with a vizard[9] at the playhouse; I have had an eye on you. If some malicious body should betray you, this kind note would hardly make your peace with her.

DORIMANT   I desire no better.

MEDLEY   Why, would her knowledge of it oblige you?

DORIMANT   Most infinitely; next to the coming to a good understanding with a new mistress, I love a quarrel with an old one. But the devil's in't, there has been such a calm in my affairs of late, I have not had the pleasure of making a woman so much as break her fan, to be sullen, or forswear herself, these three days.

MEDLEY   A very great misfortune! Let me see, I love mischief well enough to forward this business myself. I'll about it presently, and though I know the truth of what y'ave done will set her a-raving, I'll heighten it a little with invention, leave her in a fit o' the mother,[1] and be here again before y'are ready.

DORIMANT   Pray, stay; you may spare yourself the labor. The business is undertaken already by one who will manage it with as much address and, I think, with a little more malice than you can.

MEDLEY   Who i' the devil's name can this be?

8. Last resort.
9. Masked woman, often a whore.
1. Hysteria.

DORIMANT   Why, the vizard, that very vizard you saw me with.

MEDLEY   Does she love mischief so well as to betray herself to spite another?

DORIMANT   Not so neither, Medley; I will make you comprehend the mystery. This mask, for a farther confirmation of what I have been these two days swearing to her, made me yesterday at the playhouse make her a promise, before her face, utterly to break off with Loveit; and because she tenders my reputation and would not have me do a barbarous thing, has contrived a way to give me a handsome occasion.

MEDLEY   Very good.

DORIMANT   She intends, about an hour before me this afternoon, to make Loveit a visit; and (having the privilege by reason of a professed friendship between 'em to talk of her concerns)—

MEDLEY   Is she a friend?

DORIMANT   Oh, an intimate friend!

MEDLEY   Better and better! Pray proceed.

DORIMANT   She means insensibly to insinuate a discourse of me and artificially raise her jealousy to such a height that, transported with the first motions of her passion, she shall fly upon me with all the fury imaginable as soon as ever I enter. The quarrel being thus happily begun, I am to play my part: confess and justify all my roguery, swear her impertinence and ill humor makes her intolerable, tax her with the next fop that comes into my head, and in a huff march away, slight her, and leave her to be taken by whosoever thinks it worth his time to lie down before her.

MEDLEY   This vizard is a spark, and has a genius that makes her worthy of yourself, Dorimant.

Enter HANDY, SHOEMAKER, *and* FOOTMAN.

DORIMANT *[to* FOOTMAN]   You rogue there, who sneak like a dog that has flung down a dish! If you do not mend your waiting, I'll uncase[2] you and turn you loose to the wheel of fortune.—Handy, seal this and let him run with it presently.

Exit FOOTMAN.

MEDLEY   Since y'are resolved on a quarrel, why do you send her this kind note?

DORIMANT   To keep her at home in order to the business. [*To the* SHOE-MAKER.] How now, you drunken sot?

SHOEMAKER   'Zbud, you have no reason to talk. I have not had a bottle of sack of yours in my belly this fortnight.

MEDLEY   The orange-woman says your neighbors take notice what a heathen you are, and design to inform the bishop and have you burned for an atheist.

---

2. Strip you of your livery.

SHOEMAKER   Damn her, dunghill! If her husband does not remove her, she stinks so, the parish intend to indict him for a nuisance.

MEDLEY   I advise you like a friend, reform your life. You have brought the envy of the world upon you by living above yourself. Whoring and swearing are vices too genteel for a shoemaker.

SHOEMAKER   'Zbud, I think you men of quality will grow as unreasonable as the women: you would engross[3] the sins o' the nation. Poor folks can no sooner be wicked but th'are railed at by their betters.

DORIMANT   Sirrah, I'll have you stand i' the pillory for this libel.

SHOEMAKER   Some of you deserve it, I'm sure. There are so many of 'em that our journeymen nowadays, instead of harmless ballads, sing nothing but your damned lampoons.

DORIMANT   Our lampoons, you rogue?

SHOEMAKER   Nay, good master, why should not you write your own commentaries[4] as well as Caesar?

MEDLEY   The rascal's read, I perceive.

SHOEMAKER   You know the old proverb, ale and history.[5]

DORIMANT   Draw on my shoes, sirrah.

SHOEMAKER   Here's a shoe—

DORIMANT   Sits with more wrinkles than there are in an angry bully's forehead.

SHOEMAKER   'Zbud, as smooth as your mistress's skin does upon her. So, strike your foot in home. 'Zbud, if e'er a monsieur of 'em all make more fashionable ware, I'll be content to have my ears whipped off with my own paring knife.

MEDLEY   And served up in a ragout, instead of coxcombs, to a company of French shoemakers for a collation.

SHOEMAKER   Hold, hold! Damn 'em caterpillars, let 'em feed upon cabbage!—Come master, your health this morning next my heart now.[6]

DORIMANT   Go, get you home, and govern your family better! Do not let your wife follow you to the alehouse, beat your whore, and lead you home in triumph.

SHOEMAKER   'Zbud, there's never a man i' the town lives more like a gentleman with his wife than I do. I never mind her motions; she never inquires into mine. We speak to one another civilly, hate one another heartily, and because 'tis vulgar to lie and soak[7] together, we have each of us our several settle-bed.

DORIMANT [to HANDY]   Give him half a crown.

MEDLEY   Not without he will promise to be bloody drunk.

---

3. Monopolize.
4. A pun. *Commentary* could mean *treatise* or *satiric "comment."*
5. "Truth is in ale as in history."
6. He is asking for money.
7. Drink.

SHOEMAKER   Tope's the word, i' the eye of the world. [*To* HANDY.] For my master's honor, Robin![8]

DORIMANT   Do not debauch my servants, sirrah.

SHOEMAKER   I only tip him the wink; he knows an alehouse from a hovel.

Exit SHOEMAKER.

DORIMANT [*to* HANDY]   My clothes, quickly!

MEDLEY   Where shall we dine today?

Enter YOUNG BELLAIR.

DORIMANT   Where you will. Here comes a good third man.

YOUNG BELLAIR   Your servant, gentlemen.

MEDLEY   Gentle sir, how will you answer this visit to your honorable mistress? 'Tis not her interest you should keep company with men of sense, who will be talking reason.

YOUNG BELLAIR   I do not fear her pardon, do you but grant me yours for my neglect of late.

MEDLEY   Though y'ave made us miserable by the want of your good company, to show you I am free from all resentment, may the beautiful cause of our misfortune give you all the joys happy lovers have shared ever since the world began.

YOUNG BELLAIR   You wish me in heaven, but you believe me on my journey to hell.

MEDLEY   You have a good strong faith, and that may contribute much towards your salvation. I confess I am but of an untoward constitution, apt to have doubts and scruples; and in love they are no less distracting than in religion. Were I so near marriage, I should cry out by fits as I ride in my coach, "Cuckold, cuckold!" with no less fury than the mad fanatic does "Glory!" in Bethlem.[9]

YOUNG BELLAIR   Because religion makes some run mad, must I live an atheist?

MEDLEY   Is it not great indiscretion for a man of credit, who may have money enough on his word, to go and deal with Jews, who for little sums make men enter into bonds and give judgments?[1]

YOUNG BELLAIR   Preach no more on this text; I am determined, and there is no hope of my conversion.

DORIMANT [*to* HANDY, *who is fiddling about him*]   Leave your unnecessary fiddling. A wasp that's buzzing about a man's nose at dinner is not more troublesome than thou art.

HANDY   You love to have your clothes hang just, sir.

---

8. "Robin" is colloquial for *servant*—i.e., Handy. "Tope" is a more polite version of Medley's "bloody drunk."

9. Bethlehem Hospital, the insane asylum.

1. Securities.

DORIMANT   I love to be well-dressed, sir, and think it no scandal to my understanding.

HANDY   Will you use the essence, or orange-flower water?

DORIMANT   I will smell as I do today, no offense to the ladies' noses.

HANDY   Your pleasure, sir.

Exit HANDY.

DORIMANT   That a man's excellency should lie in neatly tying of a ribbon or a cravat! How careful's nature in furnishing the world with necessary coxcombs!

YOUNG BELLAIR   That's a mighty pretty suit of yours, Dorimant.

DORIMANT   I am glad 't has your approbation.

YOUNG BELLAIR   No man in town has a better fancy in his clothes than you have.

DORIMANT   You will make me have an opinion of my genius.

MEDLEY   There is a great critic, I hear, in these matters lately arrived piping hot from Paris.

YOUNG BELLAIR   Sir Fopling Flutter, you mean.

MEDLEY   The same.

YOUNG BELLAIR   He thinks himself the pattern of modern gallantry.

DORIMANT   He is indeed the pattern of modern foppery.

MEDLEY   He was yesterday at the play, with a pair of gloves up to his elbows and a periwig more exactly curled than a lady's head newly dressed for a ball.

YOUNG BELLAIR   What a pretty lisp he has!

DORIMANT   Ho, that he affects in imitation of the people of quality of France.

MEDLEY   His head stands for the most part on one side, and his looks are more languishing than a lady's when she lolls at stretch in her coach or leans her head carelessly against the side of a box 'i the playhouse.

DORIMANT   He is a person indeed of great acquired follies.

MEDLEY   He is like many others, beholding to his education for making him so eminent a coxcomb. Many a fool had been lost to the world, had their indulgent parents wisely bestowed neither learning nor good breeding on 'em.

YOUNG BELLAIR   He has been, as the sparkish word is, brisk upon the ladies already. He was yesterday at my Aunt Townley's and gave Mrs. Loveit a catalogue of his good qualities, under the character of a complete gentleman, who (according to Sir Fopling) ought to dress well, dance well, fence well, have a genius for love letters, an agreeable voice for a chamber, be very amorous, something discreet, but not overconstant.

MEDLEY   Pretty ingredients to make an accomplished person!

DORIMANT   I am glad he pitched upon Loveit.

YOUNG BELLAIR   How so?

DORIMANT   I wanted a fop to lay to her charge; and this is as pat as may be.

YOUNG BELLAIR   I am confident she loves no man but you.

DORIMANT   The good fortune were enough to make me vain, but that I am in my nature modest.

YOUNG BELLAIR   Hark you, Dorimant.—With your leave, Mr. Medley. 'Tis only a secret concerning a fair lady.

MEDLEY   Your good breeding, sir, gives you too much trouble. You might have whispered without all this ceremony.

YOUNG BELLAIR [*to* DORIMANT]   How stand your affairs with Bellinda of late?

DORIMANT   She's a little jilting baggage.

YOUNG BELLAIR   Nay, I believe her false enough, but she's ne'er the worse for your purpose. She was with you yesterday in a disguise at the play.

DORIMANT   There we fell out and resolved never to speak to one another more.

YOUNG BELLAIR   The occasion?

DORIMANT   Want of courage to meet me at the place appointed. These young women apprehend loving as much as the young men do fighting at first; but once entered, like them too, they all turn bullies straight.

Enter HANDY.

HANDY [*to* YOUNG BELLAIR]   Sir, your man without desires to speak with you.

YOUNG BELLAIR   Gentlemen, I'll return immediately.

Exit YOUNG BELLAIR.

MEDLEY   A very pretty fellow, this.

DORIMANT   He's handsome, well-bred, and by much the most tolerable of all the young men that do not abound in wit.

MEDLEY   Ever well-dressed, always complaisant, and seldom impertinent; you and he are grown very intimate, I see.

DORIMANT   It is our mutual interest to be so. It makes the women think the better of his understanding and judge more favorably of my reputation; it makes him pass upon some for a man of very good sense, and I upon others for a very civil person.

MEDLEY   What was that whisper?

DORIMANT   A thing which he would fain have known, but I did not think it fit to tell him. It might have frighted him from his honorable intentions of marrying.

MEDLEY   Emilia, give her her due, has the best reputation of any young woman about the town who has beauty enough to provoke detraction. Her carriage is unaffected, her discourse modest—not at all censorious nor pretending, like the counterfeits of the age.

DORIMANT She's a discreet maid, and I believe nothing can corrupt her but a husband.

MEDLEY A husband?

DORIMANT Yes, a husband. I have known many women make a difficulty of losing a maidenhead, who have afterwards made none of making a cuckold.

MEDLEY This prudent consideration, I am apt to think, has made you confirm poor Bellair in the desperate resolution he has taken.

DORIMANT Indeed, the little hope I found there was of her, in the state she was in, has made me by my advice contribute something towards the changing of her condition.

Enter YOUNG BELLAIR.

Dear Bellair, by heavens I thought we had lost thee! Men in love are never to be reckoned on when we would form a company.

YOUNG BELLAIR Dorimant, I am undone. My man has brought the most surprising news i' the world.

DORIMANT Some strange misfortune is befall'n your love?

YOUNG BELLAIR My father came to town last night and lodges i' the very house where Emilia lies.

MEDLEY Does he know it is with her you are in love?

YOUNG BELLAIR He knows I love, but knows not whom, without some officious sot has betrayed me.

DORIMANT Your Aunt Townley is your confidante and favors the business.

YOUNG BELLAIR I do not apprehend any ill office from her. I have received a letter, in which I am commanded by my father to meet him at my aunt's this afternoon. He tells me farther he has made a match for me, and bids me resolve to be obedient to his will or expect to be disinherited.

MEDLEY Now's your time, Bellair. Never had lover such an opportunity of giving a generous proof of his passion.

YOUNG BELLAIR As how, I pray?

MEDLEY Why, hang an estate, marry Emilia out of hand, and provoke your father to do what he threatens. 'Tis but despising a coach, humbling yourself to a pair of galoshes, being out of countenance when you meet your friends, pointed at and pitied wherever you go by all the amorous fops that know you, and your fame will be immortal.

YOUNG BELLAIR I could find in my heart to resolve not to marry at all.

DORIMANT Fie, fie! That would spoil a good jest and disappoint the well-natured town of an occasion of laughing at you.

YOUNG BELLAIR The storm I have so long expected hangs o'er my head and begins to pour down upon me. I am on the rack and can have no rest till I'm satisfied in what I fear. Where do you dine?

DORIMANT At Long's or Locket's.[2]

---

2. Fashionable taverns.

MEDLEY   At Long's let it be.

YOUNG BELLAIR   I'll run and see Emilia and inform myself how matters stand. If my misfortunes are not so great as to make me unfit for company, I'll be with you.

Exit YOUNG BELLAIR.

Enter a FOOTMAN, *with a letter.*

FOOTMAN [*to* DORIMANT]   Here's a letter, sir.

DORIMANT   The superscripiton's right: "For Mr. Dorimant."

MEDLEY   Let's see. The very scrawl and spelling of a true-bred whore.

DORIMANT   I know the hand. The style is admirable, I assure you.

MEDLEY   Prithee, read it.

DORIMANT [*reads*]   "I told a you you dud not love me, if you dud, you would have seen me again ere now. I have no money and am very malicolly. Pray send me a guynie to see the operies. Your servant to command, Molly."

MEDLEY   Pray let the whore have a favorable answer, that she may spark it in a box and do honor to her profession.

DORIMANT   She shall, and perk up i' the face of quality. [*To* HANDY.]   Is the coach at door?

HANDY   You did not bid me send for it.

DORIMANT   Eternal blockhead!

HANDY *offers to go out.*

Hey, sot!

HANDY   Did you call me, sir?

DORIMANT   I hope you have no just exception to the name, sir?

HANDY   I have sense, sir.

DORIMANT   Not so much as a fly in winter.—How did you come, Medley?

MEDLEY   In a chair.

FOOTMAN   You may have a hackney coach if you please, sir.

DORIMANT   I may ride the elephant if I please, sir. Call another chair and let my coach follow to Long's.

Exeunt FOOTMAN *and* HANDY.

"Be calm, ye great parents, etc."[3]

Exeunt, singing.

Act II. Scene i. LADY TOWNLEY's *house.*

Enter my LADY TOWNLEY *and* EMILIA.

LADY TOWNLEY   I was afraid, Emilia, all had been discovered.

EMILIA   I tremble with the apprehension still.

3. Apparently a contemporary song.

LADY TOWNLEY   That my brother should take lodgings i' the very house where you lie!

EMILIA   'Twas lucky we had timely notice to warn the people to be secret. He seems to be a mighty good-humoured old man.

LADY TOWNLEY   He ever had a notable smirking way with him.

EMILIA   He calls me rogue, tells me he can't abide me, and does so bepat me.

LADY TOWNLEY   On my word, you are much in his favor then.

EMILIA   He has been very inquisitive, I am told, about my family, my reputation, and my fortune.

LADY TOWNLEY   I am confident he does not i' the least suspect you are the woman his son's in love with.

EMILIA   What should make him then inform himself so particularly of me?

LADY TOWNLEY   He was always of a very loving temper himself. It may be he has a doting fit upon him, who knows?

EMILIA   It cannot be.

Enter YOUNG BELLAIR.

LADY TOWNLEY   Here comes my nephew.—Where did you leave your father?

YOUNG BELLAIR   Writing a note within.—Emilia, this early visit looks as if some kind jealousy would not let you rest at home.

EMILIA   The knowledge I have of my rival gives me a little cause to fear your constancy.

YOUNG BELLAIR   My constancy! I vow—

EMILIA   Do not vow. Our love is frail as is our life, and full as little in our power; and are you sure you shall outlive this day?

YOUNG BELLAIR   I am not, but when we are in perfect health, 'twere an idle thing to fright ourselves with the thoughts of sudden death.

LADY TOWNLEY   Pray, what has passed between you and your father i' the garden?

YOUNG BELLAIR   He's firm in his resolution, tells me I must marry Mrs. Harriet, or swears he'll marry himself and disinherit me. When I saw I could not prevail with him to be more indulgent, I dissembled an obedience to his will, which has composed his passion and will give us time—and I hope opportunity—to deceive him.

Enter OLD BELLAIR, *with a note in his hand.*

LADY TOWNLEY   Peace, here he comes.

OLD BELLAIR   Harry, take this and let your man carry it for me to Mr. Fourbe's[4] chamber—my lawyer, i' the Temple.[5]

Exit YOUNG BELLAIR.

---

4. From *fourbe* (French), a cheat.
5. Center of the legal profession in London.

[*To* EMILIA.] Neighbor, adod I am glad to see thee here.—Make much of her, sister. She's one of the best of your acquaintance. I like her countenance and behavior well; she has a modesty that is not common i' this age, adod she has.

LADY TOWNLEY   I know her value, brother, and esteem her accordingly.

OLD BELLAIR   Advise her to wear a little more mirth in her face. Adod, she's too serious.

LADY TOWNLEY   The fault is very excusable in a young woman.

OLD BELLAIR   Nay, adod, I like her ne'er the worse; a melancholy beauty has her charms. I love a pretty sadness in a face which varies now and then, like changeable colors, into a smile.

LADY TOWNLEY   Methinks you speak very feelingly, brother.

OLD BELLAIR   I am but five-and-fifty, sister, you know—an age not altogether insensible. [*To* EMILIA.] Cheer up, sweetheart, I have a secret to tell thee may chance to make thee merry. We three will make collation together anon. I' the meantime, mum, I can't abide you; go, I can't abide you.

    Enter YOUNG BELLAIR.

Harry! Come, you must along with me to my Lady Woodvill's.—I am going to slip the boy at a mistress.

YOUNG BELLAIR   At a wife, sir, you would say.

OLD BELLAIR   You need not look so glum, sir. A wife is no curse when she brings the blessing of a good estate with her. But an idle town flirt, with a painted face, a rotten reputation, and a crazy fortune, adod, is the devil and all; and such a one I hear you are in league with.

YOUNG BELLAIR   I cannot help detraction, sir.

OLD BELLAIR   Out, a pize[6] o' their breeches, there are keeping fools enough for such flaunting baggages, and they are e'en too good for 'em. [*To* EMILIA.] Remember night. [*Aloud.*] Go, y'are a rogue, y'are a rogue. Fare you well, fare you well. [*To* YOUNG BELLAIR.] Come, come, come along, sir.

    Exeunt OLD *and* YOUNG BELLAIR.

LADY TOWNLEY   On my word, the old man comes on apace. I'll lay my life he's smitten.

EMILIA   This is nothing but the pleasantness of his humour.

LADY TOWNLEY   I know him better than you. Let it work; it may prove lucky.

    Enter a PAGE.

PAGE   Madam, Mr. Medley has sent to know whether a visit will not be troublesome this afternoon?

---

6. An imprecation, as in *a pox*.

LADY TOWNLEY   Send him word his visits never are so.

Exit PAGE.

EMILIA   He's a very pleasant man.

LADY TOWNLEY   He's a very necessary man among us women. He's not
scandalous i' the least, perpetually contriving to bring good company
together, and always ready to stop up a gap at ombre.[7] Then, he
knows all the little news o' the town.

EMILIA   I love to hear him talk o' the intrigues. Let 'em be never so
dull in themselves, he'll make 'em pleasant i' the relation.

LADY TOWNLEY   But he improves things so much one can take no measure of the truth from him. Mr. Dorimant swears a flea or a maggot
is not made more monstrous by a magnifying glass than a story is by
his telling it.

   Enter MEDLEY.

EMILIA   Hold, here he comes.

LADY TOWNLEY   Mr. Medley.

MEDLEY   Your servant, madam.

LADY TOWNLEY   You have made yourself a stranger of late.

EMILIA   I believe you took a surfeit of ombre last time you were here.

MEDLEY   Indeed I had my bellyful of that termagant, Lady Dealer.
There never was so insatiable a carder; an old gleeker[8] never loved to
sit to 't like her. I have played with her, now at least a dozen times,
till she 'as worn out all her fine complexion and her tour[9] would keep
in curl no longer.

LADY TOWNLEY   Blame her not, poor woman. She loves nothing so well
as a black ace.

MEDLEY   The pleasure I have seen her in when she has had hope in
drawing for a matador![1]

EMILIA   'Tis as pretty sport to her as persuading masks off is to you, to
make discoveries.

LADY TOWNLEY   Pray, where's your friend Mr. Dorimant?

MEDLEY   Soliciting his affairs. He's a man of great employment—has
more mistresses now depending than the most eminent lawyer in
England has causes.

EMILIA   Here has been Mrs. Loveit so uneasy and out of humor these
two days.

LADY TOWNLEY   How strangely love and jealousy rage in that poor
woman!

MEDLEY   She could not have picked out a devil upon earth so proper
to torment her. H'as made her break a dozen or two of fans already,

7. Card game, often for three players.
8. Gleek was a card game.
9. Front of false hair.
1. High trump—such as a black ace.

tear half a score points in pieces, and destroy hoods and knots without number.

LADY TOWNLEY   We heard of a pleasant serenade he gave her t'other night.

MEDLEY   A Danish serenade, with kettledrums and trumpets.

EMILIA   Oh, barbarous!

MEDLEY   What, you are of the number of the ladies whose ears are grown so delicate since our operas, you can be charmed with nothing but *flûtes* douces and French hautboys?[2]

EMILIA   Leave your raillery and tell us, is there any new wit come forth—songs, or novels?

MEDLEY   A very pretty piece of gallantry, by an eminent author, called *The Diversions of Brussels*[3]—very necessary to be read by all old ladies who are desirous to improve themselves at questions and commands, blindman's buff, and the like fashionable recreations.

EMILIA   Oh, ridiculous!

MEDLEY   Then there is *The Art of Affectation*, written by a late beauty of quality, teaching you how to draw up your breasts, stretch up your neck, to thrust out your breech, to play with your head, to toss up your nose, to bite your lips, to turn up your eyes, to speak in a silly soft tone of a voice, and use all the foolish French words that will infallibly make your person and conversation charming; with a short apology at the latter end, in the behalf of young ladies who notoriously wash and paint, though they have naturally good complexions.

EMILIA   What a deal of stuff you tell us!

MEDLEY   Such as the town affords, madam. The Russians, hearing the great respect we have for foreign dancing, have lately sent over some of their best balladines, who are now practicing a famous ballet which will be suddenly danced at the Bear Garden.[4]

LADY TOWNLEY   Pray forbear your idle stories, and give us an account of the state of love as it now stands.

MEDLEY   Truly there has been some revolutions in those affairs: great chopping and changing among the old, and some new lovers, whom malice, indiscretion, and misfortune have luckily brought into play.

LADY TOWNLEY   What think you of walking into the next room and sitting down, before you engage in this business?

MEDLEY   I wait upon you; and I hope (though women are commonly unreasonable) by the plenty of scandal I shall discover, to give you very good content, ladies.

Exeunt.

---

2. High-pitched flutes and French oboes.
3. Medley's book titles are imaginary.
4. Theater for bear-baiting. Medley is still carrying on.

Act II. Scene ii. MRS. LOVEIT'S.

Enter MRS. LOVEIT *and* PERT; MRS. LOVEIT *putting up a letter, then pulling out her pocket glass and looking in it.*

MRS. LOVEIT   Pert.

PERT   Madam?

MRS. LOVEIT   I hate myself, I look so ill today.

PERT   Hate the wicked cause on't, that base man Mr. Dorimant, who makes you torment and vex yourself continually.

MRS. LOVEIT   He is to blame, indeed.

PERT   To blame to be two days without sending, writing, or coming near you, contrary to his oath and covenant! 'Twas to much purpose to make him swear! I'll lay my life there's not an article but he has broken: talked to the vizards i' the pit, waited upon the ladies from the boxes to their coaches, gone behind the scenes and fawned upon those little insignificant creatures, the players. 'Tis impossible for a man of his inconstant temper to forbear, I'm sure.

MRS. LOVEIT   I know he is a devil, but he has something of the angel yet undefaced in him, which makes him so charming and agreeable that I must love him, be he never so wicked.

PERT   I little thought, madam, to see your spirit tamed to this degree, who banished poor Mr. Lackwit but for taking up another lady's fan in your presence.

MRS. LOVEIT   My knowing of such odious fools contributes to the making of me love Dorimant the better.

PERT   Your knowing of Mr. Dorimant, in my mind, should rather make you hate all mankind.

MRS. LOVEIT   So it does, besides himself.

PERT   Pray, what excuse does he make in his letter?

MRS. LOVEIT   He has had business.

PERT   Business in general terms would not have been a current excuse for another. A modish man is always very busy when he is in pursuit of a new mistress.

MRS. LOVEIT   Some fop has bribed you to rail at him. He had business; I will believe it and will forgive him.

PERT   You may forgive him anything, but I shall never forgive him his turning me into ridicule, as I hear he does.

MRS. LOVEIT   I perceive you are of the number of those fools his wit had made his enemies.

PERT   I am of the number of those he's pleased to rally, madam; and if we may believe Mr. Wagfan and Mr. Caperwell, he sometimes makes merry with yourself, too, among his laughing companions.

MRS. LOVEIT   Blockheads are as malicious to witty men as ugly women are to the handsome; 'tis their interest, and they make it their business to defame 'em.

PERT   I wish Mr. Dorimant would not make it his business to defame you.

MRS. LOVEIT   Should he, I had rather be made infamous by him than owe my reputation to the dull discretion of those fops you talk of.

Enter BELLINDA.

Bellinda!

Running to her.

BELLINDA   My dear!

MRS. LOVEIT   You have been unkind of late.

BELLINDA   Do not say unkind, say unhappy.

MRS. LOVEIT   I could chide you. Where have you been these two days?

BELLINDA   Pity me rather, my dear, where I have been so tired with two or three country gentlewomen, whose conversation has been more insufferable than a country fiddle.

MRS. LOVEIT   Are they relations?

BELLINDA   No, Welsh acquaintance I made when I was last year at St. Winifred's.[5] They have asked me a thousand questions of the modes and intrigues of the town, and I have told 'em almost as many things for news that hardly were so when their gowns were in fashion.

MRS. LOVEIT   Provoking creatures, how could you endure 'em?

BELLINDA [*aside*]   Now to carry on my plot; nothing but love could make me capable of so much falsehood. 'Tis time to begin, lest Dorimant should come before her jealousy has stung her.

Laughs and then speaks on.

I was yesterday at a play with 'em, where I was fain to show 'em the living, as the man at Westminster does the dead. That is Mrs. Such-a-one, admired for her beauty; this is Mr. Such-a-one, cried up for a wit; that is sparkish Mr. Such-a-one, who keeps reverend Mrs. Such-a-one; and there sits fine Mrs. Such-a-one, who was lately cast off by my Lord Such-a-one.

MRS. LOVEIT   Did you see Dorimant there?

BELLINDA   I did; and imagine you were there with him and have no mind to own it.

MRS. LOVEIT   What should make you think so?

BELLINDA   A lady masked, in a pretty *déshabillé*,[6] whom Dorimant entertained with more respect than the gallants do a common vizard.

MRS. LOVEIT [*aside*]   Dorimant at a play entertaining a mask! Oh, heavens!

---

5. In Wales. The town of Holywell takes its name from St. Winifred's well, which supposedly arose where St. Winifred was killed by a pagan.
6. Revealing dress.

BELLINDA [*aside*] Good!

MRS. LOVEIT Did he stay all the while?

BELLINDA Till the play was done, and then led her out; which confirms me it was you.

MRS. LOVEIT Traitor!

PERT Now you may believe he had business, and you may forgive him too.

MRS. LOVEIT Ungrateful, perjured man!

BELLINDA You seem so much concerned, my dear, I fear I have told you unawares what I had better have concealed for your quiet.

MRS. LOVEIT What manner of shape had she?

BELLINDA Tall and slender. Her motions were very genteel. Certainly she must be some person of condition.

MRS. LOVEIT Shame and confusion be ever in her face when she shows it!

BELLINDA I should blame your discretion for loving that wild man, my dear; but they say he has a way so bewitching that few can defend their hearts who know him.

MRS. LOVEIT I will tear him from mine, or die i' the attempt!

BELLINDA Be more moderate.

MRS. LOVEIT Would I had daggers, darts, or poisoned arrows in my breast, so I could but remove the thoughts of him from thence!

BELLINDA Fie, fie, your transports are too violent, my dear. This may be but an accidental gallantry, and 'tis likely ended at her coach.

PERT Should it proceed farther, let your comfort be, the conduct Mr. Dorimant affects will quickly make you know your rival, ten to one let you see her ruined, her reputation exposed to the town—a happiness none will envy her but yourself, madam.

MRS. LOVEIT Whoe'er she be, all the harm I wish her is, may she love him as well as I do, and may he give her as much cause to hate him!

PERT Never doubt the latter end of your curse, madam.

MRS. LOVEIT May all the passions that are raised by neglected love— jealousy, indignation, spite, and thirst of revenge—eternally rage in her soul, as they do now in mine!

> *Walks up and down with a distracted air.*
> *Enter a* PAGE.

PAGE Madam, Mr. Dorimant—

MRS. LOVEIT I will not see him.

PAGE I told him you were within, madam.

MRS. LOVEIT Say you lied, say I'm busy—shut the door—say anything!

PAGE He's here, madam.

> *Enter* DORIMANT.

Exit PAGE.

DORIMANT

> "They taste of death who do at heaven arrive;
> But we this paradise approach alive."[7]

[*To* MRS. LOVEIT.]   What, dancing the galloping nag[8] without a fiddle?

Offers to catch her by the hand; she flings away and walks on.

I fear this restlessness of the body, madam, [*pursuing her*] proceeds from an unquietness of the mind. What unlucky accident puts you out of humour—a point ill-washed, knots spoiled i' the making up, hair shaded awry, or some other little mistake in setting you in order?

PERT   A trifle, in my opinion, sir, more inconsiderable than any you mention.

DORIMANT   Oh, Mrs. Pert! I never knew you sullen enough to be silent. Come, let me know the business.

PERT   The business, sir, the business that has taken you up these two days. How have I seen you laugh at men of business, and now to become a man of business yourself!

DORIMANT   We are not masters of our own affections; our inclinations daily alter. Now we love pleasure, and anon we shall dote on business. Human frailty will have it so, and who can help it?

MRS. LOVEIT   Faithless, inhuman, barbarous man—

DORIMANT [*aside*]   Good. Now the alarm strikes.

MRS. LOVEIT   —Without sense of love, of honor, or of gratitude! Tell me, for I will know, what devil masked she was, you were with at the play yesterday.

DORIMANT   Faith, I resolved as much as you, but the devil was obstinate and would not tell me.

MRS. LOVEIT   False in this as in your vows to me! You do know!

DORIMANT   The truth is, I did all I could to know.

MRS. LOVEIT   And dare you own it to my face? Hell and furies!

Tears her fan in pieces.

DORIMANT   Spare your fan, madam. You are growing hot and will want it to cool you.

MRS. LOVEIT   Horror and distraction seize you! Sorrow and remorse gnaw your soul and punish all your perjuries to me!

Weeps.

DORIMANT [*turning to* BELLINDA]

> "So thunder breaks the cloud in twain.
> And makes a passage for the rain."[9]

7. Opening lines of Waller's "Of Her Chamber."
8. Country dance.
9. Matthew Roydon, "An Elegy . . . for his Astrophel" (i.e., Sir Philip Sidney), lines 59–60.

[*To* BELLINDA.] Bellinda, you are the devil that have raised this storm. You were at the play yesterday and have been making discoveries to your dear.

BELLINDA   Y'are the most mistaken man i' the world.

DORIMANT   It must be so, and here I vow revenge—resolve to pursue and persecute you more impertinently than ever any loving fop did his mistress, hunt you i' the Park, trace you i' the Mall,[1] dog you in every visit you make, haunt you at the plays and i' the drawing room, hang my nose in your neck and talk to you whether you will or no, and ever look upon you with such dying eyes till your friends grow jealous of me, send you out of town, and the world suspect your reputation. [*In a lower voice.*] At my Lady Townley's when we go from hence.

    He looks kindly on BELLINDA.

BELLINDA   I'll meet you there.

DORIMANT   Enough.

MRS. LOVEIT [*pushing* DORIMANT *away*]   Stand off! You sha' not stare upon her so.

DORIMANT   Good, there's one made jealous already.

MRS. LOVEIT   Is this the constancy you vowed?

DORIMANT   Constancy at my years? 'Tis not a virtue in season; you might as well expect the fruit the autumn ripens i' the spring.

MRS. LOVEIT   Monstrous principle!

DORIMANT   Youth has a long journey to go, madam. Should I have set up my rest at the first inn I lodged at, I should never have arrived at the happiness I now enjoy.

MRS. LOVEIT   Dissembler, damned dissembler!

DORIMANT   I am so, I confess. Good nature and good manners corrupt me. I am honest in my inclinations and would not, wer't not to avoid offense, make a lady a little in years believe I think her young, wilfully mistake art for nature, and seem as fond of a thing I am weary of as when I doted on't in earnest.

MRS. LOVEIT   False man!

DORIMANT   True woman.

MRS. LOVEIT   Now you begin to show yourself.

DORIMANT   Love gilds us over and makes us show fine things to one another for a time; but soon the gold wears off, and then again the native brass appears.

MRS. LOVEIT   Think on your oaths, your vows, and protestations, perjured man!

DORIMANT   I made 'em when I was in love.

MRS. LOVEIT   And therefore ought they not to bind? Oh, impious!

DORIMANT   What we swear at such a time may be a certain proof of a

---

1. A fashionable walk in St. James's Park.

present passion; but to say truth, in love there is no security to be
given for the future.

MRS. LOVEIT   Horrid and ungrateful, begone! And never see me more!

DORIMANT   I am not one of those troublesome coxcombs who, because
they were once well-received, take the privilege to plague a woman
with their love ever after. I shall obey you, madam, though I do myself
some violence.

He offers to go, and MRS. LOVEIT *pulls him back.*

MRS. LOVEIT   Come back, you sha' not go! Could you have the ill
nature to offer it?

DORIMANT   When love grows diseased, the best thing we can do is to
put it to a violent death. I cannot endure the torture of a ling'ring and
consumptive passion.

MRS. LOVEIT   Can you think mine sickly?

DORIMANT   Oh, 'tis desperately ill! What worse symptoms are there
than your being always uneasy when I visit you, your picking quarrels
with me on slight occasions, and in my absence kindly list'ning to the
impertinences of every fashionable fool that talks to you?

MRS. LOVEIT   What fashionable fool can you lay to my charge?

DORIMANT   Why, the very cock-fool of all those fools, Sir Fopling
Flutter.

MRS. LOVEIT   I never saw him in my life but once.

DORIMANT   The worse woman you, at first sight to put on all your
charms, to entertain him with that softness in your voice and all that
wanton kindness in your eyes you so notoriously affect when you
design a conquest.

MRS. LOVEIT   So damned a lie did never malice yet invent. Who told
you this?

DORIMANT   No matter. That ever I should love a woman that can dote
on a senseless caper, a tawdry French ribbon, and a formal cravat!

MRS. LOVEIT   You make me mad!

DORIMANT   A guilty conscience may do much. Go on, be the game-
mistress of the town and enter[2] all our young fops, as fast as they come
from travel.

MRS. LOVEIT   Base and scurrilous!

DORIMANT   A fine mortifying reputation 'twill be for a woman of your
pride, wit, and quality!

MRS. LOVEIT   This jealousy's a mere pretense, a cursed trick of your
own devising. I know you.

DORIMANT   Believe it and all the ill of me you can. I would not have a
woman have the least good thought of me that can think well of
Fopling. Farewell. Fall to, and much good may do you with your
coxcomb.

2. Train.

MRS. LOVEIT   Stay! Oh stay, and I will tell you all.
DORIMANT   I have been told too much already.

Exit DORIMANT.

MRS. LOVEIT   Call him again!
PERT   E'en let him go. A fair riddance!
MRS. LOVEIT   Run, I say, call him again. I will have him called!
PERT   The devil should carry him away first, were it my concern.

Exit PERT.

BELLINDA   H'as frighted me from the very thoughts of loving men. For heav'n's sake, my dear, do not discover what I told you. I dread his tongue as much as you ought to have done his friendship.

Enter PERT.

PERT   He's gone, madam.
MRS. LOVEIT   Lightining blast him!
PERT   When I told him you desired him to come back, he smiled, made a mouth at me, flung into his coach and said—
MRS. LOVEIT   What did he say?
PERT   "Drive away"; and then repeated verses.
MRS. LOVEIT   Would I had made a contract to be a witch when first I entertained this greater devil. Monster, barbarian! I could tear myself in pieces. Revenge, nothing but revenge can ease me. Plague, war, famine, fire, all that can bring universal ruin and misery on mankind—with joy I'd perish to have you in my power but this moment!

Exit MRS. LOVEIT.

PERT   Follow, madam. Leave her not in this outrageous passion.

PERT *gathers up the things.*

BELLINDA   H'as given me the proof which I desired of his love; but 'tis a proof of his ill nature too. I wish I had not seen him use her so.

> I sigh to think that Dorimant may be
> One day as faithless and unkind to me.

Exeunt.

Act III. Scene i. LADY WOODVILL'S *lodgings.*

Enter HARRIET *and* BUSY, *her woman.*

BUSY   Dear madam, let me set that curl in order.
HARRIET   Let me alone, I will shake 'em all out of order!
BUSY   Will you never leave this wildness?

HARRIET   Torment me not.

BUSY   Look, there's a knot falling off.

HARRIET   Let it drop.

BUSY   But one pin, dear madam.

HARRIET   How do I daily suffer under thy officious fingers!

BUSY   Ah, the difference that is between you and my Lady Dapper! How uneasy she is if the least thing be amiss about her!

HARRIET   She is indeed most exact. Nothing is ever wanting to make her ugliness remarkable.

BUSY   Jeering people say so.

HARRIET   Her powdering, painting, and her patching never fail in public to draw the tongues and eyes of all the men upon her.

BUSY   She is indeed a little too pretending.

HARRIET   That women should set up for beauty as much in spite of nature as some men have done for wit!

BUSY   I hope without offense one may endeavor to make one's self agreeable.

HARRIET   Not when 'tis impossible. Women then ought to be no more fond of dressing than fools should be of talking. Hoods and modesty, masks and silence, things that shadow and conceal—they should think of nothing else.

BUSY   Jesu, madam! What will your mother think is become of you? For heav'n's sake, go in again.

HARRIET   I won't.

BUSY   This is the extravagant'st thing that ever you did in your life, to leave her and a gentleman who is to be your husband.

HARRIET   My husband! Hast thou so little wit to think I spoke what I meant when I overjoyed her in the country with a low curtsy and "What you please, madam; I shall ever be obedient"?

BUSY   Nay, I know not, you have so many fetches.[3]

HARRIET   And this was one, to get her up to London. Nothing else, I assure thee.

BUSY   Well! The man, in my mind, is a fine man.

HARRIET   The man indeed wears his clothes fashionably and has a pretty, negligent way with him, very courtly and much affected. He bows, and talks, and smiles so agreeably as he thinks.

BUSY   I never saw anything so genteel.

HARRIET   Varnished over with good breeding, many a blockhead makes a tolerable show.

BUSY   I wonder you do not like him.

HARRIET   I think I might be brought to endure him, and that is all a reasonable woman should expect in a husband; but there is duty i' the case, and like the haughty Merab, I

---

3. Tricks.

"Find much aversion in my stubborn mind,"

which

"Is bred by being promised and designed."[4]

BUSY   I wish you do not design your own ruin. I partly guess your inclinations, madam. That Mr. Dorimant—

HARRIET   Leave your prating and sing some foolish song or other.

BUSY   I will—the song you love so well ever since you saw Mr. Dorimant.

SONG

When   first   Amintas   charmed   my
heart,
    My heedless sheep began to stray;
The wolves soon stole the greatest part,
    and all will now be made a prey.
Ah, let not love your thoughts possess,
    'Tis fatal to a shepherdess;
The dang'rous passion you must shun,
    Or else like me be quite undone.

HARRIET   Shall I be paid down by a covetous parent for a purchase? I need no land. No, I'll lay myself out all in love. It is decreed.

Enter YOUNG BELLAIR.

YOUNG BELLAIR   What generous resolution are you making, madam?

HARRIET   Only to be disobedient, sir.

YOUNG BELLAIR   Let me join hands with you in that.

HARRIET   With all my heart. I never thought I should have given you mine so willingly. Here.

They join hands.

I, Harriet—

YOUNG BELLAIR   And I, Harry—

HARRIET   Do solemnly protest—

YOUNG BELLAIR   And vow—

HARRIET   That I with you—

YOUNG BELLAIR   And I with you—

HARRIET, YOUNG BELLAIR   Will never marry.

HARRIET   A match!

YOUNG BELLAIR   And no match! How do you like this indifference now?

HARRIET   You expect I should take it ill, I see.

YOUNG BELLAIR   'Tis not unnatural for you women to be a little angry,

---

4. Merab (see 1 Samuel) was promised to David but then married to Adriel. The couplet is based upon Abraham Cowley's description of Merab in *Davideis*, Book III.

you miss a conquest—though you would slight the poor man were he in your power.

HARRIET   There are some, it may be, have an eye like Bart'lomew, big enough for the whole fair;[5] but I am not of the number, and you may keep your gingerbread.[6] 'Twill be more acceptable to the lady whose dear image it wears.

YOUNG BELLAIR   I must confess, madam, you came a day after the fair.

HARRIET   And own then you are in love?

YOUNG BELLAIR   I do.

HARRIET   The confidence is generous, and in return I could almost find in my heart to let you know my inclinations.

YOUNG BELLAIR   Are you in love?

HARRIET   Yes—with this dear town, to that degree I can scarce endure the country in landscapes and in hangings.

YOUNG BELLAIR   What a dreadful thing 'twould be to be hurried back to Hampshire!

HARRIET   Ah, name it not.

YOUNG BELLAIR   As for us, I find we shall agree well enough. Would we could do something to deceive the grave people!

HARRIET   Could we delay their quick proceeding, 'twere well. A reprieve is a good step towards the getting of a pardon.

YOUNG BELLAIR   If we give over the game, we are undone. What think you of playing it on booty?[7]

HARRIET   What do you mean?

YOUNG BELLAIR   Pretend to be in love with one another. 'Twill make some dilatory excuses we may feign pass the better.

HARRIET   Let us do't, if it be but for the dear pleasure of dissembling.

YOUNG BELLAIR   Can you play your part?

HARRIET   I know not what it is to love, but I have made pretty remarks by being now and then where lovers meet. Where did you leave their gravities?

YOUNG BELLAIR   I' th' next room. Your mother was censuring our modern gallant.

Enter OLD BELLAIR *and* LADY WOODVILL.

HARRIET   Peace, here they come. I will lean against this wall and look bashfully down upon my fan while you, like an amorous spark, modishly entertain me.

LADY WOODVILL [*to* OLD BELLAIR]   Never go about to excuse 'em. Come, come, it was not so when I was a young woman.

OLD BELLAIR   Adod, they're something disrespectful—

LADY WOODVILL   Quality was then considered and not rallied by every fleering fellow.

---

5. An allusion to Bartholomew Cokes in Jonson's *Bartholomew Fair*, who wants to buy everything in sight. The fair was held annually in August.
6. A popular item at the fair.
7. Conspiring against the others.

OLD BELLAIR   Youth will have its jest, adod it will.

LADY WOODVILL   'Tis good breeding now to be civil to none but players and Exchange women.[8] They are treated by 'em as much above their condition as others are below theirs.

OLD BELLAIR   Out, a pize on 'em! Talk no more: the rogues ha' got an ill habit of preferring beauty, no matter where they find it.

LADY WOODVILL   See your son and my daughter. They have improved their acquaintance since they were within.

OLD BELLAIR   Adod, methinks they have! Let's keep back and observe.

YOUNG BELLAIR [to HARRIET]   Now for a look and gestures that may persuade 'em I am saying all the passionate things imaginable.

HARRIET   Your head a little more on one side. Ease yourself on your left leg and play with your right hand.

YOUNG BELLAIR   Thus, is it not?

HARRIET   Now set your right leg firm on the ground, adjust your belt, then look about you.

YOUNG BELLAIR   A little exercising will make me perfect.

HARRIET   Smile, and turn to me again very sparkish.

YOUNG BELLAIR   Will you take your turn and be instructed?

HARRIET   With all my heart.

YOUNG BELLAIR   At one motion play your fan, roll your eyes, and then settle a kind look upon me.

HARRIET   So.

YOUNG BELLAIR   Now spread your fan, look down upon it, and tell the sticks with a finger.

HARRIET   Very modish.

YOUNG BELLAIR   Clap your hand upon your bosom, hold down your gown. Shrug a little, draw up your breasts and let 'em fall again, gently, with a sigh or two, *etc.*

HARRIET   By the good instructions you give, I suspect you for one of those malicious observers who watch people's eyes, and from innocent looks make scandalous conclusions.

YOUNG BELLAIR   I know some, indeed, who out of mere love to mischief are as vigilant as jealousy itself, and will give you an account of every glance that passes at a play and i' th' Circle.[9]

HARRIET   'Twill not be amiss now to seem a little pleasant.

YOUNG BELLAIR   Clap your fan then in both your hands, snatch it to your mouth, smile, and with a lively motion fling your body a little forwards. So! Now spread it, fall back on the sudden, cover your face with it, and break out into a loud laughter.—Take up! Look grave and fall a-fanning to yourself. Admirably well acted!

HARRIET   I think I am pretty apt at these matters.

OLD BELLAIR [to LADY WOODVILL]   Adod, I like this well.

8. Shopkeepers at the New Exchange.
9. Circular path in Hyde Park.

LADY WOODVILL   This promises something.

OLD BELLAIR   Come, there is love i' th' case, adod there is, or will be. [*To* HARRIET]—What say you, young lady?

HARRIET   All in good time, sir. You expect we should fall to and love as gamecocks fight, as soon as we are set together. Adod, y'are unreasonable!

OLD BELLAIR   Adod, sirrah, I like thy wit well.

Enter a SERVANT.

SERVANT   The coach is at the door, madam.

OLD BELLAIR   Go, get you and take the air together.

LADY WOODVILL   Will not you go with us?

OLD BELLAIR   Out a pize! Adod, I ha' business and cannot. We shall meet at night at my sister Townley's.

YOUNG BELLAIR [*aside*]   He's going to Emilia. I overheard him talk of a collation.

Exeunt.

Act III. Scene ii. LADY TOWNLEY's

Enter LADY TOWNLEY, EMILIA, *and* MEDLEY.

LADY TOWNLEY   I pity the young lovers we last talked of, though to say truth, their conduct has been so indiscreet they deserve to be unfortunate.

MEDLEY   Y' have an exact account, from the great lady i' th' box down to the little orange-wench.

EMILIA   Y'are a living libel, a breathing lampoon. I wonder you are not torn in pieces.

MEDLEY   What think you of setting up an office of intelligence for these matters? The project may get money.

LADY TOWNLEY   You would have great dealings with country ladies.

MEDLEY   More than Muddiman[1] has with their husbands!

Enter BELLINDA.

LADY TOWNLEY   Bellinda, what has been become of you? We have not seen you here of late with your friend Mrs. Loveit.

BELLINDA   Dear creature, I left her but now so sadly afflicted.

LADY TOWNLEY   With her old distemper, jealousy?

MEDLEY   Dorimant has played her some new prank.

BELLINDA   Well, that Dorimant is certainly the worst man breathing.

EMILIA   I once thought so.

BELLINDA   And do you not think so still?

EMILIA   No, indeed.

1. Henry Muddiman, contemporary writer of "newsletters."

BELLINDA   Oh, Jesu!

EMILIA   The town does him a great deal of injury, and I will never believe what it says of a man I do not know, again, for his sake.

BELLINDA   You make me wonder.

LADY TOWNLEY   He's a very well-bred man.

BELLINDA   But strangely ill-natured.

EMILIA   Then he's a very witty man.

BELLINDA   But a man of no principles.

MEDLEY   Your man of principles is a very fine thing, indeed!

BELLINDA   To be preferred to men of parts by women who have regard to their reputation and quiet. Well, were I minded to play the fool, he should be the last man I'd think of.

MEDLEY   He has been the first in many ladies' favors, though you are so severe, madam.

LADY TOWNLEY   What he may be for a lover, I know not; but he's a very pleasant acquaintance, I am sure.

BELLINDA   Had you seen him use Mrs. Loveit as I have done, you would never endure him more.

EMILIA   What, he has quarreled with her again?

BELLINDA   Upon the slightest occasion. He's jealous of Sir Fopling.

LADY TOWNLEY   She never saw him in her life but yesterday; and that was here.

EMILIA   On my conscience, he's the only man in town that's her aversion. How horribly out of humour she was all the while he talked to her!

BELLINDA   And somebody has wickedly told him—

Enter DORIMANT.

EMILIA   Here he comes.

MEDLEY   Dorimant, you are luckily come to justify yourself. Here's a lady—

BELLINDA   —Has a word or two to say to you from a disconsolate person.

DORIMANT   You tender your reputation too much, I know, madam, to whisper with me before this good company.

BELLINDA   To serve Mrs. Loveit, I'll make a bold venture.

DORIMANT   Here's Medley, the very spirit of scandal.

BELLINDA   No matter.

EMILIA   'Tis something you are unwilling to hear, Mr. Dorimant.

LADY TOWNLEY   Tell him, Bellinda, whether he will or no.

BELLINDA   [*aloud*]   Mrs. Loveit—

DORIMANT   Softly, these are laughers; you do not know 'em.

BELLINDA   [*to* DORIMANT, *apart*]   In a word, y'ave made me hate you, which I thought you never could have done.

DORIMANT   In obeying your commands?

BELLINDA   'Twas a cruel part you played. How could you act it?

DORIMANT   Nothing is cruel to a man who could kill himself to please you. Remember, five o'clock tomorrow morning.

BELLINDA   I tremble when you name it.

DORIMANT   Be sure you come.

BELLINDA   I sha' not.

DORIMANT   Swear you will.

BELLINDA   I dare not.

DORIMANT   Swear, I say!

BELLINDA   By my life, by all the happiness I hope for—

DORIMANT   You will.

BELLINDA   I will.

DORIMANT   Kind.

BELLINDA   I am glad I've sworn. I vow I think I should have failed you else.

DORIMANT   Surprisingly kind! In what temper did you leave Loveit?

BELLINDA   Her raving was prettily over, and she began to be in a brave way of defying you and all your works. Where have you been since you went from thence?

DORIMANT   I looked in at the play.

BELLINDA   I have promised and must return to her again.

DORIMANT   Persuade her to walk in the Mall this evening.

BELLINDA   She hates the place and will not come.

DORIMANT   Do all you can to prevail with her.

BELLINDA   For what purpose?

DORIMANT   Sir Fopling will be here anon. I'll prepare him to set upon her there before me.

BELLINDA   You persecute her too much. But I'll do all you'll ha' me.

DORIMANT   [aloud] Tell her plainly, 'tis grown so dull a business I can drudge on no longer.

EMILIA   There are afflictions in love, Mr. Dorimant.

DORIMANT   You women make 'em, who are commonly as unreasonable in that as you are at play: without the advantage be on your side, a man can never quietly give over when he's weary.

MEDLEY   If you would play without being obliged to complaisance, Dorimant, you should play in public places.

DORIMANT   Ordinaries[2] were a very good thing for that, but gentlemen do not of late frequent 'em. The deep play is now in private houses.

BELLINDA *offering to steal away.*

LADY TOWNLEY   Bellinda, are you leaving us so soon?

BELLINDA   I am to go to the Park with Mrs. Loveit, madam.

Exit BELLINDA.

---

2. Taverns.

LADY TOWNLEY   This confidence[3] will go nigh to spoil this young creature.

MEDLEY   'Twill do her good, madam. Young men who are brought up
under practicing lawyers prove the abler counsel when they come to
be called to the bar themselves.

DORIMANT   The town has been very favorable to you this afternoon, my
Lady Townley. You use to have an *embarras*[4] of chairs and coaches at
your door, an uproar of footmen in your hall, and a noise of fools
above here.

LADY TOWNLEY   Indeed, my house is the general rendezvous and, next
to the playhouse, is the common refuge of all the young idle people.

EMILIA   Company is a very good thing, madam, but I wonder you do
not love it a little more chosen.

LADY TOWNLEY   'Tis good to have an universal taste. We should love
wit, but for variety be able to divert ourselves with the extravagancies
of those who want it.

MEDLEY   Fools will make you laugh.

EMILIA   For once or twice; but the repetition of their folly after a visit
or two grows tedious and insufferable.

LADY TOWNLEY   You are a little too delicate, Emilia.

Enter a PAGE.

PAGE   Sir Fopling Flutter, madam, desires to know if you are to be
seen.

LADY TOWNLEY   Here's the freshest fool in town, and one who has not
cloyed you yet. — Page!

PAGE   Madam?

LADY TOWNLEY   Desire him to walk up.

Exit PAGE.

DORIMANT   Do not you fall on him, Medley, and snub him. Soothe
him up in his extravagance. He will show the better.

MEDLEY   You know I have a natural indulgence for fools and need not
this caution, sir.

Enter SIR FOPLING, *with his* PAGE *after him.*

SIR FOPLING   Page, wait without.

Exit PAGE.

[*To* LADY TOWNLEY.]   Madam, I kiss your hands. I see yesterday was
nothing of chance; the *belles assemblées*[5] form themselves here every
day. [*To* EMILIA.] Lady, your servant. — Dorimant, let me embrace
thee. Without lying, I have not met with any of my acquaintance who
retain so much of Paris as thou dost — the very air thou hadst when

3. Confiding.
4. Congestion.
5. Fashionable gatherings.

the marquise mistook thee i' th' Tuileries[6] and cried "Hé, chevalier!" and then begged thy pardon.

DORIMANT   I would fain wear in fashion as long as I can, sir. 'Tis a thing to be valued in men as well as baubles.

SIR FOPLING   Thou art a man of wit and understands the town. Prithee let thee and I be intimate. There is no living without making some good man the confidant of our pleasures.

DORIMANT   'Tis true; but there is no man so improper for such a business as I am.

SIR FOPLING   Prithee, why hast thou so modest an opinion of thyself?

DORIMANT   Why, first, I could never keep a secret in my life; and then, there is no charm so infallibly makes me fall in love with a woman as my knowing a friend loves her. I deal honestly with you.

SIR FOPLING.   Thy humour's very gallant, or let me perish. I knew a French count so like thee.

LADY TOWNLEY   Wit, I perceive, has more power over you than beauty, Sir Fopling, else you would not have let this lady stand so long neglected.

SIR FOPLING [to EMILIA]   A thousand pardons, madam. Some civility's due of course upon the meeting a long absent friend. The éclat[7] of so much beauty, I confess, ought to have charmed me sooner.

EMILIA   The brillant[8] of so much good language, sir, has much more power than the little beauty I can boast.

SIR FOPLING   I never saw anything prettier than this high work on your point d'Espaigne.[9]

EMILIA   'Tis not so rich as point de Venise.

SIR FOPLING   Not altogether, but looks cooler, and is more proper for the season. —Dorimant, is not that Medley?

DORIMANT   The same, sir.

SIR FOPLING [to MEDLEY]   Forgive me, sir; in this embarras of civilities I could not come to have you in my arms sooner. You understand an equipage the best of any man in town, I hear.

MEDLEY   By my own you would not guess it.

SIR FOPLING   There are critics who do not write, sir.

MEDLEY   Our peevish poets will scarce allow it.

SIR FOPLING   Damn 'em, they'll allow no man wit who does not play the fool like themselves and show it! Have you taken notice of the gallesh[1] I brought over?

MEDLEY   Oh, yes! 'T has quite another air than th' English makes.

SIR FOPLING   'Tis as easily known from an English tumbril[2] as an Inns of Court man is from one of us.

---

6. The famous gardens in Paris.
7. Brilliance.
8. Glitter.
9. Spanish lace. In the next line, Venetian lace.
1. Calèche (French), a light carriage.
2. Cart, often for dung.

DORIMANT   Truly there is a *bel air*[3] in galleshes as well as men.

MEDLEY   But there are few so delicate to observe it.

SIR FOPLING   The world is generally very *grossier*[4] here, indeed.

LADY TOWNLEY [*to* EMILIA]   He's very fine.

EMILIA   Extreme proper!

SIR FOPLING   A slight suit I made to appear in at my first arrival—not worthy your consideration, ladies.

DORIMANT   The pantaloon is very well mounted.

SIR FOPLING   The tassels are new and pretty.

MEDLEY   I never saw a coat better cut.

SIR FOPLING   It makes me show long-waisted, and I think slender.

DORIMANT   That's the shape our ladies dote on.

MEDLEY   Your breech, though, is a handful too high, in my eye, Sir Fopling.

SIR FOPLING   Peace, Medley, I have wished it lower a thousand times; but a pox on't, 'twill not be!

LADY TOWNLEY   His gloves are well fringed, large and graceful.

SIR FOPLING   I was always eminent for being *bien ganté.*[5]

EMILIA   He wears nothing but what are originals of the most famous hands in Paris.

SIR FOPLING   You are in the right, madam.

LADY TOWNLEY   The suit?

SIR FOPLING   Barroy.[6]

EMILIA   The garniture?

SIR FOPLING   Le Gras.

MEDLEY   The shoes?

SIR FOPLING   Piccar.

DORIMANT   The periwig?

SIR FOPLING   Chedreux.

LADY TOWNLEY, EMILIA   The gloves?

SIR FOPLING   Orangerie.[7] You know the smell, ladies. —Dorimant, I could find in my heart for an amusement to have a gallantry with some of our English ladies.

DORIMANT   'Tis a thing no less necessary to confirm the reputation of your wit than a duel will be to satisfy the town of your courage.

SIR FOPLING   Here was a woman yesterday—

DORIMANT   Mistress Loveit.

SIR FOPLING   You have named her!

DORIMANT   You cannot pitch on a better for your purpose.

SIR FOPLING   Prithee, what is she?

DORIMANT   A person of quality, and one who has a rest of reputation

---

3. Fine style.
4. Crude.
5. Well gloved.
6. Sir Fopling names a series of fashionable Parisian merchants.
7. Scented with orange.

enough to make the conquest considerable. Besides, I hear she likes you too.

SIR FOPLING Methoughts she seemed, though, very reserved and uneasy all the time I entertained her.

DORIMANT Grimace and affectation! You will see her i' th' Mall tonight.

SIR FOPLING Prithee, let thee and I take the air together.

DORIMANT I am engaged to Medley, but I'll meet you at Saint James's[8] and give you some information upon the which you may regulate your proceedings.

SIR FOPLING All the world will be in the Park tonight. —Ladies, 'twere pity to keep so much beauty longer within doors and rob the Ring of all those charms that should adorn it. —Hey, page!

Enter PAGE.

See that all my people be ready.

PAGE *goes out again.*

Dorimant, *a revoir.*[9]

Exit SIR FOPLING.

MEDLEY A fine-mettled coxcomb.

DORIMANT Brisk and insipid.

MEDLEY Pert and dull.

EMILIA However you despise him, gentlemen, I'll lay my life he passes for a wit with many.

DORIMANT That may very well be. Nature has her cheats, stums[1] a brain, and puts sophisticate dullness often on the tasteless multitude for true wit and good humour. —Medley, come.

MEDLEY I must go a little way; I will meet you i' the Mall.

DORIMANT I'll walk through the garden thither. [*To the women.*] We shall meet anon and bow.

LADY TOWNLEY Not tonight. We are engaged about a business, the knowledge of which may make you laugh hereafter.

MEDLEY Your servant, ladies.

DORIMANT A *revoir,* as Sir Fopling says.

Exeunt MEDLEY *and* DORIMANT.

LADY TOWNLEY The old man will be here immediately.

EMILIA Let's expect him i' th' garden.

LADY TOWNLEY Go, you are a rogue!

EMILIA I can't abide you!

Exeunt.

8. St. James's Park.
9. Sir Fopling mispronounces *au revoir.* At the end of the scene, Dorimant mimics him.
1. Renews, as wine is fermented by the addition of stum, i.e., partly fermented grape juice.

Act III. Scene iii. The Mall.

Enter HARRIET *and* YOUNG BELLAIR, *she pulling him.*

HARRIET   Come along!

YOUNG BELLAIR   And leave your mother?

HARRIET   Busy will be sent with a hue and cry after us; but that's no matter.

YOUNG BELLAIR   'Twill look strangely in me.

HARRIET   She'll believe it a freak of mine and never blame your manners.

YOUNG BELLAIR [*pointing*]   What reverend acquaintance is that she has met?

HARRIET   A fellow beauty of the last king's time, though by the ruins you would hardly guess it.

Exeunt.

Enter DORIMANT *and crosses the stage.*
Enter YOUNG BELLAIR *and* HARRIET.

YOUNG BELLAIR   By this time your mother is in a fine taking.

HARRIET   If your friend Mr. Dorimant were but here now, that she might find me talking with him!

YOUNG BELLAIR   She does not know him but dreads him, I hear, of all mankind.

HARRIET   She concludes if he does but speak to a woman, she's undone—is on her knees every day to pray heav'n defend me from him.

YOUNG BELLAIR   You do not apprehend him so much as she does?

HARRIET   I never saw anything in him that was frightful.

YOUNG BELLAIR   On the contrary, have you not observed something extreme delightful in his wit and person?

HARRIET   He's agreeable and pleasant, I must own, but he does so much affect being so, he displeases me.

YOUNG BELLAIR   Lord, madam, all he does and says is so easy and so natural.

HARRIET   Some men's verses seem so to the unskilful; but labor i' the one and affectation in the other to the judicious plainly appear.

YOUNG BELLAIR   I never heard him accused of affectation before.

Enter DORIMANT *and stares upon her.*

HARRIET   It passes on the easy town, who are favorably pleased in him to call it humour.

Exeunt YOUNG BELLAIR *and* HARRIET.

DORIMANT   'Tis she! It must be she—that lovely hair, that easy shape, those wanton eyes, and all those melting charms about her mouth which Medley spoke of. I'll follow the lottery and put in for a prize with my friend Bellair.

Exit DORIMANT, *repeating:*

"In love the victors from the vanquished fly;
They fly that wound, and they pursue that die."[2]

Enter YOUNG BELLAIR *and* HARRIET; *and after them* DORIMANT, *standing at a distance.*

YOUNG BELLAIR   Most people prefer High Park to this place.

HARRIET   It has the better reputation, I confess; but I abominate the dull diversions there—the formal bows, the affected smiles, the silly by-words and amorous tweers[3] in passing. Here one meets with a little conversation now and then.

YOUNG BELLAIR   These conversations have been fatal to some of your sex, madam.

HARRIET   It may be so. Because some who want temper have been undone by gaming, must others who have it wholly deny themselves the pleasure of play?

DORIMANT   [*coming up gently and bowing to her*]   Trust me, it were unreasonable, madam.

She starts and looks grave.

HARRIET   Lord, who's this?

YOUNG BELLAIR   Dorimant.

DORIMANT   Is this the woman your father would have you marry?

YOUNG BELLAIR   It is.

DORIMANT   Her name?

YOUNG BELLAIR   Harriet.

DORIMANT   [*aside*]   I am not mistaken. —She's handsome.

YOUNG BELLAIR   Talk to her; her wit is better than her face. We were wishing for you but now.

DORIMANT   [*to* HARRIET]   Overcast with seriousness o' the sudden! A thousand smiles were shining in the face but now. I never saw so quick a change of weather.

HARRIET   [*aside*]   I feel as great a change within, but he shall never know it.

DORIMANT   You were talking of play, madam. Pray, what may be your stint?[4]

HARRIET   A little harmless discourse in public walks or at most an appointment in a box, barefaced, at the playhouse. You are for masks and private meetings, where women engage for all they are worth, I hear.

2. From Waller's "To a Friend, of the Different Success of their Loves," lines 27–28.
3. Leers.
4. Limit.

DORIMANT   I have been used to deep play, but I can make one at small game when I like my gamester well.

HARRIET   And be so unconcerned you'll ha' no pleasure in't.

DORIMANT   Where there is a considerable sum to be won, the hope of drawing people in makes every trifle considerable.

HARRIET   The sordidness of men's natures, I know, makes 'em willing to flatter and comply with the rich, though they are sure never to be the better for 'em.

DORIMANT   'Tis in their power to do us good, and we despair not but at some time or other they may be willing.

HARRIET   To men who have fared in this town like you, 'twould be a great mortification to live on hope. Could you keep a Lent for a mistress?

DORIMANT   In expectation of a happy Easter; and though time be very precious, think forty days well lost to gain your favor.

HARRIET   Mr. Bellair! Let us walk, 'tis time to leave him. Men grow dull when they begin to be particular.

DORIMANT   Y'are mistaken: flattery will not ensue, though I know y'are greedy of the praises of the whole Mall.

HARRIET   You do me wrong.

DORIMANT   I do not. As I followed you, I observed how you were pleased when the fops cried "She's handsome, very handsome, by God she is!" and whispered aloud your name—the thousand several forms you put your face into; then, to make yourself more agreeable, how wantonly you played with your head, flung back your locks, and looked smilingly over your shoulder at 'em.

HARRIET   I do not go begging men's, as you do the ladies' good liking, with a sly softness in your looks and a gentle slowness in your bows as you pass by 'em. As thus, sir. [*Acts him.*] Is not this like you?

      Enter LADY WOODVILL *and* BUSY.

YOUNG BELLAIR   Your mother, madam!

      Pulls HARRIET. *She composes herself.*

LADY WOODVILL   Ah, my dear child Harriet!

BUSY [*aside*]   Now is she so pleased with finding her again, she cannot chide her.

LADY WOODVILL   Come away!

DORIMANT   'Tis now but high Mall,[5] madam—the most entertaining time of all the evening.

HARRIET   I would fain see that Dorimant, mother, you so cry out of for a monster. He's in the Mall, I hear.

LADY WOODVILL   Come away, then! The plague is here, and you should dread the infection.

---

5. The fashionable hour on the Mall.

YOUNG BELLAIR   You may be misinformed of the gentleman.

LADY WOODVILL   Oh, no! I hope you do not know him. He is the prince of all the devils in the town—delights in nothing but in rapes and riots.

DORIMANT   If you did but hear him speak, madam—

LADY WOODVILL   Oh, he has a tongue, they say, would tempt the angels to a second fall.

Enter SIR FOPLING *with his equipage, six footmen and a page.*

SIR FOPLING   Hey, Champagne, Norman, La Rose, La Fleur, La Tour, La Verdure!—Dorimant!—

LADY WOODVILL   Here, here he is among this rout! He names him! Come away, Harriet, come away!

Exeunt LADY WOODVILL, HARRIET, BUSY, *and* YOUNG BELLAIR.

DORIMANT   This fool's coming has spoiled all: she's gone. But she has left a pleasing image of herself behind that wanders in my soul. It must not settle there.

SIR FOPLING   What reverie is this? Speak, man.

DORIMANT

> "Snatched from myself, how far behind
> Already I behold the shore!"[6]

Enter MEDLEY.

MEDLEY   Dorimant, a discovery! I met with Bellair—

DORIMANT   You can tell me no news, sir. I know all.

MEDLEY   How do you like the daughter?

DORIMANT   You never came so near truth in your life as you did in her description.

MEDLEY   What think you of the mother?

DORIMANT   Whatever I think of her, she thinks very well of me, I find.

MEDLEY   Did she know you?

DORIMANT   She did not. Whether she does now or no, I know not. Here was a pleasant scene towards, when in came Sir Fopling, mustering up his equipage, and at the latter end named me and frighted her away.

MEDLEY   Loveit and Bellinda are not far off. I saw 'em alight at St. James's.[7]

DORIMANT   Sir Fopling, hark you, a word or two. [*Whispers.*] Look you do not want assurance.

SIR FOPLING   I never do on these occasions.

---

6. From Waller's "Of Loving at First Sight," lines 3–4.
7. The palace, opposite St. James's Park and to the west end of the Mall.

DORIMANT   Walk on; we must not be seen together. Make your advantage of what I have told you. The next turn you will meet the lady.

SIR FOPLING   Hey! Follow me all.

Exeunt SIR FOPLING *and his equipage.*

DORIMANT   Medley, you shall see good sport anon between Loveit and this Fopling.

MEDLEY   I thought there was something toward, by that whisper.

DORIMANT   You know a worthy principle of hers?

MEDLEY   Not to be so much as civil to a man who speaks to her in the presence of him she professes to love.

DORIMANT   I have encouraged Fopling to talk to her tonight.

MEDLEY   Now you are here, she will go nigh to beat him.

DORIMANT   In the humour she's in, her love will make her do some very extravagant thing, doubtless.

MEDLEY   What was Bellinda's business with you at my Lady Townley's?

DORIMANT   To get me to meet Loveit here in order to an *éclaircissement*[8]. I made some difficulty of it and have prepared, this rencounter to make good my jealousy.

Enter MRS. LOVEIT, BELLINDA, *and* PERT.

MEDLEY   Here they come.

DORIMANT   I'll meet her and provoke her with a deal of dumb civility in passing by, then turn short and be behind her when Sir Fopling sets upon her.

Bows to MRS. LOVEIT.

"See how unregarded now
That piece of beauty passes."[9]

Exeunt DORIMANT *and* MEDLEY.

BELLINDA   How wonderful respectfully he bowed!

PERT   He's always over-mannerly when he has done a mischief.

BELLINDA   Methoughts, indeed, at the same time he had a strange, despising countenance.

PERT   The unlucky look he thinks becomes him.

BELLINDA   I was afraid you would have spoke to him, my dear.

MRS. LOVEIT   I would have died first. He shall no more find me the loving fool he has done.

BELLINDA   You love him still!

MRS. LOVEIT   No.

PERT   I wish you did not.

MRS. LOVEIT   I do not, and I will have you think so!—What made you hale me to this odious place, Bellinda?

---

8. Clarification.
9. Opening lines of Sir John Suckling's "Sonnet I."

BELLINDA   I hate to be hulched up in a coach. Walking is much better.

MRS. LOVEIT   Would we could meet Sir Fopling now!

BELLINDA   Lord, would you not avoid him?

MRS. LOVEIT   I would make him all the advances that may be.

BELLINDA   That would confirm Dorimant's suspicion, my dear.

MRS. LOVEIT   He is not jealous; but I will make him so, and be revenged a way he little thinks on.

BELLINDA   [aside]   If she should make him jealous, that may make him fond of her again. I must dissuade her from it. —Lord, my dear, this will certainly make him hate you.

MRS. LOVEIT   'Twill make him uneasy, though he does not care for me. I know the effects of jealousy on men of his proud temper.

BELLINDA   'Tis a fantastic remedy: its operations are dangerous and uncertain.

MRS. LOVEIT   'Tis the strongest cordial we can give to dying love. It often brings it back when there's no sign of life remaining. But I design not so much the reviving his, as my revenge.

Enter SIR FOPLING *and his equipage.*

SIR FOPLING   Hey! Bid the coachman send home four of his horses and bring the coach to Whitehall.[1] I'll walk over the Park. [*To* MRS. LOVEIT.] Madam, the honor of kissing your fair hands is a happiness I missed this afternoon at my Lady Townley's.

MRS. LOVEIT   You were very obliging, Sir Fopling, the last time I saw you there.

SIR FOPLING   The preference was due to your wit and beauty. [*To* BELLINDA.] Madam, your servant. There never was so sweet an evening.

BELLINDA   'T has drawn all the rabble of the town hither.

SIR FOPLING   'Tis pity there's not an order made that none but the *beau monde* should walk here.

MRS. LOVEIT   'Twould add much to the beauty of the place. See what a sort of nasty fellows are coming!

Enter four ill-fashioned fellows singing:

" 'Tis not for kisses alone, etc."[2]

MRS. LOVEIT   Foh! Their periwigs are scented with tobacco so strong—

SIR FOPLING   —It overcomes our pulvilio. Methinks I smell the coffe-house they come from.

FIRST MAN   Dorimant's convenient, Madam Loveit.

SECOND MAN   I like the oily buttock[3] with her.

THIRD MAN   [*pointing to* SIR FOPLING]   What spruce prig is that?

FIRST MAN   A caravan,[4] lately come from Paris.

1. Whitehall Palace, across the park from the Mall.
2. From a popular song, "Tell me no more you love," published in the same year as the play.
3. Smooth wench. *Pulvilio:* scented powder.
4. Dupe, fit for plunder.

SECOND MAN   Peace, they smoke![5]

> *All of them coughing; exeunt singing:*

"There's something else to be done, etc."

Enter DORIMANT *and* MEDLEY.

DORIMANT   They're engaged.

MEDLEY   She entertains him as if she liked him.

DORIMANT   Let us go forward, seem earnest in discourse, and show our-selves. Then you shall see how she'll use him.

BELLINDA   Yonder's Dorimant, my dear.

MRS. LOVEIT   I see him. [*Aside.*] He comes insulting, but I will disap-point him in his expectation. [*To* SIR FOPLING.] I like this pretty, nice humour of yours, Sir Fopling. [*To* BELLINDA.] With what a loathing eye he looked upon those fellows!

SIR FOPLING   I sat near one of 'em at a play today and was almost poi-soned with a pair of cordovan gloves he wears.

MRS. LOVEIT   Oh, filthy cordovan! How I hate the smell!

> *Laughs in a loud, affected way.*

SIR FOPLING   Did you observe, madam, how their cravats hung loose an inch from their neck, and what a frightful air it gave 'em?

MRS. LOVEIT   Oh! I took particular notice of one that is always spruced up with a deal of dirty, sky-colored ribbon.

BELLINDA   That's one of the walking flageolets[6] who haunt the Mall o' nights.

MRS. LOVEIT   Oh, I remember him. H' has a hollow tooth, enough to spoil the sweetness of an evening.

SIR FOPLING   I have seen the tallest walk the streets with a dainty pair of boxes,[7] neatly buckled on.

MRS. LOVEIT   And a little footboy at his heels, pocket-high, with a flat cap, a dirty face—

SIR FOPLING   —And a snotty nose.

MRS. LOVEIT   Oh, odious! There's many of my own sex, with that Hol-born equipage, trig[8] to Gray's Inn Walks, and now and then travel hither on a Sunday.

MEDLEY [*to* DORIMANT]   She takes no notice of you.

DORIMANT   Damn her! I am jealous of a counterplot.

MRS. LOVEIT   Your liveries are the finest, Sir Fopling. Oh, that page! That page is the prettily'st dressed. They are all Frenchmen?

SIR FOPLING   There's one damned English blockhead among 'em. You may know him by his mien.

---

5. Notice.
6. Flutes; or perhaps tall, thin persons.
7. Clogs or overshoes.
8. Walk briskly, trip along. "*Holborn equipage*" means middle-class attendants; *Gray's Inn Walks* were gardens at one of the Inns of Court in Holborn.

MRS. LOVEIT   Oh, that's he, that's he! What do you call him?

SIR FOPLING   [*calling* FOOTMAN]   Hey!—I know not what to call him.

MRS. LOVEIT   What's your name?

FOOTMAN   John Trott, madam.

SIR FOPLING   Oh, insufferable! Trott, Trott, Trott! There's nothing so barbarous as the names of our English servants. What countryman are you, sirrah?

FOOTMAN   Hampshire, sir.

SIR FOPLING   Then Hampshire be your name. Hey, Hampshire!

MRS. LOVEIT   Oh, that sound! That sound becomes the mouth of a man of quality.

MEDLEY   Dorimant, you look a little bashful on the matter.

DORIMANT   She dissembles better than I thought she could have done.

MEDLEY   You have tempted her with too luscious a bait. She bites at the coxcomb.

DORIMANT   She cannot fall from loving me to that?

MEDLEY   You begin to be jealous in earnest.

DORIMANT   Of one I do not love?

MEDLEY   You did love her.

DORIMANT   The fit has long been over.

MEDLEY   But I have known men fall into dangerous relapses when they have found a woman inclining to another.

DORIMANT   [*to himself*]   He guesses the secret of my heart. I am concerned but dare not show it, lest Bellinda should mistrust all I have done to gain her.

BELLINDA   [*aside*]   I have watched his look and find no alteration there. Did he love her, some signs of jealousy would have appeared.

DORIMANT   [*to* MRS. LOVEIT]   I hope this happy evening, madam, has reconciled you to the scandalous Mall. We shall have you now hankering here again.

MRS. LOVEIT   Sir Fopling, will you walk?

SIR FOPLING   I am all obedience, madam.

MRS. LOVEIT   Come along then, and let's agree to be malicious on all the ill-fashioned things we meet.

SIR FOPLING   We'll make a critique on the whole Mall, madam.

MRS. LOVEIT   Bellinda, you shall engage.

BELLINDA   To the reserve of our friends, my dear.

MRS. LOVEIT   No! No exceptions.

SIR FOPLING   We'll sacrifice all to our diversion.

MRS. LOVEIT   All, all.

SIR FOPLING   All!

BELLINDA   All? Then let it be.

Exeunt SIR FOPLING, MRS. LOVEIT, BELLINDA, *and* PERT, *laughing.*

MEDLEY   Would you had brought some more of your friends, Dorimant, to have been witnesses of Sir Fopling's disgrace and your triumph!

DORIMANT   'Twere unreasonable to desire you not to laugh at me; but pray do not expose me to the town this day or two.

MEDLEY   By that time you hope to have regained your credit?

DORIMANT   I know she hates Fopling and only makes use of him in hope to work me on again. Had it not been for some powerful considerations which will be removed tomorrow morning, I had made her pluck off this mask and show the passion that lies panting under.

Enter a FOOTMAN.

MEDLEY   Here comes a man from Bellair, with news of your last adventure.

DORIMANT   I am glad he sent him. I long to know the consequence of our parting.

FOOTMAN   Sir, my master desires you to come to my Lady Townley's presently and bring Mr. Medley with you. My Lady Woodvill and her daughter are there.

MEDLEY   Then all's well, Dorimant.

FOOTMAN   They have sent for the fiddles and mean to dance. He bid me to tell you, sir, the old lady does not know you; and would have you own yourself to be Mr. Courtage. They are all prepared to receive you by that name.

DORIMANT   That foppish admirer of quality, who flatters the very meat at honorable tables and never offers love to a woman below a lady-grandmother!

MEDLEY   You know the character you are to act, I see.

DORIMANT   This is Harriet's contrivance—wild, witty, lovesome, beautiful and young.[9] —Come along, Medley.

MEDLEY   This new woman would well supply the loss of Loveit.

DORIMANT   That business must not end so. Before tomorrow sun is set, I will revenge and clear it.

And you and Loveit, to her cost, shall find
I fathom all the depths of womankind.

Exeunt.

Act IV. Scene i. LADY TOWNLEY'S.

The scene opens with the fiddlers playing a country dance. Enter DORIMANT *and* LADY WOODVILL, YOUNG BELLAIR *and* MRS. HARRIET, OLD BELLAIR *and* EMILIA, MR. MEDLEY *and* LADY TOWNLEY, *as having just ended the dance.*

OLD BELLAIR   So, so, so! A smart bout, a very smart bout, adod!

LADY TOWNLEY   How do you like Emilia's dancing, brother?

9. Loosely derived from Waller's "Of the Danger his Majesty (Being Prince) Escaped . . . ," lines 13–14.

OLD BELLAIR   Not at all, not at all!

LADY TOWNLEY   You speak not what you think, I am sure.

OLD BELLAIR   No matter for that; go, bid her dance no more. It don't become her, it don't become her. Tell her I say so. [*Aside.*] Adod, I love her.

DORIMANT [*to* LADY WOODVILLE]   All people mingle nowadays, madam. And in public places women of quality have the least respect showed 'em.

LADY WOODVILL   I protest you say the truth, Mr. Courtage.

DORIMANT   Forms and ceremonies, the only things that uphold quality and greatness, are now shamefully laid aside and neglected.

LADY WOODVILL   Well, this is not the women's age, let 'em think what they will. Lewdness is the business now; love was the bus'ness in my time.

DORIMANT   The women, indeed, are little beholding to the young men of this age. They're generally only dull admirers of themselves and make their court to nothing but their periwigs and their cravats—and would be more concerned for the disordering of 'em, though on a good occasion, than a young maid would be for the tumbling of her head or handkercher.

LADY WOODVILL   I protest you hit 'em.

DORIMANT   They are very assiduous to show themselves at court, well-dressed, to the women of quality; but their bus'ness is with the stale mistresses of the town, who are prepared to receive their lazy addresses by industrious old lovers who have cast 'em off and made 'em easy.

HARRIET [*to* MEDLEY]   He fits my mother's humour so well, a little more and she'll dance a kissing dance with him anon.

MEDLEY   Dutifully observed, madam.

DORIMANT   They pretend to be great critics in beauty—by their talk you would think they liked no face—and yet can dote on an ill one if it belong to a laundress or a tailor's daughter. They cry a woman's past her prime at twenty, decayed at four-and-twenty, old and insufferable at thirty.

LADY WOODVILL   Insufferable at thirty! That they are in the wrong, Mr. Courtage, at five-and-thirty there are living proofs enough to convince 'em.

DORIMANT   Ay, madam; there's Mrs. Setlooks, Mrs. Droplip, and my Lady Loud. Show me among all our opening buds a face that promises so much beauty as the remains of theirs.

LADY WOODVILL   The depraved appetite of this vicious age tastes nothing but green fruit and loathes it when 'tis kindly[1] ripened.

DORIMANT   Else so many deserving women, madam, would not be so untimely neglected.

1. Naturally.

LADY WOODVILL   I protest, Mr. Courtage, a dozen such good men as you would be enough to atone for that wicked Dorimant and all the under-debauchees of the town.

> HARRIET, EMILIA, YOUNG BELLAIR, MEDLEY, *and* LADY TOWNLEY *break out into a laughter.*

What's the matter there?

MEDLEY   A pleasant mistake, madam, that a lady has made occasions a little laughter.

OLD BELLAIR [*to* DORIMANT *and* LADY WOODVILL]   Come, come, you keep 'em idle! They are impatient till the fiddles play again.

DORIMANT   You are not weary, madam?

LADY WOODVILL   One dance more. I cannot refuse you, Mr. Courtage.

> *They dance. After the dance,* OLD BELLAIR *singing and dancing up to* EMILIA.

EMILIA   You are very active, sir.

OLD BELLAIR   Adod, sirrah, when I was a young fellow, I could ha' capered up to my woman's gorget.[2]

DORIMANT [*to* LADY WOODVILL]   You are willing to rest yourself, madam?

LADY TOWNLEY [*to* DORIMANT *and* LADY WOODVILL]   We'll walk into my chamber and sit down.

MEDLEY   Leave us Mr. Courtage; he's a dancer, and the young ladies are not weary yet.

LADY WOODVILL   We'll send him out again.

HARRIET   If you do not quickly, I know where to send for Mr. Dorimant.

LADY WOODVILL   This girl's head, Mr. Courtage, is ever running on that wild fellow.

DORIMANT   'Tis well you have got her a good husband, madam. That will settle it.

> *Exeunt* LADY TOWNLEY, LADY WOODVILL, *and* DORIMANT.

OLD BELLAIR [*to* EMILIA]   Adod, sweetheart, be advised and do not throw thyself away on a young idle fellow.

EMILIA   I have no such intention, sir.

OLD BELLAIR   Have a little patience! Thou shalt have the man I spake of. Adod, he loves thee and will make a good husband. But no words—

EMILIA   But, sir—

OLD BELLAIR   No answer, out a pize! Peace, and think on't.

---

2. "I could have kicked as high as my partner's neck-scarf."

Enter DORIMANT.

DORIMANT   Your company is desired within, sir.

OLD BELLAIR   I go, I go! Good Mr. Courtage, fare you well. [*To* EMI-
LIA.] Go, I'll see you no more!

EMILIA   What have I done, sir?

OLD BELLAIR   You are ugly, you are ugly!—Is she not, Mr. Courtage?

EMILIA   Better words, or I shan't abide you!

OLD BELLAIR   Out a pize! Adod, what does she say?—Hit her a pat for
me there.

Exit OLD BELLAIR.

MEDLEY [*to* DORIMANT]   You have charms for the whole family.

DORIMANT   You'll spoil all with some unseasonable jest, Medley.

MEDLEY   You see I confine my tongue and am content to be a bare
spectator, much contrary to my nature.

EMILIA   Methinks, Mr. Dorimant, my Lady Woodvill is a little fond of
you.

DORIMANT   Would her daughter were.

MEDLEY   It may be you may find her so. Try her. You have an opportunity.

DORIMANT   And I will not lose it.—Bellair, here's a lady has something
to say to you.

YOUNG BELLAIR   I wait upon her.—Mr. Medley, we have both business
with you.

DORIMANT   Get you all together, then.

He bows to HARRIET; *she curtsies.*

[*To* HARRIET.] That demure curtsy is not amiss in jest, but do not
think in earnest it becomes you.

HARRIET   Affectation is catching, I find. From your grave bow I got it.

DORIMANT   Where had you all that scorn and coldness in your look?

HARRIET   From nature, sir; pardon my want of art. I have not learnt
those softnesses and languishings which now in faces are so much in
fashion.

DORIMANT   You need 'em not. You have a sweetness of your own, if you
would but calm your frowns and let it settle.

HARRIET   My eyes are wild and wand'ring like my passions, and cannot
yet be tied to rules of charming.

DORIMANT   Women, indeed, have commonly a method of managing
those messengers of love. Now they will look as if they would kill, and
anon they will look as if they were dying. They point and rebate[3] their
glances, the better to invite us.

HARRIET   I like this variety well enough, but hate the set face that

3. Blunt.

always looks as it would say, "Come love me"—a woman who at plays makes the *doux yeux*[4] to a whole audience and at home cannot forbear 'em to her monkey.

DORIMANT   Put on a gentle smile and let me see how well it will become you.

HARRIET   I am sorry my face does not please you as it is; but I shall not be complacent and change it.

DORIMANT   Though you are obstinate, I know 'tis capable of improvement, and shall do you justice, madam, if I chance to be at court when the critics of the circle pass their judgment; for thither you must come.

HARRIET   And expect to be taken in pieces, have all my features examined, every motion censured, and on the whole be condemned to be but pretty—or a beauty of the lowest rate. What think you?

DORIMANT   The women—nay, the very lovers who belong to the drawing room—will maliciously allow you more than that. They always grant what is apparent, that they may the better be believed when they name concealed faults they cannot easily be disproved in.

HARRIET   Beauty runs as great a risk exposed at court as wit does on the stage, where the ugly and the foolish all are free to censure.

DORIMANT   [*aside*]   I love her and dare not let her know it. I fear sh'as an ascendant o'er me and may revenge the wrongs I have done her sex. [*To her.*] Think of making a party, madam; love will engage.

HARRIET   You make me start. I did not think to have heard of love from you.

DORIMANT   I never knew what 'twas to have a settled ague yet, but now and then have had irregular fits.

HARRIET   Take heed; sickness after long health is commonly more violent and dangerous.

DORIMANT   [*aside*]   I have took the infection from her and feel the disease now spreading in me. [*To her.*] Is the name of love so frightful that you dare not stand it?

HARRIET   'Twill do little execution out of your mouth on me, I am sure.

DORIMANT   It has been fatal—

HARRIET   To some easy women, but we are not all born to one destiny. I was informed you use to laugh at love, and not make it.

DORIMANT   The time has been, but now I must speak.

HARRIET   If it be on that idle subject, I will put on my serious look, turn my head carelessly from you, drop my lip, let my eyelids fall and hang half o'er my eyes—thus, while you buzz a speech of an hour long in my ear and I answer never a word. Why do you not begin?

DORIMANT   That the company may take notice how passionately I made advances of love and how disdainfully you receive 'em.

HARRIET   When your love's grown strong enough to make you bear

---

4. Makes eyes at.

being laughed at, I'll give you leave to trouble me with it. Till when, pray forbear, sir.

Enter SIR FOPLING *and others in masks.*

DORIMANT   What's here—masquerades?

HARRIET   I thought foppery had been left off, and people might have been in private with a fiddle.

DORIMANT   'Tis endeavored to be kept on foot still by some who find themselves more acceptable, the less they are known.

YOUNG BELLAIR   This must be Sir Fopling.

MEDLEY   That extraordinary habit[5] shows it.

YOUNG BELLAIR   What are the rest?

MEDLEY   A company of French rascals whom he picked up in Paris and has brought over to be his dancing equipage on these occasions. Make him own himself; a fool is very troublesome when he presumes he is incognito.

SIR FOPLING   [*to* HARRIET]   Do you know me?

HARRIET   Ten to one but I guess at you.

SIR FOPLING   Are you women as fond of a vizard as we men are?

HARRIET   I am very fond of a vizard that covers a face I do not like, sir.

YOUNG BELLAIR   Here are no masks, you see, sir, but those which came with you. This was intended a private meeting; but because you look like a gentleman, if you will discover yourself and we know you to be such, you shall be welcome.

SIR FOPLING   [*pulling off his mask*]   Dear Bellair.

MEDLEY   Sir Fopling! How came you hither?

SIR FOPLING   Faith, as I was coming late from Whitehall, after the King's *couchée,*[6] one of my people told me he had heard fiddles at my Lady Townley's, and—

DORIMANT   You need not say any more, sir.

SIR FOPLING   Dorimant, let me kiss thee.

DORIMANT   Hark you, Sir Fopling—

Whispers.

SIR FOPLING   Enough, enough, Courtage. —[*Glancing at* HARRIET.] A pretty kind of young woman that, Medley. I observed her in the Mall, more *evelie*[7] than our English women commonly are. Prithee, what is she?

MEDLEY   The most noted *coquetté*[8] in town. Beware of her.

SIR FOPLING   Let her be what she will, I know how to take my measures. In Paris the mode is to flatter the *prudè,* laugh at the *faux-prudè,* make serious love to the *demi-prudè,* and only rally with the *coquetté.* Medley, what think you?

5. Clothing.
6. Evening reception.
7. Sprightly. Sir Fopling mispronounces *éveillée.*
8. Medley mocks Sir Fopling by accenting the final *e.* See Sir Fopling's next speech.

MEDLEY   That for all this smattering of the mathematics, you may be out in your judgment at tennis.

SIR FOPLING   What a *coq-à-l'âne*[9] is this? I talk of women, and thou answer'st tennis.

MEDLEY   Mistakes will be, for want of apprehension.

SIR FOPLING   I am very glad of the acquaintance I have with this family.

MEDLEY   My lady truly is a good woman.

SIR FOPLING   Ah, Dorimant—Courtage, I would say—would thou hadst spent the last winter in Paris with me. When thou wert there, La Corneus and Sallyes[1] were the only habitudes we had; a comedian would have been a *bonne fortune*.[2] No stranger ever passed his time so well as I did some months before I came over. I was well received in a dozen families, where all the women of quality used to visit. I have intrigues to tell thee more pleasant than ever thou read'st in a novel.

HARRIET   Write 'em, sir, and oblige us women. Our language wants such little stories.

SIR FOPLING   Writing, madam, 's a mechanic part of wit. A gentleman should never go beyond a song or a *billet*.

HARRIET   Bussy was a gentleman.

SIR FOPLING   Who, d'Ambois?[3]

MEDLEY [*aside*]   Was there ever such a brisk blockhead?

HARRIET   Not d'Ambois, sir, but Rabutin: he who writ the *Loves of France*.

SIR FOPLING   That may be, madam; many gentlemen do things that are below 'em. —Damn your authors, Courtage. Women are the prettiest things we can fool away our time with.

HARRIET   I hope ye have wearied yourself tonight at court, sir, and will not think of fooling with anybody here.

SIR FOPLING   I cannot complain of my fortune there, madam.—Dorimant—

DORIMANT   Again!

SIR FOPLING   Courtage, a pox on't! I have something to tell thee. When I had made my court within, I came out and flung myself upon the mat under the state[4] i' th' outward room, i' th' midst of half a dozen beauties who were withdrawn to jeèr among themselves, as they called it.

DORIMANT   Did you know 'em?

SIR FOPLING   Not one of 'em, by heav'ns, not I! But they were all your friends.

DORIMANT   How are you sure of that?

---

9. Lot of nonsense.
1. Probably Mesdames Cornuel and Selles, literary ladies.
2. Piece of good luck.
3. Sir Fopling confuses Bussy d'Ambois, hero of a play by George Chapman, with the French author Roger de Rabutin, Comte de Bussy.
4. Canopy.

SIR FOPLING   Why, we laughed at all the town—spared nobody but yourself. They found me a man for their purpose.

DORIMANT   I know you are malicious to your power.

SIR FOPLING   And, faith, I had occasion to show it; for I never saw more gaping fools at a ball or on a birthday.

DORIMANT   You learned who the women were?

SIR FOPLING   No matter; they frequent the drawing room.

DORIMANT   And entertain themselves at the expense of all the fops who come there.

SIR FOPLING   That's their bus'ness. Faith, I sifted 'em and find they have a sort of wit among them.

>   *Pinches a tallow candle.*

Ah, filthy!

DORIMANT   Look, he has been pinching the tallow candle.

SIR FOPLING   How can you breathe in a room where there's grease frying? Dorimant, thou art intimate with my lady: advise her, for her own sake and the good company that comes hither, to burn wax lights.

HARRIET   What are these masquerades who stand so obsequiously at a distance?

SIR FOPLING   A set of balladines, whom I picked out of the best in France and brought over with a *flute douce* or two—my servants. They shall entertain you.

HARRIET   I had rather see you dance yourself, Sir Fopling.

SIR FOPLING   And I had rather do it—all the company knows it. But, madam—

MEDLEY   Come, come, no excuses, Sir Fopling!

SIR FOPLING   By heav'ns, Medley—

MEDLEY   Like a woman I find you must be struggled with before one brings you what you desire.

HARRIET [*aside*]   Can he dance?

EMILIA   And fence and sing too, if you'll believe him.

DORIMANT   He has no more excellence in his heels than in his head. He went to Paris a plain, bashful English blockhead and is returned a fine, undertaking French fop.

MEDLEY [*to* HARRIET]   I cannot prevail.

SIR FOPLING   Do not think it want of complaisance, madam.

HARRIET   You are too well-bred to want that, Sir Fopling. I think it want of power.

SIR FOPLING   By heav'ns, and so it is! I have sat up so damned late and drunk so cursed hard since I came to this lewd town that I am fit for nothing but low dancing now—a *courante*, a *bourrée* or a *menuet*.[5] But St. André[6] tells me, if I will but be regular, in one month I shall rise again.

5. Stately dances.
6. French dancing master.

Endeavors at a caper.

Pox on this debauchery!

EMILIA   I have heard your dancing much commended.

SIR FOPLING   It had the good fortune to please in Paris. I was judged to rise within an inch as high as the basqué[7] in an entry I danced there.

HARRIET [*to* EMILIA]   I am mightily taken with this fool. Let us sit. — Here's a seat, Sir Fopling.

SIR FOPLING   At your feet, madam. I can be nowhere so much at ease. —By your leave, gown.

Sits.

HARRIET, EMILIA   Ah, you'll spoil it!

SIR FOPLING   No matter, my clothes are my creatures. I make 'em to make my court to you ladies.—Hey, *qu'on commencè!*[8]

Dance.

To an English dancer, English motions! I was forced to entertain[9] this fellow [*pointing to* JOHN TROTT], one of my set miscarrying. — Oh, horrid! Leave your damned manner of dancing and put on the French air. Have you not a pattern before you?—Pretty well! Imitation in time may bring him to something.

After the dance, enter OLD BELLAIR, LADY WOODVILL, *and* LADY TOWNLEY.

OLD BELLAIR   Hey, adod, what have we here? A mumming?

LADY WOODVILL   Where's my daughter? —Harriet!

DORIMANT   Here, here, madam. I know not but under these disguises there may be dangerous sparks. I gave the lady warning.

LADY WOODVILL   Lord, I am so obliged to you, Mr. Courtage.

HARRIET   Lord, how you admire this man!

LADY WOODVILL   What have you to except against him?

HARRIET   He's a fop.

LADY WOODVILL   He's not a Dorimant, a wild, extravagant fellow of the times.

HARRIET   He's a man made up of forms and commonplaces, sucked out of the remaining lees of the last age.

LADY WOODVILL   He's so good a man that were you not engaged—

LADY TOWNLEY   You'll have but little night to sleep in.

LADY WOODVILL   Lord, 'tis perfect day!

DORIMANT [*aside*]   The hour is almost come I appointed Bellinda, and I am not so foppishly in love here to forget. I am flesh and blood yet.

LADY TOWNLEY   I am very sensible, madam.

LADY WOODVILL   Lord, madam—

7. Skirt of a coat.
8. Begin.
9. Hire.

HARRIET Look, in what a struggle is my poor mother yonder!

YOUNG BELLAIR She has much ado to bring out the compliment.

DORIMANT She strains hard for it.

HARRIET See, see—her head tottering, her eyes staring, and her underlip trembling.

DORIMANT Now, now she's in the very convulsions of her civility. [*Aside.*] 'Sdeath, I shall lose Bellinda! I must fright her hence. She'll be an hour in this fit of good manners else. [*To* LADY WOODVILL.] Do you not know Sir Fopling, madam?

LADY WOODVILL I have seen that face. Oh heav'n, 'tis the same we met in the Mall! How came he here?

DORIMANT A fiddle in this town is a kind of fop-call. No sooner it strikes up, but the house is besieged with an army of masquerades straight.

LADY WOODVILL Lord, I tremble, Mr. Courtage. For certain Dorimant is in the company.

DORIMANT I cannot confidently say he is not. You had best begone; I will wait upon you. Your daughter is in the hands of Mr. Bellair.

LADY WOODVILL I'll see her before me. —Harriet, come away!

Exeunt LADY WOODVILL *and* HARRIET.

YOUNG BELLAIR Lights, lights!

LADY TOWNLEY Light, down there!

OLD BELLAIR Adod, it needs not—

Exeunt LADY TOWNLEY *and* YOUNG BELLAIR.

DORIMANT [*calling to the servants outside*] Call my Lady Woodvill's coach to the door! Quickly!

Exit DORIMANT.

OLD BELLAIR Stay, Mr. Medley; let the young fellows do that duty. We will drink a glass of wine together. 'Tis good after dancing. [*Looks at* SIR FOPLING.] What mumming spark is that?

MEDLEY He is not to be comprehended in few words.

SIR FOPLING Hey, La Tour!

MEDLEY Whither away, Sir Fopling?

SIR FOPLING I have bus'ness with Courtage.

MEDLEY He'll but put the ladies into their coach and come up again.

OLD BELLAIR In the meantime I'll call for a bottle.

Exit OLD BELLAIR.

Enter YOUNG BELLAIR.

MEDLEY Where's Dorimant?

YOUNG BELLAIR Stol'n home. He has had business waiting for him there all this night, I believe, by an impatience I observed in him.

MEDLEY Very likely. 'Tis but dissembling drunkenness, railing at his friends, and the kind soul will embrace the blessing and forget the tedious expectation.

SIR FOPLING   I must speak with him before I sleep.

YOUNG BELLAIR [*to* MEDLEY]   Emilia and I are resolved on that business.

MEDLEY   Peace, here's your father.

Enter OLD BELLAIR *and butler with a bottle of wine.*

OLD BELLAIR   The women are all gone to bed. Fill, boy! —Mr. Medley, begin a health.

MEDLEY [*whispers*]   To Emilia.

OLD BELLAIR   Out a pize! She's a rogue, and I'll not pledge you.

MEDLEY   I know you will.

OLD BELLAIR   Adod, drink it, then!

SIR FOPLING   Let us have the new bachique.

OLD BELLAIR   Adod, that is a hard word! What does it mean, sir?

MEDLEY   A catch or drinking song.

OLD BELLAIR   Let us have it, then.

SIR FOPLING   Fill the glasses round, and draw up in a body. —Hey, music!

They sing.

> The pleasures of love and the joys of good wine,
> To perfect our happiness wisely we join.
> We to beauty all day
> Give the sovereign sway
> And her favorite nymphs devoutly obey;
> At the plays we are constantly making our court,
> And when they are ended, we follow the sport
> To the Mall and the Park,
> Where we love till 'tis dark.
> Then sparkling champagne
> Puts an end to their reign:
> It quickly recovers
> Poor languishing lovers,
> Makes us frolic and gay, and drowns all our sorrow;
> But alas, we relapse again on the morrow.
>   Let every man stand
>   With his glass in his hand,
> And briskly discharge at the word of command.
>   Here's a health to all those
>   Whom tonight we depose.
> Wine and beauty by turns great souls should inspire;
> Present all together; and now, boys, give fire!

They drink.

OLD BELLAIR   Adod, a pretty bus'ness and very merry!

SIR FOPLING   Hark you, Medley, let you and I take the fiddles and go waken Dorimant.

MEDLEY   We shall do him a courtesy, if it be as I guess. For after the fatigue of this night, he'll quickly have his belly full and be glad of an occasion to cry, "Take away, Handy!"

YOUNG BELLAIR   I'll go with you; and there we'll consult about affairs, Medley.

OLD BELLAIR   [*looks on his watch*]   Adod, 'tis six o'clock!

SIR FOPLING   Let's away, then.

OLD BELLAIR   Mr. Medley, my sister tells me you are an honest man. And, adod, I love you. — Few words and hearty, that's the way with old Harry, old Harry.

SIR FOPLING   [*to his servants*]   Light your flambeaux![1] Hey!

OLD BELLAIR   What does the man mean?

MEDLEY   'Tis day, Sir Fopling.

SIR FOPLING   No matter; our serenade will look the greater.

Exeunt omnes.

Act IV. Scene ii. DORIMANT's *lodging; a table, a candle, a toilet, etc.*

HANDY *tying up linen. Enter* DORIMANT *in his gown, and* BEL-LINDA.

DORIMANT   Why will you be gone so soon?

BELLINDA   Why did you stay out so late?

DORIMANT   Call a chair, Handy.

Exit HANDY.

—What makes you tremble so?

BELLINDA   I have a thousand fears about me. Have I not been seen, think you?

DORIMANT   By nobody but myself and trusty Handy.

BELLINDA   Where are all your people?

DORIMANT   I have dispersed 'em on sleeveless[2] errands. What does that sigh mean?

BELLINDA   Can you be so unkind to ask me? Well [*sighs*], were it to do again—

DORIMANT   We should do it, should we not?

BELLINDA   I think we should: the wickeder man you, to make me love so well. Will you be discreet now?

DORIMANT   I will.

BELLINDA   You cannot.

1. Torches.
2. Useless.

DORIMANT   Never doubt it.

BELLINDA   I will not expect it.

DORIMANT   You do me wrong.

BELLINDA   You have no more power to keep the secret than I had not to trust you with it.

DORIMANT   By all the joys I have had and those you keep in store —

BELLINDA   —You'll do for my sake what you never did before.

DORIMANT   By that truth thou hast spoken, a wife shall sooner betray herself to her husband.

BELLINDA   Yet I had rather you should be false in this than in another thing you promised me.

DORIMANT   What's that?

BELLINDA   That you would never see Loveit more but in public places—in the Park, at court and plays.

DORIMANT   'Tis not likely a man should be fond of seeing a damned old play when there is a new one acted.

BELLINDA   I dare not trust your promise.

DORIMANT   You may.

BELLINDA   This does not satisfy me. You shall swear you never will see her more.

DORIMANT   I will, a thousand oaths. By all—

BELLINDA   Hold! You shall not, now I think on't better.

DORIMANT   I will swear!

BELLINDA   I shall grow jealous of the oath and think I owe your truth to that, not to your love.

DORIMANT   Then, by my love! No other oath I'll swear.

Enter HANDY.

HANDY   Here's a chair.

BELLINDA   Let me go.

DORIMANT   I cannot.

BELLINDA   Too willingly, I fear.

DORIMANT   Too unkindly feared. When will you promise me again?

BELLINDA   Not this fortnight.

DORIMANT   You will be better than your word.

BELLINDA   I think I shall. Will it not make you love me less?

Fiddles without.

[*Starting.*] Hark, what fiddles are these?

DORIMANT   Look out, Handy.

Exit HANDY *and returns.*

HANDY   Mr. Medley, Mr. Bellair, and Sir Fopling. They are coming up.

DORIMANT   How got they in?

HANDY   The door was open for the chair.

BELLINDA   Lord, let me fly!

DORIMANT   Here, here, down the back stairs. I'll see you into your chair.

BELLINDA   No, no, stay and receive 'em. And be sure you keep your word and never see Loveit more. Let it be a proof of your kindness.

DORIMANT   It shall. —Handy, direct her. —[*Kissing her hand.*] Everlasting love go along with thee.

Exeunt BELLINDA *and* HANDY.

Enter YOUNG BELLAIR, MEDLEY, *and* SIR FOPLING *with his page.*

YOUNG BELLAIR   Not abed yet?

MEDLEY   You have had an irregular fit, Dorimant.

DORIMANT   I have.

YOUNG BELLAIR   And it is off already?

DORIMANT   Nature has done her part, gentlemen. When she falls kindly to work, great cures are effected in little time, you know.

SIR FOPLING   We thought there was a wench in the case, by the chair that waited. Prithee, make us a *confidencé.*

DORIMANT   Excuse me.

SIR FOPLING   *Lè sagè*[3] Dorimant. Was she pretty?

DORIMANT   So pretty she may come to keep her coach and pay parish duties, if the good humour of the age continue.

MEDLEY   And be of the number of ladies kept by public-spirited men for the good of the whole town.

SIR FOPLING   Well said, Medley.

SIR FOPLING *dancing by himself.*

YOUNG BELLAIR   See Sir Fopling dancing.

DORIMANT   You are practicing and have a mind to recover, I see.

SIR FOPLING   Prithee, Dorimant, why hast not thou a glass hung up here? A room is the dullest thing without one.

YOUNG BELLAIR   Here is company to entertain you.

SIR FOPLING   But I mean in case of being alone. In a glass a man may entertain himself—

DORIMANT   The shadow of himself, indeed.

SIR FOPLING   —Correct the errors of his motions and his dress.

MEDLEY   I find, Sir Fopling, in your solitude you remember the saying of the wise man, and study yourself.

SIR FOPLING   'Tis the best diversion in our retirements. Dorimant, thou art a pretty fellow and wear'st thy clothes well, but I never saw thee have a handsome cravat. Were they made up like mine, they'd give another air to thy face. Prithee, let me send my man to dress thee but one day. By heav'ns, an Englishman cannot tie a ribbon!

DORIMANT   They are something clumsy-fisted.

SIR FOPLING   I have brought over the prettiest fellow that ever spread a

3. Prudent.

toilet. He served some time under Merille,[4] the greatest genie in the world for a *valet de chambré.*

DORIMANT   What, he who formerly belonged to the Duke of Candale?[5]

SIR FOPLING   The same, and got him his immortal reputation.

DORIMANT   Y' have a very fine brandenburgh on, Sir Fopling.

SIR FOPLING   It serves to wrap me up, after the fatigue of a ball.

MEDLEY   I see you often in it, with your periwig tied up.

SIR FOPLING   We should not always be in a set dress. 'Tis more *en cavalier* to appear now and then in a *déshabillé.*[6]

MEDLEY   Pray, how goes your business with Loveit?

SIR FOPLING   You might have answered yourself in the Mall last night. —Dorimant, did you not see the advances she made me? I have been endeavoring at a song.

DORIMANT   Already?

SIR FOPLING   'Tis my *coup d'essai*[7] in English. I would fain have thy opinion of it.

DORIMANT   Let's see it.

SIR FOPLING   Hey, page, give me my song. —Bellair, here. Thou hast a pretty voice; sing it.

YOUNG BELLAIR   Sing it yourself, Sir Fopling.

SIR FOPLING   Excuse me.

YOUNG BELLAIR   You learnt to sing in Paris.

SIR FOPLING   I did—of Lambert,[8] the greatest master in the world; but I have his own fault, a weak voice, and care not to sing out of a *ruelle.*[9]

DORIMANT   A *ruelle* is a pretty cage for a singing fop, indeed.

YOUNG BELLAIR *reads the song.*

> How charming Phillis is, how fair!
>   Ah, that she were as willing
> To ease my wounded heart of care,
>   And make her eyes less killing.
> I sigh, I sigh, I languish now,
>   And love will not let me rest;
> I drive about the Park and bow,
>   Still as I meet my dearest.

SIR FOPLING   Sing it, sing it, man! It goes to a pretty new tune which I am confident was made by Baptiste.[1]

MEDLEY   Sing it yourself, Sir Fopling. He does not know the tune.

SIR FOPLING   I'll venture.

---

4. Valet to the Duke of Orléans.
5. Famous French general and courtier.
6. " 'Tis more dashing to appear now and then casually dressed."
7. First effort.
8. Musician in the court of Louis XIV.
9. Lady's bedchamber.
1. Another musician to Louis XIV.

SIR FOPLING *sings*.

DORIMANT   Ay, marry, now 'tis something. I shall not flatter you, Sir Fopling: there is not much thought in't, but 'tis passionate and well-turned.

MEDLEY   After the French way.

SIR FOPLING   That I aimed at. Does it not give you a lively image of the thing? Slap, down goes the glass,[2] and thus we are at it.

DORIMANT   It does indeed. I perceive, Sir Fopling, you'll be the very head of the sparks who are lucky in compositions of this nature.

Enter SIR FOPLING'S FOOTMAN.

SIR FOPLING   La Tour, is the bath ready?

FOOTMAN   Yes, sir.

SIR FOPLING   *Adieu donc, mes chers.*

Exit SIR FOPLING *with attendants.*

MEDLEY   When have you your revenge on Loveit, Dorimant?

DORIMANT   I will but change my linen and about it.

MEDLEY   The powerful considerations which hindered have been removed, then?

DORIMANT   Most luckily, this morning. You must along with me; my reputation lies at stake there.

MEDLEY   I am engaged to Bellair.

DORIMANT   What's your business?

MEDLEY   Ma-tri-mony, an't like you.

DORIMANT   It does not, sir.

YOUNG BELLAIR   It may in time, Dorimant. What think you of Mrs. Harriet?

DORIMANT   What does she think of me?

YOUNG BELLAIR   I am confident she loves you.

DORIMANT   How does it appear?

YOUNG BELLAIR   Why, she's never well but when she's talking of you, but then she finds all the faults in you she can. She laughs at all who commend you; but then she speaks ill of all who do not.

DORIMANT   Women of her temper betray themselves by their over-cunning. I had once a growing love with a lady who would always quarrel with me when I came to see her, and yet was never quiet if I stayed a day from her.

YOUNG BELLAIR   My father is in love with Emilia.

DORIMANT   That is a good warrant for your proceedings. Go on and prosper; I must to Loveit. —Medley, I am sorry you cannot be a witness.

MEDLEY   Make her meet Sir Fopling again in the same place and use him ill before me.

2. Coach window.

DORIMANT   That may be brought about, I think. —I'll be at your aunt's anon and give you joy, Mr. Bellair.

YOUNG BELLAIR   You had best not think of Mrs. Harriet too much. Without church security, there's no taking up there.

DORIMANT   I may fall into the snare, too. But,

> The wise will find a difference in our fate:
> You wed a woman, I a good estate.

Exeunt.

Act IV. Scene iii. *The Mall; in front of* MRS. LOVEIT's.

Enter the chair with BELLINDA; *the men set it down and open it.* BELLINDA *starting.*

BELLINDA [*surprised*]   Lord, where am I? In the Mall! Whither have you brought me?

FIRST CHAIRMAN   You gave us no directions, madam.

BELLINDA [*aside*]   The fright I was in made me forget it.

FIRST CHAIRMAN   We used to carry a lady from the squire's hither.

BELLINDA [*aside*]   This is Loveit! I am undone if she sees me. —Quickly, carry me away!

FIRST CHAIRMAN   Whither, an't like your honor?

BELLINDA   Ask no questions!

Enter MRS. LOVEIT's FOOTMAN.

FOOTMAN   Have you seen my lady, madam?

BELLINDA   I am just come to wait upon her.

FOOTMAN   She will be glad to see you, madam. She sent me to you this morning to desire your company, and I was told you went out by five o'clock.

BELLINDA [*aside*]   More and more unlucky!

FOOTMAN   Will you walk in, madam?

BELLINDA   I'll discharge my chair and follow. Tell your mistress I am here.

Exit FOOTMAN.

GIVES THE CHAIRMEN *money.*

Take this; and if ever you should be examined, be sure you say you took me up in the Strand, over against the Exchange—as you will answer it to Mr. Dorimant.

CHAIRMEN   We will, an't like your honor.

Exeunt CHAIRMEN.

BELLINDA   Now to come off, I must on:

> In confidence and lies some hope is left;
> 'Twere hard to be found out in the first theft.

Exit.

Act V. Scene i. MRS. LOVEIT's.

Enter MRS. LOVEIT *and* PERT, *her woman.*

PERT   Well! In my eyes, Sir Fopling is no such despicable person.

MRS. LOVEIT   You are an excellent judge.

PERT   He's as handsome a man as Mr. Dorimant, and as great a gallant.

MRS. LOVEIT   Intolerable! Is't not enough I submit to his impertinences, but must I be plagued with yours too?

PERT   Indeed, madam—

MRS. LOVEIT   'Tis false, mercenary malice—

Enter her FOOTMAN.

FOOTMAN   Mrs. Bellinda, madam.

MRS. LOVEIT   What of her?

FOOTMAN   She's below.

MRS. LOVEIT   How came she?

FOOTMAN   In a chair; ambling Harry brought her.

MRS. LOVEIT [*aside*]   He bring her! His chair stands near Dorimant's door and always brings me from thence. —Run and ask him where he took her up. Go!

Exit FOOTMAN.

There is no truth in friendship neither. Women as well as men, all are false, or all are so to me at least.

PERT   You are jealous of her too?

MRS. LOVEIT   You had best tell her I am. 'Twill become the liberty you take of late. [*Aside.*] This fellow's bringing of her, her going out by five o'clock—I know not what to think.

Enter BELLINDA.

Bellinda, you are grown an early riser, I hear.

BELLINDA   Do you not wonder, my dear, what made me abroad so soon?

MRS. LOVEIT   You do not use to be so.

BELLINDA   The country gentlewomen I told you of—Lord, they have the oddest diversions—would never let me rest till I promised to go with them to the markets this morning to eat fruit and buy nosegays.

MRS. LOVEIT   Are they so fond of a filthy nosegay?

BELLINDA   They complain of the stinks of the town and are never well
but when they have their noses in one.

MRS. LOVEIT   There are essences and sweet waters.

BELLINDA   Oh, they cry out upon perfumes, they are unwholesome.
One of 'em was falling into a fit with the smell of these *narolii*.[3]

MRS. LOVEIT   Methinks, in complaisance you should have had a nosegay too.

BELLINDA   Do you think, my dear, I could be so loathsome to trick
myself up with carnations and stock-gillyflowers? I begged their pardon and told them I never wore anything but orange-flowers and
tuberose. That which made me willing to go was a strange desire I
had to eat some fresh nectarines.

MRS. LOVEIT   And had you any?

BELLINDA   The best I ever tasted.

MRS. LOVEIT   Whence came you now?

BELLINDA   From their lodgings, where I crowded out of a coach and
took a chair to come and see you, my dear.

MRS. LOVEIT   Whither did you send for that chair?

BELLINDA   'Twas going by empty.

MRS. LOVEIT   Where do these country gentlewomen lodge, I pray?

BELLINDA   In the Strand, over against the Exchange.

PERT   That place is never without a nest of 'em. They are always, as
one goes by, fleering in balconies or staring out of windows.

Enter FOOTMAN.

MRS. LOVEIT [*to the* FOOTMAN]   Come hither.

Whispers.

BELLINDA [*aside*]   This fellow by her order has been questioning the
chairmen. I threatened 'em with the name of Dorimant. If they
should have told truth, I am lost forever.

MRS. LOVEIT   In the Strand, said you?

FOOTMAN   Yes, madam, over against the Exchange.

Exit FOOTMAN.

MRS. LOVEIT   She's innocent, and I am much to blame.

BELLINDA [*aside*]   I am so frighted, my countenance will betray me.

MRS. LOVEIT   Bellinda, what makes you look so pale?

BELLINDA   Want of my usual rest and jolting up and down so long in
an odious hackney.

FOOTMAN *returns.*

FOOTMAN   Madam, Mr. Dorimant.

Exit FOOTMAN.

---

3. Essences of orange.

MRS. LOVEIT   What makes him here?

BELLINDA [*aside*]   Then I am betrayed indeed. H' has broke his word, and I love a man that does not care for me.

MRS. LOVEIT   Lord, you faint, Bellinda.

BELLINDA   I think I shall—such an oppression here on the sudden.

PERT   She has eaten too much fruit, I warrant you.

MRS. LOVEIT   Not unlikely.

PERT   'Tis that lies heavy on her stomach.

MRS. LOVEIT   Have her into my chamber, give her some surfeitwater, and let her lie down a little.

PERT   Come, madam. I was a strange devourer of fruit when I was young—so ravenous.

Exeunt BELLINDA *and* PERT, *leading her off.*

MRS. LOVEIT   Oh, that my love would but be calm awhile, that I might receive this man with all the scorn and indignation he deserves!

Enter DORIMANT.

DORIMANT   Now for a touch of Sir Fopling to begin with. —Hey, page! Give positive order that none of my people stir. Let the *canaille*[4] wait, as they should do. —Since noise and nonsense have such pow'rful charms,

> "I, that I may successful prove,
> Transform myself to what you love."[5]

MRS. LOVEIT   If that would do, you need not change from what you are: you can be vain and loud enough.

DORIMANT   But not with so good a grace as Sir Fopling. —"Hey, Hampshire!"—Oh, that sound! That sound becomes the mouth of a man of quality.

MRS. LOVEIT   Is there a thing so hateful as a senseless mimic?

DORIMANT   He's a great grievance, indeed, to all who—like yourself, madam—love to play the fool in quiet.

MRS. LOVEIT   A ridiculous animal, who has more of the ape than the ape has of the man in him.

DORIMANT   I have as mean an opinion of a sheer mimic as yourself; yet were he all ape, I should prefer him to the gay, the giddy, brisk, insipid, noisy fool you dote on.

MRS. LOVEIT   Those noisy fools, however you despise 'em, have good qualities which weigh more (or ought, at least) with us women than all the pernicious wit you have to boast of.

DORIMANT   That I may hereafter have a just value of their merit, pray do me the favor to name 'em.

4. Rabble.
5. From Waller's "To the Mutable Fair," lines 5–6.

MRS. LOVEIT   You'll despise 'em as the dull effects of ignorance and vanity, yet I care not if I mention some. First, they really admire us, while you at best but flatter us well.

DORIMANT   Take heed; fools can dissemble too.

MRS. LOVEIT   They may—but not so artificially as you. There is no fear they should deceive us. Then, they are assiduous, sir. They are ever offering us their service and always waiting on our will.

DORIMANT   You owe that to their excessive idleness. They know not how to entertain themselves at home, and find so little welcome abroad, they are fain to fly to you who countenance 'em, as a refuge against the solitude they would be otherwise condemned to.

MRS. LOVEIT   Their conversation, too, diverts us better.

DORIMANT   Playing with your fan, smelling to your gloves, commending your hair, and taking notice how 'tis cut and shaded after the new way—

MRS. LOVEIT   Were it sillier than you can make it, you must allow 'tis pleasanter to laugh at others than to be laughed at ourselves, though never so wittily. Then, though they want skill to flatter us, they flatter themselves so well, they save us the labor. We need not take that care and pains to satisfy 'em of our love, which we so often lose on you.

DORIMANT   They commonly, indeed, believe too well of themselves—and always better of you than you deserve.

MRS. LOVEIT   You are in the right: they have an implicit faith in us, which keeps 'em from prying narrowly into our secrets and saves us the vexatious trouble of clearing doubts which your subtle and causeless jealousies every moment raise.

DORIMANT   There is an inbred falsehood in women which inclines 'em still to them whom they may most easily deceive.

MRS. LOVEIT   The man who loves above his quality does not suffer more from the insolent impertinence of his mistress than the woman who loves above her understanding does from the arrogant presumptions of her friend.

DORIMANT   You mistake the use of fools: they are designed for properties and not for friends. You have an indifferent stock of reputation left yet. Lose it all like a frank gamester on the square. 'Twill then be time to turn rook and cheat it up again on a good, substantial bubble.[6]

MRS. LOVEIT   The old and the ill-favored are only fit for properties, indeed; but young and handsome fools have met with kinder fortunes.

DORIMANT   They have, to the shame of your sex be it spoken. 'Twas this, the thought of this, made me by a timely jealousy endeavor to

6. Dupe.

prevent the good fortune you are providing for Sir Fopling. But against a woman's frailty all our care is vain.

MRS. LOVEIT   Had I not with a dear experience bought the knowledge of your falsehood, you might have fooled me yet. This is not the first jealousy you have feigned to make a quarrel with me, and get a week to throw away on some such unknown, inconsiderable slut as you have been lately lurking with at plays.

DORIMANT   Women, when they would break off with a man, never want th'address to turn the fault on him.

MRS. LOVEIT   You take a pride of late in using of me ill, that the town may know the power you have over me, which now (as unreasonably as yourself) expects that I, do me all the injuries you can, must love you still.

DORIMANT   I am so far from expecting that you should, I begin to think you never did love me.

MRS. LOVEIT   Would the memory of it were so wholly worn out in me that I did doubt it too. What made you come to disturb my growing quiet?

DORIMANT   To give you joy of your growing infamy.

MRS. LOVEIT   Insupportable! Insulting devil! This from you, the only author of my shame! This from another had been justice; but from you, 'tis a hellish and inhuman outrage. What have I done?

DORIMANT   A thing that puts you below my scorn and makes my anger as ridiculous as you have made my love.

MRS. LOVEIT   I walked last night with Sir Fopling.

DORIMANT   You did, madam; and you talked and laughed aloud, "Ha, ha, ha." Oh, that laugh! That laugh becomes the confidence of a woman of quality.

MRS. LOVEIT   You, who have more pleasure in the ruin of a woman's reputation than in the endearments of her love, reproach me not with yourself and I defy you to name the man can lay a blemish on my fame.

DORIMANT   To be seen publicly so transported with the vain follies of that notorious fop, to me is an infamy below the sin of prostitution with another man.

MRS. LOVEIT   Rail on! I am satisfied in the justice of what I did: you had provoked me to it.

DORIMANT   What I did was the effect of a passion whose extravagancies you have been willing to forgive.

MRS. LOVEIT   And what I did was the effect of a passion you may forgive if you think fit.

DORIMANT   Are you so indifferent grown?

MRS. LOVEIT   I am.

DORIMANT   Nay, then 'tis time to part. I'll send you back your letters you have so often asked for. [*Looks in his pockets.*] I have two or three of 'em about me.

MRS. LOVEIT   Give 'em me.

DORIMANT   You snatch as if you thought I would not.

Gives her the letters.

There. And may the perjuries in 'em be mine if e'er I see you more.

Offers to go; she catches him.

MRS. LOVEIT   Stay!

DORIMANT   I will not.

MRS. LOVEIT   You shall!

DORIMANT   What have you to say?

MRS. LOVEIT   I cannot speak it yet.

DORIMANT   Something more in commendation of the fool. Death, I want patience! Let me go.

MRS. LOVEIT   I cannot. [*Aside.*] I can sooner part with the limbs that hold him. —I hate that nauseous fool, you know I do.

DORIMANT   Was it the scandal you were fond of, then?

MRS. LOVEIT   Y' had raised my anger equal to my love, a thing you ne'er could do before; and in revenge I did—I know not what I did. Would you would not think on't any more.

DORIMANT   Should I be willing to forget it, I shall be daily minded of it. 'Twill be a commonplace for all the town to laugh at me, and Medley, when he is rhetorically drunk, will ever be declaiming on it in my ears.

MRS. LOVEIT   'Twill be believed a jealous spite. Come, forget it.

DORIMANT   Let me consult my reputation; you are too careless of it. [*Pauses.*] You shall meet Sir Fopling in the Mall again tonight.

MRS. LOVEIT   What mean you?

DORIMANT   I have thought on it, and you must. 'Tis necessary to justify my love to the world. You can handle a coxcomb as he deserves when you are not out of humour, madam.

MRS. LOVEIT   Public satisfaction for the wrong I have done you? This is some new device to make me more ridiculous.

DORIMANT   Hear me.

MRS. LOVEIT   I will not.

DORIMANT   You will be persuaded.

MRS. LOVEIT   Never!

DORIMANT   Are you so obstinate?

MRS. LOVEIT   Are you so base?

DORIMANT   You will not satisfy my love?

MRS. LOVEIT   I would die to satisfy that; but I will not, to save you from a thousand racks, do a shameless thing to please your vanity.

DORIMANT   Farewell, false woman.

MRS. LOVEIT   Do! Go!

DORIMANT   You will call me back again.

MRS. LOVEIT   Exquisite fiend! I knew you came but to torment me.

Enter BELINDA *and* PERT.

DORIMANT [*surprised*]   Bellinda here!

BELLINDA [*aside*]   He starts and looks pale. The sight of me has touched his guilty soul.

PERT   'Twas but a qualm, as I said, a little indigestion. The surfeit-water did it, madam, mixed with a little mirabilis.[7]

DORIMANT [*aside*]   I am confounded, and cannot guess how she came hither.

MRS. LOVEIT   'Tis your fortune, Bellinda, ever to be here when I am abused by this prodigy of ill nature.

BELLINDA   I am amazed to find him here. How has he the face to come near you?

DORIMANT [*aside*]   Here is fine work towards! I never was at such a loss before.

BELLINDA   One who makes a public profession of breach of faith and ingratitude—I loathe the sight of him.

DORIMANT [*aside*]   There is no remedy. I must submit to their tongues now and some other time bring myself off as well as I can.

BELLINDA   Other men are wicked, but then they have some sense of shame. He is never well but when he triumphs—nay, glories—to a woman's face in his villainies.

MRS. LOVEIT   You are in the right, Bellinda; but methinks your kindness for me makes you concern yourself too much with him.

BELLINDA   It does indeed, my dear. His barbarous carriage to you yesterday made me hope you ne'er would see him more, and the very next day to find him here again provokes me strangely. But because I know you love him, I have done.

DORIMANT   You have reproached me handsomely, and I deserve it for coming hither, but—

PERT   You must expect it, sir. All women will hate you for my lady's sake.

DORIMANT [*aside*]   Nay, if she begins too, 'tis time to fly. I shall be scolded to death, else. [*To* BELLINDA.] I am to blame in some circumstances, I confess; but as to the main, I am not so guilty as you imagine. [*Aloud.*] I shall seek a more convenient time to clear myself.

MRS. LOVEIT   Do it now! What impediments are here?

DORIMANT   I want time, and you want temper.

MRS. LOVEIT   These are weak pretenses.

DORIMANT   You were never more mistaken in your life; and so farewell.

DORIMANT *flings off.*

MRS. LOVEIT   Call a footman, Pert. Quickly! I will have him dogged.

PERT   I wish you would not, for my quiet and your own.

7. Drink made with wine and spices.

MRS. LOVEIT   I'll find out the infamous cause of all our quarrels, pluck her mask off, and expose her bare-faced to the world!

Exit PERT.

BELLINDA [*aside*]   Let me but escape this time, I'll never venture more.
MRS. LOVEIT   Bellinda, you shall go with me.
BELLINDA   I have such a heaviness hangs on me with what I did this morning, I would fain go home and sleep, my dear.
MRS. LOVEIT   Death and eternal darkness! I shall never sleep again. Raging fevers seize the world and make mankind as restless all as I am!

Exit MRS. LOVEIT.

BELLINDA   I knew him false and helped to make him so. Was not her ruin enough to fright me from the danger? It should have been, but love can take no warning.

Exit BELLINDA.

Act V. Scene ii. LADY TOWNLEY's *house.*

Enter MEDLEY, YOUNG BELLAIR, LADY TOWNLEY, EMILIA, *and* SMIRK, *a chaplain.*

MEDLEY   Bear up, Bellair, and do not let us see that repentance in thine we daily do in married faces.
LADY TOWNLEY   This wedding will strangely surprise my brother when he knows it.
MEDLEY   Your nephew ought to conceal it for a time, madam. Since marriage has lost its good name, prudent men seldom expose their own reputations till 'tis convenient to justify their wives'.
OLD BELLAIR [*without*]   Where are you all there? Out, adod, will nobody hear?
LADY TOWNLEY   My brother! Quickly, Mr. Smirk, into this closet. You must not be seen yet.

SMIRK *goes into the closet.*
Enter OLD BELLAIR *and* LADY TOWNLEY'S PAGE.

OLD BELLAIR [*to* PAGE]   Desire Mr. Fourbe to walk into the lower parlor. I will be with him presently.

Exit PAGE.

[*To* YOUNG BELLAIR.] Where have you been, sir, you could not wait on me today?
YOUNG BELLAIR   About a business.
OLD BELLAIR   Are you so good at business? Adod, I have a business too, you shall dispatch out of hand, sir. —Send for a parson, sister. My Lady Woodvill and her daughter are coming.

LADY TOWNLEY   What need you huddle up[8] things thus?

OLD BELLAIR   Out a pize! Youth is apt to play the fool, and 'tis not good it should be in their power.

LADY TOWNLEY   You need not fear your son.

OLD BELLAIR   H' has been idling this morning, and adod, I do not like him. [*to* EMILIA.] How dost thou do, sweetheart?

EMILIA   You are very severe, sir. Married in such haste!

OLD BELLAIR   Go to, thou'rt a rogue, and I will talk with thee anon.

Enter LADY WOODVILL, HARRIET, *and* BUSY.

Here's my Lady Woodvill come. —Welcome, madam. Mr. Fourbe's below with the writings.

LADY WOODVILL   Let us down and make an end, then.

OLD BELLAIR   Sister, show the way. [*To* YOUNG BELLAIR, *who is talking to* HARRIET.]   Harry, your business lies not there yet. —Excuse him till we have done, lady, and then, adod, he shall be for thee. —Mr. Medley, we must trouble you to be a witness.

MEDLEY   I luckily came for that purpose, sir.

Exeunt OLD BELLAIR, MEDLEY, YOUNG BELLAIR, LADY TOWNLEY, *and*
LADY WOODVILL.

BUSY [*to* HARRIET]   What will you do, madam?

HARRIET   Be carried back and mewed up in the country again, run away here—anything rather than be married to a man I do not care for. —Dear Emilia, do thou advise me.

EMILIA   Mr. Bellair is engaged, you know.

HARRIET   I do, but know not what the fear of losing an estate may fright him to.

EMILIA   In the desp'rate conditions you are in, you should consult with some judicious man. What think you of Mr. Dorimant?

HARRIET   I do not think of him at all.

BUSY [*aside*]   She thinks of nothing else, I am sure.

EMILIA   How fond your mother was of Mr. Courtage.

HARRIET   Because I contrived the mistake to make a little mirth, you believe I like the man.

EMILIA   Mr. Bellair believes you love him.

HARRIET   Men are seldom in the right when they guess at a woman's mind. Would she whom he loves loved him no better!

BUSY [*aside*]   That's e'en well enough, on all conscience.

EMILIA   Mr. Dorimant has a great deal of wit.

HARRIET   And takes a great deal of pains to show it.

EMILIA   He's extremely well-fashioned.

HARRIET   Affectedly grave, or ridiculously wild and apish.

BUSY   You defend him still against your mother.

8. Rush.

HARRIET I would not, were he justly rallied; but I cannot hear anyone undeservedly railed at.

EMILIA Has your woman learnt the song you were so taken with?

HARRIET I was fond of a new thing. 'Tis dull at second hearing.

EMILIA Mr. Dorimant made it.

BUSY She knows it, madam, and has made me sing it at least a dozen times this morning.

HARRIET Thy tongue is as impertinent as thy fingers.

EMILIA [to BUSY] You have provoked her.

BUSY 'Tis but singing the song and I shall appease her.

EMILIA Prithee, do.

HARRIET She has a voice will grate your ears worse than a catcall, and dresses so ill she's scarce fit to trick up a yeoman's daughter on a holiday.

> BUSY *sings.*

Song, by Sir C. S. [9]

As Amoret with Phillis sat
One evening on the plain,
And saw the charming Strephon wait
    To tell the nymph his pain,

The threat'ning danger to remove,
    She whispered in her ear,
"Ah, Phillis, if you would not love,
    This shepherd do not hear:

None ever had so strange an art,
    His passion to convey
Into a list'ning virgin's heart
    And steal her soul away.

Fly, fly betimes, for fear you give
    Occasion for your fate."
"In vain," said she, "in vain I strive.
    Alas, 'tis now too late."

> *Enter* DORIMANT.

DORIMANT

"Music so softens and disarms the mind—"

HARRIET

"That not one arrow does resistance find."[1]

---

9. Either Sir Car Scroope (who wrote the prologue) or Sir Charles Sedley.
1. From Waller's "Of My Lady Isabella, Playing on the Lute," lines 11–12.

DORIMANT   Let us make use of the lucky minute, then.

HARRIET [*aside, turning from* DORIMANT]   My love springs with my blood into my face. I dare not look upon him yet.

DORIMANT   What have we here—the picture of celebrated beauty giving audience in public to a declared lover?

HARRIET   Play the dying fop and make the piece complete, sir.

DORIMANT   What think you if the hint were well improved—the whole mystery of making love pleasantly designed and wrought in a suit of hangings?

HARRIET   'Twere needless to execute fools in effigy who suffer daily in their own persons.

DORIMANT [*to* EMILIA, *aside*]   Mrs. Bride, for such I know this happy day has made you—

EMILIA   Defer the formal joy you are to give me, and mind your business with her. [*Aloud.*] Here are dreadful preparations, Mr. Dorimant—writings sealing, and a parson sent for.

DORIMANT   To marry this lady?

BUSY   Condemned she is; and what will become of her I know not, without you generously engage in a rescue.

DORIMANT   In this sad condition, madam, I can do no less than offer you my service.

HARRIET   The obligation is not great: you are the common sanctuary for all young women who run from their relations.

DORIMANT   I have always my arms open to receive the distressed. But I will open my heart and receive you where none yet did ever enter. You have filled it with a secret, might I but let you know it.

HARRIET   Do not speak it if you would have me believe it. Your tongue is so famed for falsehood, 'twill do the truth an injury.

Turns away her head.

DORIMANT   Turn not away, then, but look on me and guess it.

HARRIET   Did you not tell me there was no credit to be given to faces—that women nowadays have their passions as much at will as they have their complexions, and put on joy and sadness, scorn and kindness, with the same ease they do their paint and patches? Are they the only counterfeits?

DORIMANT   You wrong your own while you suspect my eyes. By all the hope I have in you, the inimitable color in your cheeks is not more free from art than are the sighs I offer.

HARRIET   In men who have been long hardened in sin, we have reason to mistrust the first signs of repentance.

DORIMANT   The prospect of such a heav'n will make me persevere and give you marks that are infallible.

HARRIET   What are those?

DORIMANT   I will renounce all the joys I have in friendship and in wine, sacrifice to you all the interest I have in other women—

HARRIET   Hold! Though I wish you devout, I would not have you turn fanatic. Could you neglect these a while and make a journey into the country?

DORIMANT   To be with you, I could live there and never send one thought to London.

HARRIET   Whate'er you say, I know all beyond High Park's a desert to you, and that no gallantry can draw you farther.

DORIMANT   That has been the utmost limit of my love; but now my passion knows no bounds, and there's no measure to be taken of what I'll do for you from anything I ever did before.

HARRIET   When I hear you talk thus in Hampshire, I shall begin to think there may be some little truth enlarged upon.

DORIMANT   Is this all? Will you not promise me—

HARRIET   I hate to promise. What we do then is expected from us and wants much of the welcome it finds when it surprises.

DORIMANT   May I not hope?

HARRIET   That depends on you and not on me; and 'tis to no purpose to forbid it.

Turns to BUSY.

BUSY   Faith, madam, now I perceive the gentleman loves you too. E'en let him know your mind, and torment yourselves no longer.

HARRIET   Dost think I have no sense of modesty?

BUSY   Think, if you lose this, you may never have another opportunity.

HARRIET   May he hate me—a curse that frights me when I speak it—if ever I do a thing against the rules of decency and honor.

DORIMANT   [*to* EMILIA]   I am beholding to you for your good intentions, madam.

EMILIA   I thought the concealing of our marriage from her might have done you better service.

DORIMANT   Try her again.

EMILIA   [*to* HARRIET]   What have you resolved, madam? The time draws near.

HARRIET   To be obstinate and protest against this marriage.

Enter LADY TOWNLEY *in haste.*

LADY TOWNLEY   [*to* EMILIA]   Quickly, quickly, let Mr. Smirk out of the closet!

SMIRK *comes out of the closet.*

HARRIET   A parson! [*To* DORIMANT.] Had you laid him in here?

DORIMANT   I knew nothing of him.

HARRIET   Should it appear you did, your opinion of my easiness may cost you dear.

Enter OLD BELLAIR, YOUNG BELLAIR, MEDLEY, *and* LADY WOODVILL.

OLD BELLAIR   Out a pize, the canonical hour[2] is almost past! Sister, is the man of God come?

LADY TOWNLEY   He waits your leisure.

OLD BELLAIR [*to* SMIRK]   By your favor, sir. —Adod, a pretty spruce fellow. What may we call him?

LADY TOWNLEY   Mr. Smirk—my Lady Biggot's chaplain.

OLD BELLAIR   A wise woman, adod she is; the man will serve for the flesh as well as the spirit. —Please you, sir, to commission a young couple to go to bed together a God's name? —Harry!

YOUNG BELLAIR   Here, sir.

OLD BELLAIR   Out a pize! Without your mistress in your hand?

SMIRK   Is this the gentleman?

OLD BELLAIR   Yes, sir.

SMIRK   Are you not mistaken, sir?

OLD BELLAIR   Adod, I think not, sir!

SMIRK   Sure you are, sir.

OLD BELLAIR   You look as if you would forbid the banns, Mr. Smirk. I hope you have no pretension to the lady.

SMIRK   Wish him joy, sir. I have done him the good office today already.

OLD BELLAIR   Out a pize! What do I hear?

LADY TOWNLEY   Never storm, brother. The truth is out.

OLD BELLAIR   How say you, sir? Is this your wedding day?

YOUNG BELLAIR   It is, sir.

OLD BELLAIR   And, adod, it shall be mine too. [*To* EMILIA.] Give me thy hand, sweetheart. [*She refuses.*] What dost thou mean? Give me thy hand, I say!

EMILIA *kneels and* YOUNG BELLAIR.

LADY TOWNLEY   Come, come, give her your blessing. This is the woman your son loved and is married to.

OLD BELLAIR   Ha! Cheated! Cozened! And by your contrivance, sister!

LADY TOWNLEY   What would you do with her? She's a rogue, and you can't abide her.

MEDLEY   Shall I hit her a pat for you, sir?

OLD BELLAIR   Adod, you are all rogues, and I never will forgive you.

Flinging away.

LADY TOWNLEY   Whither? Whither away?

MEDLEY   Let him go and cool awhile.

LADY WOODVILL [*to* DORIMANT]   Here's a business broke out now, Mr. Courtage. I am made a fine fool of.

DORIMANT   You see the old gentleman knew nothing of it.

LADY WOODVILL   I find he did not. I shall have some trick put upon

2. When marriages could be legally performed.

me, if I stay in this wicked town any longer. —Harriet, dear child, where art thou? I'll into the country straight.

OLD BELLAIR   Adod, madam, you shall hear me first.

Enter MRS. LOVEIT *and* BELLINDA.

MRS. LOVEIT   Hither my man dogged him.

BELLINDA   Yonder he stands, my dear.

MRS. LOVEIT   I see him, [*aside*] and with him the face that has undone me. Oh, that I were but where I might throw out the anguish of my heart! Here it must rage within and break it.

LADY TOWNLEY   Mrs. Loveit! Are you afraid to come forward?

MRS. LOVEIT   I was amazed to see so much company here in a morning. The occasion sure is extraordinary.

DORIMANT [*aside*]   Loveit and Bellinda! The devil owes me a share today, and I think never will have done paying it.

MRS. LOVEIT   Married! Dear Emilia, how am I transported with the news!

HARRIET [*to* DORIMANT]   I little thought Emilia was the woman Mr. Bellair was in love with. I'll chide her for not trusting me with the secret.

DORIMANT   How do you like Mrs. Loveit?

HARRIET   She's a famed mistress of yours, I hear.

DORIMANT   She has been, on occasion.

OLD BELLAIR [*to* LADY WOODVILL]   Adod, madam, I cannot help it.

LADY WOODVILL   You need make no more apologies, sir.

EMILIA [*to* MRS. LOVEIT]   The old gentleman's excusing himself to my Lady Woodvill.

MRS. LOVEIT   Ha, ha, ha! I never heard of anything so pleasant.

HARRIET [*to* DORIMANT]   She's extremely overjoyed at something.

DORIMANT   At nothing. She is one of those hoiting[3] ladies who gaily fling themselves about and force a laugh when their aching hearts are full of discontent and malice.

MRS. LOVEIT   Oh heav'n, I was never so near killing myself with laughing. —Mr. Dorimant, are you a brideman?

LADY WOODVILL   Mr. Dorimant! Is this Mr. Dorimant, madam?

MRS. LOVEIT   If you doubt it, your daughter can resolve you, I suppose.

LADY WOODVILL   I am cheated too, basely cheated!

OLD BELLAIR   Out a pize, what's here? More knavery yet?

LADY WOODVILL   Harriet! On my blessing, come away, I charge you.

HARRIET   Dear mother, do but stay and hear me.

LADY WOODVILL   I am betrayed! And thou art undone, I fear.

HARRIET   Do not fear it. I have not, nor never will, do anything against my duty. Believe me, dear mother, do!

DORIMANT [*to* MRS. LOVEIT]   I had trusted you with this secret but that

3. Romping.

I knew the violence of your nature would ruin my fortune—as now unluckily it has. I thank you, madam.

MRS. LOVEIT She's an heiress, I know, and very rich.

DORIMANT To satisfy you, I must give up my interest wholly to my love. Had you been a reasonable woman, I might have secured 'em both and been happy.

MRS. LOVEIT You might have trusted me with anything of this kind; you know you might. Why did you go under a wrong name?

DORIMANT The story is too long to tell you now. Be satisfied; this is the business, this is the mask has kept me from you.

BELLINDA [aside] He's tender of my honor, though he's cruel to my love.

MRS. LOVEIT Was it no idle mistress, then?

DORIMANT Believe me—a wife, to repair the ruins of my estate that needs it.

MRS. LOVEIT The knowledge of this makes my grief hang lighter on my soul, but I shall never more be happy.

DORIMANT Bellinda—

BELLINDA Do not think of clearing yourself with me. It is impossible. Do all men break their words thus?

DORIMANT Th'extravagant words they speak in love. 'Tis as unreasonable to expect we should perform all we promise then, as do all we threaten when we are angry. When I see you next—

BELLINDA Take no notice of me, and I shall not hate you.

DORIMANT How came you to Mrs. Loveit?

BELLINDA By a mistake the chairmen made for want of my giving them directions.

DORIMANT 'Twas a pleasant one. We must meet again.

BELLINDA Never.

DORIMANT Never?

BELLINDA When we do, may I be as infamous as you are false.

LADY TOWNLEY [to LADY WOODVILL] Men of Mr. Dorimant's character always suffer in the general opinion of the world.

MEDLEY You can make no judgment of a witty man from common fame, considering the prevailing faction, madam.

OLD BELLAIR Adod, he's in the right.

MEDLEY Besides, 'tis a common error among women to believe too well of them they know and too ill of them they don't.

OLD BELLAIR Adod, he observes well.

LADY TOWNLEY Believe me, madam, you will find Mr. Dorimant as civil a gentleman as you thought Mr. Courtage.

HARRIET If you would but know him better—

LADY WOODVILL You have a mind to know him better? Come away! You shall never see him more.

HARRIET Dear mother, stay!

LADY WOODVILL I wo' not be consenting to your ruin.

HARRIET   Were my fortune in your power—

LADY WOODVILL   Your person is.

HARRIET   Could I be disobedient, I might take it out of yours and put it into his.

LADY WOODVILL   'Tis that you would be at! You would marry this Dorimant!

HARRIET   I cannot deny it. I would, and never will marry any other man.

LADY WOODVILL   Is this the duty that you promised?

HARRIET   But I will never marry him against your will.

LADY WOODVILL   [aside]   She knows the way to melt my heart. [To HARRIET.] Upon yourself light your undoing.

MEDLEY   [to OLD BELLAIR]   Come, sir, you have not the heart any longer to refuse your blessing.

OLD BELLAIR   Adod, I ha' not. —Rise, and God bless you both. Make much of her, Harry; she deserves thy kindness. [To EMILIA.] Adod, sirrah, I did not think it had been in thee.

 Enter SIR FOPLING *and's* PAGE.

SIR FOPLING   'Tis a damned windy day. Hey, page! Is my periwig right?

PAGE   A little out of order, sir.

SIR FOPLING   Pox o' this apartment! It wants an antechamber to adjust oneself in. [To MRS. LOVEIT.] Madam, I came from your house, and your servants directed me hither.

MRS. LOVEIT   I will give order hereafter they shall direct you better.

SIR FOPLING   The great satisfaction I had in the Mall last night has given me much disquiet since.

MRS. LOVEIT   'Tis likely to give me more than I desire.

SIR FOPLING   [aside]   What the devil makes her so reserved?—Am I guilty of an indiscretion, madam?

MRS. LOVEIT   You will be of a great one, if you continue your mistake, sir.

SIR FOPLING   Something puts you out of humour.

MRS. LOVEIT   The most foolish, inconsiderable thing that ever did.

SIR FOPLING   Is it in my power?

MRS. LOVEIT   To hang or drown it. Do one of 'em, and trouble me no more.

SIR FOPLING   So *fieré? Serviteur*, madam.[4] —Medley, where's Dorimant?

MEDLEY   Methinks the lady has not made you those advances today she did last night, Sir Fopling.

SIR FOPLING   Prithee, do not talk of her.

MEDLEY   She would be a *bonne fortune.*

SIR FOPLING   Not to me at present.

MEDLEY   How so?

---

4. "So haughty? Your servant, madam."

SIR FOPLING   An intrigue now would be but a temptation to me to
throw away that vigor on one which I mean shall shortly make my
court to the whole sex in a ballet.

MEDLEY   Wisely considered, Sir Fopling.

SIR FOPLING   No one woman is worth the loss of a cut in a caper.

MEDLEY   Not when 'tis so universally designed.

LADY WOODVILL   Mr. Dorimant, everyone has spoke so much in your
behalf that I can no longer doubt but I was in the wrong.

MRS. LOVEIT [*to* BELLINDA]   There's nothing but falsehood and impertinence in this world. All men are villains or fools. Take example
from my misfortunes. Bellinda, if thou wouldst be happy, give thyself
wholly up to goodness.

HARRIET [*to* MRS. LOVEIT]   Mr. Dorimant has been your God almighty
long enough. 'Tis time to think of another.

MRS. LOVEIT [*to* BELLINDA]   Jeered by her! I will lock myself up in my
house and never see the world again.

HARRIET   A nunnery is the more fashionable place for such a retreat
and has been the fatal consequence of many a *belle passion*.

MRS. LOVEIT [*aside*]   Hold, heart, till I get home! Should I answer,
'twould make her triumph greater.

   Is going out.

DORIMANT   Your hand, Sir Fopling—

SIR FOPLING   Shall I wait upon you, madam?

MRS. LOVEIT   Legion of fools, as many devils take thee!

                                        Exit MRS. LOVEIT.

MEDLEY   Dorimant, I pronounce thy reputation clear; and henceforward, when I would know anything of woman, I will consult no other
oracle.

SIR FOPLING   Stark mad, by all that's handsome! —Dorimant, thou
hast engaged me in a pretty business.

DORIMANT   I have not leisure now to talk about it.

OLD BELLAIR   Out a pize, what does this man of mode do here again?

LADY TOWNLEY   He'll be an excellent entertainment within, brother,
and is luckily come to raise the mirth of the company.

LADY WOODVILL   Madam, I take my leave of you.

LADY TOWNLEY   What do you mean, madam?

LADY WOODVILL   To go this afternoon part of my way to Hartly.

OLD BELLAIR   Adod, you shall stay and dine first! Come, we will all be
good friends; and you shall give Mr. Dorimant leave to wait upon you
and your daughter in the country.

LADY WOODVILL   If his occasions bring him that way, I have now so
good an opinion of him, he shall be welcome.

HARRIET   To a great, rambling, lone house that looks as it were not
inhabited, the family's so small. There you'll find my mother, an old
lame aunt, and myself, sir, perched up on chairs at a distance in a

large parlor, sitting moping like three or four melancholy birds in a
spacious volary.[5] Does not this stagger your resolution?

DORIMANT   Not at all, madam. The first time I saw you, you left me
with the pangs of love upon me; and this day my soul has quite given
up her liberty.

HARRIET   This is more dismal than the country. —Emilia, pity me who
am going to that sad place. Methinks I hear the hateful noise of rooks
already—kaw, kaw, kaw. There's music in the worst cry[6] in London.
"My dill and cucumbers to pickle."

OLD BELLAIR   Sister, knowing of this matter, I hope you have provided
us some good cheer.

LADY TOWNLEY   I have, brother, and the fiddles too.

OLD BELLAIR   Let 'em strike up then. The young lady shall have a
dance before she departs.

Dance.

[*After the dance.*] So now we'll in, and make this an arrant wedding
day.

To the pit.

And if these honest gentlemen rejoice,
Adod, the boy has made a happy choice.

Exeunt omnes.

The Epilogue

By Mr. Dryden

Most modern wits such monstrous fools have shown,
They seemed not of heav'n's making, but their own.
Those nauseous harlequins in farce may pass,
But there goes more to a substantial ass;
Something of man must be exposed to view,
That, gallants, they may more resemble you.
Sir Fopling is a fool so nicely writ,
The ladies would mistake him for a wit
And when he sings, talks loud, and cocks,[7] would cry:
"I vow, methinks he's pretty company—
So brisk, so gay, so traveled, so refined,
As he took pains to graft upon his kind."[8]
True fops help nature's work, and go to school
To file and finish God a'mighty's fool.
Yet none Sir Fopling him, or him, can call:

5. Aviary.
6. Street-vendor's cry.
7. Struts.
8. "To improve his natural type."

He's knight o' th' shire[9] and represents ye all.
From each he meets, he culls whate'er he can;
Legion's his name, a people in a man.
His bulky folly gathers, as it goes,
And, rolling o'er you, like a snowball grows.
His various modes from various fathers follow;
One taught the toss,[1] and one the new French wallow.[2]
His sword-knot, this; his cravat, this designed;
And this, the yard-long snake[3] he twirls behind.
From one, the sacred periwig he gained,
Which wind ne'er blew, nor touch of hat prophaned;
Another's diving bow he did adore,
Which with a shog[4] casts all the hair before,
Till he with full decorum brings it back
And rises with a water spaniel shake.
As for his songs (the ladies' dear delight),
Those sure he took from most of you who write.
Yet every man is safe from what he feared,
For no one fool is hunted from the herd.

FINIS

9. Member of Parliament.
1. Toss of the head.
2. Rolling gait.
3. Curl or tail of a wig.
4. Shake.

APHRA BEHN

The Rover

Prologue

Wits, like physicians, never can agree,
When of a different society.
And Rabel's drops[1] were never more cried down
By all the learned doctors of the town,
Than a new play whose author is unknown.
Nor can those doctors with more malice sue
(And powerful purses) the dissenting few,
Than those, with an insulting pride, do rail
At all who are not of their own cabal.
    If a young poet hit your humour right,
You judge him then out of revenge and spite.
So amongst men there are ridiculous elves,
Who monkeys hate for being too like themselves.
So that the reason of the grand debate
Why wit so oft is damned when good plays take,
Is that you censure as you love, or hate.
    Thus like a learned conclave poets sit,
Catholic judges both of sense and wit,
And damn or save as they themselves think fit.
Yet those who to others' faults are so severe,
Are not so perfect but themselves may err.
Some write correct, indeed, but then the whole
(Bating[2] their own dull stuff i'th' play) is stole:
As bees do suck from flowers their honeydew,
So they rob others striving to please you.
    Some write their characters genteel and fine,
But then they do so toil for every line,
That what to you does easy seem, and plain,
Is the hard issue of their laboring brain.

† First performed in 1677, at Dorset Garden, and published in the same year. "Rovers" were
  Royalist gallants in exile during the Inter-regnum, 1642–60. Many returned with Charles II,
  and some were in the audience for this play.
1. Well-known medicine of the time.
2. Except.

And some th'effects of all their pains, we see,
Is but to mimic good extempore.
Others, by long converse about the town,
Have wit enough to write a lewd lampoon,
But their chief skill lies in a bawdy song.
In short, the only wit that's now in fashion,
Is but the gleanings of good conversation.
As for the author of this coming play,
I asked him what he thought fit I should say
In thanks for your good company today:
He called me fool, and said it was well known
You came not here for our sakes, but your own.
New plays are stuffed with wits, and with deboches,[3]
That crowd and sweat like cits in May-Day coaches.[4]

                                                   WRITTEN BY A PERSON OF QUALITY

The Actors' Names[5]

DON ANTONIO, the Viceroy's son	Mr. Jevon
DON PEDRO, a noble Spaniard, his friend	Mr. Medbourne
BELVILE, an English colonel in love with Florinda	Mr. Betterton
WILLMORE, the Rover	Mr. Smith
FREDERICK, an English gentleman, and friend to Belvile and Blunt	Mr. Crosby
BLUNT, an English country gentleman	Mr. Underhill
STEPHANO, servant to Don Pedro	Mr. Richards
PHILIPPO, Lucetta's gallant	Mr. Percival
SANCHO, pimp to Lucetta	Mr. John Lee
BISKEY and SEBASTIAN, two bravos to Angellica	
OFFICER and SOLDIERS	
Page to Don Antonio	
FLORINDA, sister to Don Pedro	Mrs. Betterton
HELLENA, a gay young woman designed for a nun, and sister to Florinda	Mrs. Barry
VALERIA, a kinswoman to Florinda	Mrs. Hughes
ANGELLICA BIANCA, a famous courtesan	Mrs. Quin

3. Debauches.
4. May Day was a time for parading around Hyde Park. *Cits:* ordinary citizens—a slur.
5. *The Rover* had a brilliant cast of actresses. Florinda, Valeria, Angellica, and Callis were played by four of the first women to perform on the Restoration stage. By 1677 they were well-known and successful. Hellena was one of the first roles played by a newcomer, Elizabeth Barry, who went on to become the first famous tragic actress in the English theatre. She would also excell as Mrs. Marwood in *The Way of the World*, as Mrs. Loveit in revivals of *The Man of Mode*, and as Angellica in revivals of *The Rover*. The original Moretta, Elinor Leigh, became famous in "spinster" comic roles and originated Lady Wishfort in *The Way of the World*.
   Among the men, Betterton was the leading actor of his time: he had been Dorimant in *The Man of Mode* and would play Fainall in *The Way of the World*. Cave Underhill was a well-known comedian who would later play Sir Wilfull Witwoud in *The Way of the World*.

MORETTA, her woman   *Mrs. Leigh*
CALLIS, governess to Florinda and   *Mrs. Norris*
   Hellena
LUCETTA, a jilting wench   *Mrs. Gillow*
   SERVANTS, OTHER MASQUERADERS, MEN AND WOMEN

The scene: *Naples, in Carnival time*

The Rover
or
The Banished Cavaliers

Act I. Scene i.

A Chamber.
Enter FLORINDA *and* HELLENA.

FLORINDA   What an impertinent thing is a young girl bred in a nunnery! How full of questions! Prithee no more, Hellena; I have told
thee more than thou understand'st already.

HELLENA   The more's my grief. I would fain know as much as you,
which makes me so inquisitive; nor is't enough I know you're a lover,
unless you tell me too who 'tis you sigh for.

FLORINDA   When you're a lover I'll think you fit for a secret of that
nature.

HELLENA   'Tis true, I never was a lover yet, but I begin to have a shrewd
guess what 'tis to be so, and fancy it very pretty to sigh, and sing, and
blush, and wish, and dream and wish, and long and wish to see the
man, and when I do, look pale and tremble, just as you did when my
brother brought home the fine English colonel to see you. What do
you call him? Don Belvile?

FLORINDA   Fie, Hellena.

HELLENA   That blush betrays you. I am sure 'tis so. Or is it Don Antonio the Viceroy's son? Or perhaps the rich old Don Vincentio, whom
my father designs you for a husband? Why do you blush again?

FLORINDA   With indignation; and how near soever my father thinks I
am to marrying that hated object, I shall let him see I understand
better what's due to my beauty, birth, and fortune, and more to my
soul, than to obey those unjust commands.

HELLENA   Now hang me, if I don't love thee for that dear disobedience.
I love mischief strangely, as most of our sex do who are come to
love nothing else. But tell me, dear Florinda, don't you love that fine
Anglese?[6] For I vow, next to loving him myself, 'twill please me most
that you do so, for he is so gay and so handsome.

6. Englishman.

FLORINDA   Hellena, a maid designed for a nun ought not to be so curious in a discourse of love.

HELLENA   And dost thou think that ever I'll be a nun? Or at least till
I'm so old I'm fit for nothing else? Faith no, sister; and that which
makes me long to know whether you love Belvile, is because I hope
he has some mad companion or other that will spoil my devotion.
Nay, I'm resolved to provide myself this Carnival, if there be e'er a
handsome proper fellow of my humour above ground, though I ask
first.

FLORINDA   Prithee be not so wild.

HELLENA   Now you have provided yourself of a man you take no care
of poor me. Prithee tell me, what dost thou see about me that is unfit
for love? Have I not a world of youth? A humour gay? A beauty passable? A vigor desirable? Well shaped? Clean limbed? Sweet breathed?
And sense enough to know how all these ought to be employed to the
best advantage? Yes, I do and will; therefore lay aside your hopes of
my fortune by my being a devote,[7] and tell me how you came
acquainted with this Belvile. For I perceive you knew him before he
came to Naples.

FLORINDA   Yes, I knew him at the siege of Pamplona;[8] he was then a
colonel of French horse, who when the town was ransacked, nobly
treated my brother and myself, preserving us from all insolences. And
I must own, besides great obligations, I have I know not what that
pleads kindly for him about my heart, and will suffer no other to
enter. But see, my brother.

> *Enter* DON PEDRO, STEPHANO *with a masking habit, and* CALLIS.

PEDRO   Good morrow, sister. Pray when saw you your lover Don Vincentio?

FLORINDA   I know not, sir. Callis, when was he here? For I consider it
so little I know not when it was.

PEDRO   I have a command from my father here to tell you you ought
not to despise him, a man of so vast a fortune, and such a passion for
you. —Stephano, my things.

> *Puts on his masking habit.*

FLORINDA   A passion for me? 'Tis more than e'er I saw, or he had a
desire should be known. I hate Vincentio, sir, and I would not have
a man so dear to me as my brother follow the ill customs of our
country and make a slave of his sister. And, sir, my father's will I'm
sure you may divert.

PEDRO   I know not how dear I am to you, but I wish only to be ranked
in your esteem equal with the English colonel Belvile. Why do you
frown and blush? Is there any guilt belongs to the name of that cavalier?

7. Nun.
8. Spanish city often under siege.

FLORINDA I'll not deny I value Belvile. When I was exposed to such dangers as the licenced lust of common soldiers threatened, when rage and conquest flew through the city, then Belvile, this criminal for my sake, threw himself into all dangers to save my honor. And will you not allow him my esteem?

PEDRO Yes, pay him what you will in honor, but you must consider Don Vincentio's fortune, and the jointure[9] he'll make you.

FLORINDA Let him consider my youth, beauty, and fortune, which ought not to be thrown away on his age and jointure.

PEDRO 'Tis true, he's not so young and fine a gentleman as that Belvile. But what jewels will that cavalier present you with? Those of his eyes and heart?

HELLENA And are not those better than any Don Vincentio has brought from the Indies?

PEDRO Why, how now! Has your nunnery breeding taught you to understand the value of hearts and eyes?

HELLENA Better than to believe Vincentio's deserve value from any woman. He may perhaps increase her bags, but not her family.

PEDRO This is fine! Go! Up to your devotion! You are not designed for the conversation of lovers.

HELLENA [aside] Nor saints yet a while, I hope. —Is't not enough you make a nun of me, but you must cast my sister away too, exposing her to a worse confinement than a religious life?

PEDRO The girl's mad! It is a confinement to be carried into the country to an ancient villa belonging to the family of the Vincentios these five hundred years, and have no other prospect than that pleasing one of seeing all her own that meets her eyes: a fine air, large fields, and gardens where she may walk and gather flowers?

HELLENA When, by moonlight? For I am sure she dares not encounter with the heat of the sun; that were a task only for Don Vincentio and his Indian breeding, who loves it in the dog days. And if these be her daily divertissements, what are those of the night? To lie in a wide moth-eaten bedchamber with furniture in fashion in the reign of King Sancho the First; the bed, that which his forefathers lived and died in.

PEDRO Very well.

HELLENA This apartment, new furbished and fitted out for the young wife, he out of freedom makes his dressing room; and being a frugal and a jealous coxcomb, instead of a valet to uncase his feeble carcass, he desires you to do that office. Signs of favor, I'll assure you, and such as you must not hope for unless your woman be out of the way.

PEDRO Have you done yet?

HELLENA That honor being past, the giant stretches itself, yawns and sighs a belch or two loud as a musket, throws himself into bed, and expects you in his foul sheets; and ere you can get yourself undressed,

---

9. Estate settled on women in consideration of marriage.

calls you with a snore or two. And are not these fine blessings to a young lady?

PEDRO   Have you done yet?

HELLENA   And this man you must kiss, nay you must kiss none but him too, and nuzzle through his beard to find his lips. And this you must submit to for threescore years, and all for a jointure.

PEDRO   For all your character of Don Vincentio, she is as like to marry him as she was before.

HELLENA   Marry Don Vincentio! Hang me, such a wedlock would be worse than adultery with another man. I had rather see her in the *Hostel de Dieu*,[1] to waste her youth there in vows, and be a handmaid to lazars and cripples, than to lose it in such a marriage.

PEDRO   You have considered, sister, that Belvile has no fortune to bring you to; banished his country, despised at home, and pitied abroad.

HELLENA   What then? The Viceroy's son is better than that old Sir Fifty. Don Vincentio! Don Indian! He thinks he's trading to Gambo[2] still, and would barter himself—that bell and bauble—for your youth and fortune.

PEDRO   Callis, take her hence and lock her up all this Carnival, and at Lent she shall begin her everlasting penance in a monastery.

HELLENA   I care not; I had rather be a nun than be obliged to marry as you would have me if I were designed for't.

PEDRO   Do not fear the blessing of that choice. You shall be a nun.

HELLENA [*aside*]   Shall I so? You may chance to be mistaken in my way of devotion. A nun! Yes, I am like to make a fine nun! I have an excellent humour for a grate![3] No, I'll have a saint of my own to pray to shortly, if I like any that dares venture on me.

PEDRO   Callis, make it your business to watch this wildcat. —As for you, Florinda, I've only tried you all this while and urged my father's will; but mine is that you would love Antonio: he is brave and young, and all that can complete the happiness of a gallant maid. This absence of my father will give us opportunity to free you from Vincentio by marrying here, which you must do tomorrow.

FLORINDA   Tomorrow!

PEDRO   Tomorrow, or 'twill be too late. 'Tis not my friendship to Antonio which makes me urge this, but love to thee and hatred to Vincentio; therefore resolve upon tomorrow.

FLORINDA   Sir, I shall strive to do as shall become your sister.

PEDRO   I'll both believe and trust you. Adieu.

Exeunt PEDRO *and* STEPHANO.

HELLENA   As becomes his sister! That is to be as resolved your way as he is his.

HELLENA *goes to* CALLIS.

1. Hospital run by a religious order.
2. Gambia, a British colony in West Africa.
3. Latticework on a convent window.

FLORINDA
    I ne'er till now perceived my ruin near.
    I've no defence against Antonio's love,
    For he has all the advantages of nature,
    The moving arguments of youth and fortune.

HELLENA   But hark you, Callis, you will not be so cruel to lock me up indeed, will you?

CALLIS   I must obey the commands I have. Besides, do you consider what a life you are going to lead?

HELLENA   Yes, Callis, that of a nun; and till then I'll be indebted a world of prayers to you if you'll let me now see what I never did, the divertissements of a Carnival.

CALLIS   What, go in masquerade? 'Twill be a fine farewell to the world, I take it. Pray what would you do there?

HELLENA   That which all the world does, as I am told: be as mad as the rest and take all innocent freedoms. Sister, you'll go too, will you not? Come, prithee be not sad. We'll outwit twenty brothers if you'll be ruled by me. Come, put off this dull humour with your clothes, and assume one as gay and as fantastic as the dress my cousin Valeria and I have provided, and let's ramble.

FLORINDA   Callis, will you give us leave to go?

CALLIS [*aside*]   I have a youthful itch of going myself. —Madam, if I thought your brother might not know it, and I might wait on you; for by my troth I'll not trust young girls alone.

FLORINDA   Thou seest my brother's gone already, and thou shalt attend and watch us.

    Enter STEPHANO.

STEPHANO   Madam, the habits are come, and your cousin Valeria is dressed and stays for you.

FLORINDA [*aside*]   'Tis well. I'll write a note, and if I chance to see Belvile and want an opportunity to speak to him, that shall let him know what I've resolved in favor of him.

HELLENA   Come, let's in and dress us.

                                       Exeunt.

Act I. Scene ii.

    A *long street.*
    Enter BELVILE, *melancholy;* BLUNT *and* FREDERICK.

FREDERICK   Why, what the devil ails the colonel, in a time when all the world is gay, to look like mere Lent thus? Hadst thou been long enough in Naples to have been in love, I should have sworn some such judgment had befallen thee.

BELVILE   No, I have made no new amours since I came to Naples.

FREDERICK   You have left none behind you in Paris?

BELVILE Neither.

FREDERICK I cannot divine the cause then, unless the old cause, the want of money.

BLUNT And another old cause, the want of a wench. Would not that revive you?

BELVILE You are mistaken, Ned.

BLUNT Nay, 'adsheartlikins, then thou'rt past cure.

FREDERICK I have found it out: thou hast renewed thy acquaintance with the lady that cost thee so many sighs at the siege of Pamplona— pox on't, what d'ye call her—her brother's a noble Spaniard, nephew to the dead general. Florinda. Ay, Florinda. And will nothing serve thy turn but that damned virtuous woman, whom on my conscience thou lov'st in spite too, because thou seest little or no possibility of gaining her.

BELVILE Thou art mistaken; I have int'rest enough in that lovely virgin's heart to make me proud and vain, were it not abated by the severity of a brother, who, perceiving my happiness—

FREDERICK Has civilly forbid thee the house?

BELVILE 'Tis so, to make way for a powerful rival, the Viceroy's son, who has the advantage of me in being a man of fortune, a Spaniard, and her brother's friend; which gives him liberty to make his court, whilst I have recourse only to letters and distant looks from her window, which are as soft and kind as those which heaven sends down on penitents.

BLUNT Heyday! 'Adsheartlikins, simile! By this light the man is quite spoiled. Fred, what the devil are we made of that we cannot be thus concerned for a wench? 'Adsheartlikins, our Cupids are like the cooks of the camp: they can roast or boil a woman, but they have none of the fine tricks to set 'em off; no hogoes[4] to make the sauce pleasant and the stomach sharp.

FREDERICK I dare swear I have had a hundred as young, kind, and handsome as this Florinda; and dogs eat me if they were not as troublesome to me i'th' morning as they were welcome o'er night.

BLUNT And yet I warrant he would not touch another woman if he might have her for nothing.

BELVILE That's thy joy, a cheap whore.

BLUNT Why, 'adsheartlikins, I love a frank soul. When did you ever hear of an honest woman that took a man's money? I warrant 'em good ones. But gentlemen, you may be free; you have been kept so poor with parliaments and protectors that the little stock you have is not worth preserving. But I thank my stars I had more grace than to forfeit my estate by cavaliering.[5]

BELVILE Methinks only following the court should be sufficient to entitle 'em to that.

---

4. Relishes.
5. Cromwell confiscated many royalist estates.

BLUNT   'Adsheartlikins, they know I follow it to do it no good, unless
they pick a hole in my coat for lending you money now and then,
which is a greater crime to my conscience, gentlemen, than to the
commonwealth.

Enter WILLMORE.

WILLMORE   Ha! Dear Belvile! Noble colonel!

BELVILE   Willmore! Welcome ashore, my dear rover! What happy
wind blew us this good fortune?

WILLMORE   Let me salute my dear Fred, and then command me.
—How is't, honest lad?

FREDERICK   Faith, sir, the old compliment, infinitely the better to see
my dear mad Willmore again. Prithee, why camest thou ashore? And
where's the Prince?[6]

WILLMORE   He's well, and reigns still lord of the wat'ry element. I must
aboard again within a day or two, and my business ashore was only to
enjoy myself a little this Carnival.

BELVILE   Pray know our new friend, sir; he's but bashful, a raw traveler,
but honest, stout, and one of us.

Embraces BLUNT.

WILLMORE   That you esteem him gives him an int'rest here.

BLUNT   Your servant, sir.

WILLMORE   But well, faith, I'm glad to meet you again in a warm climate, where the kind sun has its godlike power still over the wine and
women. Love and mirth are my business in Naples, and if I mistake
not the place, here's an excellent market for chapmen[7] of my humour.

BELVILE   See, here be those kind merchants of love you look for.

*Enter several men in masking habits, some playing on music, oth-
ers dancing after; women dressed like courtesans, with papers
pinned on their breasts, and baskets of flowers in their hands.*

BLUNT   'Adsheartlikins, what have we here?

FREDERICK   Now the game begins.

WILLMORE   Fine pretty creatures! May a stranger have leave to look
and love? What's here? "Roses for every month"?

Reads the papers.

BLUNT   Roses for every month? What means that?

BELVILE   They are, or would have you think they're courtesans, who
here in Naples are to be hired by the month.

WILLMORE   Kind and obliging to inform us, pray where do these roses
grow? I would fain plant some of 'em in a bed of mine.

WOMAN   Beware such roses, sir.

6. Charles II.
7. Merchants.

WILLMORE   A pox of fear: I'll be baked with thee between a pair of
    sheets, and that's thy proper still[8]; so I might but strew such roses over
    me and under me. Fair one, would you would give me leave to gather
    at your bush this idle month; I would go near to make somebody
    smell of it all the year after.
BELVILE   And thou hast need of such a remedy, for thou stink'st of tar
    and ropes' ends like a dock or pesthouse.[9]

   The Woman puts herself into the hands of a man and exeunt.

WILLMORE   Nay, nay, you shall not leave me so.
BELVILE   By all means use no violence here.
WILLMORE   Death! Just as I was going to be damnably in love, to have
    her led off! I could pluck that rose out of his hand, and even kiss the
    bed the bush grew in.
FREDERICK   No friend to love like a long voyage at sea.
BLUNT   Except a nunnery, Fred.
WILLMORE   Death! But will they not be kind? Quickly be kind? Thou
    know'st I'm no tame sigher, but a rampant lion of the forest.

   *Advances from the farther end of the scenes two men dressed all
   over with horns of several sorts, making grimaces at one another,
   with papers pinned on their backs.*

BELVILE   Oh the fantastical rogues, how they're dressed! 'Tis a satire
    against the whole sex.
WILLMORE   Is this a fruit that grows in this warm country?
BELVILE   Yes, 'tis pretty to see these Italians start, swell, and stab at the
    word cuckold, and yet stumble at horns on every threshold.[1]
WILLMORE   See what's on their back. (*Reads*). "Flowers of every night."
    Ah, rogue! And more sweet than roses of every month! This is a gar-
    dener of Adam's own breeding.

                                        They dance.

BELVILE   What think you of these grave people? Is a wake in Essex half
    so mad or extravagant?
WILLMORE   I like their sober grave way; 'tis a kind of legal authorized
    fornication, where the men are not chid for't, nor the women
    despised, as amongst our dull English. Even the monsieurs want that
    part of good manners.
BELVILE   But here in Italy, a monsieur is the humblest best-bred gen-
    tleman: duels are so baffled by bravos[2] that an age shows not one but
    between a Frenchman and a hangman, who is as much too hard for

8. As in the distillation of roses.
9. Hospital for those suffering from pestilence.
1. Horns were the sign of a cuckold.
2. Ruffians or assassins.

him on the Piazza as they are for a Dutchman on the New Bridge.[3]
But see, another crew.

> *Enter* FLORINDA, HELLENA, *and* VALERIA, *dressed like gipsies;*
> CALLIS *and* STEPHANO, LUCETTA, PHILIPPO *and* SANCHO *in mas-*
> *querade.*

HELLENA   Sister, there's your Englishman, and with him a handsome
proper fellow. I'll to him, and instead of telling him his fortune, try
my own.

WILLMORE   Gipsies, on my life. Sure these will prattle if a man cross
their hands. (*Goes to* HELLENA.) —Dear, pretty, and, I hope, young
devil, will you tell an amorous stranger what luck he's like to have?

HELLENA   Have a care how you venture with me, sir, lest I pick your
pocket, which will more vex your English humour than an Italian
fortune will please you.

WILLMORE   How the devil cam'st thou to know my country and
humour?

HELLENA   The first I guess by a certain forward impudence, which
does not displease me at this time; and the loss of your money will
vex you because I hope you have but very little to lose.

WILLMORE   Egad, child, thou'rt i'th' right; it is so little I dare not offer
it thee for a kindness. But cannot you divine what other things of
more value I have about me that I would more willingly part with?

HELLENA   Indeed no, that's the business of a witch, and I am but a
gipsy yet. Yet without looking in your hand, I have a parlous guess 'tis
some foolish heart you mean, an inconstant English heart, as little
worth stealing as your purse.

WILLMORE   Nay, then thou dost deal with the devil, that's certain.
Thou hast guessed as right as if thou hadst been one of that number
it has languished for. I find you'll be better acquainted with it, nor
can you take it in a better time; for I am come from sea, child, and
Venus not being propitious to me in her own element, I have a world
of love in store. Would you would be good-natured and take some
on't off my hands.

HELLENA   Why, I could be inclined that way, but for a foolish vow I
am going to make to die a maid.

WILLMORE   Then thou art damned without redemption, and as I am a
good Christian, I ought in charity to divert so wicked a design. Therefore prithee, dear creature, let me know quickly when and where I
shall begin to set a helping hand to so good a work.

HELLENA   If you should prevail with my tender heart, as I begin to fear
you will, for you have horrible loving eyes, there will be difficulty in't
that you'll hardly undergo for my sake.

WILLMORE   Faith, child, I have been bred in dangers, and wear a sword
that has been employed in a worse cause than for a handsome kind

---

3. An allusion to French victories in the Low Countries.

woman. Name the danger; let it be anything but a long siege, and I'll undertake it.

HELLENA   Can you storm?

WILLMORE   Oh, most furiously.

HELLENA   What think you of a nunnery wall? For he that wins me must gain that first.

WILLMORE   A nun! Oh, now I love thee for't! There's no sinner like a young saint. Nay, now there's no denying me; the old law had no curse to a woman like dying a maid: witness Jeptha's daughter.[4]

HELLENA   A very good text this, if well handled; and I perceive, Father Captain, you would impose no severe penance on her who were inclined to console herself before she took orders.[5]

WILLMORE   If she be young and handsome.

HELLENA   Ay, there's it. But if she be not—

WILLMORE   By this hand, child, I have an implicit faith, and dare venture on thee with all faults. Besides, 'tis more meritorious to leave the world when thou hast tasted and proved the pleasure on't. Then 'twill be a virtue in thee, which now will be pure ignorance.

HELLENA   I perceive, good Father Captain, you design only to make me fit for heaven. But if, on the contrary, you should quite divert me from it, and bring me back to the world again, I should have a new man to seek, I find. And what a grief that will be; for when I begin, I fancy I shall love like anything; I never tried yet.

WILLMORE   Egad, and that's kind! Prithee, dear creature, give me credit for a heart, for faith, I'm a very honest fellow. Oh, I long to come first to the banquet of love! And such a swinging appetite I bring. Oh, I'm impatient. Thy lodging, sweetheart, thy lodging, or I'm a dead man!

HELLENA   Why must we be either guilty of fornication or murder if we converse with you men? And is there no difference between leave to love me, and leave to lie with me?

WILLMORE   Faith, child, they were made to go together.

LUCETTA   [pointing to BLUNT]   Are you sure this is the man?

SANCHO   When did I mistake your game?

LUCETTA   This is a stranger, I know by his gazing; if he be brisk he'll venture to follow me, and then, if I understand my trade, he's mine. He's English, too, and they say that's a sort of good-natured loving people, and have generally so kind an opinion of themselves that a woman with any wit may flatter 'em into any sort of fool she pleases.

   She often passes by BLUNT *and gazes on him; he struts and cocks, and walks and gazes on her.*

BLUNT   'Tis so, she is taken; I have beauties which my false glass at home did not discover.

4. Judges 11.37–40. Jeptha allowed his daughter two months to bewail her virginity before sacrificing her according to a vow he had made to God.
5. Became a nun.

FLORINDA [*aside*] This woman watches me so, I shall get no opportunity to discover myself to him, and so miss the intent of my coming. —[*To* BELVILE.] But as I was saying, sir, by this line you should
be a lover.

Looking in his hand.

BELVILE I thought how right you guessed: all men are in love, or pretend to be so. Come, let me go; I'm weary of this fooling.

Walks away.

FLORINDA I will not, sir, till you have confessed whether the passion
that you have vowed Florinda be true or false.

She holds him; he strives to get from her.

BELVILE Florinda!

Turns quick towards her.

FLORINDA Softly.
BELVILE Thou hast nam'd one will fix me here forever.
FLORINDA She'll be disappointed then, who expects you this night at
the garden gate. And if you fail not, as— [*Looks on* CALLIS, *who
observes 'em.*] Let me see the other hand—you will go near to do, she
vows to die or make you happy.
BELVILE What canst thou mean?
FLORINDA That which I say. Farewell.

Offers to go.

BELVILE Oh charming sybil, stay; complete that joy which as it is will
turn into distraction! Where must I be? At the garden gate? I know it.
At night, you say? I'll sooner forfeit heaven than disobey.

Enter DON PEDRO *and other maskers, and pass over the stage.*

CALLIS Madam, your brother's here.
FLORINDA Take this to instruct you farther.

Gives him a letter, and goes off.

FREDERICK Have a care, sir, what you promise; this may be a trap laid
by her brother to ruin you.
BELVILE Do not disturb my happiness with doubts.

Opens the letter.

WILLMORE My dear pretty creature, a thousand blessings on thee! Still
in this habit, you say? And after dinner at this place?
HELLENA Yes, if you will swear to keep your heart and not bestow it
between this and that.

WILLMORE   By all the little gods of love, I swear; I'll leave it with you, and if you run away with it, those deities of justice will revenge me.

Exeunt all the women [except LUCETTA].

FREDERICK   Do you know the hand?

BELVILE   'Tis Florinda's. All blessings fall upon the virtuous maid.

FREDERICK   Nay, no idolatry; a sober sacrifice I'll allow you.

BELVILE   Oh friends, the welcom'st news! The softest letter! Nay, you shall all see it! And could you now be serious, I might be made the happiest man the sun shines on!

WILLMORE   The reason of this mighty joy?

BELVILE   See how kindly she invites me to deliver her from the threatened violence of her brother. Will you not assist me?

WILLMORE   I know not what thou mean'st, but I'll make one at any mischief where a woman's concerned. But she'll be grateful to us for the favor, will she not?

BELVILE   How mean you?

WILLMORE   How should I mean? Thou know'st there's but one way for a woman to oblige me.

BELVILE   Do not profane; the maid is nicely virtuous.

WILLMORE   Who, pox, then she's fit for nothing but a husband. Let her e'en go, colonel.

FREDERICK   Peace, she's the colonel's mistress, sir.

WILLMORE   Let her be the devil; if she be thy mistress, I'll serve her. Name the way.

BELVILE   Read here this postscript.

Gives him a letter.

WILLMORE [*reads*]   "At ten at night, at the garden gate, of which, if I cannot get the key, I will contrive a way over the wall. Come attended with a friend or two." — Kind heart, if we three cannot weave a string to let her down a garden wall, 'twere pity but the hangman wove one for us all.

FREDERICK   Let her alone for that; your woman's wit, your fair kind woman, will out-trick a broker or a Jew, and contrive like a Jesuit in chains. But see, Ned Blunt is stolen out after the lure of a damsel.

Exeunt BLUNT *and* LUCETTA.

BELVILE   So, he'll scarce find his way home again unless we get him cried by the bellman in the market place. And 'twould sound prettily: "A lost English boy of thirty."

FREDERICK   I hope 'tis some common crafty sinner, one that will fit him. It may be she'll sell him for Peru: the rogue's sturdy, and would work well in a mine. At least I hope she'll dress him for our mirth, cheat him of all, then have him well-favoredly banged, and turned out at midnight.

WILLMORE   Prithee what humour is he of, that you wish him so well?

BELVILE   Why, of an English elder brother's humour: educated in a nursery, with a maid to tend him till fifteen, and lies with his grandmother till he's of age; one that knows no pleasure beyond riding to the next fair, or going up to London with his right worshipful father in parliament time, wearing gay clothes, or making honorable love to his lady mother's laundry maid; gets drunk at a hunting match, and ten to one then gives some proofs of his prowess. A pox upon him, he's our banker, and has all our cash about him; and if he fail, we are all broke.

FREDERICK   Oh, let him alone for that matter; he's of a damned stingy quality that will secure our stock. I know not in what danger it were indeed if the jilt should pretend she's in love with him, for 'tis a kind believing coxcomb; otherwise, if he part with more than a piece of eight,[6] geld him—for which offer he may chance to be beaten if she be a whore of the first rank.

BELVILE   Nay, the rogue will not be easily beaten; he's stout enough. Perhaps if they talk beyond his capacity he may chance to exercise his courage upon some of them, else I'm sure they'll find it as difficult to beat as to please him.

WILLMORE   'Tis a lucky devil to light upon so kind a wench!

FREDERICK   Thou hadst a great deal of talk with thy little gipsy; couldst thou do no good upon her? For mine was hardhearted.

WILLMORE   Hang her, she was some damned honest person of quality, I'm sure, she was so very free and witty. If her face be but answerable to her wit and humour, I would be bound to constancy this month to gain her. In the meantime, have you made no kind acquaintance since you came to town? You do not use to be honest so long, gentlemen.

FREDERICK   Faith, love has kept us honest: we have been all fir'd with a beauty newly come to town, the famous Paduana[7] Angellica Bianca.

WILLMORE   What, the mistress of the dead Spanish general?

BELVILE   Yes, she's now the only ador'd beauty of all the youth in Naples, who put on all their charms to appear lovely in her sight: their coaches, liveries, and themselves all gay as on a monarch's birthday to attract the eyes of this fair charmer, while she has the pleasure to behold all languish for her that see her.

FREDERICK   'Tis pretty to see with how much love the men regard her, and how much envy the women.

WILLMORE   What gallant has she?

BELVILE   None; she's exposed to sale, and four days in the week she's yours, for so much a month.

WILLMORE   The very thought of it quenches all manner of fire in me. Yet prithee, let's see her.

6. Spanish dollar.
7. Native of Padua.

BELVILE   Let's first to dinner, and after that we'll pass the day as you
please. But at night ye must all be at my devotion.

WILLMORE   I will not fail you.

[*Exeunt.*]

The End of the First Act.

Act II. Scene i.

The long street.
Enter BELVILE *and* FREDERICK *in masking habits, and* WILLMORE
in his own clothes, with a vizard[8] in his hand.

WILLMORE   But why thus disguised and muzzled?

BELVILE   Because whatever extravagances we commit in these faces,
our own may not be obliged to answer 'em.

WILLMORE   I should have changed my eternal buff,[9] too; but no matter,
my little gipsy would not have found me out then. For if she should
change hers, it is impossible I should know her unless I should hear
her prattle. A pox on't, I cannot get her out of my head. Pray heaven,
if ever I do see her again, she prove damnably ugly, that I may fortify
myself against her tongue.

BELVILE   Have a care of love, for o' my conscience she was not of a
quality to give thee any hopes.

WILLMORE   Pox on 'em, why do they draw a man in then? She has
played with my heart so, that 'twill never lie still till I have met with
some kind wench that will play the game out with me. Oh, for my
arms full of soft, white, kind woman—such as I fancy Angellica.

BELVILE   This is her house, if you were but in stock to get admittance.
They have not dined yet; I perceive the picture is not out.

Enter BLUNT.

WILLMORE   I long to see the shadow of the fair substance; a man may
gaze on that for nothing.

BLUNT   Colonel, thy hand. And thine, Fred. I have been an ass, a
deluded fool, a very coxcomb from my birth till this hour, and heartily repent my little faith.

BELVILE   What the devil's the matter with thee, Ned?

BLUNT   Oh, such a mistress, Fred! Such a girl!

WILLMORE   Ha! Where?

FREDERICK   Ay, where?

BLUNT   So fond, so amorous, so toying, and so fine! And all for sheer
love, ye rogue! Oh, how she looked and kissed! And soothed my heart
from my bosom! I cannot think I was awake, and yet methinks I see

8. Face mask.
9. Leather coat.

and feel her charms still. Fred, try if she have not left the taste of her
balmy kisses upon my lips.

Kisses him.

BELVILE   Ha! Ha! Ha!

WILLMORE   Death, man, where is she?

BLUNT   What a dog was I to stay in dull England so long! How have I
laughed at the colonel when he sighed for love! But now the little
archer has revenged him! And by this one dart I can guess at all his
joys, which then I took for fancies, mere dreams and fables. Well, I'm
resolved to sell all in Essex and plant here forever.

BELVILE   What a blessing 'tis, thou hast a mistress thou dar'st boast of;
for I know thy humour is rather to have a proclaimed clap than a
secret amour.

WILLMORE   Dost know her name?

BLUNT   Her name? No, 'adsheartlikins. What care I for names? She's
fair, young, brisk and kind, even to ravishment! And what a pox care
I for knowing her by any other title?

WILLMORE   Didst give her anything?

BLUNT   Give her? Ha! Ha! Ha! Why, she's a person of quality. That's a
good one! Give her? 'Adsheartlikins, dost think such creatures are to
be bought? Or are we provided for such a purchase? Give her, quoth
ye? Why, she presented me with this bracelet for the toy of a diamond
I used to wear. No, gentlemen, Ned Blunt is not everybody. She
expects me again tonight.

WILLMORE   Egad, that's well; we'll all go.

BLUNT   Not a soul! No, gentlemen, you are wits; I am a dull country
rogue, I.

FREDERICK   Well, sir, for all your person of quality, I shall be very glad
to understand your purse be secure; 'tis our whole estate at present,
which we are loath to hazard in one bottom. Come sir, unlade.

BLUNT   Take the necessary trifle useless now to me, that am beloved by
such a gentlewoman. 'Adsheartlikins, money! Here, take mine too.

FREDERICK   No, keep that to be cozened, that we may laugh.

WILLMORE   Cozened? Death! Would I could meet with one that would
cozen me of all the love I could spare tonight.

FREDERICK   Pox, 'tis some common whore, upon my life.

BLUNT   A whore? Yes, with such clothes, such jewels, such a house,
such furniture, and so attended! A whore!

BELVILE   Why yes, sir, they are whores, though they'll neither entertain
you with drinking, swearing, or bawdry; are whores in all those gay
clothes and right jewels; are whores with those great houses richly
furnished with velvet beds, store of plate, handsome attendance, and
fine coaches; are whores, and errant[1] ones.

1. Wide-ranging, thorough.

WILLMORE   Pox on't, where do these fine whores live?

BELVILE   Where no rogues in office, ycleped[2] constables, dare give 'em laws, nor the wine-inspired bullies of the town break their windows; yet they are whores though this Essex calf believe 'em persons of quality.

BLUNT   'Adsheartlikins, y'are all fools. There are things about this Essex calf[3] that shall take with the ladies, beyond all your wit and parts. This shape and size, gentlemen, are not to be despised; my waist, too, tolerably long, with other inviting signs that shall be nameless.

WILLMORE   Egad, I believe he may have met with some person of quality that may be kind to him.

BELVILE   Dost thou perceive any such tempting things about him that should make a fine woman, and of quality, pick him out from all mankind to throw away her youth and beauty upon; nay, and her dear heart, too? No, no, Angellica has raised the price too high.

WILLMORE   May she languish for mankind till she die, and be damned for that one sin alone.

> *Enter two* BRAVOS *and hang up a great picture of Angellica's against the balcony, and two little ones at each side of the door.*

BELVILE   See there the fair sign to the inn where a man may lodge that's fool enough to give her price.

> WILLMORE *gazes on the picture.*

BLUNT   'Adsheartlikins, gentlemen, what's this?

BELVILE   A famous courtesan, that's to be sold.

BLUNT   How? To be sold? Nay, then I have nothing to say to her. Sold? What impudence is practiced in this country; with what order and decency whoring's established here by virtue of the Inquisition! Come, let's be gone; I'm sure we're no chapmen for this commodity.

FREDERICK   Thou art none, I'm sure, unless thou couldst have her in thy bed at a price of a coach in the street.

WILLMORE   How wondrous fair she is! A thousand crowns a month? By heaven, as many kingdoms were too little! A plague of this poverty, of which I ne'er complain but when it hinders my approach to beauty which virtue ne'er could purchase.

> *Turns from the picture.*

BLUNT   What's this? [*Reads.*] "A thousand crowns a month"! 'Adsheartlikins, here's a sum! Sure 'tis a mistake. —[*To one of the* BRAVOS.] Hark you, friend, does she take or give so much by the month?

FREDERICK   A thousand crowns! Why, 'tis a portion for the Infanta![4]

---

2. Called.
3. Slang for a fool.
4. Dowry for the Spanish princess.

BLUNT   Hark ye, friends, won't she trust?

BRAVO   This is a trade, sir, that cannot live by credit.

Enter DON PEDRO *in masquerade, followed by* STEPHANO.

BELVILE   See, here's more company; let's walk off a while.

Exeunt English; PEDRO *reads.*

PEDRO   Fetch me a thousand crowns; I never wished to buy this beauty at an easier rate.

Passes off.

Enter ANGELLICA *and* MORETTA *in the balcony, and draw a silk curtain.*

ANGELLICA   Prithee, what said those fellows to thee?

BRAVO   Madam, the first were admirers of beauty only, but no purchasers; they were merry with your price and picture, laughed at the sum, and so passed off.

ANGELLICA   No matter, I'm not displeased with their rallying; their wonder feeds my vanity, and he that wishes but to buy gives me more pride than he that gives my price can make my pleasure.

BRAVO   Madam, the last I knew through all his disguises to be Don Pedro, nephew to the general, and who was with him in Pamplona.

ANGELLICA   Don Pedro? My old gallant's nephew? When his uncle died he left him a vast sum of money; it is he who was so in love with me at Padua, and who used to make the general so jealous.

MORETTA   Is this he that used to prance before our window, and take such care to show himself an amorous ass? If I am not mistaken, he is the likeliest man to give your price.

ANGELLICA   The man is brave and generous, but of a humour so uneasy and inconstant that the victory over his heart is as soon lost as won; a slave that can add little to the triumph of the conqueror. But inconstancy's the sin of all mankind, therefore I'm resolved that nothing but gold shall charm my heart.

MORETTA   I'm glad on't; 'tis only interest that women of our profession ought to consider, though I wonder what has kept you from that general disease of our sex so long; I mean, that of being in love.

ANGELLICA   A kind but sullen star under which I had the happiness to be born. Yet I have had no time for love; the bravest and noblest of mankind have purchased my favors at so dear a rate, as if no coin but gold were current with our trade. But here's Don Pedro again; fetch me my lute, for 'tis for him or Don Antonio the Viceroy's son that I have spread my nets.

Enter at one door DON PEDRO, STEPHANO; DON ANTONIO *and* DIEGO [*his page*] *at the other door, with people following him in masquerade, anticly attired, some with music. They both go up to the picture.*

ANTONIO   A thousand crowns! Had not the painter flattered her, I should not think it dear.

PEDRO   Flattered her? By heaven, he cannot. I have seen the original, nor is there one charm here more than adorns her face and eyes; all this soft and sweet, with a certain languishing air that no artist can represent.

ANTONIO   What I heard of her beauty before had fired my soul, but this confirmation of it has blown it to a flame.

PEDRO   Ha!

PAGE   Sir, I have known you throw away a thousand crowns on a worse face, and though y'are near your marriage, you may venture a little love here; Florinda will not miss it.

PEDRO [aside]   Ha! Florinda! Sure 'tis Antonio.

ANTONIO   Florinda! Name not those distant joys; there's not one thought of her will check my passion here.

PEDRO [aside]   Florinda scorned! [A noise of a lute above.] And all my hopes defeated of the possession of Angellica! [ANTONIO gazes up.] Her injuries, by heaven, he shall not boast of!

Song to a lute above.

SONG

[I]

When Damon first began to love
He languished in a soft desire,
And knew not how the gods to move,
To lessen or increase his fire.
For Caelia in her charming eyes
Wore all love's sweets, and all his cruelties.

II

But as beneath a shade he lay,
Weaving of flowers for Caelia's hair,
She chanced to lead her flock that way,
And saw the am'rous shepherd there.
She gazed around upon the place,
And saw the grove, resembling night,
To all the joys of love invite,
Whilst guilty smiles and blushes dressed her face.
At this the bashful youth all transport grew,
And with kind force he taught the virgin how
To yield what all his sighs could never do.

ANGELLICA throws open the curtains and bows to ANTONIO, who pulls off his vizard and bows and blows up kisses. PEDRO, unseen, looks in's face.

ANTONIO   By heaven, she's charming fair!
PEDRO [*aside*]   'Tis he, the false Antonio!
ANTONIO [*to the bravo*]
  Friend, where must I pay my off'ring of love?
  My thousand crowns I mean.
PEDRO
  That off'ring I have designed to make,
  And yours will come too late.
ANTONIO
  Prithee begone; I shall grow angry else,
  And then thou art not safe.
PEDRO
  My anger may be fatal, sir, as yours,
  And he that enters here may prove this truth.
ANTONIO   I know not who thou art, but I am sure thou'rt worth my
    killing, for aiming at Angellica.

They draw and fight.

Enter WILLMORE *and* BLUNT, *who draw and part'em.*

BLUNT   'Adsheartlikins, here's fine doings.
WILLMORE   Tilting for the wench, I'm sure. Nay, gad, if that would win
    her I have as good a sword as the best of ye. Put up, put up, and take
    another time and place, for this is designed for lovers only.

They all put up.

PEDRO
  We are prevented; dare you meet me tomorrow on the Molo?[5]
  For I've a title to a better quarrel,
  That of Florinda, in whose credulous heart
  Thou'st made an int'rest, and destroyed my hopes.
ANTONIO   Dare! I'll meet thee there as early as the day.
PEDRO   We will come thus disguised, that whosoever chance to get the
    better, he may escape unknown.
ANTONIO   It shall be so.

Exeunt PEDRO *and* STEPHANO.

  —Who should this rival be? Unless the English colonel, of whom
  I've often heard Don Pedro speak. It must be he, and time he were
  removed who lays a claim to all my happiness.

> WILLMORE, *having gazed all this while on the picture, pulls down
> a little one.*

WILLMORE
  This posture's loose and negligent;
  The sight on't would beget a warm desire

5. Mall.

In souls whom impotence and age had chilled.
This must along with me.

BRAVO   What means this rudeness, sir? Restore the picture.

ANTONIO   Ha! Rudeness committed to the fair Angellica! —Restore the picture, sir.

WILLMORE   Indeed I will not, sir.

ANTONIO   By heaven, but you shall.

WILLMORE   Nay, do not show your sword; if you do, by this dear beauty, I will show mine too.

ANTONIO   What right can you pretend to't?

WILLMORE   That of possession, which I will maintain. You, perhaps, have a thousand crowns to give for the original.

ANTONIO   No matter, sir, you shall restore the picture.

ANGELLICA   Oh, Moretta, what's the matter?

> ANGELLICA *and* MORETTA *above.*

ANTONIO   Or leave your life behind.

WILLMORE   Death! You lie; I will do neither.

> *They fight. The Spaniards join with* ANTONIO, BLUNT *laying on like mad.*

ANGELLICA   Hold, I command you, if for me you fight.

> *They leave off and bow.*

WILLMORE [*aside*]   How heavenly fair she is! Ah, plague of her price!

ANGELLICA   You sir, in buff, you that appear a soldier, that first began this insolence—

WILLMORE   'Tis true, I did so, if you call it insolence for a man to preserve himself. I saw your charming picture and was wounded; quite through my soul each pointed beauty ran; and wanting a thousand crowns to procure my remedy, I laid this little picture to my bosom, which, if you cannot allow me, I'll resign.

ANGELLICA   No, you may keep the trifle.

ANTONIO   You shall first ask me leave, and this.

> *Fight again as before.*

> *Enter* BELVILE *and* FREDERICK, *who join with the English.*

ANGELLICA   Hold! Will you ruin me? —Biskey! Sebastian! Part 'em!

> *The Spaniards are beaten off.*

MORETTA   Oh, madam, we're undone. A pox upon that rude fellow; he's set on to ruin us. We shall never see good days again till all these fighting poor rogues are sent to the galleys.

> *Enter* BELVILE, BLUNT, FREDERICK, *and* WILLMORE *with's shirt bloody.*

BLUNT   'Adsheartlikins, beat me at this sport and I'll ne'er wear sword more.

BELVILE [*to* WILLMORE]   The devil's in thee for a mad fellow; thou art always one at an unlucky adventure. Come, let's be gone whilst we're safe, and remember these are Spaniards, a sort of people that know how to revenge an affront.

FREDERICK   You bleed! I hope you are not wounded.

WILLMORE   Not much. A plague on your dons; if they fight no better they'll ne'er recover Flanders. What the devil was't to them that I took down the picture?

BLUNT   Took it! 'Adsheartlikins, we'll have the great one too; 'tis ours by conquest. Prithee help me up and I'll pull it down.

ANGELLICA [*to* WILLMORE]   Stay, sir, and ere you affront me farther let me know how you durst commit this outrage. To you I speak, sir, for you appear a gentleman.

WILLMORE   To me, madam? —Gentlemen, your servant.

      BELVILE *stays him.*

BELVILE   Is the devil in thee? Dost know the danger of ent'ring the house of an incensed courtesan?

WILLMORE   I thank you for your care, but there are other matters in hand, there are, though we have no great temptation. Death! Let me go!

FREDERICK   Yes, to your lodging if you will, but not in here. Damn these gay harlots; by this hand I'll have as sound and handsome a whore for a patacoon.[6] Death, man, she'll murder thee!

WILLMORE   Oh, fear me not. Shall I not venture where a beauty calls? A lovely charming beauty! For fear of danger? When, by heaven, there's none so great as to long for her whilst I want money to purchase her.

FREDERICK   Therefore 'tis loss of time unless you had the thousand crowns to pay.

WILLMORE   It may be she may give a favor; at least I shall have the pleasure of saluting her when I enter and when I depart.

BELVILE   Pox, she'll as soon lie with thee as kiss thee, and sooner stab than do either. You shall not go.

ANGELLICA   Fear not, sir, all I have to wound with is my eyes.

BLUNT   Let him go. 'Adsheartlikins, I believe the gentlewoman means well.

BELVILE   Well, take thy fortune; we'll expect you in the next street. Farewell, fool, farewell.

WILLMORE   'Bye, colonel.

                                            Goes in.

FREDERICK   The rogue's stark mad for a wench.

                                            Exeunt.

6. Spanish or Portuguese silver coin, worth about four shillings.

Act II. Scene ii.

A *fine chamber.*
Enter WILLMORE, ANGELLICA, *and* MORETTA.

ANGELLICA   Insolent sir, how durst you pull down my picture?

WILLMORE   Rather, how durst you set it up to tempt poor am'rous mortals with so much excellence, which I find you have but too well consulted by the unmerciful price you set upon't. Is all this heaven of beauty shown to move despair in those that cannot buy? And can you think th'effects of that despair should be less extravagant than I have shown?

ANGELLICA   I sent for you to ask my pardon, sir, not to aggravate your crime. I thought I should have seen you at my feet imploring it.

WILLMORE   You are deceived. I came to rail at you, and rail such truths too, as shall let you see the vanity of that pride which taught you how to set such price on sin.
For such it is whilst that which is love's due
Is meanly bartered for.

ANGELLICA   Ha! Ha! Ha! Alas, good captain, what pity 'tis your edifying doctrine will do no good upon me. Moretta, fetch the gentleman a glass, and let him survey himself to see what charms he has. —[*Aside, in a soft tone.*] And guess my business.

MORETTA   He knows himself of old: I believe those breeches and he have been acquainted ever since he was beaten at Worcester.[7]

ANGELLICA   Nay, do not abuse the poor creature.

MORETTA   Good weatherbeaten corporal, will you march off? We have no need of your doctrine, though you have of our charity. But at present we have no scraps; we can afford no kindness for God's sake. In fine, sirrah, the price is too high i'th' mouth for you, therefore troop, I say.

WILLMORE   Here, good forewoman of the shop, serve me and I'll be gone.

MORETTA   Keep it to pay your laundress; your linen stinks of the gun room. For here's no selling by retail.

WILLMORE   Thou hast sold plenty of thy stale ware at a cheap rate.

MORETTA   Ay, the more silly kind heart I, but this is an age wherein beauty is at higher rates. In fine, you know the price of this.

WILLMORE   I grant you 'tis here set down, a thousand crowns a month. Pray, how much may come to my share for a pistole?[8] Bawd, take your black lead and sum it up, that I may have a pistole's worth of this vain gay thing, and I'll trouble you no more.

MORETTA   Pox on him, he'll fret me to death! Abominable fellow, I tell thee we only sell by the whole piece.

---

7. Where Charles II was defeated by Cromwell in 1651.
8. Spanish coin worth about sixteen shillings.

WILLMORE   'Tis very hard, the whole cargo or nothing. Faith, madam, my stock will not reach it; I cannot be your chapman. Yet I have countrymen in town, merchants of love like me; I'll see if they'll put in for a share. We cannot lose much by it, and what we have no use for, we'll sell upon the Friday's mart at "Who gives more?" —I am studying, madam, how to purchase you, though at present I am unprovided of money.

ANGELLICA [*aside*]   Sure this from any other man would anger me; nor shall he know the conquest he has made. —Poor angry man, how I despise this railing.

WILLMORE

Yes, I am poor. But I'm a gentleman,
And one that scorns this baseness which you practice.
Poor as I am I would not sell myself,
No, not to gain your charming high-prized person.
Though I admire you strangely for your beauty,
Yet I contemn your mind.
And yet I would at any rate enjoy you;
At your own rate; but cannot. See here
The only sum I can command on earth:
I know not where to eat when this is gone.
Yet such a slave I am to love and beauty
This last reserve I'll sacrifice to enjoy you.
Nay, do not frown, I know you're to be bought,
And would be bought by me. By me,
For a meaning trifling sum, if I could pay it down.
Which happy knowledge I will still repeat,
And lay it to my heart: it has a virtue in't,
And soon will cure those wounds your eyes have made.
And yet, there's something so divinely powerful there—
Nay, I will gaze, to let you see my strength.

Holds her, looks on her, and pauses and sighs.

By heav'n, bright creature, I would not for the world
Thy fame were half so fair as is thy face.

Turns her away from him.

ANGELLICA [*aside*]

His words go through me to the very soul.—
If you have nothing else to say to me—

WILLMORE

Yes, you shall hear how infamous you are—
For which I do not hate thee—
But that secures my heart, and all the flames it feels
Are but so many lusts:
I know it by their sudden bold intrusion.
The fire's impatient and betrays; 'tis false.

For had it been the purer flame of love,
I should have pined and languished at your feet,
Ere found the impudence to have discovered it.
I now dare stand your scorn and your denial.

MORETTA   Sure she's bewitched, that she can stand thus tamely and hear his saucy railing. —Sirrah, will you be gone?

ANGELLICA [to MORETTA]   How dare you take this liberty! Withdraw! —Pray tell me, sir, are not you guilty of the same mercenary crime? When a lady is proposed to you for a wife, you never ask how fair, discreet, or virtuous she is, but what's her fortune; which, if but small, you cry "She will not do my business," and basely leave her, though she languish for you. Say, is not this as poor?

WILLMORE   It is a barbarous custom, which I will scorn to defend in our sex, and do despise in yours.

ANGELLICA
Thou'rt a brave fellow! Put up thy gold, and know,
That were thy fortune as large as is thy soul,
Thou shouldst not buy my love
Couldst thou forget those mean effects of vanity
Which set me out to sale,
And as a lover prize my yielding joys.
Canst thou believe they'll be entirely thine,
Without considering they were mercenary?

WILLMORE
I cannot tell, I must bethink me first.
[Aside.] Ha! Death, I'm going to believe her.

ANGELLICA
Prithee confirm that faith, or if thou canst not,
Flatter me a little: 'twill please me from thy mouth.

WILLMORE [aside]
Curse on thy charming tongue! Dost thou return
My feigned contempt with so much subtlety?—
Thou'st found the easiest way into my heart,
Though I yet know that all thou say'st is false.

Turning from her in rage.

ANGELLICA
By all that's good, 'tis real;
I never loved before, though oft a mistress.
Shall my first vows be slighted?

WILLMORE [aside]   What can she mean?

ANGELLICA [in an angry tone]   I find you cannot credit me.

WILLMORE
I know you take me for an errant ass,
An ass that may be soothed into belief,
And then be used at pleasure;

But, madam, I have been so often cheated
By perjured, soft, deluding hypocrites,
That I've no faith left for the cozening sex,
Especially for women of your trade.

ANGELLICA

The low esteem you have of me perhaps
May bring my heart again:
For I have pride that yet surmounts my love.

She turns with pride; he holds her.

WILLMORE

Throw off this pride, this enemy to bliss,
And show the power of love: 'tis with those arms
I can be only vanquished, made a slave.

ANGELLICA

Is all my mighty expectation vanished?
No, I will not hear thee talk; thou hast a charm
In every word that draws my heart away,
And all the thousand trophies I designed
Thou hast undone. Why art thou soft?
Thy looks are bravely rough, and meant for war.
Couldst thou not storm on still?
I then perhaps had been as free as thou.

WILLMORE [*aside*]

Death, how she throws her fire about my soul!—
Take heed, fair creature, how you raise my hopes,
Which once assumed pretends to all dominion:
There's not a joy thou hast in store
I shall not then command.
For which I'll pay you back my soul, my life!
Come, let's begin th'account this happy minute!

ANGELLICA   And will you pay me then the price I ask?

WILLMORE

Oh, why dost thou draw me from an awful[9] worship,
By showing thou art no divinity.
Conceal the fiend, and show me all the angel!
Keep me but ignorant, and I'll be devout
And pay my vows forever at this shrine.

Kneels and kisses her hand.

ANGELLICA

The pay I mean is but thy love for mine.
Can you give that?

_____

9. Full of awe.

WILLMORE   Entirely. Come, let's withdraw where I'll renew my vows, and breathe 'em with such ardor thou shalt not doubt my zeal.

ANGELLICA   Thou hast a power too strong to be resisted.

Exeunt WILLMORE *and* ANGELLICA.

MORETTA   Now my curse go with you! Is all our project fallen to this? To love the only enemy to our trade? Nay, to love such a shameroon, a very beggar; nay, a pirate beggar, whose business is to rifle and be gone; a no-purchase, no-pay tatterdemalion, and English picaroon;[1] a rogue that fights for daily drink, and takes a pride in being loyally lousy? Oh, I could curse now, if I durst. This is the fate of most whores.

Trophies, which from believing fops we win,
Are spoils to those who cozen us again.

Exit.

The End of the Second Act.

Act III. Scene i.

A street.

Enter FLORINDA, VALERIA, HELLENA, *in antic different dresses from what they were in before;* CALLIS *attending.*

FLORINDA   I wonder what should make my brother in so ill a humour? I hope he has not found out our ramble this morning.

HELLENA   No, if he had, we should have heard on't at both ears, and have been mewed up[2] this afternoon, which I would not for the world should have happened. Hey ho, I'm as sad as a lover's lute.

VALERIA   Well, methinks we have learnt this trade of gipsies as readily as if we had been bred upon the road to Loretto; and yet I did so fumble when I told the stranger his fortune that I was afraid I should have told my own and yours by mistake. But methinks Hellena has been very serious ever since.

FLORINDA   I would give my garters she were in love, to be revenged upon her for abusing me. How is't, Hellena?

HELLENA   Ah, would I had never seen my mad monsieur. And yet, for all your laughing, I am not in love. And yet this small acquaintance, o' my conscience, will never out of my head.

VALERIA   Ha! Ha! Ha! I laugh to think how thou art fitted with a lover, a fellow that I warrant loves every new face he sees.

HELLENA   Hum, he has not kept his word with me here, and may be taken up. That thought is not very pleasant to me. What the deuce should this be now that I feel?

1. Rogue, pirate. *Shameroon:* shameful person.
2. Confined.

VALERIA   What is't like?

HELLENA   Nay, the Lord knows, but if I should be hanged I cannot choose but be angry and afraid when I think that mad fellow should be in love with anybody but me. What to think of myself I know not: would I could meet with some true damned gipsy, that I might know my fortune.

VALERIA   Know it! Why there's nothing so easy: thou wilt love this wand'ring inconstant till thou find'st thyself hanged about his neck, and then be as mad to get free again.

FLORINDA   Yes, Valeria, we shall see her bestride his baggage horse and follow him to the campaign.

HELLENA   So, so, now you are provided for there's no care taken of poor me. But since you have set my heart a-wishing, I am resolved to know for what; I will not die of the pip, so I will not.

FLORINDA   Art thou mad to talk so? Who will like thee well enough to have thee, that hears what a mad wench thou art?

HELLENA   Like me? I don't intend every he that likes me shall have me, but he that I like. I should have stayed in the nunnery still if I had liked my lady abbess as well as she liked me. No, I came thence not, as my wise brother imagines, to take an eternal farewell of the world, but to love and to be beloved; and I will be beloved, or I'll get one of your men, so I will.

VALERIA   Am I put into the number of lovers?

HELLENA   You? Why, coz, I know thou'rt too good-natured to leave us in any design; thou wouldst venture a cast[3] though thou comest off a loser, especially with such a gamester. I observe your man, and your willing ear incline that way; and if you are not a lover, 'tis an art soon learnt—that I find.

Sighs.

FLORINDA   I wonder how you learnt to love so easily. I had a thousand charms to meet my eyes and ears ere I could yield, and 'twas the knowledge of Belvile's merit, not the surprising person, took my soul. Thou art too rash, to give a heart at first sight.

HELLENA   Hang your considering lover! I never thought beyond the fancy that 'twas a very pretty, idle, silly kind of pleasure to pass one's time with: to write little soft nonsensical billets, and with great difficulty and danger receive answers in which I shall have my beauty praised, my wit admired, though little or none, and have the vanity and power to know I am desirable. Then I have the more inclination that way because I am to be a nun, and so shall not be suspected to have any such earthly thoughts about me; but when I walk thus—and sigh thus—they'll think my mind's upon my monastery, and cry, "How happy 'tis she's so resolved." But not a word of man.

FLORINDA   What a mad creature's this!

3. Throw the dice.

HELLENA   I'll warrant, if my brother hears either of you sigh, he cries gravely, "I fear you have the indiscretion to be in love, but take heed of the honor of our house, and your own unspotted fame"; and so he conjures on till he has laid the soft winged god in your hearts, or broke the bird's nest. But see, here comes your lover, but where's my inconstant? Let's step aside, and we may learn something.

Go aside.

Enter BELVILE, FREDERICK, *and* BLUNT.

BELVILE   What means this! The picture's taken in.

BLUNT   It may be the wench is good-natured, and will be kind gratis. Your friend's a proper handsome fellow.

BELVILE   I rather think she has cut his throat and is fled; I am mad he should throw himself into dangers. Pox on't, I shall want him, too, at night. Let's knock and ask for him.

HELLENA   My heart goes a-pit, a-pat, for fear 'tis my man they talk of.

Knock; MORETTA *above.*

MORETTA   What would you have?

BELVILE   Tell the stranger that entered here about two hours ago that his friends stay here for him.

MORETTA   A curse upon him for Moretta: would he were at the devil! But he's coming to you.

Enter WILLMORE.

HELLENA   Ay, ay 'tis he. Oh, how this vexes me!

BELVILE   And how and how, dear lad, has fortune smiled? Are we to break her windows, or raise up altars to her, hah?

WILLMORE   Does not my fortune sit triumphant on my brow? Dost not see the little wanton god there all gay and smiling? Have I not an air about my face and eyes that distinguish me from the crowd of common lovers? By heaven, Cupid's quiver has not half so many darts as her eyes! Oh, such a *bona roba*![4] To sleep in her arms is lying *in fresco*,[5] all perfumed air about me.

HELLENA [*aside*]   Here's fine encouragement for me to fool on!

WILLMORE   Hark'ee, where didst thou purchase that rich Canary[6] we drank today? Tell me, that I may adore the spigot and sacrifice to the butt. The juice was divine; into which I must dip my rosary, and then bless all things that I would have bold or fortunate.

BELVILE   Well, sir, let's go take a bottle and hear the story of your success.

FREDERICK   Would not French wine do better?

4. Courtesan.
5. In fresh air.
6. Sweet wine from the Canary Islands, resembling sherry.

WILLMORE   Damn the hungry balderdash! Cheerful sack[7] has a gener-
    ous virtue in't inspiring a successful confidence, gives eloquence to
    the tongue and vigor to the soul, and has in a few hours completed
    all my hopes and wishes! There's nothing left to raise a new desire in
    me. Come, let's be gay and wanton. And, gentlemen, study; study
    what you want, for here are friends that will supply gentlemen. [*Jin-
    gles gold.*] Hark what a charming sound they make! 'Tis the he and
    the she gold whilst here, and shall beget new pleasures every
    moment.
BLUNT   But hark'ee, sir, you are not married, are you?
WILLMORE   All the honey of matrimony but none of the sting, friend.
BLUNT   'Adsheartlikins, thou'rt a fortunate rogue!
WILLMORE   I am so, sir: let these inform you! Ha, how sweetly they
    chime! Pox of poverty: it makes a man a slave, makes wit and honor
    sneak. My soul grew lean and rusty for want of credit.
BLUNT   'Adsheartlikins, this I like well; it looks like my lucky bargain!
    Oh, how I long for the approach of my squire, that is to conduct me
    to her house again. Why, here's two provided for!
FREDERICK   By this light, y'are happy men.
BLUNT   Fortune is pleased to smile on us, gentlemen, to smile on us.

Enter SANCHO *and pulls down* BLUNT *by the sleeve; they go aside.*

SANCHO   Sir, my lady expects you. She has removed all that might
    oppose your will and pleasure, and is impatient till you come.
BLUNT   Sir, I'll attend you. —Oh the happiest rogue! I'll take no leave,
    lest they either dog me or stay me.

Exit with SANCHO.

BELVILE   But then the little gipsy is forgot?
WILLMORE   A mischief on thee for putting her into my thoughts! I had
    quite forgot her else, and this night's debauch had drunk her quite
    down.
HELLENA   Had it so, good captain!

Claps him on the back.

WILLMORE [*aside*]   Ha! I hope she did not hear me!
HELLENA   What, afraid of such a champion?
WILLMORE   Oh, you're a fine lady of your word, are you not? To make
    a man languish a whole day—
HELLENA   In tedious search of me.
WILLMORE   Egad, child, thou'rt in the right. Hadst thou seen what a
    melancholy dog I have been ever since I was a lover, how I have
    walked the streets like a Capuchin,[8] with my hands in my sleeves—
    faith, sweetheart, thou wouldst pity me.

7. Sherry. Willmore has a touch of Shakespeare's Falstaff when it comes to drink. See *2 Henry
    IV* 4.3.
8. Austere monk.

HELLENA [*aside*]   Now if I should be hanged I can't be angry with him,
he dissembles so heartily. —Alas, good captain, what pains you have
taken; now were I ungrateful not to reward so true a servant.

WILLMORE   Poor soul, that's kindly said; I see thou barest a conscience.
Come then, for a beginning show me thy dear face.

HELLENA   I'm afraid, my small acquaintance, you have been staying
that swinging stomach you boasted of this morning. I then remember
my little collation[9] would have gone down with you without the sauce
of a handsome face. Is your stomach so queasy now?

WILLMORE   Faith, long fasting, child, spoils a man's appetite. Yet if you
durst treat, I could so lay about me still—

HELLENA   And would you fall to before a priest says grace?

WILLMORE   Oh fie, fie, what an old out-of-fashioned thing hast thou
named? Thou couldst not dash me more out of countenance shouldst
thou show me an ugly face.

> *Whilst he is seemingly courting* HELLENA, *enter* ANGELLICA, MOR-
> ETTA, BISKEY, *and* SEBASTIAN, *all in masquerade.* ANGELLICA *sees*
> WILLMORE *and stares.*

ANGELLICA   Heavens, 'tis he! And passionately fond to see another
woman!

MORETTA   What could you less expect from such a swaggerer?

ANGELLICA
Expect? As much as I paid him: a heart entire,
Which I had pride enough to think when'er I gave,
It would have raised the man above the vulgar,
Made him all soul, and that all soft and constant.

HELLENA   You see, captain, how willing I am to be friends with you,
till time and ill luck make us lovers; and ask you the question first
rather than put your modesty to the blush by asking me. For alas, I
know you captains are such strict men, and such severe observers of
your vows to chastity, that 'twill be hard to prevail with your tender
conscience to marry a young willing maid.

WILLMORE   Do not abuse me, for fear I should take thee at thy word
and marry thee indeed, which I'm sure will be revenge sufficient.

HELLENA   O' my conscience, that will be our destiny, because we are
both of one humour: I am as inconstant as you, for I have considered,
captain, that a handsome woman has a great deal to do whilst her
face is good. For then is our harvesttime to gather friends, and should
I in these days of my youth catch a fit of foolish constancy, I were
undone: 'tis loitering by daylight in our great journey. Therefore, I
declare I'll allow but one year for love, one year for indifference, and
one year for hate; and then go hang yourself, for I profess myself the
gay, the kind, and the inconstant. The devil's in't if this won't please
you!

9. Light meal.

WILLMORE   Oh, most damnably. I have a heart with a hole quite through it too; no prison mine, to keep a mistress in.

ANGELLICA [*aside*]   Perjured man! How I believe thee now!

HELLENA   Well, I see our business as well as humours are alike: yours to cozen as many maids as will trust you, and I as many men as have faith. See if I have not as desperate a lying look as you can have for the heart of you. [*Pulls off her vizard; he starts.*] How do you like it, captain?

WILLMORE   Like it! By heaven, I never saw so much beauty! Oh, the charms of those sprightly black eyes! That strangely fair face, full of smiles and dimples! Those soft round melting cherry lips and small even white teeth! Not to be expressed, but silently adored! [*She replaces her mask.*] Oh, one look more, and strike me dumb, or I shall repeat nothing else till I'm mad.

He seems to court her to pull off her vizard; she refuses.

ANGELLICA   I can endure no more. Nor is it fit to interrupt him, for if I do, my jealousy has so destroyed my reason I shall undo him. Therefore I'll retire, and you, Sebastian [*to one of her bravos*], follow that woman and learn who 'tis; while you [*to the other bravo*] tell the fugitive I would speak to him instantly.

Exit.

This while FLORINDA *is talking to* BELVILE, *who stands sullenly;* FREDERICK *courting* VALERIA.

VALERIA [*to* BELVILE]   Prithee, dear stranger, be not so sullen, for though you have lost your love you see my friend frankly offers you hers to play with in the meantime.

BELVILE   Faith, madam, I am sorry I can't play at her game.

FREDERICK [*to* VALERIA]   Pray leave your intercession and mind your own affair. They'll better agree apart: he's a modest sigher in company, but alone no woman 'scapes him.

FLORINDA [*aside*]   Sure he does but rally. Yet, if it should be true? I'll tempt him farther. —Believe me, noble stranger, I'm no common mistress. And for a little proof on't, wear this jewel. Nay, take it, sir, 'tis right, and bills of exchange may sometimes miscarry.

BELVILE   Madam, why am I chose out of all mankind to be the object of your bounty?

VALERIA   There's another civil question asked.

FREDERICK [*aside*]   Pox of's modesty; it spoils his own markets and hinders mine.

FLORINDA   Sir, from my window I have often seen you, and women of my quality have so few opportunities for love that we ought to lose none.

FREDERICK [*to* VALERIA]   Ay, this is something! Here's a woman! When shall I be blest with so much kindness from your fair mouth? —[*Aside to* BELVILE.] Take the jewel, fool!

BELVILE   You tempt me strangely, madam, every way—

FLORINDA [*aside*]   So, if I find him false, my whole repose is gone.

BELVILE   And but for a vow I've made to a very fair lady, this goodness had subdued me.

FREDERICK [*aside to* BELVILE]   Pox on't, be kind, in pity to me be kind. For I am to thrive here but as you treat her friend.

HELLENA   Tell me what you did in yonder house, and I'll unmask.

WILLMORE   Yonder house? Oh, I went to a—to—why, there's a friend of mine lives there.

HELLENA   What, a she or a he friend?

WILLMORE   A man, upon honor, a man. A she friend? No, no, madam, you have done my business, I thank you.

HELLENA   And was't your man friend that had more darts in's eyes than Cupid carries in's whole budget[1] of arrows?

WILLMORE   So—

HELLENA   "Ah, such a *bona roba*! To be in her arms is lying *in fresco*, all perfumed air about me." Was this your man friend too?

WILLMORE   So—

HELLENA   That gave you the he and the she gold, that begets young pleasures?

WILLMORE   Well, well, madam, then you can see there are ladies in the world that will not be cruel. There are, madam, there are.

HELLENA   And there be men, too, as fine, wild, inconstant fellows as yourself. There be, captain, there be, if you go to that now. Therefore, I'm resolved—

WILLMORE   Oh!

HELLENA   To see your face no more—

WILLMORE   Oh!

HELLENA   Till tomorrow.

WILLMORE   Egad, you frighted me.

HELLENA   Nor then neither, unless you'll swear never to see that lady more.

WILLMORE   See her! Why, never to think of womankind again.

HELLENA   Kneel, and swear.

Kneels; she gives him her hand.

WILLMORE   I do, never to think, to see, to love, nor lie, with any but thyself.

HELLENA   Kiss the book.

WILLMORE   Oh, most religiously.

Kisses her hand.

HELLENA   Now what a wicked creature am I, to damn a proper fellow.

CALLIS [*to* FLORINDA]   Madam, I'll stay no longer: 'tis e'en dark.

FLORINDA [*to* BELVILE]   However, sir, I'll leave this with you, that

1. Quiver.

when I'm gone you may repent the opportunity you have lost by your modesty.

Gives him the jewel, which is her picture, and exit. He gazes after her.

WILLMORE [*to* HELLENA] 'Twill be an age till tomorrow, and till then I will most impatiently expect you. Adieu, my dear pretty angel.

Exeunt all the women.

BELVILE Ha! Florinda's picture! 'Twas she herself. What a dull dog was I! I would have given the world for one minute's discourse with her.

FREDERICK This comes of your modesty. Ah, pox o' your vow; 'twas ten to one but we had lost the jewel by't.

BELVILE Willmore, the blessed'st opportunity lost! Florinda, friends, Florinda!

WILLMORE Ah, rogue! Such black eyes! Such a face! Such a mouth! Such teeth! And so much wit!

BELVILE All, all, and a thousand charms besides.

WILLMORE Why, dost thou know her?

BEVILE Know her! Ay, ay, and a pox take me with all my heart for being so modest.

WILLMORE But hark'ee, friend of mine, are you my rival? And have I been only beating the bush all this while?

BELVILE I understand thee not. I'm mad! See here—

Shows the picture.

WILLMORE Ha! Whose picture's this? 'Tis a fine wench!

FREDERICK The colonel's mistress, sir.

WILLMORE Oh, oh, here. [*Gives the picture back.*] I thought't had been another prize. Come, come, a bottle will set thee right again.

BELVILE I am content to try, and by that time 'twill be late enough for our design.

WILLMORE Agreed.

Love does all day the soul's great empire keep,
But wine at night lulls the soft god asleep.

Exeunt.

Act III. Scene ii.

LUCETTA'S *house.*
Enter BLUNT *and* LUCETTA *with a light.*

LUCETTA Now we are safe and free: no fears of the coming home of my old jealous husband, which made me a little thoughtful when you came in first. But now love is all the business of my soul.

BLUNT   I am transported!—[*Aside.*] Pox on't, that I had but some fine things to say to her, such as lovers use. I was a fool not to learn of Fred a little by heart before I came. Something I must say. —'Adsheartlikins, sweet soul, I am not used to compliment, but I'm an honest gentleman, and thy humble servant.

LUCETTA   I have nothing to pay for so great a favor, but such a love as cannot but be great, since at first sight of that sweet face and shape it made me your absolute captive.

BLUNT [*aside*]   Kind heart, how prettily she talks! Egad, I'll show her husband a Spanish trick: send him out of the world and marry her; she's damnably in love with me, and will ne'er mind settlements, and so there's that saved.

LUCETTA   Well, sir, I'll go and undress me, and be with you instantly.

BLUNT   Make haste then, for 'adsheartlikins, dear soul, thou canst not guess at the pain of a longing lover when his joys are drawn within the compass of a few minutes.

LUCETTA   You speak my sense, and I'll make haste to prove it.

Exit.

BLUNT   'Tis a rare girl, and this one night's enjoyment with her will be worth all the days I ever passed in Essex. Would she would go with me into England, though to say truth, there's plenty of whores already. Put a box on 'em, they are such mercenary prodigal whores that they want such a one as this, that's free and generous, to give 'em good examples. Why, what a house she has, how rich and fine!

Enter SANCHO.

SANCHO   Sir, my lady has sent me to conduct you to her chamber.

BLUNT   Sir, I shall be proud to follow.—[*Aside.*] Here's one of her servants too; 'adsheartlikins, by this garb and gravity he might be a justice of peace in Essex, and is but a pimp here.

Exeunt.

Act III. Scene iii.

The scene changes to a chamber with an alcove bed in't, a table, etc.; LUCETTA *in bed. Enter* SANCHO *and* BLUNT, *who takes the candle of* SANCHO *at the door.*

SANCHO   Sir, my commission reaches no farther.

BLUNT   Sir, I'll excuse your compliment.

[*Exit* SANCHO.]

—What, in bed, my sweet mistress?

LUCETTA   You see, I still outdo you in kindness.

BLUNT   And thou shalt see what haste I'll make to quit scores. Oh, the luckiest rogue!

He undresses himself.

LUCETTA   Should you be false or cruel now—
BLUNT   False! 'Adsheartlikins, what dost thou take me for, a Jew? An insensible heathen? A pox of thy old jealous husband: an he were dead, egad, sweet soul, it should be none of my fault if I did not marry thee.
LUCETTA   It never should be mine.
BLUNT   Good soul! I'm the fortunatest dog!
LUCETTA   Are you not undressed yet?
BLUNT   As much as my impatience will permit.

Goes toward the bed in his shirt, drawers, etc.

LUCETTA   Hold, sir, put out the light; it may betray us else.
BLUNT   Anything; I need no other light but that of thine eyes.—[*Aside.*] 'Adsheartlikins, there I think I had it.

Puts out the candle; the bed descends; he gropes about to find it.

Why, why, where am I got? What, not yet? Where are you, sweetest? —Ah, the rogue's silent now. A pretty love-trick this; how she'll laugh at me anon! —You need not, my dear rogue, you need not! I'm all on fire already; come, come, now call me, in pity.—Sure I'm enchanted! I have been round the chamber, and can find neither woman nor bed. I locked the door; I'm sure she cannot go that way, or if she could, the bed could not. —Enough, enough, my pretty wanton; do not carry the jest too far! [*Lights on a trap, and is let down.*] —Ha! Betrayed! Dogs! Rogues! Pimps! Help! Help!

Enter LUCETTA, PHILLIPO, *and* SANCHO *with a light.*

PHILLIPO   Ha! Ha! Ha! He's dispatched finely.
LUCETTA   Now, sir, had I been coy, we had missed of this booty.
PHILLIPO   Nay, when I saw 'twas a substantial fool, I was mollified. But when you dote upon a serenading coxcomb, upon a face, fine clothes, and a lute, it makes me rage.
LUCETTA   You know I was never guilty of that folly, my dear Phillipo, but with yourself. But come, let's see what we have got by this.
PHILLIPO   A rich coat; sword and hat; these breeches, too, are well lined! See here, a gold watch! A purse—Ha! Gold! At least two hundred pistoles! A bunch of diamond rings, and one with the family arms! A gold box, with a medal of his king, and his lady mother's picture! These were sacred relics, believe me. See, the waistband of his breeches have a mine of gold—old queen Bess's! We have a quar-

rel to her ever since eighty-eight,[2] and may therefore justify the theft:
the Inquisition might have committed it.

LUCETTA   See, a bracelet of bowed gold! These his sisters tied about his
arm at parting. But well, for all this, I fear his being a stranger may
make a noise and hinder our trade with them hereafter.

PHILLIPO   That's our security: he is not only a stranger to us, but to the
country too. The common shore[3] into which he is descended, thou
know'st, conducts him into another street, which this light will hinder
him from ever finding again. He knows neither your name, nor that
of the street where your house is; nay, nor the way to his own lodgings.

LUCETTA   And art thou not an unmerciful rogue, not to afford him one
night for all this? I should not have been such a Jew.

PHILLIPO   Blame me not, Lucetta, to keep as much of thee as I can to
myself. Come, that thought makes me wanton; let's to bed. —Sancho, lock up these.

> This is the fleece which fools do bear,
> Designed for witty men to shear.

Exeunt.

Act III. Scene iv.

The scene changes, and discovers BLUNT *creeping out of a common shore; his face, etc., all dirty.*

BLUNT [*climbing up*]   Oh, Lord, I am got out at last, and, which is a
miracle, without a clue. And now to damning and cursing! But if that
would ease me, where shall I begin? With my fortune, myself, or the
quean[4] that cozened me? What a dog was I to believe in woman!
Oh, coxcomb! Ignorant conceited coxcomb! To fancy she could be
enamored with my person! At first sight enamored! Oh, I'm a cursed
puppy! 'Tis plain, fool was writ upon my forehead! She perceived it;
saw the Essex calf there. For what allurements could there be in this
countenance, which I can endure because I'm acquainted with it.
Oh dull, silly dog, to be thus soothed into a cozening! Had I been
drunk, I might fondly have credited the young quean; but as I was in
my right wits to be thus cheated, confirms it: I am a dull believing
English country fop. But my comrades! Death and the devil, there's
the worst of all! Then a ballad will be sung tomorrow on the Prado,[5]
to a lousy tune of the enchanted squire and the annihilated damsel.
But Fred—that rogue—and the colonel will abuse me beyond all
Christian patience. Had she left me my clothes, I have a bill of
exchange at home would have saved my credit. But now all hope is

2. The reference is to 1588, when the Spanish Armada was defeated by Queen Elizabeth's navy.
3. Sewer.
4. Slut.
5. Fashionable promenade.

taken from me. Well, I'll home, if I can find the way, with this consolation: that I am not the first kind believing coxcomb; but there are,
gallants, many such good natures amongst ye.

> And though you've better arts to hide your follies,
> 'Adsheartlikins, y'are all as errant cullies.[6]

Exit.

Act III. Scene v.

Scene, the garden in the night.
Enter FLORINDA *in an undress, with a key and a little box.*

FLORINDA   Well, thus far I'm in my way to happiness. I have got myself
free from Callis; my brother too, I find by yonder light, is got into his
cabinet,[7] and thinks not of me; I have by good fortune got the key of
the garden back door. I'll open it to prevent Belvile's knocking: a little
noise will now alarm my brother. Now am I as fearful as a young
thief. [*Unlocks the door.*] Hark! What noise is that? Oh, 'twas the wind
that played amongst the boughs. Belvile stays long, methinks; it's
time. Stay, for fear of a surprise, I'll hide these jewels in yonder jas-
mine.

She goes to lay down the box.

Enter WILLMORE, *drunk.*

WILLMORE   What the devil is become of these fellows Belvile and Frederick? They promised to stay at the next corner for me, but who the
devil knows the corner of a full moon? Now, whereabouts am I? Ha,
what have we here? A garden! A very convenient place to sleep in.
Ha! What has God sent us here? A female! By this light, a woman!
I'm a dog if it be not a very wench!

FLORINDA   He's come! Ha! Who's there?

WILLMORE   Sweet soul, let me salute thy shoestring.

FLORINDA [*aside*]   'Tis not my Belvile. Good heavens, I know him
not!—Who are you, and from whence come you?

WILLMORE   Prithee, prithee, child, not so many hard questions! Let it
suffice I am here, child. Come, come kiss me.

FLORINDA   Good gods! What luck is mine?

WILLMORE   Only good luck, child, parlous[8] good luck. Come
hither. —'Tis a delicate shining wench. By this hand, she's perfumed,
and smells like any nosegay. —Prithee, dear soul, let's not play the
fool and lose time—precious time. For as Gad shall save me, I'm as
honest a fellow as breathes, though I'm a little disguised[9] at present.

6. Dupes.
7. Private room.
8. Exceedingly.
9. Tipsy.

Come, I say. Why, thou mayst be free with me: I'll be very secret. I'll not boast who 'twas obliged me, not I; for hang me if I know thy name.

FLORINDA   Heavens! What a filthy beast is this!

WILLMORE   I am so, and thou ought'st the sooner to lie with me for that reason. For look you, child, there will be no sin in't, because 'twas neither designed nor premeditated: 'tis pure accident on both sides. That's a certain thing now. Indeed, should I make love to you, and you vow fidelity, and swear and lie till you believed and yielded— that were to make it wilful fornication, the crying sin of the nation. Thou art, therefore, as thou art a good Christian, obliged in conscience to deny me nothing. Now, come be kind without any more idle prating.

FLORINDA   Oh, I am ruined! Wicked man, unhand me!

WILLMORE   Wicked? Egad, child, a judge, were he young and vigorous, and saw those eyes of thine, would know 'twas they gave the first blow, the first provocation. Come, prithee let's lose no time, I say. This is a fine convenient place.

FLORINDA   Sir, let me go, I conjure you, or I'll call out.

WILLMORE   Ay, ay, you were best to call witness to see how finely you treat me. Do!

FLORINDA   I'll cry murder, rape, or anything, if you do not instantly let me go!

WILLMORE   A rape! Come, come, you lie, you baggage, you lie. What! I'll warrant you would fain have the world believe now that you are not so forward as I. No, not you. Why at this time of night was your cobweb door set open, dear spider, but to catch flies? Ha! Come, or I shall be damnably angry. Why, what a coil[1] is here!

FLORINDA   Sir, can you think—

WILLMORE   That you would do't for nothing? Oh, oh, I find what you would be at. Look here, here's a pistole for you. Here's a work indeed! Here, take it, I say!

FLORINDA   For heaven's sake, sir, as you're a gentleman—

WILLMORE   So now, now, she would be wheedling me for more! What, you will not take it then? You are resolved you will not? Come, come, take it or I'll put it up again, for look ye, I never give more. Why, how now, mistress, are you so high i'th' mouth a pistole won't down with you? Ha! Why, what a work's here! In good time! Come, no struggling to be gone. But an y'are good at a dumb wrestle, I'm for ye. Look ye, I'm for ye.

She struggles with him.

Enter BELVILE *and* FREDERICK.

BELVILE   The door is open. A pox of this mad fellow! I'm angry that we've lost him; I durst have sworn he had followed us.

1. Difficulty.

FREDERICK   But you were so hasty, colonel, to be gone.

FLORINDA   Help! Help! Murder! Help! Oh, I am ruined!

BELVILE   Ha! Sure that's Florinda's voice! [*Comes up to them.*] A
man! —Villain, let go that lady!

A noise; WILLMORE *turns and draws;* FREDERICK *interposes.*

FLORINDA   Belvile! Heavens! My brother too is coming, and 'twill be
impossible to escape. Belvile, I conjure you to walk under my chamber window, from whence I'll give you some instructions what to do.
This rude man has undone us.

Exit.

WILLMORE   Belvile!

Enter PEDRO, STEPHANO, *and other servants, with lights.*

PEDRO   I'm betrayed! Run, Stephano, and see if Florinda be safe.

Exit STEPHANO.

They fight, and PEDRO'S *party beats 'em out.*

—So, whoe'er they be, all is not well. I'll to Florinda's chamber.

Going out, meets STEPHANO.

STEPHANO   You need not, sir: the poor lady's fast asleep, and thinks no
harm. I would not awake her, sir, for fear of frighting her with your
danger.

PEDRO   I'm glad she's there. —Rascals, how came the garden door
open?

STEPHANO   That question comes too late, sir. Some of my fellow servants masquerading, I'll warrant.

PEDRO   Masquerading! A lewd custom to debauch our youth! There's
something more in this than I imagine.

Exeunt.

Act III. Scene vi.

Scene changes to the street.
Enter BELVILE *in rage,* FREDERICK *holding him,* WILLMORE *melancholy.*

WILLMORE   Why, how the devil should I know Florinda?

BELVILE   Ah, plague of your ignorance! If it had not been Florinda,
must you be a beast? A brute? A senseless swine?

WILLMORE   Well, sir, you see I am endued with patience: I can bear.
Though egad, y'are very free with me, methinks. I was in good hopes
the quarrel would have been on my side, for so uncivilly interrupting
me.

BELVILE   Peace, brute, whilst thou'rt safe. Oh, I'm distracted!

WILLMORE   Nay, nay, I'm an unlucky dog, that's certain.

BELVILE   Ah, curse upon the star that ruled my birth, or whatsoever other influence that makes me still so wretched.

WILLMORE   Thou break'st my heart with these complaints. There is no star in fault, no influence but sack, the cursed sack I drunk.

FREDERICK   Why, how the devil came you so drunk?

WILLMORE   Why, how the devil came you so sober?

BELVILE   A curse upon his thin skull, he was always beforehand that way.

FREDERICK   Prithee, dear colonel, forgive him; he's sorry for his fault.

BELVILE   He's always so after he has done a mischief. A plague on all such brutes!

WILLMORE   By this light, I took her for an errant harlot.

BELVILE   Damn your debauched opinion! Tell me, sot, hadst thou so much sense and light about thee to distinguish her woman, and couldst not see something about her face and person to strike an awful reverence into thy soul?

WILLMORE   Faith no, I considered her as mere a woman as I could wish.

BELVILE   'Sdeath, I have no patience. Draw, or I'll kill you!

WILLMORE   Let that alone till tomorrow, and if I set not all right again, use your pleasure.

BELVILE

Tomorrow! Damn it,
The spiteful light will lead me to no happiness.
Tomorrow is Antonio's, and perhaps
Guides him to my undoing. Oh, that I could meet
This rival, this powerful fortunate!

WILLMORE   What then?

BELVILE   Let thy own reason, or my rage, instruct thee.

WILLMORE   I shall be finely informed then, no doubt. Hear me, colonel, hear me; show me the man and I'll do his business.

BELVILE   I know him no more than thou, or if I did I should not need thy aid.

WILLMORE   This you say is Angellica's house; I promised the kind baggage to lie with her tonight.

Offers to go in.

Enter ANTONIO *and his* PAGE. ANTONIO *knocks on the hilt of's sword.*

ANTONIO   You paid the thousand crowns I directed?

PAGE   To the lady's old woman, sir, I did.

WILLMORE   Who the devil have we here?

BELVILE   I'll now plant myself under Florinda's window, and if I find no comfort there, I'll die.

Exeunt BELVILE *and* FREDERICK.

Enter MORETTA.

MORETTA   Page?
PAGE   Here's my lord.
WILLMORE   How is this? A picaroon going to board my frigate? — Here's
one chase gun[2] for you!

Drawing his sword, justles ANTONIO, *who turns and draws. They
fight;* ANTONIO *falls.*

MORETTA   Oh, bless us! We're all undone!

Runs in and shuts the door.

PAGE   Help! Murder!

BELVILE *returns at the noise of fighting.*

BELVILE   Ha! The mad rogue's engaged in some unlucky adventure
again.

Enter two or three MASQUERADERS.

MASQUERADER   Ha! A man killed!
WILLMORE   How, a man killed? Then I'll go home to sleep.

Puts up and reels out. Exeunt MASQUERADERS *another way.*

BELVILE   Who should it be? Pray heaven the rogue is safe, for all my
quarrel to him.

As BELVILE *is groping about, enter an* OFFICER *and six* SOLDIERS.

SOLDIER   Who's there?
OFFICER   So, here's one dispatched. Secure the murderer.
BELVILE   Do not mistake my charity for murder! I came to his assis-
tance!

Soldiers seize on BELVILE.

OFFICER   That shall be tried, sir. St. Jago! Swords drawn in the Carnival
time!

Goes to ANTONIO.

ANTONIO   Thy hand, prithee.
OFFICER   Ha! Don Antonio! Look well to the villain there. — How is
it, sir?
ANTONIO   I'm hurt.
BELVILE   Has my humanity made me a criminal?
OFFICER   Away with him!
BELVILE   What a curst chance is this!

Exeunt soldiers with BELVILE.

2. Bow gun.

ANTONIO [*aside*]   This is the man that has set upon me twice. —[*To the officer.*] Carry him to my apartment till you have farther orders from me.

Exit ANTONIO, *led.*

The End of the Third Act.

Act IV. Scene i.

A fine room.
Discovers BELVILE *as by dark alone.*

BELVILE   When shall I be weary of railing on fortune, who is resolved never to turn with smiles upon me? Two such defeats in one night none but the devil and that mad rogue could have contrived to have plagued me with. I am here a prisoner. But where, heaven knows. And if there be murder done, I can soon decide the fate of a stranger in a nation without mercy. Yet this is nothing to the torture my soul bows with when I think of losing my fair, my dear Florinda. Hark, my door opens. A light! A man, and seems of quality. Armed, too! Now shall I die like a dog, without defense.

Enter ANTONIO *in a nightgown, with a light; his arm in a scarf, and a sword under his arm. He sets the candle on the table.*

ANTONIO   Sir, I come to know what injuries I have done you, that could provoke you to so mean an action as to attack me basely without allowing time for my defense?

BELVILE   Sir, for a man in my circumstances to plead innocence would look like fear. But view me well, and you will find no marks of coward on me, nor anything that betrays that brutality you accuse me with.

ANTONIO   In vain, sir, you impose upon my sense. You are not only he who drew on me last night, but yesterday before the same house, that of Angellica. Yet there is something in your face and mien that makes me wish I were mistaken.

BELVILE   I own I fought today in the defense of a friend of mine with whom you, if you're the same, and your party were first engaged. Perhaps you think this crime enough to kill me, but if you do, I cannot fear you'll do it basely.

ANTONIO   No sir, I'll make you fit for a defense with this.

Gives him the sword.

BELVILE   This gallantry surprises me, nor know I how to use this present, sir, against a man so brave.

ANTONIO   You shall not need. For know, I come to snatch you from a danger that is decreed against you: perhaps your life, or long imprisonment. And 'twas with so much courage you offended, I cannot see you punished.

BELVILE   How shall I pay this generosity?

ANTONIO   It had been safer to have killed another than have attempted me. To show your danger, sir, I'll let you know my quality: and 'tis the Viceroy's son whom you have wounded.

BELVILE   The Viceroy's son! —[*Aside.*] Death and confusion! Was this plague reserved to complete all the rest? Obliged by him, the man of all the world I would destroy!

ANTONIO   You seem disordered, sir.

BELVILE   Yes, trust me, I am, and 'tis with pain that man receives such bounties who wants the power to pay 'em back again.

ANTONIO   To gallant spirits 'tis indeed uneasy, but you may quickly overpay me, sir.

BELVILE   [*aside*]   Then I am well. Kind heaven, but set us even, that I may fight with him and keep my honor safe. —Oh, I'm impatient, sir, to be discounting the mighty debt I owe you. Command me quickly.

ANTONIO   I have a quarrel with a rival, sir, about the maid we love.

BELVILE   [*aside*]   Death, 'tis Florinda he means! That thought destroys my reason, and I shall kill him.

ANTONIO   My rival, sir, is one has all the virtues man can boast of—

BELVILE   [*aside*]   Death, who should this be?

ANTONIO   He challenged me to meet him on the Molo as soon as day appeared, but last night's quarrel has made my arm unfit to guide a sword.

BELVILE   I apprehend you, sir. You'd have me kill the man that lays a claim to the maid you speak of. I'll do't. I'll fly to do't!

ANTONIO   Sir, do you know her?

BELVILE   No, sir, but 'tis enough she is admired by you.

ANTONIO   Sir, I shall rob you of the glory on't, for you must fight under my name and dress.

BELVILE   That opinion must be strangely obliging that makes you think I can personate the brave Antonio, whom I can but strive to imitate.

ANTONIO   You say too much to my advantage. Come, sir, the day appears that calls you forth. Within, sir, is the habit.

Exit ANTONIO.

BELVILE

Fantastic fortune, thou deceitful light,
That cheats the wearied traveler by night,
Though on a precipice each step you tread,
I am resolved to follow where you lead.

Exit.

Act IV. Scene ii.

The Molo.
Enter FLORINDA *and* CALLIS *in masks, with* STEPHANO.

FLORINDA [*aside*] I'm dying with my fears: Belvile's not coming as I expected under my window makes me believe that all those fears are true. —Canst thou not tell with whom my brother fights?

STEPHANO No, madam, they were both in masquerade. I was by when they challenged one another, and they had decided the quarrel then, but were prevented by some cavaliers; which made 'em put it off till now. But I am sure 'tis about you they fight.

FLORINDA [*aside*] Nay, then, 'tis with Belvile, for what other lover have I that dares fight for me except Antonio, and he is too much in favor with my brother. If it be he, for whom shall I direct my prayers to heaven?

STEPHANO Madam, I must leave you, for if my master see me, I shall be hanged for being your conductor. I escaped narrowly for the excuse I made for you last night i'th' garden.

FLORINDA And I'll reward thee for't. Prithee, no more.

Exit STEPHANO.

Enter DON PEDRO *in his masking habit.*

PEDRO Antonio's late today; the place will fill, and we may be prevented.

Walks about.

FLORINDA [*aside*] Antonio? Sure I heard amiss.

PEDRO
But who will not excuse a happy lover
When soft fair arms confine the yielding neck,
And the kind whisper languishingly breathes
"Must you be gone so soon?"
Sure I had dwelt forever on her bosom—
But stay, he's here.

Enter BELVILE *dressed in Antonio's clothes.*

FLORINDA [*aside*] 'Tis not Belvile; half my fears are vanished.

PEDRO Antonio!

BELVILE [*aside*] This must be he. —You're early, sir; I do not use to be outdone this way.

PEDRO The wretched, sir, are watchful, and 'tis enough you've the advantage of me in Angellica.

BELVILE [*aside*] Angellica! Or I've mistook my man, or else Antonio! Can he forget his interest in Florinda and fight for common prize?

PEDRO Come, sir, you know our terms.

BELVILE [*aside*] By heaven, not I. —No talking; I am ready, sir.

Offers to fight; FLORINDA *runs in.*

FLORINDA [*to* BELVILE] Oh, hold! Whoe'er you be, I do conjure you hold! If you strike here, I die!

PEDRO   Florinda!

BELVILE   Florinda imploring for my rival!

PEDRO   Away; this kindness is unseasonable.

Puts her by; they fight; she runs in just as BELVILE *disarms* PEDRO.

FLORINDA   Who are you, sir, that dares deny my prayers?

BELVILE   Thy prayers destroy him; if thou wouldst preserve him, do that thou'rt unacquainted with, and curse him.

She holds him.

FLORINDA
By all you hold most dear, by her you love,
I do conjure you, touch him not.

BELVILE
By her I love?
See, I obey, and at your feet resign
The useless trophy of my victory.

Lays his sword at her feet.

PEDRO   Antonio, you've done enough to prove you love Florinda.

BELVILE   Love Florinda! Does heaven love adoration, prayer, or penitence? Love her? Here, sir, your sword again.

Snatches up the sword and gives it to him.

Upon this truth I'll fight my life away.

PEDRO   No, you've redeemed my sister, and my friendship.

He gives him FLORINDA, *and pulls off his vizard to show his face, and puts it on again.*

BELVILE   Don Pedro!

PEDRO   Can you resign your claims to other women, and give your heart entirely to Florinda?

BELVILE
Entire, as dying saints' confessions are!
I can delay my happiness no longer:
This minute let me make Florinda mine.

PEDRO   This minute let it be. No time so proper: this night my father will arrive from Rome, and possibly may hinder what we purpose.

FLORINDA   Oh, heavens! This minute?

Enter masqueraders and pass over.

BELVILE   Oh, do not ruin me!

PEDRO   The place begins to fill, and that we may not be observed, do you walk off to St. Peter's church, where I will meet you and conclude your happiness.

BELVILE   I'll meet you there. —[*Aside.*] If there be no more saints' churches in Naples.

FLORINDA

Oh, stay, sir, and recall your hasty doom!
Alas, I have not yet prepared my heart
To entertain so strange a guest.

PEDRO   Away; this silly modesty is assumed too late.

BELVILE   Heaven, madam, what do you do?

FLORINDA

Do? Despise the man that lays a tyrant's claim
To what he ought to conquer by submission.

BELVILE   You do not know me. Move a little this way.

Draws her aside.

FLORINDA

Yes, you may force me even to the altar,
But not the holy man that offers there
Shall force me to be thine.

PEDRO *talks to* CALLIS *this while.*

BELVILE

Oh, do not lose so blest an opportunity!

Pulls off his vizard.

See, 'tis your Belvile, not Antonio,
Whom your mistaken scorn and anger ruins.

FLORINDA

Belvile!
Where was my soul it could not meet thy voice,
And take this knowledge in.

As they are talking, enter WILLMORE, *finely dressed, and* FRED-
ERICK.

WILLMORE   No intelligence? No news of Belvile yet? Well, I am the
most unlucky rascal in nature. Ha! Am I deceived, or is it he? Look,
Fred! 'Tis he, my dear Belvile!

Runs and embraces him; BELVILE'S *vizard falls out on's hand.*

BELVILE   Hell and confusion seize thee!

PEDRO   Ha! Belvile! I beg your pardon, sir.

Takes FLORINDA *from him.*

BELVILE

Nay, touch her not. She's mine by conquest, sir;
I won her by my sword.

WILLMORE   Didst thou so? And egad, child, we'll keep her by the
sword.

Draws on PEDRO; BELVILE *goes between.*

BELVILE

Stand off!

Thou'rt so profanely lewd, so curst by heaven,

All quarrels thou espousest must be fatal.

WILLMORE

Nay, an you be so hot, my valor's coy,

And shall be courted when you want it next.

Puts up his sword.

BELVILE [*to* PEDRO]

You know I ought to claim a victor's right,

But you're the brother to divine Florinda,

To whom I'm such a slave. To purchase her

I durst not hurt the man she holds so dear.

PEDRO

'Twas by Antonio's, not by Belvile's sword

This question should have been decided, sir.

I must confess much to your bravery's due,

Both now and when I met you last in arms;

But I am nicely punctual in my word,

As men of honor ought, and beg your pardon:

For this mistake another time shall clear.

Aside to FLORINDA *as they are going out.*

—This was some plot between you and Belvile,

But I'll prevent you.

[*Exeunt* PEDRO *and* FLORINDA.]

BELVILE *looks after her and begins to walk up and down in rage.*

WILLMORE   Do not be modest now and lose the woman. But if we shall fetch her back so—

BELVILE   Do not speak to me!

WILLMORE   Not speak to you? Egad, I'll speak to you, and will be answered, too.

BELVILE   Will you, sir?

WILLMORE   I know I've done some mischief, but I'm so dull a puppy that I'm the son of a whore if I know how or where. Prithee inform my understanding.

BELVILE   Leave me, I say, and leave me instantly!

WILLMORE   I will not leave you in this humour, nor till I know my crime.

BELVILE   Death, I'll tell you, sir—

Draws and runs at WILLMORE; *he runs out,* BELVILE *after him;* FREDERICK *interposes.*

Enter ANGELLICA, MORETTA, *and* SEBASTIAN.

ANGELLICA   Ha! Sebastian, is that not Willmore? Haste! haste and
bring him back.

[*Exit* SEBASTIAN.]

FREDERICK [*aside*]   The colonel's mad: I never saw him thus before.
I'll after 'em lest he do some mischief, for I am sure Willmore will
not draw on him.

Exit.

ANGELLICA
I am all rage! My first desires defeated!
For one for aught he knows that has no
Other merit than her quality,
Her being Don Pedro's sister. He loves her!
I know 'tis so. Dull, dull, insensible,
He will not see me now, though oft invited,
And broke his word last night. False perjured man!
He that but yesterday fought for my favors,
And would have made his life a sacrifice
To've gained one night with me,
Must now be hired and courted to my arms.
MORETTA   I told you what would come on't, but Moretta's an old dot-
ing fool. Why did you give him five hundred crowns, but to set him-
self out for other lovers? You should have kept him poor if you had
meant to have had any good from him.
ANGELLICA
Oh, name not such mean trifles! Had I given him all
My youth has earned from sin,
I had not lost a thought nor sigh upon't.
But I have given him my eternal rest,
My whole repose, my future joys, my heart!
My virgin heart, Moretta! Oh, 'tis gone!
MORETTA   Curse on him, here he comes. How fine she has made him,
too.

Enter WILLMORE *and* SEBASTIAN; ANGELLICA *turns and walks
away.*

WILLMORE
How now, turned shadow?
Fly when I pursue, and follow when I fly?

Sings.

Stay, gentle shadow of my dove,
    And tell me ere I go,

Whether the substance may not prove
A fleeting thing like you.

As she turns she looks on him.

There's a soft kind look remaining yet.

ANGELLICA   Well, sir, you may be gay: all happiness, all joys pursue you still. Fortune's your slave, and gives you every hour choice of new hearts and beauties, till you are cloyed with the repeated bliss which others vainly languish for. But know, false man, that I shall be revenged. [*Turns away in rage.*]

WILLMORE   So, gad, there are of those faint-hearted lovers, whom such a sharp lesson next their hearts would make as impotent as fourscore. Pox o' this whining; my business is to laugh and love. A pox on't, I hate your sullen lover: a man shall lose as much time to put you in humour now as would serve to gain a new woman.

ANGELLICA
I scorn to cool that fire I cannot raise,
Or do the drudgery of your virtuous mistress.

WILLMORE   A virtuous mistress? Death, what a thing thou hast found out for me! Why, what the devil should I do with a virtuous woman, a sort of ill-natured creatures that take a pride to torment a lover. Virtue is but an infirmity in woman, a disease that renders even the handsome ungrateful; whilst the ill-favored, for want of solicitations and address, only fancy themselves so. I have lain with a woman of quality who has all the while been railing at whores.

ANGELLICA
I will not answer for your mistress's virtue,
Though she be young enough to know no guilt;
And I could wish you would persuade my heart
'Twas the two hundred thousand crowns you courted.

WILLMORE   Two hundred thousand crowns! What story's this? What trick? What woman, ha?

ANGELLICA   How strange you make it. Have you forgot the creature you entertained on the Piazzo last night?

WILLMORE [*aside*]   Ha! My gipsy worth two hundred thousand crowns! Oh, how I long to be with her! Pox, I knew she was of quality.

ANGELLICA
False man! I see my ruin in thy face.
How many vows you breathed upon my bosom
Never to be unjust. Have you forgot so soon?

WILLMORE   Faith, no; I was just coming to repeat 'em. But here's a humour indeed would make a man a saint. —[*Aside.*] Would she would be angry enough to leave me, and command me not to wait on her.

Enter HELLENA *dressed in man's clothes.*

HELLENA   This must be Angellica: I know it by her mumping[3] matron
here. Ay, ay, 'tis she. My mad captain's with her, too, for all his swearing. How this unconstant humour makes me love him! —Pray, good
grave gentlewoman, is not this Angellica?

MORETTA   My too young sir, it is. —[*Aside.*] I hope 'tis one from Don
Antonio.

    Goes to ANGELLICA.

HELLENA [*aside*]   Well, something I'll do to vex him for this.

ANGELLICA   I will not speak with him. Am I in humour to receive a
lover?

WILLMORE   Not speak with him? Why, I'll be gone, and wait your
idler minutes. Can I show less obedience to the thing I love so
fondly?

    Offers to go.

ANGELLICA   A fine excuse this! Stay—

WILLMORE   And hinder your advantage? Should I repay your bounties
so ungratefully?

ANGELLICA [*to* HELLENA]
Come hither, boy. —[*To* WILLMORE.] That I may let you see
How much above the advantages you name
I prize one minute's joy with you.

WILLMORE [*impatient to be gone*]   Oh, you destroy me with this
endearment.—[*Aside.*] Death, how shall I get away?—Madam, 'twill
not be fit I should be seen with you. Besides, it will not be convenient.
And I've a friend—that's dangerously sick.

ANGELLICA   I see you're impatient. Yet you shall stay.

WILLMORE [*aside*]   And miss my assignation with my gipsy.

    Walks about impatiently; MORETTA *brings* HELLENA, *who
addresses herself to* ANGELLICA.

HELLENA
Madam,
You'll hardly pardon my instrusion
When you shall know my business,
And I'm too young to tell my tale with art;
But there must be a wondrous store of goodness
Where so much beauty dwells.

ANGELLICA
A pretty advocate, whoever sent thee.
Prithee proceed.

    To WILLMORE, *who is stealing off.*

        —Nay, sir, you shall not go.

3. Sullen.

WILLMORE [*aside*]   Then I shall lose my dear gipsy forever. Pox on't, she stays me out of spite.

HELLENA

I am related to a lady, madam,
Young, rich, and nobly born, but has the fate
To be in love with a young English gentleman.
Strangely she loves him, at first sight she loved him,
But did adore him when she heard him speak;
For he, she said, had charms in every word
That failed not to surprise, to wound and conquer.

WILLMORE [*aside*]   Ha! Egad, I hope this concerns me.

ANGELLICA [*aside*]

'Tis my false man he means. Would he were gone:
This praise will raise his pride, and ruin me.
     [*To* WILLMORE.]   —Well,
Since you are so impatient to be gone,
I will release you, sir.

WILLMORE [*aside*]   Nay, then I'm sure 'twas me he spoke of: this cannot be the effects of kindness in her. —No, Madam, I've considered better on't, and will not give you cause of jealousy.

ANGELLICA   But sir, I've business that—

WILLMORE   This shall not do; I know 'tis but to try me.

ANGELLICA   Well, to your story, boy. —[*Aside*]. Though 'twill undo me.

HELLENA

With this addition to his other beauties,
He won her unresisting tender heart.
He vowed, and sighed, and swore he loved her dearly;
And she believed the cunning flatterer,
And thought herself the happiest maid alive.
Today was the appointed time by both
To consummate their bliss:
The virgin, altar, and the priest were dressed;
And whilst she languished for th'expected bridegroom,
She heard he paid his broken vows to you.

WILLMORE [*aside*]   So, this is some dear rogue that's in love with me, and this way lets me know it. Or, if it be not me, she means someone whose place I may supply.

ANGELLICA

Now I perceive
The cause of thy impatience to be gone,
And all the business of this glorious dress.

WILLMORE   Damn the young prater; I know not what he means.

HELLENA

Madam,
In your fair eyes I read too much concern
To tell my farther business.

ANGELLICA

Prithee, sweet youth, talk on: thou mayst perhaps
Raise here a storm that may undo my passion,
And then I'll grant thee anything.

HELLENA

Madam, 'tis to entreat you (oh unreasonable)
You would not see this stranger.
For if you do, she vows you are undone;
Though nature never made a man so excellent,
And sure he 'ad been a god, but for inconstancy.

WILLMORE [*aside*]   Ah, rogue, how finely he's instructed! 'Tis plain, some woman that has seen me *en passant*.

ANGELLICA   Oh, I shall burst with jealousy! Do you know the man you speak of?

HELLENA   Yes, madam, he used to be in buff and scarlet.

ANGELLICA [*to* Willmore]   Thou false as hell, what canst thou say to this?

WILLMORE   By heaven—

ANGELLICA   Hold, do not damn thyself—

HELLENA   Nor hope to be believed.

He walks about; they follow.

ANGELLICA

Oh perjured man!
Is't thus you pay my generous passion back?

HELLENA   Why would you, sir, abuse my lady's faith?

ANGELLICA   And use me so unhumanely.

HELLENA   A maid so young, so innocent—

WILLMORE   Ah, young devil!

ANGELLICA   Dost thou not know thy life is in my power?

HELLENA   Or think my lady cannot be revenged?

WILLMORE [*aside*]   So, so, the storm comes finely on.

ANGELLICA

Now thou art silent: guilt has struck thee dumb.
Oh, hadst thou still been so, I'd lived in safety.

She turns away and weeps.

WILLMORE [*aside* to Hellena]   Sweetheart, the lady's name and house—quickly! I'm impatient to be with her.

Looks toward ANGELLICA *to watch her turning, and as she comes towards them he meets her.*

HELLENA [*aside*]   So, now is he for another woman.

WILLMORE   The impudent'st young thing in nature: I cannot persuade him out of his error, madam.

ANGELLICA
  I know he's in the right; yet thou'st a tongue
  That would persuade him to deny his faith.

In rage walks away.

WILLMORE [*said softly to* HELLENA] Her name, her name, dear boy!
HELLENA Have you forgot it, sir?
WILLMORE [*aside*] Oh, I perceive he's not to know I am a stranger to
  his lady. —Yes, yes, I do know, but I have forgot the—[ANGELLICA
  turns.] —By heaven, such early confidence I never saw.
ANGELLICA
  Did I not charge you with this mistress, sir?
  Which you denied, though I beheld your perjury.
  This little generosity of thine has rendered back my heart.

Walks away.

WILLMORE [*to* HELLENA] So, you have made sweet work here, my little
  mischief. Look your lady be kind and good-natured now, or I shall
  have but a cursed bargain on't. [ANGELLICA *turns toward them.*] —
  The rogue's bred up to mischief; art thou so great a fool to credit
  him?
ANGELLICA Yes, I do, and you in vain impose upon me. Come hither,
  boy. Is not this he you spake of?
HELLENA I think it is. I cannot swear, but I vow he has just such
  another lying lover's look.

    HELLENA *looks in his face; he gazes on her.*

WILLMORE [*aside*] Ha! Do I not know that face? By heaven, my little
  gipsy! What a dull dog was I: had I but looked that way I'd known
  her. Are all my hopes of a new woman banished?—Egad, if I do not
  fit thee for this, hang me. —[*To* ANGELLICA.] Madam, I have found
  out the plot.
HELLENA [*aside*] Oh lord, what does he say? Am I discovered now?
WILLMORE Do you see this young spark here?
HELLENA [*aside*] He'll tell her who I am.
WILLMORE Who do you think this is?
HELLENA [*aside*] Ay, ay, he does know me. —Nay, dear captain, I am
  undone if you discover me.
WILLMORE Nay, nay, no cogging[4]; she shall know what a precious mis-
  tress I have.
HELLENA Will you be such a devil?
WILLMORE Nay, nay, I'll teach you to spoil sport you will not make. —
  This small ambassador comes not from a person of quality, as you
  imagine and he says, but from a very errant gipsy: the talking'st, prat-
  ing'st, canting'st little animal thou ever saw'st.

4. Begging.

ANGELLICA   What news you tell me, that's the thing I mean.

HELLENA [*aside*]   Would I were well off the place! If ever I go a-captain-hunting again—

WILLMORE   Mean that thing? That gipsy thing? Thou mayst as well be jealous of thy monkey or parrot as of her. A German motion[5] were worth a dozen of her, and a dream were a better enjoyment—a creature of a constitution fitter for heaven than man.

HELLENA [*aside*]   Though I'm sure he lies, yet this vexes me.

ANGELLICA   You are mistaken: she's a Spanish woman made up of no such dull materials.

WILLMORE   Materials? Egad, an she be made of any that will either dispense or admit of love, I'll be bound to continence.

HELLENA [*aside to him*]   Unreasonable man, do you think so?

WILLMORE   You may return, my little brazen head, and tell your lady, that till she be handsome enough to be beloved, or I dull enough to be religious, there will be small hopes of me.

ANGELLICA   Did you not promise, then, to marry her?

WILLMORE   Not I, by heaven.

ANGELLICA   You cannot undeceive my fears and torments, till you have vowed you will not marry her.

HELLENA [*aside*]   If he swears that, he'll be revenged on me indeed for all my rogueries.

ANGELLICA   I know what arguments you'll bring against me: fortune and honor.

WILLMORE   Honor! I tell you, I hate it in your sex; and those that fancy themselves possessed of that foppery are the most impertinently troublesome of all womankind, and will transgress nine commandments to keep one. And to satisfy your jealousy, I swear—

HELLENA [*aside to him*]   Oh, no swearing, dear captain.

WILLMORE   If it were possible I should ever be inclined to marry, it should be some kind young sinner: one that has generosity enough to give a favor handsomely to one that can ask it discreetly, one that has wit enough to manage an intrigue of love. Oh, how civil such a wench is to a man that does her the honor to marry her.

ANGELLICA   By heaven, there's no faith in anything he says.

   Enter SEBASTIAN.

SEBASTIAN   Madam, Don Antonio—

ANGELLICA   Come hither.

HELLENA [*aside*]   Ha! Antonio! He may be coming hither, and he'll certainly discover me. I'll therefore retire without a ceremony.

                                             Exit HELLENA.

ANGELLICA   I'll see him. Get my coach ready.

SEBASTIAN   It waits you, madam.

---

5. Puppet show.

WILLMORE [*aside*] This is lucky. —What, madam, now I may be gone
and leave you to the enjoyment of my rival?

ANGELLICA
Dull man, that canst not see how ill, how poor,
That false dissimulation looks. Be gone,
And never let me see thy cozening face again,
Lest I relapse and kill thee.

WILLMORE Yes, you can spare me now. Farewell, till you're in better
humour. —[*Aside.*] I'm glad of this release. Now for my gipsy:
For though to worse we change, yet still we find
New joys, new charms, in a new miss that's kind.

Exit WILLMORE.

ANGELLICA
He's gone, and in this ague of my soul
The shivering fit returns.
Oh, with what willing haste he took his leave,
As if the longed-for minute were arrived
Of some blest assignation.
In vain I have consulted all my charms,
In vain this beauty prized, in vain believed
My eyes could kindle any lasting fires;
I had forgot my name, my infamy,
And the reproach that honor lays on those
That dare pretend a sober passion here.
Nice[6] reputation, though it leave behind
More virtues than inhabit where that dwells,
Yet that once gone, those virtues shine no more.
Then since I am not fit to be beloved,
I am resolved to think on a revenge
On him that soothed[7] me thus to my undoing.

Exeunt.

Act IV. Scene iii.

A street.
Enter FLORINDA *and* VALERIA *in habits different from what they
have been seen in.*

FLORINDA We're happily escaped, and yet I tremble still.

VALERIA A lover, and fear? Why, I am but half an one, and yet I have
courage for any attempt. Would Hellena were here: I would fain have
had her as deep in this mischief as we; she'll fare but ill else, I doubt.

FLORINDA She pretended a visit to the Augustine nuns; but I believe

6. Strict.
7. Flattered.

some other design carried her out; pray heaven we light on her. Prithee, what didst do with Callis?

VALERIA When I saw no reason would do good on her, I followed her into the wardrobe, and as she was looking for something in a great chest, I toppled her in by the heels, snatched the key of the apartment where you were confined, locked her in, and left her bawling for help.

FLORINDA 'Tis well you resolve to follow my fortunes, for thou darest never appear at home again after such an action.

VALERIA That's according as the young stranger and I shall agree. But to our business. I delivered your note to Belvile when I got out under pretense of going to mass. I found him at his lodging, and believe me it came seasonably, for never was man in so desperate a condition. I told him of your resolution of making your escape today if your brother would be absent long enough to permit you; if not, to die rather than be Antonio's.

FLORINDA Thou should'st have told him I was confined to my chamber upon my brother's suspicion that the business on the Molo was a plot laid between him and I.

VALERIA I said all this, and told him your brother was now gone to his devotion; and he resolves to visit every church till he find him, and not only undeceive him in that, but caress him so as shall delay his return home.

FLORINDA Oh heavens! He's here, and Belvile with him, too.

They put on their vizards.
Enter DON PEDRO, BELVILE, WILLMORE; BELVILE *and* DON PEDRO *seeming in serious discourse.*

VALERIA Walk boldly by them, and I'll come at a distance, lest he suspect us.

She walks by them and looks back on them.

WILLMORE Ha! A woman, and of excellent mien!

PEDRO She throws a kind look back on you.

WILLMORE Death, 'tis a likely wench, and that kind look shall not be cast away. I'll follow her.

BELVILE Prithee do not.

WILLMORE Do not? By heavens, to the antipodies,[8] with such an invitation.

She goes out, and WILLMORE *follows her.*

BELVILE 'Tis a mad fellow for a wench.

Enter FREDERICK.

8. Opposite places on the earth.

FREDERICK   Oh, colonel, such news!

BELVILE   Prithee what?

FREDERICK   News that will make you laugh in spite of fortune.

BELVILE   What, Blunt has had some damned trick put upon him? Cheated, banged, or clapped?

FREDERICK   Cheated, sir, rarely cheated of all but his shirt and drawers; the unconscionable whore too turned him out before consummation, so that, traversing the streets at midnight, the watch found him in this *fresco* and conducted him home. By heaven, 'tis such a sight, and yet I durst as well been hanged as laughed at him or pity him: he beats all that do but ask him a question, and is in such an humour.

PEDRO   Who is't has met with this ill usage, sir?

BELVILE   A friend of ours whom you must see for mirth's sake. — [*Aside.*] I'll employ him to give Florinda time for an escape.

PEDRO   What is he?

BELVILE   A young countryman of ours, one that has been educated at so plentiful a rate he yet ne'er knew the want of money; and 'twill be a great jest to see how simply he'll look without it. For my part, I'll lend him none: and the rogue know not how to put on a borrowing face and ask first, I'll let him see how good 'tis to play our parts whilst I play his. Prithee, Fred, do you go home and keep him in that posture till we come.

Exeunt.

Enter FLORINDA *from the farther end of the scene, looking behind her.*

FLORINDA   I am followed still. Ha! My brother too advancing this way! Good heavens defend me from being seen by him!

She goes off.

Enter WILLMORE, *and after him* VALERIA, *at a little distance.*

WILLMORE   Ah, there she sails! She looks back as she were willing to be boarded; I'll warrant her prize.

He goes out, VALERIA *following.*

Enter HELLENA, *just as he goes out, with a page.*

HELLENA   Ha, is not that my captain that has a woman in chase? 'Tis not Angellica.—Boy, follow those people at a distance, and bring me an account where they go in.

Exit page.

—I'll find his haunts, and plague him everywhere. Ha! My brother!

BELVILE, WILLMORE, PEDRO *cross the stage;* HELLENA *runs off.*

Act IV. Scene iv.

Scene changes to another street. Enter FLORINDA.

FLORINDA   What shall I do? My brother now pursues me. Will no kind power protect me from his tyranny? Ha! Here's a door open; I'll venture in, since nothing can be worse than to fall into his hands. My life and honor are at stake, and my necessity has no choice.

She goes in.

Enter VALERIA, *and* HELLENA'S PAGE *peeping after* FLORINDA.

PAGE   Here she went in; I shall remember this house.

Exit boy.

VALERIA   This is Belvile's lodging; she's gone in as readily as if she knew it. Ha! Here's that mad fellow again; I dare not venture in. I'll watch my opportunity.

Goes aside.

Enter WILLMORE, *gazing about him.*

WILLMORE   I have lost her hereabouts. Pox on't, she must not 'scape me so.

Goes out.

Act IV. Scene v.

Scene changes to BLUNT'S *chamber, discovers him sitting on a couch in his shirt and drawers, reading.*

BLUNT   So, now my mind's a little at peace, since I have resolved revenge. A pox on this tailor, though, for not bringing home the clothes I bespoke. And a pox of all poor cavaliers: a man can never keep a spare suit for 'em, and I shall have these rogues come in and find me naked, and then I'm undone. But I'm resolved to arm myself: the rascals shall not insult over me too much. [*Puts on an old rusty sword and buff belt.*] Now, how like a morris dancer I am equipped! A fine ladylike whore to cheat me thus without affording me a kindness for my money! A pox light on her, I shall never be reconciled to the sex more; she has made me as faithless as a physician, as uncharitable as a churchman, and as ill-natured as a poet. Oh, how I'll use all womankind hereafter! What would I give to have one of 'em within my reach now! Any mortal thing in petticoats, kind fortune, send me, and I'll forgive thy last night's malice. —Here's a cursed book, too—a warning to all young travelers—that can instruct me how to prevent such mischiefs now 'tis too late. Well, 'tis a rare convenient thing to read a little now and then, as well as hawk and hunt.

Sits down again and reads.
Enter to him FLORINDA.

FLORINDA   This house is haunted, sure: 'tis well furnished, and no living thing inhabits it. Ha! A man! Heavens, how he's attired! Sure 'tis some rope dancer, or fencing master. I tremble now for fear, and yet I must venture now to speak to him. —Sir, if I may not interrupt your meditations—

He starts up and gazes.

BLUNT   Ha, what's here? Are my wishes granted? And is not that a she creature? 'Adsheartlikins, 'tis. —What wretched thing art thou, ha?

FLORINDA   Charitable sir, you've told yourself already what I am: a very wretched maid, forced by a strange unlucky accident to seek a safety here, and must be ruined if you do not grant it.

BLUNT   Ruined! Is there any ruin so inevitable as that which now threatens thee? Dost thou know, miserable woman, into what den of mischiefs thou art fallen; what abyss of confusion, ha? Dost not see something in my looks that frights thy guilty soul, and makes thee wish to change that shape of woman for any humble animal, or devil? For those were safer for thee, and less mischievous.

FLORINDA   Alas, what mean you, sir? I must confess, your looks have something in 'em makes me fear, but I beseech you, as you seem a gentleman, pity a harmless virgin that takes your house for sanctuary.

BLUNT   Talk on, talk on; and weep, too, till my faith return. Do, flatter me out of my senses again. A harmless virgin with a pox; as much one as t'other, 'adsheartlikins. Why, what the devil, can I not be safe in my house for you, not in my chamber? Nay, not even being naked too cannot secure me? This is an impudence greater than has invaded me yet. Come, no resistance.

Pulls her rudely.

FLORINDA   Dare you be so cruel?

BLUNT   Cruel? 'Adsheartlikins, as a galley slave, or a Spanish whore. Cruel? Yes, I will kiss and beat thee all over, kiss and see thee all over; thou shalt lie with me too, not that I care for the enjoyment, but to let thee see I have ta'en deliberated malice to thee, and will be revenged on one whore for the sins of another. I will smile and deceive thee; flatter thee, and beat thee; embrace thee and rob thee, as she did me; fawn on thee, and strip thee stark naked; then hang thee out at my window by the heels, with a paper of scurvy verses fastened to thy breast in praise of damnable women. Come, come, along.

FLORINDA   Alas, sir, must I be sacrificed for the crimes of the most infamous of my sex? I never understood the sins you name.

BLUNT   Do, persuade the fool you love him, or that one of you can be just or honest; tell me I was not an easy coxcomb, or any strange impossible tale: it will be believed sooner than thy false showers or protestations. A generation of damned hypocrites! To flatter my very clothes from my back! Dissembling witches! Are these the returns you make an honest gentleman that trusts, believes, and loves you? But if I be not even with you—Come along, or I shall—

Pulls her again.
Enter FREDERICK.

FREDERICK   Ha, what's here to do?

BLUNT   'Adsheartlikins, Fred, I am glad thou art come, to be a witness of my dire revenge.

FREDERICK   What's this, a person of quality too, who is upon the ramble to supply the defects of some grave impotent husband?

BLUNT   No, this has another pretense: some very unfortunate accident brought her hither, to save a life pursued by I know not who or why, and forced to take sanctuary here at fool's haven. 'Adsheartlikins, to me of all mankind for protection? Is the ass to be cajoled again, think ye? No, young one, no prayers or tears shall mitigate my rage; therefore prepare for both my pleasures of enjoyment and revenge. For I am resolved to make up my loss here on thy body: I'll take it out in kindness and in beating.

FREDERICK   Now, mistress of mine, what do you think of this?

FLORINDA   I think he will not, dares not be so barbarous.

FREDERICK   Have a care, Blunt, she fetched a deep sigh; she is enamoured with thy shirt and drawers. She'll strip thee even of that; there are of her calling such unconscionable baggages and such dexterous thieves, they'll flay a man and he shall ne'er miss his skin till he feels the cold. There was a countryman of ours robbed of a row of teeth whilst he was a-sleeping, which the jilt made him buy again when he waked. You see, lady, how little reason we have to trust you.

BLUNT   'Adsheartlikins, why this is most abominable!

FLORINDA   Some such devils there may be, but by all that's holy, I am none such. I entered here to save a life in danger.

BLUNT   For no goodness, I'll warrant her.

FREDERICK   Faith, damsel, you had e'en confessed the plain truth, for we are fellows not to be caught twice in the same trap. Look on that wreck: a tight vessel when he set out of haven, well trimmed and laden. And see how a female picaroon of this island of rogues has shattered him, and canst thou hope for any mercy?

BLUNT   No, no, gentlewoman, come along; 'adsheartlikins, we must be better acquainted.—We'll both lie with her, and then let me alone to bang her.

FREDERICK   I'm ready to serve you in matters of revenge that has a double pleasure in't.

BLUNT   Well said.—You hear, little one, how you are condemned by public vote to the bed within; there's no resisting your destiny, sweetheart.

Pulls her.

FLORINDA   Stay, sir. I have seen you with Belvile, an English cavalier. For his sake, use me kindly. You know him, sir.

BLUNT   Belvile? Why yes, sweeting, we do know Belvile, and wish he were with us now. He's a cormorant at whore and bacon: he'd have a limb or two of thee, my virgin pullet. But 'tis no matter; we'll leave him the bones to pick.

FLORINDA   Sir, if you have any esteem for that Belvile, I conjure you to treat me with more gentleness; he'll thank you for the justice.

FREDERICK   Hark'ee, Blunt, I doubt we are mistaken in this matter.

FLORINDA   Sir, if you find me not worth Belvile's care, use me as you please. And that you may think I merit better treatment than you threaten, pray take this present.

Gives him a ring; he looks on it.

BLUNT   Hum, a diamond! Why, 'tis a wonderful virtue now that lies in this ring, a mollifying virtue. 'Adsheartlikins, there's more persuasive rhetoric in't than all her sex can utter.

FREDERICK   I begin to suspect something, and 'twould anger us vilely to be trussed up for a rape upon a maid of quality, when we only believe we ruffle a harlot.

BLUNT   Thou art a credulous fellow, but 'adsheartlikins, I have no faith yet. Why, my saint prattled as parlously as this does; she gave me a bracelet, too, a devil on her! But I sent my man to sell it today for necessaries, and it proved as counterfeit as her vows of love.

FREDERICK   However, let it reprieve her till we see Belvile.

BLUNT   That's hard, yet I will grant it.

Enter a SERVANT.

SERVANT   Oh, sir, the colonel is just come in with his new friend and a Spaniard of quality, and talks of having you to dinner with 'em.

BLUNT   'Adsheartlikins, I'm undone! I would not see 'em for the world. Hark'ee, Fred, lock up the wench in your chamber.

FREDERICK   Fear nothing, madam: whate'er he threatens, you are safe whilst in my hands.

Exeunt FREDERICK *and* FLORINDA.

BLUNT   And sirrah, upon your life, say I am not at home, or that I'm asleep, or—or—anything. Away; I'll prevent their coming this way.

Locks the door, and exeunt.

The End of the Fourth Act.

Act V. Scene i.

BLUNT'S *chamber.*

After a great knocking as at his chamber door, enter BLUNT *softly crossing the stage, in his shirt and drawers as before.*

VOICES (CALL WITHIN)   Ned! Ned Blunt! Ned Blunt!

BLUNT   The rogues are up in arms. 'Adsheartlikins, this villainous Frederick has betrayed me: they have heard of my blessed fortune.

VOICES [*and knocking within*]   Ned Blunt! Ned! Ned!

BELVILE [*within*]   Why, he's dead, sir, without dispute dead; he has not been seen today. Let's break open the door. Here, boy—

BLUNT   Ha, break open the door? 'Adsheartlikins, that mad fellow will be as good as his word.

BELVILE [*within*]   Boy, bring something to force the door.

A great noise within, at the door again.

BLUNT   So, now must I speak in my own defense; I'll try what rhetoric will do.—Hold, hold! What do you mean, gentlemen, what do you mean?

BELVILE [*within*]   Oh, rogue, art alive? Prithee open the door and convince us.

BLUNT   Yes, I am alive, gentlemen, but at present a little busy.

BELVILE [*within*]   How, Blunt grown a man of business? Come, come, open and let's see this miracle.

BLUNT   No, no, no, no, gentlemen, 'tis no great business. But—I am—at—my devotion. 'Adsheartlikins, will you not allow a man time to pray?

BELVILE [*within*]   Turned religious? A greater wonder than the first! Therefore open quickly, or we shall unhinge, we shall.

BLUNT [*aside*]   This won't do.—Why hark'ee, colonel, to tell you the truth, I am about a necessary affair of life: I have a wench with me. You apprehend me?—The devil's in't if they be so uncivil as to disturb me now.

WILLMORE [*within*]   How, a wench? Nay then, we must enter and partake. No resistance. Unless it be your lady of quality, and then we'll keep our distance.

BLUNT   So, the business is out.

WILLMORE [*within*]   Come, come, lend's more hands to the door. Now heave, all together. [*Breaks open the door.*] So, well done, my boys.

Enter BELVILE [*and his* PAGE], WILLMORE, FREDERICK, *and* PEDRO. BLUNT *looks simply,*[9] *they all laugh at him; he lays his hand on his sword, and comes up to* WILLMORE.

9. Foolishly.

BLUNT   Hark'ee, sir, laugh out your laugh quickly, d'ye hear, and be
gone. I shall spoil your sport else, 'adsheartlikins, sir, I shall. The jest
has been carried on too long.—[*Aside.*] A plague upon my tailor!

WILLMORE   'Sdeath, how the whore has dressed him! Faith, sir, I'm
sorry.

BLUNT   Are you so, sir? Keep't to yourself then, sir, I advise you, d'ye
hear, for I can as little endure your pity as his mirth.

Lays his hand on's sword.

BELVILE   Indeed, Willmore, thou wert a little too rough with Ned
Blunt's mistress. Call a person of quality whore, and one so young, so
handsome, and so eloquent? Ha, ha, he.

BLUNT   Hark'ee, sir, you know me, and know I can be angry. Have a
care, for 'adsheartlikins, I can fight, too, I can, sir. Do you mark me?
No more.

BELVILE   Why so peevish, good Ned? Some disappointments, I'll warrant. What, did the jealous count, her husband, return just in the
nick?

BLUNT   Or the devil, sir. [*They laugh.*] D'ye laugh? Look ye settle me
a good sober countenance, and that quickly, too, or you shall know
Ned Blunt is not—

BELVILE   Not everybody, we know that.

BLUNT   Not an ass to be laughed at, sir.

WILLMORE   Unconscionable sinner! To bring a lover so near his happiness—a vigorous passionate lover—and then not only cheat him of
his movables, but his very desires, too.

BELVILE   Ah, sir, a mistress is a trifle with Blunt; he'll have a dozen the
next time he looks abroad. His eyes have charms not to be resisted;
there needs no more than to expose that taking person to the view of
the fair, and he leads 'em all in triumph.

PEDRO   Sir, though I'm a stranger to you, I am ashamed at the rudeness
of my nation; and could you learn who did it, would assist you to
make an example of 'em.

BLUNT   Why ay, there's one speaks sense now, and handsomely. And
let me tell you, gentlemen, I should not have showed myself like a
jack pudding[1] thus to have made you mirth, but that I have revenge
within my power. For know, I have got into my possession a female,
who had better have fallen under any curse than the ruin I design
her. 'Adsheartlikins, she assaulted me here in my own lodgings, and
had doubtless committed a rape upon me, had not this sword
defended me.

FREDERICK   I know not that, but o' my conscience thou had ravished
her, had she not redeemed herself with a ring. Let's see't, Blunt.

Blunt shows the ring.

1. Buffoon.

BELVILE [*aside*]   Ha! The ring I gave Florinda when we exchanged our
vows! —Hark'ee, Blunt—

   Goes to whisper to him.

WILLMORE   No whispering, good colonel, there's a woman in the case.
No whispering.

BELVILE [*aside to* BLUNT]   Hark'ee, fool, be advised, and conceal both
the ring and the story for your reputation's sake. Do not let people
know what despised cullies we English are; to be cheated and abused
by one whore, and another rather bribe thee than be kind to thee, is
an infamy to our nation.

WILLMORE   Come, come, where's the wench? We'll see her; let her be
what she will, we'll see her.

PEDRO   Ay, ay, let us see her. I can soon discover whether she be of
quality, or for your diversion.

BLUNT   She's in Fred's custody.

WILLMORE   Come, come, the key—

   To FREDERICK, *who gives him the key; they are going.*

BELVILE [*aside*]   Death, what shall I do?—Stay, gentlemen. —[*Aside.*]
Yet if I hinder 'em, I shall discover all. —Hold, let's go one at once.
Give me the key.

WILLMORE   Nay, hold there, colonel, I'll go first.

FREDERICK   Nay, no dispute, Ned and I have the propriety of her.

WILLMORE   Damn propriety! Then we'll draw cuts. [BELVILE *goes to
whisper* WILLMORE.] Nay, no corruption, good colonel. Come, the
longest sword carries her.

   They all draw, forgetting DON PEDRO, *being a Spaniard, had the
longest.*

BLUNT   I yield up my interest to you, gentlemen, and that will be
revenge sufficient.

WILLMORE [*to* PEDRO]   The wench is yours. —[*Aside.*] Pox of his
Toledo,[2] I had forgot that.

FREDERICK   Come, sir, I'll conduct you to the lady.

                              Exeunt FREDERICK *and* PEDRO.

BELVILE [*aside*]   To hinder him will certainly discover her. —Dost
know, dull beast, what mischief thou hast done?

                    WILLMORE *walking up and down, out of humour.*

WILLMORE   Ay, ay, to trust our fortune to lots! A devil on't, 'twas madness, that's the truth on't.

BELVILE   Oh, intolerable sot—

———————
2. Fine Spanish blades were made at Toledo.

Enter FLORINDA *running, masked,* PEDRO *after her;* WILLMORE *gazing round her.*

FLORINDA [*aside*]   Good heaven defend me from discovery!

PEDRO   'Tis but in vain to fly me; you're fallen to my lot.

BELVILE [*aside*]   Sure she's undiscovered yet, but now I fear there is no way to bring her off.

WILLMORE [*aside*]   Why, what a pox, is not this my woman, the same I followed but now?

PEDRO talking to FLORINDA, *who walks up and down.*

PEDRO   As if I did not know ye, and your business here.

FLORINDA [*aside*]   Good heaven, I fear he does indeed!

PEDRO   Come, pray be kind; I know you meant to be so when you entered here, for these are proper gentlemen.

WILLMORE   But sir, perhaps the lady will not be imposed upon: she'll choose her man.

PEDRO   I am better bred than not to leave her choice free.

Enter VALERIA, *and is surprised at sight of* DON PEDRO.

VALERIA [*aside*]   Don Pedro here! There's no avoiding him.

FLORINDA [*aside*]   Valeria! Then I'm undone.

VALERIA [*to* PEDRO, *running to him*]   Oh, I have found you, sir! The strangest accident—if I had breath—to tell it.

PEDRO   Speak! Is Florinda safe? Hellena well?

VALERIA   Ay, ay, sir. Florinda is safe. —[*Aside.*] From any fears of you.

PEDRO   Why, where's Florinda? Speak!

VALERIA   Ay, where indeed, sir; I wish I could inform you. But to hold you no longer in doubt—

FLORINDA [*aside*]   Oh, what will she say?

VALERIA   She's fled away in the habit—of one of her pages, sir. But Callis thinks you may retrieve her yet, if you make haste away. She'll tell you, sir, the rest. —[*Aside.*] If you can find her out.

PEDRO   Dishonorable girl, she has undone my aim. —[*To* BELVILE.] Sir, you see my necessity of leaving you, and I hope you'll pardon it. My sister, I know, will make her flight to you; and if she do, I shall expect she should be rendered back.

BELVILE   I shall consult my love and honor, sir.

Exit PEDRO.

FLORINDA [*to* VALERIA]   My dear preserver, let me embrace thee.

WILLMORE   What the devil's all this?

BLUNT   Mystery, by this light.

VALERIA   Come, come, make haste and get yourselves married quickly, for your brother will return again.

BELVILE   I'm so surprised with fears and joys, so amazed to find you here in safety, I can scarce persuade my heart into a faith of what I see.

WILLMORE   Hark'ee, colonel, is this that mistress who has cost you so many sighs, and me so many quarrels with you?

BELVILE   It is. — [*To* FLORINDA.] Pray give him the honor of your hand.

WILLMORE   Thus it must be received, then. [*Kneels and kisses her hand.*] And with it give your pardon, too.

FLORINDA   The friend to Belvile may command me anything.

WILLMORE   [*aside*]   Death, would I might; 'tis a surprising beauty.

BELVILE   Boy, run and fetch a father instantly.

Exit BOY.

FREDERICK   So, now do I stand like a dog, and have not a syllable to plead my own cause with. By this hand, madam, I was never thoroughly confounded before, nor shall I ever more dare look up with confidence, till you are pleased to pardon me.

FLORINDA   Sir, I'll be reconciled to you on one condition: that you'll follow the example of your friend in marrying a maid that does not hate you, and whose fortune, I believe, will not be unwelcome to you.

FREDERICK   Madam, had I no inclinations that way, I should obey your kind commands.

BELVILE   Who, Fred marry? He has so few inclinations for womankind that had he been possessed of paradise he might have continued there to this day, if no crime but love could have disinherited him.

FREDERICK   Oh, I do not use to boast of my intrigues.

BELVILE   Boast! Why, thou dost nothing but boast. And I dare swear, wert thou as innocent from the sin of the grape as thou art from the apple, thou might'st yet claim that right in Eden which our first parents lost by too much loving.

FREDERICK   I wish this lady would think me so modest a man.

VALERIA   She would be sorry then, and not like you half so well. And I should be loath to break my word with you, which was, that if your friend and mine agreed, it should be a match between you and I.

She gives him her hand.

FREDERICK   Bear witness, colonel, 'tis a bargain.

Kisses her hand.

BLUNT   [*to* FLORINDA]   I have a pardon to beg, too; but 'adsheartlikins, I am so out of countenance that I'm a dog if I can say anything to purpose.

FLORINDA   Sir, I heartily forgive you all.

BLUNT   That's nobly said, sweet lady.—Belvile, prithee present her her ring again, for I find I have not courage to approach her myself.

Gives him the ring; he gives it to FLORINDA.

Enter BOY.

BOY   Sir, I have brought the father that you sent for.

[Exit BOY.]

BELVILE   'Tis well. And now, my dear Florinda, let's fly to complete
that mighty joy we have so long wished and sighed for.—Come, Fred,
you'll follow?

FREDERICK   Your example, sir, 'twas ever my ambition in war, and must
be so in love.

WILLMORE   And must not I see this juggling³ knot tied?

BELVILE   No, thou shalt do us better service and be our guard, lest Don
Pedro's sudden return interrupt the ceremony.

WILLMORE   Content; I'll secure this pass.

Exeunt BELVILE, FLORINDA, FREDERICK, *and* VALERIA.

Enter BOY.

BOY [*to* WILLMORE]   Sir, there's a lady without would speak to you.

WILLMORE   Conduct her in; I dare not quit my post.

BOY [*to* BLUNT]   And sir, your tailor waits you in your chamber.

BLUNT   Some comfort yet: I shall not dance naked at the wedding.

Exeunt BLUNT *and* BOY.

Enter again the BOY, *conducting in* ANGELLICA *in a masking
habit and a vizard.* WILLMORE *runs to her.*

WILLMORE [*aside*]   This can be none but my pretty gipsy.—Oh, I see
you can follow as well as fly. Come, confess thyself the most malicious
devil in nature; you think you have done my business with
Angellica—

ANGELLICA   Stand off, base villain!

She draws a pistol and holds it to his breast.

WILLMORE   Ha, 'tis not she! Who art thou, and what's thy business?

ANGELLICA   One thou hast injured, and who comes to kill thee for't.

WILLMORE   What the devil canst thou mean?

ANGELLICA   By all my hopes to kill thee—

*Holds still the pistol to his breast; he going back, she following
still.*

WILLMORE   Prithee, on what acquaintance? For I know thee not.

ANGELLICA   Behold this face so lost to thy remembrance,

Pulls off her vizard.

And then call all thy sins about thy soul,
And let 'em die with thee.

3. Deception.

WILLMORE   Angellica!

ANGELLICA   Yes, traitor! Does not thy guilty blood run shivering
through thy veins? Hast thou no horror at this sight, that tells thee
thou hast not long to boast thy shameful conquest?

WILLMORE   Faith, no, child. My blood keeps its old ebbs and flows still,
and that usual heat too, that could oblige thee with a kindness, had I
but opportunity.

ANGELLICA   Devil! Dost wanton with my pain? Have at thy heart!

WILLMORE   Hold, dear virago![4] Hold thy hand a little; I am not now at
leisure to be killed. Hold and hear me. —[*Aside.*] Death, I think she's
in earnest.

ANGELLICA [*aside, turning from him*]   Oh, if I take not heed, my coward heart will leave me to his mercy. —What have you, sir, to say? —
But should I hear thee, thoud'st talk away all that is brave about me,
and I have vowed thy death by all that's sacred.

Follows him with the pistol to his breast.

WILLMORE   Why then, there's an end of a proper handsome fellow,
that might 'a lived to have done good service yet. That's all I can say
to't.

ANGELLICA [*pausingly*]   Yet—I would give thee time for—penitence.

WILLMORE   Faith, child, I thank God I have ever took care to lead a
good, sober, hopeful life, and am of a religion that teaches me to
believe I shall depart in peace.

ANGELLICA
So will the devil! Tell me,
How many poor believing fools thou hast undone?
How many hearts thou hast betrayed to ruin?
Yet these are little mischiefs to the ills
Thou'st taught mine to commit: thou'st taught it love.

WILLMORE   Egad, 'twas shrewdly hurt the while.

ANGELLICA
Love, that has robbed it of its unconcern,
Of all that pride that taught me how to value it.
And in its room
A mean submissive passion was conveyed,
That made me humbly bow, which I ne'er did
To anything but heaven.
Thou, perjured man, didst this; and with thy oaths,
Which on thy knees thou didst devoutly make,
Softened my yielding heart, and then I was a slave.
Yet still had been content to've worn my chains,
Worn 'em with vanity and joy forever,

4. Intimidating woman.

Hadst thou not broke those vows that put them on.
'Twas then I was undone.

All this while follows him with the pistol to his breast.

WILLMORE   Broke my vows? Why, where hast thou lived? Amongst the
gods? For I never heard of mortal man that has not broke a thousand
vows.

ANGELLICA   Oh, impudence!

WILLMORE   Angellica, that beauty has been too long tempting, not to
have made a thousand lovers languish; who, in the amorous fever, no
doubt have sworn like me. Did they all die in that faith, still adoring?
I do not think they did.

ANGELLICA   No, faithless man; had I repaid their vows, as I did thine, I
would have killed the ingrateful that had abandoned me.

WILLMORE   This old general has quite spoiled thee: nothing makes a
woman so vain as being flattered. Your old lover ever supplies the
defects of age with intolerable dotage, vast charge, and that which
you call constancy; and attributing all this to your own merits, you
domineer, and throw your favors in's teeth, upbraiding him still with
the defects of age, and cuckold him as often as he deceives your
expectations. But the gay, young, brisk lover, that brings his equal
fires, and can give you dart for dart, he'll be as nice as you sometimes.

ANGELLICA

All this thou'st made me know, for which I hate thee.
Had I remained in innocent security,
I should have thought all men were born my slaves,
And worn my power like lightning in my eyes,
To have destroyed at pleasure when offended.
But when love held the mirror, the undeceiving glass
Reflected all the weakness of my soul, and made me know
My richest treasure being lost, my honor,
All the remaining spoil could not be worth
The conqueror's care or value.
Oh, how I fell, like a long-worshiped idol,
Discovering all the cheat.
Would not the incense and rich sacrifice
Which blind devotion offered at my altars
Have fallen to thee?
Why wouldst thou then destroy my fancied power?

WILLMORE

By heaven, thou'rt brave, and I admire thee strangely.
I wish I were that dull, that constant thing
Which thou wouldst have, and nature never meant me.
I must, like cheerful birds, sing in all groves,
And perch on every bough,
Billing the next kind she that flies to meet me;

Yet, after all, could build my nest with thee,
Thither repairing when I'd loved my round,
And still reserve a tributary flame.
To gain your credit, I'll pay you back your charity,
And be obliged for nothing but for love.

Offers her a purse of gold.

ANGELLICA
  Oh, that thou wert in earnest!
  So mean a thought of me
  Would turn my rage to scorn, and I should pity thee,
  And give thee leave to live;
  Which for the public safety of our sex,
  And my own private injuries, I dare not do.
  Prepare—   [*Follows still, as before.*]
  I will no more be tempted with replies.
WILLMORE   Sure—
ANGELLICA   Another word will damn thee! I've heard thee talk too
  long.

> *She follows him with the pistol ready to shoot; he retires, still
> amazed. Enter* DON ANTONIO, *his arm in a scarf, and lays hold on
> the pistol.*

ANTONIO   Ha! Angellica!
ANGELLICA   Antonio! What devil brought thee hither?
ANTONIO   Love and curiosity, seeing your coach at door. Let me disarm
  you of this unbecoming instrument of death. [*Takes away the pistol.*]
  Amongst the number of your slaves was there not one worthy the
  honor to have fought your quarrel? —[*To* WILLMORE.] Who are you,
  sir, that are so very wretched to merit death from her?
WILLMORE   One, sir, that could have made a better end of an amorous
  quarrel without you, than with you.
ANTONIO   Sure 'tis some rival. Ha! The very man took down her picture
  yesterday; the very same that set on me last night! Blessed opportunity—

Offers to shoot him.

ANGELLICA   Hold, you're mistaken, sir.
ANTONIO   By heavens, the very same! —Sir, what pretensions have you
  to this lady?
WILLMORE   Sir, I do not use to be examined, and am ill at all disputes
  but this—

Draws; ANTONIO *offers to shoot.*

ANGELLICA [*To* WILLMORE]
  Oh, hold! You see he's armed with certain death.

—And you, Antonio, I command you hold,
By all the passion you've so lately vowed me.

Enter DON PEDRO, *sees* ANTONIO, *and stays.*

PEDRO [*aside*]   Ha! Antonio! And Angellica!
ANTONIO
    When I refuse obedience to your will,
    May you destroy me with your mortal hate.
    By all that's holy, I adore you so,
    That even my rival, who has charms enough
    To make him fall a victim to my jealousy,
    Shall live; nay, and have leave to love on still.
PEDRO [*aside*]   What's this I hear?
ANGELLICA [*pointing to* WILLMORE]
    Ah thus, 'twas thus he talked, and I believed.
    Antonio, yesterday
    I'd not have sold my interest in his heart
    For all the sword has won and lost in battle.
    —But now, to show my utmost of contempt,
    I give thee life; which, if thou wouldst preserve,
    Live where my eyes may never see thee more.
    Live to undo someone whose soul may prove
    So bravely constant to revenge my love.

Goes out. ANTONIO *follows, but* PEDRO *pulls him back.*

PEDRO   Antonio, stay.
ANTONIO   Don Pedro!
PEDRO   What coward fear was that prevented thee from meeting me
    this morning on the Molo?
ANTONIO   Meet thee?
PEDRO   Yes, me; I was the man that dared thee to't.
ANTONIO   Hast thou so often seen me fight in war, to find no better
    cause to excuse my absence? I sent my sword and one to do thee
    right, finding myself uncapable to use a sword.
PEDRO   But 'twas Florinda's quarrel that we fought, and you, to show
    how little you esteemed her, sent me your rival, giving him your inter-
    est. But I have found the cause of this affront, and when I meet you
    fit for the dispute, I'll tell you my resentment.
ANTONIO   I shall be ready, sir, ere long, to do you reason.

Exit ANTONIO.

PEDRO   If I could find Florinda, now whilst my anger's high, I think I
    should be kind, and give her to Belvile in revenge.
WILLMORE   Faith, sir, I know not what you would do, but I believe the
    priest within has been so kind.
PEDRO   How? My sister married?

WILLMORE   I hope by this time he is, and bedded too, or he has not my longings about him.

PEDRO   Dares he do this? Does he not fear my power?

WILLMORE   Faith, not at all; if you will go in and thank him for the favor he has done your sister, so; if not, sir, my power's greater in this house than yours: I have a damned surly crew here that will keep you till the next tide, and then clap you on board for prize. My ship lies but a league off the Molo, and we shall show your donship a damned Tramontana rover's[5] trick.

Enter BELVILE.

BELVILE   This rogue's in some new mischief. Ha! Pedro returned!

PEDRO   Colonel Belvile, I hear you have married my sister.

BELVILE   You have heard truth then, sir.

PEDRO   Have I so? Then, sir, I wish you joy.

BELVILE   How?

PEDRO   By this embrace I do, and I am glad on't.

BELVILE   Are you in earnest?

PEDRO   By our long friendship and my obligations to thee, I am; the sudden change I'll give you reasons for anon. Come, lead me to my sister, that she may know I now approve her choice.

Exit BELVILE *with* PEDRO.

WILLMORE *goes to follow them. Enter* HELLENA, *as before in boy's clothes, and pulls him back.*

WILLMORE   Ha! My gipsy! Now a thousand blessings on thee for this kindness. Egad, child, I was e'en in despair of ever seeing thee again; my friends are all provided for within, each man his kind woman.

HELLENA   Ha! I thought they had served me some such trick!

WILLMORE   And I was e'en resolved to go aboard, and condemn myself to my lone cabin, and the thoughts of thee.

HELLENA   And could you have left me behind? Would you have been so ill natured?

WILLMORE   Why, 'twould have broke my heart, child. But since we are met again, I defy foul weather to part us.

HELLENA   And would you be a faithful friend now, if a maid should trust you?

WILLMORE   For a friend I cannot promise: thou art of a form so excellent, a face and humour too good for cold dull friendship. I am parlously afraid of being in love, child; and you have not forgotten how severely you have used me?

HELLENA   That's all one; such usage you must still look for: to find out all your haunts, to rail at you to all that love you, till I have made

5. Pirate from north of the Alps.

you love only me in your own defense, because nobody else will love you.

WILLMORE   But hast thou no better quality to recommend thyself by?

HELLENA   Faith, none, captain. Why, 'twill be the greater charity to take me for thy mistress. I am a lone child, a kind of orphan lover; and why I should die a maid, and in a captain's hands too, I do not understand.

WILLMORE   Egad, I was never clawed away with broadsides from any female before. Thou hast one virtue I adore—good nature. I hate a coy demure mistress, she's as troublesome as a colt; I'll break none. No, give me a mad mistress when mewed,[6] and in flying, one I dare trust upon the wing, that whilst she's kind will come to the lure.

HELLENA   Nay, as kind as you will, good captain, whilst it lasts. But let's lose no time.

WILLMORE   My time's as precious to me as thine can be. Therefore, dear creature, since we are so well agreed, let's retire to my chamber; and if ever thou wert treated with such savory love! Come, my bed's prepared for such a guest all clean and sweet as thy fair self. I love to steal a dish and a bottle with a friend, and hate long graces. Come, let's retire and fall to.

HELLENA   'Tis but getting my consent, and the business is soon done. Let but old gaffer[7] Hymen and his priest say amen to't, and I dare lay my mother's daughter by as proper a fellow as your father's son, without fear or blushing.

WILLMORE   Hold, hold, no bug words, child. Priest and Hymen? Prithee add a hangman to 'em to make up the consort. No, no, we'll have no vows but love, child, nor witness but the lover: the kind deity enjoins naught but love and enjoy. Hymen and priest wait still upon portion and jointure; love and beauty have their own ceremonies. Marriage is as certain a bane to love as lending money is to friendship. I'll neither ask nor give a vow, though I could be content to turn gipsy and become a left-handed bridegroom to have the pleasure of working that great miracle of making a maid a mother, if you durst venture. 'Tis upse[8] gipsy that, and if I miss I'll lose my labor.

HELLENA   And if you do not lose, what shall I get? A cradle full of noise and mischief, with a pack of repentance at my back? Can you teach me to weave incle[9] to pass my time with? 'Tis upse gipsy that, too.

WILLMORE   I can teach thee to weave a true love's knot better.

HELLENA   So can my dog.

WILLMORE   Well, I see we are both upon our guards, and I see there's no way to conquer good nature but by yielding. Here, give me thy hand: one kiss, and I am thine.

---

6. Caged.
7. Master or old fellow. Hymen, the god of marriage, was often thought to be young.
8. In the manner of.
9. Linen braid.

HELLENA   One kiss! How like my page he speaks! I am resolved you
   shall have none, for asking such a sneaking sum. He that will be
   satisfied with one kiss will never die of that longing. Good friend
   single-kiss, is all your talking come to this? A kiss, a caudle![1] Farewell,
   captain single-kiss.

   Going out; he stays her.

WILLMORE   Nay, if we part so, let me die like a bird upon a bough, at
   the sheriff's charge. By heaven, both the Indies shall not buy thee
   from me. I adore thy humour and will marry thee, and we are so of
   one humour it must be a bargain. Give me thy hand. [*Kisses her
   hand.*] And now let the blind ones, love and fortune, do their worst.

HELLENA   Why, god-a-mercy, captain!

WILLMORE   But hark'ee: the bargain is now made, but is it not fit we
   should know each other's names, that when we have reason to curse
   one another hereafter, and people ask me who 'tis I give to the devil,
   I may at least be able to tell what family you came of?

HELLENA   Good reason, captain; and where I have cause, as I doubt
   not but I shall have plentiful, that I may know at whom to throw
   my—blessings, I beseech ye your name.

WILLMORE   I am called Robert the Constant.

HELLENA   A very fine name! Pray was it your faulkner[2] or butler that
   christened you? Do they not use to whistle when they call you?

WILLMORE   I hope you have a better, that a man may name without
   crossing himself—you are so merry with mine.

HELLENA   I am called Hellena the Inconstant.

   Enter PEDRO, BELVILE, FLORINDA, FREDERICK, VALERIA.

PEDRO   Ha! Hellena!

FLORINDA   Hellena!

HELLENA   The very same. Ha! My brother! Now, captain, show your
   love and courage; stand to your arms and defend me bravely, or I am
   lost forever.

PEDRO   What's this I hear? False girl, how came you hither, and what's
   your business? Speak!

   Goes roughly to her.

WILLMORE   Hold off, sir; you have leave to parley only.

   Puts himself between.

HELLENA   I had e'en as good tell it, as you guess it. Faith, brother, my
   business is the same with all living creatures of my age: to love and
   be beloved—and here's the man.

PEDRO   Perfidious maid, hast thou deceived me too; deceived thyself
   and heaven?

1. Warm drink for the sick.
2. Hawk-keeper.

HELLENA   'Tis time enough to make my peace with that. Be you but kind, let me alone with heaven.

PEDRO   Belvile, I did not expect this false play from you. Was't not enough you'd gain Florinda, which I pardoned, but your lewd friends too must be enriched with the spoils of a noble family?

BELVILE   Faith, sir, I am as much surprised at this as you can be. Yet, sir, my friends are gentlemen, and ought to be esteemed for their misfortunes, since they have the glory to suffer with the best of men and kings. 'Tis true, he's a rover of fortune, yet a prince aboard his little wooden world.

PEDRO   What's this to the maintenance of a woman of her birth and quality?

WILLMORE   Faith, sir, I can boast of nothing but a sword which does me right where'er I come, and has defended a worse cause than a woman's; and since I loved her before I either knew her birth or name, I must pursue my resolution and marry her.

PEDRO   And is all your holy intent of becoming a nun debauched into a desire of man?

HELLENA   Why, I have considered the matter, brother, and find the three hundred thousand crowns my uncle left me, and you cannot keep from me, will be better laid out in love than in religion, and turn to as good an account. Let most voices carry it: for heaven or the captain?

ALL CRY   A captain! A captain!

HELLENA   Look ye, sir, 'tis a clear case.

PEDRO   Oh, I am mad! —[*Aside.*] If I refuse, my life's in danger. — Come, there's one motive induces me. Take her; I shall now be free from fears of her honor. Guard it you now, if you can; I have been a slave to't long enough.

> *Gives her to him.*

WILLMORE   Faith, sir, I am of a nation that are of opinion a woman's honor is not worth guarding when she has a mind to part with it.

HELLENA   Well said, captain.

PEDRO [*to* VALERIA]   This was your plot, mistress, but I hope you have married one that will revenge my quarrel to you.

VALERIA   There's no altering destiny, sir.

PEDRO   Sooner than a woman's will; therefore I forgive you all, and wish you may get my father's pardon as easily, which I fear.

> *Enter* BLUNT *dressed in a Spanish habit, looking very ridiculously; his* MAN *adjusting his band.*

MAN   'Tis very well, sir.

BLUNT   Well, sir! 'Adsheartlikins, I tell you 'tis damnable ill, sir. A Spanish habit! Good Lord! Could the devil and my tailor devise no other punishment for me but the mode of a nation I abominate?

BELVILE   What's the matter, Ned?

BLUNT   Pray view me round, and judge.

> *Turns round.*

BELVILE   I must confess thou art a kind of an odd figure.

BLUNT   In a Spanish habit with a vengeance! I had rather be in the Inquisition for Judaism than in this doublet and breeches; a pillory were an easy collar to this, three handfuls high; and these shoes, too, are worse than the stocks, with the sole an inch shorter than my foot. In fine, gentlemen, methinks I look like a bag of bays[3] stuffed full of fool's flesh.

BELVILE   Methinks 'tis well, and makes thee look e'en cavalier. Come, sir, settle your face and salute our friends. Lady—

BLUNT   [*to* HELLENA]   Ha! Sayst thou so, my little rover? Lady, if you be one, give me leave to kiss your hand, and tell you, 'adsheartlikins, for all I look so, I am your humble servant. A pox of my Spanish habit!

> *Music is heard to play.*

WILLMORE   Hark! What's this?

> *Enter* BOY.

BOY   Sir, as the custom is, the gay people in masquerade, who make every man's house their own, are coming up.

> *Enter several men and women in masking habits, with music; they put themselves in order and dance.*

BLUNT   'Adsheartlikins, would 'twere lawful to pull off their false faces, that I might see if my doxy[4] were not amongst 'em.

BELVILE   [*to the maskers*]   Ladies and gentlemen, since you are come so *a propos*, you must take a small collation with us.

WILLMORE   [*to* HELLENA]   Whilst we'll to the good man within, who stays to give us a cast[5] of his office. Have you no trembling at the near approach?

HELLENA   No more than you have in an engagement or a tempest.

WILLMORE   Egad, thou'rt a brave girl, and I admire thy love and courage.

> Lead on; no other dangers they can dread,
> Who venture in the storms o'th' marriage bed.

> *Exeunt.*

THE END

---

3. Bag of spices used in cooking.
4. Whore.
5. Sample.

Epilogue

The banished cavaliers! A roving blade!
A popish carnival! A masquerade!
The devil's in't if this will please the nation
In these our blessed times of reformation,
When conventickling[6] is so much in fashion.
And yet—
That mutinous tribe less factions do beget,
Than your continual differing in wit.
Your judgment's, as your passion's, a disease:
Nor muse nor miss your appetite can please;
You're grown as nice as queasy consciences,
Whose each convulsion, when the spirit moves,
Damns everything that maggot[7] disapproves.
    With canting rule you would the stage refine,
And to dull method all our sense confine.
With th'insolence of commonwealths you rule,
Where each gay fop and politic grave fool
On monarch wit impose, without control.
As for the last, who seldom sees a play,
Unless it be the old Blackfriars way;
Shaking his empty noddle o'er bamboo,[8]
He cries, "Good faith, these plays will never do!
Ah, sir, in my young days, what lofty wit,
What high-strained scenes of fighting there were writ.
These are slight airy toys. But tell me, pray,
What has the House of Commons done today?"
Then shows his politics, to let you see
Of state affairs he'll judge as notably
As he can do of wit and poetry.
The younger sparks, who hither do resort,
Cry,
"Pox o' your genteel things! Give us more sport!
Damn me, I'm sure 'twill never please the court."
    Such fops are never pleased, unless the play
Be stuffed with fools as brisk and dull as they.
Such might the half-crown spare, and in a glass
At home behold a more accomplished ass.
Where they may set their cravats, wigs, and faces,
And practice all their buffoonry grimaces:
See how this huff becomes, this damny,[9] stare,
Which they at home may act because they dare,

6. Pun on conventicle—a gathering of religious dissenters.
7. I.e., the spirit of dissent.
8. Over a cane.
9. "Damn me!"

But must with prudent caution do elsewhere.
Oh that our Nokes, or Tony Lee,[1] could show
A fop but half so much to th' life as you.

Postscript

This play had been sooner in print, but for a report about the town
(made by some either very malicious or very ignorant) that 'twas *Thomaso*[2] altered; which made the booksellers fear some trouble from the
proprietor of that admirable play, which indeed has wit enough to stock
a poet, and is not to be pieced or mended by any but the excellent
author himself. That I have stolen some hints from it, may be a proof
that I valued it more than to pretend to alter it, had I the dexterity of
some poets, who are not more expert in stealing than in the art of concealing, and who even that way outdo the Spartan boys. I might have
appropriated all to myself; but I, vainly proud of my judgment, hang out
the sign of Angellica (the only stolen object) to give notice where a great
part of the wit dwelt; though if the *Play of the Novella*[3] were as well
worth remembering as *Thomaso*, they might (bating the name) have as
well said I took it from thence. I will only say the plot and business (not
to boast on't) is my own; as for the words and characters, I leave the
reader to judge and compare 'em with *Thomaso*, to whom I recommend
the great entertainment of reading it. Though had this succeeded ill, I
should have had no need of imploring that justice from the critics, who
are naturally so kind to any that pretend to usurp their dominion, especially of our sex:[4] they would doubtless have given me the whole honor
on't. Therefore I will only say in English what the famous Virgil does
in Latin: I make verses, and others have the fame.[5]

FINIS

---

1. James Nokes and Anthony Lee (Leigh), well-known comic actors. Neither was in the original
   production of *The Rover*. Leigh played Old Bellair in *The Man of Mode* with the Dorset
   Garden company.
2. Play of 1654 by Thomas Killigrew, of which *The Rover* is a substantial rewriting.
3. Play of 1632 by Richard Brome, from which *The Rover* borrows a little.
4. "Especially of our sex" was omitted in the first issue and appears in some copies of the second
   issue.
5. Virgil's claim after having a distich of his own claimed by a hack writer.

The Way of the World, National Theatre at the old Vic, 1969. Haxel Hughes as Lady Wishfort and Suzanne Vasey as Peg. By permission of Zoe Dominick.

The Way of the World, National Theatre at the old Vic, 1969. Jane Wenham as Mrs. Marwood and Geraldine McEwan as Milliamant. By permission of Zoe Dominick.

WILLIAM CONGREVE

The Way of the World

Audire est operae pretium, procedere recte
Qui maechis non vultis—
—Metuat doti deprensa.—[1]

To the Right Honorable
Ralph, Earl of Montague, G.

My Lord,

Whether the world will arraign me of vanity or not, that I have presumed to dedicate this comedy to your Lordship, I am yet in doubt, though it may be it is some degree of vanity even to doubt of it. One who has at any time had the honor of your Lordship's conversation, cannot be supposed to think very meanly of that which he would prefer to your perusal; yet it were to incur the imputation of too much sufficiency, to pretend to such a merit as might abide that test of your Lordship's censure.

Whatever value may be wanting to this play while yet it is mine, will be sufficiently made up to it when it is once become your Lordship's; and it is my security that I cannot have overrated it more by my dedication than your Lordship will dignify it by your patronage.

That it succeeded on the stage was almost beyond my expectation; for but little of it was prepared for that general taste which seems now to be predominant in the palates of our audience.

Those characters which are meant to be ridiculous in most of our comedies are of fools so gross that, in my humble opinion, they should rather disturb than divert the well-natured and reflecting part of an audience; they are rather objects of charity than contempt; and instead of moving our mirth, they ought very often to excite our compassion.

This reflection moved me to design some characters which should appear ridiculous, not so much through a natural folly (which is incorri-

† First performed in 1700, at the Lincoln's Inn Fields Theatre, and published in the same year.
1. Horace, *Satires*, II.i.37–38 and 131: "You who wish trouble to the affairs of adulterers, it is worth your while to hear how they fare badly on every side.—Seized in the act, she fears for her dowry."

gible, and therefore not proper for the stage) as through an affected wit; a wit, which, at the same time that it is affected, is also false. As there is some difficulty in the formation of a character of this nature, so there is some hazard which attends the progress of its success upon the stage; for many come to a play so overcharged with criticism that they very often let fly their censure, when through their rashness they have mistaken their aim. This I had occasion lately to observe; for this play had been acted two or three days before some of these hasty judges could find the leisure to distinguish betwixt the character of a Witwoud and a Truewit.[2]

I must beg your Lordship's pardon for this digression from the true course of this epistle; but that it may not seem altogether impertinent, I beg that I may plead the occasion of it, in part of that excuse of which I stand in need, for recommending this comedy to your protection. It is only by the countenance of your Lordship, and the *few* so qualified, that such who write with care and pains can hope to be distinguished; for the prostituted name of *poet* promiscuously levels all that bear it.

Terence, the most correct writer in the world, had a Scipio and a Laelius,[3] if not to assist him, at least to support him in his reputation; and notwithstanding his extraordinary merit, it may be their countenance was not more than necessary.

The purity of his style, the delicacy of his turns, and the justness of his characters were all of them beauties which the greater part of his audience were incapable of tasting; some of the coarsest strokes of Plautus, so severely censured by Horace, were more likely to affect the multitude, such who come with expectation to laugh out the last act of a play, and are better entertained with two or three unseasonable jests than with the artful solution of the *fable*.

As Terence excelled in his performances, so had he great advantages to encourage his undertakings, for he built most on the foundations of Menander;[4] his plots were generally modeled, and his characters ready drawn to his hand. He copied Menander, and Menander had no less light in the formation of his characters from the observations of Theophrastus,[5] of whom he was a disciple; and Theophrastus, it is known, was not only the disciple, but the immediate successor of Aristotle, the first and greatest judge of poetry. These were great models to design by; and the further advantage which Terence possessed, towards giving his plays the due ornaments of purity of style and justness of manners, was not less considerable from the freedom of conversation which was permitted him with Laelius and Scipio, two of the greatest and most polite men of his age. And indeed the privilege of such a

2. Witwoud, a pretender to wit, appears in this play. Truewit, a possessor of wit, appears in Ben Jonson's *Epicoene*.
3. Patrons of the Roman comic dramatist Terence.
4. Greek comic dramatist.
5. Greek author, known for "character writing."

conversation is the only certain means of attaining to the perfection of dialogue.

If it has happened in any part of this comedy that I have gained a turn of style or expression more correct, or at least more corrigible, than in those which I have formerly written, I must, with equal pride and gratitude, ascribe it to the honor of your Lordship's admitting me into your conversation, and that of a society where everybody else was so well worthy of you, in your retirement last summer from the town; for it was immediately after that this comedy was written. If I have failed in my performance, it is only to be regretted, where there were so many not inferior either to a Scipio or a Laelius, that there should be one wanting equal to the capacity of a Terence.

If I am not mistaken, poetry is almost the only art which has not yet laid claim to your Lordship's patronage. Architecture and painting, to the great honor of our country, have flourished under your influence and protection. In the meantime, poetry, the eldest sister of all arts, and parent of most, seems to have resigned her birthright, by having neglected to pay her duty to your Lordship, and by permitting others of a later extraction to prepossess that place in your esteem to which none can pretend a better title. Poetry, in its nature, is sacred to the good and great; the relation between them is reciprocal, and they are ever propitious to it. It is the privilege of poetry to address to them, and it is their prerogative alone to give it protection.

This received maxim is a general apology for all writers who consecrate their labors to great men; but I could wish at this time that this address were exempted from the common pretense of all dedications; and that, as I can distinguish your Lordship even among the most deserving, so this offering might become remarkable by some particular instance of respect, which should assure your Lordship that I am, with all due sense of your extreme worthiness and humanity,

My Lord,

Your Lordship's most obedient

and most obliged humble servant

WILL. CONGREVE

Prologue

Spoken by Mr. Betterton[6]

Of those few fools, who with ill stars are cursed,
Sure scribbling fools, called poets, fare the worst;
For they're a sort of fools which Fortune makes,
And after she has made 'em fools, forsakes.
With Nature's oafs 'tis quite a different case.
For Fortune favors all her idiot race;

6. Who played Fainall.

In her own nest the cuckoo eggs we find,
O'er which she brooks to hatch the changeling kind.[7]
No portion for her own she has to spare,
So much she dotes on her adopted care.

Poets are bubbles,[8] by the town drawn in,
Suffered at first some trifling stakes to win;
But what unequal hazards do they run!
Each time they write they venture all they've won;
The squire that's buttered still is sure to be undone.
This author, heretofore, has found your favor,
But pleads no merit from his past behavior.
To build on that might prove a vain presumption,
Should grants to poets made admit resumption;
And in Parnassus[9] he must lose his seat
If that be found a forfeited estate.

He owns, with toil he wrote the following scenes,
But if they're naught ne'er spare him for his pains.
Damn him the more; have no commiseration
For dullness on mature deliberation.
He swears he'll not resent one hissed-off scene,
Nor, like those peevish wits, his play maintain,
Who, to assert their sense, your taste arraign.
Some plot we think he has, and some new thought,
Some humour too, no farce—but that's a fault.
Satire, he thinks, you ought not to expect;
For so reformed a town who dares correct?[1]
To please this time has been his sole pretense;
He'll not instruct, lest it should give offense.
Should he by chance a knave or fool expose
That hurts none here; sure here are none of those.
In short, our play shall (with your leave to show it)
Give you one instance of a passive poet,
Who to your judgments yields all resignation;
So save or damn, after your own discretion.

Dramatis Personae

MEN

FAINALL, in love with MRS. MARWOOD	*Mr. Betterton*
MIRABELL, in love with MRS. MILLAMANT	*Mr. Verbruggen*
WITWOUD, Followers of MRS. MILLAMANT }	{ *Mr. Bowen*
PETULANT,	{ *Mr. Bowman*

7. The cuckoo was known to lay eggs in the nests of other birds. *Changeling* means (1) *an idiot*, and (2) *a child substituted for another.*
8. Dupes.
9. Greek mountain, sacred to Apollo and the Muses.
1. A reference to moralistic efforts to reform manners; more particularly to Jeremy Collier's attack on the licentiousness of the stage—see p. 491.

SIR WILFULL WITWOUD, Half-brother to ⎤
  WITWOUD, and Nephew to LADY WISHFORT ⎦   *Mr. Underhill*

WAITWELL, Servant to MIRABELL   *Mr. Bright*

WOMEN

LADY WISHFORT, Enemy to MIRABELL, for ⎤
  having falsely pretended love to her ⎦   *Mrs. Leigh*

MRS. MILLAMANT, A fine Lady, Niece to ⎤
  LADY WISHFORT, and loves MIRABELL ⎦   *Mrs. Bracegirdle*

MRS. MARWOOD, Friend to MR. FAINALL, and ⎤
  likes MIRABELL   ⎦   *Mrs. Barry*

MRS. FAINALL, Daughter to LADY WISHFORT, ⎤
  and Wife to FAINALL, formerly Friend to ⎦   *Mrs. Bowman*
  MIRABELL

FOIBLE, Woman to LADY WISHFORT   *Mrs. Willis*

MINCING, Woman to MRS. MILLAMANT   *Mrs. Prince*

        Dancers, Footmen, and Attendants

SCENE — LONDON

The time equal to that of the presentation.

The Way of the World

Act I. A Chocolate-house.

MIRABELL *and* FAINALL, *rising from cards*; BETTY *waiting.*

MIRABELL   You are a fortunate man, Mr. Fainall.

FAINALL   Have we done?

MIRABELL   What you please. I'll play on to entertain you.

FAINALL   No, I'll give you your revenge another time, when you are not so indifferent; you are thinking of something else now, and play too negligently. The coldness of a losing gamester lessens the pleasure of the winner. I'd no more play with a man that slighted his ill fortune than I'd make love to a woman who undervalued the loss of her reputation.

MIRABELL   You have a taste extremely delicate and are for refining on your pleasures.

FAINALL   Prithee, why so reserved? Something has put you out of humour.

MIRABELL   Not at all; I happen to be grave today, and you are gay; that's all.

FAINALL   Confess, Millamant and you quarreled last night, after I left you; my fair cousin has some humours that would tempt the patience of a stoic. What, some coxcomb came in, and was well received by her, while you were by.

MIRABELL   Witwoud and Petulant, and what was worse, her aunt, your wife's mother, my evil genius; or to sum up all in her own name, my old Lady Wishfort came in.

FAINALL   Oh, there it is then! She has a lasting passion for you, and with reason. What, then my wife was there?

MIRABELL   Yes, and Mrs. Marwood and three or four more, whom I never saw before. Seeing me, they all put on their grave faces, whispered one another; then complained aloud of the vapors,[2] and after fell into a profound silence.

FAINALL   They had a mind to be rid of you.

MIRABELL   For which reason I resolved not to stir. At last the good old lady broke through her painful taciturnity, with an invective against long visits. I would not have understood her, but Millamant joining in the argument, I rose and with a constrained smile told her, I thought nothing was so easy as to know when a visit began to be troublesome. She reddened and I withdrew, without expecting her reply.

FAINALL   You were to blame to resent what she spoke only in compliance with her aunt.

MIRABELL   She is more mistress of herself than to be under the necessity of such a resignation.

FAINALL   What? though half her fortune depends upon her marrying with my lady's approbation?

MIRABELL   I was then in such a humour, that I should have been better pleased if she had been less discreet.

FAINALL   Now I remember, I wonder not they were weary of you. Last night was one of their cabal-nights; they have 'em three times a week, and meet by turns, at one another's apartments, where they come together like the coroner's inquest, to sit upon the murdered reputations of the week. You and I are excluded; and it was once proposed that all the male sex should be excepted; but somebody moved that, to avoid scandal, there might be one man of the community; upon which motion Witwoud and Petulant were enrolled members.

MIRABELL   And who may have been the foundress of this sect? My Lady Wishfort, I warrant, who publishes her detestation of mankind, and full of the vigor of fifty-five, declares for a friend and ratafia;[3] and let posterity shift for itself, she'll breed no more.

FAINALL   The discovery of your sham addresses to her, to conceal your love to her niece, has provoked this separation. Had you dissembled better, things might have continued in the state of nature.

MIRABELL   I did as much as a man could, with any reasonable conscience. I proceeded to the very last act of flattery with her, and was guilty of a song in her commendation. Nay, I got a friend to put her into a lampoon, and compliment her with the imputation of an affair with a young fellow, which I carried so far, that I told her the malicious town took notice that she was grown fat of a sudden; and when

2. Depression.
3. A liqueur, fruit flavored.

she lay in of a dropsy, persuaded her she was reported to be in labor. The devil's in't, if an old woman is to be flattered further, unless a man should endeavor downright personally to debauch her; and that my virtue forbade me. But for the discovery of that amour, I am indebted to your friend, or your wife's friend, Mrs. Marwood.

FAINALL   What should provoke her to be your enemy, unless she has made you advances, which you have slighted? Women do not easily forgive omissions of that nature.

MIRABELL   She was always civil to me, till of late. I confess I am not one of those coxcombs who are apt to interpret a woman's good manners to her prejudice, and think that she who does not refuse 'em everything can refuse 'em nothing.

FAINALL   You are a gallant man, Mirabell; and though you may have cruelty enough not to satisfy a lady's longing, you have too much generosity not to be tender of her honor. Yet you speak with an indifference which seems to be affected, and confesses you are conscious of a negligence.

MIRABELL   You pursue the argument with a distrust that seems to be unaffected, and confesses you are conscious of a concern for which the lady is more indebted to you than your wife.

FAINALL   Fie, fie, friend! If you grow censorious, I must leave you. I'll look upon the gamesters in the next room.

MIRABELL   Who are they?

FAINALL   Petulant and Witwoud. [*To* BETTY.] Bring me some chocolate.

Exit.

MIRABELL   Betty, what says your clock?

BETTY   Turned of the last canonical hour, sir.[4]

MIRABELL   How pertinently the jade answers me! [*Looking on his watch.*] Ha? almost one o'clock! Oh, y'are come!

Enter a SERVANT.

Well, is the grand affair over? You have been something tedious.

SERVANT   Sir, there's such coupling at Pancras,[5] that they stand behind one another, as 'twere in a country dance. Ours was the last couple to lead up; and no hopes appearing of dispatch, besides the parson growing hoarse, we were afraid his lungs would have failed before it came to our turn; so we drove round to Duke's Place, and there they were riveted in a trice.

MIRABELL   So, so, you are sure they are married.

SERVANT   Married and bedded, sir; I am witness.

MIRABELL   Have you the certificate?

SERVANT   Here it is, sir.

4. Noon, the last hour when marriages could be legally performed.
5. At St. Pancras Church (and at St. James's Church in Duke's Place, mentioned later in this speech) weddings were quick and a license was not always required.

MIRABELL   Has the tailor brought Waitwell's clothes home, and the new liveries?

SERVANT   Yes, sir.

MIRABELL   That's well. Do you go home again, d'ye hear, and adjourn the consummation till farther order; bid Waitwell shake his ears, and Dame Partlet[6] rustle up her feathers, and meet me at one o'clock by Rosamond's Pond,[7] that I may see her before she returns to her lady; and as you tender your ears, be secret.

Exit SERVANT.

Re-enter FAINALL *and* BETTY.

FAINALL   Joy of your success, Mirabell; you look pleased.

MIRABELL   Aye, I have been engaged in a matter of some sort of mirth, which is not yet ripe for discovery. I am glad this is not a cabal-night. I wonder, Fainall, that you who are married, and of consequence should be discreet, will suffer your wife to be of such a party.

FAINALL   Faith, I am not jealous. Besides, most who are engaged are women and relations; and for the men, they are of a kind too contemptible to give scandal.

MIRABELL   I am of another opinion. The greater the coxcomb, always the more scandal; for a woman who is not a fool can have but one reason for associating with a man that is.

FAINALL   Are you jealous as often as you see Witwoud entertained by Millamant?

MIRABELL   Of her understanding I am, if not of her person.

FAINALL   You do her wrong; for, to give her her due, she has wit.

MIRABELL   She has beauty enough to make any man think so, and complaisance enough not to contradict him who shall tell her so.

FAINALL   For a passionate lover, methinks you are a man somewhat too discerning in the failings of your mistress.

MIRABELL   And for a discerning man, somewhat too passionate a lover; for I like her with all her faults; nay, like her for her faults. Her follies are so natural, or so artful, that they become her; and those affectations which in another woman would be odious, serve but to make her more agreeable. I'll tell thee, Fainall, she once used me with that insolence, that in revenge I took her to pieces; sifted her and separated her failings; I studied 'em, and got 'em by rote. The catalogue was so large that I was not without hopes one day or other to hate her heartily: to which end I so used myself to think of 'em that at length, contrary to my design and expectation, they gave me every hour less and less disturbance; till in a few days it became habitual to me to remember 'em without being displeased. They are now grown as familiar to me as my own frailties; and in all probability, in a little time longer I shall like 'em as well.

6. Pertelote, a hen (and wife of Chauntecleer in Chaucer's *Nun's Priest's Tale*).
7. A pond in St. James's Park.

FAINALL   Marry her, marry her! Be half as well acquainted with her charms as you are with her defects, and my life on't, you are your own man again.

MIRABELL   Say you so?

FAINALL   Aye, aye, I have experience: I have a wife, and so forth.

Enter MESSENGER.

MESSENGER   Is one Squire Witwoud here?

BETTY   Yes; what's your business?

MESSENGER   I have a letter for him, from his brother Sir Wilfull, which I am charged to deliver into his own hands.

BETTY   He's in the next room, friend; that way.

Exit MESSENGER.

MIRABELL   What, is the chief of that noble family in town, Sir Wilfull Witwoud?

FAINALL   He is expected today. Do you know him?

MIRABELL   I have seen him. He promises to be an extraordinary person; I think you have the honor to be related to him.

FAINALL   Yes, he is half brother to this Witwoud by a former wife, who was sister to my Lady Wishfort, my wife's mother. If you marry Millamant, you must call cousins too.

MIRABELL   I had rather be his relation than his acquaintance.

FAINALL   He comes to town in order to equip himself for travel.

MIRABELL   For travel! Why the man I mean is above forty.

FAINALL   No matter for that; 'tis for the honor of England that all Europe should know we have blockheads of all ages.

MIRABELL   I wonder there is not an act of parliament to save the credit of the nation, and prohibit the exportation of fools.

FAINALL   By no means; 'tis better as 'tis. 'Tis better to trade with a little loss, than to be quite eaten up with being overstocked.

MIRABELL   Pray, are the follies of this knight-errant and those of the squire his brother anything related?

FAINALL   Not at all; Witwoud grows by the knight, like a medlar grafted on a crab.[8] Once will melt in your mouth, and t'other set your teeth on edge; one is all pulp, and the other all core.

MIRABELL   So one will be rotten before he be ripe, and the other will be rotten without ever being ripe at all.

FAINALL   Sir Wilfull is an odd mixture of bashfulness and obstinancy. But when he's drunk, he's as loving as the monster in *The Tempest*,[9] and much after the same manner. To give t'other his due, he has something of good nature and does not always want wit.

MIRABELL   Not always; but as often as his memory fails him, and his commonplace of comparisons.[1] He is a fool with a good memory and

8. A pulpy, overripe fruit grafted on a crabapple.
9. Caliban, in Dryden and D'Avenant's adaptation of Shakespeare's *The Tempest*.
1. Commonplace book, for copying witty remarks.

some few scraps of other folks' wit. He is one whose conversation can never be approved, yet it is now and then to be endured. He has indeed one good quality, he is not exceptious,[2] for he so passionately affects the reputation of understanding raillery, that he will construe an affront into a jest, and call downright rudeness and ill language satire and fire.

FAINALL   If you have a mind to finish his picture, you have an opportunity to do it at full length. Behold the original!

Enter WITWOUD.

WITWOUD   Afford me your compassion, my dears! Pity me, Fainall! Mirabell, pity me!

MIRABELL   I do from my soul.

FAINALL   Why, what's the matter?

WITWOUD   No letters for me, Betty?

BETTY   Did not the messenger bring you one but now, sir?

WITWOUD   Aye, but no other?

BETTY   No, sir.

WITWOUD   That's hard, that's very hard. A messenger, a mule, a beast of burden! He has brought me a letter from the fool my brother, as heavy as a panegyric in a funeral sermon, or a copy of commendatory verses from one poet to another. And what's worse, 'tis as sure a forerunner of the author as an epistle dedicatory.

MIRABELL   A fool, and your brother, Witwoud!

WITWOUD   Aye, aye, my half brother. My half brother he is, no nearer upon honor.

MIRABELL   Then 'tis possible he may be but half a fool.

WITWOUD   Good, good, Mirabell, *le drôle*![3] Good, good; hang him, don't let's talk of him. Fainall, how does your lady? Gad, I say anything in the world to get this fellow out of my head. I beg pardon that I should ask a man of pleasure, and the town, a question at once so foreign and domestic. But I talk like an old maid at a marriage, I don't know what I say; but she's the best woman in the world.

FAINALL   'Tis well you don't know what you say, or else your commendation would go near to make me either vain or jealous.

WITWOUD   No man in town lives well with a wife but Fainall. Your judgment, Mirabell.

MIRABELL   You had better step and ask his wife, if you would be credibly informed.

WITWOUD   Mirabell.

MIRABELL   Aye.

WITWOUD   My dear, I ask ten thousand pardons. Gad, I have forgot what I was going to say to you!

MIRABELL   I thank you heartily, heartily.

WITWOUD   No, but prithee excuse me: my memory is such a memory.

2. Quarrelsome.
3. The amusing fellow.

MIRABELL   Have a care of such apologies, Witwoud; for I never knew a fool but he affected to complain, either of the spleen or his memory.

FAINALL   What have you done with Petulant?

WITWOUD   He's reckoning his money, my money it was. I have no luck today.

FAINALL   You may allow him to win of you at play, for you are sure to be too hard for him at repartee; since you monopolize the wit that is between you, the fortune must be his of course.

MIRABELL   I don't find that Petulant confesses the superiority of wit to be your talent, Witwoud.

WITWOUD   Come, come, you are malicious now, and would breed debates. Petulant's my friend, and a very honest fellow, and a very pretty fellow, and has a smattering—faith and troth, a pretty deal of an odd sort of a small wit: nay, I'll do him justice. I'm his friend, I won't wrong him neither. And if he had but any judgment in the world, he would not be altogether contemptible. Come, come, don't detract from the merits of my friend.

FAINALL   You don't take your friend to be over-nicely bred?

WITWOUD   No, no, hang him, the rogue has no manners at all, that I must own. No more breeding than a bum-baily,[4] that I grant you. 'Tis pity, faith; the fellow has fire and life.

MIRABELL   What, courage?

WITWOUD   Hum, faith, I don't know as to that, I can't say as to that. Yes, faith, in a controversy he'll contradict anybody.

MIRABELL   Though 'twere a man whom he feared, or a woman whom he loved.

WITWOUD   Well, well, he does not always think before he speaks; we have all our failings. You're too hard upon him, you are, faith. Let me excuse him. I can defend most of his faults, except one or two. One he has, that's the truth on't; if he were my brother, I could not acquit him. That, indeed, I could wish were otherwise.

MIRABELL   Aye, marry, what's that, Witwoud?

WITWOUD   Oh, pardon me! Expose the infirmities of my friend! No, my dear, excuse me there.

FAINALL   What, I warrant he's unsincere, or 'tis some such trifle.

WITWOUD   No, no, what if he be? 'Tis no matter for that, his wit will excuse that. A wit should no more be sincere than a woman constant; one argues a decay of parts, as t'other of beauty.

MIRABELL   Maybe you think him too positive?

WITWOUD   No, no, his being positive is an incentive to argument, and keeps up conversation.

FAINALL   Too illiterate?

WITWOUD   That! that's his happiness; his want of learning gives him the more opportunities to show his natural parts.

MIRABELL   He wants words?

---

4. Low-ranking bailiff.

WITWOUD Aye, but I like him for that now; for his want of words gives me the pleasure very often to explain his meaning.

FAINALL He's impudent?

WITWOUD No, that's not it.

MIRABELL Vain?

WITWOUD No.

MIRABELL What! he speaks unseasonable truths sometimes, because he has not wit enough to invent an evasion?

WITWOUD Truths! ha! ha! ha! No, no, since you will have it, I mean he never speaks truth at all, that's all. He will lie like a chambermaid, or a woman of quality's porter. Now that is a fault.

Enter COACHMAN.

COACHMAN Is Master Petulant here, mistress?

BETTY Yes.

COACHMAN Three gentlewomen in the coach would speak with him.

FAINALL Oh brave Petulant! Three!

BETTY I'll tell him.

COACHMAN You must bring two dishes of chocolate and a glass of cinnamon-water.

Exeunt BETTY *and* COACHMAN.

WITWOUD That should be for two fasting strumpets, and a bawd troubled with wind. Now you may know what the three are.

MIRABELL You are very free with your friend's acquaintance.

WITWOUD Aye, aye, friendship without freedom is as dull as love without enjoyment, or wine without toasting; but to tell you a secret, these are trulls that he allows coach-hire, and something more by the week, to call on him once a day at public places.

MIRABELL How!

WITWOUD You shall see he won't go to 'em because there's no more company here to take notice of him. Why, this is nothing to what he used to do: before he found out this way, I have known him call for himself.

FAINALL Call for himself? What dost thou mean?

WITWOUD Mean! Why, he would slip you out of this chocolate-house, just when you had been talking to him. As soon as your back was turned, whip, he was gone! Then trip to his lodging, clap on a hood and scarf, and mask, slap into a hackney-coach, and drive hither to the door again in a trice, where he would send in for himself; that I mean, call for himself, wait for himself; nay, and what's more, not finding himself, sometimes leave a letter for himself.

MIRABELL I confess this is something extraordinary. I believe he waits for himself now, he is so long a-coming. Oh! I ask his pardon.

Enter PETULANT *and* BETTY.

BETTY   Sir, the coach stays.

PETULANT   Well, well; I come. 'Sbud, a man had as good be a professed midwife as a professed whoremaster, at this rate! To be knocked up and raised at all hours, and in all places! Pox on 'em, I won't come! D'ye hear, tell 'em I won't come. Let 'em snivel and cry their hearts out.

FAINALL   You are very cruel, Petulant.

PETULANT   All's one, let it pass. I have a humour to be cruel.

MIRABELL   I hope they are not persons of condition that you use at this rate.

PETULANT   Condition! Condition's a dried fig, if I am not in humour! By this hand, if they were your—a—a—your what'd'ye-call-'ems themselves, they must wait or rub off, if I want appetite.

MIRABELL   What-d'ye-call-'ems! What are they, Witwoud?

WITWOUD   Empresses, my dear; by your what-d'ye-call-'ems he means sultana queens.

PETULANT   Aye, Roxolanas.[5]

MIRABELL   Cry you mercy.

FAINALL   Witwoud says they are—

PETULANT   What does he say th'are?

WITWOUD   I? Fine ladies, I say.

PETULANT   Pass on, Witwoud. Harkee, by this light his relations: two co-heiresses his cousins, and an old aunt, that loves caterwauling better than a conventicle.[6]

WITWOUD   Ha! ha! ha! I had a mind to see how the rogue would come off. Ha! ha! ha! Gad, I can't be angry with him, if he had said they were my mother and my sisters.

MIRABELL   No!

WITWOUD   No; the rogue's wit and readiness of invention charm me. Dear Petulant!

BETTY   They are gone, sir, in great anger.

PETULANT   Enough, let 'em trundle. Anger helps complexion, saves paint.

FAINALL   This continence is all dissembled; this is in order to have something to brag of the next time he makes court to Millamant, and swear he has abandoned the whole sex for her sake.

MIRABELL   Have you not left off your impudent pretensions there yet? I shall cut your throat some time or other, Petulant, about that business.

PETULANT   Aye, aye, let that pass. There are other throats to be cut.

MIRABELL   Meaning mine, sir?

PETULANT   Not I. I mean nobody; I know nothing. But there are uncles and nephews in the world, and they may be rivals. What then? All's one for that.

5. Prostitutes, as "Empresses" and "sultana queens" above. D'Avenant's *The Siege of Rhodes* made the name Roxolana famous.
6. Meeting of nonconformists.

MIRABELL   How! Harkee Petulant, come hither. Explain, or I shall call your interpreter.[7]

PETULANT   Explain! I know nothing. Why, you have an uncle, have you not, lately come to town, and lodges by my Lady Wishfort's?

MIRABELL   True.

PETULANT   Why, that's enough. You and he are not friends; and if he should marry and have a child, you may be disinherited, ha?

MIRABELL   Where hast thou stumbled upon all this truth?

PETULANT   All's one for that; why, then say I know something.

MIRABELL   Come, thou art an honest fellow, Petulant, and shalt make love to my mistress, thou sha't, faith. What hast thou heard of my uncle?

PETULANT   I? Nothing I. If throats are to be cut, let swords clash! Snug's the word; I shrug and am silent.

MIRABELL   Oh, raillery, raillery! Come, I know thou art in the women's secrets. What, you're a cabalist; I know you stayed at Millamant's last night, after I went. Was there any mention made of my uncle or me? Tell me. If thou hadst but good nature equal to thy wit, Petulant, Tony Witwoud, who is now thy competitor in fame, would show as dim by thee as a dead whiting's eye by a pearl of orient; he would no more be seen by thee than Mercury is by the sun. Come, I'm sure thou wo't tell me.

PETULANT   If I do, will you grant me common sense then for the future?

MIRABELL   Faith, I'll do what I can for thee; and I'll pray that Heaven may grant it thee in the meantime.

PETULANT   Well, harkee.

>   MIRABELL *and* PETULANT *talk apart.*

FAINALL   Petulant and you both will find Mirabell as warm a rival as a lover.

WITWOUD   Pshaw! pshaw! That she laughs at Petulant is plain. And for my part, but that it is almost a fashion to admire her, I should— harkee, to tell you a secret, but let it go no further; between friends, I shall never break my heart for her.

FAINALL   How!

WITWOUD   She's handsome; but she's a sort of an uncertain woman.

FAINALL   I thought you had died for her.

WITWOUD   Umh—no—

FAINALL   She has wit.

WITWOUD   'Tis what she will hardly allow anybody else. Now, demme,[8] I should hate that, if she were as handsome as Cleopatra. Mirabell is not so sure of her as he thinks for.

FAINALL   Why do you think so?

WITWOUD   We stayed pretty late there last night, and heard something

---

7. One who explains difficult texts. Witwoud, ironically.
8. Damn me.

of an uncle to Mirabell, who is lately come to town, and is between him and the best part of his estate. Mirabell and he are at some distance, as my Lady Wishfort has been told; and you know she hates Mirabell worse than a Quaker hates a parrot, or than a fishmonger hates a hard frost. Whether this uncle has seen Mrs. Millamant or not, I cannot say; but there were items of such a treaty being in embryo, and if it should come to life, poor Mirabell would be in some sort unfortunately fobbed,[9] i'faith.

FAINALL   'Tis impossible Millamant should hearken to it.

WITWOUD   Faith, my dear, I can't tell; she's a woman and a kind of a humorist.[1]

MIRABELL   And is this the sum of what you could collect last night?

PETULANT   The quintessence. Maybe Witwoud knows more; he stayed longer. Besides, they never mind him; they say anything before him.

MIRABELL   I thought you had been the greatest favorite.

PETULANT   Aye, *tête à tête*, but not in public, because I make remarks.

MIRABELL   You do?

PETULANT   Aye, aye, pox, I'm malicious, man! Now he's soft, you know, they are not in awe of him. The fellow's well-bred, he's what you call a—what-d'ye-call-'em, a fine gentleman, but he's silly withal.

MIRABELL   I thank you. I know as much as my curiosity requires. Fainall, are you for the Mall?[2]

FAINALL   Aye, I'll take a turn before dinner.

WITWOUD   Aye, we'll all walk in the park; the ladies talked of being there.

MIRABELL   I thought you were obliged to watch for your brother Sir Wilfull's arrival.

WITWOUD   No, no, he comes to his aunt's, my Lady Wishfort. Pox on him! I shall be troubled with him too; what shall I do with the fool?

PETULANT   Beg him for his estate, that I may beg you afterwards; and so have but one trouble with you both.

WITWOUD   Oh, rare Petulant! Thou art as quick as a fire in a frosty morning; thou shalt to the Mall with us, and we'll be very severe.

PETULANT   Enough, I'm in a humour to be severe.

MIRABELL   Are you? Pray then walk by yourselves. Let not us be accessory to your putting the ladies out of countenance with your senseless ribaldry, which you roar out aloud as often as they pass by you; and when you have made a handsome woman blush, then you think you have been severe.

PETULANT   What, what? Then let 'em show their innocence by not understanding what they hear, or else show their discretion by not hearing what they would not be thought to understand.

MIRABELL   But hast not thou then sense enough to know that thou

9. Tricked.
1. Whimsical person.
2. A fashionable promenade adjoining St. James's Park.

ought'st to be most ashamed thyself, when thou hast put another out of countenance?

PETULANT Not I, by this hand! I always take blushing either for a sign of guilt or ill-breeding.

MIRABELL I confess you ought to think so. You are in the right, that you may plead the error of your judgment in defense of your practice.

> Where modesty's ill manners, 'tis but fit
> That impudence and malice pass for wit.

Exeunt.

Act II. St. James's Park.

Enter MRS. FAINALL *and* MRS. MARWOOD.

MRS. FAINALL Aye, aye, dear Marwood, if we will be happy, we must find the means in ourselves, and among ourselves. Men are ever in extremes, either doting or averse. While they are lovers, if they have fire and sense, their jealousies are insupportable. And when they cease to love (we ought to think at least) they loathe; they look upon us with horror and distaste; they meet us like the ghosts of what we were, and as such, fly from us.

MRS. MARWOOD True, 'tis an unhappy circumstance of life, that love should ever die before us; and that the man so often should outlive the lover. But say what you will, 'tis better to be left than never to have been loved. To pass our youth in dull indifference, to refuse the sweets of life because they once must leave us, is as preposterous as to wish to have been born old, because we one day must be old. For my part, my youth may wear and waste, but it shall never rust in my possession.

MRS. FAINALL Then it seems you dissemble an aversion to mankind, only in compliance with my mother's humour.

MRS. MARWOOD Certainly. To be free, I have no taste of those insipid dry discourses with which our sex of force must entertain themselves, apart from men. We may affect endearments to each other, profess eternal friendships, and seem to dote like lovers; but 'tis not in our natures long to persevere. Love will resume his empire in our breasts; and every heart, or soon or late, receive and readmit him as its lawful tyrant.

MRS. FAINALL Bless me, how have I been deceived! Why you profess a libertine!

MRS. MARWOOD You see my friendship by my freedom. Come, be as sincere, acknowledge that your sentiments agree with mine.

MRS. FAINALL Never!

MRS. MARWOOD You hate mankind?

MRS. FAINALL Heartily, inveterately.

MRS. MARWOOD Your husband?

MRS. FAINALL   Most transcendently; aye, though I say it, meritoriously.

MRS. MARWOOD   Give me your hand upon it.

MRS. FAINALL   There.

MRS. MARWOOD   I join with you; what I have said has been to try you.

MRS. FAINALL   Is it possible? Dost thou hate those vipers, men?

MRS. MARWOOD   I have done hating 'em, and am now come to despise 'em; the next thing I have to do, is eternally to forget 'em.

MRS. FAINALL   There spoke the spirit of an Amazon, a Penthesilea.[3]

MRS. MARWOOD   And yet I am thinking sometimes to carry my aversion further.

MRS. FAINALL   How?

MRS. MARWOOD   Faith, by marrying; if I could but find one that loved me very well and would be thoroughly sensible of ill usage, I think I should do myself the violence of undergoing the ceremony.

MRS. FAINALL   You would not make him a cuckold?

MRS. MARWOOD   No, but I'd make him believe I did, and that's as bad.

MRS. FAINALL   Why had not you as good do it?

MRS. MARWOOD   Oh, if he should ever discover it, he would then know the worst, and be out of his pain; but I would have him ever to continue upon the rack of fear and jealousy.

MRS. FAINALL   Ingenious mischief! Would thou wert married to Mirabell.

MRS. MARWOOD   Would I were!

MRS. FAINALL   You change color.

MRS. MARWOOD   Because I hate him.

MRS. FAINALL   So do I; but I can hear him named. But what reason have you to hate him in particular?

MRS. MARWOOD   I never loved him; he is, and always was, insufferably proud.

MRS. FAINALL   By the reason you give for your aversion, one would think it dissembled; for you have laid a fault to his charge of which his enemies must acquit him.

MRS. MARWOOD   Oh, then it seems you are one of his favorable enemies! Methinks you look a little pale, and now you flush again.

MRS. FAINALL   Do I? I think I am a little sick o' the sudden.

MRS. MARWOOD   What ails you?

MRS. FAINALL   My husband. Don't you see him? He turned short upon me unawares, and has almost overcome me.

Enter FAINALL *and* MIRABELL.

MRS. MARWOOD   Ha! ha! ha! He comes opportunely for you.

MRS. FAINALL   For you, for he has brought Mirabell with him.

FAINALL   My dear!

MRS. FAINALL   My soul!

FAINALL   You don't look well today, child.

---

3. Queen of the Amazons, a legendary race of female warriors.

MRS. FAINALL   D'ye think so?

MIRABELL   He is the only man that does, madam.

MRS. FAINALL   The only man that would tell me so at least; and the only man from whom I could hear it without mortification.

FAINALL   Oh my dear, I am satisfied of your tenderness; I know you cannot resent anything from me, especially what is an effect of my concern.

MRS. FAINALL   Mr. Mirabell, my mother interrupted you in a pleasant relation last night; I would fain hear it out.

MIRABELL   The persons concerned in that affair have yet a tolerable reputation. I am afraid Mr. Fainall will be censorious.

MRS. FAINALL   He has a humour more prevailing than his curiosity, and will willingly dispense with the hearing of one scandalous story, to avoid giving an occasion to make another by being seen to walk with his wife. This way, Mr. Mirabell, and I dare promise you will oblige us both.

Exeunt MRS. FAINALL *and* MIRABELL.

FAINALL   Excellent creature! Well, sure if I should live to be rid of my wife, I should be a miserable man.

MRS. MARWOOD   Aye!

FAINALL   For having only that one hope, the accomplishment of it, of consequence must put an end to all my hopes; and what a wretch is he who must survive his hopes! Nothing remains when that day comes, but to sit down and weep like Alexander, when he wanted other worlds to conquer.

MRS. MARWOOD   Will you not follow 'em?

FAINALL   Faith, I think not.

MRS. MARWOOD   Pray let us; I have a reason.

FAINALL   You are not jealous?

MRS. MARWOOD   Of whom?

FAINALL   Of Mirabell.

MRS. MARWOOD   If I am, is it inconsistent with my love to you that I am tender of your honor?

FAINALL   You would intimate then, as if there were a fellow-feeling between my wife and him.

MRS. MARWOOD   I think she does not hate him to that degree she would be thought.

FAINALL   But he, I fear, is too insensible.

MRS. MARWOOD   It may be you are deceived.

FAINALL   It may be so. I do now begin to apprehend it.

MRS. MARWOOD   What?

FAINALL   That I have been deceived, madam, and you are false.

MRS. MARWOOD   That I am false? What mean you?

FAINALL   To let you know I see through all your little arts. Come, you both love him; and both have equally dissembled your aversion. Your mutual jealousies of one another have made you clash till you have both struck fire. I have seen the warm confession reddening on your cheeks, and sparkling from your eyes.

MRS. MARWOOD   You do me wrong.

FAINALL   I do not. 'Twas for my ease to oversee[4] and wilfully neglect the gross advances made him by my wife; that by permitting her to be engaged, I might continue unsuspected in my pleasures, and take you oftener to my arms in full security. But could you think, because the nodding husband would not wake, that e'er the watchful lover slept?

MRS. MARWOOD   And wherewithal can you reproach me?

FAINALL   With infidelity, with loving of another, with love of Mirabell.

MRS. MARWOOD   'Tis false. I challenge you to show an instance that can confirm your groundless accusation. I hate him.

FAINALL   And wherefore do you hate him? He is insensible, and your resentment follows his neglect. An instance? The injuries you have done him are a proof, your interposing in his love. What cause had you to make discoveries of his pretended passion? To undeceive the credulous aunt, and be the officious obstacle of his match with Milla-mant?

MRS. MARWOOD   My obligations to my lady urged me; I had professed a friendship to her, and could not see her easy nature so abused by that dissembler.

FAINALL   What, was it conscience then? Professed a friendship! Oh, the pious friendships of the female sex!

MRS. MARWOOD   More tender, more sincere, and more enduring, than all the vain and empty vows of men, whether professing love to us, or mutual faith to one another.

FAINALL   Ha! ha! ha! you are my wife's friend too.

MRS. MARWOOD   Shame and ingratitude! Do you reproach me? You, you upbraid me! Have I been false to her, through strict fidelity to you, and sacrificed my friendship to keep my love inviolate? And have you the baseness to charge me with the guilt, unmindful of the merit! To you it should be meritorious, that I have been vicious; and do you reflect that guilt upon me, which should lie buried in your bosom?

FAINALL   You misinterpret my reproof. I meant but to remind you of the slight account you once could make of strictest ties, when set in comparison with your love to me.

MRS. MARWOOD   'Tis false; you urged it with deliberate malice! 'Twas spoke in scorn, and I never will forgive it.

FAINALL   Your guilt, not your resentment, begets your rage. If yet you loved, you could forgive a jealousy; but you are stung to find you are discovered.

MRS. MARWOOD   It shall be all discovered. You too shall be discovered; be sure you shall. I can but be exposed. If I do it myself, I shall prevent[5] your baseness.

4. Overlook.
5. Anticipate.

FAINALL   Why, what will you do?

MRS. MARWOOD   Disclose it to your wife; own what has passed between us.

FAINALL   Frenzy!

MRS. MARWOOD   By all my wrongs I'll do't! I'll publish to the world the injuries you have done me, both in my fame and fortune! With both I trusted you, you bankrupt in honor, as indigent of wealth.

FAINALL   Your fame I have preserved. Your fortune has been bestowed as the prodigality of your love would have it, in pleasures which we both have shared. Yet had not you been false, I had ere this repaid it. 'Tis true, had you permitted Mirabell with Millamant to have stolen their marriage, my lady had been incensed beyond all means of reconcilement; Millamant had forfeited the moiety[6] of her fortune, which then would have descended to my wife. And wherefore did I marry, but to make a lawful prize of a rich widow's wealth, and squander it on love and you?

MRS. MARWOOD   Deceit and frivolous pretense!

FAINALL   Death, am I not married? What's pretense? Am I not imprisoned, fettered? Have I not a wife? Nay a wife that was a widow, a young widow, a handsome widow; and would be again a widow, but that I have a heart of proof, and something of a constitution to bustle through the ways of wedlock and this world. Will you yet be reconciled to truth and me?

MRS. MARWOOD   Impossible. Truth and you are inconsistent. I hate you, and shall for ever.

FAINALL   For loving you?

MRS. MARWOOD   I loathe the name of love after such usage; and next to the guilt with which you would asperse me, I scorn you most. Farewell!

FAINALL   Nay, we must not part thus.

MRS. MARWOOD   Let me go.

FAINALL   Come, I'm sorry.

MRS. MARWOOD   I care not, let me go. Break my hands, do! I'd leave 'em to get loose.

FAINALL   I would not hurt you for the world. Have I no other hold to keep you here?

MRS. MARWOOD   Well, I have deserved it all.

FAINALL   You know I love you.

MRS. MARWOOD   Poor dissembling! Oh, that—Well, it is not yet—

FAINALL   What? what is it not? What is it not yet? It is not yet too late—

MRS. MARWOOD   No, it is not yet too late; I have that comfort.

FAINALL   It is, to love another.

MRS. MARWOOD   But not to loathe, detest, abhor mankind, myself, and the whole treacherous world.

FAINALL   Nay, this is extravagance, Come, I ask your pardon. No tears. I was to blame; I could not love you and be easy in my doubts. Pray,

6. Half.

forbear. I believe you. I'm convinced I've done you wrong; and any way, every way will make amends. I'll hate my wife yet more, damn her! I'll part with her, rob her of all she's worth, and we'll retire somewhere, anywhere, to another world. I'll marry thee; be pacified. 'Sdeath, they come; hide your face, your tears. You have a mask; wear it a moment. This way, this way. Be persuaded.

Exeunt.

Enter MIRABELL *and* MRS. FAINALL.

MRS. FAINALL   They are here yet.

MIRABELL   They are turning into the other walk.

MRS. FAINALL   While I only hated my husband, I could bear to see him; but since I have despised him, he's too offensive.

MIRABELL   Oh, you should hate with prudence.

MRS. FAINALL   Yes, for I have loved with indiscretion.

MIRABELL   You should have just so much disgust for your husband as may be sufficient to make you relish your lover.

MRS. FAINALL   You have been the cause that I have loved without bounds, and would you set limits to that aversion of which you have been the occasion? Why did you make me marry this man?

MIRABELL   Why do we daily commit disagreeable and dangerous actions? To save that idol, reputation. If the familiarities of our loves had produced that consequence of which you were apprehensive, where could you have fixed a father's name with credit, but on a husband? I knew Fainall to be a man lavish of his morals, an interested[7] and professing friend, a false and a designing lover; yet one whose wit and outward fair behavior have gained a reputation with the town enough to make that woman stand excused who has suffered herself to be won by his addresses. A better man ought not to have been sacrificed to the occasion; a worse had not answered to the purpose. When you are weary of him, you know your remedy.

MRS. FAINALL   I ought to stand in some degree of credit with you, Mirabell.

MIRABELL   In justice to you, I have made you privy to my whole design, and put it in your power to ruin or advance my fortune.

MRS. FAINALL   Whom have you instructed to represent your pretended uncle?

MIRABELL   Waitwell, my servant.

MRS. FAINALL   He is an humble servant to Foible, my mother's woman, and may win her to your interest.

MIRABELL   Care is taken for that. She is won and worn by this time. They were married this morning.

MRS. FAINALL   Who?

MIRABELL   Waitwell and Foible. I would not tempt my servant to betray me by trusting him too far. If your mother, in hopes to ruin me,

7. Self-interested.

should consent to marry my pretended uncle, he might, like Mosca in *The Fox*, stand upon terms[8] so I made him sure beforehand.

MRS. FAINALL   So, if my poor mother is caught in a contract, you will discover the imposture betimes, and release her by producing a certificate of her gallant's former marriage.

MIRABELL   Yes, upon condition she consent to my marriage with her niece, and surrender the moiety of her fortune in her possession.

MRS. FAINALL   She talked last night of endeavoring at a match between Millamant and your uncle.

MIRABELL   That was by Foible's direction, and my instruction, that she might seem to carry it more privately.

MRS. FAINALL   Well, I have an opinion of your success, for I believe my lady will do anything to get a husband; and when she has this, which you have provided for her, I suppose she will submit to anything to get rid of him.

MIRABELL   Yes, I think the good lady would marry anything that resembled a man, though 'twere no more than what a butler could pinch out of a napkin.

MRS. FAINALL   Female frailty! We must all come to it, if we live to be old and feel the craving of a false appetite when the true is decayed.

MIRABELL   An old woman's appetite is depraved like that of a girl. 'Tis the green sickness[9] of a second childhood; and like the faint offer of a latter spring, serves but to usher in the fall, and withers in an affected bloom.

MRS. FAINALL   Here's your mistress.

Enter MRS. MILLAMANT, WITWOUD, *and* MINCING.

MIRABELL   Here she comes, i'faith, full sail, with her fan spread and her streamers out, and a shoal of fools for tenders. Ha, no, I cry her mercy!

MRS. FAINALL   I see but one poor empty sculler; and he tows her woman after him.

MIRABELL   You seem to be unattended, madam. You used to have the beau monde throng after you, and a flock of gay fine perukes[1] hovering round you.

WITWOUD   Like moths about a candle. I had like to have lost my comparison for want of breath.

MILLAMANT   Oh, I have denied myself airs today. I have walked as fast through the crowd—

WITWOUD   As a favorite in disgrace, and with as few followers.

MILLAMANT   Dear Mr. Witwoud, truce with your similitudes; for I am as sick of 'em—

8. Mosca is the scheming servant in Ben Jonson's *Volpone, or The Fox*; "standing upon terms" in that play amounts to blackmail.
9. The anemia that sometimes affects girls at puberty.
1. Wigs.

WITWOUD   As a physician of a good air. I cannot help it, madam, though 'tis against myself.

MILLAMANT   Yet again! Mincing, stand between me and his wit.

WITWOUD   Do, Mrs. Mincing, like a screen before a great fire. I confess I do blaze today; I am too bright.

MRS. FAINALL   But, dear Millamant, why were you so long?

MILLAMANT   Long! Lord, have I not made violent haste? I have asked every living thing I met for you; I have inquired after you, as after a new fashion.

WITWOUD   Madam, truce with your similitudes. No, you met her husband, and did not ask him for her.

MIRABELL   By your leave, Witwoud, that were like inquiring after an old fashion, to ask a husband for his wife.

WITWOUD   Hum, a hit! a hit! a palpable hit![2] I confess it.

MRS. FAINALL   You were dressed before I came abroad.

MILLAMANT   Aye, that's true. Oh, but then I had—Mincing, what had I? Why was I so long?

MINCING   O mem, your la'ship stayed to peruse a pecquet[3] of letters.

MILLAMANT   Oh, aye, letters; I had letters. I am persecuted with letters. I hate letters. Nobody knows how to write letters; and yet one has 'em, one does not know why. They serve one to pin up one's hair.

WITWOUD   Is that the way? Pray, madam, do you pin up your hair with all your letters? I find I must keep copies.

MILLAMANT   Only with those in verse, Mr. Witwoud. I never pin up my hair with prose. I fancy one's hair would not curl if it were pinned up with prose. I think I tried once, Mincing.

MINCING   O mem, I shall never forget it.

MILLAMANT   Aye, poor Mincing tift[4] and tift all the morning.

MINCING   'Till I had the cremp in my fingers, I'll vow, mem. And all to no purpose. But when your la'ship pins it up with poetry, it sits so pleasant the next day as anything, and is so pure and so crips.[5]

WITWOUD   Indeed, so crips?

MINCING   You're such a critic, Mr. Witwoud.

MILLAMANT   Mirabell, did not you take exceptions last night? Oh, aye, and went away. Now I think on't, I'm angry. No, now I think on't, I'm pleased; for I believe I gave you some pain.

MIRABELL   Does that please you?

MILLAMANT   Infinitely; I love to give pain.

MIRABELL   You would affect a cruelty which is not in your nature; your true vanity is in the power of pleasing.

MILLAMANT   Oh, I ask your pardon for that. One's cruelty is one's power; and when one parts with one's cruelty, one parts with one's power; and when one has parted with that, I fancy one's old and ugly.

---

2. From the dueling scene in *Hamlet* V.ii.
3. Packet. Mincing's speech is affected.
4. Arranged, set the hair.
5. A variation of "crisp."

MIRABELL   Aye, aye, suffer your cruelty to ruin the object of your
power, to destroy your lover, and then how vain, how lost a thing
you'll be! Nay, 'tis true: you are no longer handsome when you've lost
your lover; your beauty dies upon the instant. For beauty is the lover's
gift; 'tis he bestows your charms, your glass is all a cheat. The ugly
and the old, whom the looking glass mortifies, yet after commendation can be flattered by it, and discover beauties in it; for that reflects
our praises, rather than your face.

MILLAMANT   Oh, the vanity of these men! Fainall, d'ye hear him? If
they did not commend us, we were not handsome! Now you must
know they could not commend one, if one was not handsome. Beauty
the lover's gift! Lord, what is a lover, that it can give? Why, one makes
lovers as fast as one pleases, and they live as long as one pleases, and
they die as soon as one pleases; and then, if one pleases, one makes
more.

WITWOUD   Very pretty. Why, you make no more of making of lovers,
madam, than of making so many card-matches.[6]

MILLAMANT   One no more owes one's beauty to a lover than one's wit
to an echo. They can but reflect what we look and say; vain empty
things if we are silent or unseen, and want a being.

MIRABELL   Yet to those two vain empty things you owe two [of] the
greatest pleasures of your life.

MILLAMANT   How so?

MIRABELL   To your lover you owe the pleasure of hearing yourselves
praised; and to an echo the pleasure of hearing yourselves talk.

WITWOUD   But I know a lady that loves talking so incessantly, she won't
give an echo fair play; she has that everlasting rotation of tongue, that
an echo must wait till she dies, before it can catch her last words.

MILLAMANT   Oh, fiction! Fainall, let us leave these men.

MIRABELL   Draw off Witwoud. [Aside to MRS. FAINALL.]

MRS. FAINALL   Immediately. I have a word or two for Mr. Witwoud.

Exeunt WITWOUD *and* MRS. FAINALL.

MIRABELL   I would beg a little private audience too. You had the tyranny to deny me last night, though you knew I came to impart a
secret to you that concerned my love.

MILLAMANT   You saw I was engaged.

MIRABELL   Unkind! You had the leisure to entertain a herd of fools;
things who visit you from their excessive idleness, bestowing on your
easiness that time which is the incumbrance of their lives. How can
you find delight in such society? It is impossible they should admire
you; they are not capable. Or if they were, it should be to you as a
mortification, for sure to please a fool is some degree of folly.

MILLAMANT   I please myself. Besides, sometimes to converse with fools
is for my health.

6. Matches made by dipping cardboard strips in melted sulphur.

MIRABELL   Your health! Is there a worse disease than the conversation of fools?

MILLAMANT   Yes, the vapors; fools are physic for it, next to assafoetida.[7]

MIRABELL   You are not in a course of fools?

MILLAMANT   Mirabell, if you persist in this offensive freedom, you'll displease me. I think I must resolve, after all, not to have you; we shan't agree.

MIRABELL   Not in our physic, it may be.

MILLAMANT   And yet our distemper, in all likelihood, will be the same; for we shall be sick of one another. I shan't endure to be reprimanded nor instructed; 'tis so dull to act always by advice, and so tedious to be told of one's faults—I can't bear it. Well, I won't have you, Mirabell—I'm resolved—I think—you may go.—Ha! ha! ha! What would you give that you could help loving me?

MIRABELL   I would give something that you did not know I could not help it.

MILLAMANT   Come, don't look grave then. Well, what do you say to me?

MIRABELL   I say that a man may as soon make a friend by his wit, or a fortune by his honesty, as win a woman with plain dealing and sincerity.

MILLAMANT   Sententious Mirabell! Prithee, don't look with that violent and inflexible wise face, like Solomon at the dividing of the child in an old tapestry hanging.[8]

MIRABELL   You are merry, madam, but I would persuade you for one moment to be serious.

MILLAMANT   What, with that face? No, if you keep your countenance, 'tis impossible I should hold mine. Well, after all, there is something very moving in a love-sick face. Ha! ha! ha!—Well, I won't laugh, don't be peevish—Heighho! Now I'll be melancholy, as melancholy as a watch-light.[9] Well, Mirabell, if ever you will win me, woo me now. —Nay, if you are so tedious, fare you well. —I see they are walking away.

MIRABELL   Can you not find in the variety of your disposition one moment—

MILLAMANT   To hear you tell me Foible's married, and your plot like to speed? —No.

MIRABELL   But how came you to know it?

MILLAMANT   Unless by the help of the devil, you can't imagine; unless she should tell me herself. Which of the two it may have been, I will leave you to consider; and when you have done thinking of that, think of me.

Exit with MINCING.

7. A sort of smelling salts.
8. From 1 Kings 3.16–28.
9. Nightlight, as in a sickroom.

MIRABELL   I have something more—Gone! Think of you! To think of
a whirlwind, though 'twere in a whirlwind, were a case of more steady
contemplation; a very tranquility of mind and mansion. A fellow that
lives in a windmill has not a more whimsical dwelling than the heart
of a man that is lodged in a woman. There is no point of the compass
to which they cannot turn, and by which they are not turned; and by
one as well as another, for motion, not method, is their occupation.
To know this, and yet continue to be in love, is to be made wise from
the dictates of reason, and yet persevere to play the fool by the force
of instinct.—Oh, here come my pair of turtles![1] —What, billing so
sweetly! Is not Valentine's Day over with you yet?

> *Enter* WAITWELL *and* FOIBLE.

Sirrah, Waitwell, why sure you think you were married for your own
recreation, and not for my conveniency.

WAITWELL   Your pardon, sir. With submission, we have indeed been
solacing in lawful delights; but still with an eye to business, sir. I have
instructed her as well as I could. If she can take your directions as
readily as my instructions, sir, your affairs are in a prosperous way.

MIRABELL   Give you joy, Mrs. Foible.

FOIBLE   O las, sir, I'm so ashamed! I'm afraid my lady has been in a
thousand inquietudes for me. But I protest, sir, I made as much haste
as I could.

WAITWELL   That she did indeed, sir. It was my fault that she did not
make more.

MIRABELL   That I believe.

FOIBLE   But I told my lady as you instructed me, sir, that I had a prospect of seeing Sir Rowland, your uncle; and that I would put her
ladyship's picture in my pocket to show him, which I'll be sure to say
has made him so enamored of her beauty, that he burns with impatience to lie at her ladyship's feet and worship the original.

MIRABELL   Excellent Foible! Matrimony has made you eloquent in
love.

WAITWELL   I think she has profited, sir. I think so.

FOIBLE   You have seen Madam Millamant, sir?

MIRABELL   Yes.

FOIBLE   I told her, sir, because I did not know that you might find an
opportunity; she had so much company last night.

MIRABELL   Your diligence will merit more. In the meantime—

> *Gives money.*

FOIBLE   O dear sir, your humble servant.

WAITWELL   Spouse.

MIRABELL   Stand off, sir, not a penny! Go on and prosper, Foible; the
lease shall be made good and the farm stocked, if we succeed.

---

1. Turtledoves.

FOIBLE   I don't question your generosity, sir; and you need not doubt of success. If you have no more commands, sir, I'll be gone; I'm sure my lady is at her toilet and can't dress till I come.—Oh dear, I'm sure that [*looking out*] was Mrs. Marwood that went by in a mask; if she has seen me with you I'm sure she'll tell my lady. I'll make haste home and prevent her. Your servant, sir. B'w'y,[2] Waitwell.

Exit.

WAITWELL   Sir Rowland, if you please. The jade's so pert upon her preferment she forgets herself.

MIRABELL   Come, sir, will you endeavor to forget yourself, and transform into Sir Rowland?

WAITWELL   Why, sir, it will be impossible I should remember myself. Married, knighted, and attended all in one day! 'Tis enough to make any man forget himself. The difficulty will be how to recover my acquaintance and familiarity with my former self, and fall from my transformation to a reformation into Waitwell. Nay, I shan't be quite the same Waitwell neither; for now I remember me, I am married and can't be my own man again.

> Aye, there's the grief; that's the sad change of life,
> To lose my title, and yet keep my wife.

Exeunt.

Act III. *A Room in* LADY WISHFORT'S *House.*

LADY WISHFORT *at her toilet,* PEG *waiting.*

LADY WISHFORT   Merciful! no news of Foible yet?

PEG   No, madam.

LADY WISHFORT   I have no more patience. If I have not fretted myself till I am pale again, there's no veracity in me! Fetch me the red; the red, do you hear, sweetheart? An arrant ash-color, as I'm a person! Look you how this wench stirs! Why dost thou not fetch me a little red? Didst thou not hear me, mopus?

PEG   The red ratafia does your ladyship mean, or the cherry brandy?

LADY WISHFORT   Ratafia, fool! No, fool! Not the ratafia, fool. Grant me patience! I mean the Spanish paper,[3] idiot; complexion, darling. Paint, paint, paint, dost thou understand that, changeling, dangling thy hands like bobbins before thee? Why dost thou not stir, puppet? thou wooden thing upon wires!

PEG   Lord, madam, your ladyship is so impatient! I cannot come at the paint, madam; Mrs. Foible has locked it up and carried the key with her.

LADY WISHFORT   A pox take you both! Fetch me the cherry brandy then. [*Exit* PEG.] I'm as pale and as faint, I look like Mrs. Qualmsick,

2. Good-by.
3. For applying rouge.

the curate's wife, that's always breeding. Wench, come, come, wench, what art thou doing? sipping? tasting? Save thee, dost thou not know the bottle?

Re-enter PEG *with a bottle and china cup.*

PEG   Madam, I was looking for a cup.

LADY WISHFORT   A cup, save thee! and what a cup hast thou brought! Dost thou take me for a fairy, to drink out of an acorn? Why didst thou not bring thy thimble? Hast thou ne'er a brass thimble clinking in thy pocket with a bit of nutmeg? I warrant thee. Come, fill, fill! So; again. [*One knocks.*] See who that is. Set down the bottle first. Here, here, under the table. What, wouldst thou go with the bottle in thy hand, like a tapster? As I'm a person, this wench has lived in an inn upon the road, before she came to me, like Maritornes the Asturian in *Don Quixote*![4] No Foible yet?

PEG   No, madam, Mrs. Marwood.

LADY WISHFORT   Oh, Marwood, let her come in. Come in, good Marwood.

Enter MRS. MARWOOD.

MRS. MARWOOD   I'm surprised to find your ladyship in dishabillé at this time of day.

LADY WISHFORT   Foible's a lost thing; has been abroad since morning, and never heard of since.

MRS. MARWOOD   I saw her but now, as I came masked through the park, in conference with Mirabell.

LADY WISHFORT   With Mirabell! You call my blood into my face with mentioning that traitor. She durst not have the confidence! I sent her to negotiate an affair in which, if I'm detected, I'm undone. If that wheedling villain has wrought upon Foible to detect me, I'm ruined. Oh my dear friend, I'm a wretch of wretches if I'm detected.

MRS. MARWOOD   O madam, you cannot suspect Mrs. Foible's integrity.

LADY WISHFORT   Oh, he carries poison in his tongue that would corrupt integrity itself! If she has given him an opportunity, she has as good as put her integrity into his hands. Ah, dear Marwood, what's integrity to an opportunity? Hark! I hear her! Go, you thing, and send her in. [*Exit* PEG.] Dear friend, retire into my closet,[5] that I may examine her with more freedom. You'll pardon me, dear friend; I can make bold with you. There are books over the chimney. Quarles and Prynne, and the *Short View of the Stage*, with Bunyan's works, to entertain you.[6]

Exit MRS. MARWOOD.

4. Chambermaid in *Dox Quixote*, Part I, xvi.
5. Small, private room.
6. Lady Wishfort's bookshelf seems to include such Puritan works as Francis Quarles's *Emblems, Divine and Moral* (1635) and William Prynne's *Histriomastix* (1632), along with Jeremy Collier's *Short View of the Immorality and Profaneness of the English Stage* (1698).

Enter FOIBLE.

Oh Foible, where hast thou been? What hast thou been doing?

FOIBLE   Madam, I have seen the party.

LADY WISHFORT   But what hast thou done?

FOIBLE   Nay, 'tis your ladyship has done, and are to do; I have only promised. But a man so enamored, so transported! Well, here it is, all that is left; all that is not kissed away. Well, if worshiping of pictures be a sin, poor Sir Rowland, I say.

LADY WISHFORT   The miniature has been counted like. But hast thou not betrayed me, Foible? Hast thou not detected me to that faithless Mirabell? What hadst thou to do with him in the Park? Answer me, has he got nothing out of thee?

FOIBLE   [*aside*]   So the devil has been beforehand with me. What shall I say?—Alas, madam, could I help it, if I met that confident thing? Was I in fault? If you had heard how he used me, and all upon your ladyship's account, I'm sure you would not suspect my fidelity. Nay, if that had been the worst, I could have borne; but he had a fling at your ladyship too. And then I could not hold; but i'faith I gave him his own.

LADY WISHFORT   Me? What did the filthy fellow say?

FOIBLE   O madam! 'tis a shame to say what he said, with his taunts and his fleers, tossing up his nose. Humph! (says he), what, you are a hatching some plot (says he), you are so early abroad, or catering (says he), ferreting for some disbanded officer, I warrant. Half-pay is but thin subsistence (says he). Well, what pension does your lady propose? Let me see (says he), what, she must come down pretty deep now, she's superannuated (says he) and—

LADY WISHFORT   Ods my life, I'll have him, I'll have him murdered. I'll have him poisoned. Where does he eat? I'll marry a drawer to have him poisoned in his wine. I'll send for Robin from Locket's[7] immediately.

FOIBLE   Poison him? Poisoning's too good for him. Starve him, madam, starve him; marry Sir Rowland and get him disinherited. Oh, you would bless yourself to hear what he said!

LADY WISHFORT   A villain! superannuated!

FOIBLE   Humph! (says he), I hear you are laying designs against me too (says he), and Mrs. Millamant is to marry my uncle (he does not suspect a word of your ladyship); but (says he) I'll fit you for that. I warrant you (says he), I'll hamper you for that (says he), you and your old frippery[8] too (says he), I'll handle you—

LADY WISHFORT   Audacious villain! Handle me! would he durst! Frippery? old frippery! Was there ever such a foulmouthed fellow? I'll be married tomorrow; I'll be contracted tonight.

FOIBLE   The sooner the better, madam.

7. A fashionable tavern.
8. Cast-off clothes.

LADY WISHFORT   Will Sir Rowland be here, say'st thou? When, Foible?

FOIBLE   Incontinently, madam. No new sheriff's wife expects the return of her husband after knighthood with that impatience in which Sir Rowland burns for the dear hour of kissing your ladyship's hands after dinner.

LADY WISHFORT   Frippery? superannuated frippery! I'll frippery the villain; I'll reduce him to frippery and rags! A tatterdemalion! I hope to see him hung with tatters, like a Long Lane penthouse[9] or a gibbet thief. A slander-mouthed railer! I warrant the spendthrift prodigal's in debt as much as the million lottery,[1] or the whole court upon a birthday. I'll spoil his credit with his tailor. Yes, he shall have my niece with her fortune, he shall!

FOIBLE   He! I hope to see him lodge in Ludgate[2] first, and angle into Blackfriars for brass farthings with an old mitten.

LADY WISHFORT   Aye, dear Foible; thank thee for that, dear Foible. He has put me out of all patience. I shall never recompose my features to receive Sir Rowland with any economy of face. This wretch has fretted me that I am absolutely decayed. Look, Foible.

FOIBLE   Your ladyship has frowned a little too rashly, indeed, madam. There are some cracks discernible in the white varnish.

LADY WISHFORT   Let me see the glass. Cracks, say'st thou? Why I am arrantly flayed; I look like an old peeled wall. Thou must repair me, Foible, before Sir Rowland comes, or I shall never keep up to my picture.

FOIBLE   I warrant you, madam, a little art once made your picture like you; and now a little of the same art must make you like your picture. Your picture must sit for you, madam.

LADY WISHFORT   But art thou sure Sir Rowland will not fail to come? Or will he not fail when he does come? Will he be importunate, Foible, and push? For if he should not be importunate, I shall never break decorums. I shall die with confusion, if I am forced to advance. Oh no, I can never advance! I shall swoon if he should expect advances. No, I hope Sir Rowland is better bred than to put a lady to the necessity of breaking her forms. I won't be too coy neither. I won't give him despair; but a little disdain is not amiss, a little scorn is alluring.

FOIBLE   A little scorn becomes your ladyship.

LADY WISHFORT   Yes, but tenderness becomes me best, a sort of a dyingness. You see that picture has a short of a—ha, Foible? a swimminess in the eyes. Yes, I'll look so. My niece affects it; but she wants features. Is Sir Rowland handsome? Let my toilet be removed. I'll dress above. I'll receive Sir Rowland here. Is he handsome? Don't answer me. I won't know; I'll be surprised, I'll be taken by surprise.

---

9. Stall in Long Lane, Smithfield, where old clothes and rags were sold.
1. A government lottery of 1694 to raise a million pounds.
2. Debtors' prison. Prisoners would beg by dropping a mitten on a string from their gratings to the street below.

FOIBLE   By storm, madam. Sir Rowland's a brisk man.

LADY WISHFORT   Is he! Oh, then he'll importune, if he's a brisk man. I
shall save decorums if Sir Rowland importunes. I have a mortal terror
at the apprehension of offending against decorums. Nothing but
importunity can surmount decorums. Oh, I'm glad he's a brisk man.
Let my things be removed, good Foible.

Exit.

Enter MRS. FAINALL.[3]

MRS. FAINALL   O Foible, I have been in a fright, lest I should come too
late! That devil Marwood saw you in the Park with Mirabell, and I'm
afraid will discover it to my lady.

FOIBLE   Discover what, madam?

MRS. FAINALL   Nay, nay, put not on that strange face. I am privy to the
whole design, and know that Waitwell, to whom thou wert this morning married, is to personate Mirabell's uncle, and as such, winning
my lady, to involve her in those difficulties from which Mirabell only
must release her, by his making his conditions to have my cousin and
her fortune left to her own disposal.

FOIBLE   O dear madam, I beg your pardon. It was not my confidence
in your ladyship that was deficient; but I thought the former good
correspondence between your ladyship and Mr. Mirabell might have
hindered his communicating this secret.

MRS. FAINALL   Dear Foible, forget that.

FOIBLE   O dear madam, Mr. Mirabell is such a sweet, winning gentleman, but your ladyship is the pattern of generosity. Sweet lady, to be
so good! Mr. Mirabell cannot choose but be grateful. I find your
ladyship has his heart still. Now, madam, I can safely tell your ladyship our success. Mrs. Marwood had told my lady; but I warrant I
managed myself. I turned it all for the better. I told my lady that Mr.
Mirabell railed at her. I laid horrid things to his charge, I'll vow; and
my lady is so incensed that she'll be contracted to Sir Rowland
tonight, she says. I warrant I worked her up, that he may have her for
asking for, as they say of a Welsh maidenhead.

MRS. FAINALL   O rare Foible!

FOIBLE   Madam, I beg your ladyship to acquaint Mr. Mirabell of his
success. I would be seen as little as possible to speak to him; besides,
I believe Madame Marwood watches me. She has a month's mind;[4]
but I know Mr. Mirabell can't abide her. [*Enter* FOOTMAN.] John,
remove my lady's toilet. Madam, your servant. My lady is so impatient, I fear she'll come for me, if I stay.

MRS. FAINALL   I'll go with you up the backstairs, lest I should meet her.

Exeunt.

3. Sometimes staged so that Mrs. Marwood is visible, overhearing the following from one of the
stage doors.
4. Strong inclination.

Enter MRS. MARWOOD.

MRS. MARWOOD   Indeed, Mrs. Engine, is it thus with you? Are you
become a go-between of this importance? Yes, I shall watch you. Why
this wench is the *passe-partout,* a very master key to everybody's
strongbox. My friend Fainall, have you carried it so swimmingly? I
thought there was something in it; but it seems it's over with you.
Your loathing is not from a want of appetite then, but from a surfeit.
Else you could never be so cool to fall from a principal to be an
assistant; to procure for him! A pattern of generosity, that I confess.
Well, Mr. Fainall, you have met with your match. O man, man!
woman, woman! The devil's an ass; if I were a painter, I would draw
him like an idiot, a driveler with a bib and bells. Man should have
his head and horns, and woman the rest of him. Poor simple fiend!
Madam Marwood has a month's mind, but he can't abide her. 'Twere
better for him you had not been his confessor in that affair, without
you could have kept his counsel closer. I shall not prove another
pattern of generosity and stalk for him, till he takes his stand to aim
at a fortune. He has not obliged me to that, with those excesses of
himself; and now I'll have none of him. Here comes the good lady,
panting ripe; with a heart full of hope, and a head full of care, like
any chemist upon the day of projection.[5]

Enter LADY WISHFORT.

LADY WISHFORT   O dear Marwood, what shall I say, for this rude forgetfulness? But my dear friend is all goodness.

MRS. MARWOOD   No apologies, dear madam. I have been very well
entertained.

LADY WISHFORT   As I'm a person, I am in a very chaos to think I should
so forget myself; but I have such an olio[6] of affairs, really I know not
what to do. —[*Calls.*] Foible! —I expect my nephew, Sir Wilfull,
every moment too. —Why, Foible! —He means to travel for improvement.

MRS. MARWOOD   Methinks Sir Wilfull should rather think of marrying
than traveling at his years. I hear he is turned of forty.

LADY WISHFORT   Oh, he's in less danger of being spoiled by his travels.
I am against my nephew's marrying too young. It will be time enough
when he comes back and has acquired discretion to choose for himself.

MRS. MARWOOD   Methinks Mrs. Millamant and he would make a very
fit match. He may travel afterwards. 'Tis a thing very usual with young
gentlemen.

LADY WISHFORT   I promise you I have thought on't; and since 'tis your
judgment, I'll think on't again. I assure you I will; I value your judgment extremely. On my word, I'll propose it.

5. When an alchemist added the final element in hopes of changing base metal to gold.
6. Hodgepodge.

Enter FOIBLE.

Come, come, Foible, I had forgot my nephew will be here before dinner. I must make haste.

FOIBLE   Mr. Witwoud and Mr. Petulant are come to dine with your ladyship.

LADY WISHFORT   Oh dear, I can't appear till I'm dressed. Dear Marwood, shall I be free with you again, and beg you to entertain 'em? I'll make all imaginable haste. Dear friend, excuse me.

Exeunt LADY WISHFORT *and* FOIBLE.

Enter MRS. MILLAMANT *and* MINCING.

MILLAMANT   Sure never anything was so unbred as that odious man! Marwood, your servant.

MRS. MARWOOD   You have a color, what's the matter?

MILLAMANT   That horrid fellow, Petulant, has provoked me into a flame. I have broke my fan. Mincing, lend me yours; is not all the powder out of my hair?

MRS. MARWOOD   No, what has he done?

MILLAMANT   Nay, he has done nothing; he has only talked. Nay, he has said nothing neither; but he has contradicted everything that has been said. For my part, I thought Witwoud and he would have quarreled.

MINCING   I vow, mem, I thought once they would have fit.[7]

MILLAMANT   Well, 'tis a lamentable thing, I'll swear, that one has not the liberty of choosing one's acquaintance as one does one's clothes.

MRS. MARWOOD   If we had the liberty, we should be as weary of one set of acquaintance, though never so good, as we are of one suit, though never so fine. A fool and a doily stuff[8] would now and then find days of grace, and be worn for variety.

MILLAMANT   I could consent to wear 'em, if they would wear alike; but fools never wear out—they are such *drap-de-Berry*[9] things without one could give 'em to one's chambermaid after a day or two!

MRS. MARWOOD   'Twere better to indeed. Or what think you of the playhouse? A fine, gay, glossy fool should be given there, like a new masking habit, after the masquerade is over, and we have done with the disguise. For a fool's visit is always a disguise, and never admitted by a woman of wit, but to blind her affair with a lover of sense. If you would but appear barefaced now, and own Mirabell, you might as easily put off Petulant and Witwoud as your hood and scarf. And indeed 'tis time, for the town has found it; the secret is grown too big for the pretense. 'Tis like Mrs. Primly's great belly; she may lace it down before, but it burnishes on her hips. Indeed, Millamant, you can no more conceal it than my Lady Strammel can her face, that

7. Fought.
8. Cheap woolen cloth.
9. Heavy, coarse woolens.

goodly face, which, in defiance of her Rhenish wine tea,[1] will not be comprehended in a mask.

MILLAMANT   I'll take my death, Marwood, you are more censorious than a decayed beauty, or a discarded toast.[2] Mincing, tell the men they may come up. My aunt is not dressing.—Their folly is less provoking than your malice. [*Exit* MINCING.] The town has found it! What has it found? That Mirabell loves me is no more a secret than it is a secret that you discovered it to my aunt, or than the reason why you discovered it is a secret.

MRS. MARWOOD   You are nettled.

MILLAMANT   You're mistaken. Ridiculous!

MRS. MARWOOD   Indeed, my dear, you'll tear another fan, if you don't mitigate those violent airs.

MILLAMANT   O silly! Ha! ha! ha! I could laugh immoderately. Poor Mirabell! His constancy to me has quite destroyed his complaisance for all the world beside. I swear, I never enjoined it him to be so coy. If I had the vanity to think he would obey me, I would command him to show more gallantry. 'Tis hardly well-bred to be so particular on one hand, and so insensible on the other. But I despair to prevail, and so let him follow his own way. Ha! ha! ha! Pardon me, dear creature, I must laugh, ha! ha! ha!—though I grant you 'tis a little barbarous, ha! ha! ha!

MRS. MARWOOD   What pity 'tis, so much fine raillery, and delivered with so significant gesture, should be so unhappily directed to miscarry.

MILLAMANT   Ha? Dear creature, I ask your pardon. I swear I did not mind you.

MRS. MARWOOD   Mr. Mirabell and you both may think it a thing impossible, when I shall tell him by telling you—

MILLAMANT   Oh dear, what? For it is the same thing, if I hear it, ha! ha! ha!

MRS. MARWOOD   That I detest him, hate him, madam.

MILLAMANT   O madam, why so do I—and yet the creature loves me, ha! ha! ha! How can one forbear laughing to think of it! I am a sybil if I am not amazed to think what he can see in me. I'll take my death, I think you are handsomer—and within a year or two as young. If you could but stay for me, I should overtake you—but that cannot be. —Well, that thought makes me melancholy. —Now I'll be sad.

MRS. MARWOOD   Your merry note may be changed sooner than you think.

MILLAMANT   D'ye say so? Then I'm resolved to have a song to keep up my spirits.

Enter MINCING.

MINCING   The gentlemen stay but to comb, madam, and will wait on you.

1. White Rhenish wine was supposed to benefit the figure and complexion.
2. Lady to whom toasts are no longer drunk.

MILLAMANT   Desire Mrs. ——, that is in the next room, to sing the song
I would have learned yesterday. You shall hear it, madam, not that
there's any great matter in it, but 'tis agreeable to my humour.

SONG

Set by Mr. John Eccles and sung by Mrs. Hodgson.

I

Love's but the frailty of the mind,
When 'tis not with ambition joined;
A sickly flame, which, if not fed, expires,
And feeding, wastes in self-consuming fires.

II

'Tis not to wound a wanton boy
Or amorous youth, that gives the joy;
But 'tis the glory to have pierced a swain,
For whom inferior beauties sighed in vain.

III

Then I alone the conquest prize,
When I insult a rival's eyes;
If there's delight in love, 'tis when I see
That heart, which others bleed for, bleed for me.

Enter PETULANT *and* WITWOUD.

MILLAMANT   Is your animosity composed, gentlemen?
WITWOUD   Raillery, raillery, madam; we have no animosity. We hit off
a little wit now and then, but no animosity. The falling-out of wits is
like the falling-out of lovers; we agree in the main,[3] like treble and
bass. Ha, Petulant?
PETULANT   Aye, in the main, but when I have a humour to contradict.
WITWOUD   Aye, when he has a humour to contradict, then I contradict
too. What, I know my cue. Then we contradict one another like two
battledores,[4] for contradictions beget one another like Jews.
PETULANT   If he says black's black, if I have a humour to say 'tis blue,
let that pass; all's one for that. If I have a humour to prove it, it must
be granted.
WITWOUD   Not positively must, but it may, it may.
PETULANT   Yes, it positively must, upon proof positive.
WITWOUD   Aye, upon proof positive it must; but upon proof presump-
tive it only may. That's a logical distinction now, madam.

---

3. Mainly. Also a musical term for the middle voice in a song.
4. Small rackets in a game of shuttlecock (badminton).

MRS. MARWOOD   I perceive your debates are of importance and very learnedly handled.

PETULANT   Importance is one thing, and learning's another; but a debate's a debate, that I assert.

WITWOUD   Petulant's an enemy to learning; he relies altogether on his parts.

PETULANT   No, I'm no enemy to learning; it hurts not me.

MRS. MARWOOD   That's a sign indeed it's no enemy to you.

PETULANT   No, no, it's no enemy to anybody but them that have it.

MILLAMANT   Well, an illiterate man's my aversion. I wonder at the impudence of any illiterate man to offer to make love.

WITWOUD   That I confess I wonder at too.

MILLAMANT   Ah! to marry an ignorant that can hardly read or write!

PETULANT   Why should a man be ever the further from being married, though he can't read, any more than he is from being hanged? The ordinary's[5] paid for setting the psalm, and the parish priest for reading the ceremony. And for the rest which is to follow in both cases, a man may do it without book; so all's one for that.

MILLAMANT   D'ye hear the creature? Lord, here's company, I'll be gone.

Exeunt MILLAMANT *and* MINCING.

WITWOUD   In the name of Bartlemew and his fair,[6] what have we here?

MRS. MARWOOD   'Tis your brother, I fancy. Don't you know him?

WITWOUD   Not I. Yes, I think it is he. I've almost forgot him; I have not seen him since the Revolution.[7]

Enter SIR WILFULL WITWOUD *in a country riding habit, and a* SERVANT *to* LADY WISHFORT.

SERVANT   Sir, my lady's dressing. Here's company; if you please to walk in, in the meantime.

SIR WILFULL   Dressing! What, it's but morning here, I warrant, with you in London; we should count it towards afternoon in our parts, down in Shropshire. Why then, belike my aunt han't dined yet, ha, friend?

SERVANT   Your aunt, sir?

SIR WILFULL   My aunt, sir! Yes, my aunt, sir, and your lady, sir; your lady is my aunt, sir. Why, what, dost thou not know me, friend? Why then, send somebody here that does. How long hast thou lived with thy lady, fellow, ha?

SERVANT   A week, sir; longer than anybody in the house, except my lady's woman.

SIR WILFULL   Why then, belike thou dost not know thy lady, if thou seest her, ha, friend?

5. Clergyman who ministered to condemned prisoners.
6. Bartholomew Fair, held annually in Smithfield around 24 August.
7. Bloodless Revolution of 1688.

SERVANT   Why truly, sir, I cannot safely swear to her face in a morning, before she is dressed. 'Tis like I may give a shrewd guess at her by this time.

SIR WILFULL   Well, prithee try what thou canst do; if thou canst not guess, inquire her out, dost hear, fellow? And tell her, her nephew, Sir Wilfull Witwoud, is in the house.

SERVANT   I shall, sir.

SIR WILFULL   Hold ye, hear me, friend; a word with you in your ear. Prithee who are these gallants?

SERVANT   Really, sir, I can't tell; here come so many here, 'tis hard to know 'em all.

Exit SERVANT.

SIR WILFULL   Oons, this fellow knows less than a starling; I don't think a'knows his own name.

MRS. MARWOOD   Mr. Witwoud, your brother is not behindhand in forgetfulness; I fancy he has forgot you too.

WITWOUD   I hope so. The devil take him that remembers first, I say.

SIR WILFULL   Save you, gentlemen and lady!

MRS. MARWOOD   For shame, Mr. Witwoud; why won't you speak to him? And you, sir.

WITWOUD   Petulant, speak.

PETULANT   And you, sir.

SIR WILFULL   No offense, I hope.

Salutes MARWOOD.

MRS. MARWOOD   No sure, sir.

WITWOUD   This is a vile dog, I see that already. No offense! Ha! ha! ha! to him; to him, Petulant, smoke him.

PETULANT   It seems as if you had come a journey, sir; hem, hem.

Surveying him round.

SIR WILFULL   Very likely, sir, that it may seem so.

PETULANT   No offense, I hope, sir.

WITWOUD   Smoke the boots, the boots; Petulant, the boots, ha! ha! ha!

SIR WILFULL   May be not, sir; thereafter as 'tis meant, sir.

PETULANT   Sir, I presume upon the information of your boots.

SIR WILFULL   Why, 'tis like you may, sir. If you are not satisfied with the information of my boots, sir, if you will step to the stable, you may inquire further of my horse, sir.

PETULANT   Your horse, sir! Your horse is an ass, sir!

SIR WILFULL   Do you speak by way of offense, sir?

MRS. MARWOOD   The gentleman's merry, that's all, sir. —[*Aside.*] 'Slife, we shall have a quarrel betwixt an horse and an ass, before they find one another out. —[*Aloud.*] You must not take anything amiss from your friends, sir. You are among your friends here, though it may be you don't know it. If I am not mistaken, you are Sir Wilfull Witwoud.

SIR WILFULL   Right, lady; I am Sir Wilfull Witwoud, so I write myself; no offense to anybody, I hope; and nephew to the Lady Wishfort of this mansion.

MRS. MARWOOD   Don't you know this gentleman, sir?

SIR WILFULL   Hum! What, sure 'tis not—yea by'r Lady, but 'tis. 'Sheart, I know not whether 'tis or no. Yea, but 'tis, by the Wrekin.[8] Brother Anthony! What, Tony, i'faith! What, dost thou not know me? By'r Lady, nor I thee, thou art so be-cravated and be-periwigged. 'Sheart, why dost not speak? Art thou o'er-joyed?

WITWOUD   Ods, brother, is it you? Your servant, brother.

SIR WILFULL   Your servant! Why, yours, sir. Your servant again, 'sheart, and your friend and servant to that, and a—[puff] and a flapdragon for your service, sir! and a hare's foot, and a hare's scut for your service, sir, an you be so cold and so courtly!

WITWOUD   No offense, I hope, brother.

SIR WILFULL   'Sheart, sir, but there is, and much offense! A pox, is this your Inns o'Court[9] breeding, not to know your friends and your relations, your elders and your betters?

WITWOUD   Why, brother Wilfull of Salop,[1] you may be as short as a Shrewsbury cake, if you please. But I tell you, 'tis not modish to know relations in town. You think you're in the country, where great lubberly brothers slabber and kiss one another when they meet, like a call of serjeants. 'Tis not the fashion here; 'tis not indeed, dear brother.

SIR WILFULL   The fashion's a fool; and you're a fop, dear brother. 'Sheart, I've suspected this. By'r Lady, I conjectured you were a fop, since you began to change the style of your letters and write in a scrap of paper, gilt round the edges, no broader than a subpoena. I might expect this when you left off Honored Brother, and hoping you are in good health, and so forth—to begin with a Rat me,[2] knight, I'm so sick of a last night's debauch—ods heart, and then tell a familiar tale of a cock and a bull, and a whore and a bottle, and so conclude. You could write news before you were out of your time,[3] when you lived with honest Pumple Nose, the attorney of Furnival's Inn,[4] you could entreat to be remembered then to your friends round the Wrekin. We could have gazettes then, and Dawks's Letter, and the Weekly Bill,[5] till of late days.

PETULANT   'Slife, Witwoud, were you ever an attorney's clerk? of the family of the Furnivals? Ha! ha! ha!

WITWOUD   Aye, aye, but that was for a while, not long, not long. Pshaw!

8. A famous hill in Shropshire.
9. The legal societies in London.
1. Shropshire.
2. Contraction of may God rot me.
3. While you were still apprentice to an attorney.
4. A subordinate Inn of Court.
5. Newspapers. Dawks's Letter was a weekly news-sheet; the Weekly Bill was the official list of deaths in and around London.

I was not in my own power then; an orphan, and this fellow was my guardian. Aye, aye, I was glad to consent to that man to come to London. He had the disposal of me then. If I had not agreed to that, I might have been bound prentice to a felt-maker in Shrewsbury; this fellow would have bound me to a maker of felts.

SIR WILFULL 'Sheart, and better than to be bound to a maker of fops, where, I suppose, you have served your time; and now you may set up for yourself.

MRS. MARWOOD You intend to travel, sir, as I'm informed.

SIR WILFULL Belike I may, madam. I may chance to sail upon the salt seas, if my mind hold.

PETULANT And the wind serve.

SIR WILFULL Serve or not serve, I shan't ask license of you, sir; nor the weathercock your companion. I direct my discourse to the lady, sir. 'Tis like my aunt may have told you, madam. Yes, I have settled my concerns, I may say now, and am minded to see foreign parts. If an how that the peace holds,[6] whereby, that is, taxes abate.

MRS. MARWOOD I thought you had designed for France at all adventures.

SIR WILFULL I can't tell that; 'tis like I may, and 'tis like I may not. I am somewhat dainty in making a resolution, because when I make it, I keep it. I don't stand shill I, shall I, then; if I say't, I'll do't. But I have thoughts to tarry a small matter in town, to learn somewhat of your lingo first, before I cross the seas. I'd gladly have a spice of your French, as they say, whereby to hold discourse in foreign countries.

MRS. MARWOOD Here is an academy in town for that use.

SIR WILFULL There is? 'Tis like there may.

MRS. MARWOOD No doubt you will return very much improved.

WITWOUD Yes, refined, like a Dutch skipper from a whale-fishing.

Enter LADY WISHFORT *and* FAINALL.

LADY WISHFORT Nephew, you are welcome.

SIR WILFULL Aunt, your servant.

FAINALL Sir Wilfull, your most faithful servant.

SIR WILFULL Cousin Fainall, give me your hand.

LADY WISHFORT Cousin Witwoud, your servant; Mr. Petulant, your servant. Nephew, you are welcome again. Will you drink anything after your journey, nephew, before you eat? Dinner's almost ready.

SIR WILFULL I'm very well, I thank you, aunt; however, I thank you for your courteous offer. 'Sheart, I was afraid you would have been in the fashion too, and have remembered to have forgot your relations. Here's your cousin Tony; belike I mayn't call him brother for fear of offense.

6. The Peace of Ryswick in 1697 interrupted war with France.

LADY WISHFORT   Oh, he's a rallier, nephew. My cousin's a wit; and your great wits always rally their best friends to choose.[7] When you have been abroad, nephew, you'll understand raillery better.

    FAINALL *and* MRS. MARWOOD *talk apart.*

SIR WILFULL   Why then, let him hold his tongue in the meantime, and rail when that day comes.

    Enter MINCING.

MINCING   Mem, I come to acquaint your la'ship that dinner is impatient.

SIR WILFULL   Impatient? Why then, belike it won't stay till I pull off my boots. Sweetheart, can you help me to a pair of slippers? My man's with his horses, I warrant.

LADY WISHFORT   Fie, fie, nephew, you would not pull off your boots here. Go down into the hall; dinner shall stay for you. My nephew's a little unbred; you'll pardon him, madam. Gentlemen, will you walk? Marwood?

MRS. MARWOOD   I'll follow you, madam, before Sir Wilfull is ready.

    Exeunt all but MRS. MARWOOD *and* FAINALL.

FAINALL   Why then, Foible's a bawd, an arrant, rank, matchmaking bawd. And I, it seems, am a husband, a rank husband; and my wife a very arrant, rank wife, all in the way of the world. 'Sdeath, to be an anticipated cuckold, a cuckold in embryo! Sure I was born with budding antlers, like a young satyr, or a citizen's child.[8] 'Sdeath, to be outwitted, to be out-jilted, out-matrimonied! If I had kept my speed like a stag, 'twere somewhat; but to crawl after, with my horns like a snail, and outstripped by my wife, 'tis scurvy wedlock.

MRS. MARWOOD   Then shake it off. You have often wished for an opportunity to part; and now you have it. But first prevent their plot; the half of Millamant's fortune is too considerable to be parted with, to a foe, to Mirabell.

FAINALL   Damn him! that had been mine, had you not made that fond discovery. That had been forfeited, had they been married. My wife had added luster to my horns by that increase of fortune; I could have worn 'em tipt with gold, though my forehead had been furnished like a deputy lieutenant's hall.[9]

MRS. MARWOOD   They may prove a cap of maintenance[1] to you still, if you can away with[2] your wife. And she's no worse than when you had her. I dare swear she had given up her game before she was married.

7. Make fun of their friends at will.
8. Fainall would think that the child of a citizen (a London merchant) was born to be cuckolded by rakes of higher social class.
9. With antlers—i.e., the cuckold's horns.
1. In heraldry, a cap with two points (i.e., the cuckold's horns again), worn as a sign of dignity.
2. Endure.

FAINALL   Hum! That may be. She might throw up her cards; but I'll be hanged if she did not put Pam in her pocket.[3]

MRS. MARWOOD   You married her to keep you; and if you can contrive to have her keep you better than you expected, why should you not keep her longer than you intended?

FAINALL   The means, the means.

MRS. MARWOOD   Discover to my lady your wife's conduct; threaten to part with her. My lady loves her, and will come to any composition to save her reputation. Take the opportunity of breaking it, just upon the discovery of this imposture. My lady will be enraged beyond bounds, and sacrifice niece and fortune and all, at that conjuncture. And let me alone to keep her warm; if she should flag in her part, I will not fail to prompt her.

FAINALL   Faith, this has an appearance.

MRS. MARWOOD   I'm sorry I hinted to my lady to endeavor a match between Millamant and Sir Wilfull; that may be an obstacle.

FAINALL   Oh, for that matter leave me to manage him; I'll disable him for that. He will drink like a Dane; after dinner, I'll set his hand in.

MRS. MARWOOD   Well, how do you stand affected towards your lady?

FAINALL   Why, faith, I'm thinking of it. Let me see. I am married already, so that's over. My wife has played the jade with me; well, that's over too. I never loved her, or if I had, why that would have been over too by this time. Jealous of her I cannot be, for I am certain; so there's an end of jealousy. Weary of her I am, and shall be. No, there's no end of that; no, no, that were too much to hope. Thus far concerning my repose; now for my reputation. As to my own, I married not for it; so that's out of the question. And as to my part in my wife's, why she had parted with hers before; so bringing none to me, she can take none from me. 'Tis against all rule of play that I should lose to one who has not wherewithal to stake.

MRS. MARWOOD   Besides, you forget, marriage is honorable.

FAINALL   Hum! Faith, and that's well thought on. Marriage is honorable, as you say; and if so, wherefore should cuckoldom be a discredit, being derived from so honorable a root?

MRS. MARWOOD   Nay, I know not; if the root be honorable, why not the branches?[4]

FAINALL   So, so; why this point's clear. Well, how do we proceed?

MRS. MARWOOD   I will contrive a letter which shall be delivered to my lady at the time when that rascal who is to act Sir Rowland is with her. It shall come as from an unknown hand, for the less I appear to know of the truth, the better I can play the incendiary. Besides, I would not have Foible provoked if I could help it, because you know she knows some passages. Nay, I expect all will come out; but let the mine be sprung first, and then I care not if I'm discovered.

---

3. She has an ace up her sleeve (Mirabell). Pam is the highest card in the game of loo.
4. Of the cuckold's horns.

FAINALL   If the worst came to the worst, I'll turn my wife to grass.[5] I have already a deed of settlement of the best part of her estate, which I have wheedled out of her; and that you shall partake at least.

MRS. MARWOOD   I hope you are convinced that I hate Mirabell; now you'll be no more jealous.

FAINALL   Jealous! No, by this kiss. Let husbands be jealous; but let the lover still believe. Or if he doubt, let it be only to endear his pleasure, and prepare the joy that follows, when he proves his mistress true. But let husbands' doubts convert to endless jealousy; or if they have belief, let it corrupt to superstition and blind credulity. I am single, and will herd no more with 'em. True, I wear the badge, but I'll disown the order. And since I take my leave of 'em, I care not if I leave 'em a common motto to their common crest:

> All husbands must or pain or shame endure;
> The wise too jealous are, fools too secure.

Exeunt.

Act IV. *Scene continues.*

Enter LADY WISHFORT *and* FOIBLE.

LADY WISHFORT   Is Sir Rowland coming, say'st thou, Foible? and are things in order?

FOIBLE   Yes, madam, I have put wax lights in the sconces, and placed the footmen in a row in the hall, in their best liveries, with the coachman and postilion to fill up the equipage.

LADY WISHFORT   Have you pulvilled[6] the coachman and postilion that they may not stink of the stable when Sir Rowland comes by?

FOIBLE   Yes, madam.

LADY WISHFORT   And are the dancers and the music ready, that he may be entertained in all points with correspondence to his passion?

FOIBLE   All is ready, madam.

LADY WISHFORT   And—well—and how do I look, Foible?

FOIBLE   Most killing well, madam.

LADY WISHFORT   Well, and how shall I receive him? In what figure shall I give his heart the first impression? There is a great deal in the first impression. Shall I sit? —No, I won't sit—I'll walk—aye, I'll walk from the door upon his entrance; and then turn full upon him. —No, that will be too sudden. I'll lie—aye, I'll lie down—I'll receive him in my little dressing-room; there's a couch—yes, yes, I'll give the first impression on a couch. —I won't lie neither, but loll and lean upon one elbow, with one foot a little dangling off, jogging in a thoughtful way—yes—and then as soon as he appears, start, aye, start and be surprised, and rise to meet him in a pretty disorder—yes—

5. Turn her out to pasture.
6. Powdered with scent.

oh, nothing is more alluring than a levee[7] from a couch in some confusion. —It shows the foot to advantage, and furnishes with blushes, and recomposing airs beyond comparison. Hark! There's a coach.

FOIBLE   'Tis he, madam.

LADY WISHFORT   Oh dear, has my nephew made his addresses to Millamant? I ordered him.

FOIBLE   Sir Wilfull is set in to drinking, madam, in the parlor.

LADY WISHFORT   Ods my life, I'll send him to her. Call her down, Foible; bring her hither. I'll send him as I go. When they are together, then come to me, Foible, that I may not be too long alone with Sir Rowland.

Exit.

Enter MRS. MILLAMANT *and* MRS. FAINALL.

FOIBLE   Madam, I stayed here, to tell your ladyship that Mr. Mirabell has waited this half hour for an opportunity to talk with you, though my lady's orders were to leave you and Sir Wilfull together. Shall I tell Mr. Mirabell that you are at leisure?

MILLAMANT   No—what would the dear man have? I am thoughtful and would amuse myself—bid him come another time.

> There never yet was woman made,
> Nor shall, but to be cursed.[8]

Repeating and walking about.

That's hard!

MRS. FAINALL   You are very fond of Sir John Suckling today, Millamant, and the poets.

MILLAMANT   He? Aye, and filthy verses; so I am.

FOIBLE   Sir Wilfull is coming, madam. Shall I send Mr. Mirabell away?

MILLAMANT   Aye, if you please, Foible, send him away—or send him hither—just as you will, dear Foible—I think I'll see him—shall I? Aye, let the wretch come.

Exit FOIBLE.

> Thyrsis, a youth of the inspired train.[9]

Repeating.

Dear Fainall, entertain Sir Wilfull. Thou hast philosophy to undergo a fool; thou art married and hast patience. I would confer with my own thoughts.

7. A rising.
8. The opening lines of an untitled poem by Sir John Suckling. The poems which Millamant calls to mind—on the brevity of love and the falseness of men—reflect concern for her own situation and perhaps the depth of her feeling for Mirabell.
9. The first line of Edmund Waller's *The Story of Phoebus and Daphne, Applied.*

MRS. FAINALL   I am obliged to you, that you would make me your proxy
in this affair; but I have business of my own.

> *Enter* SIR WILFULL.

O Sir Wilfull, you are come at the critical instant. There's your mistress up to the ears in love and contemplation; pursue your point,
now or never.

SIR WILFULL   Yes; my aunt would have it so. I would gladly have been
encouraged with a bottle or two, because I'm somewhat wary at first,
before I am acquainted. [*This while* MILLAMANT *walks about repeating
to herself.*] But I hope, after a time, I shall break my mind; that is,
upon further acquaintance. So for the present, cousin, I'll take my
leave. If so be you'll be so kind to make my excuse, I'll return to my
company.

MRS. FAINALL   Oh, fie, Sir Wilfull! What, you must not be daunted.

SIR WILFULL   Daunted! No, that's not it. It is not so much for that; for
if so be that I set on't, I'll do't. But only for the present; 'tis sufficient
till further acquaintance, that's all. Your servant.

MRS. FAINALL   Nay, I'll swear you shall never lose so favorable an
opportunity, if I can help it. I'll leave you together and lock the door.

> *Exit.*

SIR WILFULL   Nay, nay, cousin. I have forgot my gloves. What d'ye do?
'Sheart, 'a has locked the door indeed, I think. Nay, Cousin Fainall,
open the door! Pshaw, what a vixen trick is this? Nay, now 'a has seen
me too. Cousin, I made bold to pass through as it were. I think this
door's enchanted!

MILLAMANT [*repeating*]

> I prithee spare me, gentle boy,
> Press me no more for that slight toy—[1]

SIR WILFULL   Anan?[2] Cousin, your servant.

MILLAMANT [*repeating*]

> That foolish trifle of a heart—

Sir Wilfull!

SIR WILFULL   Yes. Your servant. No offense, I hope, cousin.

MILLAMANT [*repeating*]

> I swear it will not do its part,
> Though thou dost thine, employ'st thy power and art.

Natural, easy Suckling!

SIR WILFULL   Anan? Suckling! No such suckling neither, cousin, nor
stripling; I thank heaven, I'm no minor.

MILLAMANT   Ah, rustic! ruder than Gothic!

---

1. The opening lines of an untitled song by Suckling.
2. "How's that?" A provincial term.

SIR WILFULL   Well, well, I shall understand your lingo one of these days, cousin; in the meanwhile, I must answer in plain English.

MILLAMANT   Have you any business with me, Sir Wilfull?

SIR WILFULL   Not at present, cousin. Yes, I made bold to see, to come and know if that how you were disposed to fetch a walk this evening, if so be that I might not be troublesome, I would have fought[3] a walk with you.

MILLAMANT   A walk! What then?

SIR WILFULL   Nay, nothing. Only for the walk's sake, that's all.

MILLAMANT   I nauseate walking; 'tis a country diversion. I loathe the country and everything that relates to it.

SIR WILFULL   Indeed! Ha! Look ye, look ye, you do? Nay, 'tis like you may. Here are choice of pastimes here in town, as plays and the like; that must be confessed indeed.

MILLAMANT   Ah, *l'étourdie!*[4] I hate the town too.

SIR WILFULL   Dear heart, that's much. Ha! that you should hate 'em both! Ha! 'tis like you may; there are some can't relish the town, and others can't away with the country. 'Tis like you may be one of those, cousin.

MILLAMANT   Ha! ha! ha! Yes, 'tis like I may. You have nothing further to say to me?

SIR WILFULL   Not at present, cousin. 'Tis like when I have an opportunity to be more private, I may break my mind in some measure. I conjecture you partly guess.—However, that's as time shall try; but spare to speak and spare to speed, as they say.

MILLAMANT   If it is of no great importance, Sir Wilfull, you will oblige me to leave me; I have just now a little business—

SIR WILFULL   Enough, enough, cousin, yes, yes, all a case; when you're disposed, when you're disposed. Now's as well as another time; and another time as well as now. All's one for that. Yes, yes, if your concerns call you, there's no haste; it will keep cold, as they say. Cousin, your servant. I think this door's locked.

MILLAMANT   You may go this way, sir.

SIR WILFULL   Your servant; then with your leave I'll return to my company.

Exit.

MILLAMANT   Aye, aye; ha! ha! ha!

Like Phoebus sung the no less amorous boy.[5]

Enter MIRABELL.

MIRABELL

Like Daphne she, as lovely and as coy.

3. A provincial form of *fetched.*
4. "Ah, the giddy town!"
5. From Waller's *Phoebus and Daphne*, line 3. Mirabell completes the couplet in the next line.

Do you lock yourself up from me, to make my search more curious?[6] Or is this pretty artifice contrived, to signify that here the chase must end and my pursuit be crowned, for you can fly no further?

MILLAMANT   Vanity! No. I'll fly and be followed to the last moment. Though I am upon the very verge of matrimony, I expect you should solicit me as much as if I were wavering at the grate of a monastery, with one foot over the threshold. I'll be solicited to the very last, nay and afterwards.

MIRABELL   What, after the last?

MILLAMANT   Oh, I should think I was poor and had nothing to bestow, if I were reduced to an inglorious ease and freed from the agreeable fatigues of solicitation.

MIRABELL   But do not you know that when favors are conferred upon instant and tedious solicitation, that they diminish in their value, and that both the giver loses the grace, and the receiver lessens his pleasure?

MILLAMANT   It may be in things of common application; but never sure in love. Oh, I hate a lover that can dare to think he draws a moment's air independent on the bounty of his mistress. There is not so impudent a thing in nature as the saucy look of an assured man, confident of success. The pedantic arrogance of a very husband has not so pragmatical an air. Ah! I'll never marry, unless I am first made sure of my will and pleasure.

MIRABELL   Would you have 'em both before marriage? Or will you be contented with the first now, and stay for the other till after grace?

MILLAMANT   Ah! don't be impertinent. —My dear liberty, shall I leave thee? My faithful solitude, my darling contemplation, must I bid you then adieu? Ay-h adieu —my morning thoughts, agreeable wakings, indolent slumbers, all ye *douceurs*, ye *sommeils du matin*,[7] adieu? —I can't do't, 'tis more than impossible. Positively, Mirabell, I'll lie abed in a morning as long as I please.

MIRABELL   Then I'll get up in a morning as early as I please.

MILLAMANT   Ah! Idle creature, get up when you will. —And d'ye hear, I won't be called names after I'm married; positively I won't be called names.

MIRABELL   Names!

MILLAMANT   Aye, as wife, spouse, my dear, joy, jewel, love, sweetheart, and the rest of that nauseous cant, in which men and their wives are so fulsomely familiar—I shall never bear that. —Good Mirabell, don't let us be familiar or fond, nor kiss before folks, like my Lady Fadler and Sir Francis; nor go to Hyde Park together the first Sunday in a new chariot, to provoke eyes and whispers; and then never to be seen there together again; as if we were proud of one another the first week, and ashamed of one another ever after. Let us be very strange

6. Complicated.
7. Sweetnesses and morning naps.

and well-bred; let us be as strange[8] as if we had been married a great
while, and as well-bred as if we were not married at all.

MIRABELL   Have you any more conditions to offer? Hitherto your
demands are pretty reasonable.

MILLAMANT   Trifles! —As liberty to pay and receive visits to and from
whom I please; to write and receive letters, without interrogatories or
wry faces on your part; to wear what I please; and choose conversation
with regard only to my own taste; to have no obligation upon me to
converse with wits that I don't like, because they are your acquaintance; or to be intimate with fools, because they may be your relations. Come to dinner when I please; dine in my dressing room when
I'm out of humour, without giving a reason. To have my closet inviolate; to be sole empress of my tea table, which you must never presume to approach without first asking leave. And lastly, wherever I
am, you shall always knock at the door before you come in. These
articles subscribed, if I continue to endure you a little longer, I may
be degrees dwindle into a wife.

MIRABELL   Your bill of fare is something advanced in this latter account.
Well, have I liberty to offer conditions—that when you are dwindled
into a wife, I may not be beyond measure enlarged into a husband?

MILLAMANT   You have free leave. Propose your utmost; speak and spare
not.

MIRABELL   I thank you. *Imprimis*[9] then, I covenant that your acquaintance be general; that you admit no sworn confidante, or intimate of
your own sex; no she-friend to screen her affairs under your countenance, and tempt you to make trial of a mutual secrecy. No decoy-
duck to wheedle you a fop, scrambling to the play in a mask; then
bring you home in a pretended fright, when you think you shall be
found out, and rail at me for missing the play, and disappointing the
frolic which you had, to pick me up and prove my constancy.

MILLAMANT   Detestable *imprimis*! I go to the play in a mask!

MIRABELL   *Item*, I article that you continue to like your own face as
long as I shall; and while it passes current with me, that you endeavor
not to new-coin it. To which end, together with all vizards[1] for the
day, I prohibit all masks for the night, made of oiled skins and I know
not what—hog's bones, hare's gall, pig-water, and the marrow of a
roasted cat. In short, I forbid all commerce with the gentlewoman in
What-d'ye-call-it Court. *Item*, I shut my doors against all bawds with
baskets, and pennyworths of muslin, china, fans, atlases,[2] etc. —*Item*,
when you shall be breeding—

MILLAMANT   Ah! name it not.

MIRABELL   Which may be presumed, with a blessing on our
endeavors—

---

8. Reserved.
9. *In the first place*; the phrasing of legal documents.
1. Masks.
2. Satins.

MILLAMANT   Odious endeavors!

MIRABELL   I denounce against all strait-lacing, squeezing for a shape, till you mold my boy's head like a sugar loaf, and instead of a man-child, make me the father to a crooked billet.[3] Lastly, to the dominion of the tea table I submit, but with proviso, that you exceed not in your province, but restrain yourself to native and simple tea-table drinks, as tea, chocolate, and coffee. As likewise to genuine and authorized tea-table talk—such as mending of fashions, spoiling reputations, railing at absent friends, and so forth; but that on no account you encroach upon the men's prerogative, and presume to drink healths, or toast fellows; for prevention of which, I banish all foreign forces, all auxiliaries to the tea table, as orange brandy, all aniseed, cinnamon, citron, and Barbadoes waters, together with ratafia and the most noble spirit of clary.[4] But for cowslip-wine, poppy-water, and all dormitives, those I allow. These provisos admitted, in other things I may prove a tractable and complying husband.

MILLAMANT   Oh, horrid provisos! filthy strong waters! I toast fellows, odious men! I hate your odious provisos.

MIRABELL   Then we're agreed. Shall I kiss your hand upon the contract? And here comes one to be a witness to the sealing of the deed.

   Enter MRS. FAINALL.

MILLAMANT   Fainall, what shall I do? Shall I have him? I think I must have him.

MRS. FAINALL   Aye, aye, take him, take him, what should you do?

MILLAMANT   Well then—I'll take my death I'm in a horrid fright—Fainall, I shall never say it—well—I think—I'll endure you.

MRS. FAINALL   Fie, fie! have him, have him, and tell him so in plain terms; for I am sure you have a mind to him.

MILLAMANT   Are you? I think I have—and the horrid man looks as if he thought so too. —Well, you ridiculous thing you, I'll have you—I won't be kissed, nor I won't be thanked—here, kiss my hand though. —So, hold your tongue now, and don't say a word.

MRS. FAINALL   Mirabell, there's a necessity for your obedience; you have neither time to talk nor stay. My mother is coming; and in my conscience, if she should see you, would fall into fits and maybe not recover time enough to return to Sir Rowland, who, as Foible tells me, is in a fair way to succeed. Therefore spare your ecstasies for another occasion, and slip down the backstairs, where Foible waits to consult you.

MILLAMANT   Aye, go, go. In the meantime I suppose you have said something to please me.

MIRABELL   I am all obedience.

                                                                              Exit.

3. Stick of wood.
4. These are all alcoholic drinks.

MRS. FAINALL   Yonder Sir Wilfull's drunk, and so noisy that my mother
has been forced to leave Sir Rowland to appease him; but he answers
her only with singing and drinking. What they have done by this time
I know not; but Petulant and he were quarreling as I came by.

MILLAMANT   Well, if Mirabell should not make a good husband, I am
a lost thing—for I find I love him violently.

MRS. FAINALL   So it seems, when you mind not what's said to you. If
you doubt him, you had best take up with Sir Wilfull.

MILLAMANT   How can you name that superannuated lubber? foh!

Enter WITWOUD *from drinking.*

MRS. FAINALL   So, is the fray made up, that you left 'em?

WITWOUD   Left 'em? I could stay no longer. I have laughed like ten
christenings; I am tipsy with laughing. If I had stayed any longer I
should have burst; I must have been let out and pieced in the sides
like an unsized camlet.[5] Yes, yes, the fray is composed; my lady came
in like a *nolle prosequi*[6] and stopped their proceedings.

MILLAMANT   What was the dispute?

WITWOUD   That's the jest; there was no dispute. They could neither of
'em speak for rage, and so fell a-sputtering at one another like two
roasting apples.

Enter PETULANT *drunk.*

Now Petulant, all's over, all's well. Gad, my head begins to whim it
about. Why dost thou not speak? Thou art both as drunk and as mute
as a fish.

PETULANT   Look you, Mrs. Millamant, if you can love me, dear
nymph, say it, and that's the conclusion. Pass on, or pass off; that's all.

WITWOUD   Thou hast uttered volumes, folios, in less than *decimo sexto*,
my dear Lacedemonian.[7] Sirrah Petulant, thou art an epitomizer of
words.

PETULANT   Witwoud, you are an annihilator of sense.

WITWOUD   Thou art a retailer of phrases and dost deal in remnants of
remnants, like a maker of pincushions; thou art in truth (metaphori-
cally speaking) a speaker of shorthand.

PETULANT   Thou are (without a figure) just one half of an ass, and
Baldwin[8] yonder, thy half brother, is the rest. A gemini[9] of asses split
would make just four of you.

WITWOUD   Thou dost bite, my dear mustard seed; kiss me for that.

PETULANT   Stand off! I'll kiss no more males. I have kissed your twin
yonder in a humour of reconciliation, till he [*hiccup*] rises upon my
stomach like a radish.

MILLAMANT   Eh! filthy creature! What was the quarrel?

5. An unstiffened fabric.
6. Legal phrase for ending a lawsuit.
7. *Decimo sexto* means *a small book.* Lacedemonians (Spartans) were men of few words.
8. The ass in the beast epic *Reynard the Fox.*
9. Twins, from the Roman deities Castor and Pollux.

PETULANT   There was no quarrel; there might have been a quarrel.

WITWOUD   If there had been words enow between 'em to have expressed provocation, they had gone together by the ears like a pair of castanets.

PETULANT   You were the quarrel.

MILLAMANT   Me!

PETULANT   If I have a humour to quarrel, I can make less matters conclude premises. If you are not handsome, what then, if I have a humour to prove it? If I shall have my reward, say so; if not, fight for your face the next time yourself. I'll go sleep.

WITWOUD   Do, wrap thyself up like a wood louse, and dream revenge; and hear me, if thou canst learn to write by tomorrow morning, pen me a challenge. I'll carry it for thee.

PETULANT   Carry your mistress's monkey a spider! Go flea dogs, and read romances! I'll go to bed to my maid.

Exit.

MRS. FAINALL   He's horridly drunk. How came you all in this pickle?

WITWOUD   A plot! a plot! to get rid of the knight. Your husband's advice; but he sneaked off.

Enter LADY WISHFORT, *and* SIR WILFULL *drunk.*

LADY WISHFORT   Out upon't, out upon't! At years of discretion, and comport yourself at this rantipole[1] rate!

SIR WILFULL   No offense, aunt.

LADY WISHFORT   Offense! As I'm a person, I'm ashamed of you—foh! how you stink of wine! D'ye think my niece will ever endure such a borachio! you're an absolute borachio.[2]

SIR WILFULL   Borachio!

LADY WISHFORT   At a time when you should commence an amour and put your best foot foremost—

SIR WILFULL   'Sheart, an you grutch me your liquor, make a bill. Give me more drink, and take my purse.

Sings.

> Prithee fill me the glass,
> Till it laugh in my face,
> With ale that is potent and mellow;
> He that whines for a lass
> Is an ignorant ass,
> For a bumper has not its fellow.

But if you would have me marry my cousin, say the word, and I'll do't. Wilfull will do't; that's the word. Wilfull will do't; that's my crest. My motto I have forgot.

1. Ill-mannered.
2. Drunkard.

LADY WISHFORT   My nephew's a little overtaken, cousin, but 'tis with drinking your health. O' my word you are obliged to him.

SIR WILFULL   *In vino veritas,*[3] aunt. If I drunk your health today, cousin, I am a borachio. But if you have a mind to be married, say the word, and send for the piper; Wilfull will do't. If not, dust it away, and let's have t'other round. —Tony! —Odsheart, where's Tony? —Tony's an honest fellow; but he spits after a bumper, and that's a fault.

   Sings.

> We'll drink, and we'll never ha' done, boys,
>   Put the glass then around with the sun, boys;
> Let Apollo's example invite us;
>   For he's drunk every night,
>   And that makes him so bright,
> That he's able next morning to light us.

The sun's a good pimple, an honest soaker; he has a cellar at your Antipodes. If I travel, aunt, I touch at your Antipodes;[4] your Antipodes are a good, rascally sort of topsy-turvy fellows. If I had a bumper, I'd stand upon my head and drink a health to 'em. A match, or no match, cousin with the hard name? Aunt, Wilfull will do't. If she has her maidenhead, let her look to't; if she has not, let her keep her own counsel in the meantime, and cry out at the nine months' end.

MILLAMANT   Your pardon, madam, I can stay no longer. Sir Wilfull grows very powerful. Egh! how he smells! I shall be overcome if I stay. Come, cousin.

   Exeunt MILLAMANT *and* MRS. FAINALL.

LADY WISHFORT   Smells! he would poison a tallow chandler[5] and his family. Beastly creature, I know not what to do with him! Travel, quotha! aye, travel, travel, get thee gone, get thee but far enough, to the Saracens, or the Tartars, or the Turks, for thou art not fit to live in a Christian commonwealth, thou beastly pagan!

SIR WILFULL   Turks, no; no Turks, aunt; your Turks are infidels, and believe not in the grape. Your Mahometan, your Mussulman, is a dry stinkard. No offense, aunt. My map says that your Turk is not so honest a man as your Christian. I cannot find by the map that your Mufti[6] is orthodox; whereby it is a plain case that orthodox is a hard word, aunt, and [*hiccup*] Greek for claret.

   Sings.

> To drink is a Christian diversion,
> Unknown to the Turk and the Persian:
>   Let Mahometan fools

3. "In wine there is truth."
4. Opposite places of the earth. *Pimple:* good friend.
5. A maker or seller of candles.
6. Mohammedan priest.

> Live by heathenish rules,
> And be damned over tea cups and coffee!
> But let British lads sing,
> Crown a health to the king,
> And a fig for your sultan and sophy![7]

Ah, Tony!

Enter FOIBLE, *and whispers* LADY WISHFORT.

LADY WISHFORT [*aside to* FOIBLE]   Sir Rowland impatient? Good lack!
What shall I do with this beastly tumbril?[8] [*Aloud.*] Go lie down and
sleep, you sot! or, as I'm a person, I'll have you bastinadoed[9] with
broomsticks. Call up the wenches.

Exit FOIBLE.

SIR WILFULL   Ahey! Wenches, where are the wenches?
LADY WISHFORT   Dear Cousin Witwoud, get him away, and you will
bind me to you inviolably. I have an affair of moment that invades
me with some precipitation. You will oblige me to all futurity.
WITWOUD   Come, knight. Pox on him, I don't know what to say to him.
Will you go to a cock-match?
SIR WILFULL   With a wench, Tony? Is she a shake-bag,[1] Sirrah? Let me
bite your cheek for that.
WITWOUD   Horrible! He has a breath like a bagpipe! Aye, aye, come,
will you march, my Salopian?[2]
SIR WILFULL   Lead on, little Tony; I'll follow thee, my Anthony, my
Tantony.[3] Sirrah, thou shalt be my Tantony, and I'll be thy pig.

And a fig for your sultan and sophy.

Exit singing with WITWOUD.

LADY WISHFORT   This will never do. It will never make a match—at
least before he has been abroad.

Enter WAITWELL, *disguised as for* SIR ROWLAND.

Dear Sir Rowland, I am confounded with confusion at the retrospec-
tion of my own rudeness! I have more pardons to ask than the Pope
distributes in the Year of Jubilee. But I hope, where there is likely to
be so near an alliance, we may unbend the severity of decorum and
dispense with a little ceremony.
WAITWELL   My impatience, madam, is the effect of my transport; and
till I have the possession of your adorable person, I am tantalized on
a rack, and do but hang, madam, on the tenter of expectation.

7. The Shah of Persia.
8. Dung cart.
9. Beaten on the soles of the feet.
1. Gamecock.
2. Native of Shropshire.
3. St. Anthony, the patron of swineherds.

LADY WISHFORT   You have an excess of gallantry, Sir Rowland, and press things to a conclusion with a most prevailing vehemence. But a day or two for decency of marriage—

WAITWELL   For decency of funeral, madam! The delay will break my heart; or, if that should fail, I shall be poisoned. My nephew will get an inkling of my designs and poison me; and I would willingly starve him before I die; I would gladly go out of the world with that satisfaction. That would be some comfort to me, if I could but live so long as to be revenged on that unnatural viper.

LADY WISHFORT   Is he so unnatural, say you? Truly I would contribute much both to the saving of your life, and the accomplishment of your revenge. Not that I respect[4] myself, though he has been a perfidious wretch to me.

WAITWELL   Perfidious to you!

LADY WISHFORT   O Sir Rowland, the hours that he has died away at my feet, the tears that he has shed, the oaths that he has sworn, the palpitations that he has felt, the trances and the tremblings, the ardors and the ecstasies, the kneelings and the risings, the heart-heavings, and the hand-grippings, the pangs and the pathetic regards of his protesting eyes! Oh, no memory can register.

WAITWELL   What, my rival! Is the rebel my rival? 'A dies.

LADY WISHFORT   No, don't kill him at once, Sir Rowland; starve him gradually, inch by inch.

WAITWELL   I'll do't. In three weeks he shall be barefoot; in a month out at knees with begging an alms. He shall starve upward and upward, till he has nothing living but his head, and then go out in a stink like a candle's end upon a save-all.[5]

LADY WISHFORT   Well, Sir Rowland, you have the way. You are no novice in the labyrinth of love; you have the clue. But as I am a person, Sir Rowland, you must not attribute my yielding to any sinister appetite, or indigestion of widowhood; nor impute my complacency to any lethargy of continence. I hope you do not think me prone to any iteration of nuptials.

WAITWELL   Far be it from me—

LADY WISHFORT   If you do, I protest I must recede, or think that I have made a prostitution of decorums; but in the vehemence of compassion, and to save the life of a person of so much importance—

WAITWELL   I esteem it so.

LADY WISHFORT   Or else you wrong my condescension.

WAITWELL   I do not, I do not!

LADY WISHFORT   Indeed you do.

WAITWELL   I do not, fair shrine of virtue!

LADY WISHFORT   If you think the least scruple of carnality was an ingredient—

---

4. Consider.
5. A device for burning candles to the end.

WAITWELL   Dear madam, no. You are all camphire[6] and frankincense, all chastity and odor.

LADY WISHFORT   Or that—

Enter FOIBLE.

FOIBLE   Madam, the dancers are ready, and there's one with a letter, who must deliver it into your own hands.

LADY WISHFORT   Sir Rowland, will you give me leave? Think favorably, judge candidly, and conclude you have found a person who would suffer racks in honor's cause, dear Sir Rowland, and will wait on you incessantly.[7]

WAITWELL   Fie, fie! What a slavery have I undergone! Spouse, hast thou any cordial! I want spirits.

FOIBLE   What a washy rogue art thou, to pant thus for a quarter of an hour's lying and swearing to a fine lady!

WAITWELL   Oh, she is the antidote to desire! Spouse, thou wilt fare the worse for't. I shall have no appetite to iteration of nuptials this eight-and-forty hours. By this hand I'd rather be a chairman in the dog-days[8] than act Sir Rowland till this time tomorrow!

Enter LADY WISHFORT, *with a letter.*

LADY WISHFORT   Call in the dancers. Sir Rowland, we'll sit, if you please, and see the entertainment.

Dance.

Now, with your permission, Sir Rowland, I will peruse my letter. I would open it in your presence, because I would not make you uneasy. If it should make you uneasy, I would burn it. Speak, if it does. But you may see by the superscription it is like a woman's hand.

FOIBLE [*aside to* WAITWELL]   By heaven! Mrs. Marwood's; I know it. My heart aches. Get it from her.

WAITWELL   A woman's hand? No, madam, that's no woman's hand; I see that already. That's somebody whose throat must be cut.

LADY WISHFORT   Nay, Sir Rowland, since you give me a proof of your passion by your jealousy, I promise you I'll make you a return, by a frank communication. You shall see it; we'll open it together. Look you here. [*Reads.*] "Madam, though unknown to you"—Look you there, 'tis from nobody that I know—"I have that honor for your character, that I think myself obliged to let you know you are abused. He who pretends to be Sir Rowland is a cheat and a rascal." —Oh, heavens! what's this?

FOIBLE [*aside*]   Unfortunate! all's ruined!

WAITWELL   How, how, let me see, let me see! [*Reading.*] "A rascal, and

6. Camphor was supposed to reduce sexual desire.
7. Instantly.
8. Bearer of a sedan chair in the hottest time of summer.

disguised and suborned for that imposture." —O villainy! O villainy—"by the contrivance of—"

LADY WISHFORT   I shall faint. I shall die, I shall die, oh!

FOIBLE [*aside to* WAITWELL]   Say 'tis your nephew's hand. Quickly, his plot, swear, swear it!

WAITWELL   Here's a villain! Madam, don't you perceive it? don't you see it?

LADY WISHFORT   Too well, too well! I have seen too much.

WAITWELL   I told you at first I knew the hand. A woman's hand? The rascal writes a sort of a large hand, your Roman hand. I saw there was a throat to be cut presently. If he were my son, as he is my nephew, I'd pistol him!

FOIBLE   Oh, treachery! But are you sure, Sir Rowland, it is his writing?

WAITWELL   Sure? Am I here? Do I live? Do I love this pearl of India? I have twenty letters in my pocket from him in the same character.

LADY WISHFORT   How!

FOIBLE   Oh, what luck it is, Sir Rowland, that you were present at this juncture! This was the business that brought Mr. Mirabell disguised to Madam Millamant this afternoon. I thought something was contriving, when he stole by me and would have hid his face.

LADY WISHFORT   How, how! I heard the villain was in the house indeed; and now I remember, my niece went away abruptly, when Sir Wilfull was to have made his addresses.

FOIBLE   Then, then, madam, Mr. Mirabell waited for her in her chamber, but I would not tell your ladyship to discompose you when you were to receive Sir Rowland.

WAITWELL   Enough, his date is short.

FOIBLE   No, good Sir Rowland, don't incur the law.

WAITWELL   Law? I care not for law. I can but die, and 'tis in a good cause. My lady shall be satisfied of my truth and innocence, though it cost me my life.

LADY WISHFORT   No, dear Sir Rowland, don't fight; if you should be killed, I must never show my face; or hanged—oh, consider my reputation, Sir Rowland! No, you shan't fight. I'll go in and examine my niece; I'll make her confess. I conjure you, Sir Rowland, by all your love, not to fight.

WAITWELL   I am charmed, madam; I obey. But some proof you must let me give you; I'll go for a black box, which contains the writings of my whole estate, and deliver that into your hands.

LADY WISHFORT   Aye, dear Sir Rowland, that will be some comfort; bring the black box.

WAITWELL   And may I presume to bring a contract to be signed this night? May I hope so far?

LADY WISHFORT   Bring what you will; but come alive, pray come alive. Oh, this is a happy discovery!

WAITWELL   Dead or alive I'll come, and married we will be in spite of treachery; aye, and get an heir that shall defeat the last remaining glimpse of hope in my abandoned nephew. Come, my buxom widow.

> Ere long you shall substantial proof receive
> That I'm an errant knight—

FOIBLE [*aside*]

> Or arrant knave.

Exeunt.

Act V. *Scene continues.*

Enter LADY WISHFORT *and* FOIBLE.

LADY WISHFORT   Out of my house, out of my house, thou viper! thou serpent, that I have fostered! thou bosom traitress that I raised from nothing! Begone! begone! begone! go! go! That I took from washing of old gauze and weaving of dead hair,[9] with a bleak blue nose, over a chafing dish of starved embers, and dining behind a traverse rag, in a shop no bigger than a birdcage! Go, go! starve again, do, do!

FOIBLE   Dear madam, I'll beg pardon on my knees.

LADY WISHFORT   Away! out! out! Go set up for yourself again! Do, drive a trade, do, with your three-pennyworth of small ware, flaunting upon a pack-thread, under a brandy-seller's bulk, or against a dead wall by a ballad-monger! Go, hang out an old frisoneer gorget, with a yard of yellow colberteen again.[1] Do! an old gnawed mask, two rows of pins, and a child's fiddle; a glass necklace with the beads broken, and a quilted nightcap with one ear. Go, go, drive a trade! These were your commodities, you treacherous trull! This was your merchandise you dealt in, when I took you into my house, placed you next myself, and made you governante of my whole family! You have forgot this, have you, now you have feathered your nest?

FOIBLE   No, no, dear madam. Do but hear me; have but a moment's patience. I'll confess all. Mr. Mirabell seduced me; I am not the first that he has wheedled with his dissembling tongue. Your ladyship's own wisdom has been deluded by him; then how should I, a poor ignorant, defend myself? O madam, if you knew but what he promised me, and how he assured me your ladyship should come to no damage! Or else the wealth of the Indies should not have bribed me to conspire against so good, so sweet, so kind a lady as you have been to me.

LADY WISHFORT   No damage? What, to betray me, to marry me to a cast servingman? to make me a receptacle, an hospital for a decayed pimp? No damage? O thou frontless[2] impudence, more than a big-bellied actress.

9. Wig-making.
1. *Gorget*, a woolen neckpiece; *colberteen*, cheap lace.
2. Shameless.

FOIBLE   Pray do but hear me, madam; he could not marry your ladyship, madam. No indeed; his marriage was to have been void in law,
for he was married to me first, to secure your ladyship. He could not
have bedded your ladyship; for if he had consummated with your
ladyship, he must have run the risk of the law and been put upon his
clergy.[3] Yes indeed; I inquired of the law in that case before I would
meddle or make.

LADY WISHFORT   What, then I have been your property, have I? I have
been convenient to you, it seems! While you were catering for Mirabell, I have been broker for you? What, have you made a passive bawd
of me? This exceeds all precedent; I am brought to fine uses, to
become a botcher of secondhand marriages between Abigails and
Andrews![4] I'll couple you! Yes, I'll baste you together, you and your
Philander![5] I'll Duke's Place you, as I'm a person! Your turtle is in
custody already; you shall coo in the same cage, if there be constable
or warrant in the parish.

Exit.

FOIBLE   Oh, that ever I was born! Oh, that I was ever married! A bride!
aye, I shall be a Bridewell-bride.[6] Oh!

Enter MRS. FAINALL.

MRS. FAINALL   Poor Foible, what's the matter?

FOIBLE   O madam, my lady's gone for a constable. I shall be had to a
justice, and put to Bridewell to beat hemp. Poor Waitwell's gone to
prison already.

MRS. FAINALL   Have a good heart, Foible; Mirabell's gone to give security for him. This is all Marwood's and my husband's doing.

FOIBLE   Yes, yes, I know it, madam; she was in my lady's closet, and
overheard all that you said to me before dinner. She sent the letter to
my lady; and that missing effect, Mr. Fainall laid this plot to arrest
Waitwell, when he pretended to go for the papers; and in the meantime Mrs. Marwood declared all to my lady.

MRS. FAINALL   Was there no mention made of me in the letter? My
mother does not suspect my being in the confederacy? I fancy Marwood has not told her, though she has told my husband.

FOIBLE   Yes, madam; but my lady did not see that part. We stifled the
letter before she read so far. Has that mischievous devil told Mr. Fainall of your ladyship then?

MRS. FAINALL   Aye, all's out, my affair with Mirabell, everything discovered. This is the last day of our living together; that's my comfort.

FOIBLE   Indeed, madam, and so 'tis a comfort if you knew all. He has

---

3. First offenders could sometimes escape penal sentence by showing an ability to read and
write. The privilege was called "benefit of clergy" because it had originally been restricted to
clergymen.
4. Generic names for maids and servants. *Botcher:* a mender of old clothes.
5. Lover.
6. Bridewell was the women's prison in London.

been even with your ladyship; which I could have told you long enough since, but I love to keep peace and quietness by my good will. I had rather bring friends together than set 'em at distance. But Mrs. Marwood and he are nearer related than ever their parents thought for.

MRS. FAINALL   Say'st thou so, Foible? Canst thou prove this?

FOIBLE   I can take my oath of it, madam; so can Mrs. Mincing. We have had many a fair word from Madam Marwood, to conceal something that passed in our chamber one evening when you were at Hyde Park and we were thought to have gone a-walking; but we went up unawares, though we were sworn to secrecy too. Madam Marwood took a book and swore us upon it, but it was a book of verses and poems. So as long as it was not a Bible oath, we may break it with a safe conscience.

MRS. FAINALL   This discovery is the most opportune thing I could wish. Now, Mincing?

Enter MINCING.

MINCING   My lady would speak with Mrs. Foible, mem. Mr. Mirabell is with her; he has set your spouse at liberty, Mrs. Foible, and would have you hide yourself in my lady's closet till my old lady's anger is abated. Oh, my old lady is in a perilous passion at something Mrs. Fainall has said; he swears, and my old lady cries. There's a fearful hurricane, I vow. He says, mem, how that he'll have my lady's fortune made over to him, or he'll be divorced.

MRS. FAINALL   Does your lady or Mirabell know that?

MINCING   Yes, mem; they have sent me to see if Sir Wilfull be sober and to bring him to them. My lady is resolved to have him, I think, rather than lose such a vast sum as six thousand pound. Oh, come, Mrs. Foible, I hear my lady.

MRS. FAINALL   Foible, you must tell Mincing that she must prepare to vouch when I call her.

FOIBLE   Yes, yes, madam.

MINCING   O yes, mem, I'll vouch anything for your ladyship's service, be what it will.

Exeunt MINCING *and* FOIBLE.

Enter LADY WISHFORT *and* MARWOOD.

LADY WISHFORT   O my dear friend, how can I enumerate the benefits that I have received from your goodness? To you I owe the timely discovery of the false vows of Mirabell; to you the detection of the imposter Sir Rowland. And now you are become an intercessor with my son-in-law, to save the honor of my house, and compound[7] for the frailties of my daughter. Well, friend, you are enough to reconcile me to the bad world, or else I would retire to deserts and solitudes,

7. Make a settlement, often in monetary terms.

and feed harmless sheep by groves and purling streams. Dear Marwood, let us leave the world, and retire by ourselves and be shepherdesses.

MRS. MARWOOD   Let us first dispatch the affair in hand, madam. We shall have leisure to think of retirement afterwards. Here is one who is concerned in the treaty.

LADY WISHFORT   O daughter, daughter, is it possible thou shouldst be my child, bone of my bone, and flesh of my flesh, and, as I may say, another me, and yet transgress the most minute particle of severe virtue? Is it possible you should lean aside to iniquity, who have been cast in the direct mold of virtue? I have not only been a mold but a pattern for you, and a model for you, after you were brought into the world.

MRS. FAINALL   I don't understand your ladyship.

LADY WISHFORT   Not understand? Why, have you not been naught? Have you not been sophisticated?[8] Not understand? Here I am ruined to compound for your caprices and your cuckoldoms. I must pawn my plate and my jewels, and ruin my niece, and all little enough.

MRS. FAINALL   I am wronged and abused, and so are you. 'Tis a false accusation, as false as hell, as false as your friend here, aye, or your friend's friend, my false husband.

MRS. MARWOOD   My friend, Mrs. Fainall? Your husband my friend? What do you mean?

MRS. FAINALL   I know what I mean, madam, and so do you; and so shall the world at a time convenient.

MRS. MARWOOD   I am sorry to see you so passionate, madam. More temper[9] would look more like innocence. But I have done. I am sorry my zeal to serve your ladyship and family should admit of misconstruction, or make me liable to affronts. You will pardon me, madam, if I meddle no more with an affair in which I am not personally concerned.

LADY WISHFORT   O dear friend, I am so ashamed that you should meet with such returns! [*To* MRS. FAINALL.] You ought to ask pardon on your knees, ungrateful creature; she deserves more from you than all your life can accomplish. [*To* MRS. MARWOOD.] Oh, don't leave me destitute in this perplexity! No, stick to me, my good genius.

MRS. FAINALL   I tell you, madam, you're abused. Stick to you! Aye, like a leech, to suck your best blood; she'll drop off when she's full. Madam, you shan't pawn a bodkin, nor part with a brass counter,[1] in composition for me. I defy 'em all. Let 'em prove their aspersions; I know my own innocence, and dare stand by a trial.

Exit.

8. Corrupted. *Naught*: immoral.
9. Moderation.
1. An imitation coin. *Bodkin*: ornamental hairpin.

LADY WISHFORT   Why, if she should be innocent, if she should be
wronged after all, ha? I don't know what to think—and, I promise
you, her education has been unexceptionable. I may say it; for I
chiefly made it my own care to initiate her very infancy in the rudi-
ments of virtue, and to impress upon her tender years a young odium
and aversion to the very sight of men—aye, friend, she would ha'
shrieked if she had but seen a man, till she was in her teens. As I'm a
person, 'tis true. She was never suffered to play with a male child,
though but in coats; nay, her very babies[2] were of the feminine gender. Oh, she never looked a man in the face but her own father, or
the chaplain, and him we made a shift to put upon her for a woman,
by the help of his long garments and his sleek face, till she was going
in her fifteen.

MRS. MARWOOD   'Twas much she should be deceived so long.

LADY WISHFORT   I warrant you, or she would never have borne to have
been catechized by him; and have heard his long lectures against
singing and dancing, and such debaucheries; and going to filthy
plays, and profane music-meetings, where the lewd trebles squeak
nothing but bawdy, and the basses roar blasphemy. Oh, she would
have swooned at the sight or name of an obscene playbook! And can
I think, after all this, that my daughter can be naught? What, a whore?
And thought it excommunication to set her foot within the door of a
playhouse! O my dear friend, I can't believe it, no, no! As she says,
let him prove it, let him prove it.

MRS. MARWOOD   Prove it, madam? What, and have your name prostituted in a public court! Yours and your daughter's reputation worried
at the bar by a pack of bawling lawyers! To be ushered in with an
Oyez[3] of scandal, and have your case opened by an old fumbling
lecher in a quoif[4] like a man midwife; to bring your daughter's infamy
to light; to be a theme for legal punsters and quibblers by the statute,
and become a jest against a rule of court, where there is no precedent
for a jest in any record, not even in Doomsday Book;[5] to discompose
the gravity of the bench, and provoke naughty interrogatories in more
naughty law Latin, while the good judge, tickled with the proceeding,
simpers under a gray beard, and fidges off and on his cushion as if he
had swallowed cantharides, or sat upon cow-itch.[6]

LADY WISHFORT   Oh, 'tis very hard!

MRS. MARWOOD   And then to have my young revelers of the Temple[7]
take notes, like prentices at a conventicle; and after, talk it all over
again in commons, or before drawers in an eating house.

LADY WISHFORT   Worse and worse!

---

2. Dolls.
3. "Hear ye" (French), a court-cry to gain silence.
4. Cap of a sergeant-at-law.
5. In which a survey of English lands was recorded in 1085–86.
6. Cantharides (Spanish fly) and cow-itch (the plant cowhage) would both cause the judge to
"fidge" (fidget).
7. Law students. The Inner and Middle Temples were Inns of the Court.

MRS. MARWOOD   Nay, this is nothing; if it would end here, 'twere well. But it must, after this, be consigned by the shorthand writers to the public press; and from thence be transferred to the hands, nay into the throats and lungs of hawkers, with voices more licentious than the loud flounder-man's, or the woman that cries gray peas. And this you must hear till you are stunned; nay, you must hear nothing else for some days.

LADY WISHFORT   Oh, 'tis insupportable! No, no, dear friend; make it up, make it up; aye, aye, I'll compound. I'll give up all, myself and my all, my niece and her all, anything, everything for composition.

MRS. MARWOOD   Nay, madam, I advise nothing; I only lay before you, as a friend, the inconveniences which perhaps you have overseen.[8] Here comes Mr. Fainall. If he will be satisfied to huddle up all in silence, I shall be glad. You must think I would rather congratulate than condole with you.

Enter FAINALL.

LADY WISHFORT   Aye, aye, I do not doubt it, dear Marwood; no, no, I do not doubt it.

FAINALL   Well, madam, I have suffered myself to be overcome by the importunity of this lady your friend, and am content that you shall enjoy your own proper estate during life, on condition you oblige yourself never to marry, under such penalty as I think convenient.

LADY WISHFORT   Never to marry?

FAINALL   No more Sir Rowlands; the next imposture may not be so timely detected.

MRS. MARWOOD   That condition, I dare answer, my lady will consent to, without difficulty; she has already but too much experienced the perfidiousness of men. Besides, madam, when we retire to our pastoral solitude, we shall bid adieu to all other thoughts.

LADY WISHFORT   Aye, that's true; but in case of necessity, as of health, or some such emergency—

FAINALL   Oh, if you are prescribed marriage, you shall be considered; I will only reserve to myself the power to choose for you. If your physic be wholesome, it matters not who is your apothecary. Next, my wife shall settle on me the remainder of her fortune, not made over already; and for her maintenance depend entirely on my discretion.

LADY WISHFORT   This is inhumanly savage, exceeding the barbarity of a Muscovite husband.

FAINALL   I learned it from his Czarish majesty's retinue,[9] in a winter evening's conference over brandy and pepper, amongst other secrets of matrimony and policy, as they are at present practiced in the northern hemisphere. But this must be agreed unto, and that positively. Lastly, I will be endowed, in right of my wife, with that six thousand

8. Overlooked.
9. Peter the Great had visited London in 1698.

pound, which is the moiety of Mrs. Millamant's fortune in your possession; and which she has forfeited (as will appear by the last will and testament of your deceased husband, Sir Jonathan Wishfort) by her disobedience in contracting herself against your consent or knowledge, and by refusing the offered match with Sir Wilfull Witwoud, which you, like a careful aunt, had provided for her.

LADY WISHFORT   My nephew was *non compos*,[1] and could not make his addresses.

FAINALL   I come to make demands. I'll hear no objections.

LADY WISHFORT   You will grant me time to consider?

FAINALL   Yes, while the instrument is drawing, to which you must set your hand till more sufficient deeds can be perfected; which I will take care shall be done with all possible speed. In the meanwhile, I will go for the said instrument, and till my return you may balance this matter in your own discretion.

Exit.

LADY WISHFORT   This insolence is beyond all precedent, all parallel. Must I be subject to this merciless villain?

MRS. MARWOOD   'Tis severe indeed, madam, that you should smart for your daughter's wantonness.

LADY WISHFORT   'Twas against my consent that she married this barbarian, but she would have him, though her year was not out.[2]—Ah! her first husband, my son Languish, would not have carried it thus. Well, that was my choice, this is hers; she is matched now with a witness.[3] I shall be mad! Dear friend, is there no comfort for me? Must I live to be confiscated at this rebel rate? —Here come two more of my Egyptian plagues, too.[4]

Enter MILLAMANT *and* SIR WILFULL WITWOUD.

SIR WILFULL   Aunt, your servant.

LADY WISHFORT   Out, caterpillar, call me not aunt! I know thee not!

SIR WILFULL   I confess I have been a little in disguise,[5] as they say. 'Sheart! and I'm sorry for't. What would you have? I hope I committed no offense, aunt, and, if I did, I am willing to make satisfaction; and what can a man say fairer? If I have broke anything, I'll pay for't, an it cost a pound. And so let that content for what's past, and make no more words. For what's to come, to pleasure you I'm willing to marry my cousin. So pray let's all be friends; she and I are agreed upon the matter before a witness.

LADY WISHFORT   How's this, dear niece? Have I any comfort? Can this be true?

1. Not in his right mind.
2. Her first year of widowhood, the conventional period of mourning.
3. With a vengeance.
4. Plagues were visited upon Pharaoh until he agreed to release the Israelites (Exodus 7–12).
5. Drunk.

MILLAMANT   I am content to be a sacrifice to your repose, madam; and
to convince you that I had no hand in the plot, as you were misinformed, I have laid my commands on Mirabell to come in person,
and be a witness that I give my hand to this flower of knighthood; and
for the contract that passed between Mirabell and me, I have obliged
him to make a resignation of it in your ladyship's presence. He is
without, and waits your leave for admittance.

LADY WISHFORT   Well, I'll swear I am something revived at this testimony of your obedience; but I cannot admit that traitor. I fear I cannot fortify myself to support his appearance. He is as terrible to me as
a Gorgon;[6] if I see him, I fear I shall turn to stone, petrify incessantly.

MILLAMANT   If you disoblige him, he may resent your refusal and insist
upon the contract still. Then 'tis the last time he will be offensive to
you.

LADY WISHFORT   Are you sure it will be the last time? If I were sure of
that! Shall I never see him again?

MILLAMANT   Sir Wilfull, you and he are to travel together, are you not?

SIR WILFULL   'Sheart, the gentleman's a civil gentleman, aunt; let him
come in. Why, we are sworn brothers and fellow travelers. We are to
be Pylades and Orestes,[7] he and I. He is to be my interpreter in foreign parts. He has been overseas once already; and with proviso that
I marry my cousin, will cross 'em once again, only to bear me company. 'Sheart, I'll call him in. An I set on't once, he shall come in;
and see who'll hinder him.

Exit.

MRS. MARWOOD   This is precious fooling, if it would pass; but I'll know
the bottom of it.

LADY WISHFORT   O dear Marwood, you are not going?

MRS. MARWOOD   Not far, madam; I'll return immediately.

Exit.

Re-enter SIR WILFULL *and* MIRABELL.

SIR WILFULL   Look up, man, I'll stand by you; 'sbud an she do frown,
she can't kill you; besides—harkee, she dare not frown desperately,
because her face is none of her own. 'Sheart, an she should, her
forehead would wrinkle like the coat of a cream cheese; but mum for
that, fellow traveler.

MIRABELL   If a deep sense of the many injuries I have offered to so
good a lady, with a sincere remorse and a hearty contrition, can but
obtain the least glance of compassion, I am too happy. Ah, madam,
there was a time! But let it be forgotten. I confess I have deservedly
forfeited the high place I once held, of sighing at your feet. Nay, kill
me not, by turning from me in disdain. I come not to plead for favor;

6. Whose glance turned men to stone.
7. Devoted friends, especially in hard traveling.

nay, not for pardon. I am a suppliant only for your pity. I am going
where I never shall behold you more.

SIR WILFULL   How, fellow traveler! You shall go by yourself then.

MIRABELL   Let me be pitied first, and afterwards forgotten—I ask no
more.

SIR WILFULL   By'r Lady, a very reasonable request, and will cost you
nothing, aunt. Come, come, forgive and forget, aunt; why you must,
an you are a Christian.

MIRABELL   Consider, madam, in reality you could not receive much
prejudice; it was an innocent device, though I confess it had a face of
guiltiness. It was at most an artifice which love contrived, and errors
which love produces have ever been accounted venial. At least think
it is punishment enough that I have lost what in my heart I hold most
dear, that to your cruel indignation I have offered up this beauty, and
with her my peace and quiet; nay, all my hopes of future comfort.

SIR WILFULL   An he does not move me, would I might never be o' the
quorum![8] An it were not as good a deed as to drink, to give her to
him again, I would I might never take shipping! Aunt, if you don't
forgive quickly, I shall melt, I can tell you that. My contract went no
farther than a little mouth-glue, and that's hardly dry; one doleful sigh
more from my fellow traveler, and 'tis dissolved.

LADY WISHFORT   Well, nephew, upon your account—ah, he has a false
insinuating tongue! Well, sir, I will stifle my just resentment at my
nephew's request. I will endeavor what I can to forget, but on proviso
that you resign the contract with my niece immediately.

MIRABELL   It is in writing and with papers of concern; but I have sent
my servant for it, and will deliver it to you, with all acknowledgments
for your transcendent goodness.

LADY WISHFORT [aside]   Oh, he has witchcraft in his eyes and tongue!
When I did not see him, I could have bribed a villain to his assassination; but his appearance rakes the embers which have so long lain
smothered in my breast.

Enter FAINALL and MRS. MARWOOD.

FAINALL   Your date of deliberation, madam, is expired. Here is the
instrument; are you prepared to sign?

LADY WISHFORT   If I were prepared, I am not empowered. My niece
exerts a lawful claim, having matched herself by my direction to Sir
Wilfull.

FAINALL   That sham is too gross to pass on me, though 'tis imposed on
you, madam.

MILLAMANT   Sir, I have given my consent.

MIRABELL   And, sir, I have resigned my pretensions.

SIR WILFULL   And, sir, I assert my right; and will maintain it in defiance
of you, sir, and of your instrument. 'Sheart, an you talk of an instru-

---

8. The quorum of justices of the peace at a court session.

ment, sir, I have an old fox[9] by my thigh shall hack your instrument of ram vellum to shreds, sir! It shall not be sufficient for a mittimus[1] or a tailor's measure. Therefore, withdraw your instrument, sir, or by'r Lady, I shall draw mine.

LADY WISHFORT   Hold, nephew, hold!

MILLAMANT   Good Sir Wilfull, respite your valor.

FAINALL   Indeed? Are you provided of a guard, with your single beef-eater[2] there? But I'm prepared for you, and insist upon my first proposal. You shall submit your own estate to my management and absolutely make over my wife's to my sole use, as pursuant to the purport and tenor of this other covenant. [To MILLAMANT.] I suppose, madam, your consent is not requisite in this case; nor, Mr. Mirabell, your resignation; nor, Sir Wilfull, your right. You may draw your fox if you please, sir, and make a bear-garden[3] flourish somewhere else; for here it will not avail. This, my Lady Wishfort, must be subscribed, or your darling daughter's turned adrift, like a leaky hulk, to sink or swim, as she and the current of this lewd town can agree.

LADY WISHFORT   Is there no means, no remedy to stop my ruin? Ungrateful wretch! dost thou not owe thy being, thy subsistence, to my daughter's fortune?

FAINALL   I'll answer you when I have the rest of it in my possession.

MIRABELL   But that you would not accept of a remedy from my hands—I own I have not deserved you should owe any obligation to me; or else perhaps I could advise—

LADY WISHFORT   Oh, what? what? to save me and my child from ruin, from want, I'll forgive all that's past; nay, I'll consent to anything to come, to be delivered from this tyranny.

MIRABELL   Aye, madam, but that is too late; my reward is intercepted. You have disposed of her who only could have made me a compensation for all my services. But be it as it may, I am resolved I'll serve you; you shall not be wronged in this savage manner.

LADY WISHFORT   How! Dear Mr. Mirabell, can you be so generous at last? But it is not possible. Harkee, I'll break my nephew's match; you shall have my niece yet, and all her fortune, if you can but save me from this imminent danger.

MIRABELL   Will you? I take you at your word. I ask no more. I must have leave for two criminals to appear.

LADY WISHFORT   Aye, aye; anybody, anybody!

MIRABELL   Foible is one, and a penitent.

Enter MRS. FAINALL, FOIBLE, *and* MINCING.

MRS. MARWOOD [*to* FAINALL]   Oh, my shame! These corrupt things are bought and brought hither to expose me.

9. Sword.
1. Warrant of arrest.
2. Yeoman of the guard.
3. Arena for bear-baiting.

MIRABELL *and* LADY WISHFORT *go to* MRS. FAINALL *and* FOIBLE.

FAINALL   If it must all come out, why let 'em know it; 'tis but the way of the world. That shall not urge me to relinquish or abate one title of my terms; no, I will insist the more.

FOIBLE   Yes indeed, madam; I'll take my Bible oath of it.

MINCING   And so will I, mem.

LADY WISHFORT   O Marwood, Marwood, art thou false? my friend deceive me? Hast thou been a wicked accomplice with that profligate man?

MRS. MARWOOD   Have you so much ingratitude and injustice, to give credit against your friend to the aspersions of two such mercenary trulls?

MINCING   Mercenary, mem? I scorn your words. 'Tis true we found you and Mr. Fainall in the blue garret; by the same token, you swore us to secrecy upon Messalina's poems[4]. Mercenary? No, if we would have been mercenary, we should have held our tongues; you would have bribed us sufficiently.

FAINALL   Go, you are an insignificant thing! Well, what are you the better for this? Is this Mr. Mirabell's expedient? I'll be put off no longer. You thing, that was a wife, shall smart for this! I will not leave thee wherewithal to hide thy shame; your body shall be as naked as your reputation.

MRS. FAINALL   I despise you, and defy your malice! You have aspersed me wrongfully. I have proved your falsehood. Go you and your treacherous—I will not name it, but starve together, perish!

FAINALL   Not while you are worth a groat, indeed, my dear. Madam, I'll be fooled no longer.

LADY WISHFORT   Ah, Mr. Mirabell, this is small comfort, the detection of this affair.

MIRABELL   Oh, in good time. Your leave for the other offender and penitent to appear, madam.

Enter WAITWELL *with a box of writings.*

LADY WISHFORT   O Sir Rowland! Well, rascal?

WAITWELL   What your ladyship pleases. I have brought the black box at last, madam.

MIRABELL   Give it to me. Madam, you remember your promise.

LADY WISHFORT   Aye, dear sir.

MIRABELL   Where are the gentlemen?

WAITWELL   At hand, sir, rubbing their eyes; just risen from sleep.

FAINALL   'Sdeath, what's this to me? I'll not wait your private concerns.

Enter PETULANT *and* WITWOUD.

PETULANT   How now? What's the matter? Whose hand's out?

---

4. Mincing misunderstands the term "Miscellany," a collection of poems by various writers.

WITWOUD   Heyday! what, are you all got together, like players at the end of the last act?

MIRABELL   You may remember, gentlemen, I once requested your hands as witnesses to a certain parchment.

WITWOUD   Aye, I do; my hand I remember. Petulant set his mark.

MIRABELL   You wrong him; his name is fairly written, as shall appear. You do not remember, gentlemen, anything of what that parchment contained?

Undoing the box.

WITWOUD   No.

PETULANT   Not I. I writ. I read nothing.

MIRABELL   Very well; now you shall know. Madam, your promise.

LADY WISHFORT   Aye, aye, sir, upon my honor.

MIRABELL   Mr. Fainall, it is now time that you should know that your lady, while she was at her own disposal, and before you had by your insinuations wheedled her out of a pretended settlement of the greatest part of her fortune—

FAINALL   Sir! pretended!

MIRABELL   Yes, sir. I say that this lady, while a widow, having, it seems, received some cautions respecting your inconstancy and tyranny of temper, which from her own partial opinion and fondness of you she could never have suspected—she did, I say, by the wholesome advice of friends and of sages learned in the laws of this land, deliver this same as her act and deed to me in trust, and to the uses within mentioned. You may read if you please [*Holding out the parchment.*]—though perhaps what is inscribed on the back may serve your occasions.

FAINALL   Very likely, sir. What's here? Damnation! [*Reads.*] "A deed of conveyance of the whole estate real of Arabella Languish, widow, in trust to Edward Mirabell." Confusion!

MIRABELL   Even so, sir; 'tis the way of the world, sir, of the widows of the world. I suppose this deed may bear an elder date than what you have obtained from your lady.

FAINALL   Perfidious fiend! then thus I'll be revenged.

Offers to run at MRS. FAINALL.

SIR WILFULL   Hold, sir! Now you may make your bear-garden flourish somewhere else, sir.

FAINALL   Mirabell, you shall hear of this, sir; be sure you shall. Let me pass, oaf!

Exit.

MRS. FAINALL   Madam, you seem to stifle your resentment; you had better give it vent.

MRS. MARWOOD   Yes, it shall have vent, and to your confusion; or I'll perish in the attempt.

Exit.

LADY WISHFORT   O daughter, daughter, 'tis plain thou hast inherited thy mother's prudence.

MRS. FAINALL   Thank Mr. Mirabell, a cautious friend, to whose advice all is owing.

LADY WISHFORT   Well, Mr. Mirabell, you have kept your promise, and I must perform mine. First, I pardon, for your sake, Sir Rowland there and Foible. The next thing is to break the matter to my nephew, and how to do that—

MIRABELL   For that, madam, give yourself no trouble; let me have your consent. Sir Wilfull is my friend; he has had compassion upon lovers, and generously engaged a volunteer in this action for our service, and now designs to prosecute his travels.

SIR WILFULL   'Sheart, aunt, I have no mind to marry. My cousin's a fine lady, and the gentleman loves her, and she loves him, and they deserve one another; my resolution is to see foreign parts. I have set on't, and when I'm set on't, I must do't. And if these two gentlemen would travel too, I think they may be spared.

PETULANT   For my part, I say little; I think things are best off or on.

WITWOUD   I gad, I understand nothing of the matter; I'm in a maze yet, like a dog in a dancing school.

LADY WISHFORT   Well, sir, take her, and with her all the joy I can give you.

MILLAMANT   Why does not the man take me? Would you have me give myself to you over again?

MIRABELL   Aye, and over and over again; for I would have you as often as possibly I can. [Kisses her hand.] Well, heaven grant I love you not too well; that's all my fear.

SIR WILFULL   'Sheart, you'll have time enough to toy after you're married; or if you will toy now, let us have a dance in the meantime, that we who are not lovers may have some other employment besides looking on.

MIRABELL   With all my heart, dear Sir Wilfull. What shall we do for music?

FOIBLE   Oh, sir, some that were provided for Sir Rowland's entertainment are yet within call.

A dance.

LADY WISHFORT   As I am a person, I can hold out no longer. I have wasted my spirits so today already that I am ready to sink under the fatigue; and I cannot but have some fears upon me yet that my son Fainall will pursue some desperate course.

MIRABELL   Madam, disquiet not yourself on that account; to my knowledge his circumstances are such, he must of force comply. For my part, I will contribute all that in me lies to a reunion. In the meantime, madam [to MRS. FAINALL], let me before these witnesses restore to you this deed of trust; it may be a means, well-managed, to make you live easily together.

From hence let those be warned, who mean to wed,
Lest mutual falsehood stain the bridal bed;
For each deceiver to his cost may find,
That marriage frauds too oft are paid in kind.

Exeunt omnes.

Epilogue

Spoken by Mrs. Bracegirdle[5]

After our Epilogue this crowd dismisses,
I'm thinking how this play'll be pulled to pieces.
But pray consider, ere you doom its fall,
How hard a thing 'twould be to please you all.
There are some critics so with spleen diseased,
They scarcely come inclining to be pleased;
And sure he must have more than mortal skill,
Who pleases any one against his will.
Then, all bad poets we are sure are foes,
And how their number's swelled, the town well knows;
In shoals I've marked 'em judging in the pit;
Though they're on no pretense for judgment fit,
But that they have been damned for want of wit.
Since when, they, by their own offenses taught,
Set up spies on plays, and finding fault.
Others there are whose malice we'd prevent;
Such who watch plays with scurrilous intent
To mark out who by characters are meant.
And though no perfect likeness they can trace,
Yet each pretends to know the copied face.
These with false glosses feed their own ill nature,
And turn to libel what was meant a satire.
May such malicious fops this fortune find,
To think themselves alone the fools designed;
If any are so arrogantly vain,
To think they singly can support a scene,
And furnish fool enough to entertain.
For well the learned and the judicious know
That satire scorns to stoop so meanly low
As any one abstracted fop to show.
For, as when painters form a matchless face,
They from each fair one catch some different grace;
And shining features in one portrait blend,
To which no single beauty must pretend;
So poets oft do in one piece expose
Whole *belles assemblées* of coquettes and beaux.

5. Who played Millamant.

RICHARD STEELE

The Conscious Lovers†

Illud genus narrationis quod in personis positum est debet habere sermonis festivitatem, animorum dissimilitudinem, gravitatem lenitatem, spem metum, suspicionem disiderium, dissimulationem misericordiam, rerum varietates, fortunae commutationem, insperatum incommodum, subitam laetitiam, iucundum exitum rerum.[1]

To the King[2]

May it please your Majesty,

After having aspired to the highest and most laudable ambition, that of following the cause of liberty, I should not have humbly petitioned your Majesty for a direction of the theater[3] had I not believed success in that province an happiness much to be wished by an honest man and highly conducing to the prosperity of the Commonwealth. It is in this view I lay before your Majesty a comedy, which the audience, in justice to themselves, has supported and encouraged, and is the prelude of what, by your Majesty's influence and favor, may be attempted in future representations.

The imperial mantle, the royal vestment, and the shining diadem are what strike ordinary minds; but your Majesty's native goodness, your passion for justice and her constant assessor mercy is what continually surrounds you, in the view of intelligent spirits, and gives hope to the suppliant, who sees he has more than succeeded in giving Your Majesty an opportunity of doing good. Our King is above the greatness of royalty, and every act of his will which makes another man happy has ten times more charms in it than one that makes himself appear raised above the condition of others. But even this carries unhappiness with it; for calm

---

† First performed in 1722, at Drury Lane, and published in the same year (with 1723 on the title page).
1. *Rhetorica ad Herennium* (formerly attributed to Cicero) I.viii: "A narrative based on characters should have a lively style and diverse traits of personality, such as gravity and gentleness, hope and fear, distrust and desire, hypocrisy and compassion, and a variety of events, such as reversal of fortune, unexpected disaster, sudden joy, and a happy ending."
2. George I.
3. Steele was governor of Drury Lane Theatre, where the play was first produced.

dominion, equal[4] grandeur, and familiar greatness do not easily affect the imagination of the vulgar, who cannot see power but in terror; and as fear moves mean spirits and love prompts great ones to obey, the insinuations of malcontents are directed accordingly, and the unhappy people are ensnared, from want of reflection, into disrespectful ideas of their gracious and amiable Sovereign, and then only begin to apprehend the greatness of their master when they have incurred his displeasure.

As your Majesty was invited to the throne of a willing people for their own sakes and has ever enjoyed it with contempt of the ostentation of it, we beseech you to protect us who revere your title as we love your person. 'Tis to be a savage to be a rebel, and they who have fallen from you have not so much forfeited their allegiance as lost their humanity. And therefore, if it were only to preserve myself from the imputation of being amongst the insensible and abandoned, I would beg permission in the most public manner possible to profess myself, with the utmost sincerity and zeal.

SIRE,

Your MAJESTY'S
Most Devoted Subject and Servant,
RICHARD STEELE

The Preface

This comedy has been received with universal acceptance, for it was in every part excellently performed; and there needs no other applause of the actors but that they excelled according to the dignity and difficulty of the character they represented. But this great favor done to the work in acting renders the expectation still the greater from the author to keep up the spirit in the representation of the closet[5] or any other circumstance of the reader, whether alone or in company. To which I can only say that it must be remembered a play is to be seen and is made to be represented with the advantage of action nor can appear but with half the spirit without it; for the greatest effect of a play in reading is to excite the reader to go see it; and when he does so, it is then a play has the effect of example and precept.

The chief design of this was to be an innocent performance, and the audience have abundantly showed how ready they are to support what is visibly intended that way; nor do I make any difficulty to acknowledge that the whole was writ for the sake of the scene of the fourth act, wherein Mr. Bevil evades the quarrel with his friend, and hope it may have some effect upon the Goths and Vandals that frequent the theaters, or a more polite audience may supply their absence.

But this incident and the case of the father and daughter are

4. Calm.
5. Small room or study.

esteemed by some people no subjects of comedy; but I cannot be of their mind, for anything that has its foundation in happiness and success must be allowed to be the object of comedy, and sure it must be an improvement of it to introduce a joy too exquisite for laughter, that can have no spring but in delight, which is the case of this young lady. I must therefore contend that the tears which were shed on that occasion flowed from reason and good sense and that men ought not to be laughed at for weeping till we are come to a more clear notion of what is to be imputed to the hardness of the head and the softness of the heart; and I think it was very politely said of Mr. Wilks[6] to one who told him there was a general[7] weeping for Indiana, "I'll warrant he'll fight ne'er the worse for that." To be apt to give way to the impressions of humanity is the excellence of a right disposition and the natural working of a well-turned spirit. But as I have suffered by critics who are got no farther than to inquire whether they ought to be pleased or not, I would willingly find them properer matter for their employment, and revive here a song which was omitted for want of a performer and designed for the entertainment of Indiana; Signor Carbonelli[8] instead of it played on the fiddle, and it is for want of a singer that such advantageous things are said of an instrument which were designed for a voice. The song is the distress of a love-sick maid and may be a fit entertainment for some small critics to examine whether the passion is just or the distress male or female.

I

From place to place forlorn I go,
    With downcast eyes, a silent shade;
Forbidden to declare my woe;
    To speak, till spoken to, afraid.

II

My inward pangs, my secret grief,
    My soft consenting looks betray:
He loves, but gives me no relief:
    Why speaks not he who may?

It remains to say a word concerning Terence, and I am extremely surprised to find what Mr. Cibber[9] told me prove a truth, that what I valued myself so much upon, the translation of him,[1] should be imputed to me as a reproach. Mr. Cibber's zeal for the work, his care and application

---

6. Actor-manager of Drury Lane who played the role of Myrtle.
7. General Charles Churchill. Indiana was played by his mistress, Anne Oldfield.
8. A virtuoso violinist.
9. Actor-manager at Drury Lane.
1. Steele's play is an adaptation of Terence's *Andria*.

in instructing the actors and altering the disposition of the scenes when I was, through sickness, unable to cultivate such things myself, has been a very obliging favor and friendship to me. For this reason, I was very hardly persuaded to throw away Terence's celebrated funeral and take only the bare authority of the young man's character,[2] and how I have worked it into an Englishman and made use of the same circumstances of discovering a daughter when we least hoped for one is humbly submitted to the learned reader.

Prologue

By Mr. Welsted[3]

Spoken by Mr. Wilks

To win your hearts, and to secure your praise,
The comic-writers strive by various ways:
By subtle stratagems they act their game,
And leave untried no avenue to fame.
One writes the spouse a beating from his wife;
And says, "Each stroke was copied from the life."
Some fix all wit and humour in grimace,
And make a livelihood of Pinkey's[4] face.
Here one gay show and costly habits tries,
Confiding to the judgment of your eyes.
Another smuts his scene, a cunning shaver,
Sure of the rakes' and of the wenches' favor.
Oft have these arts prevailed; and one may guess,
If practiced o'er again, would find success.
But the bold sage, the poet of tonight,
By new and desp'rate rules resolved to write;
Fain would he give more just applauses rise,
And please by wit that scorns the aids of vice;
The praise he seeks, from worthier motives springs,
Such praise as praise to those that give it brings.
    Your aid, most humbly sought, then, Britons, lend,
And lib'ral mirth like lib'ral men defend:
No more let ribaldry, with license writ,
Usurp the name of eloquence or wit;
No more let lawless farce uncensured go,
The lewd dull gleanings of a Smithfield show.[5]
'Tis yours with breeding to refine the age,

2. "Terence's celebrated funeral" is a scene in the *Andria*. The "young man's character" refers to Terence's Pamphilus, who slightly resembles Bevil Junior.
3. Leonard Welsted, a contemporary poet.
4. William Pinkethman, a comedian.
5. An amusement at the annual Bartholomew Fair.

To chasten wit, and moralize the stage.
　　Ye modest, wise and good, ye fair, ye brave,
Tonight the champion of your virtues save,
Redeem from long contempt the comic name,
And judge politely for your country's fame.

Dramatis Personae

MEN

SIR JOHN BEVIL	*Mr. Mills*
MR. SEALAND	*Mr. Williams*
BEVIL JUNIOR, in love with Indiana	*Mr. Booth*
MYRTLE, in love with Lucinda	*Mr. Wilks*
CIMBERTON, a coxcomb	*Mr. Griffin*
HUMPHREY, an old servant to Sir John	*Mr. Shepard*
TOM, servant to Bevil Junior	*Mr. Cibber*
DANIEL, a country boy, servant to Indiana	*Mr. Theophilus Cibber*

WOMEN

MRS. SEALAND, second wife to Sealand	*Mrs. Moore*
ISABELLA, sister to Sealand	*Mrs. Thurmond*
INDIANA, Sealand's daughter by his first wife	*Mrs. Oldfield*
LUCINDA, Sealand's daughter by his second wife	*Mrs. Booth*
PHILLIS, maid to Lucinda	*Mrs. Younger*

Scene: *London*

The Conscious Lovers

Act I. Scene i.

Scene, SIR JOHN BEVIL's *house.*
Enter SIR JOHN BEVIL *and* HUMPHREY.

SIR JOHN BEVIL　Have you ordered that I should not be interrupted while I am dressing?

HUMPHREY　Yes, sir. I believed you had something of moment to say to me.

SIR JOHN BEVIL　Let me see, Humphrey; I think it is now full forty years since I first took thee to be about myself.

HUMPHREY   I thank you, sir, it has been an easy forty years, and I have passed 'em without much sickness, care, or labor.

SIR JOHN BEVIL   Thou hast a brave constitution; you are a year or two older than I am, sirrah.

HUMPHREY   You have ever been of that mind, sir.

SIR JOHN BEVIL   You knave, you know it; I took thee for thy gravity and sobriety in my wild years.

HUMPHREY   Ah sir, our manners were formed from our different fortunes, not our different age. Wealth gave a loose to your youth, and poverty put a restraint upon mine.

SIR JOHN BEVIL   Well, Humphrey, you know I have been a kind master to you; I have used you, for the ingenuous nature I observed in you from the beginning, more like an humble friend than a servant.

HUMPHREY   I humbly beg you'll be so tender of me as to explain your commands, sir, without any farther preparation.

SIR JOHN BEVIL   I'll tell thee then. In the first place, this wedding of my son's, in all probability—shut the door—will never be at all.

HUMPHREY   How, sir! Not be at all? For what reason is it carried on in appearance?

SIR JOHN BEVIL   Honest Humphrey, have patience, and I'll tell thee all in order. I have myself, in some part of my life, lived, indeed, with freedom, but, I hope, without reproach. Now I thought liberty would be as little injurious to my son; therefore, as soon as he grew towards man, I indulged him in living after his own manner. I knew not how, otherwise, to judge of his inclination; for what can be concluded from a behavior under restraint and fear? But what charms me above all expression is that my son has never in the least action, the most distant hint or word, valued himself upon that great estate of his mother's, which, according to our marriage settlement, he has had ever since he came to age.

HUMPHREY   No, sir; on the contrary, he seems afraid of appearing to enjoy it before you or any belonging to you. He is as dependent and resigned to your will as if he had not a farthing but what must come from your immediate bounty. You have ever acted like a good and generous father, and he like an obedient and grateful son.

SIR JOHN BEVIL   Nay, his carriage is so easy to all with whom he converses that he is never assuming, never prefers himself to others, nor ever is guilty of that rough sincerity which a man is not called to and certainly disobliges most of his acquaintance. To be short, Humphrey, his reputation was so fair in the world that old Sealand, the great India merchant, has offered his only daughter and sole heiress to that vast estate of his as a wife for him. You may be sure I made no difficulties, the match was agreed on, and this very day named for the wedding.

HUMPHREY   What hinders the proceeding?

SIR JOHN BEVIL   Don't interrupt me. You know I was last Thursday at the masquerade; my son, you may remember, soon found us out. He knew his grandfather's habit, which I then wore; and though it was the mode in the last age, yet the maskers, you know, followed us as if we had been the most monstrous figures in that whole assembly.

HUMPHREY   I remember indeed a young man of quality in the habit of a clown that was particularly troublesome.

SIR JOHN BEVIL   Right. He was too much what he seemed to be. You remember how impertinently he followed, and teased us, and would know who we were.

HUMPHREY [*aside*]   I know he has a mind to come into that particular.

SIR JOHN BEVIL   Ay, he followed us till the gentlemen who led the lady in the Indian mantle presented that gay creature to the rustic and bid him like Cymon in the fable[6] grow polite by falling in love and let that worthy old gentleman alone, meaning me. The clown was not reformed but rudely persisted and offered to force off my mask; with that the gentleman, throwing off his own, appeared to be my son, and in his concern for me tore off that of the nobleman. At this they seized each other, the company called the guards, and in the surprise the lady swooned away, upon which my son quitted his adversary and had now no care but of the lady, when raising her in his arms, "Art thou gone," cried he, "forever? —Forbid it heaven!" She revives at his known voice, and with the most familiar though modest gesture hangs in safety over his shoulder weeping, but wept as in the arms of one before whom she could give herself a loose were she not under observation. While she hides her face in his neck, he carefully conveys her from the company.

HUMPHREY   I have observed this accident has dwelt upon you very strongly.

SIR JOHN BEVIL   Her uncommon air, her noble modesty, the dignity of her person, and the occasion itself drew the whole assembly together; and I soon heard it buzzed about, she was the adopted daughter of a famous sea-officer, who had served in France. Now this unexpected and public discovery of my son's so deep concern for her—

HUMPHREY   Was what I suppose alarmed Mr. Sealand, in behalf of his daughter, to break off the match.

SIR JOHN BEVIL   You are right. He came to me yesterday and said he thought himself disengaged from the bargain, being credibly informed my son was already married, or worse, to the lady at the masquerade. I palliated matters and insisted on our agreement, but we parted with little less than a direct breach between us.

HUMPHREY   Well, sir, and what notice have you taken of all this to my young master?

SIR JOHN BEVIL   That's what I wanted to debate with you. I have said nothing to him yet. But look you, Humphrey, if there is so much in this amour of his that he denies upon my summons to marry, I have cause enough to be offended; and then by my insisting upon his mar-

6. Cymon, a slow-witted fellow who learned politeness when he fell in love with the sleeping Iphigenia. The tale appears in Boccaccio's *Decameron and* Dryden's *Fables.*

rying today, I shall know how far he is engaged to this lady in masquerade and from thence only shall be able to take my measures. In
the meantime I would have you find out how far that rogue his man
is let into his secret. He, I know, will play tricks, as much to cross me
as to serve his master.

HUMPHREY   Why do you think so of him, sir? I believe he is no worse
than I was for you, at your son's age.

SIR JOHN BEVIL   I see it in the rascal's looks. But I have dwelt on these
things too long; I'll go to my son immediately, and while I'm gone,
your part is to convince his rogue Tom that I am in earnest. I'll leave
him to you.

Exit SIR JOHN BEVIL.

HUMPHREY   Well, though this father and son live as well together as
possible, yet their fear of giving each other pain is attended with constant mutual uneasiness. I'm sure I have enough to do to be honest
and yet keep well with them both. But they know I love 'em, and that
makes the task less painful however.

Enter TOM, *singing.*

Oh, here's the prince of poor coxcombs, the representative of all the
better fed than taught. —Ho! ho! Tom, whither so gay and so airy this
morning?

TOM   Sir, we servants of single gentlemen are another kind of people
than you domestic ordinary drudges that do business. We are raised
above you. The pleasures of board-wages, tavern-dinners, and many a
clear gain—vails,[7] alas, you never heard or dreamt of.

HUMPHREY   Thou hast follies and vices enough for a man of ten thousand a year, though 'tis but as t'other day that I sent for you to town,
to put you into Mr. Sealand's family, that you might learn a little
before I put you to my young master, who is too gentle for training
such a rude thing as you were into proper obedience. You then pulled
off your hat to everyone you met in the street, like a bashful great
awkward cub as you were. But your great oaken cudgel when you
were a booby became you much better than that dangling stick at
your button now you are a fop.[8] That's fit for nothing, except it hangs
there to be ready for your master's hand when you are impertinent.

TOM   Uncle Humphrey, you know my master scorns to strike his servants. You talk as if the world was now just as it was when my old
master and you were in your youth—when you went to dinner
because it was so much a clock, when the great blow[9] was given in
the hall at the pantry-door, and all the family came out of their holes
in such strange dresses and formal faces as you see in the pictures in
our long gallery in the country.

7. Tips.
8. A servant trying for fashion would sometimes attach his walking stick to a coat button.
9. Upon the dinner gong.

HUMPHREY   Why, you wild rogue!

TOM   You could not fall to your dinner till a formal fellow in a black gown said something over the meat, as if the cook had not made it ready enough.

HUMPHREY   Sirrah, who do you prate after? Despising men of sacred characters! I hope you never heard my good young master talk so like a profligate!

TOM   Sir, I say you put upon me, when I first came to town, about being orderly, and the doctrine of wearing shams[1] to make linen last clean a fortnight, keeping my clothes fresh, and wearing a frock within doors.

HUMPHREY   Sirrah, I gave you those lessons because I supposed at that time your master and you might have dined at home every day and cost you nothing; then you might have made a good family servant. But the gang you have frequented since at chocolate-houses and taverns in a continual round of noise and extravagance—

TOM   I don't know what you heavy inmates call noise and extravagance, but we gentlemen who are well fed and cut a figure, sir, think it a fine life, and that we must be very pretty fellows who are kept only to be looked at.

HUMPHREY   Very well, sir. I hope the fashion of being lewd and extravagant, despising of decency and order, is almost at an end, since it is arrived at persons of your quality.

TOM   Master Humphrey, ha! ha! you were an unhappy lad to be sent up to town in such queer days as you were. Why now, sir, the lackeys are the men of pleasure of the age, the top-gamesters and many a laced coat about town have had their education in our parti-colored regiment.[2] We are false lovers, have a taste of music, poetry, billet-doux, dress, politics, ruin damsels, and when we are weary of this lewd town and have a mind to take up,[3] whip into our masters' wigs and linen and marry fortunes.

HUMPHREY   Hey-day!

TOM   Nay, sir, our order is carried up to the highest dignities and distinctions; step but into the Painted Chamber,[4] and by our titles you'd take us all for men of quality. Then again, come down to the Court of Requests, and you see us all laying our broken heads together for the good of the nation. And though we never carry a question *nemine contradicente*,[5] yet this I can say with a safe conscience—and I wish every gentleman of our cloth could lay his hand upon his heart and say the same—that I never took so much as a single mug of beer for my vote in all my life.

1. False shirt-fronts.
2. I.e., of menservants.
3. Reform.
4. Room in Parliament where servants waited for their masters. The Court of Requests, mentioned below, was nearby. Servants were in the habit of imitating the roles and titles of their masters. See Steele's discussion in *The Spectator*, No. 88.
5. Unanimously.

HUMPHREY Sirrah, there is no enduring your extravagance; I'll hear you prate no longer. I wanted to see you to inquire how things go with your master, as far as you understand them; I suppose he knows he is to be married today.

TOM Ay, sir, he knows it and is dressed as gay as the sun; but, between you and I, my dear, he has a very heavy heart under all that gaiety. As soon as he was dressed, I retired, but overheard him sigh in the most heavy manner. He walked thoughtfully to and fro in the room, then went into his closet; when he came out, he gave me this for his mistress, whose maid you know—

HUMPHREY Is passionately fond of your fine person.

TOM The poor fool is so tender, and loves to hear me talk of the world, and the plays, operas, and ridottos[6] for the winter; the parks and Belsize[7] for our summer diversions; and "Lard!" says she, "You are so wild—but you have a world of humour—"

HUMPHREY Coxcomb! Well, but why don't you run with your master's letter to Mrs. Lucinda, as he ordered you?

TOM Because Mrs. Lucinda is not so easily come at as you think for.

HUMPHREY Not easily come at? Why sirrah, are not her father and my old master agreed that she and Mr. Bevil are to be one flesh before tomorrow morning?

TOM It's no matter for that; her mother, it seems, Mrs. Sealand, has not agreed to it, and you must know, Mr. Humphrey, that in that family the gray mare is the better horse.

HUMPHREY What dost thou mean?

TOM In one word, Mrs. Sealand pretends to have a will of her own and has provided a relation of hers, a stiff, starched philosopher and a wise fool, for her daughter; for which reason, for these ten past days, she has suffered no message nor letter from my master to come near her.

HUMPHREY And where had you this intelligence?

TOM From a foolish fond soul, that can keep nothing from me—one that will deliver this letter too, if she is rightly managed.

HUMPHREY What? Her pretty handmaid, Mrs. Phillis?

TOM Even she, sir; this is the very hour, you know, she usually comes hither, under a pretense of a visit to your housekeeper forsooth, but in reality to have a glance at—

HUMPHREY Your sweet face, I warrant you.

TOM Nothing else in nature; you must know, I love to fret and play with the little wanton—

HUMPHREY Play with the little wanton! What will this world come to?

TOM I met her this morning in a new manteau and petticoat,[8] not a bit the worse for her lady's wearing, and she has always new thoughts and new airs with new clothes. Then she never fails to steal some

6. Musical entertainments, popular in 1722.
7. An estate near London, used for public amusements.
8. A gown open in front, revealing an underskirt.

glance or gesture from every visitant at their house, and is indeed the whole town of coquettes at second hand. But here she comes; in one motion she speaks and describes herself better than all the words in the world can.

HUMPHREY Then I hope, dear sir, when your own affair is over, you will be so good as to mind your master's with her.

TOM Dear Humphrey, you know my master is my friend, and those are people I never forget.

HUMPHREY Sauciness itself! But I'll leave you to do your best for him.

Enter PHILLIS.

PHILLIS Oh, Mr. Thomas, is Mrs. Sugar-key at home? Lard, one is almost ashamed to pass along the streets. The town is quite empty and nobody of fashion left in it; and the ordinary people do so stare to see anything—dressed like a woman of condition—as it were on the same floor with them pass by. Alas! Alas! It is a sad thing to walk! Oh Fortune! Fortune!

TOM What? A sad thing to walk? Why, Madame Phillis, do you wish yourself lame?

PHILLIS No, Mr. Tom, but I wish I were generally carried in a coach or chair, and of a fortune neither to stand nor go, but to totter, or slide, to be short-sighted, or stare, to fleer[9] in the face, to look distant, to observe, to overlook, yet all become me; and, if I was rich, I could twire[1] and loll as well as the best of them. Oh Tom! Tom! Is it not a pity that you should be so great a coxcomb and I so great a coquette and yet be such poor devils as we are?

TOM Mrs. Phillis, I am your humble servant for that—

PHILLIS Yes, Mr. Thomas, I know how much you are my humble servant, and know what you said to Mrs. Judy, upon seeing her in one of her lady's cast manteaus; that anyone would have thought her the lady, and that she had ordered the other to wear it till it sat easy, for now only it was becoming; to my lady it was only a covering, to Mrs. Judy it was a habit. This you said, after somebody or other. Oh, Tom! Tom! Thou art as false and as base as the best gentleman of them all; but, you wretch, talk to me no more on the old odious subject. Don't, I say.

TOM [*in a submissive tone, retiring*] I know not how to resist your commands, madam.

PHILLIS Commands about parting are grown mighty easy to you of late.

TOM [*aside*] Oh, I have her; I have nettled and put her into the right temper to be wrought upon, and set a-prating. —Why truly, to be plain with you, Mrs. Phillis, I can take little comfort of late in frequenting your house.

9. Smile scornfully.
1. Leer.

PHILLIS   Pray, Mr. Thomas, what is it all of a sudden offends your nicety at our house?

TOM   I don't care to speak particulars, but I dislike the whole.

PHILLIS   I thank you, sir, I am a part of that whole.

TOM   Mistake me not, good Phillis.

PHILLIS   Good Phillis! Saucy enough. But however—

TOM   I say, it is that thou art a part which gives me pain for the disposition of the whole. You must know, madam, to be serious, I am a man, at the bottom, of prodigious nice honor. You are too much exposed to company at your house. To be plain, I don't like so many that would be your mistress's lovers whispering to you.

PHILLIS   Don't think to put that upon me. You say this because I wrung you to the heart when I touched your guilty conscience about Judy.

TOM   Ah Phillis! Phillis! If you but knew my heart!

PHILLIS   I know too much on't.

TOM   Nay then, poor Crispo's[2] fate and mine are one. Therefore give me leave to say, or sing at least, as he does upon the same occasion—

    Sings "Se vedete," &c.

PHILLIS   What, do you think I'm to be fobbed off with a song? I don't question but you have sung the same to Mrs. Judy too.

TOM   Don't disparage your charms, good Phillis, with jealousy of so worthless an object; besides, she is a poor hussy, and if you doubt the sincerity of my love, you will allow me true to my interest. You are a fortune, Phillis—

PHILLIS   [*aside*]   What would the fop be at now?—In good time, indeed, you shall be setting up for a fortune!

TOM   Dear Mrs. Phillis, you have such a spirit that we shall never be dull in marriage when we come together. But I tell you, you are a fortune, and you have an estate in my hands.

    He pulls out a purse; she eyes it.

PHILLIS   What pretense have I to what is in your hands, Mr. Tom?

TOM   As thus: there are hours, you know, when a lady is neither pleased or displeased, neither sick or well, when she lolls or loiters, when she's without desires from having more of everything than she knows what to do with.

PHILLIS   Well, what then?

TOM   When she has not life enough to keep her bright eyes quite open to look at her own dear image in the glass.

PHILLIS   Explain thyself, and don't be so fond of thy own prating.

TOM   There are also prosperous and good-natured moments, as when a knot or a patch is happily fixed, when the complexion particularly flourishes.

2. Hero of an opera by Giovanni Bononcini, popular in London in 1722. Crispo sings "*Se vedete*" when he is unjustly accused of deceit.

PHILLIS Well, what then? I have not patience!

TOM Why then, or on the like occasions, we servants who have skill to know how to time business, see when such a pretty folded thing as this [*shows a letter*] may be presented, laid, or dropped, as best suits the present humour. And, madam, because it is a long wearisome journey to run through all the several stages of a lady's temper, my master, who is the most reasonable man in the world, presents you this to bear your charges on the road.

> *Gives her the purse.*

PHILLIS Now you think me a corrupt hussy.

TOM Oh fie, I only think you'll take the letter.

PHILLIS Nay, I know you do, but I know my own innocence; I take it for my mistress's sake.

TOM I know it, my pretty one, I know it.

PHILLIS Yes, I say I do it, because I would not have my mistress deluded by one who gives no proof of his passion; but I'll talk more of this, as you see me on my way home. No, Tom, I assure thee, I take this trash of thy master's, not for the value of the thing but as it convinces me he has a true respect for my mistress. I remember a verse to the purpose:

> They may be false who languish and complain,
> But they who part with money never feign.

> *Exeunt.*

Act I. Scene ii.

BEVIL JUNIOR's *lodgings.*
BEVIL JUNIOR, *reading.*

BEVIL JUNIOR These moral writers practice virtue after death.[3] This charming Vision of Mirza! Such an author consulted in a morning sets the spirit for the vicissitudes of the day better than the glass does a man's person. But what a day have I to go through! To put on an easy look with an aching heart—if this lady my father urges me to marry should not refuse me, my dilemma is insupportable. But why should I fear it? Is not she in equal distress with me? Has not the letter I have sent her this morning confessed my inclination to another? Nay, have I not moral assurances of her engagements too to my friend Myrtle? It's impossible but she must give in to it, for, sure, to be denied is a favor any man may pretend to. It must be so. Well then, with the assurance of being rejected, I think I may confidently say to my father I am ready to marry her. Then let me resolve upon what I am not very good at, though it is an honest dissimulation.

---

3. Addison had died in 1719. His *Vision of Mirza* appeared in *The Spectator*, No. 159.

Enter TOM.

TOM   Sir John Bevil, sir, is in the next room.

BEVIL JUNIOR   Dunce! Why did not you bring him in?

TOM   I told him, sir, you were in your closet.[4]

BEVIL JUNIOR   I thought you had known, sir, it was my duty to see my father anywhere.

Going himself to the door.

TOM [*aside*]   The Devil's in my master! He has always more wit than I have.

BEVIL JUNIOR *introducing* SIR JOHN BEVIL.

BEVIL JUNIOR   Sir, you are the most gallant, the most complaisant of all parents. Sure 'tis not a compliment to say these lodgings are yours. Why would you not walk in, sir?

SIR JOHN BEVIL   I was loath to interrupt you unseasonably on your wedding day.

BEVIL JUNIOR   One to whom I am beholden for my birthday might have used less ceremony.

SIR JOHN BEVIL   Well, son, I have intelligence you have writ to your mistress this morning. It would please my curiosity to know the contents of a wedding-day letter, for courtship must then be over.

BEVIL JUNIOR   I assure you, sir, there was no insolence in it upon the prospect of such a vast fortune's being added to our family but much acknowledgment of the lady's greater desert.

SIR JOHN BEVIL   But, dear Jack, are you in earnest in all this? And will you really marry her?

BEVIL JUNIOR   Did I ever disobey any command of yours, sir? Nay, any inclination that I saw you bent upon?

SIR JOHN BEVIL   Why, I can't say you have, son; but methinks in this whole business you have not been so warm as I could have wished you. You have visited her, it's true, but you have not been particular. Everyone knows you can say and do as handsome things as any man, but you have done nothing but lived in the general, been complaisant only.

BEVIL JUNIOR   As I am ever prepared to marry if you bid me, so I am ready to let it alone if you will have me.

HUMPHREY *enters unobserved.*

SIR JOHN BEVIL   Look you there now! Why, what am I to think of this so absolute and so indifferent a resignation?

BEVIL JUNIOR   Think? That I am still your son, sir. Sir, you have been married, and I have not. And you have, sir, found the inconvenience

4. Small, private room.

there is when a man weds with too much love in his head. I have been told, sir, that at the time you married, you made a mighty bustle on the occasion. There was challenging and fighting, scaling walls, locking up the lady, and the gallant under an arrest for fear of killing all his rivals. Now, sir, I suppose you having found the ill consequences of these strong passions and prejudices in preference of one woman to another in case of a man's becoming a widower—

SIR JOHN BEVIL   How is this?

BEVIL JUNIOR   I say, sir, experience has made you wiser in your care of me. For sir, since you lost my dear mother, your time has been so heavy, so lonely, and so tasteless that you are so good as to guard me against the like unhappiness by marrying me prudentially by way of bargain and sale. For, as you well judge, a woman that is espoused for a fortune is yet a better bargain if she dies; for then a man still enjoys what he did marry, the money, and is disencumbered of what he did not marry, the woman.

SIR JOHN BEVIL   But pray, sir, do you think Lucinda then a woman of such little merit?

BEVIL JUNIOR   Pardon me, sir, I don't carry it so far neither; I am rather afraid I shall like her too well; she has, for one of her fortune, a great many needless and superfluous good qualities.

SIR JOHN BEVIL   I am afraid, son, there's something I don't see yet, something that's smothered under all this raillery.

BEVIL JUNIOR   Not in the least, sir. If the lady is dressed and ready, you see I am. I suppose the lawyers are ready too.

HUMPHREY [aside]   This may grow warm, if I don't interpose.—Sir, Mr. Sealand is at the coffeehouse and has sent to speak with you.

SIR JOHN BEVIL   Oh! That's well! Then I warrant the lawyers are ready. Son, you'll be in the way, you say—

BEVIL JUNIOR   If you please, sir, I'll take a chair and go to Mr. Sealand's, where the young lady and I will wait your leisure.

SIR JOHN BEVIL   By no means. The old fellow will be so vain if he sees—

BEVIL JUNIOR   Ay, but the young lady, sir, will think me so indifferent—

HUMPHREY [aside to BEVIL JUNIOR]   Ay, there you are right. Press your readiness to go to the bride—he won't let you.

BEVIL JUNIOR [aside to HUMPHREY]   Are you sure of that?

HUMPHREY [aside]   How he likes being prevented.

SIR JOHN BEVIL [looking on his watch]   No, no. You are an hour or two too early.

BEVIL JUNIOR   You'll allow me, sir, to think it too late to visit a beautiful, virtuous young woman in the pride and bloom of life, ready to give herself to my arms; and to place her happiness or misery for the future in being agreeable or displeasing to me is a—call a chair.

SIR JOHN BEVIL   No, no, no, dear Jack; this Sealand is a moody old fellow. There's no dealing with some people but by managing with indifference. We must leave to him the conduct of this day. It is the last of his commanding his daughter.

BEVIL JUNIOR   Sir, he can't take it ill that I am impatient to be hers.

SIR JOHN BEVIL   Pray let me govern in this matter. You can't tell how humorsome old fellows are. There's no offering reason to some of 'em, especially when they are rich. [*Aside.*] If my son should see him before I've brought old Sealand into better temper, the match would be impracticable.

HUMPHREY   Pray, sir, let me beg you to let Mr. Bevil go. [*Aside to* SIR JOHN BEVIL.] See whether he will or not. [*Then to* BEVIL JUNIOR.] Pray, sir, command yourself; since you see my master is positive, it is better you should not go.

BEVIL JUNIOR   My father commands me as to the object of my affections, but I hope he will not as to the warmth and height of them.

SIR JOHN BEVIL [*aside*]   So! I must even leave things as I found them. And in the meantime, at least, keep old Sealand out of his sight.— Well, son, I'll go myself and take orders in your affair. You'll be in the way, I suppose, if I send to you. I'll leave your old friend with you. [*Aside to* HUMPHREY.] Humphrey, don't let him stir, d'ye hear? — Your servant, your servant.

Exit SIR JOHN BEVIL.

HUMPHREY   I have a sad time on't, sir, between you and my master. I see you are unwilling, and I know his violent inclinations for the match. I must betray neither and yet deceive you both for your common good. Heav'n grant a good end of this matter. But there is a lady, sir, that gives your father much trouble and sorrow—you'll pardon me.

BEVIL JUNIOR   Humphrey, I know thou art a friend to both, and in that confidence, I dare tell thee—that lady—is a woman of honor and virtue. You may assure yourself I never will marry without my father's consent. But give me leave to say too, this declaration does not come up to a promise that I will take whomsoever he pleases.

HUMPHREY   Come, sir, I wholly understand you. You would engage my services to free you from this woman whom my master intends you, to make way, in time, for the woman you have really a mind to.

BEVIL JUNIOR   Honest Humphrey, you have always been an useful friend to my father and myself; I beg you continue your good offices, and don't let us come to the necessity of a dispute; for, if we should dispute, I must either part with more than life or lose the best of fathers.

HUMPHREY   My dear master, were I but worthy to know this secret that so near concerns you, my life, my all should be engaged to serve you. This, sir, I dare promise, that I am sure I will and can be secret. Your trust, at worst, but leaves you where you were; and if I cannot serve you, I will at once be plain and tell you so.

BEVIL JUNIOR   That's all I ask. Thou hast made it now my interest to trust thee. Be patient then, and hear the story of my heart.

HUMPHREY   I am all attention, sir.

BEVIL JUNIOR   You may remember, Humphrey, that in my last travels my father grew uneasy at my making so long a stay at Toulon.

HUMPHREY   I remember it; he was apprehensive some woman had laid hold of you.

BEVIL JUNIOR   His fears were just, for there I first saw this lady. She is of English birth: her father's name was Danvers, a younger brother of an ancient family, and originally an eminent merchant of Bristol, who, upon repeated misfortunes, was reduced to go privately to the Indies. In this retreat Providence again grew favorable to his industry and, in six years' time, restored him to his former fortunes. On this he sent directions over that his wife and little family should follow him to the Indies. His wife, impatient to obey such welcome orders, would not wait the leisure of a convoy, but took the first occasion of a single ship, and with her husband's sister only and this daughter, then scarce seven years old, undertook the fatal voyage. For here, poor creature, she lost her liberty, and life; she and her family, with all they had, were unfortunately taken by a privateer from Toulon. Being thus made a prisoner, though as such not ill treated, yet the fright, the shock, and cruel disappointment seized with such violence upon her unhealthy frame, she sickened, pined, and died at sea.

HUMPHREY   Poor soul! Oh the helpless infant!

BEVIL JUNIOR   Her sister yet survived and had the care of her. The captain too proved to have humanity and became a father to her; for having himself married an English woman, and being childless, he brought home into Toulon this her little countrywoman, presenting her, with all her dead mother's movables of value, to his wife, to be educated as his own adopted daughter.

HUMPHREY   Fortune here seemed, again, to smile on her.

BEVIL JUNIOR   Only to make her frowns more terrible. For, in his height of fortune, this captain too, her benefactor, unfortunately was killed at sea, and dying intestate, his estate fell wholly to an advocate, his brother, who coming soon to take possession, there found among his other riches this blooming virgin, at his mercy.

HUMPHREY   He durst not, sure, abuse his power!

BEVIL JUNIOR   No wonder if his pampered blood was fired at the sight of her—in short, he loved. But when all arts and gentle means had failed to move, he offered too his menaces in vain, denouncing vengeance on her cruelty, demanding her to account for all her maintenance from her childhood, seized on her little fortune as his own inheritance, and was dragging her by violence to prison when Providence at the instant interposed and sent me, by miracle, to relieve her.

HUMPHREY   'Twas Providence indeed. But pray, sir, after all this trouble, how came this lady at last to England?

BEVIL JUNIOR   The disappointed advocate, finding she had so unexpected a support, on cooler thoughts descended to a composition,[5] which I, without her knowledge, secretly discharged.

HUMPHREY   That generous concealment made the obligation double.

BEVIL JUNIOR   Having thus obtained her liberty, I prevailed, not without some difficulty, to see her safe to England; where no sooner arrived, but my father, jealous of my being imprudently engaged, immediately proposed this other fatal match that hangs upon my quiet.

HUMPHREY   I find, sir, you are irrecoverably fixed upon this lady.

BEVIL JUNIOR   As my vital life dwells in my heart. And yet you see what I do to please my father: walk in this pageantry of dress, this splendid covering of sorrow. But, Humphrey, you have your lesson.

HUMPHREY   Now, sir, I have but one material question—

BEVIL JUNIOR   Ask it freely.

HUMPHREY   Is it, then, your own passion for this secret lady or hers for you that gives you this aversion to the match your father has proposed you?

BEVIL JUNIOR   I shall appear, Humphrey, more romantic in my answer than in all the rest of my story. For though I dote on her to death and have no little reason to believe she has the same thoughts for me, yet in all my acquaintance and utmost privacies with her, I never once directly told her that I loved.

HUMPHREY   How was it possible to avoid it?

BEVIL JUNIOR   My tender obligations to my father have laid so inviolable a restraint upon my conduct that, till I have his consent to speak, I am determined on that subject to be dumb forever.

HUMPHREY   Well, sir, to your praise be it spoken, you are certainly the most unfashionable lover in Great Britain.

   Enter TOM.

TOM   Sir, Mr. Myrtle's at the next door, and if you are at leisure, will be glad to wait on you.

BEVIL JUNIOR   Whenever he pleases—hold, Tom! Did you receive no answer to my letter?

TOM   Sir, I was desired to call again; for I was told her mother would not let her be out of her sight; but about an hour hence, Mrs. Lettice said, I should certainly have one.

BEVIL JUNIOR   Very well.

                                        Exit TOM.

HUMPHREY   Sir, I will take another opportunity. In the meantime, I only think it proper to tell you that from a secret I know, you may appear to your father as forward as you please to marry Lucinda, with-

5. Compromise.

out the least hazard of its coming to a conclusion—sir, your most obedient servant.

BEVIL JUNIOR   Honest Humphrey, continue but my friend in this exigence, and you shall always find me yours.

Exit HUMPHREY.

I long to hear how my letter has succeeded with Lucinda. But I think it cannot fail; for, at worst, were it possible she could take it ill, her resentment of my indifference may as probably occasion a delay as her taking it right. Poor Myrtle, what terrors must he be in all this while? Since he knows she is offered to me and refused to him, there is no conversing or taking any measures with him for his own service. But I ought to bear with my friend and use him as one in adversity:

> All his disquiets by my own I prove,
> The greatest grief's perplexity in love.

Exit.

Act II. Scene i.

Scene continues.
Enter BEVIL JUNIOR *and* TOM.

TOM   Sir, Mr. Myrtle.

BEVIL JUNIOR   Very well, do your step again and wait for an answer to my letter.

Exit TOM.

Enter MYRTLE.

Well, Charles, why so much care in thy countenance? Is there anything in this world deserves it? You, who used to be so gay, so open, so vacant![6]

MYRTLE   I think we have of late changed complexions. You, who used to be much the graver man, are now all air in your behavior. But the cause of my concern may, for aught I know, be the same object that gives you all this satisfaction. In a word, I am told that you are this very day—and your dress confirms me in it—to be married to Lucinda.

BEVIL JUNIOR   You are not misinformed. Nay, put not on the terrors of a rival till you hear me out. I shall disoblige the best of fathers if I don't seem ready to marry Lucinda. And you know I have ever told you, you might make use of my secret resolution never to marry her, for your own service, as you please. But I am now driven to the

6. Relaxed.

extremity of immediately refusing or complying unless you help me to escape the match.

MYRTLE   Escape? Sir, neither her merit or her fortune are below your acceptance. Escaping, do you call it!

BEVIL JUNIOR   Dear sir, do you wish I should desire the match?

MYRTLE   No—but such is my humorous and sickly state of mind, since it has been able to relish nothing but Lucinda, that though I must owe my happiness to your aversion to this marriage, I can't bear to hear her spoken of with levity or unconcern.

BEVIL JUNIOR   Pardon me, sir; I shall transgress that way no more. She has understanding, beauty, shape, complexion, wit—

MYRTLE   Nay, dear Bevil, don't speak of her as if you loved her, neither.

BEVIL JUNIOR   Why then, to give you ease at once, though I allow Lucinda to have good sense, wit, beauty, and virtue, I know another in whom these qualities appear to me more amiable than in her.

MYRTLE   There you spoke like a reasonable and good-natured friend. When you acknowledge her merit and own your prepossession for another at once, you gratify my fondness and cure my jealousy.

BEVIL JUNIOR   But all this while you take no notice, you have no apprehension of another man that has twice the fortune of either of us.

MYRTLE   Cimberton! Hang him, a formal, philosophical, pedantic coxcomb! For the sot, with all these crude notions of diverse things, under the direction of great vanity and very little judgment, shows his strongest bias is avarice, which is so predominant in him that he will examine the limbs of his mistress with the caution of a jockey and pays no more compliment to her personal charms than if she were a mere breeding animal.

BEVIL JUNIOR   Are you sure that is not affected? I have known some women sooner set on fire by that sort of negligence than by—

MYRTLE   No, no; hang him, the rogue has no art; it is pure simple insolence and stupidity.

BEVIL JUNIOR   Yet, with all this, I don't take him for a fool.

MYRTLE   I own the man is not a natural;[7] he has a very quick sense, though very slow understanding. He says indeed many things that want only the circumstances of time and place to be very just and agreeable.

BEVIL JUNIOR   Well, you may be sure of me if you can disappoint him; but my intelligence says the mother has actually sent for the conveyancer[8] to draw articles for his marriage with Lucinda, though those for mine with her are, by her father's order, ready for signing; but it seems she has not thought fit to consult either him or his daughter in the matter.

MYRTLE   Pshaw! A poor troublesome woman. Neither Lucinda nor her father will ever be brought to comply with it. Besides, I am sure

7. Half-wit.
8. Lawyer.

Cimberton can make no settlement upon her without the concur-
rence of his great uncle Sir Geoffry in the West.

BEVIL JUNIOR   Well sir, and I can tell you, that's the very point that is
now laid before her counsel, to know whether a firm settlement can
be made without his uncle's actual joining in it. Now pray consider,
sir, when my affair with Lucinda comes, as it soon must, to an open
rupture, how are you sure that Cimberton's fortune may not then
tempt her father too hear his proposals?

MYRTLE   There you are right indeed, that must be provided against. Do
you know who are her counsel?

BEVIL JUNIOR   Yes, for your service I have found out that too; they are
Serjeant Bramble and old Target. By the way, they are neither of 'em
known in the family; now I was thinking why you might not put a
couple of false counsel upon her to delay and confound matters a
little. Besides, it may probably let you into the bottom of her whole
design against you.

MYRTLE   As how, pray?

BEVIL JUNIOR   Why, can't you slip on a black wig and a gown and be
old Bramble yourself?

MYRTLE   Ha! I don't dislike it—but what shall I do for a brother in the
case?

BEVIL JUNIOR   What think you of my fellow, Tom? The rogue's intelligent and is a good mimic; all his part will be but to stutter heartily,
for that's old Target's case. Nay, it would be an immoral thing to mock
him, were it not that his impertinence is the occasion of its breaking
out to that degree. The conduct of the scene will chiefly lie upon
you.

MYRTLE   I like it of all things. If you'll send Tom to my chambers, I will
give him full instructions. This will certainly give me occasion to
raise difficulties, to puzzle or confound her project for a while at least.

BEVIL JUNIOR   I'll warrant you success. So far we are right then. And
now, Charles, your apprehension of my marrying her is all you have
to get over.

MYRTLE   Dear Bevil! Though I know you are my friend, yet when I
abstract myself from my own interest in the thing, I know no objection she can make to you or you to her, and therefore hope—

BEVIL JUNIOR   Dear Myrtle, I am as much obliged to you for the cause
of your suspicion as I am offended at the effect. But be assured, I am
taking measures for your certain security and that all things with
regard to me will end in your entire satisfaction.

MYRTLE [going]   Well, I'll promise you to be as easy and as confident
as I can, though I cannot but remember that I have more than life at
stake on your fidelity.

BEVIL JUNIOR   Then depend upon it, you have no chance against you.

MYRTLE   Nay, no ceremony, you know I must be going.

Exit MYRTLE.

BEVIL JUNIOR   Well! This is another instance of the perplexities which
    arise too in faithful friendship. We must often, in this life, go on in
    our good offices even under the displeasure of those to whom we do
    them, in compassion to their weaknesses and mistakes. But all this
    while poor Indiana is tortured with the doubt of me! She has no
    support or comfort but in my fidelity, yet sees me daily pressed to
    marriage with another! How painful, in such a crisis, must be every
    hour she thinks on me! I'll let her see, at least, my conduct to her is
    not changed. I'll take this opportunity to visit her; for though the
    religious vow I have made to my father restrains me from ever mar-
    rying without his approbation, yet that confines me not from seeing a
    virtuous woman that is the pure delight of my eyes and the guiltless
    joy of my heart. But the best condition of human life is but a gentler
    misery.

> To hope for perfect happiness is vain,
> And Love has ever its allays[9] of pain.

Exit.

Act II. Scene ii.

Enter ISABELLA *and* INDIANA *in her own lodgings.*

ISABELLA   Yes, I say 'tis artifice, dear child; I say to thee again and
    again, 'tis all skill and management.
INDIANA   Will you persuade me there can be an ill design in supporting
    me in the condition of a woman of quality? Attended, dressed, and
    lodged like one; in my appearance abroad and my furniture at home,
    every way in the most sumptuous manner, and he that does it has an
    artifice, a design in it?
ISABELLA   Yes, yes.
INDIANA   And all this without so much as explaining to me that all
    about me comes from him?
ISABELLA   Ay, ay, the more for that—that keeps the title to all you have
    the more in him.
INDIANA   The more in him! He scorns the thought—
ISABELLA   Then he—he—he—
INDIANA   Well, be not so eager. If he is an ill man, let us look into his
    stratagems. Here is another of them. [*Showing a letter.*] Here's two
    hundred and fifty pound in bank notes with these words, "To pay for
    the set of dressing-plate, which will be brought home tomorrow."
    Why, dear aunt, now here's another piece of skill for you which I own
    I cannot comprehend; and it is with a bleeding heart I hear you say
    anything to the disadvantage of Mr. Bevil. When he is present, I look
    upon him as one to whom I owe my life and the support of it, then
    again, as the man who loves me with sincerity and honor. When his

9. Alloys.

eyes are cast another way and I dare survey him, my heart is painfully divided between shame and love. Oh, could I tell you—

ISABELLA   Ah, you need not. I imagine all this for you.

INDIANA   This is my state of mind in his presence; and when he is absent, you are ever dinning my ears with notions of the arts of men; that his hidden bounty, his respectful conduct, his careful provision for me after his preserving me from utmost misery are certain signs he means nothing but to make I know not what of me.

ISABELLA   Oh! You have a sweet opinion of him, truly.

INDIANA   I have, when I am with him, ten thousand things besides my sex's natural decency and shame to suppress my heart that yearns to thank, to praise, to say it loves him. I say, thus it is with me while I see him; and in his absence I am entertained with nothing but your endeavors to tear this amiable image from my heart and, in its stead, to place a base dissembler, an artful invader of my happiness, my innocence, my honor.

ISABELLA   Ah, poor soul! Has not his plot taken? Don't you die for him? Has not the way he has taken been the most proper with you? Oh ho! He has sense and has judged the thing right.

INDIANA   Go on then, since nothing can answer you; say what you will of him. Heigh ho!

ISABELLA   Heigh ho, indeed. It is better to say so as you are now than as many others are. There are, among the destroyers of women, the gentle, the generous, the mild, the affable, the humble, who all, soon after their success in their designs, turn to the contrary of those characters. I will own to you Mr. Bevil carries his hypocrisy the best of any man living, but still he is a man and therefore a hypocrite. They have usurped an exemption from shame for any baseness, any cruelty towards us. They embrace without love; they make vows without conscience of obligation; they are partners, nay, seducers to the crime wherein they pretend to be less guilty.

INDIANA [*aside*]   That's truly observed. —But what's all this to Bevil?

ISABELLA   This it is to Bevil and all mankind. Trust not those who will think the worse of you for your confidence in them. Serpents who lie in wait for doves! Won't you be on your guard against those who would betray you? Won't you doubt those who would condemn you for believing 'em? Take it from me, fair and natural dealing is to invite injuries; 'tis bleating to escape wolves who would devour you. Such is the world—[*aside*] and such, since the behavior of one man to myself, have I believed all the rest of the sex.

INDIANA   I will not doubt the truth of Bevil, I will not doubt it. He has not spoken it by an organ that is given to lying: his eyes are all that have ever told me that he was mine. I know his virtue, I know his filial piety, and ought to trust his management with a father to whom he has uncommon obligations. What have I to be concerned for? My lesson is very short. If he takes me forever, my purpose of life is only to please him. If he leaves me, which Heaven avert, I know he'll do it nobly, and I shall have nothing to do but to learn to die after worse than death has happened to me.

ISABELLA Ay do, persist in your credulity! Flatter yourself that a man of his figure and fortune will make himself the jest of the town and marry a handsome beggar for love.

INDIANA The town! I must tell you, madam, the fools that laugh at Mr. Bevil will but make themselves more ridiculous. His actions are the result of thinking, and he has sense enough to make even virtue fashionable.

ISABELLA O' my conscience, he has turned her head. —Come, come; if he were the honest fool you take him for, why has he kept you here these three weeks without sending you to Bristol in search of your father, your family, and your relations?

INDIANA I am convinced he still designs it and that nothing keeps him here but the necessity of not coming to a breach with his father in regard to the match he has proposed him. Beside, has he not writ to Bristol? And has not he advice that my father has not been heard of there almost these twenty years?

ISABELLA All sham, mere evasion; he is afraid if he should carry you thither, your honest relations may take you out of his hands and so blow up all his wicked hopes at once.

INDIANA Wicked hopes! Did I ever give him any such?

ISABELLA Has he ever given you any honest ones? Can you say, in your conscience, he has ever once offered to marry you?

INDIANA No! But by his behavior I am convinced he will offer it the moment 'tis in his power or consistent with his honor to make such a promise good to me.

ISABELLA His honor!

INDIANA I will rely upon it; therefore desire you will not make my life uneasy by these ungrateful jealousies of one to whom I am and wish to be obliged. For from his integrity alone I have resolved to hope for happiness.

ISABELLA Nay, I have done my duty; if you won't see, at your peril be it—

INDIANA Let it be. This is his hour of visiting me.

ISABELLA Oh, to be sure, keep up your form; don't see him in a bed-chamber. [*Apart.*] This is pure prudence when she is liable, wherever he meets her, to be conveyed where'er he pleases.

INDIANA All the rest of my life is but waiting till he comes. I live only when I'm with him.

Exit.

ISABELLA Well, go thy ways, thou willful innocent! I once had almost as much love for a man who poorly left me to marry an estate. And I am now, against my will, what they call an old maid. But I will not let the peevishness of that condition grow upon me, only keep up the suspicion of it, to prevent this creature's being any other than a virgin except upon proper terms.

Exit.

Re-enter INDIANA, *speaking to a* SERVANT.

INDIANA   Desire Mr. Bevil to walk in.

Exit SERVANT.

Design! Impossible! A base, designing mind could never think of what he hourly puts in practice. And yet, since the late rumor of his marriage, he seems more reserved than formerly. He sends in, too, before he sees me, to know if I am at leisure. Such new respect may cover coldness in the heart. It certainly makes me thoughtful. I'll know the worst at once; I'll lay such fair occasions in his way that it shall be impossible to avoid an explanation. For these doubts are insupportable! But see, he comes, and clears them all.

Enter BEVIL JUNIOR.

BEVIL JUNIOR   Madam, your most obedient—I am afraid I broke in upon your rest last night. 'Twas very late before we parted, but 'twas your own fault: I never saw you in such agreeable humour.

INDIANA   I am extremely glad we were both pleased, for I thought I never saw you better company.

BEVIL JUNIOR   Me, madam! You rally. I said very little.

INDIANA   But I am afraid you heard me say a great deal; and when a woman is in the talking vein, the most agreeable thing a man can do, you know, is to have patience to hear her.

BEVIL JUNIOR   Then it's pity, madam, you should ever be silent, that we might be always agreeable to one another.

INDIANA   If I had your talent or power to make my actions speak for me, I might indeed be silent and yet pretend to something more than the agreeable.

BEVIL JUNIOR   If I might be vain of anything in my power, madam, 'tis that my understanding from all your sex has marked you out as the most deserving object of my esteem.

INDIANA   Should I think I deserve this, 'twere enough to make my vanity forfeit the very esteem you offer me.

BEVIL JUNIOR   How so, madam?

INDIANA   Because esteem is the result of reason, and to deserve it from good sense, the height of human glory. Nay, I had rather a man of honor should pay me that than all the homage of a sincere and humble love.

BEVIL JUNIOR   You certainly distinguish right, madam; love often kindles from external merit only—

INDIANA   But esteem arises from a higher source, the merit of the soul—

BEVIL JUNIOR   True. And great souls only can deserve it.

   Bowing respectfully.

INDIANA   Now I think they are greater still that can so charitably part with it.

BEVIL JUNIOR   Now, madam, you make me vain since the utmost pride and pleasure of my life is that I esteem you—as I ought.

INDIANA [*aside*]   As he ought! Still more perplexing! He neither saves nor kills my hope.

BEVIL JUNIOR   But madam, we grow grave methinks. Let's find some other subject. Pray, how did you like the opera last night?

INDIANA   First give me leave to thank you for my tickets.

BEVIL JUNIOR   Oh, your servant, madam. But pray tell me, you now who are never partial to the fashion I fancy must be the properest judge of a mighty dispute among the ladies, that is, whether *Crispo* or *Griselda*[1] is the more agreeable entertainment.

INDIANA   With submission now, I cannot be a proper judge of this question.

BEVIL JUNIOR   How so, madam?

INDIANA   Because I find I have a partiality for one of them.

BEVIL JUNIOR   Pray, which is that?

INDIANA   I do not know—there's something in that rural cottage of Griselda, her forlorn condition, her poverty, her solitude, her resignation, her innocent slumbers, and that lulling *"Dolce Sogno"*[2] that's sung over her; it had an effect upon me that—in short, I never was so well deceived at any of them.

BEVIL JUNIOR   Oh! Now then, I can account for the dispute: *Griselda*, it seems, is the distress of an injured innocent woman; *Crispo*, that only of a man in the same condition. Therefore the men are mostly concerned for Crispo, and, by a natural indulgence, both sexes for Griselda.

INDIANA   So that judgment, you think, ought to be for one though fancy and complaisance have got ground for the other. Well, I believe you will never give me leave to dispute with you on any subject, for I own *Crispo* has its charms for me too, though in the main, all the pleasure the best opera gives us is but mere sensation. Methinks it's pity the mind can't have a little more share in the entertainment. The music's certainly fine, but in my thoughts there's none of your composers come up to old Shakespeare and Otway.

BEVIL JUNIOR   How, madam! Why if a woman of your sense were to say this in the drawing room—

---

1. Operas by Giovanni Bononcini, both popular in London in 1722.
2. "Sweet Dream," sung to the sleeping Griselda by her husband.

Enter a SERVANT.

SERVANT   Sir, here's Signor Carbonelli says he waits your commands in the next room.

BEVIL JUNIOR   A propos! You were saying yesterday, madam, you had a mind to hear him. Will you give him leave to entertain you now?

INDIANA   By all means. Desire the gentleman to walk in.

Exit SERVANT.

BEVIL JUNIOR   I fancy you will find something in this hand that is uncommon.

INDIANA   You are always finding ways, Mr. Bevil, to make life seem less tedious to me.

Enter MUSIC MASTER.

When the gentleman pleases.

After a sonata[3] is played, BEVIL JUNIOR *waits on the* MASTER *to the door, etc.*

BEVIL JUNIOR   You smile, madam, to see me so complaisant to one whom I pay for his visit. Now I own I think it is not enough barely to pay those whose talents are superior to our own—I mean such talents as would become our condition if we had them. Methinks we ought to do something more than barely gratify them for what they do at our command only because their fortune is below us.

INDIANA   You say I smile. I assure you it was a smile of approbation, for indeed I cannot but think it the distinguishing part of a gentleman to make his superiority of fortune as easy to his inferiors as he can. [*Aside.*] Now once more to try him. —I was saying just now I believed you would never let me dispute with you, and I dare say it will always be so. However I must have your opinion upon a subject which created a debate between my aunt and me just before you came hither. She would needs have it that no man ever does any extraordinary kindness or service for a woman but for his own sake.

BEVIL JUNIOR   Well, madam! Indeed I can't but be of her mind.

INDIANA   What, though he should maintain and support her without demanding anything of her on her part?

BEVIL JUNIOR   Why, madam, is making an expense in the service of a valuable woman—for such I must suppose her—though she should never do him any favor, nay, though she should never know who did her such service, such a mighty heroic business?

INDIANA   Certainly! I should think he must be a man of an uncommon mold.

BEVIL JUNIOR   Dear madam, why so? 'Tis but, at best, a better taste in

3. Originally, any composition for instruments (as distinguished from vocal music).

expense. To bestow upon one whom he may think one of the ornaments of the whole creation, to be conscious that from his superfluity
an innocent, a virtuous spirit is supported above the temptations and
sorrows of life! That he sees satisfaction, health, and gladness in her
countenance while he enjoys the happiness of seeing her—as that I
will suppose too, or he must be too abstracted, too insensible. I say, if
he is allowed to delight in that prospect, alas, what mighty matter is
there in all this?

INDIANA   No mighty matter in so disinterested a friendship!

BEVIL JUNIOR   Disinterested! I can't think him so. Your hero, madam,
is no more than what every gentleman ought to be, and I believe very
many are. He is only one who takes more delight in reflections than
in sensations. He is more pleased with thinking than eating. That's
the utmost you can say of him. Why, madam, a greater expense than
all this men lay out upon an unnecessary stable of horses.

INDIANA   Can you be sincere in what you say?

BEVIL JUNIOR   You may depend upon it, if you know any such man, he
does not love dogs inordinately.

INDIANA   No, that he does not.

BEVIL JUNIOR   Nor cards, nor dice.

INDIANA   No.

BEVIL JUNIOR   Nor bottle companions.

INDIANA   No.

BEVIL JUNIOR   Nor loose women.

INDIANA   No, I'm sure he does not.

BEVIL JUNIOR   Take my word then, if your admired hero is not liable to
any of these kinds of demands, there's no such pre-eminence in this
as you imagine. Nay, this way of expense you speak of is what exalts
and raises him that has a taste for it. And at the same time his delight
is incapable of satiety, disgust, or penitence.

INDIANA   But still I insist his having no private interest in the action
makes it prodigious, almost incredible.

BEVIL JUNIOR   Dear madam, I never knew you more mistaken. Why,
who can be more an usurer than he who lays out his money in such
valuable purchases? If pleasure be worth purchasing, how great a
pleasure is it to him who has a true taste of life to ease an aching
heart, to see the human countenance lighted up into smiles of joy on
the receipt of a bit of ore which is superfluous and otherwise useless
in a man's own pocket? What could a man do better with his cash?
This is the effect of an humane disposition where there is only a
general tie of nature and common necessity. What then must it be
when we serve an object of merit, of admiration!

INDIANA   Well, the more you argue against it, the more I shall admire
the generosity.

BEVIL JUNIOR   Nay, nay. Then, madam, 'tis time to fly, after a declaration that my opinion strengthens my adversary's argument. I had best

hasten to my appointment with Mr. Myrtle and begone while we are friends and—before things are brought to an extremity—

Exit carelessly.

Enter ISABELLA.

ISABELLA   Well, madam, what think you of him now, pray?

INDIANA   I protest I begin to fear he is wholly disinterested in what he does for me. On my heart, he has no other view but the mere pleasure of doing it and has neither good or bad designs upon me.

ISABELLA   Ah, dear niece! Don't be in fear of both! I'll warrant you, you will know time enough that he is not indifferent.

INDIANA   You please me when you tell me so. For if he has any wishes towards me, I know he will not pursue them but with honor.

ISABELLA   I wish I were as confident of one as t'other. I saw the respectful downcast of his eye when you catcht him gazing at you during the music. He, I warrant, was surprised, as if he had been taken stealing your watch. Oh, the undissembled guilty look!

INDIANA   But did you observe any such thing, really? I thought he looked most charmingly graceful! How engaging is modesty in a man when one knows there is a great mind within. So tender a confusion! And yet, in other respects, so much himself, so collected, so dauntless, so determined!

ISABELLA   Ah, niece! There is a sort of bashfulness which is the best engine to carry on a shameless purpose. Some men's modesty serves their wickedness, as hypocrisy gains the respect due to piety. But I will own to you, there is one hopeful symptom, if there could be such a thing as a disinterested lover. But it's all a perplexity, till—till—till—

INDIANA   Till what?

ISABELLA   Till I know whether Mr. Myrtle and Mr. Bevil are really friends or foes. And that I will be convinced of before I sleep, for you shall not be deceived.

INDIANA   I'm sure I never shall if your fears can guard me. In the meantime, I'll wrap myself up in the integrity of my own heart, nor dare to doubt of his.

As conscious honor all his actions steers:
So conscious innocence dispels my fears.

Exeunt.

Act III. Scene i.

Scene, SEALAND's *house.*
Enter TOM *meeting* PHILLIS.

TOM   Well, Phillis! What, with a face as if you had never seen me before? [*Aside.*] What a work have I to do now! She has seen some new visitant at their house whose airs she has catched and is resolved to practice them upon me. Numberless are the changes she'll dance through before she'll answer this plain question, *videlicit*,[4] have you delivered my master's letter to your lady? Nay, I know her too well to ask an account of it in an ordinary way; I'll be in my airs as well as she. —Well, madam, as unhappy as you are at present pleased to make me, I would not, in the general, be any other than what I am. I would not be a bit wiser, a bit richer, a bit taller, a bit shorter than I am at this instant.

Looking steadfastly at her.

PHILLIS Did ever anybody doubt, Master Thomas, but that you were extremely satisfied with your sweet self?

TOM I am indeed. The thing I have least reason to be satisfied with is my fortune, and I am glad of my poverty. Perhaps if I were rich, I should overlook the finest woman in the world that wants nothing but riches to be thought so.

PHILLIS [*aside*] How prettily was that said! But I'll have a great deal more before I'll say one word.

TOM I should, perhaps, have been stupidly above her, had I not been her equal; and by not being her equal, never had opportunity of being her slave. I am my master's servant for hire; I am my mistress's from choice, would she but approve my passion.

PHILLIS I think it's the first time I ever heard you speak of it with any sense of the anguish, if you really do suffer any.

TOM Ah, Phillis, can you doubt, after what you have seen?

PHILLIS I know not what I have seen, nor what I have heard. But since I'm at leisure, you may tell me when you fell in love with me, how you fell in love with me, and what you have suffered or are ready to suffer for me.

TOM [*aside*] Oh, the unmerciful jade! When I'm in haste about my master's letter! But I must go through it. —Ah! Too well I remember when and how and on what occasion I was first surprised. It was on the first of April, one thousand seven hundred and fifteen, I came into Mr. Sealand's service. I was then a hobbledehoy, and you a pretty little tight[5] girl, a favorite handmaid of the housekeeper. At that time, we neither of us knew what was in us. I remember I was ordered to get out of the window, one pair of stairs,[6] to rub the sashes clean. The person employed on the innerside was your charming self, whom I had never seen before.

PHILLIS I think I remember the silly accident. What made ye, you oaf, ready to fall down into the street?

TOM You know not, I warrant you. You could not guess what surprised me. You took no delight when you immediately grew wanton in your

4. Namely; from *videre licet*: it is permitted to see, as in a list.
5. Trim.
6. On the second floor.

conquest and put your lips close and breathed upon the glass, and when my lips approached, a dirty cloth you rubbed against my face and hid your beauteous form; when I again drew near, you spit and rubbed and smiled at my undoing.

PHILLIS   What silly thoughts you men have!

TOM   We were Pyramus and Thisbe.[7] But ten times harder was my fate. Pyramus could peep only through a wall; I saw her, saw my Thisbe in all her beauty but as much kept from her as if a hundred walls between, for there was more, there was her will against me. Would she but yet relent! Oh, Phillis! Phillis! Shorten my torment and declare you pity me.

PHILLIS   I believe it's very sufferable; the pain is not so exquisite but that you may bear it a little longer.

TOM   Oh, my charming Phillis, if all depended on my fair one's will, I could with glory suffer. But, dearest creature, consider our miserable state.

PHILLIS   How! Miserable!

TOM   We are miserable to be in love and under the command of others than those we love—with that generous passion in the heart, to be sent to and fro on errands, called, checked and rated for the meanest trifles. Oh, Phillis! You don't know how many china cups and glasses my passion for you has made me break. You have broke my fortune as well as my heart.

PHILLIS   Well, Mr. Thomas, I cannot but own to you that I believe your master writes and you speak the best of any men in the world. Never was woman so well pleased with a letter as my young lady was with his, and this is an answer to it.

Gives him a letter.

TOM   This was well done, my dearest. Consider, we must strike out some pretty livelihood for ourselves by closing their affairs. It will be nothing for them to give us a little being of our own, some small tenement out of their large possessions. Whatever they give us, 'twill be more than what they keep for themselves: one acre, with Phillis, would be worth a whole country without her.

PHILLIS   O, could I but believe you!

TOM   If not the utterance, believe the touch of my lips.

Kisses her.

PHILLIS   There's no contradicting you. How closely you argue, Tom!

TOM   And will closer, in due time. But I must hasten with this letter, to hasten toward the possession of you. Then, Phillis, consider how I must be revenged, look to it, of all your skittishness, shy looks, and at best but coy compliances.

PHILLIS   Oh, Tom, you grow wanton and sensual, as my lady calls it; I

7. See Shakespeare's *Midsummer Night's Dream*, act 5.

must not endure it. Oh! Foh! You are a man, an odious filthy male
creature. You should behave, if you had a right sense or were a man
of sense like Mr. Cimberton, with distance and indifference, or, let
me see, some other becoming hard word, with seeming in-in-inadver-
tency, and not rush on one as if you were seizing a prey. But hush—
the ladies are coming. Good Tom, don't kiss me above once and be
gone. Lard, we have been fooling and toying and not considered the
main business of our masters and mistresses.

TOM   Why, their business is to be fooling and toying as soon as the
parchments[8] are ready.

PHILLIS   Well remembered—parchments. My lady, to my knowledge,
is preparing writings between her coxcomb cousin Cimberton and
my mistress though my master has an eye to the parchments already
prepared between your master Mr. Bevil and my mistress; and I
believe my mistress herself has signed and sealed, in her heart, to Mr.
Myrtle—did I not bid you kiss me but once and be gone? But I know
you won't be satisfied.

TOM   No, you smooth creature, how should I!

> *Kissing her hand.*

PHILLIS   Well, since you are so humble, or so cool, as to ravish my
hand only, I'll take my leave of you like a great lady, and you a man
of quality.

> *They salute[9] formally*

TOM   Pox of all this state.

> *Offers to kiss her more closely.*

PHILLIS   No, prithee, Tom, mind your business. We must follow that
interest which will take, but endeavor at that which will be most for
us and we like most. Oh, here's my young mistress! [TOM *taps her
neck behind and kisses his fingers.*] Go, ye liquorish[1] fool.

> *Exit* TOM.

> *Enter* LUCINDA.

LUCINDA   Who was that you was hurrying away?

PHILLIS   One that I had no mind to part with.

LUCINDA   Why did you turn him away then?

PHILLIS   For your ladyship's service, to carry your ladyship's letter to his
master. I could hardly get the rogue away.

LUCINDA   Why, has he so little love for his master?

PHILLIS   No, but he has so much love for his mistress.

LUCINDA   But I thought I heard him kiss you. Why do you suffer that?

8. Marriage contracts.
9. Kiss.
1. Eager, lustful.

PHILLIS   Why, madam, we vulgar take it to be a sign of love. We servants, we poor people that have nothing but our persons to bestow or treat for are forced to deal and bargain by way of sample. And therefore, as we have no parchments or wax necessary in our agreements, we squeeze with our hands and seal with our lips to ratify vows and promises.

LUCINDA   But can't you trust one another without such earnest down?[2]

PHILLIS   We don't think it safe, any more than you gentry, to come together without deeds executed.

LUCINDA   Thou art a pert, merry hussy.

PHILLIS   I wish, madam, your lover and you were as happy as Tom and your servant are.

LUCINDA   You grow impertinent.

PHILLIS   I have done, madam, and I won't ask you what you intend to do with Mr. Myrtle, what your father will do with Mr. Bevil, nor what you all, especially my lady, mean by admitting Mr. Cimberton as particularly here as if he were married to you already. Nay, you are married actually as far as people of quality are.

LUCINDA   How's that?

PHILLIS   You have different beds in the same house.

LUCINDA   Pshaw! I have a very great value for Mr. Bevil but have absolutely put an end to his pretensions in the letter I gave you for him. But my father, in his heart, still has a mind to him, were it not for this woman they talk of. And I am apt to imagine he is married to her, or never designs to marry at all.

PHILLIS   Then Mr. Myrtle—

LUCINDA   He had my parents' leave to apply to me, and by that has won me and my affections; who is to have this body of mine without 'em, it seems, is nothing to me. My mother says it's indecent for me to let my thoughts stray about the person of my husband. Nay, she says a maid rigidly virtuous, though she may have been where her lover was a thousand times, should not have made observations enough to know him from another man when she sees him in a third place.

PHILLIS   That is more than the severity of a nun, for not to see when one may is hardly possible; not to see when one can't is very easy. At this rate, madam, there are a great many whom you have not seen who—

LUCINDA   Mamma says the first time you see your husband should be at that instant he is made so, when your father with the help of the minister gives you to him; then you are to see him, then you are to observe and take notice of him, because then you are to obey him.

PHILLIS   But does not my lady remember you are to love as well as obey?

LUCINDA   To love is a passion, 'tis a desire, and we must have no desires. Oh, I cannot endure the reflection! With what insensibility on my part, with what more than patience have I been exposed and offered to some awkward booby or other in every county of Great Britain!

PHILLIS   Indeed, madam, I wonder I never heard you speak of it before with this indignation.

LUCINDA   Every corner of the land has presented me with a wealthy coxcomb. As fast as one treaty has gone off, another has come on, till my name and person have been the tittle-tattle of the whole town. What is this world come to? No shame left! To be bartered for like the beasts of the fields, and that in such an instance as coming together to an entire familiarity and union of soul and body. Oh! And this without being so much as well-wishers to each other but for increase of fortune.

PHILLIS   But, madam, all these vexations will end very soon in one for all. Mr. Cimberton is your mother's kinsman and three hundred years an older gentleman than any lover you ever had, for which reason, with that of his prodigious large estate, she is resolved on him and has sent to consult the lawyers accordingly. Nay, has, whether you know it or no, been in treaty with Sir Geoffry, who, to join in the settlement, has accepted of a sum to do it and is every moment expected in town for that purpose.

LUCINDA   How do you get all this intelligence?

PHILLIS   By an art I have, I thank my stars, beyond all the waiting-maids in Great Britain, the art of list'ning, madam, for your ladyship's service.

LUCINDA   I shall soon know as much as you do. Leave me, leave me, Phillis, be gone. Here, here, I'll turn you out. My mother says I must not converse with my servants, though I must converse with no one else.

Exit PHILLIS.

How unhappy are we who are born to great fortunes! No one looks at us with indifference or acts towards us on the foot of plain dealing. Yet, by all I have been heretofore offered to or treated for, I have been used with the most agreeable of all abuses, flattery; but now, by this phlegmatic fool I am used as nothing or a mere thing. He, forsooth, is too wise, too learned to have any regard to desires, and I know not what the learned oaf calls sentiments of love and passion. Here he comes with my mother. It's much if he looks at me. Or if he does, takes no more notice of me than of any other movable in the room.

Enter MRS. SEALAND *and* MR. CIMBERTON.

MRS. SEALAND   How do I admire this noble, this learned taste of yours and the worthy regard you have to our own ancient and honorable house in consulting a means to keep the blood as pure and as regularly descended as may be.

CIMBERTON   Why, really, madam, the young women of this age are treated with discourses of such a tendency and their imaginations so bewildered in flesh and blood that a man of reason can't talk to be understood. They have no ideas of happiness but what are more gross than the gratification of hunger and thirst.

LUCINDA [*aside*]   With how much reflection he is a coxcomb!

CIMBERTON   And in truth, madam, I have considered it as a most brutal custom that persons of the first character in the world should go as ordinarily and with as little shame to bed as to dinner with one another. They proceed to the propagation of the species as openly as to the preservation of the individual.

LUCINDA [*aside*]   She that willingly goes to bed to thee must have no shame, I'm sure.

MRS. SEALAND   Oh, Cousin Cimberton! Cousin Cimberton! How abstracted, how refined is your sense of things! But, indeed, it is too true, there is nothing so ordinary as to say in the best governed families, "My master and lady are gone to bed." One does not know but it might have been said of one's self.

Hiding her face with her fan.

CIMBERTON   Lycurgus,[3] madam, instituted otherwise. Among the Lacedemonians, the whole female world was pregnant, but none but the mothers themselves knew by whom. Their meetings were secret and the amorous congress always by stealth, and no such professed doings between the sexes as are tolerated among us under the audacious word marriage.

MRS. SEALAND   Oh, had I lived in those days and been a matron of Sparta, one might with less indecency have had ten children according to that modest institution that one under the confusion of our modern, barefaced manner.

LUCINDA [*aside*]   And yet, poor woman, she has gone through the whole ceremony, and here I stand a melancholy proof of it.

MRS. SEALAND   We will talk then of business. That girl walking about the room there is to be your wife. She has, I confess, no ideas, no sentiments that speak her born of a thinking mother.

CIMBERTON   I have observed her. Her lively look, free air, and disengaged countenance speak her very—

LUCINDA   Very what?

CIMBERTON   If you please, madam, to set her a little that way.

MRS. SEALAND   Lucinda, say nothing to him; you are not a match for him. When you are married, you may speak to such a husband when you're spoken to. But I am disposing of you above yourself every way.

CIMBERTON   Madam, you cannot but observe the inconveniences I expose myself to in hopes that your ladyship will be the consort of my better part. As for the young woman, she is rather an impediment

3. The lawgiver of Lacedemonia.

than a help to a man of letters and speculation. Madam, there is no reflection, no philosophy can at all times subdue the sensitive life, but the animal shall sometimes carry away the man. Ha! Ay, the vermilion of her lips.

LUCINDA   Pray, don't talk of me thus.

CIMBERTON   The pretty enough—pant of her bosom.

LUCINDA   Sir! Madam, don't you hear him?

CIMBERTON   Her forward chest.

LUCINDA   Intolerable!

CIMBERTON   High health.

LUCINDA   The grave, easy impudence of him!

CIMBERTON   Proud heart.

LUCINDA   Stupid coxcomb!

CIMBERTON   I say, madam, her impatience while we are looking at her throws out all attractions—her arms—her neck—what a spring in her step!

LUCINDA   Don't you run me over thus, you strange unaccountable!

CIMBERTON   What an elasticity in her veins and arteries!

LUCINDA   I have no veins, no arteries.

MRS. SEALAND   Oh, child, hear him, he talks finely, he's a scholar, he knows what you have.

CIMBERTON   The speaking invitation of her shape, the gathering of herself up, and the indignation you see in the pretty little thing—now I am considering her on this occasion but as one that is to be pregnant.

LUCINDA [*aside*]   The familiar, learned, unseasonable puppy!

CIMBERTON   And pregnant undoubtedly she will be yearly. I fear I shan't for many years have discretion enough to give her one fallow season.

LUCINDA   Monster! There's no bearing it. The hideous sot! There's no enduring it, to be thus surveyed like a steed at sale.

CIMBERTON   At sale! She's very illiterate. But she's very well limbed too. Turn her in.[4] I see what she is.

MRS. SEALAND   Go, you creature, I am ashamed of you.

Exit LUCINDA *in a rage.*

CIMBERTON   No harm done. You know, madam, the better sort of people, as I observed to you, treat by their lawyers of weddings [*adjusting himself at the glass*], and the woman in the bargain, like the mansion-house in the sale of the estate, is thrown in, and what that is, whether good or bad, is not at all considered.

MRS. SEALAND   I grant it, and therefore make no demand for her youth and beauty and every other accomplishment, as the common world think 'em, because she is not polite.

CIMBERTON   Madam, I know your exalted understanding, abstracted as it is from vulgar prejudices, will not be offended when I declare to

4. Drive her in (as an animal).

you I marry to have an heir to my estate and not to beget a colony or a plantation. This young woman's beauty and constitution will demand provision for a tenth child at least.

MRS. SEALAND [*aside*] With all that wit and learning, how considerate! What an economist!—Sir, I cannot make her any other than she is, or say she is much better than the other young women of this age or fit for much besides being a mother. But I have given directions for the marriage settlements, and Sir Geoffry Cimberton's counsel is to meet ours here, at this hour, concerning his joining in the deed, which, when executed, makes you capable of settling what is due to Lucinda's fortune. Herself, as I told you, I say nothing of.

CIMBERTON No, no, no, indeed, madam, it is not usual, and I must depend upon my own reflection and philosophy not to overstock my family.

MRS. SEALAND I cannot help her, Cousin Cimberton, but she is, for aught I see, as well as the daughter of anybody else.

CIMBERTON That is very true, madam.

Enter a SERVANT, *who whispers* MRS. SEALAND.

MRS. SEALAND The lawyers are come, and now we are to hear what they have resolved as to the point whether it's necessary that Sir Geoffry should join in the settlement as being what they call in the remainder. But, good cousin, you must have patience with 'em. These lawyers, I am told, are of a different kind. One is what they call a chamber-counsel, the other a pleader.[5] The conveyancer is slow from an imperfection in his speech, and therefore shunned the bar, but extremely passionate and impatient of contradiction. The other is as warm as he but has a tongue so voluble and a head so conceited he will suffer nobody to speak but himself.

CIMBERTON You mean old Serjeant Target and Counsellor Bramble? I have heard of 'em.

MRS. SEALAND The same. Show in the gentlemen.

Exit SERVANT.

Re-enter SERVANT, *introducing* MYRTLE *and* TOM *disguised as* BRAMBLE *and* TARGET.

MRS. SEALAND Gentlemen, this is the party concerned, Mr. Cimberton. And I hope you have considered of the matter.

TARGET [TOM] Yes, madam, we have agreed that it must be by indent—dent—dent—dent—

BRAMBLE [MYRTLE] Yes, madam, Mr. Serjeant and myself have agreed, as he is pleased to inform you, that it must be an indenture tripartite, and tripartite let it be, for Sir Geoffry must needs be a party. Old Cimberton, in the year 1619, says in that ancient roll in Mr.

---

5. The chamber-counsel gives opinions in private but does not argue in court. The pleader is a trial lawyer.

Serjeant's hands, "as recourse thereto being had—will more at large appear—"

TARGET Yes, and by the deeds in your hands it appears that—

BRAMBLE Mr. Serjeant, I beg of you to make no inferences upon what is in our custody, but speak to the titles in your own deeds. I shall not show that deed till my client is in town.

CIMBERTON You know best your own methods.

MRS. SEALAND The single question is whether the entail is such that my cousin Sir Geoffry is necessary in this affair?

MYRTLE Yes, as to the lordship of Tretriplet but not as to the messuage of Grimgribber.[6]

TARGET I say that Gr—gr—that Gr—gr—Grimgribber, Grimgribber is in us. That is to say the remainder thereof, as well as that of Tr—tr—Triplet.

BRAMBLE You go upon the deed of Sir Ralph, made in the middle of the last century, precedent to that in which old Cimberton made over the remainder and made it pass to the heirs general, by which your client comes in; and I question whether the remainder even of Tre-triplet is in him. But we are willing to waive that and give him a valuable consideration. But we shall not purchase what is in us for-ever, as Grimgribber is, at the rate as we guard against the contingent of Mr. Cimberton having no son. Then we know Sir Geoffry is the first of the collateral male line in this family. Yet—

TARGET Sir, Gr—gr—ber is—

BRAMBLE I apprehend you very well, and your argument might be of force, and we would be inclined to hear that in all its parts. But sir, I see very plainly what you are going into. I tell you, it is as probable a contingent that Sir Geoffry may die before Mr. Cimberton as that he may outlive him.

TARGET Sir, we not ripe for that yet, but I must say—

BRAMBLE Sir, I allow you the whole extent of that argument, but that will go no farther than as to the claimants under old Cimberton. I am of opinion that according to the instruction of Sir Ralph, he could not dock the entail and then create a new estate for the heirs general.

TARGET Sir, I have not patience to be told that, when Gr—gr—ber—

BRAMBLE I will allow it you, Mr. Serjeant, but there must be the word "heirs forever" to make such an estate as you pretend.

CIMBERTON I must be impartial, though you are counsel for my side of the question. Were it not that you are so good as to allow him what he has not said, I should think it very hard you should answer him without hearing him. But gentlemen, I believe you have both consid-ered this matter and are firm in your different opinions. 'Twere better therefore you proceeded according to the particular sense of each of you and gave your thoughts distinctly in writing. And do you see, sirs, pray let me have a copy of what you say, in English.

---

6. Steele invented "Grimgribber," but it later came to mean *legal jargon.*

BRAMBLE   Why, what is all we have been saying? In English! Oh! But I forgot myself, you're a wit. But however, to please you sir, you shall have it in as plain terms as the law will admit of.

CIMBERTON   But I would have it, sir, without delay.

BRAMBLE   That, sir, the law will not admit of. The courts are sitting at Westminster, and I am this moment obliged to be at every one of them, and 'twould be wrong if I should not be in the Hall to attend one of 'em at least; the rest would take it ill else. Therefore, I must leave what I have said to Mr. Serjeant's consideration, and I will digest his arguments on my part, and you shall hear from me again, sir.

Exit BRAMBLE [MYRTLE].

TARGET   Agreed, agreed.

CIMBERTON   Mr. Bramble is very quick. He parted a little abruptly.

TARGET   He could not bear my argument; I pinched him to the quick about that Gr—gr—ber.

MRS. SEALAND   I saw that, for he durst not so much as hear you—I shall send to you, Mr. Serjeant, as soon as Sir Geoffry comes to town, and then I hope all may be adjusted.

TARGET   I shall be at my chambers at my usual hours.

Exit.

CIMBERTON   Madam, if you please, I'll now attend you to the tea table, where I shall hear from your ladyship reason and good sense, after all this law and gibberish.

MRS. SEALAND   'Tis a wonderful thing, sir, that men of professions do not study to talk the substance of what they have to say in the language of the rest of the world. Sure, they'd find their account[7] in it.

CIMBERTON   They might, perhaps, madam, with people of your good sense; but, with the generality 'twould never do. The vulgar would have no respect for truth and knowledge if they were exposed to naked view.

Truth is too simple, of all art bereaved:
Since the world will—why, let it be deceived.

Exeunt.

Act IV. Scene i.

Scene, BEVIL JUNIOR's *lodgings.*
BEVIL JUNIOR *with a letter in his hand, followed by* TOM.

TOM   Upon my life, sir, I know nothing of the matter; I never opened my lips to Mr. Myrtle about anything of your honor's letter to Madam Lucinda.

7. Profit.

BEVIL JUNIOR [*aside*] What's the fool in such a fright for? — I don't suppose you did. What I would know is whether Mr. Myrtle showed any suspicion or asked you any questions to lead you to say casually that you had carried any such letter for me this morning.

TOM Well, sir, if he did ask me any questions, how could I help it?

BEVIL JUNIOR I don't say you could, oaf! I am not questioning you, but him. What did he say to you?

TOM Why, sir, when I came to his chambers to be dressed for the lawyer's part your honor was pleased to put me upon, he asked me if I had been at Mr. Sealand's this morning. So I told him, sir, I often went thither, because, sir, if I had not said that, he might have thought there was something more in my going now than at another time.

BEVIL JUNIOR Very well. [*Aside.*] The fellow's caution, I find, has given him this jealousy. — Did he ask you no other questions?

TOM Yes sir, now I remember, as we came away in the hackney coach from Mr. Sealand's, "Tom," says he, "as I came in to your master this morning he bade you go for an answer to a letter he had sent. Pray did you bring him any?" says he. "Ah!" says I, "Sir, your honor is pleased to joke with me; you have a mind to know whether I can keep a secret or no?"

BEVIL JUNIOR And so, by showing him you could, you told him you had one?

TOM [*confused*] Sir—

BEVIL JUNIOR [*aside*] What mean actions does jealousy make a man stoop to! How poorly has he used art with a servant to make him betray his master! — Well! And when did he give you this letter for me?

TOM Sir, he writ it before he pulled off his lawyer's gown at his own chambers.

BEVIL JUNIOR Very well; and what did he say when you brought him my answer to it?

TOM He looked a little out of humour, sir, and said it was very well.

BEVIL JUNIOR I knew he would be grave upon't. Wait without.

TOM [*aside*] Humh! 'Gad, I don't like this; I am afraid we are all in the wrong box here.

Exit TOM.

BEVIL JUNIOR I put on a serenity while my fellow was present, but I have never been more thoroughly disturbed. This hot man! To write me a challenge on supposed artificial dealing when I professed myself his friend! I can live contented without glory, but I cannot suffer shame. What's to be done? But first, let me consider Lucinda's letter again.

Reads.

"Sir,

I hope it is consistent with the laws a woman ought to impose upon herself to acknowledge that your manner of declining a treaty of marriage in our family and desiring the refusal may come from hence has something more engaging in it than the courtship of him, who, I fear, will fall to my lot except your friend exerts himself for our common safety and happiness. I have reasons for desiring Mr. Myrtle may not know of this letter till hereafter and am your most obliged humble servant,

LUCINDA SEALAND."

Well, but the postscript.

Reads.

"I won't, upon second thoughts, hide anything from you. But my reason for concealing this is that Mr. Myrtle has a jealousy in his temper which gives me some terrors. But my esteem for him inclines me to hope that only an ill effect which sometimes accompanies a tender love, and what may be cured by a careful and unblamable conduct."

Thus has this lady made me her friend and confidant and put herself in a kind under my protection. I cannot tell him immediately the purport of her letter except I could cure him of the violent and untractable passion of jealousy and so serve him and her by disobeying her in the article of secrecy more than I should by complying with her directions. But then this dueling, which custom has imposed upon every man who would live with reputation and honor in the world—how must I preserve myself from imputations there? He'll, forsooth, call it, or think it fear if I explain without fighting. But his letter—I'll read it again.

Reads.

"Sir,

You have used me basely in corresponding and carrying on a treaty where you told me you were indifferent. I have changed my sword since I saw you, which advertisement I thought proper to send you against the next meeting between you and the injured

CHARLES MYRTLE."

Enter TOM.

TOM Mr. Myrtle, sir. Would your honor please to see him?

BEVIL JUNIOR Why you stupid creature! Let Mr. Myrtle wait at my lodgings! Show him up.

Exit TOM.

Well, I am resolved upon my carriage to him. He is in love, and in every circumstance of life a little distrustful, which I must allow for. But here he is.

Enter TOM *introducing* MYRTLE.

Sir, I am extremely obliged to you for this honor. [*To* TOM] But, sir, you, with your very discerning face, leave the room.

Exit TOM.

Well, Mr. Myrtle, your commands with me?

MYRTLE   The time, the place, our long acquaintance, and many other circumstances which affect me on this occasion oblige me, without farther ceremony or conference, to desire you would not only, as you already have, acknowledge the receipt of my letter, but also comply with the request in it. I must have farther notice taken of my message than these half lines, "I have yours—I shall be at home—"

BEVIL JUNIOR   Sir, I own I have received a letter from you in a very unusual style. But as I design everything in this matter shall be your own action, your own seeking, I shall understand nothing but what you are pleased to confirm face to face, and I have already forgot the contents of your epistle.

MYRTLE   This cool manner is very agreeable to the abuse you have already made of my simplicity and frankness, and I see your moderation tends to your own advantage and not mine, to your own safety, not consideration of your friend.

BEVIL JUNIOR   My own safety, Mr. Myrtle!

MYRTLE   Your own safety, Mr. Bevil.

BEVIL JUNIOR   Look you, Mr. Myrtle, there's no disguising that I understand what you would be at, but, sir, you know, I have often dared to disapprove of the decisions a tyrant custom has introduced to the breach of all laws, both divine and human.

MYRTLE   Mr. Bevil, Mr. Bevil, it would be a good first principle in those who have so tender a conscience that way to have as much abhorrence of doing injuries as—

BEVIL JUNIOR   As what?

MYRTLE   As fear of answering for 'em.

BEVIL JUNIOR   As fear of answering for 'em! But that apprehension is just or blamable according to the object of that fear. I have often told you in confidence of heart I abhorred the daring to defend the Author of Life and rushing into his presence—I say, by the very same act to commit the crime against him and immediately to urge on his tribunal.

MYRTLE   Mr. Bevil, I must tell you, this coolness, this gravity, this show of conscience shall never cheat me of my mistress. You have, indeed, the best excuse for life, the hopes of possessing Lucinda. But consider, sir, I have as much reason to be weary of it if I am to lose her. And my first attempt to recover her shall be to let her see the dauntless man who is to be her guardian and protector.

BEVIL JUNIOR   Sir, show me but the least glimpse of argument that I am authorized by my own hand to vindicate any lawless insult of this nature, and I will show thee—to chastise thee—hardly deserves the name of courage—slight, inconsiderate man! There is, Mr. Myrtle, no such terror in quick anger; and you shall, you know not why, be cool, as you have, you know not why, been warm.

MYRTLE Is the woman one loves so little an occasion of anger? You, perhaps, who know not what it is to love, who have your ready, your commodious, your foreign trinket for your loose hours, and from your fortune, your specious outward carriage, and other lucky circumstances, as easy a way to the possession of a woman of honor, you know nothing of what it is to be alarmed, to be distracted with anxiety and terror of losing more than life. Your marriage, happy man, goes on like common business, and in the interim you have your rambling captive, your Indian princess for your soft moments of dalliance, your convenient, your ready Indiana.

BEVIL JUNIOR You have touched me beyond the patience of a man, and I'm excusable, in the guard of innocence—or from the infirmity of human nature which can bear no more—to accept your invitation and observe your letter. Sir, I'll attend you.

> *Enter* TOM.

TOM Did you call, sir? I thought you did; I heard you speak aloud.

BEVIL JUNIOR Yes, go call a coach.

TOM Sir—master—Mr. Myrtle—friends—gentlemen—what d'ye mean? I am but a servant, or—

BEVIL JUNIOR Call a coach.

> *Exit* TOM.

> A *long pause, walking sullenly by each other.*

[*Aside.*] Shall I, though provoked to the uttermost, recover myself at the entrance of a third person, and that my servant too, and not have respect enough to all I have ever been receiving from infancy, the obligation to the best of fathers, to an unhappy virgin too, whose life depends on mine?

> *Shutting the door.*

[*To* MYRTLE.] I have, thank Heaven, had time to recollect myself, and shall not, for fear of what such a rash man as you think of me, keep longer unexplained the false appearances under which your infirmity of temper makes you suffer, when, perhaps, too much regard to a false point of honor makes me prolong that suffering.

MYRTLE I am sure Mr. Bevil cannot doubt but I had rather have satisfaction from his innocence than his sword.

BEVIL JUNIOR Why then would you ask it first that way?

MYRTLE Consider, you kept your temper yourself no longer than till I spoke to the disadvantage of her you loved.

BEVIL JUNIOR True. But let me tell you, I have saved you from the most exquisite distress though you had succeeded in the dispute. I know you so well that I am sure to have found this letter about a man you had killed would have been worse than death to yourself. Read it. [*Aside.*] When he is thoroughly mortified and shame has got the better of jealousy, when he has seen himself throughly,[8] he will deserve to be assisted towards obtaining Lucinda.

MYRTLE [*aside*]   With what a superiority has he turned the injury on me as the aggressor! I begin to fear I have been too far transported. "A treaty in our family!" Is not that saying too much? I shall relapse. But, I find, on the postscript, "something like jealousy"—with what face can I see my benefactor, my advocate, whom I have treated like a betrayer?—Oh! Bevil, with what words shall I—

BEVIL JUNIOR   There needs none; to convince is much more than to conquer.

MYRTLE   But can you—

BEVIL JUNIOR   You have o'erpaid the inquietude you gave me in the change I see in you towards me. Alas, what machines are we! Thy face is altered to that of another man, to that of my companion, my friend.

MYRTLE   That I could be such a precipitant wretch!

BEVIL JUNIOR   Pray, no more.

MYRTLE   Let me reflect how many friends have died by the hands of friends for want of temper. And you must give me leave to say again and again how much I am beholden to that superior spirit you have subdued me with. What had become of one of us, or perhaps both, had you been as weak as I was and as incapable of reason?

BEVIL JUNIOR   I congratulate to us both the escape from ourselves and hope the memory of it will make us dearer friends than ever.

MYRTLE   Dear Bevil, your friendly conduct has convinced me that there is nothing manly but what is conducted by reason and agreeable to the practice of virtue and justice. And yet, how many have been sacrificed to that idol, the unreasonable opinion of men! Nay, they are so ridiculous in it that they often use their swords against each other with dissembled anger and real fear.

> Betrayed by honor, and compelled by shame,
> They hazard being, to preserve a name:
> Nor dare inquire into the dread mistake,
> Till plunged in sad eternity they wake.

Exeunt.

Act IV. Scene ii.

Scene, St. James's Park. Enter SIR JOHN BEVIL *and* MR. SEALAND.

SIR JOHN BEVIL   Give me leave, however, Mr. Sealand, as we are upon a treaty for uniting our families, to mention only the business of an

8. Thoroughly.

ancient house. Genealogy and descent are to be of some consideration in an affair of this sort—

MR. SEALAND   Genealogy and descent! Sir, there has been in our family a very large one. There was Galfrid, the father of Edward, the father of Ptolemy, the father of Crassus, the father of Earl Richard, the father of Henry the Marquis, the father of Duke John—

SIR JOHN BEVIL   What, do you rave, Mr. Sealand? All these great names in your family?

MR. SEALAND   These? Yes sir, I have heard my father name 'em all, and more.

SIR JOHN BEVIL   Ay, sir? And did he say they were all in your family?

MR. SEALAND   Yes sir, he kept 'em all, he was the greatest cocker[9] in England. He said Duke John won him many battles and never lost one.

SIR JOHN BEVIL   Oh sir, your servant, you are laughing at my laying any stress upon descent. But I must tell you, sir, I never knew anyone but he that wanted that advantage, turn it into ridicule.

MR. SEALAND   And I never knew anyone who had many better advantages put that into his account. But, Sir John, value yourself as you please upon your ancient house, I am to talk freely of everything you are pleased to put into your bill of rates on this occasion. Yet, sir, I have made no objections to your son's family. 'Tis his morals that I doubt.

SIR JOHN BEVIL   Sir, I can't help saying that what might injure a citizen's credit may be no stain to a gentleman's honor.

MR. SEALAND   Sir John, the honor of a gentleman is liable to be tainted by as small a matter as the credit of a trader. We are talking of a marriage, and in such a case, the father of a young woman will not think it an addition to the honor or credit of her lover—that he is a keeper—

SIR JOHN BEVIL   Mr. Sealand, don't take upon you to spoil my son's marriage with any woman else.

MR. SEALAND   Sir John, let him apply to any woman else and have as many mistresses as he pleases—

SIR JOHN BEVIL   My son, sir, is a discreet and sober gentleman—

MR. SEALAND   Sir, I never saw a man that wenched soberly and discreetly that ever left it off. The decency observed in the practice hides even from the sinner the iniquity of it. They pursue it, not that their appetites hurry 'em away, but, I warrant you, because 'tis their opinion they may do it.

SIR JOHN BEVIL   Were what you suspect a truth, do you design to keep your daughter a virgin till you find a man unblemished that way?

MR. SEALAND   Sir, as much a cit[1] as you take me for, I know the town and the world. And give me leave to say that we merchants are a

---

9. Breeder of fighting cocks.
1. City tradesman; a contemptuous term for a middle-class merchant.

species of gentry that have grown into the world this last century, and
are as honorable, and almost as useful, as you landed folks that have
always thought yourselves so much above us. For your trading, forsooth, is extended no farther than a load of hay or a fat ox. You are
pleasant people, indeed, because you are generally bred up to be lazy;
therefore, I warrant you, industry is dishonorable.

SIR JOHN BEVIL   Be not offended, sir; let us go back to our point.

MR. SEALAND   Oh, not at all offended—but I don't love to leave any
part of the account unclosed. Look you, Sir John, comparisons are
odious, and more particularly so on occasions of this kind when we
are projecting races that are to be made out of both sides of the comparisons.

SIR JOHN BEVIL   But my son, sir, is, in the eye of the world, a gentleman
of merit.

MR. SEALAND   I own to you, I think him so. But, Sir John, I am a man
exercised and experienced in chances and disasters. I lost, in my earlier years, a very fine wife, and with her a poor little infant; that makes
me, perhaps, over-cautious to preserve the second bounty of Providence to me, and be as careful as I can of this child. You'll pardon
me, my poor girl, sir, is as valuable to me as your boasted son to you.

SIR JOHN BEVIL   Why, that's one very good reason, Mr. Sealand, why I
wish my son had her.

MR. SEALAND   There is nothing but this strange lady here, this *incog-
nita*, that can be objected to him. Here and there a man falls in love
with an artful creature and gives up all the motives of life to that one
passion.

SIR JOHN BEVIL   A man of my son's understanding cannot be supposed
to be one of them.

MR. SEALAND   Very wise men have been so enslaved; and when a man
marries with one of them upon his hands, whether moved from the
demand of the world or slighter reasons, such a husband soils[2] with
his wife for a month perhaps, then good b'w'y', madam—the show's
over. Ah! John Dryden points out such a husband to a hair where he
says,

> "And while abroad so prodigal the dolt is,
> Poor spouse at home as ragged as a colt is."[3]

Now in plain terms, sir, I shall not care to have my poor girl turned
a-grazing, and that must be the case when—

SIR JOHN BEVIL   But pray consider, sir, my son—

MR. SEALAND   Look you, sir, I'll make the matter short. This unknown
lady, as I told you, is all the objection I have to him. But, one way or
other, he is, or has been, certainly engaged to her. I am therefore

2. Cohabits.
3. From Dryden's epilogue to Vanbrugh's *The Pilgrim*, 1700. A similar couplet occurs in his
   prologue to Southerne's *The Disappointment*, 1684.

resolved this very afternoon to visit her. Now from her behavior or appearance, I shall soon be let into what I may fear or hope for.

SIR JOHN BEVIL   Sir, I am very confident there can be nothing inquired into, relating to my son, that will not, upon being understood, turn to his advantage.

MR. SEALAND   I hope that as sincerely as you believe it. Sir John Bevil, when I am satisfied in this great point, if your son's conduct answers the character you give him, I shall wish your alliance more than that of any gentleman in Great Britain, and so your servant.

Exit.

SIR JOHN BEVIL   He is gone in a way but barely civil. But his great wealth and the merit of his only child, the heiress of it, are not to be lost for a little peevishness.

Enter HUMPHREY.

Oh, Humphrey, you are come in a seasonable minute. I want to talk to thee and to tell thee that my head and heart are on the rack about my son.

HUMPHREY   Sir, you may trust his discretion; I am sure you may.

SIR JOHN BEVIL   Why, I do believe I may, and yet I'm in a thousand fears when I lay this vast wealth before me. When I consider his prepossessions, either generous to a folly in an honorable love or abandoned past redemption in a vicious one, and from the one or the other, his insensibility to the fairest prospect towards doubling our estate, a father, who knows how useful wealth is, and how necessary, even to those who despise it, I say a father, Humphrey, a father cannot bear it.

HUMPHREY   Be not transported, sir; you will grow incapable of taking any resolution in your perplexity.

SIR JOHN BEVIL   Yet, as angry as I am with him, I would not have him surprised in anything. This mercantile rough man may go grossly into the examination of this matter and talk to the gentlewoman so as to—

HUMPHREY   No, I hope, not in an abrupt manner.

SIR JOHN BEVIL   No, I hope not. Why, dost thou know anything of her, or of him, or of anything of it, or all of it?

HUMPHREY   My dear master, I know so much; that I told him this very day you had reason to be secretly out of humour about her.

SIR JOHN BEVIL   Did you go so far? Well, what said he to that?

HUMPHREY   His words were, looking upon me steadfastly, "Humphrey," says he, "that woman is a woman of honor."

SIR JOHN BEVIL   How! Do you think he is married to her or designs to marry her?

HUMPHREY   I can say nothing to the latter. But he says he can marry no one without your consent while you are living.

SIR JOHN BEVIL   If he said so much, I know he scorns to break his word
with me.

HUMPHREY   I am sure of that.

SIR JOHN BEVIL   You are sure of that—well, that's some comfort. Then
I have nothing to do but to see the bottom of this matter during this
present ruffle—oh, Humphrey—

HUMPHREY   You are not ill, I hope, sir.

SIR JOHN BEVIL   Yes, a man is very ill that's in a very ill humour. To be
a father is to be in care for one whom you oftener disoblige than
please by that very care. Oh, that sons could know the duty to a father
before they themselves are fathers! But, perhaps, you'll say now that I
am one of the happiest fathers in the world; but, I assure you, that of
the very happiest is not a condition to be envied.

HUMPHREY   Sir, your pain arises not from the thing itself but your particular sense of it—you are overfond, nay, give me leave to say, you
are unjustly apprehensive from your fondness. My master Bevil never
disobliged you, and he will, I know he will, do everything you ought
to expect.

SIR JOHN BEVIL   He won't take all this money with this girl. For aught
I know, he will, forsooth, have so much moderation as to think he
ought not to force his liking for any consideration.

HUMPHREY   He is to marry her, not you; he is to live with her, not you,
sir.

SIR JOHN BEVIL   I know not what to think. But I know nothing can be
more miserable than to be in this doubt. Follow me; I must come to
some resolution.

Exeunt.

Act IV. Scene iii.

Scene, BEVIL JUNIOR's *lodgings. Enter* TOM *and* PHILLIS.

TOM   Well, madam, if you must speak with Mr. Myrtle, you shall. He
is now with my master in the library.

PHILLIS   But you must leave me alone with him, for he can't make me
a present, nor I so handsomely take anything from him before you; it
would not be decent.

TOM   It will be very decent, indeed, for me to retire and leave my mistress with another man.

PHILLIS   He is a gentleman and will treat me properly.

TOM   I believe so. But, however, I won't be far off and therefore will
venture to trust you. I'll call him to you.

Exit TOM.

PHILLIS   What a deal of pother and sputter here is between my mistress
and Mr. Myrtle from mere punctilio![4] I could any hour of the day get

4. Detail of conduct.

her to her lover and would do it, but she, forsooth, will allow no plot to get him. But if he can come to her, I know she would be glad of it. I must therefore do her an acceptable violence and surprise her into his arms. I am sure I go by the best rule imaginable—if she were my maid, I should think her the best servant in the world for doing so by me.

Enter MYRTLE *and* TOM.

Oh sir, you and Mr. Bevil are fine gentlemen to let a lady remain under such difficulties as my poor mistress, and no attempt to set her at liberty or release her from the danger of being instantly married to Cimberton.

MYRTLE   Tom as been telling. But what is to be done?

PHILLIS   What is to be done—when a man can't come at his mistress! Why, can't you fire our house or the next house to us, to make us run out and you take us?

MYRTLE   How, Mrs. Phillis—

PHILLIS   Ay, let me see that rogue [*indicating* TOM] deny to fire a house, make a riot, or any other little thing, when there were no other way to come at me.

TOM   I am obliged to you, madam.

PHILLIS   Why, don't we hear every day of people's hanging themselves for love, and won't they venture the hazard of being hanged for love? Oh! Were I a man—

MYRTLE   What manly thing would you have me undertake, according to your ladyship's notion of a man?

PHILLIS   Only be at once what, one time or other, you may be, and wish to be, or must be.

MYRTLE   Dear girl, talk plainly to me, and consider, I, in my condition, can't be in very good humour. You say, to be at once what I must be.

PHILLIS   Ay, ay, I mean no more than to be an old man. I saw you do it very well at the masquerade. In a word, old Sir Geoffry Cimberton is every hour expected in town to join in the deeds and settlements for marrying Mr. Cimberton. He is half blind, half lame, half deaf, half dumb; though as to his passions and desires, he is as warm and ridiculous as when in the heat of youth—

TOM   Come to the business, and don't keep the gentleman in suspense for the pleasure of being courted, as you serve me.

PHILLIS   I saw you at the masquerade act such a one to perfection. Go and put on that very habit, and come to our house as Sir Geoffry. There is not one there but myself knows his person. I was born in the parish where he is lord of the manor. I have seen him often and often at church in the country. Do not hesitate, but come thither. They will think you bring a certain security against Mr. Myrtle, and you bring Mr. Myrtle. Leave the rest to me, I leave this with you, and expect— They don't, I told you, know you; they think you out of

town, which you had as good be forever, if you lose this opportunity.
I must be gone; I know I am wanted at home.

MYRTLE   My dear Phillis!

> *Catches and kisses her, and gives her money.*

PHILLIS   Oh fie! My kisses are not my own; you have committed violence, but I'll carry 'em to the right owner.

> TOM *kisses her.*

[*To* TOM.] Come, see me downstairs, and leave the lover to think of
his last game for the prize.

> *Exeunt* TOM *and* PHILLIS.

MYRTLE   I think I will instantly attempt this wild expedient. The extravagance of it will make me less suspected, and it will give me opportunity to assert my own right to Lucinda, without whom I cannot live.
But I am so mortified at this conduct of mine towards poor Bevil. He
must think meanly of me. I know not how to reassume myself and be
in spirit enough for such an adventure as this. Yet I must attempt it,
if it be only to be near Lucinda under her present perplexities. And
sure —

> The next delight to transport with the fair
> Is to relieve her in her hours of care.

> *Exit.*

Act V. Scene i.

> *Scene,* SEALAND's *house. Enter* PHILLIS *with lights before* MYRTLE,
> *disguised like old* SIR GEOFFRY, *supported by* MRS. SEALAND,
> LUCINDA, *and* CIMBERTON.

MRS. SEALAND   Now I have seen you thus far, Sir Geoffry, will you
excuse me a moment while I give my necessary orders for your
accommodation?

> *Exit* MRS. SEALAND.

MYRTLE   I have not seen you, Cousin Cimberton, since you were ten
years old, and as it is incumbent on you to keep up our name and
family, I shall upon very reasonable terms join with you in a settlement to that purpose. Though I must tell you, cousin, this is the first
merchant that has married into our house.

LUCINDA [*aside*]   Deuce on 'em! Am I a merchant because my father
is?

MYRTLE   But is he directly a trader at this time?

CIMBERTON   There's no hiding the disgrace, sir; he trades to all parts of
the world.

MYRTLE   We never had one of our family before who descended from persons that did anything.

CIMBERTON   Sir, since it is a girl that they have, I am, for the honor of my family, willing to take it in again and to sink her into our name and no harm done.

MYRTLE   'Tis prudently and generously resolved. Is this the young thing?

CIMBERTON   Yes sir.

PHILLIS [*aside to* LUCINDA]   Good madam, don't be out of humour but let them run to the utmost of their extravagance. Hear them out.

MYRTLE   Can't I see her nearer? My eyes are but weak.

PHILLIS [*aside to* LUCINDA]   Besides, I am sure the uncle has something worth your notice, I'll take care to get off the young one and leave you to observe what may be wrought out of the old one for your good.

Exit.

CIMBERTON   Madam, this old gentleman, your great-uncle, desires to be introduced to you and to see you nearer. Approach, sir.

MYRTLE   By your leave, young lady—[*Puts on spectacles.*] Cousin Cimberton! She has exactly that sort of neck and bosom for which my sister Gertrude was so much admired in the year sixty-one before the French dresses first discovered anything in women below the chin.

LUCINDA [*aside*]   What a very odd situation am I in! Though I cannot but be diverted at the extravagance of their humours, equally unsuitable to their age—chin, quotha—I don't believe my passionate lover there knows whether I have one or not. Ha! Ha!

MYRTLE   Madam. I would not willingly offend, but I have a better glass—[5]

Pulls out a large one.
Enter PHILLIS *to* CIMBERTON.

PHILLIS   Sir, my lady desires to show the apartment to you that she intends for Sir Geoffry.

CIMBERTON   Well sir, by that time you have sufficiently gazed and sunned yourself in the beauties of my spouse there, I will wait on you again.

Exit CIMBERTON *and* PHILLIS.

MYRTLE   Were it not, madam, that I might be troublesome, there is something of importance, though we are alone, which I would say more safe from being heard.

5. Optical instrument.

LUCINDA [*aside*]   There is something in this old fellow, methinks, that raises my curiosity.

MYRTLE   To be free, madam, I as heartily condemn this kinsman of mine as you do and am sorry to see so much beauty and merit devoted by your parents to so insensible a possessor.

LUCINDA [*aside*]   Surprising—I hope then, sir, you will not contribute to the wrong you are so generous as to pity, whatever may be the interest of your family.

MYRTLE   This hand of mine shall never be employed to sign anything against your good and happiness.

LUCINDA   I am sorry, sir, it is not in my power to make you proper acknowledgements, but there is a gentleman in the world whose gratitude will, I am sure, be worthy of the favor.

MYRTLE   All the thanks I desire, madam, are in your power to give.

LUCINDA   Name them, and command them.

MYRTLE   Only, madam, that the first time you are alone with your lover, you will, with open arms, receive him.

LUCINDA   As willingly as his heart could wish it.

MYRTLE   Thus then he claims your promise! Oh, Lucinda!

LUCINDA   Oh! A cheat! A cheat! A cheat!

MYRTLE   Hush! 'Tis I, 'tis I, your lover, Myrtle himself, madam.

LUCINDA   Oh bless me! What a rashness and folly to surprise me so— But hush—my mother—

Enter MRS. SEALAND, CIMBERTON, *and* PHILLIS.

MRS. SEALAND   How now! What's the matter?

LUCINDA   Oh madam! As soon as you left the room, my uncle fell into a sudden fit, and—and—so I cried out for help, to support him, and conduct him to his chamber.

MRS. SEALAND   That was kindly done! Alas! Sir, how do you find yourself?

MYRTLE   Never was taken in so odd a way in my life. Pray lead me! Oh! I was talking here—pray carry me—to my Cousin Cimberton's young lady—

MRS. SEALAND [*aside*]   My Cousin Cimberton's young lady! How zealous he is, even in his extremity, for the match! A right Cimberton!

CIMBERTON *and* LUCINDA *lead him, as one in pain, etc.*

CIMBERTON   Pox! Uncle, you will pull my ear off.

LUCINDA   Pray uncle! You will squeeze me to death.

MRS. SEALAND   No matter, no matter, he knows not what he does. Come, sir, shall I help you out?

MYRTLE   By no means; I'll trouble nobody but my young cousins here.

They lead him off.

PHILLIS   But pray, madam, does your ladyship intend that Mr. Cimberton shall really marry my young mistress at last? I don't think he likes her.

MRS. SEALAND   That's not material! Men of his speculation[6] are above desires. But be it as it may, now I have given old Sir Geoffry the trouble of coming up to sign and seal, with what countenance can I be off?

PHILLIS   As well as with twenty others, madam. It is the glory and honor of a great fortune to live in continual treaties and still to break off. It looks great, madam.

MRS. SEALAND   True, Phillis. Yet to return our blood again into the Cimbertons is an honor not to be rejected. But were not you saying that Sir John Bevil's creature Humphrey has been with Mr. Sealand?

PHILLIS   Yes, madam: I overheard them agree that Mr. Sealand should go himself and visit this unknown lady that Mr. Bevil is so great with; and if he found nothing there to fright him, that Mr. Bevil should still marry my young mistress.

MRS. SEALAND   How! Nay then, he shall find she is my daughter as well as his: I'll follow him this instant and take the whole family along with me. The disputed power of disposing of my own daughter shall be at an end this very night. I'll live no longer in anxiety for a little hussy that hurts my appearance wherever I carry her and for whose sake I seem to be not at all regarded, and that in the best of my days.

PHILLIS   Indeed, madam, if she were married, your ladyship might very well be taken for Mr. Sealand's daughter.

MRS. SEALAND   Nay, when the chit has not been with me, I have heard the men say as much. I'll no longer cut off the greatest pleasure of a woman's life, the shining in assemblies, by her forward anticipation of the respect that's due to her superior—she shall down to Cimberton-Hall—she shall—she shall.

PHILLIS   I hope, madam, I shall stay with your ladyship.

MRS. SEALAND   Thou shalt, Phillis, and I'll place thee then more about me. But order chairs immediately; I'll be gone this minute.

Exeunt.

Act V. Scene ii.

Scene, Charing Cross. Enter MR. SEALAND *and* HUMPHREY.

MR. SEALAND   I am very glad, Mr. Humphrey, that you agree with me that it is for our common good I should look thoroughly into this matter.

HUMPHREY   I am indeed of that opinion, for there is no artifice, nothing concealed in our family which ought in justice to be known. I need not desire you, sir, to treat the lady with care and respect.

6. Vision.

MR. SEALAND   Master Humphrey, I shall not be rude, though I design
  to be a little abrupt and come into the matter at once to see how she
  will bear upon a surprise.
HUMPHREY   That's the door, sir, I wish you success.

  While HUMPHREY *speaks,* MR. SEALAND *consults his tablebook.*[7]

[*Aside.*]   I am less concerned what happens there because I hear Mr.
Myrtle is well-lodged as old Sir Geoffry, so I am willing to let this
gentleman employ himself here to give them time at home, for I am
sure 'tis necessary for the quiet of our family Lucinda were disposed of
out of it, since Mr. Bevil's inclination is so much otherwise engaged.

Exit.

MR. SEALAND   I think this is the door.

  Knocks.

I'll carry this matter with an air of authority to inquire, though I make
an errand to begin discourse.

  Knocks again, and enter a FOOTBOY.

So young man! Is your lady within?
BOY   Alack, sir! I am but a country boy—I dan't know whether she is
  or noa. But an you'll stay a bit, I'll goa and ask the gentlewoman that's
  with her.
MR. SEALAND   Why, sirrah, though you are a country boy, you can see,
  can't you? You know whether she is at home when you see her, don't
  you?
BOY   Nay, nay, I'm not such a country lad neither, master, to think she's
  at home because I see her. I have been in town but a month, and I
  lost one place already for believing my own eyes.
MR. SEALAND   Why, sirrah! Have you learnt to lie already?
BOY   Ah, master, things that are lies in the country are not lies at London—I begin to know my business a little better than so. But an you
  please to walk in, I'll call a gentlewoman to you that can tell you for
  certain; she can make bold to ask my lady herself.
MR. SEALAND   O, then, she is within, I find, though you dare not say
  so.
BOY   Nay, nay! That's neither here nor there. What's matter whether
  she is within or no if she has not a mind to see anybody?
MR. SEALAND   I can't tell, sirrah, whether you are arch or simple, but
  however get me a direct answer and here's a shilling for you.
BOY   Will you please to walk in? I'll see what I can do for you.
MR. SEALAND   I see you will be fit for your business in time, child. But
  I expect to meet with nothing but extraordinaries in such a house.

7. Notebook.

BOY Such a house! Sir, you han't seen it yet. Pray walk in.
MR. SEALAND   Sir, I'll wait upon you.

Exeunt.

Act V. Scene iii.

Scene, INDIANA's *house. Enter* ISABELLA.

ISABELLA   What anxiety do I feel for this poor creature! What will be
the end of her? Such a languishing, unreserved passion for a man
that at last must certainly leave or ruin her, and perhaps both! Then
the aggravation of the distress is that she does not believe he will—
not but, I must own, if they are both what they would seem, they are
made for one another as much as Adam and Eve were, for there is no
other of their kind but themselves.

Enter BOY.

So, Daniel! What news with you?
BOY   Madam, there's a gentleman below would speak with my lady.
ISABELLA   Sirrah, don't you know Mr. Bevil yet?
BOY   Madam, 'tis not the gentleman who comes every day and asks for
you and won't go in till he knows whether you are with her or no.
ISABELLA [*aside*]   Ha! That's a particular I did not know before.—Well!
Be it who it will, let him come up to me.

Exit BOY *and re-enters with* MR. SEALAND. ISABELLA *looks
amazed.*

MR. SEALAND   Madam, I can't blame your being a little surprised to see
a perfect stranger make a visit and—
ISABELLA   I am indeed surprised! [*Aside.*] I see he does not know me.
MR. SEALAND   You are very prettily lodged here, madam; in troth, you
seem to have everything in plenty. [*Aside, and looking about.*] A thousand a year, I warrant you, upon this pretty nest of rooms, and the
dainty one within them.
ISABELLA [*aside*]   Twenty years, it seems, have less effect in the alteration of a man of thirty than of a girl of fourteen; he's almost still the
same. But alas! I find, by other men as well as himself, I am not what
I was. As soon as he spoke, I was convinced 'twas he. How shall I
contain my surprise and satisfaction? He must not know me yet.
MR. SEALAND   Madam, I hope I don't give you any disturbance, but
there is a young lady here with whom I have a particular business to
discourse, and I hope she will admit me to that favor.
ISABELLA   Why, sir, have you had any notice concerning her? I wonder
who could give it you.
MR. SEALAND   That, madam, is fit only to be communicated to herself.
ISABELLA   Well, sir, you shall see her. [*Aside.*] I find he knows nothing

yet nor shall from me. I am resolved I will observe this interlude, this sport of nature and of fortune. —You shall see her presently, sir; for now I am as a mother and will trust her with you.

Exit.

MR. SEALAND   As a mother! Right; that's the old phrase for one of those commode[8] ladies who lend out beauty for hire to young gentlemen that have pressing occasions. But here comes the precious lady herself. In troth, a very sightly woman—

Enter INDIANA.

INDIANA   I am told, sir, you have some affair that requires your speaking with me.

MR. SEALAND   Yes, madam. There came to my hands a bill drawn by Mr. Bevil which is payable tomorrow, and he, in the intercourse of business, sent it to me, who have cash of his, and desired me to send a servant with it, but I have made bold to bring you the money myself.

INDIANA   Sir, was that necessary?

MR. SEALAND   No, madam; but, to be free with you, the fame of your beauty and the regard which Mr. Bevil is a little too well known to have for you excited my curiosity.

INDIANA   Too well known to have for me! Your sober appearance, sir, which my friend described, made me expect no rudeness or absurdity at least—who's there? Sir, if you pay the money to a servant, 'twill be as well.

MR. SEALAND   Pray, madam, be not offended. I came hither on an innocent, nay a virtuous design; and, if you will have patience to hear me, it may be as useful to you, as you are in a friendship with Mr. Bevil, as to my only daughter, whom I was this day disposing of.

INDIANA   You make me hope, sir, I have mistaken you; I am composed again. Be free, say on—[*aside*] what I am afraid to hear—

MR. SEALAND   I feared, indeed, an unwarranted passion here, but I did not think it was in abuse of so worthy an object, so accomplished a lady as your sense and mien bespeak. But the youth of our age care not what merit and virtue they bring to shame, so they gratify—

INDIANA   Sir, you are going into very great errors. But, as you are pleased to say you see something in me that has changed, at least, the color of your suspicions, so has your appearance altered mine and made me earnestly attentive to what has any way concerned you to inquire into my affairs and character.

MR. SEALAND   [*aside*]   How sensibly, with what an air she talks!

INDIANA   Good sir, be seated, and tell me tenderly—keep all your suspicions concerning me alive that you may in a proper and prepared way—acquaint me why the care of your daughter obliges a person of your seeming worth and fortune to be thus inquisitive about a

---

8. Accommodating.

wretched, helpless, friendless—[*Weeping.*] But I beg your pardon—
though I am an orphan, your child is not; and your concern for her,
it seems, has brought you hither. I'll be composed. Pray go on, sir.

MR. SEALAND   How could Mr. Bevil be such a monster to injure such
a woman?

INDIANA   No, sir, you wrong him. He has not injured me; my support
is from his bounty.

MR. SEALAND   Bounty! When gluttons give high prices for delicates,
they are prodigious bountiful.

INDIANA   Still, still you will persist in that error. But my own fears tell
me all: you are the gentleman, I suppose, for whose happy daughter
he is designed a husband by his good father, and he has, perhaps,
consented to the overture. He was here this morning dressed beyond
his usual plainness, nay, most sumptuously, and he is to be, perhaps,
this night a bridegroom.

MR. SEALAND   I own he was intended such. But, madam, on your
account I have determined to defer my daughter's marriage till I am
satisfied from your own mouth of what nature are the obligations you
are under to him.

INDIANA   His actions, sir, his eyes have only made me think he
designed to make me the partner of his heart. The goodness and
gentleness of his demeanor made me misinterpret all. 'Twas my own
hope, my own passion, that deluded me. He never made one amorous advance to me. His large heart and bestowing hand have only
helped the miserable. Nor know I why but from his mere delight in
virtue that I have been his care, the object on which to indulge and
please himself with pouring favors.

MR. SEALAND   Madam, I know not why it is, but I, as well as you, am
methinks afraid of entering into the matter I came about; but 'tis the
same thing as if we had talked never so distinctly—he ne'er shall have
a daughter of mine.

INDIANA   If you say this from what you think of me, you wrong yourself
and him. Let not me, miserable though I may be, do injury to my
benefactor. No, sir, my treatment ought rather to reconcile you to his
virtues. If to bestow, without a prospect of return, if to delight in
supporting what might, perhaps, be thought an object of desire with
no other view than to be her guard against those who would not
be so disinterested, if these actions, sir, can in a careful parent's eye
commend him to a daughter, give yours, sir, give her to my honest,
generous Bevil. What have I to do but sigh, and weep, to rave, run
wild, a lunatic in chains, or, hid in darkness, mutter in distracted
starts and broken accents my strange, strange story!

MR. SEALAND   Take comfort, madam.

INDIANA   All my comfort must be to expostulate in madness, to relieve
with frenzy my despair, and, shrieking, to demand of fate why—why
was I born to such variety of sorrows?

MR. SEALAND   If I have been the least occasion—

INDIANA   No, 'twas Heaven's high will I should be such—to be plun-
dered in my cradle! Tossed on the seas! And even there, an infant
captive! To lose my mother, hear but of my father! To be adopted!
Lose my adopter! Then plunged again in worse calamities!

MR. SEALAND   An infant captive!

INDIANA   Yet then to find the most charming of mankind once more to
set me free from what I thought the last distress, to load me with his
services, his bounties, and his favors; to support my very life in a way
that stole at the same time my very soul itself from me.

MR. SEALAND   And has young Bevil been this worthy man?

INDIANA   Yet then again, this very man to take another! Without leaving me the right, the pretense of easing my fond heart with tears! For
oh, I can't reproach him, though the same hand that raised me to
this height now throws me down the precipice.

MR. SEALAND   Dear lady! Oh, yet one moment's patience. My heart
grows full with your affliction. But yet, there's something in your story
that—

INDIANA   My portion here is bitterness and sorrow.

MR. SEALAND   Do not think so. Pray answer me, does Bevil know your
name and family?

INDIANA   Alas, too well! Oh, could I be any other thing than what I
am—I'll tear away all traces of my former self, my little ornaments,
the remains of my first state, the hints of what I ought to have been—

In her disorder she throws away a bracelet, which MR. SEALAND
takes up, and looks earnestly on it.

MR. SEALAND   Ha! What's this? My eyes are not deceived? It is, it is
the same! The very bracelet which I bequeathed my wife at our last
mournful parting.

INDIANA   What said you, sir? Your wife! Whither does my fancy carry
me? What means this unfelt motion at my heart? And yet again my
fortune but deludes me, for if I err not, sir, your name is Sealand, but
my lost father's name was—.

MR. SEALAND   Danvers! Was it not?

INDIANA   What new amazement! That is indeed my family.

MR. SEALAND   Know then, when my misfortunes drove me to the
Indies, for reasons too tedious now to mention, I changed my name
of Danvers into Sealand.

Enter ISABELLA.

ISABELLA   If yet there wants an explanation of your wonder, examine
well this face—yours, sir, I well remember—gaze on, and read, in
me, your sister Isabella!

MR. SEALAND   My sister!

ISABELLA   But here's a claim more tender yet—your Indiana, sir, your
long lost daughter.

MR. SEALAND   Oh, my child! My child!

INDIANA   All-gracious Heavens! Is it possible? Do I embrace my father?

MR. SEALAND   And do I hold thee—these passions are too strong for utterance—rise, rise, my child, and give my tears their way—Oh, my sister!

> *Embracing her.*

ISABELLA   Now, dearest niece, my groundless fears, my painful cares no more shall vex thee. If I have wronged thy noble lover with too hard suspicions, my just concern for thee, I hope, will plead my pardon.

MR. SEALAND   Oh! Make him then the full amends and be yourself the messenger of joy. Fly this instant! Tell him all these wondrous turns of Providence in his favor! Tell him I have now a daughter to bestow which he no longer will decline, that this day he still shall be a bridegroom, nor shall a fortune, the merit which his father seeks, be wanting. Tell him the reward of all his virtues waits on his acceptance.

> *Exit* ISABELLA.

My dearest Indiana!

> *Turns, and embraces her.*

INDIANA   Have I then at last a father's sanction on my love? His bounteous hand to give and make my heart a present worthy of Bevil's generosity?

MR. SEALAND   Oh my child! How are our sorrows past o'erpaid by such a meeting! Though I have lost so many years of soft paternal dalliance with thee, yet, in one day, to find thee thus, and thus bestow thee in such perfect happiness is ample, ample reparation! And yet again the merit of thy lover—

INDIANA   Oh! Had I spirits left to tell you of his actions, how strongly filial duty has suppressed his love, and how concealment still has doubled all his obligations, the pride, the joy of his alliance, sir, would warm your heart as he has conquered mine.

MR. SEALAND   How laudable is love when born of virtue! I burn to embrace him—

INDIANA   See, sir, my aunt already has succeeded and brought him to your wishes.

> *Enter* ISABELLA, *with* SIR JOHN BEVIL, BEVIL JUNIOR, MRS. SEALAND, CIMBERTON, MYRTLE, *and* LUCINDA.

SIR JOHN BEVIL [*entering*]   Where? Where's this scene of wonder? Mr. Sealand, I congratulate, on this occasion, our mutual happiness. Your good sister, sir, has, with the story of your daughter's fortune, filled us with surprise and joy. Now all exceptions are removed. My son has now avowed his love and turned all former jealousies and doubts to approbation, and, I am told, your goodness has consented to reward him.

MR. SEALAND   If, sir, a fortune equal to his father's hopes can make this object worthy his acceptance.

BEVIL JUNIOR   I hear your mention, sir, of fortune with pleasure only as it may prove the means to reconcile the best of fathers to my love. Let him be provident, but let me be happy.—My ever-destined, my acknowledged wife!

Embracing INDIANA

INDIANA   Wife! Oh, my ever loved, my lord, my master!

SIR JOHN BEVIL [*to* INDIANA]   I congratulate myself as well as you that I had a son who could, under such disadvantages, discover your great merit.

MR. SEALAND   Oh, Sir John, how vain, how weak is human prudence! What care, what foresight, what imagination could contrive such blest events to make our children happy as Providence in one short hour has laid before us?

CIMBERTON [*to* MRS. SEALAND]   I am afraid, madam, Mr. Sealand is a little too busy for our affair. If you please, we'll take another opportunity.

MRS. SEALAND   Let us have patience, sir.

CIMBERTON   But we make Sir Geoffry wait, madam.

MYRTLE   Oh, sir! I am not in haste.

During this, BEVIL JUNIOR *presents* LUCINDA *to* INDIANA

MR. SEALAND   But here! Here's our general benefactor. Excellent young man that could be at once a lover to her beauty and a parent to her virtue.

BEVIL JUNIOR   If you think that an obligation, sir, give me leave to over-pay myself in the only instance that can now add to my felicity, by begging you to bestow this lady on Mr. Myrtle.

MR. SEALAND   She is his without reserve; I beg he may be sent for. Mr. Cimberton, notwithstanding you never had my consent, yet there is, since I last saw you, another objection to your marriage with my daughter.

CIMBERTON   I hope, sir, your lady has concealed nothing from me.

MR. SEALAND   Troth, sir, nothing but what was concealed from myself—another daughter, who has an undoubted title to half my estate.

CIMBERTON   How, Mr. Sealand! Why then if half Mrs. Lucinda's fortune is gone, you can't say that any of my estate is settled upon her. I was in treaty for the whole, but if that is not to be come at, to be sure, there can be no bargain. Sir, I have nothing to do but to take my leave of your good lady, my cousin, and beg pardon for the trouble I have given this old gentleman.

MYRTLE   That you have, Mr. Cimberton, with all my heart.

Discovers himself.

OMNES   Mr. Myrtle!

MYRTLE   And I beg pardon of the whole company that I assumed the person of Sir Geoffry only to be present at the danger of this lady's being disposed of and in her utmost exigence to assert my right to her. Which if her parents will ratify, as they once favored my pretensions, no abatement of fortune shall lessen her value to me.

LUCINDA   Generous man!

MR. SEALAND   If, sir, you can overlook the injury of being in treaty with one who as meanly left her as you have generously asserted your right in her, she is yours.

LUCINDA   Mr. Myrtle, though you have ever had my heart, yet now I find I love you more because I bring you less.

MYRTLE   We have much more than we want, and I am glad any event has contributed to the discovery of our real inclinations to each other.

MRS. SEALAND [*aside*]   Well! However I'm glad the girl's disposed of any way.

BEVIL JUNIOR   Myrtle! No longer rivals now, but brothers.

MYRTLE   Dear Bevil! You are born to triumph over me! But now our competition ceases. I rejoice in the pre-eminence of your virtue and your alliance adds charms to Lucinda.

SIR JOHN BEVIL   Now, ladies and gentlemen, you have set the world a fair example. Your happiness is owing to your constancy and merit, and the several difficulties you have struggled with evidently show

> Whate'er the generous mind itself denies
> The secret care of Providence supplies.

Exeunt.

Epilogue[9]

Spoken by Mrs. Oldfield[1]

Now, I presume, our moralizing knight
Is heartily convinced my sense was right:
   I told him, flat, his Conscious Lovers' passion
Had, many ages past, been out of fashion.
That all attempts to mend the mode were shallow,
Our man in favor now's a pretty fellow
That talks and laughs and sings, fights, dances, dresses,
Rakes with an air, and keeps his string of misses,

---

9. This epilogue, spoken on the opening night, was not printed with the play and first appeared in Benjamin Victor's *Epistle to Sir Richard Steele* (2nd edition, 1722). Welsted's epilogue, which follows, was originally published with the play.

1. Who played Indiana.

Then to his fame such courage too belongs
That when by rivals called to account for wrongs,
Ne'er stands to talk but—hah—whips 'em through the lungs. ⎫
　　Not like his Bevil—coolly waits his season,
And traps determined courage into reason;
Nor loves like him, poor soul, confined to one!
And is at vast expense—for nothing done!
To pass whole days alone and never meddle,
Treat her with senseless solo—on the fiddle!
And all this chaste restraint, forsooth, to flow
From strait obedience to a father due!
T'have shown his modern breeding, he should rather
Not have obeyed, but bit the put,[2] his father;
Or, in compliance to his daddy's courting,
Have starved his dear, and fairly took the fortune.
But to maintain her, and not let her know it—
Oh! the wild—crack-brained notions of a poet!
What though his hero never loved before,
He might have, sure, done less for her—or more.
　　With scenes of this coarse kind, he owns that plays
Too often have beguiled you of your praise:
Where sense and virtue were allowed no part,
That only touched the loose and wanton heart.
If then a diff'rent way of thinking might ⎫
Incline the chaste to hear, the learned to write, ⎬
On you it rests—to make your profit your delight. ⎭

Epilogue

By Mr. Welsted
Intended to Be Spoken by Indiana

Our author, whom entreaties cannot move,
Spite of the dear coquetry that you love,
Swears he'll not frustrate, so he plainly means,
By a loose epilogue his decent scenes.
Is it not, sirs, hard fate I meet today,
To keep me rigid[3] still beyond the play?
And yet I'm saved a world of pains that way.
I now can look, I now can move at ease,
Nor need I torture these poor limbs to please;
Nor with the hand or foot attempt surprise,
Nor wrest my features, nor fatigue my eyes.

2. "Bit the put" means "fooled the blockhead."
3. Strait-laced, moral.

Bless me! What freakish gambols have I played!
What motions tried and wanton looks betrayed!
Out of pure kindness all! to over-rule
The threatened hiss, and screen some scribbling fool.
With more respect I'm entertained tonight:
Our author thinks I can with ease delight.
My artless looks while modest graces arm,
He says, I need but to appear, and charm.
A wife so formed, by these examples bred,
Pours joy and gladness 'round the marriage bed;
Soft source of comfort, kind relief from care,
And 'tis her least perfection to be fair.
The nymph with Indiana's worth who vies
A nation will behold with Bevil's eyes.

The School for Scandal, Haymarket Theatre, London, 1962. In foreground, Ralph Richardson as Sir Peter Teazle, Charles Lloyd Pack as Crabtree, and Gwen Ffrangcon-Davies as Mrs. Candour. By permission of the Harvard Theatre Collection.

RICHARD BRINSLEY SHERIDAN

The School for Scandal

Prologue

Spoken by Mr. King[1]

Written by D. Garrick, Esq.[2]

A School for Scandal! tell me, I beseech you,
Needs there a school this modish art to teach you?
No need of lessons now, the knowing think—
We might as well be taught to eat and drink.
Caused by a dearth of scandal, should the vapors
Distress our fair ones—let 'em read the papers;
Their pow'rful mixtures such disorders hit;
Crave what they will, there's *quantum sufficit.*[3]
    "Lord!" cries my Lady Wormwood (who loves tattle,
And puts much salt and pepper in her prattle),
Just ris'n at noon, all night at cards when threshing
Strong tea and scandal—"Bless me, how refreshing!
Give me the papers, Lisp—how bold and free! (*Sips.*)
Last night Lord L—— (*sips*) *was caught with Lady D——*
For aching heads what charming sal volatile! (*Sips.*)
If Mrs. B.——will still continue flirting,
We hope she'll DRAW, *or we'll* UNDRAW *the curtain.*
Fine satire, poz[4]—in public all abuse it,
But, by ourselves (*sips*), our praise we can't refuse it.
Now, Lisp, *read you*—there, at that dash and star."[5]
    "Yes, ma'am.—*A certain Lord had best beware,*
Who lives not twenty miles from Grosv'nor Square;

---

† First performed in 1777, at Drury Lane. Sheridan did not authorize publication, and the versions printed during his lifetime were in various degrees spurious. The most authoritative texts occur in manuscripts with corrections in Sheridan's hand, especially in a copy which Sheridan presented to Lady Crewe in 1777.
1. Who played Sir Peter Teazle.
2. David Garrick, the most famous actor of his age.
3. As much as suffices.
4. Slang for "positively."
5. With a dash and star the middle letters of a person's name were obscured in published gossip columns, as a way of avoiding libel suits.

For should he Lady W——find willing,
WORMWOOD *is bitter"* — "Oh! that's me! the villain!
Throw it behind the fire, and never more
Let that vile paper come within my door." —
   Thus at our friends we laugh, who feel the dart;
   To reach our feelings, we ourselves must smart.
   Is our young bard so young, to think that he
   Can stop the full spring-tide of calumny?
   Knows he the world so little, and its trade?
   Alas! the devil is sooner raised than laid.
   So strong, so swift, the monster there's no gagging:
   Cut Scandal's head off—still the tongue is wagging.
   Proud of your smiles once lavishly bestow'd,
   Again your young Don Quixote takes the road:
   To show his gratitude, he draws his pen,
   And seeks this hydra,[6] Scandal, in his den.
For your applause all perils he would through—⎫
He'll fight—that's *write*—a cavalliero true,   ⎬
Till every drop of blood—that's *ink*—is spilt for you.⎭

Dramatis Personae

MEN

SIR PETER TEAZLE	*Mr. King*
SIR OLIVER SURFACE	*Mr. Yates*
JOSEPH SURFACE	*Mr. Palmer*
CHARLES SURFACE	*Mr. Smith*
CRABTREE	*Mr. Parsons*
SIR BENJAMIN BACKBITE	*Mr. Dodd*
ROWLEY	*Mr. Aickin*
TRIP	*Mr. LaMash*
MOSES	*Mr. Baddeley*
SNAKE	*Mr. Packer*
CARELESS	*Mr. Farren*

and other Companions to CHARLES [SURFACE],
Servants, etc.

WOMEN

LADY TEAZLE	*Mrs. Abington*
MARIA	*Miss P. Hopkins*
LADY SNEERWELL	*Miss Sherry*
MRS. CANDOUR	*Miss Pope*

6. A fabled snake whose many heads grew again as soon as they were cut off.

The School for Scandal

Act I. Scene i.

[LADY SNEERWELL's *house*.]
LADY SNEERWELL *at the dressing-table*—SNAKE *drinking choco-late*.

LADY SNEERWELL   The paragraphs, you say, Mr. Snake, were all inserted?

SNAKE   They were, madam, and as I copied them myself in a feigned hand, there can be no suspicion whence they came.

LADY SNEERWELL   Did you circulate the reports of Lady *Brittle's* intrigue with Captain *Boastall?*

SNAKE   That is in as fine a train as your ladyship could wish,—in the common sense of things, I think it must reach Mrs. *Clackit's* ears within four-and-twenty hours; and then, you know, the business is as good as done.

LADY SNEERWELL   Why, truly, Mrs. *Clackit* has a very pretty talent, and a great deal of industry.

SNAKE   True, madam, and has been tolerably successful in her day: — to my knowledge, she has been the cause of six matches being broken off, and three sons being disinherited, of four forced elopements, as many close confinements, nine separate maintenances, and two divorces;—nay, I have more than once traced her causing a *Tête-à-Tête* in the *Town and Country Magazine*,[7] when the parties perhaps had never seen each other's faces before in the course of their lives.

LADY SNEERWELL   She certainly has talents, but her manner is gross.

SNAKE   'Tis very true,—she generally designs well, has a free tongue, and a bold invention; but her coloring is too dark, and her outline often extravagant. She wants that *delicacy* of *hint*, and *mellowness* of *sneer*, which distinguish your ladyship's scandal.

LADY SNEERWELL   Ah! you are partial, Snake.

SNAKE   Not in the least; everybody allows that Lady *Sneerwell* can do more with a *word* or a *look* than many can with the most labored detail, even when they happen to have a little truth on their side to support it.

LADY SNEERWELL   Yes, my dear Snake; and I am no hypocrite to deny the satisfaction I reap from the success of my efforts. Wounded myself, in the early part of my life, by the envenomed tongue of slander, I confess I have since known no pleasure equal to the reducing others to the level of my own injured reputation.

SNAKE   Nothing can be more natural. But, Lady Sneerwell, there is one affair in which you have lately employed me, wherein, I confess, I am at a loss to guess your motives.

---

7. The scandal column in this magazine was entitled "Tête-à-Tête."

LADY SNEERWELL   I conceive you mean with respect to my neighbor, Sir Peter Teazle, and his family?

SNAKE   I do; here are two young men, to whom Sir Peter has acted as a kind of guardian since their father's death; the elder possessing the most amiable character, and universally well spoken of; the youngest, the most dissipated and extravagant young fellow in the kingdom, without friends or character,—the former an avowed admirer of your ladyship, and apparently your favorite; the latter attached to Maria, Sir Peter's ward, and confessedly beloved by her. Now, on the face of these circumstances, it is utterly unaccountable to me, why you, the widow of a city knight, with a good jointure,[8] should not close with the passion of a man of such character and expectations as Mr. *Surface*; and more so why you should be so uncommonly earnest to destroy the mutual attachment subsisting between his brother *Charles* and *Maria*.

LADY SNEERWELL   Then, at once to unravel this mystery, I must inform you that love has no share whatever in the intercourse between Mr. *Surface* and me.

SNAKE   No!

LADY SNEERWELL   His real attachment is to *Maria*, or her fortune; but, finding in his brother a favored rival, he has been obliged to mask his pretensions, and profit by my assistance.

SNAKE   Yet still I am more puzzled why you should interest yourself in his success.

LADY SNEERWELL   Heav'ns! how dull you are! Cannot you surmise the weakness which I hitherto, through shame, have concealed even from *you*? Must I confess that *Charles*—that libertine, that extravagant, that bankrupt fortune and reputation—that he it is for whom I am thus anxious and malicious, and to gain whom I would sacrifice everything?

SNAKE   Now, indeed, your conduct appears consistent; but how came you and Mr. *Surface* so confidential?

LADY SNEERWELL   For our mutual interest. I have found him out a long time since—I know him to be artful, selfish, and malicious—in short, a sentimental knave.

SNAKE   Yet, Sir Peter vows he has not his equal in England—and, above all, he praises him as a man of sentiment.

LADY SNEERWELL   True; and with the assistance of his sentiment and hypocrisy he has brought him [Sir Peter] entirely into his interest with regard to *Maria*.

Enter SERVANT.

SERVANT   Mr. Surface.

LADY SNEERWELL   Show him up.

Exit SERVANT.

8. Property settled upon a woman at marriage which becomes hers in widowhood.

He generally calls about this time. I don't wonder at people's giving him to me for a lover.

    Enter JOSEPH SURFACE.

JOSEPH SURFACE   My dear Lady Sneerwell, how do you do to-day? Mr. Snake, your most obedient.

LADY SNEERWELL   Snake has just been arraigning me on our mutual attachment, but I have informed him of our real views; you know how useful he has been to us; and, believe me, the confidence is not ill placed.

JOSEPH SURFACE   Madam, it is impossible for me to suspect a man of Mr. *Snake*'s sensibility and discernment.

LADY SNEERWELL   Well, well, no compliments now;—but tell me when you saw your mistress, *Maria*—or, what is more material to me, your brother.

JOSEPH SURFACE   I have not seen either since I left you; but I can inform you that they never meet. Some of your stories have taken a good effect on Maria.

LADY SNEERWELL   Ah, my dear Snake! the merit of this belongs to you. But do your brother's distresses increase?

JOSEPH SURFACE   Every hour;—I am told he has had another execution[9] in the house yesterday; in short, his dissipation and extravagance exceed any thing I ever heard of.

LADY SNEERWELL   Poor Charles!

JOSEPH SURFACE   True, madam;—notwithstanding his vices, one can't help feeling for him.—Aye, poor Charles! I'm sure I wish it was in *my* power to be of any essential service to him.—For the man who does not share in the distress of a brother, even though merited by his own misconduct, deserves——

LADY SNEERWELL   O lud! you are going to be moral, and forget that you are among friends.

JOSEPH SURFACE   Egad, that's true!—I'll keep that sentiment till I see Sir Peter. However, it is certainly a charity to rescue Maria from such a libertine, who, if he is to be reclaimed, can be so only by a person of your ladyship's superior accomplishments and understanding.

SNAKE   I believe, Lady Sneerwell, here's company coming,—I'll go and copy the letter I mentioned to you.—Mr. Surface, your most obedient.

    Exit SNAKE.

JOSEPH SURFACE   Sir, your very devoted.—Lady Sneerwell, I am very sorry you have put any further confidence in that fellow.

LADY SNEERWELL   Why so?

JOSEPH SURFACE   I have lately detected him in frequent conference

---

9. Legal seizure of a debtor's goods in default of payment.

with old *Rowley*, who was formerly my father's steward, and has never, you know, been a friend of mine.

LADY SNEERWELL   And do you think he would betray us?

JOSEPH SURFACE   Nothing more likely: take my word for't, Lady Sneerwell, that fellow hasn't virtue enough to be faithful even to his own villainy.—Hah! Maria!

Enter MARIA.

LADY SNEERWELL   Maria, my dear, how do you do?—What's the matter?

MARIA   Oh! there is that disagreeable lover of mine, Sir *Benjamin Backbite*, has just called at my guardian's, with his odious uncle, *Crabtree*; so I slipped out, and ran hither to avoid them.

LADY SNEERWELL   Is that all?

JOSEPH SURFACE   If my brother *Charles* had been of the party, ma'am, perhaps you would not have been so much alarmed.

LADY SNEERWELL   Nay, now you are severe; for I dare swear the truth of the matter is, Maria heard *you* were here;—but, my dear, what has Sir Benjamin done, that you should avoid him so?

MARIA   Oh, he has done nothing—but 'tis for what he has said,—his conversation is a perpetual libel on all his acquaintance.

JOSEPH SURFACE   Aye, and the worst of it is, there is no advantage in not knowing him; for he'll abuse a stranger just as soon as his best friend—and his uncle's as bad.

LADY SNEERWELL   Nay, but we should make allowance; Sir Benjamin is a wit and a poet.

MARIA   For my part, I own, madam, wit loses its respect with me, when I see it in company with malice.—What do you think, Mr. Surface?

JOSEPH SURFACE   Certainly, madam; to smile at the jest which plants a thorn in another's breast is to become a principal in the mischief.

LADY SNEERWELL   Pshaw! there's no possibility of being witty without a little ill nature: the malice of a good thing is the barb that makes it stick.—What's your opinion, Mr. Surface?

JOSEPH SURFACE   To be sure, madam, that conversation, where the spirit of raillery is suppressed, will ever appear tedious and insipid.

MARIA   Well, I'll not debate how far scandal may be allowable; but in a man, I am sure, it is always contemptible.—We have pride, envy, rivalship, and a thousand motives to depreciate each other; but the male slanderer must have the cowardice of a woman before he can traduce one.

Enter SERVANT.

SERVANT   Madam, Mrs. Candour is below, and, if your ladyship's at leisure, will leave her carriage.

LADY SNEERWELL   Beg her to walk in.

Exit SERVANT.

Now Maria, however here is a character to your taste; for though Mrs. Candour is a little talkative, everybody allows her to be the best-natured and best sort of woman.

MARIA   Yes, with a very gross affectation of good nature and benevolence, she does more mischief than the direct malice of old Crabtree.

JOSEPH SURFACE   I'faith 'tis very true, Lady Sneerwell; whenever I hear the current running against the characters of my friends, I never think them in such danger as when Candour undertakes their defence.

LADY SNEERWELL   Hush!—here she is!

Enter MRS. CANDOUR.

MRS. CANDOUR   My dear Lady Sneerwell, how have you been this century?—Mr. Surface, what news do you hear?—though indeed it is no matter, for I think one hears nothing else but scandal.

JOSEPH SURFACE   Just so, indeed, madam.

MRS. CANDOUR   Ah, Maria! child,—what, is the whole affair off between you and Charles? His extravagance, I presume—the town talks of nothing else.

MARIA   I am very sorry, ma'am, the town has so little to do.

MRS. CANDOUR   True, true, child: but there is no stopping people's tongues.—I own I was hurt to hear it, as indeed I was to learn, from the same quarter, that your guardian, Sir Peter, and Lady Teazle have not agreed lately so well as could be wished.

MARIA   'Tis strangely impertinent for people to busy themselves so.

MRS. CANDOUR   Very true, child, but what's to be done? People will talk—there's no preventing it.—Why, it was but yesterday I was told that Miss Gadabout had eloped with Sir Filigree Flirt.—But, Lord! there's no minding what one hears—though, to be sure, I had this from very good authority.

MARIA   Such reports are highly scandalous.

MRS. CANDOUR   So they are, child—shameful, shameful! But the world is so censorious, no character escapes.—Lord, now who would have suspected your friend, Miss Prim, of an indiscretion? Yet such is the ill-nature of people, that they say her uncle stopped her last week, just as she was stepping into the York Diligence[1] with her dancing-master.

MARIA   I'll answer for't there are no grounds for the report.

MRS. CANDOUR   Oh, no foundation in the world, I dare swear; no more, probably, than for the story circulated last month, of Mrs. Festino's affair with Colonel Cassino;—though, to be sure, that matter was never rightly cleared up.

JOSEPH SURFACE   The license of invention some people take is monstrous indeed.

MARIA   'Tis so.—But, in my opinion, those who report such things are equally culpable.

---

1. The stagecoach to York.

MRS. CANDOUR   To be sure they are; tale-bearers are as bad as the tale-makers—'tis an old observation, and a very true one—but what's to be done, as I said before? how will you prevent people from talking?—To-day, Mrs. Clackit assured me Mr. and Mrs. Honeymoon were at last become mere man and wife, like the rest of their acquaintances.—She likewise hinted that a certain widow, in the next street, had got rid of her dropsy and recovered her shape in a most surprising manner. And at the same time Miss Tattle, who was by, affirmed that Lord Buffalo had discovered his lady at a house of no extraordinary fame—and that Sir Harry Bouquet and Tom Saunter were to measure swords on a similar provocation. But, Lord, do you think I would report these things! No, no! tale-bearers, as I said before, are just as bad as tale-makers.

JOSEPH SURFACE   Ah! Mrs. Candour, if everybody had your forbearance and good nature!

MRS. CANDOUR   I confess, Mr. Surface, I cannot bear to hear people attacked behind their backs, and when ugly circumstances come out against one's acquaintance I own I always love to think the best.—By the bye, I hope it is not true that your brother is absolutely ruined?

JOSEPH SURFACE   I am afraid his circumstances are very bad indeed, ma'am.

MRS. CANDOUR   Ah!—I heard so—but you must tell him to keep up his spirits—everybody almost is in the same way! Lord Spindle, Sir Thomas Splint, Captain Quinze, and Mr. Nickit—all up, I hear, within this week; so, if Charles is undone, he'll find half his acquaintances ruined too—and that, you know, is a consolation.

JOSEPH SURFACE   Doubtless, ma'am—a very great one.

    Enter SERVANT.

SERVANT   Mr. Crabtree and Sir Benjamin Backbite.

LADY SNEERWELL   So, Maria, you see your lover pursues you; positively you shan't escape.

    Enter CRABTREE *and* SIR BENJAMIN BACKBITE.

CRABTREE   Lady Sneerwell, I kiss your hands. Mrs. Candour, I don't believe you are acquainted with my nephew, Sir Benjamin Backbite? Egad, ma'am, he has a pretty wit, and is a pretty poet too; isn't he, Lady Sneerwell?

SIR BENJAMIN   O fie, uncle!

CRABTREE   Nay, egad it's true—I'll back him at a rebus[2] or a charade against the best rhymer in the kingdom. Has your ladyship heard the epigram he wrote last week on Lady Frizzle's feather catching fire?—Do, Benjamin, repeat it—or the charade you made last night extempore at Mrs. Drowzie's conversazione.— Come now; your *first* is the name of a fish, your *second* a great naval commander, and——

---

2. A riddle in which pictures represent the syllables of a word to be guessed.

SIR BENJAMIN   Uncle, now—prithee——

CRABTREE   I'faith, ma'am, 'twould surprise you to hear how ready he is at these things.

LADY SNEERWELL   I wonder, Sir Benjamin, you never publish anything.

SIR BENJAMIN   To say truth, ma'am, 'tis very vulgar to print; and, as my little productions are mostly satires and lampoons on particular people, I find they circulate more by giving copies in confidence to the friends of the parties—however, I have some love elegies, which, when favored with this lady's smiles, I mean to give to the public.

CRABTREE   'Fore heav'n, ma'am, they'll immortalize you!—you'll be handed down to posterity like Petrarch's Laura, or Waller's Sacharissa.[3]

SIR BENJAMIN   Yes, madam, I think you will like them, when you shall see them on a beautiful quarto page, where a neat rivulet of text shall murmur through a meadow of margin. 'Fore gad, they will be the most elegant things of their kind!

CRABTREE   But, ladies, that's true—have you heard the news?

MRS. CANDOUR   What, sir, do you mean the report of—

CRABTREE   No, ma'am, that's not it.—Miss Nicely is going to be married to her own footman.

MRS. CANDOUR   Impossible!

CRABTREE   Ask Sir Benjamin.

SIR BENJAMIN   'Tis very true, ma'am—everything is fixed, and the wedding liveries bespoke.

CRABTREE   Yes—and they *do* say there were pressing reasons for it.

LADY SNEERWELL   Why, I *have* heard something of this before.

MRS. CANDOUR   It can't be—and I wonder any one should believe such a story of so prudent a lady as Miss Nicely.

SIR BENJAMIN   O lud! ma'am, that's the very reason 'twas believed at once. She has always been so *cautious* and so *reserved*, that everybody was sure there was some reason for it at bottom.

MRS. CANDOUR   Why, to be sure, a tale of scandal is as fatal to the credit of a prudent lady of her stamp as a fever is generally to those of the strongest constitutions; but there is a sort of puny, sickly reputation that is always ailing, yet will outlive the robuster characters of a hundred prudes.

SIR BENJAMIN   True, madam, there are valetudinarians in reputation as well as constitution, who, being conscious of their weak part, avoid the least breath of air, and supply their want of stamina by care and circumspection.

MRS. CANDOUR   Well, but this may be all a mistake. You know, Sir Benjamin, very trifling circumstances often give rise to the most injurious tales.

CRABTREE   That they do, I'll be sworn, ma'am. Did you ever hear how

3. Laura inspired the love poems of Petrarch. "Sacharissa" was Lady Dorothy Sidney, to whom Edmund Waller addressed his love poems.

Miss Piper came to lose her lover and her character last summer at Tunbridge?[4]—Sir Benjamin, you remember it?

SIR BENJAMIN   Oh, to be sure!—the most whimsical circumstance—

LADY SNEERWELL   How was it, pray?

CRABTREE   Why, one evening, at Mrs. Ponto's assembly, the conversation happened to turn on the difficulty of breeding Nova Scotia sheep in this country. Says a young lady in company, "I have known instances of it; for Miss Letitia Piper, a first cousin of mine, had a Nova Scotia sheep that produced her twins." "What!" cries the old Dowager Lady Dundizzy (who you know is as deaf as a post), "has Miss Piper had twins?" This mistake, as you may imagine, threw the whole company into a fit of laughing. However, 'twas the next morning everywhere reported, and in a few days believed by the whole town, that Miss Letitia Piper had actually been brought to bed of a fine boy and a girl—and in less than a week there were people who could name the father, and the farm-house where the babies were put out to nurse!

LADY SNEERWELL   Strange, indeed!

CRABTREE   Matter of fact, I assure you.—O lud! Mr. Surface, pray is it true that your uncle, Sir Oliver, is coming home?

JOSEPH SURFACE   Not that I know of, indeed, sir.

CRABTREE   He has been in the East Indias a long time. You can scarcely remember him, I believe.—Sad comfort, whenever he returns, to hear how your brother has gone on!

JOSEPH SURFACE   Charles has been imprudent, sir, to be sure; but I hope no busy people have already prejudiced Sir Oliver against him,—he may reform.

SIR BENJAMIN   To be sure he may—for my part I never believed him to be so utterly void of principle as people say—and though he has lost all his friends, I am told nobody is better spoken of by the Jews.[5]

CRABTREE   That's true, egad, nephew. If the old Jewry were a ward, I believe Charles would be an alderman; no man more popular there, 'fore gad! I hear he pays as many annuities as the Irish tontine;[6] and that, whenever he's sick, they have prayers for the recovery of his health in the Synagogue.

SIR BENJAMIN   Yet no man lives in greater splendor.—They tell me, when he entertains his friends, he can sit down to dinner with a dozen of his own securities;[7] have a score [of] tradesmen waiting in the antechamber, and an officer behind every guest's chair.

JOSEPH SURFACE   This may be entertainment to you, gentlemen, but you pay very little regard to the feelings of a brother.

---

4. A fashionable resort in Kent.
5. I.e., the moneylenders.
6. A life annuity plan established in 1773 by the Irish government.
7. Men who have endorsed his notes.

MARIA [*Aside.*]   Their malice is intolerable!—Lady Sneerwell, I must wish you a good morning—I'm not very well.

Exit MARIA.

MRS. CANDOUR   O dear! She changes color very much!

LADY SNEERWELL   Do, Mrs. Candour, follow her—she may want assistance.

MRS. CANDOUR   That I will, with all my soul, ma'am.—Poor dear girl! who knows what her situation may be!

Exit MRS. CANDOUR.

LADY SNEERWELL   'Twas nothing but that she could not bear to hear Charles reflected on, notwithstanding their difference.

SIR BENJAMIN   The young lady's *penchant* is obvious.

CRABTREE   But, Benjamin, you mustn't give up the pursuit for that; follow her, and put her into good humour. Repeat her some of your own verses.—Come, I'll assist you.

SIR BENJAMIN   Mr. Surface, I did not mean to hurt you; but depend upon't your brother is utterly undone. [*Going.*]

CRABTREE   O, lud, aye! undone as ever man was—can't raise a guinea. [*Going.*]

SIR BENJAMIN   And everything sold, I'm told, that was movable. [*Going.*]

CRABTREE   I have seen one that was at his house—not a thing left but some empty bottles that were overlooked, and the family pictures, which I believe are framed in the wainscot. [*Going.*]

SIR BENJAMIN   And I am very sorry to hear also some bad stories against him. [*Going.*]

CRABTREE   Oh, he has done many mean things, that's certain. [*Going.*]

SIR BENJAMIN   But, however, as he's your brother—[*Going.*]

CRABTREE   We'll tell you all, another opportunity.

Exeunt CRABTREE *and* SIR BENJAMIN.

LADY SNEERWELL   Ha, ha! ha! 'tis very hard for them to leave a subject they have not quite run down.

JOSEPH SURFACE   And I believe the abuse was no more acceptable to your ladyship than to Maria.

LADY SNEERWELL   I doubt[8] her affections are farther engaged than we imagined; but the family are to be here this evening, so you may as well dine where you are, and we shall have an opportunity of observing farther;—in the meantime, I'll go and plot mischief, and you shall study sentiments.

Exeunt.

8. Fear.

Act I. Scene ii.

SIR PETER TEAZLE's *house.*
Enter SIR PETER.

SIR PETER   When an old bachelor takes a young wife, what is he to expect?—'Tis now six months since Lady Teazle made me the happiest of men—and I have been the miserablest dog ever since that ever committed wedlock! We tift a little going to church, and came to a quarrel before the bells were done ringing. I was more than once nearly choked with gall during the honeymoon, and had lost all comfort in life before my friends had done wishing me joy! Yet I chose with caution—a girl bred wholly in the country, who never knew luxury beyond one silk gown, nor dissipation above the annual gala of a race ball. Yet now she plays her part in all the extravagant fopperies of the fashion and the town, with as ready a grace as if she had never seen a bush nor a grassplat out of Grosvenor Square! I am sneered at by my old acquaintance—paragraphed in the newspapers. She dissipates my fortune, and contradicts all my humours; yet the worst of it is, I doubt I love her, or I should never bear all this. However, I'll never be weak enough to own it.

Enter ROWLEY.

ROWLEY   Oh! Sir Peter, your servant,—how is it with you, sir?
SIR PETER   Very bad, Master Rowley, very bad;—I meet with nothing but crosses and vexations.
ROWLEY   What can have happened to trouble you since yesterday?
SIR PETER   A good question to a married man!
ROWLEY   Nay, I'm sure your lady, Sir Peter, can't be the cause of your uneasiness.
SIR PETER   Why, has anyone told you she was dead?
ROWLEY   Come, come, Sir Peter, you love her, notwithstanding your tempers don't exactly agree.
SIR PETER   But the fault is entirely hers, Master Rowley. I am, myself, the sweetest-tempered man alive, and hate a teasing temper—and so I tell her a hundred times a day.
ROWLEY   Indeed!
SIR PETER   Aye; and what is very extraordinary, in all our disputes she is always in the wrong! But Lady Sneerwell, and the set she meets at her house, encourage the perverseness of her disposition. Then, to complete my vexations, Maria, my ward, whom I ought to have the power of a father over, is determined to turn rebel too, and absolutely refuses the man whom I have long resolved on for her husband; — meaning, I suppose, to bestow herself on his profligate brother.
ROWLEY   You know, Sir Peter, I have always taken the liberty to differ with you on the subject of these two young gentlemen. I only wish

you may not be deceived in your opinion of the elder. For Charles, my life on't! he will retrieve his errors yet. Their worthy father, once my honored master, was, at his years, nearly as wild a spark; yet, when he died, he did not leave a more benevolent heart to lament his loss.

SIR PETER   You are wrong, Master Rowley. On their father's death, you know, I acted as a kind of guardian to them both, till their uncle Sir Oliver's Eastern liberality gave them an early independence; of course, no person could have more opportunities of judging of their hearts, and I was never mistaken in my life. Joseph is indeed a model for the young men of the age. He is a man of sentiment, and acts up to the sentiments he professes; but, for the other, take my word for't, if he had any grains of virtue by descent, he has dissipated them with the rest of his inheritance. Ah! my old friend, Sir Oliver, will be deeply mortified when he finds how part of his bounty has been mis-applied.

ROWLEY   I am sorry to find you so violent against the young man, because this may be the most critical period of his fortune. I came hither with news that will surprise you.

SIR PETER   What! let me hear.

ROWLEY   Sir Oliver *is* arrived, and at this moment in town.

SIR PETER   How! you astonish me! I thought you did not expect him this month.

ROWLEY   I did not; but his passage has been remarkably quick.

SIR PETER   Egad, I shall rejoice to see my old friend,—'tis sixteen years since we met—we have had many a day together; but does he still enjoin us not to inform his nephews of his arrival?

ROWLEY   Most strictly. He means, before it is known, to make some trial of their dispositions.

SIR PETER   Ah! There needs no art to discover their merits—however, he shall have his way; but, pray, does he know I am married?

ROWLEY   Yes, and will soon wish you joy.

SIR PETER   What, as we drink health of a friend in a consumption! Ah, Oliver will laugh at me—we used to rail at matrimony together—but he has been steady to his text. Well, he must be at my house, though—I'll instantly give orders for his reception. But, Master Row-ley, don't drop a word that Lady Teazle and I ever disagree.

ROWLEY   By no means.

SIR PETER   For I should never be able to stand Noll's jokes; so I'd have him think, Lord forgive me! that we are a very happy couple.

ROWLEY   I understand you—but then you must be very careful not to differ while he's in the house with you.

SIR PETER   Egad, and so we must—and that's impossible. Ah! Master Rowley, when an old bachelor marries a young wife, he deserves—no—the crime carries the punishment along with it.

Exeunt.

Act II. Scene i.

SIR PETER TEAZLE'S *house.*
Enter SIR PETER *and* LADY TEAZLE.

SIR PETER   Lady Teazle, Lady Teazle, I'll not bear it!

LADY TEAZLE   Sir Peter, Sir Peter, you may bear it or not, as you please; but I ought to have my own way in everything, and what's more, I *will* too.—What! though I was educated in the country, I know very well that women of fashion in London are accountable to nobody after they are married.

SIR PETER   Very well, ma'am, very well,—so a husband is to have no influence, no authority?

LADY TEAZLE   Authority! No, to be sure—if you wanted authority over me, you should have adopted me, and not married me; I am sure you were old enough.

SIR PETER   Old enough!—aye, there it is!—Well, well, Lady Teazle, though my life may be made unhappy by your temper, I'll not be ruined by your extravagance.

LADY TEAZLE   My extravagance! I'm sure I'm not more extravagant than a woman of fashion ought to be.

SIR PETER   No, no, madam, you shall throw away no more sums on such unmeaning luxury. 'Slife! to spend as much to furnish your dressing-room with flowers in a winter as would suffice to turn the Pantheon[9] into a greenhouse, and give a *fête champêtre*[1] at Christmas!

LADY TEAZLE   Lord, Sir Peter, am I to blame because flowers are dear in cold weather? You should find fault with the climate, and not with me. For my part, I am sure I wish it was spring all the year round, and that roses grew under one's feet!

SIR PETER   Oons! madam—if you had been born to this, I shouldn't wonder at your talking thus.—But you forget what your situation was when I married you.

LADY TEAZLE   No, no, I don't; 'twas a very disagreeable one, or I should never have married *you.*

SIR PETER   Yes, yes, madam, you were then in somewhat an humbler style—the daughter of a plain country squire. Recollect, Lady Teazle, when I saw you first, sitting at your tambour,[2] in a pretty figured linen gown, with a bunch of keys by your side, your hair combed smooth over a roll, and your apartment hung round with fruits in worsted, of your own working.

LADY TEAZLE   O, yes! I remember it very well, and a curious life I led— my daily occupation to inspect the dairy, superintend the poultry, make extracts from the family receipt-book, and comb my aunt Deborah's lapdog.

9. A concert hall in London.
1. Outdoor entertainment.
2. Frame for embroidery.

SIR PETER Yes, yes, ma'am, 'twas so indeed.

LADY TEAZLE And then, you know, my evening amusements! To draw patterns for ruffles, which I had not the materials to make; to play Pope Joan[3] with the curate; to read a novel to my aunt; or to be stuck down to an old spinet to strum my father to sleep after a fox-chase.

SIR PETER I am glad you have so good a memory. Yes, madam, these were the recreations I took you from; but now you must have your coach—*vis-à-vis*[4]—and three powdered footmen before your chair and, in summer, a pair of white cats[5] to draw you to Kensington Gardens.—No recollection, I suppose, when you were content to ride double, behind the butler, on a docked coach-horse?

LADY TEAZLE No—I swear I never did that—I deny the butler and the coach-horse.

SIR PETER This, madam, was your situation—and what have I not done for you? I have made you a woman of fashion, of fortune, of rank—in short, I have made you my wife.

LADY TEAZLE Well, then, and there is but one thing more you can make me to add to the obligation—and that is——

SIR PETER My widow, I suppose?

LADY TEAZLE Hem! hem!

SIR PETER Thank you, madam—but don't flatter yourself; for though your ill-conduct may disturb my peace, it shall never break my heart, I promise you: however, I am equally obliged to you for the hint.

LADY TEAZLE Then why will you endeavor to make yourself so disagreeable to me, and thwart me in every little elegant expense?

SIR PETER 'Slife, madam, I say, had you any of these elegant expenses when you married me?

LADY TEAZLE Lud, Sir Peter! would you have me be out of the fashion?

SIR PETER The fashion, indeed! what had you to do with the fashion before you married me?

LADY TEAZLE For my part, I should think you would like to have your wife thought a woman of taste.

SIR PETER Aye—there again—taste! Zounds! madam, you had no taste when you married *me!*

LADY TEAZLE That's very true, indeed, Sir Peter! and *after* having married you, I am sure I should never pretend to taste again! But now, Sir Peter, if we have finished our daily jangle, I presume I may go to my engagement of Lady Sneerwell's?

SIR PETER Aye—there's another precious circumstance!—a charming set of acquaintance you have made there!

LADY TEAZLE Nay, Sir Peter, they are people of rank and fortune, and remarkably tenacious of reputation.

SIR PETER Yes, egad, they are tenacious of reputation with a vengeance; for they don't choose anybody should have a character but

3. A card game.
4. A fashionable coach in which passengers could face each other.
5. Probably ponies.

themselves! Such a crew! Ah! many a wretch has rid on a hurdle[6] who has done less mischief than those utterers of forged tales, coiners of scandal,—and clippers of reputation.

LADY TEAZLE   What! would you restrain the freedom of speech?

SIR PETER   Oh! they have made you just as bad as any one of the society.

LADY TEAZLE   Why, I believe I do bear a part with a tolerable grace. But I vow I have no malice against the people I abuse; when I say an ill-natured thing, 'tis out of pure good humour—and I take it for granted they deal exactly in the same manner with me. But, Sir Peter, you know you promised to come to Lady Sneerwell's too.

SIR PETER   Well, well, I'll call in just to look after my own character.

LADY TEAZLE   Then, indeed, you must make haste after me or you'll be too late.—So good-bye to ye.

Exit LADY TEAZLE.

SIR PETER   So—I have gained much by my intended expostulations! Yet with what a charming air she contradicts everything I say, and how pleasingly she shows her contempt of my authority. Well, though I can't make her love me, there is a great satisfaction in quarreling with her; and I think she never appears to such advantage as when she's doing everything in her power to plague me.

Exit.

Act II. Scene ii.

LADY SNEERWELL'S.

LADY SNEERWELL, MRS. CANDOUR, CRABTREE, SIR BENJAMIN BACK-BITE, *and* JOSEPH SURFACE.

LADY SNEERWELL   Nay, positively, we will hear it.

JOSEPH SURFACE   Yes, yes, the epigram, by all means.

SIR BENJAMIN   Pleague on't, uncle! 'tis mere nonsense.

CRABTREE   No, no; 'fore gad, very clever for an extempore!

SIR BENJAMIN   But, ladies, you should be acquainted with the circumstance,—you must know, that one day last week, as Lady Betty Curricle was taking the dust in Hyde Park, in a sort of duodecimo phaëton,[7] she desired me to write some verses on her ponies; upon which, I took out my pocket-book, and in one moment produced the following:

> Sure never were seen two such beautiful ponies!
> Other horses are clowns, and these macaronies!
> Nay, to give 'em this title I'm sure isn't wrong—
> Their legs are so slim, and their tails so long.

6. Cart or sledge on which traitors were hauled to execution.
7. A light open carriage. "Duodecimo" (a very small book) indicates its size.

CRABTREE   There, ladies—done in the smack of a whip, and on horse-back too!

JOSEPH SURFACE   A very Phoebus, mounted—indeed, Sir Benjamin.

SIR BENJAMIN   O dear sir—trifles—trifles.

Enter LADY TEAZLE *and* MARIA.

MRS. CANDOUR   I must have a copy.

LADY SNEERWELL   Lady Teazle, I hope we shall see Sir Peter.

LADY TEAZLE   I believe he'll wait on your ladyship presently.

LADY SNEERWELL   Maria, my love, you look grave. Come, you shall sit down to cards with Mr. Surface.

MARIA   I take very little pleasure in cards—however, I'll do as your lady-ship pleases.

LADY TEAZLE   [*Aside.*]   I am surprised Mr. Surface should sit down with *her.*—I thought he would have embraced this opportunity of speaking to me before Sir Peter came.

MRS. CANDOUR   [*coming forward*]   Now, I'll die but you are so scandal-ous, I'll forswear your society.

LADY TEAZLE   What's the matter, Mrs. Candour?

MRS. CANDOUR   They'll not allow our friend Miss Vermilion to be handsome.

LADY SNEERWELL   Oh, surely, she's a pretty woman.

CRABTREE   I am very glad you think so, ma'am.

MRS. CANDOUR   She has a charming fresh color.

LADY TEAZLE   Yes, when it is fresh put on.

MRS. CANDOUR   O fie! I'll swear her color is natural—I have seen it come and go.

LADY TEAZLE   I dare swear you have, ma'am—it goes of a night, and comes again in the morning.

MRS. CANDOUR   Ha! ha! ha! how I hate to hear you talk so! But surely, now, her sister *is,* or *was,* very handsome.

CRABTREE   Who? Mrs. Evergreen?—O Lord! she's six-and-fifty if she's an hour!

MRS. CANDOUR   Now positively you wrong her; fifty-two or fifty-three is the utmost—and I don't think she looks more.

SIR BENJAMIN   Ah! there is no judging by her looks, unless one could see her face.

LADY SNEERWELL   Well, well, if Mrs. Evergreen *does* take some pains to repair the ravages of time, you must allow she effects it with great ingenuity; and surely that's better than the careless manner in which the widow Ochre caulks her wrinkles.

SIR BENJAMIN   Nay, now, Lady Sneerwell, you are severe upon the widow. Come, come, it is not that she paints so ill—but, when she has finished her face, she joins it on so badly to her neck, that she looks like a mended statue, in which the connoisseur sees at once that the head's modern, though the trunk's antique!

CRABTREE   Ha! ha! ha! Well said, nephew!

MRS. CANDOUR   Ha! ha! ha! Well, you make me laugh, but I vow I hate you for't.—What do you think of Miss Simper?

SIR BENJAMIN   Why, she has very pretty teeth.

LADY TEAZLE   Yes; and on that account, when she is neither speaking nor laughing (which very seldom happens), she never absolutely shuts her mouth, but leaves it always on a jar, as it were.

MRS. CANDOUR   How can you be so ill-natured?

LADY TEAZLE   Nay, I allow even that's better than the pains Mrs. Prim takes to conceal her losses in front. She draws her mouth till it positively resembles the aperture of a poor's-box,[8] and all her words appear to slide out edgeways.

LADY SNEERWELL   Very well, Lady Teazle; I see you can be a little severe.

LADY TEAZLE   In defence of a friend it is but justice;—but here comes Sir Peter to spoil our pleasantry.

Enter SIR PETER TEAZLE.

SIR PETER   Ladies, your most obedient—Mercy on me, here is the whole set! a character dead at every word, I suppose. [*Aside.*]

MRS. CANDOUR   I am rejoiced you are come, Sir Peter. They have been *so* censorious. They will allow good qualities to nobody—not even good nature to our friend Mrs. Pursy.

LADY TEAZLE   What, the fat dowager who was at Mrs. Codille's last night?

MRS. CANDOUR   Nay, her bulk is her misfortune; and, when she takes such pains to get rid of it, you ought not to reflect on her.

LADY SNEERWELL   That's very true, indeed.

LADY TEAZLE   Yes, I know she almost lives on acids and small whey;[9] laces herself by pulleys; and often, in the hottest noon of summer, you may see her on a little squat pony, with her hair platted up behind like a drummer's, and puffing round the Ring[1] on a full trot.

MRS. CANDOUR   I thank you, Lady Teazle, for defending her.

SIR PETER   Yes, a good defense, truly.

MRS. CANDOUR   But Sir Benjamin is as censorious as Miss Sallow.

CRABTREE   Yes, and she is a curious being to pretend to be censorious!—an awkward gawky, without any one good point under heaven.

MRS. CANDOUR   Positively you shall not be so very servere. Miss Sallow is a relation of mine by marriage, and, as for her person, great allowance is to be made; for, let me tell you, a woman labors under many disadvantages who tries to pass for a girl at six-and-thirty.

LADY SNEERWELL   Though, surely, she is handsome still—and for the weakness in her eyes, considering how much she reads by candlelight, it is not to be wondered at.

8. A box for contributions to charity.
9. The watery part of milk.
1. Circular drive in Hyde Park.

MRS. CANDOUR   True; and then as to her manner, upon my word I
think it is particularly graceful, considering she never had the least
education; for you know her mother was a Welch milliner, and her
father a sugar-baker at Bristol.

SIR BENJAMIN   Ah! you are both of you too good-natured!

SIR PETER   Yes, damned good-natured! This their own relation! mercy
on me! [*Aside.*]

SIR BENJAMIN   And Mrs. Candour is of so moral a turn she can sit for
an hour to hear Lady Stucco talk sentiment.

LADY TEAZLE   Nay, I vow Lady Stucco is very well with the dessert after
dinner; for she's just like the French fruit one cracks for mottoes—
made up of paint and proverb.

MRS. CANDOUR   Well, I never will join in ridiculing a friend; and so I
constantly tell my cousin Ogle, and you all know what pretensions
she has to be critical in beauty.

CRABTREE   Oh, to be sure! she has herself the oddest countenance that
ever was seen; 'tis a collection of features from all the different countries of the globe.

SIR BENJAMIN   So she has, indeed—an Irish front!

CRABTREE   Caledonian locks!

SIR BENJAMIN   Dutch nose!

CRABTREE   Austrian lip!

SIR BENJAMIN   Complexion of a Spaniard!

CRABTREE   And teeth *à la Chinoise!*

SIR BENJAMIN   In short, her face resembles a *table d'hôte* at Spa[2]—
where no two guests are of a nation——

CRABTREE   Or a congress at the close of a general war—wherein all the
members, even to her eyes, appear to have a different interest, and
her nose and chin are the only parties likely to join issue.

MRS. CANDOUR   Ha! ha! ha!

SIR PETER   Mercy on my life!—a person they dine with twice a week!
[*Aside.*]

MRS. CANDOUR   Nay, but I vow you shall not carry the laugh off so—for
give me leave to say, that Mrs. Ogle—

SIR PETER   Madam, madam, I beg your pardon—there's no stopping
these good gentlemen's tongues. But when I tell *you*, Mrs. Candour,
that the lady they are abusing is a particular friend of mine—I hope
you'll not take her part.

LADY SNEERWELL   Well said, Sir Peter! but you are a cruel creature—
too phlegmatic yourself for a jest, and too peevish to allow wit on
others.

SIR PETER   Ah, madam, true wit is more nearly allied to good nature
than your ladyship is aware of.

LADY TEAZLE   True, Sir Peter; I believe they are so near akin that they
can never be united.

2. The dining table at Spa, a famous resort in Belgium.

SIR BENJAMIN Or rather, madam, suppose them man and wife, because one so seldom sees them together.

LADY TEAZLE But Sir Peter is such an enemy to scandal, I believe he would have it put down by parliament.

SIR PETER 'Fore heaven, madam, if they were to consider the sporting with reputation of as much importance as poaching on manors, and pass *An Act for the Preservation of Fame*, I believe many would thank them for the bill.

LADY SNEERWELL O lud! Sir Peter; would you deprive us of our privileges?

SIR PETER Aye, madam; and then no person should be permitted to kill characters or run down reputations, but qualified old maids and disappointed widows.

LADY SNEERWELL Go, you monster!

MRS. CANDOUR But sure you would not be quite so severe on those who only report what they hear.

SIR PETER Yes, madam, I would have law merchant[3] for them too; and in all cases of slander currency, whenever the drawer of the lie was not to be found, the injured parties should have a right to come on any of the endorsers.

CRABTREE Well, for my part, I believe there never was a scandalous tale without some foundation.

LADY SNEERWELL Come, ladies, shall we sit down to cards in the next room?

Enter SERVANT *and whispers* SIR PETER.

SIR PETER I'll be with them directly.—[*Exit* SERVANT.] I'll get away unperceived. [*Aside.*]

LADY SNEERWELL Sir Peter, you are not leaving us?

SIR PETER Your ladyship must excuse me; I'm called away by particular business—but I leave my character behind me.

Exit SIR PETER.

SIR BENJAMIN Well certainly, Lady Teazle, that lord of yours is a strange being; I could tell you some stories of him would make you laugh heartily, if he wasn't your husband.

LADY TEAZLE O pray don't mind that—come, do let's hear them.

They join the rest of the company, all talking as they are going into the next room.

JOSEPH SURFACE [*Rising with* MARIA.] Maria, I see you have no satisfaction in this society.

MARIA How is it possible I should? If to raise malicious smiles at the infirmities and misfortunes of those who have never injured us be the

3. System of commercial law. Sir Peter continues the metaphor by playing on the fact that endorsers of notes are held responsible in cases of default of payment.

province of wit or humour, heaven grant me a double portion of dulness!

JOSEPH SURFACE   Yet they appear more ill-natured than they are; they have no malice at heart.

MARIA   Then is their conduct still more contemptible; for, in my opinion, nothing could excuse the intemperance of their tongues but a natural and ungovernable bitterness of mind.

JOSEPH SURFACE   But can you, Maria, feel thus for others, and be unkind to me alone? Is hope to be denied the tenderest passion?

MARIA   Why will you distress me by renewing this subject?

JOSEPH SURFACE   Ah, Maria! you would not treat me thus, and oppose your guardian, Sir Peter's will, but that I see that profligate *Charles* is still a favored rival.

MARIA   Ungenerously urged! But, whatever my sentiments of that unfortunate young man are, be assured I shall not feel more bound to give him up, because his distresses have lost him the regard even of a brother.

LADY TEAZLE *returns.*

JOSEPH SURFACE   Nay, but, Maria, do not leave me with a frown—by all that's honest, I swear—Gad's life, here's Lady Teazle. [*Aside.*]—You must not—no, you shall not—for, though I have the greatest regard for Lady Teazle——

MARIA   Lady Teazle!

JOSEPH SURFACE   Yet were Sir Peter to suspect——

LADY TEAZLE   [*Coming forward.*]   What's this, pray? Do you take her for me?—Child, you are wanted in the next room.—

Exit MARIA.

What is all this, pray?

JOSEPH SURFACE   Oh, the most unlucky circumstance in nature! Maria has somehow suspected the tender concern I have for your happiness, and threatened to acquaint Sir Peter with her suspicions, and I was just endeavoring to reason with her when you came.

LADY TEAZLE   Indeed! but you seemed to adopt a very tender mode of reasoning—do you *usually* argue on your knees?

JOSEPH SURFACE   Oh, she's a child—and I thought a little bombast—but, Lady Teazle, when are you to give me your judgment on my library, as you promised?

LADY TEAZLE   No, no,—I begin to think it would be imprudent, and you know I admit you as a lover no further than *fashion* requires.

JOSEPH SURFACE   True—a mere Platonic cicisbeo,[4] what every London wife is *entitled* to.

LADY TEAZLE   Certainly, one must not be out of the fashion; however, I have so much of my country prejudices left, that, though Sir Peter's ill humour may vex me ever so, it never shall provoke me to——

4. The recognized gallant of a married woman.

JOSEPH SURFACE   The only revenge in your power. Well, I applaud your moderation.

LADY TEAZLE   Go—you are an insinuating wretch! But we shall be missed—let us join the company.

JOSEPH SURFACE   But we had best not return together.

LADY TEAZLE   Well, don't stay—for Maria shan't come to hear any more of your *reasoning*, I promise you.

Exit LADY TEAZLE.

JOSEPH SURFACE   A curious dilemma, truly, my politics have run me into! I wanted, at first, only to ingratiate myself with Lady Teazle, that she might not be my enemy with Maria; and I have, I don't know how, become her serious lover. Sincerely I begin to wish I had never made such a point of gaining so *very good* a character, for it has led me into so many cursed rogueries that I doubt I shall be exposed at last.

Exit.

Act II. Scene iii.

SIR PETER'S.
Enter SIR OLIVER SURFACE *and* ROWLEY.

SIR OLIVER   Ha! ha! ha! and so my old friend is married, hey?—a young wife out of the country.—Ha! ha! ha!—that he should have stood bluff[5] to old bachelor so long, and sink into a husband at last!

ROWLEY   But you must not rally him on the subject, Sir Oliver; 'tis a tender point, I assure you, though he has been married only seven months.

SIR OLIVER   Then he has been just half a year on the stool of repentance![6] Poor Peter! But you say he has entirely given up Charles—never sees him, hey?

ROWLEY   His prejudice against him is astonishing, and I am sure greatly increased by a jealousy of him with Lady Teazle, which he has been industriously led into by a scandalous society in the neighborhood, who have contributed not a little to Charles's ill name; whereas the truth is, I believe, if the lady is partial to either of them, his brother is the favorite.

SIR OLIVER   Aye,—I know there are a set of malicious, prating, prudent gossips, both male and female, who murder characters to kill time, and will rob a young fellow of his good name before he has years to know the value of it,—but I am not to be prejudiced against my nephew by such, I promise you! No, no;—if Charles has done nothing false or mean, I shall compound for his extravagance.

ROWLEY   Then, my life on't, you will reclaim him.—Ah, sir, it gives

5. Firm.
6. A seat in church where offenders do penance.

me new life to find that *your* heart is not turned against him, and that
the son of my good old master has one friend, however, left.

SIR OLIVER   What! shall I forget, Master Rowley, when I was at his
years myself? Egad, my brother and I were neither of us very *prudent*
youths—and yet, I believe, you have not seen many better men than
your old master was?

ROWLEY   Sir, 'tis this reflection gives me assurance that Charles may
yet be a credit to his family.—But here comes Sir Peter.

SIR OLIVER   Egad, so he does!—Mercy on me, he's greatly altered, and
seems to have a settled married look! One may read husband in his
face at this distance!

Enter SIR PETER TEAZLE.

SIR PETER   Hah! Sir Oliver—my old friend! Welcome to England a
thousand times!

SIR OLIVER   Thank you, thank you, Sir Peter! and i'faith I am glad to
find you well, believe me!

SIR PETER   Ah! 'tis a long time since we met—sixteen years, I doubt,
Sir Oliver, and many a cross accident in the time.

SIR OLIVER   Aye, I have had my share—but, what! I find you are married, hey, my old boy?—Well, well, it can't be helped—and so I wish
you joy with all my heart!

SIR PETER   Thank you, thank you, Sir Oliver.—Yes, I have entered into
the happy state—but we'll not talk of that now.

SIR OLIVER   True, true, Sir Peter; old friends should not begin on grievances at first meeting. No, no, no.

ROWLEY [*to* SIR OLIVER.]   Take care, pray, sir.

SIR OLIVER   Well, so one of my nephews is a wild rogue, hey?

SIR PETER   Wild! Ah! my old friend, I grieve for your disappointment
there—he's a lost young man, indeed; however, his brother will make
you amends; *Joseph* is, indeed, what a youth should be—everybody
in the world speaks well of him.

SIR OLIVER   I am sorry to hear it—he has too good a character to be an
honest fellow.—Everybody speaks well of him! Psha! then he has
bowed as low to knaves and fools as to the honest dignity of genius or
virtue.

SIR PETER   What, Sir Oliver! do you blame him for not making enemies?

SIR OLIVER   Yes, if he has merit enough to deserve them.

SIR PETER   Well, well—you'll be convinced when you know him. 'Tis
edification to hear him converse—he professes the noblest sentiments.

SIR OLIVER   Ah, plague of his sentiments! If he salutes me with a scrap
of morality in his mouth, I shall be sick directly. But, however, don't
mistake me, Sir Peter; I don't mean to defend Charles's errors—but,
before I form my judgment of either of them, I intend to make a trial
of their hearts—and my friend Rowley and I have planned something
for the purpose.

ROWLEY   And Sir Peter shall own for once he has been mistaken.

SIR PETER   Oh, my life on Joseph's honor!

SIR OLIVER   Well, come, give us a bottle of good wine, and we'll drink the lad's health, and tell you our scheme.

SIR PETER   *Allons,*[7] then!

SIR OLIVER   And don't, Sir Peter, be so severe against your old friend's son. Odds my life! I am not sorry that he has run out of the course a little; for my part, I hate to see prudence clinging to the green succors of youth; 'tis like ivy round a sapling, and spoils the growth of the tree.

Exeunt.

Act III. Scene i.

SIR PETER's.

SIR PETER TEAZLE, SIR OLIVER SURFACE, *and* ROWLEY.

SIR PETER   Well, then—we will see this fellow first, and have our wine afterwards. But how is this, Master Rowley? I don't see the jet[8] of your scheme.

ROWLEY   Why, sir, this Mr. Stanley, whom I was speaking of, is nearly related to them, by their mother; he was once a merchant in Dublin, but has been ruined by a series of undeserved misfortunes. He has applied, by letter, since his confinement, both to Mr. Surface and Charles—from the former he has received nothing but evasive promises of future service, while Charles has done all that his extravagance has left him power to do; and he is, at this time, endeavoring to raise a sum of money, part of which, in the midst of his own distresses, I know he intends for the service of poor Stanley.

SIR OLIVER   Ah! he is my brother's son.

SIR PETER   Well, but how is Sir Oliver personally to——

ROWLEY   Why, sir, I will inform Charles and his brother that Stanley has obtained permission to apply in person to his friends, and, as they have neither of them ever seen him, let Sir Oliver assume his character, and he will have a fair opportunity of judging at least of the benevolence of their dispositions; and believe me, sir, you will find in the youngest brother one who, in the midst of folly and dissipation, has still, as our immortal bard expresses it,—

> a tear for pity, and a hand
> Open as day, for melting charity.[9]

SIR PETER   Psha! What signifies his having an open hand or purse either, when he has nothing left to give? Well, well, make the trial, if you please; but where is the fellow whom you brought for Sir Oliver to examine, relative to Charles's affairs?

---

7. "Let's go."
8. Point.
9. Shakespeare's 2 *Henry IV* 4.4.31–32.

ROWLEY   Below, waiting his commands, and no one can give him better intelligence.—This, Sir Oliver, is a friendly Jew, who, to do him justice, has done everything in his power to bring your nephew to a proper sense of his extravagance.

SIR PETER   Pray let us have him in.

ROWLEY   Desire Mr. Moses to walk upstairs.

SIR PETER   But why should you suppose he will speak the truth?

ROWLEY   Oh, I have convinced him that he has no chance of recovering certain sums advanced to Charles but through the bounty of Sir Oliver, who he knows is arrived; so that you may depend on his fidelity to his interest. I have also another evidence in my power, one Snake, whom I have detected in a matter little short of forgery, and shall shortly produce to remove some of *your* prejudices, Sir Peter, relative to Charles and Lady Teazle.

SIR PETER   I have heard too much on that subject.

ROWLEY   Here comes the honest Israelite.

   Enter MOSES.

—This is Sir Oliver.

SIR OLIVER   Sir, I understand you have lately had great dealings with my nephew Charles.

MOSES   Yes, Sir Oliver—I have done all I could for him, but he was ruined before he came to me for assistance.

SIR OLIVER   That was unlucky, truly—for you have had no opportunity of showing your talents.

MOSES   None at all—I hadn't the pleasure of knowing his distresses— till he was some thousands worse than nothing.

SIR OLIVER   Unfortunate, indeed! But I suppose you have done all in your power for him, honest Moses?

MOSES   Yes, he knows that. This very evening I was to have brought him a gentleman from the city, who doesn't know him, and will, I believe, advance him some money.

SIR PETER   What, one Charles has never had money from before?

MOSES   Yes; Mr. Premium, of Crutched Friars[1]—formerly a broker.

SIR PETER   Egad, Sir Oliver, a thought strikes me!—Charles, you say, doesn't know Mr. Premium?

MOSES   Not at all.

SIR PETER   Now then, Sir Oliver, you may have a better opportunity of satisfying yourself than by an old romancing tale of a poor relation;— go with my friend Moses, and represent Mr. *Premium*, and then, I'll answer for't, you will see your nephew in all his glory.

SIR OLIVER   Egad, I like this idea better than the other, and I may visit *Joseph* afterwards, as old *Stanley*.

SIR PETER   True—so you may.

ROWLEY   Well, this is taking Charles rather at a disadvantage, to be

---

1. A street in London. *Crutched* means *having or bearing a cross.*

sure. However, Moses—you understand Sir Peter, and will be faithful?

MOSES   You may depend upon me,—this is near the time I was to have gone.

SIR OLIVER   I'll accompany you as soon as you please, Moses; but hold! I have forgot one thing—how the plague shall I be able to pass for a Jew?

MOSES   There's no need—the principal is Christian.

SIR OLIVER   Is he?—I'm sorry to hear it—but, then again, an't I rather too smartly dressed to look like a money-lender?

SIR PETER   Not at all; 'twould not be out of character, if you went in your own carriage—would it, Moses?

MOSES   Not in the least.

SIR OLIVER   Well, but how must I talk? there's certainly some cant of usury, and mode of treating, that I ought to know.

SIR PETER   Oh, there's not much to learn—the great point, as I take it, is to be exorbitant enough in your demands—hey, Moses?

MOSES   Yes, that's a very great point.

SIR OLIVER   I'll answer for't I'll not be wanting in that. I'll ask him eight or ten per cent on the loan, at least.

MOSES   If you ask him no more than that, you'll be discovered immediately.

SIR OLIVER   Hey! what the plague! how much then?

MOSES   That depends upon the circumstances. If he appears not very anxious for the supply, you should require only forty or fifty per cent; but if you find him in great distress, and want the moneys very bad— you may ask double.

SIR PETER   A good honest trade you're learning, Sir Oliver!

SIR OLIVER   Truly I think so—and not unprofitable.

MOSES   Then, you know, you haven't the moneys yourself, but are forced to borrow them for him of a friend.

SIR OLIVER   Oh! I borrow it of a friend, do I?

MOSES   Yes, and your friend is an unconscionable dog, but you can't help it.

SIR OLIVER   My friend is an unconscionable dog, is he?

MOSES   Yes, and he himself has not the moneys by him—but is forced to sell stock at a great loss.

SIR OLIVER   He is forced to sell stock, is he, at a great loss, is he? Well, that's very kind of him.

SIR PETER   I'faith, Sir Oliver—Mr. Premium, I mean—you'll soon be master of the trade. But, Moses! wouldn't you have him run out a little against the Annuity Bill?[2] That would be in character, I should think.

MOSES   Very much.

---

2. A bill to protect the property of minors. It became law during the first run of the play.

ROWLEY   And lament that a young man now must be at years of discretion before he is suffered to ruin himself?

MOSES   Aye, great pity!

SIR PETER   And abuse the public for allowing merit to an act whose only object is to snatch misfortune and imprudence from the rapacious relief of usury, and give the minor a chance of inheriting his estate without being undone by coming into possession.

SIR OLIVER   So, so—Moses shall give me further instructions as we go together.

SIR PETER   You will not have much time, for your nephew lives hard by.

SIR OLIVER   Oh, never fear! my tutor appears so able, that though Charles lived in the next street, it must be my own fault if I am not a complete rogue before I turn the corner.

Exeunt SIR OLIVER *and* MOSES.

SIR PETER   So now I think Sir Oliver will be convinced;—you are partial, Rowley, and would have prepared Charles for the other plot.

ROWLEY   No, upon my word, Sir Peter.

SIR PETER   Well, go bring me this Snake, and I'll hear what he has to say presently.—I see Maria, and want to speak with her.—

Exit ROWLEY.

I should be glad to be convinced my suspicions of Lady Teazle and Charles were unjust. I have never yet opened my mind on this subject to my friend *Joseph*—I'm determined I will do it—*he* will give me his opinion sincerely.

Enter MARIA.

So, child, has Mr. Surface returned with you?

MARIA   No, sir—he was engaged.

SIR PETER   Well, Maria, do you not reflect, the more you converse with that amiable young man, what return his partiality for you deserves?

MARIA   Indeed, Sir Peter, your frequent importunity on this subject distresses me extremely—you compel me to declare, that I know no man who has ever paid me a particular attention whom I would not prefer to Mr. Surface.

SIR PETER   So—here's perverseness! No, no, Maria, 'tis Charles only whom you would prefer—'tis evident his vices and follies have won your heart.

MARIA   This is unkind, sir—you know I have obeyed you in neither seeing nor corresponding with him; I have heard enough to convince me that he is unworthy my regard. Yet I cannot think it culpable, if, while my understanding severely condemns his vices, my heart suggests some pity for his distresses.

SIR PETER   Well, well, pity him as much as you please, but give your heart and hand to a worthier object.

MARIA   Never to his brother!

SIR PETER   Go, perverse and obstinate! But take care, madam; you have never yet known what the authority of a guardian is—don't compel me to inform you of it.

MARIA   I can only say, you shall not have *just* reason. 'Tis true, by my father's will, I am for a short period bound to regard you as his substitute, but must cease to think you so, when you compel me to be miserable.

Exit MARIA.

SIR PETER   Was ever man so crossed as I am! everything conspiring to fret me!—I had not been involved in matrimony a fortnight, before her father, a hale and hearty man, died—on purpose, I believe, for the pleasure of plaguing me with the care of his daughter. But here comes my helpmate! She appears in great good humour. How happy I should be if I could tease her into loving me, though but a little!

Enter LADY TEAZLE.

LADY TEAZLE   Lud! Sir Peter, I hope you haven't been quarreling with Maria—it isn't using me well to be ill humoured when I am not by.

SIR PETER   Ah, Lady Teazle, you might have the power to make me good humoured at all times.

LADY TEAZLE   I am sure I wish I had—for I want you to be in charming sweet temper at this moment. Do be good humoured now, and let me have two hundred pounds, will you?

SIR PETER   Two hundred pounds! what, an't I to be in a good humour without paying for it! But speak to me thus, and i'faith there's nothing I could refuse you. You shall have it; but seal me a bond for the repayment.

LADY TEAZLE   O, no—there—my note of hand will do as well.

SIR PETER [*Kissing her hand.*]   And you shall no longer reproach me with not giving you an independent settlement,—I mean shortly to surprise you; shall we always live thus, hey?

LADY TEAZLE   If you please. I'm sure I don't care how soon we leave off quarrelling, provided you'll own *you* were tired first.

SIR PETER   Well—then let our future contest be, who shall be most obliging.

LADY TEAZLE   I assure you, Sir Peter, good nature becomes you. You look now as you did before we were married!—when you used to walk with me under the elms, and tell me stories of what a gallant you were in your youth, and chuck me under the chin, you would, and ask me if I thought I could love an old fellow, who would deny me nothing—didn't you?

SIR PETER   Yes, yes, and you were as kind and attentive.

LADY TEAZLE   Aye, so I was, and would always take your part, when my acquaintance used to abuse you, and turn you into ridicule.

SIR PETER   Indeed!

LADY TEAZLE   Aye, and when my cousin Sophy has called you a stiff, peevish old bachelor, and laughed at me for thinking of marrying one who might be my father, I have always defended you—and said, I didn't think you so ugly by any means, and that I dared say you'd make a very good sort of a husband.

SIR PETER   And you prophesied right—and we shall certainly now be the happiest couple——

LADY TEAZLE   And never differ again!

SIR PETER   No, never!—though at the same time, indeed, my dear Lady Teazle, you must watch your temper very narrowly; for in all our little quarrels, my dear, if you recollect, my love, you always began first.

LADY TEAZLE   I beg your pardon, my dear Sir Peter: indeed, you always gave the provocation.

SIR PETER   Now, see, my angel! take care—*contradicting* isn't the way to keep friends.

LADY TEAZLE   Then, don't *you* begin it, my love!

SIR PETER   There, now! you—you are going on—you don't perceive, my life, that you are just doing the very thing which you know always makes me angry.

LADY TEAZLE   Nay, you know if you will be angry without any reason—

SIR PETER   There now! you want to quarrel again.

LADY TEAZLE   No, I am sure I don't—but, if you will be so peevish——

SIR PETER   There now! who begins first?

LADY TEAZLE   Why, you, to be sure. I said nothing—but there's no bearing your temper.

SIR PETER   No, no, madam, the fault's in your own temper.

LADY TEAZLE   Aye, you are just what my cousin Sophy said you would be.

SIR PETER   Your cousin Sophy is a forward, impertinent gipsy.

LADY TEAZLE   You are a great bear, I'm sure, to abuse my relations.

SIR PETER   Now may all the plagues of marriage be doubled on me, if ever I try to be friends with you any more!

LADY TEAZLE   So much the better.

SIR PETER   No, no, madam; 'tis evident you never cared a pin for me, and I was a madman to marry you—a pert, rural coquette, that had refused half the honest squires in the neighborhood!

LADY TEAZLE   And I am sure, I was a fool to marry you—an old dangling bachelor, who was single at fifty, only because he never could meet with any one who would have him.

SIR PETER   Aye, aye, madam; but you were pleased enough to listen to me—*you* never had such an offer before.

LADY TEAZLE   No! didn't I refuse Sir Twivy Tarrier, who everybody said would have been a better match—for his estate is just as good as yours—and he has broke his neck since we have been married.

SIR PETER I have done with you, madam! You are an unfeeling, ungrateful—but there's an end of everything. I believe you capable of anything that's bad. Yes, madam, I now believe the reports relative to you and Charles, madam—yes, madam, you and Charles—are not without grounds——

LADY TEAZLE Take care, Sir Peter! you had better not insinuate any such thing! I'll not be suspected with*out cause,* I promise you.

SIR PETER Very well, madam! very well! a separate maintenance as soon as you please. Yes, madam, or a divorce! I'll make an example of myself for the benefit of all old bachelors. Let us separate, madam.

LADY TEAZLE Agreed! agreed! And now, my dear Sir Peter, we are of a mind once more, we may be the *happiest couple,* and *never differ again,* you know: ha! ha! Well, you are going to be in a passion, I see, and I shall only interrupt you—so, bye! bye!

Exit.

SIR PETER Plagues and tortures! can't I make her angry neither? Oh, I am the miserablest fellow! But I'll not bear her presuming to keep her temper—no! she may break my heart, but she shan't keep her temper.

Exit.

Act III. Scene ii.

CHARLES's *house.*
Enter TRIP, MOSES, *and* SIR OLIVER SURFACE.

TRIP Here, Master Moses! if you'll stay a moment, I'll try whether— what's the gentleman's name?

SIR OLIVER Mr. Moses, what *is* my name? [*Aside.*]

MOSES Mr. Premium.

TRIP Premium—very well.

Exit TRIP, *taking snuff.*

SIR OLIVER To judge by the servants one wouldn't believe the master was ruined. But what!—sure, this was my brother's house?

MOSES Yes, sir; Mr. Charles bought it of Mr. Joseph, with the furniture, pictures, &c., just as the old gentleman left it—Sir Peter thought it a great piece of extravagance in him.

SIR OLIVER In my mind, the other's economy in *selling* it to him was more reprehensible by half.

Re-enter TRIP.

TRIP My master says you must wait, gentlemen; he has company, and can't speak with you yet.

SIR OLIVER   If he knew *who* it was wanted to see him, perhaps he wouldn't have sent such a message?

TRIP   Yes, yes, sir; he knows *you* are here—I didn't forget little Premium—no, no, no.

SIR OLIVER   Very well—and I pray, sir, what may be your name?

TRIP   Trip, sir—my name is Trip, at your service.

SIR OLIVER   Well, then, Mr. Trip, you have a pleasant sort of a place here, I guess.

TRIP   Why, yes—here are three or four of us pass our time agreeably enough; but then our wages are sometimes a little in arrear—and not very great either—but fifty pounds a year, and find our own bags and bouquets.[3]

SIR OLIVER   [*Aside.*]   Bags and bouquets! halters and bastinadoes![4]

TRIP   But *à propos*, Moses, have you been able to get me that little bill discounted?

SIR OLIVER   [*Aside.*]   Wants to raise money, too!—mercy on me! Has his distresses, I warrant, like a lord,—and affects creditors and duns.

MOSES   'Twas not to be done, indeed, Mr. Trip.

> *Gives the note.*

TRIP   Good lack, you surprise me! My friend *Brush* has endorsed it, and I thought when he put his mark on the back of a bill 'twas as good as cash.

MOSES   No, 'twouldn't do.

TRIP   A small sum—but twenty pounds. Hark'ee, Moses, do you think you couldn't get it me by way of annuity?

SIR OLIVER   [*Aside.*]   An annuity! ha! ha! a footman raise money by way of annuity! Well done, luxury, egad!

MOSES   But you must insure your place.

TRIP   Oh, with all my heart! I'll insure my place, and my life too, if you please.

SIR OLIVER   [*Aside.*]   It's more than I would your neck.

TRIP   But then, Moses, it must be done before this d——d register[5] takes place—one wouldn't like to have one's name made public, you know.

MOSES   No, certainly. But is there nothing you could deposit?

TRIP   Why, nothing capital of my master's wardrobe has dropped lately; but I could give you a mortgage on some of his winter clothes, with equity of redemption before November—or you shall have the reversion of the French velvet, or a post-obit[6] on the blue and silver;—these, I should think, Moses, with a few pair of point ruffles, as a collateral security—hey, my little fellow?

MOSES   Well, well.

---

3. Footmen's dress.
4. Cudgels.
5. The record of annuities granted according to the Annuity Bill.
6. A bond to take effect after death.

Bell rings.

TRIP   Gad, I heard the bell! I believe, gentlemen, I can now introduce you. Don't forget the annuity, little Moses! This way, gentlemen, insure my place, you know.

SIR OLIVER [*Aside.*]   If the man be a shadow of his master, this is the temple of dissipation indeed!

Exeunt.

Act III. Scene iii.

CHARLES [SURFACE], CARELESS, &c., &c. *at a table with wine,* &c.

CHARLES   'Fore heaven, 'tis true!—there's the great degeneracy of the age. Many of our acquaintance have taste, spirit, and politeness; but, plague on't, they won't drink.

CARELESS   It is so, indeed, Charles! they give in to all the substantial luxuries of the table, and abstain from nothing but wine and wit.

CHARLES   Oh, certainly society suffers by it intolerably! for now, instead of the social spirit of raillery that used to mantle over a glass of bright Burgundy, their conversation is become just like the Spa-water they drink, which has all the pertness and flatulence of champagne, without its spirit or flavor.

1 GENT   But what are *they* to do who love play better than wine?

CARELESS   True! there's Harry diets himself for gaming, and is now under a hazard[7] regimen.

CHARLES   Then he'll have the worst of it. What! you wouldn't train a horse for the course by keeping him from corn! For my part, egad, I am now never so successful as when I am a little merry—let me throw on a bottle of champagne, and I never lose—at least I never feel my losses, which is exactly the same thing.

2 GENT   Aye, that I believe.

CHARLES   And, then, what man can pretend to be a believer in love, who is an abjurer of wine? 'Tis the test by which the lover knows his own heart. Fill a dozen bumpers to a dozen beauties, and she that floats at top is the maid that has bewitched you.

CARELESS   Now then, Charles, be honest, and give us your real favorite.

CHARLES   Why, I have withheld her only in compassion to you. If I toast her, you must give a round of her peers—which is impossible—on earth.

CARELESS   Oh, then we'll find some canonised vestals or heathen goddesses that will do, I warrant!

CHARLES   Here then, bumpers, you rogues! bumpers! Maria! Maria—

Drink.

---

7. A dice game.

1 GENT   Maria who?

CHARLES   O, damn the surname!—'tis too formal to be registered in Love's calendar—but now, Sir Toby Bumper, beware—we must have beauty superlative.

CARELESS   Nay, never study, Sir Toby: we'll stand to the toast, though your mistress should want an eye—and you know you have a song will excuse you.

SIR TOBY   Egad, so I have! and I'll give him the song instead of the lady.

SONG AND CHORUS

Here's to the maiden of bashful fifteen;
    Here's to the widow of fifty;
Here's to the flaunting extravagant quean,[8]
    And here's to the housewife that's thrifty.
    Chorus.   Let the toast pass—
        Drink to the lass—
I'll warrant she'll prove an excuse for the glass.

Here's to the charmer whose dimples we prize;
    Now to the maid who has none, sir;
Here's to the girl with a pair of blue eyes,
    And here's to the nymph with but one, sir.
    Chorus.   Let the toast pass, &c.

Here's to the maid with a bosom of snow:
    Now to *her* that's as brown as a berry:
Here's to the wife with a face full of woe,
    And now for the damsel that's merry.
    Chorus.   Let the toast pass, &c.

For let 'em be clumsy, or let 'em be slim,
    Young or ancient, I care not a feather:
So fill a pint bumper quite up to the brim,
    —And let us e'en toast 'em together.
    Chorus.   Let the toast pass, &c.

ALL   Bravo! Bravo!

Enter TRIP, *and whispers* CHARLES SURFACE.

CHARLES   Gentlemen, you must excuse me a little.—Careless, take the chair, will you?

CARELESS   Nay, prithee, Charles, what now? This is one of your peerless beauties, I suppose, has dropped in by chance?

CHARLES   No, faith! To tell you the truth, 'tis a Jew and a broker, who are come by appointment.

8. Harlot or hussy.

CARELESS   Oh, damn it! let's have the Jew in—

1 GENT   Aye, and the broker too, by all means.

2 GENT   Yes, yes, the Jew and the broker.

CHARLES   Egad, with all my heart!—Trip bid the gentlemen walk in.—

[Exit TRIP.]

Though there's one of them a stranger, I can tell you.

CARELESS   Charles, let us give them some generous Burgundy, and perhaps they'll grow conscientious.

CHARLES   Oh, hang 'em, no! wine does but draw forth a man's *natural*
qualities; and to make *them* drink would only be to whet their
knavery.

Enter TRIP, SIR OLIVER SURFACE, and MOSES.

CHARLES   So, honest Moses; walk in, pray, Mr. Premium—that's the
gentleman's name, isn't it, Moses?

MOSES   Yes, sir.

CHARLES   Set chairs, Trip.—Sit down, Mr. Premium.—Glasses,
Trip.—Sit down, Moses.—Come, Mr. Premium, I'll give you a sentiment; here's "Success to usury!"—Moses, fill the gentleman a
bumper.

MOSES   Success to usury!

CARELESS   Right, Moses—usury is prudence and industry, and deserves
to succeed.

SIR OLIVER   Then here's—All the success it deserves!

CARELESS   No, no, that won't do! Mr. Premium, you have demurred to
the toast, and must drink it in a pint bumper.

1 GENT   A pint bumper, at least.

MOSES   Oh, pray, sir, consider—Mr. Premium's a gentleman.

CARELESS   And therefore loves good wine.

2 GENT   Give Moses a quart glass—this is mutiny, and a high contempt
of the chair.

CARELESS   Here, now for't! I'll see justice done, to the last drop of my
bottle.

SIR OLIVER   Nay, pray, gentlemen—I did not expect this usage.

CHARLES   No, hang it, Careless, you shan't; Mr. Premium's a stranger.

SIR OLIVER [*Aside.*]   Odd! I wish I was well out of this company.

CARELESS   Plague on 'em then! if they won't drink, we'll not sit down
with 'em. Come, Harry, the dice are in the next room.— Charles,
you'll join us—when you have finished your business with these gentlemen?

CHARLES   I will! I will!—
Careless!

Exeunt Gentlemen.

CARELESS   Well!

CHARLES   Perhaps I may want *you*.

CARELESS   Oh, you know I am always ready—word, note, or bond, 'tis all the same to me.

Exit.

MOSES   Sir, this is Mr. Premium, a gentleman of the strictest honor and secrecy; and always performs what he undertakes. Mr. Premium, this is——

CHARLES   Pshaw! have done! Sir, my friend Moses is a very honest fellow, but a little slow at expression; he'll be an hour giving us our titles. Mr. Premium, the plain state of the matter is this—I am an extravagant young fellow who want[s] money to borrow; you I take to be a prudent old fellow, who ha[s] got money to lend. I am blockhead enough to give fifty per cent sooner than not have it; and you, I presume, are rogue enough to take a hundred if you could get it. Now, sir, you see we are acquainted at once, and may proceed to business without farther ceremony.

SIR OLIVER   Exceeding frank, upon my word. I see, sir, you are not a man of many compliments.

CHARLES   Oh, no, sir! plain dealing in business I always think best.

SIR OLIVER   Sir, I like you the better for't. However, you are mistaken in one thing—I have no money to lend, but I believe I could procure some of a friend; but then he's an unconscionable dog—isn't he, Moses? And must sell stock to accommodate you—mustn't he, Moses?

MOSES   Yes, indeed! You know I always speak the truth, and scorn to tell a lie!

CHARLES   Right! People that expect truth generally do. But these are trifles, Mr. Premium. What! I know money isn't to be bought without paying for't!

SIR OLIVER   Well, but what security could you give? You have no land, I suppose?

CHARLES   Not a mole-hill, nor a twig, but what's in beau-pots[9] out at the window!

OLIVER   Nor any stock, I presume?

CHARLES   Nothing but live stock—and that's only a few pointers and ponies. But pray, Mr. Premium, are you acquainted at all with any of my connections?

SIR OLIVER   Why, to say truth, I am.

CHARLES   Then you must know that I have a devilish rich uncle in the East Indies, Sir *Oliver Surface*, from whom I have the greatest expectations.

SIR OLIVER   That you have a wealthy uncle, I have heard—but how your expectations will turn out is more, I believe, than you can tell.

CHARLES   Oh, no!—there can be no doubt—they tell me I'm a prodigious favorite—and that he talks of leaving me everything.

9. Flowerpots.

SIR OLIVER   Indeed! this is the first I've heard on't.

CHARLES   Yes, yes, 'tis just so.—Moses knows 'tis true; don't you, Moses?

MOSES   Oh, yes! I'll swear to't.

SIR OLIVER [*Aside.*]   Egad, they'll persuade me presently I'm at Bengal.

CHARLES   Now I propose, Mr. Premium, if it's agreeable to you, a post-obit on Sir Oliver's life; though at the same time the old fellow has been so liberal to me that I give you my word I should be very sorry to hear anything had happened to him.

SIR OLIVER   Not more than *I* should, I assure you. But the bond you mention happens to be just the worst security you could offer me—for I might live to a hundred and never recover the principal.

CHARLES   Oh, yes, you would!—the moment Sir Oliver dies, you know, you'd come on me for the money.

SIR OLIVER   Then I believe I should be the most unwelcome dun you ever had in your life.

CHARLES   What! I suppose you are afraid now that Sir Oliver is too good a life?

SIR OLIVER   No, indeed I am not—though I have heard he is as hale and healthy as any man of his years in Christendom.

CHARLES   There again you are misinformed. No, no, the climate has hurt him considerably, poor uncle Oliver. Yes, he breaks apace, I'm told—and so much altered lately that his nearest relations don't know him.

SIR OLIVER   No! Ha! ha! ha! so much altered lately that his relations don't know him! Ha! ha! ha! that's droll, egad—ha! ha! ha!

CHARLES   Ha! ha!—you're glad to hear that, little Premium.

SIR OLIVER   No, no, I'm not.

CHARLES   Yes, yes, you are—ha! ha! ha!—you know that mends your chance.

SIR OLIVER   But I'm told Sir Oliver is coming over—nay, some say he is actually arrived.

CHARLES   Pshaw! sure I must know better than you whether he's come or not. No, no, rely on't, he is at this moment at Calcutta, isn't he, Moses?

MOSES   Oh, yes, certainly.

SIR OLIVER   Very true, as you say, you must know better than I, though I have it from pretty good authority—haven't I, Moses?

MOSES   Yes, most undoubted!

SIR OLIVER   But, sir, as I understand you want a few hundreds immediately, is there nothing you would dispose of?

CHARLES   How do you mean?

SIR OLIVER   For instance, now—I have heard—that your father left behind him a great quantity of massy old plate.

CHARLES   O lud! that's gone long ago—Moses can tell you how better than I can.

SIR OLIVER   Good lack! all the family race-cups and corporation-bowls! [*Aside.*]—Then it was also supposed that his library was one of the most valuable and complete.

CHARLES   Yes, yes, so it was—vastly too much so for a private gentleman—for my part, I was always of a communicative disposition, so I thought it a shame to keep so much knowledge to myself.

SIR OLIVER [*Aside.*]   Mercy on me! learning that had run in the family like an heirloom!—[*Aloud.*] Pray, what are become of the books?

CHARLES   You must inquire of the auctioneer, Master Premium, for I don't believe even Moses can direct you there.

MOSES   I never meddle with books.

SIR OLIVER   So, so, nothing of the family property left, I suppose?

CHARLES   Not much, indeed; unless you have a mind to the family pictures. I have got a room full of ancestors above—and if you have a taste for old paintings, egad, you shall have 'em a bargain!

SIR OLIVER   Hey! and the devil! sure, you wouldn't sell your forefathers, would you?

CHARLES   Every man of 'em, to the best bidder.

SIR OLIVER   What! your great-uncles and aunts?

CHARLES   Aye, and my great-grandfathers and grandmothers too.

SIR OLIVER   Now I give him up!—[*Aside.*]—What the plague, have you no bowels for your own kindred? Odd's life! do you take me for Shylock in the play, that you would raise money of me on your own flesh and blood?

CHARLES   Nay, my little broker, don't be angry: what need *you* care, if you have your money's worth?

SIR OLIVER   Well, I'll be the purchaser—I think I can dispose of the family.—[*Aside.*] Oh, I'll never forgive him this! never!

Enter CARELESS.

CARELESS   Come, Charles, what keeps you?

CHARLES   I can't come yet. I'faith! we are going to have a sale above—here's little Premium will buy all my ancestors!

CARELESS   Oh, burn your ancestors!

CHARLES   No, he may do that afterwards, if he pleases. Stay, Careless, we want you; egad, you shall be auctioneer—so come along with us.

CARELESS   Oh, have with you, if that's the case.—I can handle a hammer as well as a dice box!

SIR OLIVER [*Aside.*]   Oh, the profligates!

CHARLES   Come, Moses, you shall be appraiser, if we want one. — Gad's life, little Premium, you don't seem to like the business.

SIR OLIVER   Oh, yes, I do, vastly! Ha! ha! yes, yes, I think it a rare joke to sell one's family by auction—ha! ha!—[*Aside.*] Oh, the prodigal!

CHARLES   To be sure! when a man wants money, where the plague should he get assistance, if he can't make free with his own relations?

Act IV. Scene i.

Picture-room at CHARLES's.
Enter CHARLES SURFACE, SIR OLIVER SURFACE, MOSES, *and* CARE-
LESS.

CHARLES   Walk in, gentlemen, pray walk in!—here they are, the family
of the Surfaces, up to the Conquest.[1]

SIR OLIVER   And, in my opinion, a goodly collection.

CHARLES   Aye, aye, these are done in true spirit of portrait-painting—
no volunteer grace or expression—not like the works of your modern
Raphael, who gives you the strongest resemblance, yet contrives to
make your own portrait independent of you; so that you may sink the
original and not hurt the picture. No, no; the merit of these is the
inveterate likeness—all stiff and awkward as the originals, and like
nothing in human nature beside!

SIR OLIVER   Ah! we shall never see such figures of men again.

CHARLES   I hope not. Well, you see, Master Premium, what a domestic
character I am—here I sit of an evening surrounded by my family.
But come, get to your pulpit, Mr. Auctioneer—here's an old gouty
chair of my grandfather's will answer the purpose.

CARELESS   Aye, aye, this will do. But, Charles, I have ne'er a hammer;
and what's an auctioneer without his hammer?

CHARLES   Egad, that's true. What parchment have we here? [*Takes
down a roll.*] "*Richard, heir to Thomas*"—our genealogy in full. Here,
Careless, you shall have no common bit of mahogany—here's the
family tree for you, you rogue—this shall be your hammer, and now
you may knock down my ancestors with their own pedigree.

SIR OLIVER [*Aside.*]   What an unnatural rogue!—an *ex post facto* parri-
cide![2]

CARELESS   Yes, yes, here's a list of your generation indeed;—faith,
Charles, this is the most convenient thing you could have found for
the business, for 'twill serve not only as a hammer, but a catalogue
into the bargain.—But come, begin—A-going, a-going, a-going!

CHARLES   Bravo, Careless! Well, here's my great uncle, Sir Richard
Raviline, a marvellous good general in his day, I assure you. He served
in all the Duke of Marlborough's wars, and got that cut over his eye
at the battle of Malplaquet.[3] What say you, Mr. Premium? look at
him—there's a hero for you! not cut out of his feathers, as your modern clipped captains are, but enveloped in wig and regimentals, as a
general should be. What do you bid?

MOSES   Mr. Premium would have you speak.

CHARLES   Why, then, he shall have him for ten pounds, and I am sure
that's not dear for a staff officer.

---

1. The Norman conquest of England (1066).
2. In retrospect, a murderer of his forefathers.
3. A victory over the French in 1709.

SIR OLIVER [*Aside.*]   Heaven deliver me! his famous uncle Richard for ten pounds!—Very well, sir, I take him at that.

CHARLES   Careless, knock down my uncle Richard.—Here, now, is a maiden sister of his, my great-aunt Deborah, done by Kneller,[4] thought to be in his best manner, and a very formidable likeness. There she is, you see, a shepherdess feeding her flock. You shall have her for five pounds ten—the sheep are worth the money.

SIR OLIVER [*Aside.*]   Ah! poor Deborah! a woman who set such a value on herself!—Five pound ten—she's mine.

CHARLES   Knock down my aunt Deborah! Here, now, are two that were a sort of cousins of theirs.—You see, Moses, these pictures were done some time ago, when beaux wore wigs, and the ladies wore their own hair.

SIR OLIVER   Yes, truly, head-dresses appear to have been a little lower in those days.

CHARLES   Well, take that couple for the same.

MOSES   'Tis [a] good bargain.

CHARLES   Careless!—This, now, is a grandfather of my mother's, a learned judge, well known on the western circuit.—What do you rate him at, Moses?

MOSES   Four guineas.

CHARLES   Four guineas! Gad's life, you don't bid me the price of his wig.—Mr. Premium, *you* have more respect for the woolsack;[5] do let us knock his lordship down at fifteen.

SIR OLIVER   By all means.

CARELESS   Gone!

CHARLES   And there are two brothers of his, William and Walter Blunt, Esquires, both members of Parliament, and noted speakers; and, what's very extraordinary, I believe this is the first time they were ever bought and sold.

SIR OLIVER   That's very extraordinary, indeed! I'll take them at your own price, for the honor of Parliament.

CARELESS   Well said, little Premium! I'll knock 'em down at forty.

CHARLES   Here's a jolly fellow—I don't know what relation, but he was mayor of Manchester; take him at eight pounds.

SIR OLIVER   No, no—six will do for the mayor.

CHARLES   Come, make it guineas, and I'll throw you the two aldermen there into the bargain.

SIR OLIVER   They're mine.

CHARLES   Careless, knock down the mayor and aldermen. But, plague on't! we shall be all day retailing in this manner; do let us deal whole-sale—what say you, little Premium? Give me three hundred pounds for the rest of the family in the lump.

CARELESS   Aye, aye, that will be the best way.

4. Sir Godfrey Kneller, a successful portrait painter.
5. I.e., respect for judges. The Lord Chancellor, presiding over the House of Lords, is tradition-ally seated on a woolsack.

SIR OLIVER   Well, well, anything to accommodate you; they are mine. But there is one portrait which you have always passed over.

CARELESS   What, that ill-looking little fellow over the settee?

SIR OLIVER   Yes, sir, I mean that; though I don't think him so ill-looking a little fellow, by any means.

CHARLES   What, that? Oh, that's my uncle Oliver! 'Twas done before he went to India.

CARELESS   Your uncle Oliver! Gad, then you'll never be friends, Charles. That, now, to me, is as stern a looking rogue as ever I saw— an unforgiving eye, and a damned disinheriting countenance! an inveterate knave, depend on't. Don't you think so, little Premium?

SIR OLIVER   Upon my soul, sir, I do not; I think it is as honest a looking face as any in the room, dead or alive. But I suppose your uncle Oliver goes with the rest of the lumber?

CHARLES   No, hang it! I'll not part with poor Noll. The old fellow has been very good to me, and, egad, I'll keep his picture while I've a room to put it in.

SIR OLIVER   The rogue's my nephew after all! [*Aside.*]—But, sir, I have somehow taken a fancy to that picture.

CHARLES   I'm sorry for't, for you certainly will not have it. Oons! haven't you got enough of 'em?

SIR OLIVER   I forgive him everything! [*Aside.*]—But, sir, when I take a whim in my head, I don't value money. I'll give you as much for that as for all the rest.

CHARLES   Don't tease me, master broker; I tell you I'll not part with it, and there's an end on't.

SIR OLIVER   How like his father the dog is!—[*Aloud.*] Well, well, I have done.—I did not perceive it before, but I think I never saw such a resemblance.—Well, sir—here is a draught for your sum.

CHARLES   Why, 'tis for eight hundred pounds!

SIR OLIVER   You will not let Sir Oliver go?

CHARLES   Zounds! no! I tell you, once more.

SIR OLIVER   Then never mind the difference; we'll balance another time. But give me your hand on the bargain; you are an honest fellow, Charles—I beg pardon, sir, for being so free.—Come, Moses.

CHARLES   Egad, this is a whimsical old fellow!—but hark'ee, Premium, you'll prepare lodgings for these gentlemen.

SIR OLIVER   Yes, yes, I'll send for them in a day or two.

CHARLES   But hold—do now—send a genteel conveyance for them, for, I assure you, they were most of them used to ride in their own carriages.

SIR OLIVER   I will, I will, for all but—Oliver.

CHARLES   Aye, all but the little honest nabob.[6]

SIR OLIVER   You're fixed on that?

CHARLES   Peremptorily.

6. One who has made his fortune in India.

SIR OLIVER   A dear extravagant rogue!—Good day!—Come, Moses,—
Let me hear now who dares call him profligate!

Exeunt SIR OLIVER *and* MOSES.

CARELESS   Why, this is the oddest genius of the sort I ever saw!

CHARLES   Egad, he's the prince of brokers, I think. I wonder how the
devil Moses got acquainted with so honest a fellow.—Ha! here's Rowley.—Do, Careless, say I'll join the company in a moment.

CARELESS   I will—but don't let that old blockhead persuade you to
squander any of that money on old musty debts, or any such nonsense; for tradesmen, Charles, are the most exorbitant fellows!

CHARLES   Very true, and paying them is only encouraging them.

CARELESS   Nothing else.

Exit CARELESS.

CHARLES   Aye, aye, never fear.
So! this was an odd fellow, indeed! Let me see, two-thirds of this is
mine by right—five hundred and thirty pounds. 'Fore heaven! I find
one's ancestors are more valuable relations than I took 'em for!—
Ladies and gentlemen, your most obedient and very grateful humble
servant.

Enter ROWLEY.

Ha! old Rowley! egad, you are just come in time to take leave of your
old acquaintance.

ROWLEY   Yes, I heard they were going. But I wonder you can have such
spirits under so many distresses.

CHARLES   Why, there's the point—my distresses are so many, that I
can't afford to part with my spirits; but I shall be rich and splenetic,
all in good time. However, I suppose you are surprised that I am not
more sorrowful at parting with so many near relations; to be sure, 'tis
very affecting; but, rot 'em, you see they never move a muscle, so why
should I?

ROWLEY   There's no making you serious a moment.

CHARLES   Yes, faith: I am so now. Here, my honest Rowley, here, get
me this changed, and take a hundred pounds of it immediately to old
Stanley.

ROWLEY   A hundred pounds! Consider only—

CHARLES   Gad's life, don't talk about it! poor Stanley's wants are pressing, and, if you don't make haste, we shall have some one call that
has a better right to the money.

ROWLEY   Ah! there's the point! I never will cease dunning you with the
old proverb——

CHARLES   "Be *just* before you're *generous*," hey!—Why, so I would if I
could; but Justice is an old lame hobbling beldame,[7] and I can't get
her to keep pace with Generosity, for the soul of me.

7. Hag.

ROWLEY   Yet, Charles, believe me, one hour's reflection——

CHARLES   Aye, aye, it's all very true; but hark'ee, Rowley, while I have, by heaven I'll give—so, damn your economy! and now for hazard.

Exeunt.

Act IV. Scene ii.

The parlor.
Enter SIR OLIVER SURFACE *and* MOSES.

MOSES   Well, sir, I think, as Sir Peter said, you have seen Mr. Charles in high glory; 'tis great pity he's so extravagant.

SIR OLIVER   True, but he wouldn't sell my picture.

MOSES   And loves wine and women so much.

SIR OLIVER   But he wouldn't sell my picture!

MOSES   And game[s] so deep.

SIR OLIVER   But he wouldn't sell my picture. Oh, here's Rowley.

Enter ROWLEY.

ROWLEY   So, Sir Oliver, I find you have made a purchase——

SIR OLIVER   Yes, yes, our young rake has parted with his ancestors like old tapestry.

ROWLEY   And here has he commissioned me to redeliver you part of the purchase-money—I mean, though, in your necessitous character of old *Stanley.*

MOSES   Ah! there is the pity of all: he is so damned charitable.

ROWLEY   And I left a hosier and two tailors in the hall, who, I'm sure, won't be paid, and this hundred would satisfy 'em.

SIR OLIVER   Well, well, I'll pay his debts—and his benevolence too; but now I am no more a broker, and you shall introduce me to the elder brother as old Stanley.

ROWLEY   Not yet awhile; Sir Peter, I know, means to call there about this time.

Enter TRIP.

TRIP   O gentlemen, I beg pardon for not showing you out; this way— Moses, a word.

Exeunt TRIP *and* MOSES.

SIR OLIVER   There's a fellow for you! Would you believe it, that puppy intercepted the Jew on our coming, and wanted to raise money before he got to his master!

ROWLEY   Indeed!

SIR OLIVER   Yes, they are now planning an annuity business. Ah, Master Rowley, in my days, servants were content with the follies of their masters, when they were worn a little threadbare—but now they have their vices, like their birthday clothes,[8] with the gloss on.

Exeunt.

Act IV. Scene iii.

A library [in JOSEPH SURFACE's *house.]*
JOSEPH SURFACE *and* SERVANT.

JOSEPH SURFACE   No letter from Lady Teazle?

SERVANT   No, sir.

JOSEPH SURFACE [*Aside.*]   I am surprised she hasn't sent, if she is prevented from coming. Sir Peter certainly does not suspect me. Yet I wish I may not lose the heiress, through the scrape I have drawn myself in with the wife; however, Charles's imprudence and bad character are great points in my favor.

Knocking.

SERVANT   Sir, I believe that must be Lady Teazle.

JOSEPH SURFACE   Hold! See whether it is or not, before you go to the door—I have a particular message for you, if it should be my brother.

SERVANT   'Tis her ladyship, sir; she always leaves her chair at the milliner's in the next street.

JOSEPH SURFACE   Stay, stay—draw that screen before the window—that will do;—my opposite neighbor is a maiden lady of so curious a temper.—[SERVANT *draws the screen, and exit.*] I have a difficult hand to play in this affair. Lady Teazle has lately suspected my views on Maria; but she must by no means be let into that secret,—at least, not till I have her more in my power.

Enter LADY TEAZLE.

LADY TEAZLE   What, sentiment in soliloquy! Have you been very impatient now? O lud! don't pretend to look grave. I vow I couldn't come before.

JOSEPH SURFACE   O madam, punctuality is a species of constancy, a very unfashionable quality in a lady.

LADY TEAZLE   Upon my word, you ought to pity me. Do you know that Sir Peter is grown so ill-tempered to me of late, and so jealous of *Charles* too—that's the best of the story, isn't it?

JOSEPH SURFACE [*Aside.*]   I am glad my scandalous friends keep that up.

LADY TEAZLE   I am sure I wish he would let Maria marry him, and then perhaps he would be convinced; don't you, Mr. Surface?

JOSEPH SURFACE [*Aside.*]   Indeed I do not.—Oh, certainly I do! for

8. Worn on the King's birthday.

then my dear Lady Teazle would also be convinced how wrong her suspicions were of my having any design on the silly girl.

Sit.

LADY TEAZLE   Well, well I'm inclined to believe you. But isn't it provoking, to have the most ill-natured things said to one? And there's my friend Lady Sneerwell has circulated I don't know how many scandalous tales of me! and all without any foundation, too—that's what vexes me.

JOSEPH SURFACE   Aye, madam, to be sure, that *is* the provoking circumstance—without foundation! yes, yes, there's the mortification, indeed; for, when a scandalous story is believed against one, there certainly is no comfort like the consciousness of having deserved it.

LADY TEAZLE   No, to be sure—then I'd forgive their malice; but to attack me, who am really so innocent, and who never say an ill-natured thing of anybody—that is, of any friend—and then Sir Peter, too, to have him so peevish, and so suspicious, when I know the integrity of my own heart—indeed 'tis monstrous!

JOSEPH SURFACE   But, my dear Lady Teazle, 'tis your own fault if you suffer it. When a husband entertains a groundless suspicion of his wife, and withdraws his confidence from her, the original compact is broke, and she owes it to the honor of her sex to endeavor to outwit him.

LADY TEAZLE   Indeed! So that, if he suspects me without cause, it follows that the best way of curing his jealousy is to give him reason for't?

JOSEPH SURFACE   Undoubtedly—for your husband should never be deceived in you: and in that case it becomes *you* to be frail in compliment to *his* discernment.

LADY TEAZLE   To be sure, what you say is very reasonable, and when the consciousness of my own innocence——

JOSEPH SURFACE   Ah, my dear madam, there is the great mistake; 'tis this very conscious innocence that is of the greatest prejudice to you. What is it makes you negligent of forms, and careless of the world's opinion? why, the *consciousness* of your innocence. What makes you thoughtless in your conduct, and apt to run into a thousand little imprudences? why, the *consciousness* of your innocence. What makes you impatient of Sir Peter's temper and outrageous at his suspicions? why, the *consciousness* of your own innocence!

LADY TEAZLE   'Tis very true!

JOSEPH SURFACE   Now, my dear Lady Teazle, if you would but once make a trifling *faux pas*, you can't conceive how cautious you would grow—and how ready to humour and agree with your husband.

LADY TEAZLE   Do you think so?

JOSEPH SURFACE   Oh, I'm sure on't; and then you would find all scandal would cease at once, for—in short, your character at present is like a person in a plethora, absolutely dying of too much health.

LADY TEAZLE   So, so; then I perceive your prescription is, that I must sin in my own defence, and part with my virtue to preserve my reputation?

JOSEPH SURFACE   Exactly so, upon my credit, ma'am.

LADY TEAZLE   Well, certainly that is the oddest doctrine, and the newest receipt for avoiding calumny?

JOSEPH SURFACE   An infallible one, believe me. *Prudence*, like *experience*, must be paid for.

LADY TEAZLE   Why, if my understanding were once convinced——

JOSEPH SURFACE   Oh, certainly, madam, your understanding *should* be convinced. Yes, yes—heaven forbid I should persuade you to do anything you *thought* wrong. No, no, I have too much honor to desire it.

LADY TEAZLE   Don't you think we may as well leave honor out of the argument?

JOSEPH SURFACE   Ah, the ill effects of your country education, I see, still remain with you.

LADY TEAZLE   I doubt they do, indeed; and I will fairly own to you, that if I could be persuaded to do wrong, it would be by Sir Peter's ill-usage sooner than your honorable logic, after all.

JOSEPH SURFACE   Then, by this hand, which he is unworthy of—— [*Taking her hand.*]

Re-enter SERVANT.

'Sdeath, you blockhead—what do you want?

SERVANT   I beg pardon, sir, but I thought you wouldn't choose Sir Peter to come up without announcing him.

JOSEPH SURFACE   Sir Peter!—Oons—the devil!

LADY TEAZLE   Sir Peter! O lud! I'm ruined! I'm ruined!

SERVANT   Sir, 'twasn't I let him in.

LADY TEAZLE   Oh! I'm undone! What will become of me, now, Mr. Logic?—Oh! mercy, he's on the stairs—I'll get behind here—and if ever I'm so imprudent again——

Goes behind the screen.

JOSEPH SURFACE   Give me that book.

Sits down. SERVANT *pretends to adjust his hair.*
Enter SIR PETER TEAZLE.

SIR PETER   Aye, ever improving himself!—Mr. Surface, Mr. Surface——

JOSEPH SURFACE   Oh, my dear Sir Peter, I beg your pardon. [*Gaping, and throws away the book.*] I have been dozing over a stupid book. Well, I am much obliged to you for this call. You haven't been here, I believe, since I fitted up this room. Books, you know, are the only things I am a coxcomb in.

SIR PETER   'Tis very neat indeed. Well, well, that's proper; and you make even your screen a source of knowledge—hung, I perceive, with maps.

JOSEPH SURFACE   Oh, yes, I find great use in that screen.

SIR PETER   I dare say you must—certainly—when you want to find anything in a hurry.

JOSEPH SURFACE [*Aside.*]   Aye, or to hide anything in a hurry either.

SIR PETER   Well, I have a little private business——

JOSEPH SURFACE   You needn't stay. [*To Servant.*]

SERVANT   No, sir.

Exit.

JOSEPH SURFACE   Here's a chair, Sir Peter—I beg——

SIR PETER   Well, now we are alone, there is a subject, my dear friend, on which I wish to unburden my mind to you—a point of the greatest moment to my peace: in short, my good friend, Lady Teazle's conduct of late has made me extremely unhappy.

JOSEPH SURFACE   Indeed! I am very sorry to hear it.

SIR PETER   Yes, 'tis but too plain she has not the least regard for me; but, what's worse, I have pretty good authority to suspect she must have formed an attachment to another.

JOSEPH SURFACE   You astonish me!

SIR PETER   Yes! and, between ourselves, I think I have discovered the person.

JOSEPH SURFACE   How! you alarm me exceedingly.

SIR PETER   Aye, my dear friend, I knew you would sympathize with me!

JOSEPH SURFACE   Yes, believe me, Sir Peter, such a discovery would hurt me just as much as it would you.

SIR PETER   I am convinced of it.—Ah! it is a happiness to have a friend whom one can trust even with one's family secrets. But have you no guess who I mean?

JOSEPH SURFACE   I haven't the most distant idea. It can't be Sir Benjamin Backbite!

SIR PETER   O, no! What say you to Charles?

JOSEPH SURFACE   My brother! impossible!

SIR PETER   Ah, my dear friend, the goodness of your own heart misleads you—you judge of others by yourself.

JOSEPH SURFACE   Certainly, Sir Peter, the heart that is conscious of its own integrity is ever slow to credit another's treachery.

SIR PETER   True; but your brother has no sentiment—you never hear him talk so.

JOSEPH SURFACE   Yet I can't but think Lady Teazle herself has too much principle——

SIR PETER   Aye; but what's her principle against the flattery of a handsome, lively young fellow?

JOSEPH SURFACE   That's very true.

SIR PETER   And then, you know, the difference of our ages makes it very improbable that she should have any great affection for me; and if she were to be frail, and I were to make it public, why the town would only laugh at me, the foolish old bachelor who had married a girl.

JOSEPH SURFACE   That's true, to be sure—they *would* laugh.

SIR PETER   Laugh! aye, and make ballads, and paragraphs, and the devil knows what of me.

JOSEPH SURFACE   No, you must never make it public.

SIR PETER   But then again—that the nephew of my old friend, Sir Oliver, should be the person to attempt such a wrong, hurts me more nearly.

JOSEPH SURFACE   Aye, there's the point. When ingratitude barbs the dart of injury, the wound has double danger in it.

SIR PETER   Aye—I, that was, in a manner, left his guardian—in whose house he had been so often entertained—who never in my life denied him—my advice!

JOSEPH SURFACE   Oh, 'tis not to be credited! There *may* be a man capable of such baseness, to be sure; but, for my part, till you can give me positive proofs, I cannot but doubt it. However, if it should be proved on him, he is no longer a brother of mine! I disclaim kindred with him—for the man who can break through the laws of hospitality, and attempt the wife of his friend, deserves to be branded as the pest of society.

SIR PETER   What a difference there is between you! What noble sentiments!

JOSEPH SURFACE   Yet I cannot suspect Lady Teazle's honor.

SIR PETER   I am sure I wish to think well of her, and to remove all ground of quarrel between us. She has lately reproached me more than once with having made no settlement on her; and, in our last quarrel, she almost hinted that she should not break her heart if I was dead. Now, as we seem to differ in our ideas of expense, I have resolved she shall be her own mistress in that respect for the future; and if I *were* to die, she shall find that I have not been inattentive to her interest while living. Here, my friend, are the drafts of two deeds, which I wish to have your opinion on. By one, she will enjoy eight hundred a year independent while I live; and, by the other, the bulk of my fortune after my death.

JOSEPH SURFACE   This conduct, Sir Peter, is indeed truly generous.— [*Aside.*] I wish it may not corrupt my pupil.

SIR PETER   Yes, I am determined she shall have no cause to complain, though I would not have her acquainted with the latter instance of my affection yet awhile.

JOSEPH SURFACE   Nor I, if I could help it. [*Aside.*]

SIR PETER   And now, my dear friend, if you please, we will talk over the situation of your hopes with *Maria.*

JOSEPH SURFACE   [*Softly.*]   No, no, Sir Peter; another time, if you please.

SIR PETER   I am sensibly chagrined at the little progress you seem to make in her affection.

JOSEPH SURFACE   I beg you will not mention it. What are my disappointments when your happiness is in debate! [*Softly.*]—'Sdeath, I shall be ruined every way! [*Aside.*]

SIR PETER   And though you are so averse to my acquainting Lady Teazle with your passion, I am sure she's not your enemy in the affair.

JOSEPH SURFACE   Pray, Sir Peter, now oblige me. I am really too much affected by the subject we have been speaking on to bestow a thought on my own concerns. The man who is entrusted with his friend's distresses can never——

Enter SERVANT.

Well, sir?

SERVANT   Your brother, sir, is speaking to a gentleman in the street, and says he knows you are within.

JOSEPH SURFACE   'Sdeath, blockhead—I'm not within—I'm out for the day.

SIR PETER   Stay—hold—a thought has struck me—you shall be at home.

JOSEPH SURFACE   Well, well, let him up.

Exit SERVANT.

He'll interrupt Sir Peter—however—

SIR PETER   Now, my good friend, oblige me, I entreat you. Before Charles comes, let me conceal myself somewhere; then do you tax him on the point we have been talking on, and his answers may satisfy me at once.

JOSEPH SURFACE   O, fie, Sir Peter! would you have me join in so mean a trick?—to trepan[9] my brother too?

SIR PETER   Nay, you tell me you are *sure* he is innocent; if so, you do him the greatest service by giving him an opportunity to clear himself, and you will set my heart at rest. Come, you shall not refuse me; here, behind the screen will be [*Goes to the screen.*]—Hey! what the devil! there seems to be *one* listener here already—I'll swear I saw a petticoat!

JOSEPH SURFACE   Ha! ha! ha! Well, this is ridiculous enough. I'll tell you, Sir Peter, though I hold a man of intrigue to be a most despicable character, yet you know, it doesn't follow that one is to be an absolute Joseph[1] either! Hark'ee! 'tis a little French milliner, a silly rogue that plagues me—and having some character—on your coming, she ran behind the screen.

SIR PETER   Ah, you rogue!—But, egad, she has overheard all I have been saying of my wife.

JOSEPH SURFACE   Oh, 'twill never go any further, you may depend on't!

9. Entrap.
1. I.e., one who refuses all opportunities with women. In Genesis 39.7–20, Joseph refuses the adulterous invitations of Potiphar's wife.

SIR PETER   No! then, i'faith, let her hear it out.— Here's a closet will
do as well.

JOSEPH SURFACE   Well, go in then.

SIR PETER   Sly rogue! sly rogue!

Goes into the closet.

JOSEPH SURFACE   A very narrow escape, indeed! and a curious situation
I'm in, to part man and wife in this manner.

LADY TEAZLE [*Peeping from the screen.*]   Couldn't I steal off?

JOSEPH SURFACE   Keep close, my angel!

SIR PETER [*Peeping out.*]   Joseph, tax him home.

JOSEPH SURFACE   Back, my dear friend!

LADY TEAZLE [*Peeping.*]   Couldn't you lock Sir Peter in?

JOSEPH SURFACE   Be still, my life!

SIR PETER [*Peeping.*]   You're sure the little milliner won't blab?

JOSEPH SURFACE   In, in, my dear Sir Peter!—'Fore gad, I wish I had a
key to the door.

Enter CHARLES SURFACE.

CHARLES   Hollo! brother, what has been the matter? Your fellow would
not let me up at first. What! have you had a Jew or a wench with you?

JOSEPH SURFACE   Neither, brother, I assure you.

CHARLES   But what has made Sir Peter steal off? I thought he had been
with you.

JOSEPH SURFACE   He was, brother; but, hearing *you* were coming, he
did not choose to stay.

CHARLES   What! was the old gentleman afraid I wanted to borrow
money of him!

JOSEPH SURFACE   No, sir, but I am sorry to find, Charles, that you have
lately given that worthy man grounds for great uneasiness.

CHARLES   Yes, they tell me I do that to a great many worthy men. But
how so, pray?

JOSEPH SURFACE   To be plain with you, brother, he thinks you are
endeavoring to gain Lady Teazle's affections from him.

CHARLES   Who, I? O lud! not I, upon my word. —Ha! ha! ha! so the
old fellow has found out that he has got a young wife, has he?—or,
what's worse, has her ladyship discovered that she has an old husband?

JOSEPH SURFACE   This is no subject to jest on, brother.—He who can
laugh——

CHARLES   True, true, as you were going to say—then, seriously, I never
had the least idea of what you charge me with, upon my honor.

JOSEPH SURFACE   Well, it will give Sir Peter great satisfaction to hear
this. [*Aloud.*]

CHARLES   To be sure, I once thought the lady seemed to have taken a
fancy to me; but, upon my soul, I never gave her the least encouragement. Besides, you know my attachment to Maria.

JOSEPH SURFACE   But sure, brother, even if Lady Teazle had betrayed the fondest partiality for you——

CHARLES   Why, look'ee, Joseph, I hope I shall never deliberately do a dishonorable action—but if a pretty woman were purposely to throw herself in my way—and that pretty woman married to a man old enough to be her father——

JOSEPH SURFACE   Well!

CHARLES   Why, I believe I should be obliged to borrow a little of your morality, that's all.—But, brother, do you know now that you surprise me exceedingly, by naming *me* with Lady Teazle; for, faith, I alway[s] understood *you* were her favorite.

JOSEPH SURFACE   Oh, for shame, Charles! This retort is foolish.

CHARLES   Nay, I swear I have seen you exchange such significant glances——

JOSEPH SURFACE   Nay, nay, sir, this is no jest——

CHARLES   Egad, I'm serious! Don't you remember—one day, when I called here——

JOSEPH SURFACE   Nay, prithee, Charles——

CHARLES   And found you together——

JOSEPH SURFACE   Zounds, sir, I insist——

CHARLES   And another time, when your servant——

JOSEPH SURFACE   Brother, brother, a word with you!— [*Aside.*] Gad, I must stop him.

CHARLES   Informed me, I say, that——

JOSEPH SURFACE   Hush! I beg your pardon, but Sir Peter has overheard all we have been saying—I knew you would clear yourself, or I should not have consented.

CHARLES   How, Sir Peter! Where is he?

JOSEPH SURFACE   Softly, there! [*Points to the closet.*]

CHARLES   Oh, 'fore heaven, I'll have him out.—Sir Peter, come forth!

JOSEPH SURFACE   No, no——

CHARLES   I say, Sir Peter, come into court.—[*Pulls in* SIR PETER.] What! my old guardian!—What—turn inquisitor, and take evidence, incog.?[2]

SIR PETER   Give me your hand, Charles—I believe I have suspected you wrongfully—but you mustn't be angry with Joseph—'twas my plan!

CHARLES   Indeed!

SIR PETER   But I acquit you. I promise you I don't think near so ill of you as I did. What I have heard has given me great satisfaction.

CHARLES   Egad, then, 'twas lucky you didn't hear any more. Wasn't it, Joseph? [*Half aside.*]

SIR PETER   Ah! you would have retorted on him.

CHARLES   Aye, aye, that was a joke.

SIR PETER   Yes, yes, I know his honor too well.

2. Incognito.

CHARLES   But you might as well have suspected him as me in this matter, for all that. Mightn't he, Joseph? [*Half aside.*]

SIR PETER   Well, well, I believe you.

JOSEPH SURFACE [*Aside.*]   Would they were both out of the room!

SIR PETER   And in future, perhaps, we may not be such strangers.

Enter SERVANT *who whispers* JOSEPH SURFACE.

JOSEPH SURFACE   Lady Sneerwell!—stop her by all means—[*Exit* SERVANT.] Gentlemen—I beg pardon—I must wait on you downstairs—here's a person come on particular business.

CHARLES   Well, you can see him in another room. Sir Peter and I haven't met a long time, and I have something to say to him.

JOSEPH SURFACE   They must not be left together.—I'll send Lady Sneerwell away, and return directly.—[*Aside.*] Sir Peter, not a word of the French milliner.

Exit JOSEPH SURFACE.

SIR PETER   Oh! not for the world!—Ah, Charles, if you associated more with your brother, one might indeed hope for your reformation. He is a man of sentiment.—Well, there is nothing in the world so noble as a man of sentiment!

CHARLES   Pshaw! he is too moral by half, and so apprehensive of his good name, as he calls it, that I suppose he would as soon let a priest into his house as a girl.

SIR PETER   No, no,—come, come,—you wrong him. No, no, Joseph is no rake, but he is not such a saint in that respect either,—I have a great mind to tell him—we should have a laugh! [*Aside.*]

CHARLES   Oh, hang him! he's a very anchorite, a young hermit!

SIR PETER   Hark'ee—you must not abuse him; he may chance to hear of it again, I promise you.

CHARLES   Why, you won't tell him?

SIR PETER   No—but—this way.—[*Aside.*] Egad, I'll tell him.—Hark'ee, have you a mind to have a good laugh at Joseph?

CHARLES   I should like it of all things.

SIR PETER   Then, i'faith, we will!—I'll be quit with him for discovering me. [*Aside.*]—He had a girl with him when I called.

CHARLES   What! Joseph? you jest.

SIR PETER   Hush!—a little—French milliner—[*whispers*] and the best of the jest is—she's in the room now.

CHARLES   The devil she is!

SIR PETER   Hush! I tell you. [*Points to the screen.*]

CHARLES   Behind the screen! 'Slife, let's unveil her!

SIR PETER   No, no, he's coming:—you shan't, indeed!

CHARLES   Oh, egad, we'll have a peep at the little milliner!

SIR PETER   Not for the world!—Joseph will never forgive me.

CHARLES   I'll stand by you——

SIR PETER [*Struggling with* CHARLES.]   Odds, here he is!

JOSEPH SURFACE *enters just as* CHARLES *throws down the screen.*

CHARLES   Lady Teazle, by all that's wonderful!

SIR PETER   Lady Teazle, by all that's horrible!

CHARLES   Sir Peter, this is one of the smartest French milliners I ever saw. Egad, you seem all to have been diverting yourselves here at hide and seek—and I don't see who is out of the secret. Shall I beg your ladyship to inform me?—Not a word!—Brother, will you please to explain this matter? What! Morality dumb too!—Sir Peter, though I *found* you in the dark, perhaps you are not so now! All mute! Well—though *I* can make nothing of the affair, I suppose you perfectly understand one another; so I'll leave you to yourselves.—[*Going.*] Brother, I'm sorry to find you *have given that worthy man so much uneasiness,*—Sir Peter! there's nothing *in the world* so *noble as a man of sentiment!*

Exit CHARLES.

They stand for some time looking at each other.

JOSEPH SURFACE   Sir Peter—notwithstanding I confess that appearances are against me—if you will afford me your patience—I make no doubt but I shall explain everything to your satisfaction.

SIR PETER   If you please—

JOSEPH SURFACE   The fact is, sir, Lady Teazle, knowing my pretensions to your ward Maria—I say, sir, Lady Teazle, being apprehensive of the jealousy of your temper—and knowing my friendship to the family—she, sir, I say—called here—in order that—I might explain those pretensions—but on your coming—being apprehensive—as I said—of your jealousy—she withdrew—and this, you may depend on't is the whole truth of the matter.

SIR PETER   A very clear account, upon my word; and I dare swear the lady will vouch for every article of it.

LADY TEAZLE [*Coming forward.*]   For not one word of it, Sir Peter!

SIR PETER   How! don't you think it worth while to agree in the lie?

LADY TEAZLE   There is not one syllable of truth in what the gentleman has told you.

SIR PETER   I believe you, upon my soul, ma'am!

JOSEPH SURFACE [*Aside.*]   'Sdeath, madam, will you betray me?

LADY TEAZLE   Good Mr. Hypocrite, by your leave, I will speak for myself.

SIR PETER   Aye, let her alone, sir; you'll find she'll make out a better story than *you*, without prompting.

LADY TEAZLE   Hear me, Sir Peter!—I came here on no matter relating to your ward, and even ignorant of this gentleman's pretensions to her—but I came, seduced by his insidious arguments, at least to listen to his pretended passion, if not to sacrifice *your* honor to his baseness.

SIR PETER   Now, I believe, the truth *is* coming, indeed!

JOSEPH SURFACE   The woman's mad!

LADY TEAZLE   No sir; she has recovered her senses, and your own arts have furnished her with the means.—Sir Peter, I do not expect you to credit me—but the tenderness you expressed for me, when I am sure you could not think I was a witness to it, has penetrated to my heart, and had I left the place without the shame of this discovery, my future life should have spoke[n] the sincerity of my gratitude. As for that smooth-tongue hypocrite, who would have seduced the wife of his too credulous friend, while he affected honorable addresses to his ward—I behold him now in a light so truly despicable, that I shall never again respect myself for having listened to him.

Exit.

JOSEPH   SURFACE   Notwithstanding   all   this,   Sir   Peter,   heaven knows— —

SIR PETER   That you are a villain!—and so I leave you to your conscience.

JOSEPH SURFACE   You are too rash, Sir Peter; you shall hear me. The man who shuts out conviction by refusing to——

SIR PETER   Oh!—

Exeunt, JOSEPH SURFACE *following and speaking.*

Act V. Scene i.

The library [*in* JOSEPH SURFACE'*s house.*]
Enter JOSEPH SURFACE *and* SERVANT.

JOSEPH SURFACE   Mr. Stanley! why should you think I would see him? you *must* know he comes to ask something.

SERVANT   Sir, I should not have let him in, but that Mr. Rowley came to the door with him.

JOSEPH SURFACE   Pshaw! blockhead! to suppose that I should *now* be in a temper to receive visits from poor relations!—Well, why don't you show the fellow up?

SERVANT   I will, sir.—Why, sir, it was not my fault that Sir Peter discovered my lady——

JOSEPH SURFACE   Go, fool!

Exit SERVANT.

Sure, Fortune never played a man of my policy such a trick before! My character with Sir Peter, my hopes with Maria, destroyed in a moment! I'm in a rare humour to listen to other people's distresses! I shan't be able to bestow even a benevolent sentiment on Stanley.— So! here he comes, and Rowley with him. I must try to recover myself—and put a little charity into my face, however.

Exit.

Enter SIR OLIVER SURFACE *and* ROWLEY.

SIR OLIVER   What! does he avoid us? That was he, was it not?

ROWLEY   It was, sir—but I doubt you are come a little too abruptly—his nerves are so weak, that the sight of a poor relation may be too much for him.—I should have gone first to break you to him.

SIR OLIVER   A plague of his nerves!—Yet this is he whom Sir Peter extols as a man of the most benevolent way of thinking!

ROWLEY   As to his way of thinking, I cannot pretend to decide; for, to do him justice, he appears to have as much speculative benevolence as any private gentleman in the kingdom, though he is seldom so sensual as to indulge himself in the exercise of it.

SIR OLIVER   Yet has a string of charitable sentiments, I suppose, at his fingers' ends!

ROWLEY   Or, rather, at his tongue's end, Sir Oliver; for I believe there is no sentiment he has more faith in than that "Charity begins at home."

SIR OLIVER   And his, I presume, is of that domestic sort which never stirs abroad at all.

ROWLEY   I doubt you'll find it so;—but he's coming—I mustn't seem to interrupt you; and you know, immediately as you leave him, I come in to announce your arrival in your real character.

SIR OLIVER   True; and afterwards you'll meet me at Sir Peter's.

ROWLEY   Without losing a moment.

Exit ROWLEY.

SIR OLIVER   So! I don't like the complaisance of his features.

Re-enter JOSEPH SURFACE.

JOSEPH SURFACE   Sir, I beg you ten thousand pardons for keeping you a moment waiting—Mr. Stanley, I presume.

SIR OLIVER   At your service.

JOSEPH SURFACE   Sir, I beg you will do me the honor to sit down—I entreat you, sir.

SIR OLIVER   Dear sir—there's no occasion.—Too civil by half! [*Aside.*]

JOSEPH SURFACE   I have not the pleasure of knowing you, Mr. Stanley; but I am extremely happy to see you look so well. You were nearly related to my mother, I think, Mr. Stanley?

SIR OLIVER   I was, sir—so nearly that my present poverty, I fear, may do discredit to her wealthy children—else I should not have presumed to trouble you.

JOSEPH SURFACE   Dear sir, there needs no apology: he that is in distress, though a stranger, has a right to claim kindred with the wealthy;—I am sure I wish *I* was one of that class, and had it in my power to offer you even a small relief.

SIR OLIVER   If your uncle, Sir Oliver, were here, I should have a friend.

JOSEPH SURFACE   I wish he were, sir, with all my heart: you should not want an advocate with him, believe me, sir.

SIR OLIVER   I should not *need* one—my distresses would recommend me; but I imagined his bounty had enabled *you* to become the agent of his charity.

JOSEPH SURFACE   My dear sir, you were strangely misinformed. Sir Oliver is a worthy man, a very worthy sort of man; but—avarice, Mr. Stanley, is the vice of age. I will tell you, my good sir, in confidence, what he has done for me has been a mere nothing; though people, I know, have thought otherwise, and, for my part, I never chose to contradict the report.

SIR OLIVER   What! has he never transmitted you bullion! rupees! pagodas!³

JOSEPH SURFACE   O dear sir, nothing of the kind! No, no; a few presents now and then—china—shawls—Congo tea—avadavats⁴ and India crackers⁵—little more, believe me.

SIR OLIVER [*Aside.*]   Here's gratitude for twelve thousand pounds! — Avadavats and Indian crackers!

JOSEPH SURFACE   Then, my dear sir, you have heard, I doubt not, of the extravagance of my brother; there are very few would credit what I have done for that unfortunate young man.

SIR OLIVER   Not I, for one! [*Aside.*]

JOSEPH SURFACE   The sums I have lent him! Indeed I have been exceedingly to blame—it was an amiable weakness: however, I don't pretend to defend it—and now I feel it doubly culpable, since it has deprived me of the pleasure of serving *you*, Mr. Stanley, as my heart dictates.

SIR OLIVER [*Aside.*]   Dissembler!—Then, sir, you cannot assist me?

JOSEPH SURFACE   At present, it grieves me to say, I cannot; but, whenever I have the ability, you may depend upon hearing from me.

SIR OLIVER   I am extremely sorry——

JOSEPH SURFACE   Not more than I am, believe me; to pity, without the power to relieve, is still more painful than to ask and be denied.

SIR OLIVER   Kind sir, your most obedient humble servant.

JOSEPH SURFACE   You leave me deeply affected, Mr. Stanley.—William, be ready to open the door.

SIR OLIVER   O dear sir, no ceremony.

JOSEPH SURFACE   Your very obedient.

SIR OLIVER   Sir, your most obsequious.

JOSEPH SURFACE   You may depend upon hearing from me, whenever I can be of service.

SIR OLIVER   Sweet sir, you are too good.

JOSEPH SURFACE   In the meantime I wish you health and spirits.

3. Rupees and pagodas: Indian coins.
4. Small Indian songbirds.
5. Firecrackers.

SIR OLIVER   Your ever grateful and perpetual humble servant.
JOSEPH SURFACE   Sir, yours as sincerely.
SIR OLIVER   Now I am satisfied!

Exit.

JOSEPH SURFACE [*Solus.*]   This is one bad effect of a good character; it invites applications from the unfortunate, and there needs no small degree of address to gain the reputation of benevolence without incurring the expense. The silver one of pure charity is an expensive article in the catalogue of a man's good qualities; whereas the sentimental French plate I use instead of it makes just as good a show, and pays no tax.

Enter ROWLEY.

ROWLEY   Mr. Surface, your servant—I was apprehensive of interrupting you—though my business demands immediate attention—as this note will inform you.
JOSEPH SURFACE   Always happy to see Mr. Rowley.—[*Reads.*] How! "*Oliver—Surface*"—My uncle arrived!
ROWLEY   He is, indeed—we have just parted—quite well, after a speedy voyage, and impatient to embrace his worthy nephew.
JOSEPH SURFACE   I am astonished!—William! stop Mr. Stanley, if he's not gone.
ROWLEY   Oh! he's out of reach, I believe.
JOSEPH SURFACE   Why didn't you let me know this when you came in together?
ROWLEY   I thought you had particular business. But I must be gone to inform your brother, and appoint him here to meet his uncle. He will be with you in a quarter of an hour.
JOSEPH SURFACE   So he says. Well, I am strangely overjoyed at his coming.—[*Aside.*] Never, to be sure, was anything so damned unlucky!
ROWLEY   You will be delighted to see how well he looks.
JOSEPH SURFACE   Oh! I'm rejoiced to hear it.—[*Aside.*] Just at this time!
ROWLEY   I'll tell him how impatiently you expect him.
JOSEPH SURFACE   Do, do; pray give my best duty and affection. Indeed, I cannot express the sensations I feel at the thought of seeing him.— [*Exit* ROWLEY.] Certainly his coming just at this time is the cruellest piece of ill fortune.

Exit.

Act V. Scene ii.

At SIR PETER'S.
Enter MRS. CANDOUR *and* MAID.

MAID   Indeed, ma'am, my lady will see nobody at present.
MRS. CANDOUR   Did you tell her it was her friend Mrs. Candour?

MAID   Yes, madam; but she begs you will excuse her.

MRS. CANDOUR   Do go again; I shall be glad to see her, if it be only for a moment, for I am sure she must be in great distress. —

Exit MAID.

Dear heart, how provoking; I'm not mistress of half the circumstances! We shall have the whole affair in the newspapers, with the names of the parties at length, before I have dropped the story at a dozen houses.

Enter SIR BENJAMIN BACKBITE.

O dear Sir Benjamin! you have heard, I suppose——

SIR BENJAMIN   Of Lady Teazle and Mr. Surface——

MRS. CANDOUR   And Sir Peter's discovery——

SIR BENJAMIN   Oh, the strangest piece of business, to be sure!

MRS. CANDOUR   Well, I never was so surprised in my life. I am so sorry for all parties, indeed I am.

SIR BENJAMIN   Now, I don't pity Sir Peter at all—he was so extravagantly partial to Mr. Surface.

MRS. CANDOUR   Mr. Surface! Why, 'twas with Charles Lady Teazle was detected.

SIR BENJAMIN   No such thing—Mr. Surface is the gallant.

MRS. CANDOUR   No, no—Charles is the man. 'Twas Mr. Surface brought Sir Peter on purpose to discover them.

SIR BENJAMIN   I tell you I have it from one——

MRS. CANDOUR   And I have it from one——

SIR BENJAMIN   Who had it from one, who had it——

MRS. CANDOUR   From one immediately—— But here's Lady Sneerwell; perhaps she knows the whole affair.

Enter LADY SNEERWELL.

LADY SNEERWELL   So, my dear Mrs. Candour, here's a sad affair of our friend Lady Teazle!

MRS. CANDOUR   Aye, my dear friend, who could have thought it——

LADY SNEERWELL   Well, there's no trusting appearances; though, indeed, she was always too lively for me.

MRS. CANDOUR   To be sure, her manners were a little too free—but she was very young!

LADY SNEERWELL   And had, indeed, some good qualities.

MRS. CANDOUR   So she had, indeed. But have you heard the particulars?

LADY SNEERWELL   No; but everybody says that Mr. Surface——

SIR BENJAMIN   Aye, there, I told you—Mr. Surface was the man.

MRS. CANDOUR   No, no, indeed—the assignation was with Charles.

LADY SNEERWELL   With Charles! You alarm me, Mrs. Candour.

MRS. CANDOUR   Yes, yes, he was the lover. Mr. Surface—do him justice—was only the informer.

SIR BENJAMIN   Well, I'll not dispute with you, Mrs. Candour; but, be it which it may, I hope that Sir Peter's wound will not——

MRS. CANDOUR   Sir Peter's wound! Oh, mercy! I didn't hear a word of their fighting.

LADY SNEERWELL   Nor I, a syllable.

SIR BENJAMIN   No! what, no mention of the duel?

MRS. CANDOUR   Not a word.

SIR BENJAMIN   O Lord—yes, yes—they fought before they left the room.

LADY SNEERWELL   Pray let us hear.

MRS. CANDOUR   Aye, do oblige us with the duel.

SIR BENJAMIN   "Sir," says Sir Peter—immediately after the discovery—"you are a most ungrateful fellow."

MRS. CANDOUR   Aye, to Charles——

SIR BENJAMIN   No, no—to Mr. Surface—"a most ungrateful fellow; and old as I am, sir," says he, "I insist on immediate satisfaction."

MRS. CANDOUR   Aye, that must have been to Charles; for 'tis very unlikely Mr. Surface should go to fight in his house.

SIR BENJAMIN   'Gad's life, ma'am, not at all—"giving me immediate satisfaction."—On this, madam, Lady Teazle, seeing Sir Peter in such danger, ran out of the room in strong hysterics, and Charles after her, calling out for hartshorn[6] and water! Then, madam, they began to fight with swords——

Enter CRABTREE.

CRABTREE   With pistols, nephew—I have it from undoubted authority.

MRS. CANDOUR   O Mr. Crabtree, then it is all true!

CRABTREE   Too true, indeed, ma'am, and Sir Peter's dangerously wounded——

SIR BENJAMIN   By a thrust of *in seconde*[7] quite through his left side——

CRABTREE   By a bullet lodged in the thorax.

MRS. CANDOUR   Mercy on me! Poor Sir Peter!

CRABTREE   Yes, ma'am—though Charles would have avoided the matter, if he could.

MRS. CANDOUR   I knew Charles was the person.

SIR BENJAMIN   Oh, my uncle, I see, knows nothing of the matter.

CRABTREE   But Sir Peter taxed him with the basest ingratitude——

SIR BENJAMIN   That I told you, you know.

CRABTREE   Do, nephew, let me speak!—and insisted on an immediate——

SIR BENJAMIN   Just as I said.

CRABTREE   Odds life, nephew, allow others to know something too! A pair of pistols lay on the bureau (for Mr. Surface, it seems, had come the night before late from Salt-Hill, where he had been to see the

6. Smelling-salts.
7. A standard position in fencing.

Montem[8] with a friend, who has a son at Eton), so, unluckily, the pistols were left charged.

SIR BENJAMIN   I heard nothing of this.

CRABTREE   Sir Peter forced Charles to take one, and they fired, it seems, pretty nearly together. Charles's shot took place, as I told you, and Sir Peter's missed; but, what is very extraordinary, the ball struck against a little bronze Pliny that stood over the chimney-piece, grazed out of the window at a right angle, and wounded the postman, who was just coming to the door with a double letter from Northamptonshire.

SIR BENJAMIN   My uncle's account is more circumstantial, I must confess; but I believe mine is the true one, for all that.

LADY SNEERWELL   [Aside.]   I am more interested in this affair than they imagine, and must have better information.

                                                            Exit LADY SNEERWELL.

SIR BENJAMIN   [After a pause looking at each other.]   Ah! Lady Sneerwell's alarm is very easily accounted for.

CRABTREE   Yes, yes, they certainly do say—but that's neither here nor there.

MRS. CANDOUR   But, pray, where is Sir Peter at present?

CRABTREE   Oh! they brought him home, and he is now in the house, though the servants are ordered to deny it.

MRS. CANDOUR   I believe so, and Lady Teazle, I suppose, attending him.

CRABTREE   Yes, yes; I saw one of the faculty[9] enter just before me.

SIR BENJAMIN   Hey! who comes here?

CRABTREE   Oh, this is he—the physician, depend on't.

MRS. CANDOUR   Oh, certainly! it must be the physician; and now we shall know.

        Enter SIR OLIVER SURFACE.

CRABTREE   Well, doctor, what hopes?

MRS. CANDOUR   Aye, doctor, how's your patient?

SIR BENJAMIN   Now, doctor, isn't it a wound with a small-sword?

CRABTREE   A bullet lodged in the thorax, for a hundred!

SIR OLIVER   Doctor! a wound with a small-sword! and a bullet in the thorax?—Oons! are you mad, good people?

SIR BENJAMIN   Perhaps, sir, you are not a doctor?

SIR OLIVER   Truly, I am to thank you for my degree, if I am.

CRABTREE   Only a friend of Sir Peter's, then, I presume. But, sir, you must have heard of this accident?

SIR OLIVER   Not a word!

CRABTREE   Not of his being dangerously wounded?

SIR OLIVER   The devil he is!

8. An annual festival by the students of Eton College.
9. A physician.

SIR BENJAMIN   Run through the body——
CRABTREE   Shot in the breast——
SIR BENJAMIN   By one Mr. Surface——
CRABTREE   Aye, the younger.
SIR OLIVER   Hey! what the plague! you seem to differ strangely in your accounts—however, you agree that Sir Peter is dangerously wounded.
SIR BENJAMIN   Oh, yes, we agree there.
CRABTREE   Yes, yes, I believe there can be no doubt of that.
SIR OLIVER   Then, upon my word, for a person in that situation, he is the most imprudent man alive—for here he comes, walking as if nothing at all were the matter.

Enter SIR PETER TEAZLE.

Odds heart, Sir Peter! you are come in good time, I promise you; for we had just *given you over.*
SIR BENJAMIN   Egad, uncle, this is the most sudden recovery!
SIR OLIVER   Why, man! what do you do out of bed with a small-sword through your body, and a bullet lodged in your thorax?
SIR PETER   A small-sword and a bullet?
SIR OLIVER   Aye; these gentlemen would have killed you without law or physic, and wanted to dub me a doctor—to make me an accomplice.
SIR PETER   Why, what is all this?
SIR BENJAMIN   We rejoice, Sir Peter, that the story of the duel is not true, and are sincerely sorry for your other misfortunes.
SIR PETER   So, so; all over the town already. [*Aside.*]
CRABTREE   Though, Sir Peter, you were certainly vastly to blame to marry at all, at your years.
SIR PETER   Sir, what business is that of yours?
MRS. CANDOUR   Though, indeed, as Sir Peter made so good a husband, he's very much to be pitied.
SIR PETER   Plague on your pity, ma'am! I desire none of it.
SIR BENJAMIN   However, Sir Peter, you must not mind the laughing and jests you will meet with on this occasion.
SIR PETER   Sir, I desire to be master in my own house.
CRABTREE   'Tis no uncommon case, that's one comfort.
SIR PETER   I insist on being left to myself: without ceremony, I insist on your leaving my house directly!
MRS. CANDOUR   Well, well, we are going; and depend on't, we'll make the best report of you we can.
SIR PETER   Leave my house!
CRABTREE   And tell how hardly you have been treated.
SIR PETER   Leave my house!
SIR BENJAMIN   And how patiently you bear it.
SIR PETER   Fiends! vipers! furies! Oh! that their own venom would choke them!

Exeunt MRS. CANDOUR, SIR BENJAMIN BACKBITE, CRABTREE, &c.

SIR OLIVER   They are very provoking indeed, Sir Peter.

Enter ROWLEY.

ROWLEY   I heard high words—what has ruffled you, Sir Peter?

SIR PETER   Pshaw! what signifies asking? Do I ever pass a day without my vexations?

SIR OLIVER   Well, I'm not inquisitive—I come only to tell you that I have seen both my nephews in the manner we proposed.

SIR PETER   A precious couple they are!

ROWLEY   Yes, and Sir Oliver is convinced that your judgment was right, Sir Peter.

SIR OLIVER   Yes, I find *Joseph* is indeed the man, after all.

ROWLEY   Yes, as Sir Peter says, he's a man of sentiment.

SIR OLIVER   And acts up to the sentiments he professes.

ROWLEY   It certainly is edification to hear him talk.

SIR OLIVER   Oh, he's a model for the young men of the age! But how's this, Sir Peter? you don't join in your friend Joseph's praise, as I expected.

SIR PETER   Sir Oliver, we live in a damned wicked world, and the fewer we praise the better.

ROWLEY   What! do *you* say so, Sir Peter, who were never mistaken in your life?

SIR PETER   Pshaw! plague on you both! I see by your sneering you have heard the whole affair. I shall go mad among you!

ROWLEY   Then, to fret you no longer, Sir Peter, we are indeed acquainted with it all. I met Lady Teazle coming from Mr. Surface's, so humbled that she deigned to request me to be her advocate with you.

SIR PETER   And does Sir Oliver know all too?

SIR OLIVER   Every circumstance.

SIR PETER   What, of the closet—and the screen, hey?

SIR OLIVER   Yes, yes, and the little French milliner. Oh, I have been vastly diverted with the story! ha! ha!

SIR PETER   'Twas very pleasant.

SIR OLIVER   I never laughed more in my life, I assure you: ha! ha!

SIR PETER   O, vastly diverting! ha! ha!

ROWLEY   To be sure, Joseph with his sentiments! ha! ha!

SIR PETER   Yes, yes, his sentiments! ha! ha! A hypocritical villain!

SIR OLIVER   Aye, and that rogue Charles to pull Sir Peter out of the closet: ha! ha!

SIR PETER   Ha! ha! 'twas devilish entertaining, to be sure!

SIR OLIVER   Ha! ha! Egad, Sir Peter, I should like to have seen your face when the screen was thrown down: ha! ha!

SIR PETER   Yes, yes, my face when the screen was thrown down: ha! ha! Oh, I must never show my head again!

SIR OLIVER   But come, come, it isn't fair to laugh at you neither, my old friend—though, upon my soul, I can't help it.

SIR PETER   Oh, pray don't restrain your mirth on my account—it does not hurt me at all! I laugh at the whole affair myself. Yes, yes, I think being a standing jest for all one's acquaintances a very happy situation. O yes, and then of a morning to read the paragraphs about Mr. S——, Lady T——, and Sir P——, will be so entertaining!

ROWLEY   Without affectation, Sir Peter, you may despise the ridicule of fools. But I see Lady Teazle going towards the next room; I am sure you must desire a reconciliation as earnestly as she does.

SIR OLIVER   Perhaps my being here prevents her coming to you. Well, I'll leave honest Rowley to mediate between you; but he must bring you all presently to Mr. Surface's, where I am now returning, if not to reclaim a libertine, at least to expose hypocrisy.

SIR PETER   Ah! I'll be present at your discovering yourself there with all my heart—though 'tis a vile unlucky place for discoveries!

ROWLEY   We'll follow.

[*Exit* SIR OLIVER SURFACE.]

SIR PETER   She is not coming here, you see, Rowley.

ROWLEY   No, but she has left the door of that room open, you perceive. See, she is in tears!

SIR PETER   Certainly a little mortification appears very becoming in a wife! Don't you think it will do her good to let her pine a little?

ROWLEY   Oh, this is ungenerous in you!

SIR PETER   Well, I know not what to think. You remember, Rowley, the letter I found of hers, evidently intended for Charles!

ROWLEY   A mere forgery, Sir Peter! laid in your way on purpose. This is one of the points which I intend *Snake* shall give you conviction on.

SIR PETER   I wish I were once satisfied of that. She looks this way. What a remarkably elegant turn of the head she has! Rowley, I'll go to her.

ROWLEY   Certainly.

SIR PETER   Though, when it is known that we are reconciled, people will laugh at me ten times more!

ROWLEY   Let them laugh, and retort their malice only by showing them you are happy in spite of it.

SIR PETER   I'faith, so I will! and, if I'm not mistaken, we may yet be the happiest couple in the country.

ROWLEY   Nay, Sir Peter—he who once lays aside suspicion——

SIR PETER   Hold, my dear Rowley! if you have any regard for me, never let me hear you utter anything like a sentiment—I have had enough of them to serve me the rest of my life.

Exeunt.

Act V. Scene iii.

The library [*in* JOSEPH SURFACE'S *house*].
JOSEPH SURFACE *and* LADY SNEERWELL.

LADY SNEERWELL   Impossible! Will not Sir Peter immediately be reconciled to Charles, and of consequence no longer oppose his union with Maria? The thought is distraction to me!

JOSEPH SURFACE   Can passion furnish a remedy?

LADY SNEERWELL   No, nor cunning either. Oh, I was a fool, an idiot, to league with such a blunderer!

JOSEPH SURFACE   Sure, Lady Sneerwell, *I* am the greatest sufferer; yet you see I bear the accident with calmness.

LADY SNEERWELL   Because the disappointment doesn't reach your *heart*; your *interest* only attached you to Maria. Had you felt for *her* what *I* have for that ungrateful libertine, neither your temper nor hypocrisy could prevent your showing the sharpness of your vexation.

JOSEPH SURFACE   But why should your reproaches fall on *me* for this disappointment?

LADY SNEERWELL   Are you not the cause of it? What had you to do to bate in your pursuit of Maria to pervert Lady Teazle by the way? Had you not a sufficient field for your roguery in blinding Sir Peter, and supplanting your brother? I hate such an avarice of crimes; 'tis an unfair monopoly, and never prospers.

JOSEPH SURFACE   Well, I admit I have been to blame. I confess I deviated from the direct road of wrong, but I don't think we're so totally defeated neither.

LADY SNEERWELL   No!

JOSEPH SURFACE   You tell me you have made a trial of Snake since we met, and that you still believe him faithful to us—

LADY SNEERWELL   I do believe so.

JOSEPH SURFACE   And that he has undertaken, should it be necessary, to swear and prove that Charles is at this time contracted by vows and honor to your ladyship—which some of his former letters to you will serve to support?

LADY SNEERWELL   This, indeed, might have assisted.

JOSEPH SURFACE   Come, come; it is not too late yet.— [*Knocking at the door.*] But hark! this is probably my uncle, Sir Oliver: retire to that room; we'll consult farther when he's gone.

LADY SNEERWELL   Well! but if *he* should find you out too—

JOSEPH SURFACE   Oh, I have no fear of that. Sir Peter will hold his tongue for his own credit['s] sake—and you may depend on't I shall soon discover Sir Oliver's weak side!

LADY SNEERWELL   I have no diffidence[1] of your abilities—only be constant to one roguery at a time.

Exit.

JOSEPH SURFACE   I will, I will! So! 'tis confounded hard, after such bad fortune, to be baited by one's confederate in evil. Well, at all events, my character is so much better than Charles's, that I certainly—

---

1. Doubt.

hey!—what!—this is not *Sir Oliver,* but old *Stanley* again! Plague on't! that he should return to tease me just now! We shall have Sir Oliver come and find him here—and——

> *Enter* SIR OLIVER SURFACE.

Gad's life, Mr. Stanley, why have you come back to plague me just at this time? You must not stay now, upon my word.

SIR OLIVER　Sir, I hear your uncle Oliver is expected here, and though he has been so penurious to *you,* I'll try what he'll do for *me.*

JOSEPH SURFACE　Sir, 'tis impossible for you to stay now, so I must beg——Come any other time, and I promise you you shall be assisted.

SIR OLIVER　No: Sir Oliver and I must be acquainted.

JOSEPH SURFACE　Zounds, sir! then I insist on your quitting the room directly.

SIR OLIVER　Nay, sir!

JOSEPH SURFACE　Sir, I insist on't—Here, William! show this gentleman out. Since you compel me, sir—not one moment—this is such insolence!

> *Going to push him out.*
> *Enter* CHARLES SURFACE.

CHARLES　Heyday! what's the matter now? What the devil, have you got hold of my little broker here? Zounds, brother, don't hurt little Premium. What's the matter, my little fellow?

JOSEPH SURFACE　So! he has been with you, too, has he?

CHARLES　To be sure he has! Why, 'tis as honest a little—— But sure, Joseph, you have not been borrowing money too, have you?

JOSEPH SURFACE　Borrowing! no! But, brother, you know here we expect Sir Oliver every——

CHARLES　O gad, that's true! Noll mustn't find the little broker here to be sure.

JOSEPH SURFACE　Yet, Mr. *Stanley* insists——

CHARLES　Stanley! why his name is *Premium.*

JOSEPH SURFACE　No, no, *Stanley.*

CHARLES　No, no, *Premium.*

JOSEPH SURFACE　Well, no matter which—but—

CHARLES　Aye, aye, Stanley or Premium, 'tis the same thing, as you say; for I suppose he goes by half [a] hundred names, besides A.B.'s at the coffee-houses.[2]

JOSEPH SURFACE　Death! here's Sir Oliver at the door. [*Knocking again.*] Now I beg, Mr. Stanley——

CHARLES　Aye, and I beg, Mr. Premium——

SIR OLIVER　Gentlemen——

JOSEPH SURFACE　Sir, by heaven you shall go!

---

2. Moneylenders often met their clients under assumed names at coffeehouses.

CHARLES   Aye, out with him, certainly.

SIR OLIVER   This violence——

JOSEPH SURFACE   'Tis your own fault.

CHARLES   Out with him, to be sure.

Both forcing SIR OLIVER *out.*
Enter SIR PETER *and* LADY TEAZLE, MARIA, *and* ROWLEY.

SIR PETER   My old friend, Sir Oliver—hey! What in the name of wonder!—Here are dutiful nephews!—assault their uncle at the first visit!

LADY TEAZLE   Indeed, Sir Oliver, 'twas well we came in to rescue you.

ROWLEY   Truly it was; for I perceive, Sir Oliver, the character of old
Stanley was no protection to you.

SIR OLIVER   Nor of Premium either: the necessities of the *former* could
not extort a shilling from *that* benevolent gentleman; and now, egad,
I stood a chance of faring worse than my ancestors, and being
knocked down without being bid for.

After a pause, JOSEPH *and* CHARLES *turning to each other.*

JOSEPH SURFACE   Charles! [*Aside.*]

CHARLES   Joseph!

JOSEPH SURFACE   'Tis now complete!

CHARLES   Very!

SIR OLIVER   Sir Peter, my friend, and Rowley too—look on that elder
nephew of mine. You know what he has already received from my
bounty; and you know also how gladly I would have regarded half my
fortune as held in trust for him—judge, then, my disappointment in
discovering him to be destitute of truth—charity—and gratitude!

SIR PETER   Sir Oliver, I should be more surprised at this declaration, if
I had not myself found him selfish, treacherous, and hypocritical!

LADY TEAZLE   And if the gentleman pleads not guilty to these, pray let
him call *me* to his character.

SIR PETER   Then, I believe, we need add no more.—If he knows himself, he will consider it as the most perfect punishment that he is
known to the world.

CHARLES [*Aside.*]   If they talk this way to *Honesty*, what will they say to
me, by and by?

SIR PETER, LADY TEAZLE, *and* MARIA *retire.*

SIR OLIVER   As for that prodigal, his brother, there——

CHARLES [*Aside.*]   Aye, now comes my turn: the damned family pictures will ruin me!

JOSEPH SURFACE   Sir Oliver!—uncle!—will you honor me with a
hearing?

CHARLES [*Aside.*]   Now if Joseph would make one of his long speeches,
I might recollect myself a little.

SIR OLIVER [*to* JOSEPH SURFACE.]   I suppose you would undertake to
justify yourself entirely?

JOSEPH SURFACE   I trust I could.

SIR OLIVER   Pshaw!—Well, sir! and *you* [*to* CHARLES] could justify yourself too, I suppose?

CHARLES   Not that I know of, Sir Oliver.

SIR OLIVER   What!—Little Premium has been let too much into the secret, I presume?

CHARLES   True, sir; but they were family secrets, and should never be mentioned again, you know.

ROWLEY   Come, Sir Oliver, I know you cannot speak of Charles's follies with anger.

SIR OLIVER   Odd's heart, no more I can—nor with gravity either. Sir Peter, do you know the rogue bargained with me for all his ancestors—sold me judges and generals by the foot—and maiden aunts as cheap as broken china.

CHARLES   To be sure, Sir Oliver, I did make a little free with the family canvas, that's the truth on't. My ancestors may certainly rise in evidence against me, there's no denying it; but believe me sincere when I tell you—and upon my soul I would not say it if I was not—that if I do not appear mortified at the exposure of my follies, it is because I feel at this moment the warmest satisfaction in seeing you, my liberal benefactor.

SIR OLIVER   Charles, I believe you. Give me your hand again; the ill-looking little fellow over the settee has made your peace.

CHARLES   Then, sir, my gratitude to the original is still increased.

LADY TEAZLE   [*Pointing to* MARIA.]   Yet, I believe, Sir Oliver, here is one whom Charles is still more anxious to be reconciled to.

SIR OLIVER   Oh, I have heard of his attachment there; and, with the young lady's pardon, if I construe right—that blush——

SIR PETER   Well, child, speak your sentiments.

MARIA   Sir, I have little to say, but that I shall rejoice to hear that he is happy; for me, whatever claim I had to his affection, I willingly resign it to one who has a better title.

CHARLES   How, Maria!

SIR PETER   Heyday! what's the mystery now? While he appeared an incorrigible rake, you would give your hand to no one else; and now that he is likely to reform, I warrant you won't have him.

MARIA   His own heart—and Lady Sneerwell know the cause.

CHARLES   Lady Sneerwell!

JOSEPH SURFACE   Brother, it is with great concern I am obliged to speak on this point, but my regard to justice compels me, and Lady Sneerwell's injuries can no longer be concealed.

> *Goes to the door.*
> *Enter* LADY SNEERWELL.

SIR PETER   So! another French milliner!—Egad, he has one in every room in the house, I suppose!

LADY SNEERWELL   Ungrateful Charles! Well may you be surprised, and

feel for the indelicate situation which your perfidy has forced me
into.

CHARLES   Pray, uncle, is this another plot of yours? For, as I have life, I
don't understand it.

JOSEPH SURFACE   I believe, sir, there is but the evidence of one person
more necessary to make it extremely clear.

SIR PETER   And that person, I imagine, is Mr. Snake.—Rowley, you
were perfectly right to bring him with us, and pray let him appear.

ROWLEY   Walk in, Mr. Snake.

Enter SNAKE.

I thought his testimony might be wanted; however, it happens
unluckily, that he comes to confront Lady Sneerwell, and not to support her.

LADY SNEERWELL   Villain! Treacherous to me at last! [*Aside.*]—Speak,
fellow, have *you* too conspired against me?

SNAKE   I beg your ladyship ten thousand pardons: you paid me
extremely liberally for the lie in question; but I have unfortunately
been offered double to speak the truth.

SIR PETER   Plot and counterplot, egad—I wish your ladyship joy of the
success of your negotiation.

LADY SNEERWELL   The torments of shame and disappointment on you
all!

LADY TEAZLE   Hold, Lady Sneerwell—before you go, let me thank you
for the trouble you and that gentleman have taken, in writing letters
to me from Charles, and answering them yourself; and let me also
request you to make my respects to the Scandalous College, of which
you are president, and inform them, that Lady Teazle, licentiate,[3]
begs leave to return the diploma they granted her, as she leaves off
practice, and kills characters no longer.

LADY SNEERWELL   You too, madam!—provoking—insolent! May your
husband live these fifty years!

Exit.

SIR PETER   Oons! what a fury!

LADY TEAZLE   A malicious creature, indeed!

SIR PETER   Hey! not for her last wish?

LADY TEAZLE   Oh, no!

SIR OLIVER   Well, sir, and what have you to say now?

JOSEPH SURFACE   Sir, I am so confounded, to find that Lady *Sneerwell*
could be guilty of suborning Mr. *Snake* in this manner, to impose on
us all, that I know not what to say; however, lest her revengeful spirit
should prompt her to injure my brother, I had certainly better follow
her directly.

Exit

3. Holder of a diploma.

SIR PETER   Moral to the last drop!

SIR OLIVER   Aye, and marry her, Joseph, if you can.—Oil and vinegar, egad! you'll do very well together.

ROWLEY   I believe we have no more occasion for Mr. Snake at present.

SNAKE   Before I go, I beg pardon once for all, for whatever uneasiness I have been the humble instrument of causing to the parties present.

SIR PETER   Well, well, you have made atonement by a good deed at last.

SNAKE   But I must request of the company, that it shall never be known.

SIR PETER   Hey! what the plague! are you ashamed of having done a right thing once in your life?

SNAKE   Ah, sir,—consider I live by the badness of my character—I have nothing but my infamy to depend on! and, if it were once known that I had been betrayed into an honest action, I should lose every friend I have in the world.

SIR OLIVER   Well, well—we'll not traduce you by saying anything in your praise, never fear.

Exit SNAKE.

SIR PETER   There's a precious rogue! yet that fellow is a writer and a critic!

LADY TEAZLE   See, Sir Oliver, there needs no persuasion now to reconcile your nephew and Maria.

CHARLES *and* MARIA *apart.*

SIR OLIVER   Aye, aye, that's as it should be, and, egad, we'll have the wedding to-morrow morning.

CHARLES   Thank you, my dear uncle.

SIR PETER   What, you rogue! don't you ask the girl's consent first?

CHARLES   Oh, I have done that a long time—above a minute ago—and she has looked yes.

MARIA   For shame, Charles!—I protest, Sir Peter, there has not been a word——

SIR OLIVER   Well, then, the fewer the better—may your love for each other never know abatement.

SIR PETER   And may you live as happily together as Lady Teazle and I—intend to do!

CHARLES   Rowley, my old friend, I am sure you congratulate me; and I suspect that I owe you much.

SIR OLIVER   You do, indeed, Charles.

ROWLEY   If my efforts to serve you had not succeeded you would have been in my debt for the attempt—but deserve to be happy—and you overpay me.

SIR PETER   Aye, honest Rowley always said you would reform.

CHARLES   Why as to reforming, Sir Peter, I'll make no promises, and that I take to be a proof that I intend to set about it.—But here shall be my monitor—my gentle guide.—Ah! can I leave the virtuous path those eyes illumine?

Thou thou, dear maid, shouldst waive thy *beauty's* sway,
Thou still must rule, because I *will* obey:
An humbled fugitive from Folly view,
No sanctuary near but *Love* and—YOU;

To the audience.

You can, indeed, each anxious fear remove,
For even *Scandal* dies, if *you* approve.

FINIS

Epilogue

Written by G. Colman, Esq.[4]

Spoken by Mrs. Abington[5]

I, who was late so volatile and gay,
Like a trade-wind must now blow all one way,
Bend all my cares, my studies, and my vows,
To one old rusty weathercock—my spouse!
So wills our virtuous bard—the motley Bayes[6]
Of crying epilogues and laughing plays!
Old bachelors, who marry smart young wives,
Learn from our play to regulate your lives:
Each bring his dear to town, all faults upon her—
London will prove the very source of honor.
Plunged fairly in, like a cold bath it serves,
When principles relax, to brace the nerves.
Such is my case;—and yet I might deplore
That the gay dream of dissipation's o'er;
And say, ye fair, was ever lively wife,
Born with a genius for the highest life,
Like me untimely blasted in her bloom,
Like me condemned to such a dismal doom?
Save money—when I just knew how to waste it!
Leave London—just as I began to taste it!
Must I then watch the early crowing cock,
The melancholy ticking of a clock;
In the lone rustic hall for ever pounded,
With dogs, cats, rats, and squalling brats surrounded?
With humble curates can I now retire,
(While good Sir Peter boozes with the squire,)
And at backgammon mortify my soul,

---

4. George Colman, playwright.
5. Who played Lady Teazle.
6. Poet—from the leading character (a caricature of Dryden) in Buckingham's *The Rehearsal*.

That pants for loo,[7] or flutters at a vole?[8]
Seven's the main![9] Dear sound!—that must expire,
Lost at hot cockles,[1] round a Christmas fire!
The transient hour of fashion too soon spent,
Farewell the tranquil mind, farewell content![2]
Farewell the plumèd head, the cushioned tête,
That takes the cushion from its proper seat!
That spirit-stirring drum![3]—card drums I mean,
Spadille—odd trick—pam—basto[4]—king and queen!
And you, ye knockers, that, with brazen throat,
The welcome visitors' approach denote;
Farewell! all quality of high renown,
Pride, pomp, and circumstance of glorious town!
Farewell! your revels I partake no more,
And Lady Teazle's occupation's o'er!
All this I told our bard—he smiled, and said 'twas clear,
I ought to play deep tragedy next year.
Meanwhile he drew wise morals from his play,
And in these solemn periods stalked away:—
"Blest were the fair like you; her faults who stopped,
And closed her follies when the curtain dropped!
No more in vice or error to engage,
Or play the fool at large on life's great stage."

---

7. A card game.
8. Winning all the tricks.
9. A term in hazard, a dice game.
1. A parlor game popular in the country.
2. These lines parody *Othello*, 3.3.348–58.
3. A fashionable card-party.
4. Spadille, pam, and basto were the names of cards.

CONTEXTS

On Wit, Humour, and Laughter: 1650–1775

THOMAS HOBBES

[On Laughter]†

From On Human Nature, *Chapter IX*
(1650)

There is a passion that hath *no name*; but the sign of it is that distortion of the countenance which we call *laughter,* which is always *joy:* but what joy, what we think, and wherein we triumph when we laugh, is not hitherto declared by any. That it consisteth in *wit,* or, as they call it, in the *jest,* experience *confuteth:* for men laugh at mischances and indecencies, wherein there lieth no wit nor jest at all. And forasmuch as the same thing is no more ridiculous when it groweth stale or usual, whatsoever it be that moveth laughter, it must be *new* and *unexpected.* Men laugh often, especially such as are greedy of applause from every thing they do well, at their own actions performed never so little beyond their own expectations; as also at their own *jests:* and in this case it is manifest, that the passion of laughter proceedeth from a *sudden conception* of some *ability* in himself that laugheth. Also men laugh at the *infirmities* of others, by comparison wherewith their own abilities are set off and illustrated. Also men laugh at *jests,* the *wit* whereof always consisteth in the elegant *discovering* and conveying to our minds some *absurdity* of *another:* and in this case also the passion of laughter proceedeth from the *sudden* imagination of our own odds and eminency: for what is else the recommending of ourselves to our own good opinion, by comparison with another man's infirmity or absurdity? For when a jest is broken upon ourselves, or friends of whose dishonor we participate, we never laugh thereat. I may therefore conclude, that the passion

---

† Brief definitions often prove the most lasting, especially when offered by a controversial writer. Thomas Hobbes was the most controversial English philosopher of his time, and his explanation of laughter, no more than a paragraph in his long essay *On Human Nature,* became for the next hundred years the central point of reference for other commentators—especially for those whom Hobbes alarmed.

of laughter is nothing else but *sudden glory* arising from some sudden *conception* of some *eminency* in ourselves, by *comparison* with the *infirmity* of others, or with our own formerly: for men laugh at the follies of themselves past, when they come suddenly to remembrance, except they bring with them any present dishonor. It is no wonder therefore that men take heinously to be laughed at or derided, that is, triumphed over. Laughter *without offense*, must be at *absurdities* and infirmities *abstracted* from persons, and when all the company may laugh together: for laughing to one's-self putteth all the rest into jealousy and examination of themselves. Besides, it is vain glory, and an argument of little worth, to think the infirmity of another, sufficient matter for his triumph. * * *

[On Wit]†

From Leviathan, *Part I, Chapter VIII*
(*1651*)

Virtue generally, in all sorts of subjects, is somewhat that is valued for eminence, and consists in comparison. For if all things were equal in all men, nothing would be prized. And by *virtues intellectual* are always understood such abilities of the mind as men praise, value, and desire should be in themselves and go commonly under the name of a *good wit*, though the same word *wit* be used also to distinguish one certain ability from the rest.

These *virtues* are of two sorts: *natural* and *acquired*. By natural, I mean not that which a man has from his birth, for that is nothing else but sense, wherein men differ so little one from another and from brute beasts as it is not to be reckoned among virtues. But I mean that *wit* which is gotten by use only and experience, without method, culture, or instruction. This NATURAL WIT consists principally in two things: *celerity of imagining*—that is, swift succession of one thought to another—*and steady direction* to some approved end. On the contrary, a slow imagination makes that defect or fault of the mind which is commonly called DULLNESS, *stupidity*, and sometimes by other names that signify slowness of motion or difficulty to be moved.

And this difference of quickness is caused by the difference of men's

---

† Wit is another famous Hobbesian topic, and this he treated at length in his famous *Leviathan*. Reprinted here is his basic definition, in which he divides wit into two kinds: the perception of similitudes among things commonly regarded as different (fancy); and the perception of differences among things commonly regarded as similar (judgment). Having set forth this distinction, Hobbes offers a characteristic intrigue: what causes people to have different degrees of wit is that they have different passions for power. One must know what *power* meant to Hobbes, for it is a key word in his political philosophy, and it offers some unusual implications about wit for the reader who puts things together. Part of Hobbes's discussion of power, from a different section of *Leviathan*, has therefore been joined to the section on wit.

passions that love and dislike, some one thing, some another; and there-fore some men's thoughts run one way, some another, and are held to and observe differently the things that pass through their imagination. And whereas in this succession of men's thoughts there is nothing to observe in the things they think on but either in what they be *like one another* or in what they be *unlike, or what they serve for* or *how they serve to such a purpose*, those that observe their similitudes, in case they be such as are but rarely observed by others, are said to have a *good wit*, by which, in this occasion, is meant a *good fancy*. But they that observe their differences and dissimilitudes, which is called *distinguishing* and *discerning* and *judging* between thing and thing, in case such discerning be not easy, are said to have a *good judgment*; and particularly in matter of conversation and business wherein times, places, and persons are to be discerned, this virtue is called DISCRETION.

The former—that is, fancy—without the help of judgment, is not commended as a virtue; but the latter, which is judgment and discre-tion, is commended for itself without the help of fancy. Besides the discretion of times, places, and persons necessary to a good fancy, there is required also an often application of his thoughts to their end—that is to say, to some use to be made of them. This done, he that has this virtue will be easily fitted with similitudes that will please, not only by illustrations of his discourse and adorning it with new and apt meta-phors, but also by the rarity of their invention. But without steadiness and direction to some end, a great fancy is one kind of madness, such as they have that, entering into any discourse, are snatched from their purpose by everything that comes in their thought into so many and so long digressions and parentheses that they utterly lose themselves; which kind of folly I know no particular name for; but the cause of it is some-times want of experience, whereby that seems to a man new and rare which does not so to others; sometimes pusillanimity, by which that seems great to him which other men think a trifle; and whatsoever is new or great, and therefore thought fit to be told, withdraws a man by degrees from the intended way of his discourse.

In a good poem, whether it be *epic* or *dramatic*, as also in *sonnets, epigrams*, and other pieces, both judgment and fancy are required; but the fancy must be more eminent, because they please for the extrava-gancy, but ought not to displease by indiscretion.

In a good history the judgment must be eminent, because the good-ness consists in the method, in the truth, and in the choice of the actions that are most profitable to be known. Fancy has no place, but only in adorning the style.

In orations of praise and in invectives the fancy is predominant, because the design is not truth but to honor or dishonor, which is done by noble or by vile comparisons. The judgment does not suggest what circumstances make an action laudable or culpable.

In hortatives and pleadings, as truth or disguise serves best to the design in hand, so is the judgment or the fancy most required.

In demonstration, in counsel, and all rigorous search of truth, judgment does all, except sometimes the understanding have need to be opened by some apt similitude, and then there is so much use of fancy. But for metaphors, they are in this case utterly excluded. For seeing they openly profess deceit, to admit them into counsel or reasoning were manifest folly.

And in any discourse whatsoever, if the defect of discretion be apparent, how extravagant soever the fancy be, the whole discourse will be taken for a sign of want of wit; and so will it never when the discretion is manifest, though the fancy be never so ordinary.

The secret thoughts of a man run over all things—holy, profane, clean, obscene, grave, and light—without shame or blame, which verbal discourse cannot do farther than the judgment shall approve of the time, place, and persons. An anatomist or a physician may speak or write his judgment of unclean things because it is not to please but profit; but for another man to write his extravagant and pleasant fancies of the same is as if a man, from being tumbled into the dirt, should come and present himself before good company. And it is the want of discretion that makes the difference. Again, in professed remissness of mind and familiar company, a man may play with the sounds and equivocal significations of words, and that many times with encounters of extraordinary fancy; but in a sermon, or in public, or before persons unknown or whom we ought to reverence, there is no jingling of words that will not be accounted folly; and the difference is only in the want of discretion. So that where wit is wanting, it is not fancy that is wanting but discretion. Judgment therefore without fancy is wit, but fancy without judgment not.

When the thoughts of a man that has a design in hand, running over a multitude of things, observes how they conduce to that design, or what design they may conduce unto, if his observations be such as are not easy or usual this wit of his is called PRUDENCE, and depends on much experience and memory of the like things and their consequences heretofore. In which there is not so much difference of men as there is in their fancies and judgment, because the experience of men equal in age is not much unequal as to the quantity but lies in different occasions, everyone having his private designs. To govern well a family and a kingdom are not different degrees of prudence but different sorts of business; no more than to draw a picture in little, or as great, or greater than the life are different degrees of art. A plain husbandman is more prudent in affairs of his own house than a privy councilor in the affairs of another man.

To prudence, if you add the use of unjust or dishonest means such as usually are prompted to men by fear or want, you have that crooked wisdom which is called CRAFT, which is a sign of pusillanimity. For magnanimity is contempt of unjust or dishonest helps. And that which the Latins call *versutia*—translated into English *shifting*—and is a putting off of a present danger or incommodity by engaging into a greater, as when a man robs one to pay another, is but a shorter-sighted craft, called *versutia* from *versura*, which signifies taking money at usury for the present payment of interest.

As for *acquired wit*—I mean acquired by method and instruction—there is none but reason, which is grounded on the right use of speech and produces the sciences. But of reason and science I have already spoken in the fifth and sixth chapters.

The causes of this difference of wits are in the passions, and the difference of passions proceeds partly from the different constitution of the body and partly from different education. For if the difference proceeded from the temper of the brain and the organs of sense, either exterior or interior, there would be no less difference of men in their sight, hearing, or other senses than in their fancies and discretions. It proceeds, therefore, from the passions, which are different not only from the difference of men's complexions, but also from their difference of customs and education.

The passions that most of all cause the difference of wit are principally the more or less desire of power, of riches, of knowledge, and of honor. All which may be reduced to the first—that is, desire of power. For riches, knowledge, and honor are but several sorts of power. * * *

[On Power]

From Leviathan, *Part I, Chapter X*

The POWER of a man, to take it universally, is his present means to obtain some future apparent good, and is either *original* or *instrumental.*

Natural power is the eminence of the faculties of body or mind, as extraordinary strength, form, prudence, arts, eloquence, liberality, nobility. *Instrumental* are those powers which, acquired by these or by fortune, are means and instruments to acquire more, as riches, reputation, friends, and the secret working of God, which men call good luck. For the nature of power is in this point like to fame, increasing as it proceeds; or like the motion of heavy bodies, which, the further they go, make still the more haste.

The greatest of human powers is that which is compounded of the powers of most men united by consent in one person, natural or civil, that has the use of all their powers depending on his will, such as is the power of a commonwealth; or depending on the wills of each particular, such as is the power of a faction or of divers factions leagued. Therefore to have servants is power; to have friends is power; for they are strengths united.

Also riches joined with liberality is power, because it procures friends and servants; without liberality, not so, because in this case they defend not, but expose men to envy, as a prey.

Reputation of power is power, because it draws with it the adherence of those that need protection.

So is reputation of love of a man's country, called popularity, for the same reason.

Also, what quality soever makes a man beloved or feared of many, or the reputation of such quality, is power, because it is a means to have the assistance and service of many.

Good success is power, because it makes reputation of wisdom or good fortune, which makes men either fear him or rely on him.

Affability of men already in power is increase of power, because it gains love.

Reputation of prudence in the conduct of peace or war is power, because to prudent men we commit the government of ourselves more willingly than to others.

Nobility is power, not in all places, but only in those commonwealths where it has privileges, for in such privileges consists their power.

Eloquence is power, because it is seeming prudence.

Form is power, because, being a promise of good, it recommends men to the favor of women and strangers.

The sciences are small power, because not eminent and therefore not acknowledged in any man; nor are at all but in a few, and in them but of a few things. For science is of that nature as none can understand it to be but such as in a good measure have attained it.

Arts of public use—as fortification, making of engines, and other instruments of war—because they confer to defense and victory, are power, and though the true mother of them be science—namely, the mathematics—yet, because they are brought into the light by the hand of the artificer, they be esteemed—the midwife passing with the vulgar for the mother—as his issue.

The *value* or WORTH of a man is, as of all other things, his price— that is to say, so much as would be given for the use of his power—and therefore is not absolute but a thing dependent on the need and judgment of another. An able conductor of soldiers is of great price in time of war present or imminent, but in peace not so. A learned and uncorrupt judge is much worth in time of peace, but not so much in war. And as in other things so in men, not the seller but the buyer determines the price. For let a man, as most men do, rate themselves at the highest value they can, yet their true value is no more than it is esteemed by others.

The manifestation of the value we set on one another is that which is commonly called honoring and dishonoring. To value a man at a high rate is to *honor* him, at a low rate is to *dishonor* him. But high and low, in this case, is to be understood by comparison to the rate that each man sets on himself.

The public worth of a man, which is the value set on him by the commonwealth, is that which men commonly call DIGNITY. And this value of him by the commonwealth is understood by offices of command, judicature, public employment, or by names and titles introduced for distinction of such value.

To pray to another for aid of any kind is *to* HONOR, because a sign we have an opinion he has power to help; and the more difficult the aid is, the more is the honor.

To obey is to honor, because no man obeys them whom they think have no power to help or hurt them. And consequently to disobey is to *dishonor*.

To give great gifts to a man is to honor him, because it is buying of protection and acknowledging of power. To give little gifts is to dishonor, because it is but alms, and signifies an opinion of the need of small helps.

To be sedulous in promoting another's good, also to flatter, is to honor, as a sign we seek his protection or aid. To neglect is to dishonor.

To give way or place to another in any commodity is to honor, being a confession of greater power. To arrogate is to dishonor.

To show any sign of love or fear of another is to honor, for both to love and to fear is to value. To condemn, or less to love or fear than he expects, is to dishonor, for it is undervaluing.

To praise, magnify, or call happy is to honor, because nothing but goodness, power, and felicity is valued. To revile, mock, or pity is to dishonor.

To speak to another with consideration, to appear before him with decency and humility, is to honor him, as signs of fear to offend. To speak to him rashly, to do anything before him obscenely, slovenly, impudently, is to dishonor.

To believe, to trust, to rely on another is to honor him, sign of opinion of his virtue and power. To distrust or not believe is to dishonor.

To hearken to a man's counsel or discourse of what kind soever is to honor, as a sign we think him wise or eloquent or witty. To sleep or go forth or talk the while is to dishonor.

To do those things to another which he takes for signs of honor, or which the law or custom makes so, is to honor, because in approving the honor done by others he acknowledges the power which others acknowledge. To refuse to do them is to dishonor.

To agree with in opinion is to honor, as being a sign of approving his judgment and wisdom. To dissent is dishonor, and an upbraiding of error; and, if the dissent be in many things, of folly.

To imitate is to honor, for it is vehemently to approve. To imitate one's enemy is to dishonor.

To honor those another honors is to honor him, as a sign of approbation of his judgment. To honor his enemies is to dishonor him.

To employ in counsel or in actions of difficulty is to honor, as a sign of opinion of his wisdom or other power. To deny employment in the same cases to those that seek it is to dishonor.

All these ways of honoring are natural, and as well within as without commonwealths. But in commonwealths, where he or they that have the supreme authority can make whatsoever they please to stand for signs of honor, there be other honors.

A sovereign does honor a subject with whatsoever title or office or employment or action that he himself will have taken for a sign of his will to honor him.

The king of Persia honored Mordecai when he appointed he should be conducted through the streets in the king's garment, upon one of the king's horses, with a crown on his head, and a prince before him, proclaiming *thus shall it be done to him that the king will honor*.[1] And yet another king of Persia, or the same another time, to one that demanded for some great service to wear one of the king's robes, gave him leave so to do, but with this addition, that he should wear it as the king's fool, and then it was dishonor. So that of civil honor the fountain is in the person of the commonwealth and depends on the will of the sovereign, and is therefore temporary and called *civil honor:* such as magistracy, offices, titles, and in some places coats and scutcheons painted; and men honor such as have them as having so many signs of favor in the commonwealth, which favor is power. *Honorable* is whatsoever possession, action, or quality is an argument and sign of power.

And therefore to be honored, loved, or feared of many is honorable, as arguments of power. To be honored of few or none, *dishonorable*.

Dominion and victory is honorable, because acquired by power; and servitude, for need or fear, is dishonorable.

Good fortune, if lasting, honorable, as a sign of the favor of God. Ill fortune and losses, dishonorable. Riches are honorable, for they are power. Poverty, dishonorable. Magnanimity, liberality, hope, courage, confidence are honorable, for they proceed from the conscience of power. Pusillanimity, parsimony, fear, diffidence are dishonorable.

Timely resolution, or determination of what a man is to do, is honorable, as being the contempt of small difficulties and dangers. And irresolution dishonorable, as a sign of too much valuing of little impediments

1. Esther 6.11.

and little advantages; for when a man has weighed things as long as the time permits and resolves not, the difference of weight is but little; and therefore if he resolve not, he overvalues little things, which is pusilla-nimity.

All action and speeches that proceed, or seem to proceed, from much experience, science, discretion, or wit are honorable, for all these are powers. Actions or words that proceed from error, ignorance, or folly, dishonorable.

Gravity, as far forth as it seems to proceed from a mind employed on something else, is honorable, because employment is a sign of power. But if it seem to proceed from a purpose to appear grave, it is dishonor-able. For the gravity of the former is like the steadiness of a ship laden with merchandise; but of the latter, like the steadiness of a ship ballasted with sand and other trash.

To be conspicuous—that is to say, to be known—for wealth, office, great actions, or any eminent good is honorable, as a sign of the power for which he is conspicuous. On the contrary, obscurity is dishonorable.

To be descended from conspicuous parents is honorable, because they the more easily attain the aids and friends of their ancestors. On the contrary, to be descended from obscure parentage is dishonorable.

Actions proceeding from equity, joined with loss, are honorable, as signs of magnanimity; for magnanimity is a sign of power. On the con-trary, craft, shifting, neglect of equity is dishonorable.

Covetousness of great riches and ambition of great honors are honor-able, as signs of power to obtain them. Covetousness and ambition of little gains or preferments is dishonorable.

Nor does it alter the case of honor whether an action, so it be great and difficult and consequently a sign of much power, be just or unjust, for honor consists only in the opinion of power. Therefore the ancient heathen did not think they dishonored but greatly honored the gods when they introduced them in their poems committing rapes, thefts, and other great but unjust or unclean acts; insomuch as nothing is so much celebrated in Jupiter as his adulteries, nor in Mercury as his frauds and thefts—of whose praises, in a hymn of Homer, the greatest is this: that, being born in the morning, he had invented music at noon and, before night, stolen away the cattle of Apollo from his herds-men. * * *[2]

2. Hobbes's discussion of power continues in Chapters XI and XII of *Leviathan*, culminating in his famous statement about a "war of every man against every man."

JOHN DRYDEN

Preface to *An Evening's Love: or, The Mock Astrologer*[†]
(1671)

I had thought, Reader, in this preface to have written somewhat concerning the difference betwixt the plays of our age and those of our
predecessors on the English stage: to have shown in what parts of dramatic poesy we were excelled by Ben Jonson, I mean humour and contrivance of comedy; and in what we may justly claim precedence of
Shakespeare and Fletcher, namely in heroic plays. But this design I
have waived on second considerations; at least deferred it till I publish
the *Conquest of Granada*, where the discourse will be more proper. I
have also prepared to treat of the improvement of our language since
Fletcher's and Jonson's days, and consequently of our refining the courtship, raillery, and conversation of plays: but as I am willing to decline
that envy which I should draw on myself from some old opiniatre[1]
judges of the stage; so likewise I am pressed in time so much that I have
not leisure, at present, to go through with it.

Neither, indeed, do I value a reputation gained from comedy so far
as to concern myself about it any more than I needs must in my own
defense: for I think it, in its own nature, inferior to all sorts of dramatic
writing. Low comedy especially requires, on the writer's part, much of
conversation with the vulgar: and much of ill nature in the observation
of their follies. But let all men please themselves according to their
several tastes: that which is not pleasant to me may be to others who
judge better; and, to prevent an accusation from my enemies, I am
sometimes ready to imagine that my disgust of low comedy proceeds
not so much from my judgment as from my temper; which is the reason
why I so seldom write it; and that when I succeed in it (I mean so far as

---

[†] Dryden's essays and prefaces form the central body of English criticism in the Restoration
period. No writer of the age was more influential in defining such terms as *wit* and *humour*, or
in establishing criteria for evaluating dramatic works. *An Evening's Love* was first performed in
1668, and it is important to notice that in his preface to the published version (1671) Dryden
already felt a need to defend himself against moralistic attacks of the sort that Jeremy Collier
was to enlarge upon a generation later. Indeed, Collier centered a large portion of his attack
upon this essay (see p. 491).

Along with this extended discussion of wit and comedy, two of Dryden's briefest statements
about wit are important to know: wit "is no other than the faculty of imagination in the writer
which, like a nimble spaniel, beats over and ranges through the field of memory, till it springs
the quarry it hunted after. . . . It is some lively and apt description, dressed in such colors of
speech that it sets before your eyes the absent object as perfectly and more delightfully than
nature" (Preface to *Annus Mirabilis*, 1667); and wit "is a propriety of thoughts and words; or,
in other terms, thoughts and words elegantly adapted to the subject" ("The Author's Apology,"
prefixed to *The State of Innocence*, 1677).

1. Stubborn.

to please the audience), yet I am nothing satisfied with what I have done; but am often vexed to hear the people laugh, and clap, as they perpetually do, where I intended 'em no jest; while they let pass the better things without taking notice of them. Yet even this confirms me in my opinion of slighting popular applause, and of condemning that approbation which those very people give, equally with me, to the zany of a mountebank; or to the appearance of an antic on the theater, without wit on the poet's part, or any occasion of laughter from the actor besides the ridiculousness of his habit and his grimaces.

But I have descended, before I was aware, from comedy to farce; which consists principally of grimaces. That I admire not any comedy equally with tragedy is, perhaps, from the sullenness of my humour; but that I detest those farces which are now the most frequent entertainments of the stage, I am sure I have reason on my side. Comedy consists, though of low persons, yet of natural actions and characters; I mean such humours, adventures, and designs as are to be found and met with in the world. Farce, on the other side, consists of forced humours and unnatural events. Comedy presents us with the imperfections of human nature. Farce entertains us with what is monstrous and chimerical: the one causes laughter in those who can judge of men and manners, by the lively representation of their folly or corruption; the other produces the same effect in those who can judge of neither, and that only by its extravagances. The first works on the judgment and fancy; the latter on the fancy only: there is more of satisfaction in the former kind of laughter, and in the latter more of scorn. But how it happens that an impossible adventure should cause our mirth, I cannot so easily imagine. Something there may be in the oddness of it, because on the stage it is the common effect of things unexpected to surprise us into a delight: and that is to be ascribed to the strange appetite, as I may call it, of the fancy; which, like that of a longing woman, often runs out into the most extravagant desires; and is better satisfied sometimes with loam, or with the rinds of trees, than with the wholesome nourishments of life. In short, there is the same difference betwixt farce and comedy as betwixt an empiric[2] and a true physician: both of them may attain their ends; but what the one performs by hazard, the other does by skill. And as the artist is often unsuccessful while the mountebank succeeds; so farces more commonly take the people than comedies. For to write unnatural things is the most probable way of pleasing them, who understand not nature. And a true poet often misses of applause because he cannot debase himself to write so ill as to please his audience.

*   *   *

Ben Jonson is to be admired for many excellencies; and can be taxed with fewer failings than any English poet. I know I have been accused

2. Quack.

as an enemy of his writings; but without any other reason than that I do not admire him blindly, and without looking into his imperfections. For why should he only be exempted from those frailties from which Homer and Virgil are not free? Or why should there be any *ipse dixit* in our poetry, any more than there is in our philosophy? I admire and applaud him where I ought: those who do more do but value themselves in their admiration of him; and, by telling you they extol Ben Jonson's way, would insinuate to you that they can practice it. For my part, I declare that I want judgment to imitate him; and should think it a great impudence in myself to attempt it. To make men appear pleasantly ridiculous on the stage was, as I have said, his talent; and in this he needed not the acumen of wit, but that of judgment. For the characters and representations of folly are only the effects of observation; and observation is an effect of judgment. Some ingenious men, for whom I have a particular esteem, have thought I have much injured Ben Jonson when I have not allowed his wit to be extraordinary: but they confound the notion of what is witty with what is pleasant. That Ben Jonson's plays were pleasant, he must want reason who denies: but that pleasantness was not properly wit, or the sharpness of conceit, but the natural imitation of folly: which I confess to be excellent in its kind, but not to be of that kind which they pretend. Yet if we will believe Quintilian in his chapter *De movendo risu*, he gives his opinion of both in these following words: *stulta reprehendere facillimum est; nam per se sunt ridicula: et a derisu non procul abest risus: sed rem urbanum facit aliqua ex nobis adjectio.*[3]

And some perhaps would be apt to say of Jonson as it was said of Demosthenes: *non displicuisse illi jocos, sed non contigisse.*[4]

I will not deny but that I approve most the mixed way of comedy; that which is neither all wit, nor all humour, but the result of both. Neither so little of humour as Fletcher shows, nor so little of love and wit as Jonson; neither all cheat, with which the best plays of the one are filled, nor all adventure, which is the common practice of the other. I would have the characters well chosen, and kept distant from interfering with each other; which is more than Fletcher or Shakespeare did: but I would have more of the *urbana, venusta, salsa, faceta,*[5] and the rest which Quintilian reckons up as the ornaments of wit; and these are extremely wanting in Ben Jonson. As for repartee in particular; as it is the very soul of conversation, so it is the greatest grace of comedy, where it is proper to the characters. There may be much of acuteness in a thing well said; but there is more in a quick reply: *sunt enim longe venustiora omnia in respondendo*

---

3. *Institutio Oratoria* 6.3.71: "It is easy to make fun of folly, for folly is itself ridiculous, and our response always verges on laughter; but the joke improves when we add something of our own."
4. Ibid. 6.3.2: "Not that he disliked jokes, but that he lacked the power to make them."
5. Ibid. 6.3.17–20. The four terms describe kinds of wit: *urbanitas*, urbanity and learning; *venustus*, grace and charm; *salsus*, the salt of wit; *facetus*, polished elegance.

quam in provocando.[6] Of one thing I am sure, that no man ever will decry wit but he who despairs of it himself; and who has no other quarrel to it but that which the fox had to the grapes. Yet, as Mr Cowley (who had a greater portion of it than any man I know) tells us in his character of wit, rather than all wit let there be none.[7] I think there's no folly so great in any poet of our age as the superfluity and waste of wit was in some of our predecessors: particularly we may say of Fletcher and of Shakespeare what was said of Ovid, *in omni ejus ingenio, facilius quod rejici, quam quod adjici potest, invenies.*[8] The contrary of which was true in Virgil, and our incomparable Jonson.

Some enemies of repartee have observed to us that there is a great latitude in their characters which are made to speak it: and that it is easier to write wit than humour; because, in the characters of humour, the poet is confined to make the person speak what is only proper to it. Whereas all kind of wit is proper in the character of a witty person. But, by their favor, there are as different characters in wit as in folly. Neither is all kind of wit proper in the mouth of every ingenious person. A witty coward and a witty brave must speak differently. Falstaff and the Liar speak not like Don John in the *Chances*, and Valentine in *Wit without Money*.[9] And Jonson's Truewit in the *Silent Woman* is a character different from all of them. Yet it appears that this one character of wit was more difficult to the author than all his images of humour in the play: for those he could describe and manage from his observations of men; this he has taken, at least a part of it, from books: witness the speeches in the first act, translated *verbatim* out of Ovid *De arte amandi*; to omit what afterwards he borrowed from the sixth satire of Juvenal against women.

However, if I should grant that there were a greater latitude in characters of wit than in those of humour; yet that latitude would be of small advantage to such poets who have too narrow an imagination to write it. And to entertain an audience perpetually with humour is to carry them from the conversation of gentlemen, and treat them with the follies and extravagances of Bedlam.

I find I have launched out farther than I intended in the beginning of this preface. And that, in the heat of writing, I have touched at something which I thought to have avoided. 'Tis time now to draw homeward: and to think rather of defending myself than assaulting others. I have already acknowledged that this play is far from perfect: but I do not think myself obliged to discover the imperfections of it to my adversaries, any more than a guilty person is bound to accuse himself before his judges. 'Tis charged upon me that I make debauched persons (such as, they say, my

6. Ibid. 6.3.13: "For wit always appears more successful in reply than in attack."
7. Cowley's "Ode: Of Wit," lines 35–36.
8. *Institutio Oratoria* 6.3.5: "In all his wit you will find it easier to remove than to add." The modern reading ends *possit, invenient.*
9. Comedies by John Fletcher.

Astrologer and Gamester are) my protagonists, or the chief persons of the drama; and that I make them happy in the conclusion of my play; against the law of comedy, which is to reward virtue and punish vice. I answer first, that I know no such law to have been constantly observed in comedy, either by the ancient or modern poets. Chaerea is made happy in the *Eunuch*, after having deflowered a virgin; and Terence generally does the same through all his plays, where you perpetually see not only debauched young men enjoy their mistresses, but even the courtesans themselves rewarded and honored in the catastrophe. The same may be observed in Plautus almost everywhere. Ben Jonson himself, after whom I may be proud to err, has given me more than once the example of it. That in the *Alchemist* is notorious, where Face, after having contrived and carried on the great cozenage of the play, and continued in it without repentance to the last, is not only forgiven by his master, but enriched by his consent with the spoils of those whom he had cheated. And, which is more, his master himself, a grave man and a widower, is introduced taking his man's counsel, debauching the widow first, in hope to marry her afterward. In the *Silent Woman*, Dauphine (who, with the other two gentlemen, is of the same character with my Celadon in the *Maiden Queen*, and with Wildblood in this) professes himself in love with all the Collegiate Ladies: and they likewise are all of the same character with each other, excepting only Madam Otter, who has something singular: yet this naughty Dauphine is crowned in the end with the possession of his uncle's estate, and with the hopes of enjoying all his mistresses; and his friend Mr Truewit (the best character of a gentleman which Ben Jonson ever made) is not ashamed to pimp for him. As for Beaumont and Fletcher, I need not allege examples out of them; for that were to quote almost all their comedies.

But now it will be objected that I patronize vice by the authority of former poets, and extenuate my own faults by recrimination. I answer that, as I defend myself by their example, so that example I defend by reason, and by the end of all dramatic poesy. In the first place, therefore, give me leave to show you their mistake who have accused me. They have not distinguished, as they ought, betwixt the rules of tragedy and comedy. In tragedy, where the actions and persons are great, and the crimes horrid, the laws of justice are more strictly to be observed; and examples of punishment to be made to deter mankind from the pursuit of vice. Faults of this kind have been rare amongst the ancient poets: for they have punished in Oedipus, and in his posterity, the sin which he knew not he had committed. Medea is the only example I remember at present who escapes from punishment after murder. Thus tragedy fulfils one great part of its institution: which is, by example, to instruct. But in comedy it is not so; for the chief end of it is divertisement and delight: and that so much, that it is disputed, I think, by Heinsius, before Horace his *Art of Poetry*, whether instruction be any part of its employment.[1] At least I am sure it can be but its secondary end: for the business of the poet is to make you laugh: when he writes humour, he makes folly ridiculous; when wit, he moves you, if not always to laughter, yet to a pleasure that is more noble. And if he works a cure on folly, and the small imperfections in mankind, by exposing them to public view, that cure is not performed by an immediate operation. For it works first on the ill nature of the audience; they are moved to laugh by the representation of deformity; and the shame of that laughter teaches us to amend what is ridiculous in our manners. This being, then, established, that the first end of comedy is delight, and instruction only the second, it may reasonably be inferred that comedy is not so much obliged to the punishment of faults which it represents, as tragedy. For the persons in comedy are of a lower quality, the action is little, and the faults and vices are but the sallies of youth, and the frailties of human nature, and not premeditated crimes: such to which all men are obnoxious, not such as are attempted only by few, and those abandoned to all sense of virtue: such as move pity and commiseration, not destestation and horror; such, in short, as may be forgiven, not such as must of necessity be punished. But, lest any man should think that I write this to make libertinism amiable, or that I cared not to debase the end and institution of comedy so I might thereby maintain my own errors, and those of better poets, I must further declare, both for them and for myself, that we make not vicious persons happy, but only as Heaven makes sinners so; that is, by reclaiming them first from vice. For so 'tis to be supposed they are, when they resolve to marry; for then enjoying what they desire in one, they cease to pursue the love of many. So Chaerea is made happy by Terence, in marrying her whom he had deflowered: and so are Wildblood and the Astrologer in this play.

There is another crime with which I am charged, at which I am yet much less concerned, because it does not relate to my manners, as the former did, but only to my reputation as a poet: a name of which I assure the reader I am nothing proud; and therefore cannot be very solicitous to defend it. I am taxed with stealing all my plays, and that by some who should be the last men from whom I would steal any part of 'em. There is one answer which I will not make; but it has been made for me by him to whose grace and patronage I owe all things,

  et spes et ratio studiorum in Caesare tantum,[2]

and without whose command they should no longer be troubled with any thing of mine, that he only desired that they who accused me of theft would always steal him plays like mine. But though I have reason

---

1. Daniel Heinsius was a Dutch scholar who edited Horace in 1610. Dryden is wrong to suggest that he urged delight more than teaching as the purpose of comedy.
2. Juvenal, *Satires* 7.1: "The hope and inducement of studies rest upon Caesar alone." *An Evening's Love* was dedicated to the Duke of Newcastle.

to be proud of this defense, yet I should waive it, because I have a worse opinion of my own comedies than any of my enemies can have. 'Tis true that, where ever I have liked any story in a romance, novel, or foreign play, I have made no difficulty, nor ever shall, to take the foundation of it, to build it up, and to make it proper for the English stage. And I will be so vain to say it has lost nothing in my hands: but it always cost me so much trouble to heighten it for our theater (which is incomparably more curious in all the ornaments of dramatic poesy than the French or Spanish), that when I had finished my play, it was like the hulk of Sir Francis Drake, so strangely altered that there scarcely remained any plank of the timber which first built it.[3] To witness this, I need go no farther than this play: it was first Spanish, and called *El astrologo fingido*; then made French by the younger Corneille; and is now translated into English, and in print, under the name of the *Feigned Astrologer*.[4] What I have performed in this will best appear by comparing it with those: you will see that I have rejected some adventures which I judged were not divertising; that I have heightened those which I have chosen, and that I have added others which were neither in the French nor Spanish. And besides, you will easily discover that the walk of the Astrologer is the least considerable in my play: for the design of it turns more on the parts of Wildblood and Jacinta, who are the chief persons in it. I have farther to add that I seldom use the wit and language of any romance or play, which I undertake to alter: because my own invention (as bad as it is) can furnish me with nothing so dull as what is there. Those who have called Virgil, Terence, and Tasso plagiaries (though they much injured them), had yet a better color for their accusation; for Virgil has evidently translated Theocritus, Hesiod, and Homer, in many places; besides what he has taken from Ennius in his own language. Terence was not only known to translate Menander (which he avows also in his prologues), but was said also to be helped in those translations by Scipio the African and Laelius. And Tasso, the most excellent of modern poets, and whom I reverence next to Virgil, has taken both from Homer many admirable things which were left untouched by Virgil, and from Virgil himself where Homer could not furnish him. Yet the bodies of Virgil's and Tasso's poems were their own; and so are all the ornaments of language and elocution in them. The same (if there were any thing commendable in this play) I could say for it. But I will come nearer to our own countrymen. Most of Shakespeare's plays, I mean the stories of them, are to be found in the *Hecatommithi* or *Hundred Novels* of

---

3. After Drake's circumnavigation of the globe, the *Golden Hind* became a museum for sightseers. By the middle of the seventeenth century, after many repairs, the ship had fallen apart and the pieces were carried away for souvenirs.

4. Calderón's play was the source of Corneille's *Le feint astrologue* (1651), anonymously adapted into English as *The Feigned Astrologer* (1668).

Cinthio.[5] I have myself read in his Italian that of *Romeo and Juliet,* the *Moor of Venice,* and many others of them. Beaumont and Fletcher had most of theirs from Spanish novels: witness the *Chances,* the *Spanish Curate, Rule a Wife and Have a Wife,* the *Little French Lawyer,* and so many others of them as compose the greatest part of their volume in folio. Ben Jonson, indeed, has designed his plots himself; but no man has borrowed so much from the Ancients as he has done: and he did well in it, for he has thereby beautified our language.

But these little critics do not well consider what is the work of a poet, and what the graces of a poem. The story is the least part of either: I mean the foundation of it, before it is modeled by the art of him who writes it; who forms it with more care, by exposing only the beautiful parts of it to view, than a skillful lapidary sets a jewel. On this foundation of the story the characters are raised: and, since no story can afford characters enough for the variety of the English stage, it follows that it is to be altered and enlarged with new persons, accidents, and designs, which will almost make it new. When this is done, the forming it into acts and scenes, disposing of actions and passions into their proper places, and beautifying both with descriptions, similitudes, and propriety of language, is the principal employment of the poet; as being the largest field of fancy, which is the principal quality required in him: for so much the word ποιητής implies. Judgment, indeed, is necessary in him; but 'tis fancy that gives the life-touches, and the secret graces to it; especially in the serious plays, which depend not much on observation. For to write humour in comedy (which is the theft of poets from mankind), little of fancy is required; the poet observes only what is ridiculous and pleasant folly, and by judging exactly what is so, he pleases in the representation of it.

But in general, the employment of a poet is like that of a curious gunsmith or watchmaker: the iron or silver is not his own; but they are the least part of that which gives the value: the price lies wholly in the workmanship. And he who works dully on a story, without moving laughter in a comedy, or raising concernments in a serious play, is no more to be accounted a good poet than a gunsmith of the Minories[6] is to be compared with the best workman of the town.

But I have said more of this than I intended; and more, perhaps, than I needed to have done. I shall but laugh at them hereafter who accuse me with so little reason; and withal condemn their dullness who, if they could ruin that little reputation I have got, and which I value not, yet would want both wit and learning to establish their own; or to be remembered in after ages for any thing but only that which makes them ridiculous in this.

5. Cinthio's *Hecatommithi* (1565) was a source for *Othello* and others of Shakespeare's plays, but not for *Romeo and Juliet.*
6. Location of armorers' workshops in London.

WILLIAM CONGREVE

Concerning Humour in Comedy[†]
(1695)

Dear Sir. You write to me that you have entertained yourself two or three days with reading several comedies of several authors, and your observation is that there is more of Humour in our English writers than in any of the other comic poets, ancient or modern. You desire to know my opinion, and at the same time my thought of that which is generally called Humour in comedy.

I agree with you in an impartial preference of our English writers in that particular. But if I tell you my thoughts of Humour, I must at the same time confess that what I take for true Humour has not been so often written even by them as is generally believed. And some who have valued themselves and have been esteemed by others for that kind of writing have seldom touched upon it. To make this appear to the world would require a long and labored discourse, and such as I neither am able nor willing to undertake. But such little remarks as may be continued within the compass of a letter, and such unpremeditated thoughts as may be communicated between friend and friend, without incurring the censure of the world, or setting up for a dictator, you shall have from me since you have enjoined it.

To define Humour, perhaps, were as difficult as to define Wit, for like that, it is of infinite variety. To enumerate the several Humours of men were a work as endless as to sum up their several opinions. And in my mind the *Quot homines tot Sententiae*[1] might have been more properly interpreted of Humour, since there are many men of the same opinion in many things who are yet quite different in Humours. But tho' we cannot certainly tell what Wit is, or, what Humour is, yet we may go near to show something which is not Wit or not Humour, and yet often mistaken for both. And since I have mentioned Wit and Humour together, let me make the first distinction between them and observe to you that *Wit is often mistaken for Humour*.

I have observed that when a few things have been wittily and pleasantly spoken by any character in a comedy it has been very usual for those who make their remarks on a play while it is acting to say, *Such a thing is very Humourously spoken. There is a great deal of Humour in that part.* Thus the character of the person speaking, maybe, surpris-

---

[†] This essay first appeared in a collection of *Letters on Several Occasions: Written By and Between Mr. Dryden, Mr. Wycherley, Mr. ——, Mr. Congreve, and Mr. Dennis*, published in 1696. Congreve, in his mid-twenties at the time, was already well-known as a writer of comedies. This is his most extensive critical commentary on the subject. The letter is addressed to John Dennis.

1. As many opinions as men.

ingly and pleasantly, is mistaken for a character of Humour which indeed is a character of Wit. But there is a great difference between a comedy wherein there are many things *humourously*, as they call it which is *pleasantly*, spoken, and one where there are several characters of Humour distinguished by the particular and different Humours appropriated to the several persons represented and which naturally arise from the different constitutions, complexions, and dispositions of men. The saying of humourous things does not distinguish characters, for every person in a comedy may be allowed to speak them. From a witty man they are expected, and even a fool may be permitted to stumble on 'em by chance. Tho' I make a difference betwixt Wit and Humour, yet I do not think that humourous characters exclude Wit. No, but the manner of Wit should be adapted to the Humour. As for instance, a character of splenetic and peevish Humour should have a satirical Wit. A jolly and sanguine Humour should have a facetious Wit. The former should speak positively; the latter, carelessly, for the former observes and shows things as they are; the latter, rather overlooks Nature and speaks things as he would have them; and his Wit and Humour have both of them a less alloy of judgment than the others.

As Wit, so its opposite, *folly, is sometimes mistaken for Humour.*

When a poet brings a character on the stage committing a thousand absurdities and talking impertinencies, roaring aloud and laughing immoderately on every, or rather, upon no occasion, this is a character of Humour.

Is anything more common than to have a pretended comedy stuffed with such grotesques, figures, and farce fools? Things that either are not in Nature, or if they are, are monsters and births of mischance, and consequently as such should be stifled and huddled out of the way like Sooterkins, that mankind may not be shocked with an appearing possibility of the degeneration of a God-like species. For my part, I am as willing to laugh as anybody, and am as easily diverted with an object truly ridiculous, but at the same time, I can never care for seeing things that force me to entertain low thoughts of my Nature. I don't know how it is with others, but I confess freely to you, I could never look long upon a monkey without very mortifying reflections, tho' I never heard anything to the contrary why that creature is not originally of a distinct species. As I don't think Humour exclusive of Wit, neither do I think it inconsistent with Folly, but I think the Follies should be only such as men's Humours may incline 'em to, and not Follies entirely abstracted from both Humour and Nature.

Sometimes *personal defects are misrepresented for Humours.*

I mean, sometimes characters are barbarously exposed on the stage, ridiculing natural deformities, casual defects in the senses, and infirmities of age. Sure the poet must both be very ill-natured himself and think his audience so when he proposes by showing a man deformed, or deaf, or blind, to give them an agreeable entertainment, and hopes to raise their mirth by what is truly an object of compassion. But much need not be said upon this head to anybody, especially to you, who in one of your letters to me concerning Mr. Jonson's *Fox*[2] have justly excepted against this immoral part of ridicule in Corbaccio's character; and there I must agree with you to blame him, whom otherwise I cannot enough admire for his great mastery of true Humour in comedy.

External habit of body is often mistaken for Humour.

By external habit I do not mean the ridiculous dress or clothing of a character, tho' that goes a good way in some received characters. (But undoubtedly a man's Humour may incline him to dress differently from other people.) But I mean a singularity of manners, speech, and behavior peculiar to all, or most, of the same country, trade, profession, or education. I cannot think that a Humour which is only a habit or disposition contracted by use or custom; for by a disuse or compliance with other customs it may be worn off or diversified.

Affectation is generally mistaken for Humour.

These are indeed so much alike that at a distance they may be mistaken one for the other. For what is Humour in one may be Affectation in another, and nothing is more common than for some to affect particular ways of saying and doing things peculiar to others whom they admire and would imitate. Humour is the life, Affectation the picture. He that draws a character of Affectation shows Humour at the second hand; he at best but publishes a translation and his pictures are but copies.

But as these two last distinctions are the nicest, so it may be most proper to explain them by particular instances from some author of reputation. Humour I take either to be born with us, and so of a natural growth, or else to be grafted into us by some accidental change in the constitution or revolution of the internal habit of body, by which it becomes, if I may so call it, naturalized.

Humour is from Nature, Habit from custom, and Affectation from industry.

Humour shows us as we are.

Habit shows us as we appear under a forcible impression.

Affectation shows us what we would be under a voluntary disguise.

Tho' here I would observe by the way that a continued Affectation may in time become a Habit.

The character of Morose in the *Silent Woman*[3] I take to be a character of Humour. And I choose to instance this character to you from many others of the same author because I know it has been condemned

---

2. I.e., Ben Jonson's *Volpone* (1606). Corbaccio, a foolish and greedy old man in the play, is also deaf, and Dennis had complained that turning a physical defect into ridicule is "contrary to the end of comedy, instruction."
3. Jonson's *Epicoene: or The Silent Woman*, 1609.

by many as unnatural and farce. And you have yourself hinted some dislike of it for the same reason in a letter to me concerning some of Jonson's plays.

Let us suppose Morose to be a man naturally splenetic and melancholy; is there anything more offensive to one of such a disposition than noise and clamor? Let any man that has the spleen (and there are enough in England) be judge. We see common examples of this Humour in little every day. 'Tis ten to one but three parts in four of the company that you dine with are discomposed and startled at the cutting of a cork or scratching a plate with a knife. It is a proportion of the same Humour that makes such or any other noise offensive to the person that hears it, for there are others who will not be disturbed at all by it. Well. But Morose you will say is so extravagant he cannot bear any discourse or conversation above a whisper. Why, it is his excess of this Humour that makes him become ridiculous and qualifies his character for comedy. If the poet had given him but a moderate proportion of that Humour, 'tis odds but half the audience would have sided with the character and have condemned the author for exposing a Humour which was neither remarkable nor ridiculous. Besides, the distance of the stage requires the figure represented to be something larger than the life, and sure a picture may have features larger in proportion and yet be very like the original. If this exactness of quality were to be observed in Wit, as some would have it in Humour, what would become of those characters that are designed for men of Wit? I believe if a poet should steal a dialogue of any length from the extempore discourse of the two wittiest men upon earth, he would find the scene but coldly received by the town. But to the purpose.

The character of Sir John Daw in the same play is a character of Affectation. He everywhere discovers[4] an Affectation of learning, when he is not only conscious to himself but the audience also plainly perceives that he is ignorant. Of this kind are the characters of Thraso in the *Eunuch* of Terence, and Pyrgopolinices in the *Miles Gloriosus* of Plautus. They affect to be thought valiant when both themselves and the audience know they are not. Now such boasting of valor in men who were really valiant would undoubtedly be a Humour, for a fiery disposition might naturally throw a man into the same extravagance which is only affected in the characters I have mentioned.

The character of Cob in *Every Man in His Humour* and most of the under-characters in *Bartholomew Fair*[5] discover only a singularity of manners appropriated to the several educations and professions of the persons represented. They are not Humours but Habits contracted by custom. Under this head may be ranged all country clowns, sailors,

4. Reveals.
5. Comedies by Jonson.

tradesmen, jockeys, gamesters, and such like who make use of cants or peculiar dialects in their several arts and vocations. One may almost give a receipt for the composition of such a character, for the poet has nothing to do but to collect a few proper phrases and terms of art and to make the person apply them by ridiculous metaphors in his conversation with characters of different natures. Some late characters of this kind have been very successful, but in my mind they may be painted without much art or labor, since they require little more than a good memory and superficial observation. But true Humour cannot be shown without a dissection of Nature and a narrow search to discover the first seeds from whence it has its root and growth.

If I were to write to the world, I should be obliged to dwell longer upon each of these distinctions and examples, for I know that they would not be plain enough to all readers. But a bare hint is sufficient to inform you of the notions which I have on this subject. And I hope by this time you are of my opinion that Humour is neither Wit, nor Folly, nor personal defect, nor Affectation, nor Habit, and yet that each and all of these have been both written and received for Humour.

I should be unwilling to venture even on a bare description of Humour, much more, to make a definition of it, but now my hand is in, I'll tell you what serves me instead of either. I take it to be, *A singular and unavoidable manner of doing or saying anything, peculiar and natural to one man only, by which his speech and actions are distinguished from those of other men.*

Our Humour has relation to us, and to what proceeds from us, as the accidents have to a substance; it is a color, taste, and smell diffused through all; tho' our actions are never so many and different in form, they are all splinters of the same wood and have naturally one complexion, which tho' it may be disguised by art, yet cannot be wholly changed. We may paint it with other colors, but we cannot change the grain. So the natural sound of an instrument will be distinguished, tho' the notes expressed by it are never so various and the diversions never so many. Dissimulation may, by degrees, become more easy to our practice, but it can never absolutely transubstantiate us into what we would seem. It will always be in some proportion a violence upon nature.

A man may change his opinion, but I believe he will find it a difficulty to part with his Humour, and there is nothing more provoking than the being made sensible of that difficulty. Sometimes one shall meet with those who, innocently enough, but at the same time impertinently, will ask the question, "Why are you not merry?" "Why are you not gay, pleasant, and cheerful?" Then instead of answering, could I ask such one, "Why are you not handsome? Why have you not black eyes and a better complexion?" Nature abhors to be forced.

The two famous philosophers of Ephesus and Abdera[6] have their different sects at this day. Some weep and others laugh at one and the same thing.

I don't doubt but you have observed several men laugh when they are angry, others who are silent, some that are loud. Yet I cannot suppose that it is the passion of anger which is in itself different, or more or less in one than t'other, but that it is the Humour of the man that is predominant and urges him to express it in that manner. Demonstrations of pleasure are as various; one man has a Humour of retiring from all company when anything has happened to please him beyond expectation; he hugs himself alone, and thinks it an addition to the pleasure to keep it secret. Another is upon thorns till he has made proclamation of it, and must make other people sensible of his happiness before he can be so himself. So it is in grief and other passions. Demonstrations of love and the effects of that passion upon several Humours are infinitely different, but here the ladies who abound in servants[7] are the best judges. Talking of the ladies, methinks something should be observed of the Humour of the fair sex, since they are sometimes so kind as to furnish out a character for comedy. But I must confess I have never made any observation of what I apprehend to be true Humour in women. Perhaps passions are too powerful in that sex to let Humour have its course, or maybe by reason of their natural coldness, Humour cannot exert itself to that extravagant degree which it often does in the male sex. For if ever anything does appear comical or ridiculous in a woman, I think it is little more than an acquired Folly or an Affectation. We may call them the weaker sex, but I think the true reason is because our Follies are stronger and our faults more prevailing.

One might think that the diversity of Humour, which must be allowed to be diffused throughout mankind, might afford endless matter for the support of comedies. But when we come closely to consider that point, and nicely to distinguish the difference of Humours, I believe we shall find the contrary. For tho' we allow every man something of his own and a peculiar Humour, yet every man has it not in quantity to become remarkable by it. Or if many do become remarkable by their Humours, yet all those Humours may not be diverting. Nor is it only requisite to distinguish what Humour will be diverting, but also how much of it, what part of it to show in light and what to cast in shades, how to set it off by preparatory scenes, and by opposing other Humours to it in the same scene. Thro' a wrong judgment, sometimes, men's Humours may be opposed when there is really no specific difference between them, only a greater proportion of the same in one than t'other,

6. Heraclitus of Ephesus was known as the "weeping philosopher"; Democritus of Abdera, as the "laughing philosopher."
7. Lovers.

occasioned by his having more phlegm, or choler, or whatever the constitution is, from whence their Humours derive their source.

There is infinitely more to be said on this subject, tho' perhaps I have already said too much; but I have said it to a friend, who I am sure will not expose it if he does not approve of it. I believe the subject is entirely new and was never touched upon before; and if I would have anyone to see this private essay, it should be someone who might be provoked by my errors in it to publish a more judicious treatise on the subject. Indeed I wish it were done, that the world being a little acquainted with the scarcity of true Humour, and the difficulty of finding and showing it, might look a little more favorably on the labors of them who endeavor to search into Nature for it and lay it open to the public view.

I don't say but that very entertaining and useful characters, and proper for comedy, may be drawn from Affectations and those other qualities which I have endeavored to distinguish from Humour; but I would not have such imposed on the world for Humour, nor esteemed of equal value with it. It were perhaps the work of a long life to make one comedy true in all its parts, and to give every character in it a true and distinct Humour. Therefore, every poet must be beholding to other helps to make out his number of ridiculous characters. But I think such a one deserves to be broke who makes all false musters, who does not show one true Humour in a comedy, but entertains his audience to the end of the play with everything out of nature.

I will make but one observation to you more, and have done; and that is grounded upon an observation of your own, and which I mentioned at the beginning of my letter, *viz.*, that there is more of Humour in our English comic writers than in any others. I do not at all wonder at it, for I look upon Humour to be almost of English growth; at least, it does not seem to have found such increase on any other soil. And what appears to me to be the reason of it is the great freedom, privilege, and liberty which the common people of England enjoy. Any man that has a Humour is under no restraint or fear of giving it a vent; they have a proverb among them which, maybe, will show the bent and genius of the people as well as a longer discourse. "He that will have a May Pole shall have a May Pole." This is a maxim with them and their practice is agreeable to it. I believe something considerable too may be ascribed to their feeding so much on flesh, and the grossness of their diet in general. But I have done; let the physicians agree that. Thus you have my thoughts of Humour to my power of expressing them in so little time and compass. You will be kind to show me wherein I have erred, and as you are very capable of giving me instruction, so I think I have a very just title to demand it from you, being without reserve,

Your real Friend,
and humble Servant,
W. CONGREVE

July 10, 1695

RICHARD STEELE

Epilogue to *The Lying Lover*[†]
(1704)

Our too advent'rous author soared tonight ⎤
Above the little praise, mirth to excite, ⎬
And chose with pity to chastise delight. ⎦
For laughter's a distorted passion, born
Of sudden self-esteem and sudden scorn;
Which, when 'tis o'er, the men in pleasure wise
Both him that moved it and themselves despise;
While generous pity of a painted woe
Make us ourselves both more approve and know.
What is that touch within, which nature gave
For man to man, e'er fortune made a slave?
Sure it descends from that dread power alone ⎤
Who levels thunder from His awful throne, ⎬
And shakes both worlds—yet hears the wretched groan. ⎦

'Tis what the ancient sage would ne'er define,
Wonder'd—and called, part human, part divine:
'Tis that pure joy, which guardian angels know
When timely they assist their care below,
When they the good protect, the ill oppose;
'Tis what our Sovereign feels when she bestows,
Which gives her glorious cause such high success,
That only on the stage you see distress.

The Tatler, No. 219[††]
(1710)

From my own Apartment, Sept. 1.

Never were men so perplexed as a select company of us were this evening with a couple of possessed wits, who through our ill fortune, and
their own confidence, had thought fit to pin themselves upon a gentle-

---

[†] *The Lying Lover* (first performed in 1703 and published in the following year) was Steele's
second play, and the epilogue is one of his earliest statements about the kindly feelings proper
to comedy. Together with the Preface and Prologue to *The Conscious Lovers*, it offers a fairly
complete definition of "sentimental" comedy.

[††] *The Tatler* and *The Spectator*, upon which Addison and Steele collaborated in the years 1709–
12, often commented on comedy and related literary subjects. Taken together, these essays

man who had owned to them that he was going to meet such and such persons, and named us one by one. These pert puppies immediately resolved to come with him, and from the beginning to the end of the night entertained each other with impertinences, to which we were perfect strangers. I am come home very much tired; for the affliction was so irksome to me, that it surpasses all other I ever knew, insomuch that I cannot reflect upon this sorrow with pleasure, though it is past.

An easy manner of conversation is the most desirable quality a man can have; and for that reason coxcombs will take upon them to be familiar with people whom they never saw before. What adds to the vexation of it is, that they will act upon the foot of knowing you by fame, and rally with you, as they call it, by repeating what your enemies say of you; and court you, as they think, by uttering to your face at a wrong time all the kind things your friends speak of you in your absence.

These people are the more dreadful, the more they have of what is usually called wit: for a lively imagination, when it is not governed by a good understanding, makes such miserable havoc both in conversation and business, that it lays you defenseless, and fearful to throw the least word in its way that may give it new matter for its further errors.

Tom Mercett has as quick a fancy as any one living; but there is no reasonable man can bear him half-an-hour. His purpose is to entertain, and it is of no consequence to him what is said, so it be what is called well said; as if a man must bear a wound with patience, because he that pushed at you came up with a good air and mien. That part of life which we spend in company, is the most pleasing of all our moments; and therefore I think our behavior in it should have its laws as well as the part of our being which is generally esteemed the more important. From hence it is, that from long experience I have made it a maxim, that however we may pretend to take satisfaction in sprightly mirth and high jollity, there is no great pleasure in any company where the basis of the society is not mutual good-will. When this is in the room, every trifling circumstance, the most minute accident, the absurdity of a servant, the repetition of an old story, the look of a man when he is telling it, the most indifferent and the most ordinary occurrences, are matters which produce mirth and good-humour. I went to spend an hour after this manner with some friends who enjoy it in perfection whenever they meet, when those destroyers above-mentioned came in upon us. There is not a man among them has any notion of distinction of superiority to one another, either in their fortunes or their talents, when they are in

---

indicate the spirit of sophisticated moralism which informed discussions of laughter, wit, and comedy in the early eighteenth century. Particularly for Steele, right-minded laughter is a matter of benevolent and social grace, a concern of "mutual good-will." Addison's perspective is often more formal and critical than Steele's; but even when he appears to be following Hobbes (*Spectator* No. 249), his interests return to the generous and polite possibilities of the comic impulse.

company. Or if any reflection to the contrary occurs in their thoughts, it only strikes a delight upon their minds, that so much wisdom and power is in possession of one whom they love and esteem.

In these my lucubrations, I have frequently dwelt upon this one topic. It would make short work for us reformers, for it is only want of making this a position that renders some characters bad which would otherwise be good. Tom Mercett means no man ill, but does ill to everybody. His ambition is to be witty; and to carry on that design, he breaks through all things that other people hold sacred. If he thought wit was no way to be used but to the advantage of society, that sprightliness would have a new turn, and we should expect what he is going to say with satisfaction instead of fear. It is no excuse for being mischievous, that a man is mischievous without malice: nor will it be thought an atonement that the ill was done not to injure the party concerned, but to divert the indifferent.

It is, methinks, a very great error that we should not profess honesty in conversation as much as in commerce. If we consider that there is no greater misfortune than to be ill received where we love the turning a man to ridicule among his friends, we rob him of greater enjoyments than he could have purchased by his wealth; yet he that laughs at him, would perhaps be the last man who would hurt him in this case of less consequence. It has been said, the history of Don Quixote utterly destroyed the spirit of gallantry in the Spanish nation; and I believe we may say much more truly, that the humour of ridicule has done as much injury to the true relish of company in England.

Such satisfactions as arise from the secret comparison of ourselves to others, with relation to their inferior fortunes or merit, are mean and unworthy. The true and high state of conversation is when men communicate their thoughts to each other upon such subjects, and in such a manner, as would be pleasant if there were no such thing as folly in the world; for it is but a low condition of wit in one man which depends upon folly in another. * * *

JOSEPH ADDISON

The Spectator, No. 47
(1711)

Mr. Hobbes, in his "Discourse of Human Nature," which, in my humble opinion, is much the best of all his works, after some very curious observations upon laughter, concludes thus: "The passion of laughter is nothing else but sudden glory arising from some sudden conception of some eminency in ourselves, by comparison with the infirmity of others, or with our own formerly. For men laugh at the follies of themselves past, when they come suddenly to remembrance, except they bring with them any present dishonor."

According to this author therefore, when we hear a man laugh excessively, instead of saying he is very merry, we ought to tell him he is very proud. And indeed, if we look into the bottom of this matter, we shall meet with many observations to confirm us in his opinion. Every one laughs at somebody that is in an inferior state of folly to himself. It was formerly the custom for every great house in England to keep a tame fool dressed in petticoats, that the heir of the family might have an opportunity of joking upon him, and divert himself with his absurdities. For the same reason idiots are still in request in most of the courts of Germany, where there is not a prince of any great magnificence who has not two or three dressed, distinguished, undisputed fools in his retinue, whom the rest of the courtiers are always breaking their jests upon.

The Dutch, who are more famous for their industry and application than for wit and humour, hang up in several of their streets what they call the sign of the Gaper, that is, the head of an idiot dressed in a cap and bells, and gaping in a most immoderate manner. This is a standing jest at Amsterdam.

Thus every one diverts himself with some person or other that is below him in point of understanding, and triumphs in the superiority of his genius, whilst he has such objects of derision before his eyes. Mr. Dennis has very well expressed this in a couple of humorous lines, which are part of a translation of a satire in Monsieur Boileau.[1]

> Thus one fool lolls his tongue out at another,
> And shakes his empty noddle at his brother.

Mr. Hobbes's reflection gives us the reason why the insignificant people above-mentioned are stirrers up of laughter among men of a gross taste. But as the more understanding part of mankind do not find their risibility affected by such ordinary objects, it may be worth the while to examine into the several provocatives of laughter in men of superior sense and knowledge.

In the first place I must observe, that there is a set of merry drolls, whom the common people of all countries admire, and seem to love so well, that they could eat them, according to the old proverb: I mean those circumforaneous[2] wits whom every nation calls by the name of that dish of meat which it loves best. In Holland they are termed "pickled herrings"; in France, "Jean potages"; in Italy, "maccaronies"; and in Great Britain, "Jack puddings." These merry wags, from whatsoever food they receive their titles, that they may make their audiences laugh,

1. Boileau, *Satire IV*, translated by John Dennis.
2. Strolling, vagrant.

always appear in a fool's coat, and commit such blunders and mistakes in every step they take, and every word they utter, as those who listen to them would be ashamed of.

But this little triumph of the understanding, under the disguise of laughter, is nowhere more visible than in that custom which prevails everywhere among us on the first day of the present month,[3] when everybody takes it in his head to make as many fools as he can. In proportion as there are more follies discovered, so there is more laughter raised on this day, than in any other in the whole year. A neighbor of mine, who is a haberdasher by trade, and a very shallow conceited fellow, makes his boasts that for these ten years successively he has not made less than a hundred "April fools." My landlady had a falling out with him about a fortnight ago, for sending every one of her children upon some "sleeveless errand," as she terms it. Her eldest son went to buy a halfpenny worth of inkle[4] at a shoemaker's; the eldest daughter was dispatched half a mile to see a monster; and, in short, the whole family of innocent children made "April fools." Nay, my landlady herself did not escape him. This empty fellow has laughed upon these conceits ever since.

This art of wit is well enough, when confined to one day in a twelvemonth; but there is an ingenious tribe of men sprung up of late years, who are for making "April fools" every day in the year. These gentlemen are commonly distinguished by the name of "biters"; a race of men that are perpetually employed in laughing at those mistakes which are of their own production.

Thus we see, in proportion as one man is more refined than another, he chooses his fool out of a lower or higher class of mankind; or, to speak in a more philosophical language, that secret elation and pride of heart which is generally called laughter, arises in him from his comparing himself with an object below him, whether it so happens that it be a natural or an artificial fool. It is indeed very possible, that the persons we laugh at may in the main of their characters be much wiser men than ourselves; but if they would have us laugh at them, they must fall short of us in those respects which stir up this passion.

I am afraid I shall appear too abstracted in my speculations, if I show that when a man of wit makes us laugh, it is by betraying some oddness or infirmity in his own character, or in the representation which he makes of others; and that when we laugh at a brute, or even at an inanimate thing, it is at some action or incident that bears a remote analogy to any blunder or absurdity in reasonable creatures.

But to come into common life: I shall pass by the consideration of those stage coxcombs that are able to shake a whole audience, and take

3. April.
4. Linen tape.

notice of a particular sort of men who are such provokers of mirth in conversation, that it is impossible for a club or merry meeting to subsist without them; I mean those honest gentlemen that are always exposed to the wit and raillery of their well-wishers and companions; that are pelted by men, women, and children, friends and foes, and, in a word, stand as "butts" in conversation, for every one to shoot at that pleases. I know several of these "butts" who are men of wit and sense, though by some odd turn of humour, some unlucky cast in their person or behavior, they have always the misfortune to make the company merry. The truth of it is, a man is not qualified for a "butt," who has not a good deal of wit and vivacity, even in the ridiculous side of his character. A stupid "butt" is only fit for the conversation of ordinary people; men of wit require one that will give them play, and bestir himself in the absurd part of his behavior. A "butt" with these accomplishments frequently gets the laugh of his side, and turns the ridicule upon him that attacks him. Sir John Falstaff was an hero of this species, and gives a good description of himself in his capacity of a "butt," after the following manner: "Men of all sorts," says that merry knight,[5] "take a pride to gird at me. The brain of man is not able to invent anything that tends to laughter more than I invent, or is invented on me. I am not only witty in myself, but the cause that wit is in other men."

The Spectator, No. 62
(1711)

Mr. Locke has an admirable reflection upon the difference of wit and judgment, whereby he endeavors to show the reason why they are not always the talents of the same person. His words are as follow: "And hence, perhaps, may be given some reason of that common observation, that men who have a great deal of wit and prompt memories, have not always the clearest judgment, or deepest reason. For wit lying most in the assemblage of ideas, and putting those together with quickness and variety, wherein can be found any resemblance or congruity, thereby to make up pleasant pictures and agreeable visions in the fancy; judgment, on the contrary, lies quite on the other side, in separating carefully one from another, ideas wherein can be found the least difference, thereby to avoid being misled by similitude, and by affinity to take one thing for another. This is a way of proceeding quite contrary to metaphor and allusion; wherein, for the most part, lies that entertainment and pleasantry of wit which strikes so lively on the fancy, and is therefore so acceptable to all people."[1]

5. 2 Henry IV I.2.7–12.
1. John Locke, Essay Concerning Human Understanding 2.11.2.

This is, I think, the best and most philosophical account that I have ever met with of wit, which generally, though not always, consists in such a resemblance and congruity of ideas as this author mentions. I shall only add to it, by way of explanation, that every resemblance of ideas is not that which we call wit, unless it be such an one that gives delight and surprise to the reader. These two properties seem essential to wit, more particularly the last of them. In order therefore that the resemblance in the ideas be wit, it is necessary that the ideas should not lie too near one another in the nature of things; for where the likeness is obvious, it gives no surprise. To compare one man's singing to that of another, or to represent the whiteness of any object by that of milk and snow, or the variety of its colors by those of the rainbow, cannot be called wit, unless, besides this obvious resemblance, there be some further congruity discovered in the two ideas that is capable of giving the reader some surprise. Thus when a poet tells us, the bosom of his mistress is as white as snow, there is no wit in the comparison; but when he adds, with a sigh, that it is as cold too, it then grows into wit. Every reader's memory may supply him with innumerable instances of the same nature. For this reason, the similitudes in heroic poets, who endeavor rather to fill the mind with great conceptions, than to divert it with such as are new and surprising, have seldom anything in them that can be called wit. Mr. Locke's account of wit, with this short explanation, comprehends most of the species of wit, as metaphors, similitudes, allegories, enigmas, mottoes, parables, fables, dreams, visions, dramatic writings, burlesque, and all the methods of allusion: as there are many other pieces of wit (how remote soever they may appear at first sight from the foregoing description) which upon examination will be found to agree with it.

As true wit generally consists in this resemblance and congruity of ideas, false wit chiefly consists in the resemblance and congruity sometimes of single letters, as in anagrams, chronograms, lipograms, and acrostics; sometimes of syllables, as in echoes and doggerel rhymes; sometimes of words, as in puns and quibbles; and sometimes of whole sentences or poems, cast into the figures of eggs, axes, or altars: nay, some carry the notion of wit so far as to ascribe it even to external mimicry; and to look upon a man as an ingenious person, that can resemble the tone, posture, or face of another.

As true wit consists in the resemblance of ideas, and false wit in the resemblance of words, according to the foregoing instances; there is another kind of wit which consists partly in the resemblance of ideas, and partly in the resemblance of words; which for distinction's sake I shall call mixed wit. This kind of wit is that which abounds in Cowley, more than in any author that ever wrote. Mr. Waller has likewise a great deal of it. Mr. Dryden is very sparing in it. Milton had a genius much above it. Spenser is in the same class with Milton. The Italians, even in their epic poetry, are full of it. Monsieur Boileau, who formed himself upon the ancient poets, has everywhere rejected it with scorn. If we look after mixed wit among the Greek writers, we shall find it nowhere but in the epigrammatists. There are indeed some strokes of it in the little poem ascribed to Musaeus, which by that, as well as many other marks, betrays itself to be a modern composition. If we look into the Latin writers, we find none of this mixed wit in Virgil, Lucretius, or Catullus; very little in Horace. But a great deal of it in Ovid, and scarce anything else in Martial.

Out of the innumerable branches of mixed wit, I shall choose one instance which may be met with in all the writers of this class. The passion of love in its nature has been thought to resemble fire; for which reason the words fire and flame are made use of to signify love. The witty poets therefore have taken an advantage from the doubtful meaning of the word fire, to make an infinite number of witticisms. Cowley, observing the cold regard of his mistress's eyes, and at the same time their power of producing love in him, considers them as burning-glasses made of ice; and finding himself able to live in the greatest extremities of love, concludes the torrid zone to be habitable.[2] When his mistress has read his letter written in juice of lemon by holding it to the fire, he desires her to read it over a second time by love's flames. When she weeps, he wishes it were inward heat that distilled those drops from the limbec.[3] When she is absent he is beyond eighty, that is, thirty degrees nearer the pole than when she is with him. His ambitious love is a fire that naturally mounts upwards; his happy love is the beams of heaven, and his unhappy love flames of hell. When it does not let him sleep, it is a flame that sends up no smoke; when it is opposed by counsel and advice, it is a fire that rages the more by the wind's blowing upon it. Upon the dying of a tree in which he had cut his loves, he observes that his written flames had burned up and withered the tree. When he resolves to give over his passion, he tells us that one burnt like him for ever dreads the fire. His heart is an Etna, that instead of Vulcan's shop encloses Cupid's forge in it. His endeavoring to drown his love in wine, is throwing oil upon the fire. He would insinuate to his mistress, that the fire of love, like that of the sun (which produces so many living creatures) should not only warm but beget. Love in another place cooks pleasure at his fire. Sometimes the poet's heart is frozen in every breast, and sometimes scorched in every eye. Sometimes he is drowned in tears, and burnt in love, like a ship set on fire in the middle of the sea.

The reader may observe in every one of these instances, that the poet mixes the qualities of fire with those of love; and in the same sentence

2. These examples come from Cowley's collection of lyric poems, *The Mistress* (1647).
3. Alembic, an apparatus used in distillation.

speaking of it both as a passion, and as real fire, surprises the reader with those seeming resemblances or contradictions that make up all the wit in this kind of writing. Mixed wit therefore is a composition of pun and true wit, and is more or less perfect as the resemblance lies in the ideas or in the words: its foundations are laid partly in falsehood and partly in truth: reason puts in her claim for one half of it, and extravagance for the other. The only province therefore for this kind of wit, is epigram, or those little occasional poems that in their own nature are nothing else but a tissue of epigrams. I cannot conclude this head of mixed wit, without owning that the admirable poet out of whom I have taken the examples of it, had as much true wit as any author that ever writ; and indeed all other talents of an extraordinary genius.

It may be expected, since I am upon this subject, that I should take notice of Mr. Dryden's definition of wit; which, with all the deference that is due to the judgment of so great a man, is not so properly a definition of wit, as of good writing in general. Wit, as he defines it, is "a propriety of words and thoughts adapted to the subject."[4] If this be a true definition of wit, I am apt to think that Euclid was the greatest wit that ever set pen to paper: it is certain there never was a greater propriety of words and thoughts adapted to the subject, than what that author has made use of in his elements. I shall only appeal to my reader, if this definition agrees with any notion he has of wit: if it be a true one, I am sure Mr. Dryden was not only a better poet, but a greater wit than Mr. Cowley; and Virgil a much more facetious man than either Ovid or Martial. * * *

OLIVER GOLDSMITH

An Essay on the Theater; or, A Comparison between Laughing and Sentimental Comedy[†]
(1773)

The theater, like all other amusements, has its fashions and its prejudices; and, when satiated with its excellence, mankind begin to mistake change for improvement. For some years tragedy was the reigning entertainment, but of late it has entirely given way to comedy, and our best

4. Addison omits an important word. Dryden wrote ". . . thoughts and words *elegantly* adapted to the subject." See daggered note on p. 464.
† Goldsmith's attack on sentimental comedy appeared in the *Westminster Magazine* in 1773. Within the year, his own play *She Stoops to Conquer* had scored a success; within five years, it had been joined by the major comedies of Sheridan to form a revival of what Goldsmith in his essay calls "laughing comedy."

efforts are now exerted in these lighter kinds of composition. The pomp-
ous train, the swelling phrase, and the unnatural rant are displaced for
that natural portrait of human folly and frailty, of which all are judges,
because all have sat for the picture.

But as in describing nature it is presented with a double face, either
of mirth or sadness, our modern writers find themselves at a loss which
chiefly to copy from; and it is now debated, whether the exhibition of
human distress is likely to afford the mind more entertainment than that
of human absurdity?

Comedy is defined by Aristotle to be a picture of the frailties of the
lower part of mankind, to distinguish it from tragedy, which is an exhibition of the misfortunes of the great. When comedy, therefore, ascends
to produce the characters of princes or generals upon the stage, it is out
of its walk, since low life and middle life are entirely its object. The
principal question, therefore, is, whether, in describing low or middle
life, an exhibition of its follies be not preferable to a detail of its calamities? Or, in other words, which deserves the preference—the weeping
sentimental comedy so much in fashion at present, or the laughing, and
even low comedy, which seems to have been last exhibited by Vanbrugh
and Cibber?[1]

If we apply to authorities, all the great masters in the dramatic art
have but one opinion. Their rule is, that as tragedy displays the calamities of the great, so comedy should excite our laughter by ridiculously
exhibiting the follies of the lower part of mankind. Boileau, one of the
best modern critics, asserts that comedy will not admit of tragic distress:—

> *Le comique, ennemi des soupirs et des pleurs,*
> *N'admet point dans ses vers de tragiques douleurs.*[2]

Nor is this rule without the strongest foundation in nature, as the distresses of the mean by no means affect us so strongly as the calamities
of the great. When tragedy exhibits to us some great man fallen from
his height and struggling with want and adversity, we feel his situation
in the same manner as we suppose he himself must feel, and our pity is
increased in proportion to the height from which he fell. On the contrary, we do not so strongly sympathize with one born in humbler circumstances, and encountering accidental distress: so that while we melt
for Belisarius,[3] we scarcely give halfpence to the beggar who accosts us
in the street. The one has our pity, the other our contempt. Distress,
therefore, is the proper object of tragedy, since the great excite our pity

---

1. Sir John Vanbrugh and Colley Cibber, dramatists of the 1690s and earlier eighteenth century.
2. *L'Art Poétique* 3.401–02: "Comedy, the foe of sighs and tears / Prevents all tragic sorrows from
   its lines."
3. A famous Roman general under the emperor Justinian. According to legend, he was disgraced,
   blinded, and forced to beg in the streets.

by their fall; but not equally so of comedy, since the actors employed in it are originally so mean that they sink but little by their fall.

Since the first origin of the stage, tragedy and comedy have run in distinct channels, and never till of late encroached upon the provinces of each other. Terence, who seems to have made the nearest approaches, always judiciously stops short before he comes to the downright pathetic; and yet he is even reproached by Caesar for wanting the *vis comica*. All the other comic writers of antiquity aim only at rendering folly or vice ridiculous, but never exalt their characters into buskined pomp, or make what Voltaire humourously calls *a tradesmen's tragedy*.

Yet notwithstanding this weight of authority, and the universal practice of former ages, a new species of dramatic composition has been introduced, under the name of *sentimental* comedy, in which the virtues of private life are exhibited, rather than the vices exposed; and the distresses rather than the faults of mankind make our interest in the piece. These comedies have had of late great success, perhaps from their novelty, and also from their flattering every man in his favorite foible. In these plays almost all the characters are good, and exceedingly generous; they are lavish enough of their *tin* money on the stage: and though they want humour, have abundance of sentiment and feeling. If they happen to have faults or foibles, the spectator is taught not only to pardon but to applaud them, in consideration of the goodness of their hearts; so that folly, instead of being ridiculed, is commended, and the comedy aims at touching our passions without the power of being truly pathetic. In this manner we are likely to lose one great source of entertainment on the stage; for while the comic poet is invading the province of the tragic muse, he leaves her lovely sister quite neglected. Of this, however, he is no way solicitous, as he measures his fame by his profits.

But it will be said that the theater is formed to amuse mankind, and that it matters little, if this end be answered, by what means it is obtained. If mankind find delight in weeping at comedy, it would be cruel to abridge them in that or any other innocent pleasure. If those pieces are denied the name of comedies, yet call them by any other name, and if they are delightful, they are good. Their success, it will be said, is a mark of their merit, and it is only abridging our happiness to deny us an inlet to amusement.

These objections, however, are rather specious than solid. It is true that amusement is a great object of the theater, and it will be allowed that these sentimental pieces do often amuse us, but the question is whether the true comedy would not amuse us more? The question is whether a character supported throughout a piece, with its ridicule still attending, would not give us more delight than this species of bastard tragedy, which only is applauded because it is new?

A friend of mine, who was sitting unmoved at one of these sentimental pieces, was asked how he could be so indifferent? "Why, truly," says he, "as the hero is but a tradesman, it is indifferent to me whether he be turned out of his counting-house on Fish Street Hill, since he will still have enough left to open shop in St. Giles's."

The other objection is as ill-grounded; for though we should give those pieces another name, it will not mend their efficacy. It will continue a kind of *mulish* production, with all the defects of its opposite parents, and marked with sterility. If we are permitted to make comedy weep, we have an equal right to make tragedy laugh and to set down in blank verse the jests and repartees of all the attendants in a funeral procession.

But there is one argument in favor of sentimental comedy, which will keep it on the stage in spite of all that can be said against it. It is, of all others, the most easily written. Those abilities that can hammer out a novel are fully sufficient for the production of a sentimental comedy. It is only sufficient to raise the characters a little; to deck out the hero with a riband, or give the heroine a title; then to put an insipid dialogue, without character or humour, into their mouths, give them mighty good hearts, very fine clothes, furnish a new set of scenes, make a pathetic scene or two, with a sprinkling of tender melancholy conversation through the whole, and there is no doubt but all the ladies will cry and all the gentlemen applaud.

Humour at present seems to be departing from the stage, and it will soon happen that our comic players will have nothing left for it but a fine coat and a song. It depends upon the audience whether they will actually drive those poor merry creatures from the stage, or sit at a play as gloomy as at the Tabernacle.[4] It is not easy to recover an art when once lost; and it will be but a just punishment, that when, by our being too fastidious, we have banished humour from the stage, we should ourselves be deprived of the art of laughing.

4. A Methodist chapel in London.

The Collier Controversy: 1698

JEREMY COLLIER

A Short View of the Immorality and Profaneness of the English Stage[†]
(1698)

Introduction

The business of plays is to recommend virtue and discountenance vice; to show the uncertainty of human greatness, the sudden turns of fate, and the unhappy conclusions of violence and injustice; 'tis to expose the singularities of pride and fancy, to make folly and falsehood contemptible, and to bring everything that is ill under infamy and neglect. This design has been oddly pursued by the English stage. Our poets write with a different view and are gone into another interest. 'Tis true, were their intentions fair, they might be serviceable to this purpose. They have in a great measure the springs of thought and inclination in their power. Show, music, action, and rhetoric are moving entertainments; and, rightly employed, would be very significant. But force and motion are things indifferent, and the use lies chiefly in the application. These advantages are now in the enemy's hand and under a very dangerous management. Like cannon seized, they are pointed the wrong way; and by the strength of the defense, the mischief is made the greater. That this complaint is not unreasonable I shall endeavor to prove by showing the misbehavior of the stage with respect to morality and religion. Their liberties in the following particulars are intolerable, *viz.*, their smuttiness of expression; their swearing, profaneness, and lewd application of Scripture; their abuse of the clergy, their making their top

---

[†] Collier was something of an outlaw by the time he published his *Short View*. As a non-juror (that is, a clergyman who refused to swear allegiance to William and Mary after the "bloodless revolution" of 1688), he had been deprived of his offices and briefly imprisoned; and in 1696 he became a fugitive from another charge, that of absolving on the scaffold two prisoners convicted of an assassination plot against the king. Compared to these adventures, an attack on the indecency of the stage was rather a popular effort, and Collier did not stop with one volley. Within the next decade he wrote *A Defense of the Short View* (1698), *A Second Defense of the Short View* (1700), *A Dissuasive from the Playhouse* (1703), and *A Farther Vindication of the Short View* (1707).

characters libertines and giving them success in their debauchery. This charge, with some other irregularities, I shall make good against the stage and show both the novelty and scandal of the practice. And, first, I shall begin with the rankness and indecency of their language.

Chapter I: The Immodesty of the Stage

In treating this head, I hope the reader does not expect that I should set down chapter and page and give him the citations at length. To do this would be a very unacceptable and foreign employment. Indeed the passages, many of them, are in no condition to be handled. He that is desirous to see these flowers, let him do it in their own soil. 'Tis my business rather to kill the root than transplant it. But that the poets may not complain of injustice, I shall point to the infection at a distance, and refer in general to play and person.

Now among the curiosities of this kind we may reckon Mrs. Pinchwife, Horner, and Lady Fidget in the *Country Wife*; Widow Blackacre and Olivia in the *Plain Dealer*.[1] These, though not all the exceptionable characters, are the most remarkable. I'm sorry the author should stoop his wit thus low and use his understanding so unkindly. Some people appear coarse and slovenly out of poverty. They can't well go to the charge of sense. They are offensive, like beggars, for want of necessaries. But this is none of the *Plain Dealer's* case; he can afford his Muse a better dress when he pleases. But then the rule is, where the motive is the less, the fault is the greater. To proceed. Jacinta, Elvira, Dalinda, and Lady Pliant, in the *Mock Astrologer, Spanish Friar, Love Triumphant,* and *Double Dealer*,[2] forget themselves extremely; and almost all the characters in the *Old Bachelor*[3] are foul and nauseous. *Love for Love* and the *Relapse* strike sometimes upon this sand, and so likewise does *Don Sebastian*.[4]

I don't pretend to have read the stage through; neither am I particular to my utmost. Here is quoting enough unless 'twere better. Besides, I may have occasion to mention somewhat of this kind afterwards. But from what has been hinted already, the reader may be over-furnished. Here is a large collection of debauchery; such pieces are rarely to be met with. 'Tis sometimes painted at length too and appears in great variety of progress and practice. It wears almost all sorts of dresses to engage the fancy and fasten upon the memory and keep up the charm from languishing. Sometimes you have it in image and description; sometimes by way of allusion; sometimes in disguise; and sometimes without it. And what can be the meaning of such a representation unless

1. Both plays are by Wycherley.
2. The first three plays are by Dryden, the fourth by Congreve.
3. By Congreve.
4. By Congreve, Vanbrugh, and Dryden, respectively.

it be to tincture the audience, to extinguish shame, and make lewdness a diversion? This is the natural consequence, and therefore one would think 'twas the intention too. Such licentious discourse tends to no point but to stain the imagination, to awaken folly, and to weaken the defenses of virtue. It was upon the account of these disorders that Plato banished poets his Commonwealth. And one of the Fathers calls poetry, *Vinum Daemonum*, an intoxicating draught made up of the Devil's dispensatory.

I grant the abuse of a thing is no argument against the use of it. However, young people particularly should not entertain themselves with a lewd picture, especially when 'tis drawn by a masterly hand. For such a liberty may probably raise those passions which can neither be discharged without trouble, nor satisfied without a crime. 'Tis not safe for a man to trust his virtue too far, for fear it should give him the slip! But the danger of such an entertainment is but part of the objection; 'tis all scandal and meanness into the bargain. It does in effect degrade human nature; sinks reason into appetite, and breaks down the distinctions between man and beast. Goats and monkeys, if they could speak, would express their brutality in such language as this.

To argue the matter more at large.

Smuttiness is a fault in behavior as well as in religion. 'Tis a very coarse diversion, the entertainment of those who are generally least both in sense and station. The looser part of the mob have no true relish of decency and honor, and want education and thought to furnish out a genteel conversation. Barrenness of fancy makes them often take up with those scandalous liberties. A vicious imagination may blot a great deal of paper at this rate with ease enough. And 'tis possible convenience may sometimes invite to the expedient. The modern poets seem to use smut as the old ones did machines, to relieve a fainting invention. When Pegasus is jaded and would stand still, he is apt like other tits to run into every puddle.

Obscenity in any company is a rustic, uncreditable talent, but among women 'tis particularly rude. Such talk would be very affrontive in conversation and not endured by any lady of reputation. Whence then comes it to pass that those liberties which disoblige so much in conversation should entertain upon the stage? Do women leave all the regards to decency and conscience behind them when they come to the playhouse? Or does the place transform their inclinations and turn their former aversions into pleasure? Or were their pretenses to sobriety elsewhere nothing but hypocrisy and grimace? Such suppositions as these are all satire and invective. They are rude imputations upon the whole sex. To treat the ladies with such stuff is no better than taking their money to abuse them. It supposes their imagination vicious and their memories ill-furnished, that they are practiced in the language of the stews and pleased with the scenes of brutishness. When at the same time the customs of education and the laws of decency are so very cautious and reserved in regard to women—I say so very reserved—that 'tis almost a fault for them to understand they are ill-used. They can't discover their disgust without disadvantage, nor blush without disservice to their modesty. To appear with any skill in such cant looks as if they had fallen upon ill conversation or managed their curiosity amiss. In a word, he that treats the ladies with such discourse must conclude either that they like it or they do not. To suppose the first is a gross reflection upon their virtue. And as for the latter case, it entertains them with their own aversion, which is ill-nature, and ill-manners enough in all conscience. And in this particular custom and conscience, the forms of breeding and the maxims of religion are on the same side. In other instances vice is often too fashionable. But here a man can't be a sinner without being a clown.

In this respect the stage is faulty to a scandalous degree of nauseousness and aggravation. For:

1. The poets make women speak smuttily. Of this the places beforementioned are sufficient evidence, and if there was occasion they might be multiplied to a much greater number. Indeed the comedies are seldom clear of these blemishes. And sometimes you have them in tragedy. For instance, the *Orphan's*[5] Monimia makes a very improper description, and the Royal Leonora in the *Spanish Friar* runs a strange length in the history of love. And do princesses use to make their reports with such fulsome freedoms? Certainly this Leonora was the first queen of her family. Such raptures are too luscious for Joan of Naples. Are these the tender things Mr. . Dryden says the ladies call on him for? I suppose he means the ladies that are too modest to show their faces in the pit.[6] This entertainment can be fairly designed for none but such. Indeed it hits their palate exactly. It regales their lewdness, graces their character, and keeps up their spirits for their vocation. Now to bring women under such misbehavior is violence to their native modesty, and a misrepresentation of their sex. For modesty, as Mr. Rapin[7] observes, is the character of women. To represent them without this quality is to make monsters of them and throw them out of their kind. Euripides, who was no negligent observer of human nature, is always careful of this Decorum. Thus Phaedra,[8] when possessed with an infamous passion, takes all imaginable pains to conceal it. She is as regular and reserved in her language as the most virtuous matron. 'Tis true, the force of shame and desire, the scandal of satisfying, and the difficulty of parting with her inclina-

5. A play by Thomas Otway.
6. Prostitutes sometimes wore masks to the theater.
7. René Rapin, a seventeenth-century French commentator on Aristotle.
8. In Euripides' *Hippolitus*.

tions disorder her to distraction. However, her frenzy is not lewd; she keeps her modesty even after she has lost her wits. Had Shakespeare secured this point for his young virgin, Ophelia, the play had been better contrived. Since he was resolved to drown the lady like a kitten, he should have set her a swimming a little sooner. To keep her alive only to sullen her reputation and discover the rankness of her breath was very cruel. But it may be said the freedoms of distraction go for nothing, a fever has no faults, and a man *non compos* may kill without murder. It may be so; but then such people ought to be kept in dark rooms and without company. To show them or let them loose is somewhat unreasonable. But after all, the modern stage seems to depend upon this expedient. Women are sometimes represented silly, and sometimes mad, to enlarge their liberty and screen their impudence from censure. This politic contrivance we have in Marcella, Hoyden, and Miss Prue.[9] However, it amounts to this confession, that women, when they have their understanding about them, ought to converse otherwise. In fine, modesty is the distinguishing virtue of that sex and serves both for ornament and defense; modesty was designed by providence as a guard to virtue, and that it might be always at hand 'tis wrought into the mechanism of the body. 'Tis likewise proportioned to the occasions of life and strongest in youth when passion is so too. 'Tis a quality as true to innocence as the senses are to health; whatever is ungrateful to the first is prejudicial to the latter. The enemy no sooner approaches, but the blood rises in opposition and looks defiance to an indecency. It supplies the room of reasoning and collection. Intuitive knowledge can scarcely make a quicker impression; and what, then, can be a surer guide to the unexperienced? It teaches by sudden instinct and aversion. This is both a ready and a powerful method of instruction. The tumult of the blood and spirits and the uneasiness of the sensation are of singular use. They serve to awaken reason and prevent surprise. Thus the distinctions of good and evil are refreshed, and the temptation kept at a proper distance.

2. They represent their single ladies and persons of condition under these disorders of liberty. This makes the irregularity still more monstrous and a greater contradiction to Nature and probability. But rather than not be vicious, they will venture to spoil a character. This mismanagement we have partly seen already. Jacinta and Belinda[1] are farther proof; and the *Double Dealer* is particularly remarkable. There are but four Ladies in this play, and three of the biggest of them are whores. A great compliment to quality to tell them there is not above a quarter of them honest! This was not the Roman breeding. Terence and Plautus his strumpets were little people; but of this more hereafter.

9. Characters in, respectively, Thomas D'Urfey's *Don Quixote*, Vanbrugh's *The Relapse*, and Dryden's *An Evening's Love; or, The Mock Astrologer*.
1. Characters in Dryden's *The Mock Astrologer* and Congreve's *The Old Bachelor*.

3. They have oftentimes not so much as the poor refuge of a double meaning to fly to. So that you are under a necessity either of taking ribaldry or nonsense. And when the sentence has two handles, the worst is generally turned to the audience. The matter is so contrived that the smut and scum of the thought now arises uppermost, and, like a picture drawn to sight, looks always upon the company.

4. And which is still more extraordinary, the prologues and epilogues are sometimes scandalous to the last degree. I shall discover them for once, and let them stand like rocks in the margin.[2] Now here, properly speaking, the actors quit the stage and remove from fiction into life. Here they converse with the boxes and pit and address directly to the audience. These preliminary and concluding parts are designed to justify the conduct of the play, and bespeak the favor of the company. Upon such occasions one would imagine, if ever, the ladies should be used with respect and the measures of decency observed. But here we have lewdness without shame or example. Here the poet exceeds himself. Here are such strains as would turn the stomach of an ordinary debauchee and be almost nauseous in the stews. And to make it the more agreeable, women are commonly picked out for this service. Thus the poet courts the good opinion of the audience. This is the dessert he regales the ladies with at the close of the entertainment. It seems, he thinks, they have admirable palates! Nothing can be a greater breach of manners than such liberties as these. If a man would study to outrage quality and virtue, he could not do it more effectually. But:

5. Smut is still more insufferable with respect to religion. The heathen religion was in a great measure a mystery of iniquity. Lewdness was consecrated in the temples as well as practiced in the stews. Their deities were great examples of vice and worshipped with their own inclination. 'Tis no wonder therefore their poetry should be tinctured with their belief, and that the stage should borrow some of the liberties of their theology. This made Mercury's procuring and Jupiter's adultery the more passable in *Amphytrion*.[3] Upon this score, Gimnausium is less monstrous in praying the gods to send her store of gallants. And thus Chaerea defends his adventure by the precedent of Jupiter and Danae. But the Christian religion is quite of another complexion. Both its precepts and authorities are the highest discouragement to licentiousness. It forbids the remotest tendencies to evil, banishes the follies of conversation, and obliges up to sobriety of thought. That which might pass for raillery and entertainment in heathenism is detestable in Christianity. The restraint of the precept and the quality of the Deity and the expectations of futurity quite alter the case.

---

2. In the margin Collier lists *The Mock Astrologer, The Country Wife,* Dryden's *Cleomenes (The Spartan Hero),* and *The Old Bachelor.*
3. Collier mentions Roman comedies by Plautus and Terence.

*   *   *

*From Chapter IV. The Stage-Poets Make Their Principal
Persons Vicious and Reward Them at the End of the Play*

The lines of virtue and vice are struck out by nature in very legible distinctions; they tend to a different point, and in the greater instances the space between them is easily perceived. Nothing can be more unlike than the original forms of these qualities: the first has all the sweetness, charms, and graces imaginable; the other has the air of a post ill carved into a monster, and looks both foolish and frightful together. These are the native appearances of Good and Evil. And they that endeavor to blot the distinctions, to rub out the colors or change the marks, are extremely to blame. 'Tis confessed as long as the mind is awake and conscience goes true there's no fear of being imposed on. But when vice is varnished over with pleasure and comes in the shape of convenience, then the case grows somewhat dangerous; for the fancy may be gained and the guards corrupted and reason suborned against itself. And thus a disguise often passes when the person would otherwise be stopped. To put lewdness into a thriving condition, to give it an equipage of quality, and to treat it with ceremony and respect is the way to confound the understanding, to fortify the charm, and to make the mischief invincible. Innocence is often owing to fear, and appetite is kept under by shame; but when these restraints are once taken off, when profit and liberty lie on the same side, and a man can debauch himself into credit, what can be expected in such a case, but that pleasure should grow absolute and madness carry all before it? The stage seems eager to bring matters to this issue; they have made a considerable progress and are still pushing their point with all the vigor imaginable. If this be not their aim, why is lewdness so much considered in character and success? Why are their favorites atheistical and their fine gentlemen debauched? To what purpose is vice thus preferred, thus ornamented and caressed, unless for imitation? That matter of fact stands thus, I shall make good by several instances. To begin then with their men of breeding and figure. Wildblood[4] sets up for debauchery, ridicules marriage, and swears by Mahomet. Bellamy makes sport with the Devil, and Lorenzo[5] is vicious and calls his father bawdy magistrate. Horner is horridly smutty, and Harcourt false to his friend who used him kindly. In *The Plain Dealer*, Freeman talks coarsely, cheats the widow, debauches her son, and makes him undutiful. Bellmour[6] is lewd and profane, and Mellefont[7] puts Careless in the best way he can to debauch

---

4. In Dryden's *The Mock Astrologer*, as is Bellamy, below.
5. In Dryden's *The Spanish Friar*.
6. In Congreve's *The Old Bachelor*.
7. In Congreve's *The Double-Dealer*.

Lady Plyant. These sparks generally marry the top ladies, and those that do not are brought to no penance, but go off with the character of fine gentlemen. In *Don Sebastian*,[8] Antonio, an atheistical bully, is rewarded with the Lady Moraima and half the Mufti's estate. Valentine in *Love for Love* is (if I may so call him) the hero of the play. This spark the poet would pass for a person of virtue, but he speaks too late. 'Tis true, he was hearty in his affection to Angelica. Now without question, to be in love with a fine lady of 30,000 Pounds is a great virtue! But then abating this single commendation, Valentine is altogether compounded of vice. He is a prodigal debauchee, unnatural and profane, obscene, saucy and undutiful, and yet this libertine is crowned for the man of merit, has his wishes thrown into his lap, and makes the happy exit. I perceive we should have a rare set of virtues if these poets had the making of them! How they hug a vicious character, and how profuse are they in their liberalities to lewdness! In *The Provoked Wife*,[9] Constant swears at length, solicits Lady Brute, confesses himself lewd, and prefers debauchery to marriage. He handles the last subject very notably and worth the hearing. *There is* (says he) *a poor sordid slavery in marriage that turns the flowing tide of honor and sinks it to the lowest ebb of infamy. 'Tis a corrupted soil; ill nature, avarice, sloth, cowardice, and dirt are all its product—but then constancy (alias whoring) is a brave, free, haughty, generous agent.* This is admirable stuff both for the rhetoric and the reason! The character of Young Fashion in *The Relapse* is of the same staunchness, but this the reader may have in another place.

To sum up the evidence. A fine gentleman is a fine whoring, swearing, smutty, atheistical man. These qualifications, it seems, complete the idea of honor. They are the top improvements of fortune and the distinguishing glories of birth and breeding! This is the stage-test for quality, and those that can't stand it ought to be disclaimed. The restraints of conscience and the pendantry of virtue are unbecoming a cavalier. Future securities and reaching beyond life are vulgar provisions. If he falls a-thinking at this rate, he forfeits his honor; for his head was only made to run against a post! Here you have a man of breeding and figure that burlesques the Bible, swears, and talks smut to ladies, speaks ill of his friend behind his back, and betrays his interest. A fine gentleman that has neither honesty nor honor, conscience nor manners, good nature nor civil hypocrisy; fine only in the insignificancy of life, the abuse of religion, and the scandals of conversation. These worshipful things are the poet's favorites. They appear at the head of the fashion and shine in character and equipage. If there is any sense stirring, they must have it, though the rest of the stage suffer never so much by the partiality. And what can be the meaning of this wretched distribution of

8. By Dryden.
9. By Vanbrugh.

honor? Is it not to give credit and countenance to vice and to shame young people out of all pretense to conscience and regularity? They seem forced to turn lewd in their own defense. They can't otherwise justify themselves to the fashion, nor keep up the character of gentlemen. Thus people not well-furnished with thought and experience are debauched both in practice and principle. And thus religion grows uncreditable and passes for ill education. The stage seldom gives quarter to any thing that's serviceable or significant, but persecutes worth and goodness under every appearance. He that would be safe from their satire must take care to disguise himself in vice and hang out the colors of debauchery. How often is learning, industry, and frugality ridiculed in comedy? The rich citizens are often misers and cuckolds, and the universities, schools of pedantry upon this score. In short, libertinism and profaneness, dressing, idleness, and gallantry, are the only valuable qualities. As if people were not apt enough of themselves to be lazy, lewd, and extravagant unless they were pricked forward and provoked by glory and reputation. Thus the marks of honor and infamy are misapplied, and the ideas of virtue and vice confounded. Thus monstrousness goes for proportion, and the blemishes of human nature make up the beauties of it.

The fine ladies are of the same cut with the gentlemen. Moraima is scandalously rude to her father, helps him to a beating, and runs away with Antonio.[1] Angelica talks saucily to her uncle,[2] and Belinda confesses her inclination for a gallant.[3] And, as I have observed already, the topping ladies in *The Mock Astrologer, Spanish Friar, Country Wife, Old Bachelor, Orphan, Double Dealer,* and *Love Triumphant* are smutty and sometimes profane.

❅   ❅   ❅

Thus we see what a fine time lewd people have on the English stage. No censure, no mark of infamy, no mortification must touch them. They keep their honor untarnished and carry off the advantage of their character. They are set up for the standard of behavior and the masters of ceremony and sense. And at last, that the example may work the better they generally make them rich and happy and reward them with their own desires.

Mr. Dryden, in the Preface to his *Mock Astrologer,*[4] confesses himself blamed for this practice: *for making debauched persons his protagonists or chief persons of the drama; and for making them happy in the conclusion of the play, against the law of comedy, which is to reward virtue and punish vice.* To this objection he makes a lame defense. And answers,

1. In Dryden's *Don Sebastian.*
2. In Congreve's *Love for Love.*
3. In Vanbrugh's *The Provoked Wife.*
4. Reprinted on pp. 464–71.

*that he knows no such law constantly observed in comedy by the ancient
or modern poets.* What then? Poets are not always exactly in rule. It may
be a good law though 'tis not constantly observed; some laws are constantly broken and yet ne'er the worse for all that. He goes on and pleads
the authorities of Plautus and Terence. I grant there are instances of
favor to vicious young people in those authors, but to this I reply:

1. That those poets had a greater compass of liberty in their religion.
Debauchery did not lie under those discouragements of scandal and
penalty with them, as it does with us. Unless, therefore, he can prove
heathenism and Christianity the same, his precedents will do him little
service.

2. Horace, who was as good a judge of the stage as either of those
comedians, seems to be of another opinion.[5] He condemns the obsceni-
ties of Plautus and tells you men of fortune and quality in his time
would not endure immodest satire. He continues, that poets were formerly admired for the great services they did: for teaching matters relating to religion and government; for refining the manners, tempering the
passions, and improving the understandings of mankind; for making
them more useful in domestic relations and the public capacities of life.
This is a demonstration that vice was not the inclination of the muses
in those days, and that Horace believed the chief business of a poet was
to instruct the audience. * * *

Lastly, Horace having expressly mentioned the beginning and progress of comedy, discovers himself more fully. He advises a poet to form
his work upon the precepts of Socrates and Plato and the models of
moral philosophy. This was the way to preserve decency and to assign a
proper fate and behavior to every character. Now if Horace would have
his poet governed by the maxims of morality, he must oblige him to
sobriety of conduct and a just distribution of rewards and punishments.

Mr. Dryden makes homewards and endeavors to fortify himself in
modern authority. He lets us know that *Ben Jonson, after whom he may
be proud to err, gives him more than one example of this conduct; that in
The Alchemist is notorious,* where neither Face nor his master are corrected according their demerits. But how proud soever Mr. Dryden may
be of an error, he has not so much of Ben Jonson's comedy as he pretends. His instance of Face *etc.* in *The Alchemist* is rather notorious
against his purpose than for it.

For Face did not counsel his master Lovewit to debauch the widow;
neither is it clear that the matter went thus far. He might gain her consent upon terms of honor for aught appears to the contrary. 'Tis true,
Face, who was one of the principal cheats, is pardoned and considered.
But then his master confesses himself kind to a fault. He owns this
indulgence was a breach of justice and unbecoming the gravity of an

5. Collier refers to Horace's *Ars Poetica.*

old man. And then desires the audience to excuse him upon the score of the temptation. But *Face continued in the cozenage till the last without repentance*. Under favor, I conceive this is a mistake. For does not Face make an apology before he leaves the stage? Does he not set himself at the bar, arraign his own practice, and cast the cause upon the clemency of the company? And are not all these signs of the dislike of what he had done? Thus careful the poet is to prevent the ill impressions of his play! He brings both man and master to confession; he dismisses them like malefactors and moves for their pardon before he gives them their discharge. But the Mock Astrologer has a gentler hand: Wildblood and Jacinta are more generously used. There is no acknowledgment exacted, no hardship put upon them. They are permitted to talk on in their libertine way to the last and take leave without the least appearance of reformation. The Mock Astrologer urges Ben Jonson's *Silent Woman* as another precedent to his purpose. For *there Dauphine confesses himself in love with all the collegiate ladies. And yet this naughty Dauphine is crowned in the end with the possession of his uncle's estate, and with the hopes of all his mistresses*. This charge, as I take it, is somewhat too severe. I grant Dauphine professes himself in love with the collegiate ladies at first. But when they invite him to a private visit, he makes them no promise, but rather appears tired and willing to disengage. Dauphine therefore is not altogether so naughty as this author represents him.

Ben Jonson's *Fox*[6] is clearly against Mr. Dryden. And here I have his own confession for proof. He declares the *poet's end in this play was the punishment of vice and the reward of virtue*. Ben was forced to strain for this piece of justice and break through the unity of design. This Mr. Dryden remarks upon him. However, he is pleased to commend the performance and calls it an excellent fifth act.

Ben Jonson shall speak for himself afterwards in the character of a critic; in the meantime I shall take a testimony or two from Shakespeare. And here we may observe the admired Falstaff goes off in disappointment. He is thrown out of favor as being a rake and dies like a rat behind the hangings. The pleasure he had given would not excuse him. The poet was not so partial as to let his humour compound for his lewdness. If 'tis objected that this remark is wide of the point, because Falstaff is represented in tragedy, where the laws of justice are more strictly observed. To this I answer, that you may call *Henry the Fourth* and *Fifth* tragedies if you please; but for all that, Falstaff wears no buskins; his character is perfectly comical from end to end.

The next instance shall be in Flowerdale the prodigal.[7] This spark, notwithstanding his extravagance, makes a lucky hand on't at last and marries up a rich lady. But then the poet qualifies him for his good

6. I.e., *Volpone*.
7. Collier refers to *The London Prodigal*, once thought to be Shakespeare's.

fortune and mends his manners with his circumstances. He makes him repent and leave off his intemperance, swearing, *etc.* And when his father warned him against a relapse, he answers very soberly: *Heaven helping me, I'll hate the course of Hell.*

I could give some instances of this kind out of Beaumont and Fletcher, but there's no need of any farther quotation: for Mr. Dryden is not satisfied with his apology from authority. He does as good as own that this may be construed no better than defending one ill practice by another. To prevent this very reasonable objection he endeavors to vindicate his precedents from the reason of the thing. To this purpose he *makes a wide difference between the rules of tragedy and comedy. That vice must be impartially prosecuted in the first, because the persons are great, etc.*

It seems then executions are only for greatness and quality. Justice is not to strike much lower than a prince. Private people may do what they please. They are too few for mischief and too little for punishment! This would be admirable doctrine for Newgate and give us a general Gaol-Delivery without more ado. But in *tragedy* (says the Mock Astrologer) *the crimes are likewise horrid,* so that there is a necessity for severity and example. And how stands the matter in comedy? Quite otherwise. There the *faults are but the sallies of youth and the frailties of human nature.* For instance. There is nothing but a little whoring, pimping, gaming, profaneness, etc. And who could be so hard hearted to give a man any trouble for this? Such rigors would be strangely inhumane! A poet is a better natured thing I can assure you. These little miscarriages *move pity and commiseration and are not such as must of necessity be punished.* This is comfortable casuistry! But to be serious. Is dissolution of manners such a peccadillo? Does a profligate conscience deserve nothing but commiseration? And are people damned only for human frailties? I perceive the laws of religion and those of the stage differ extremely! The strength of his defense lies in this choice maxim, that the *chief end of comedy is delight.* He questions *whether instruction has any thing to do in comedy. If it has, he is sure 'tis no more than its secondary end; for the business of the poet is to make you laugh.* Granting the truth of this principle, I somewhat question the serviceableness of it. For is there no diversion to be had unless vice appears prosperous and rides at the head of success? One would think such a preposterous distribution of rewards should rather shock the reason and raise the indignation of the audience. To laugh without reason is the pleasure of fools, and against it, of something worse. The exposing of knavery and making lewdness ridiculous is a much better occasion for laughter. And this, with submission, I take to be the end of comedy. And therefore it does not differ from tragedy in the end, but in the means. Instruction is the principal design of both. The one works by terror, the other by infamy.

'Tis true, they don't move in the same line, but they meet in the same point at last.

*   *   *

Indeed to make delight the main business of comedy is an unreasonable and dangerous principle, opens the way to all licentiousness, and confounds the distinction between mirth and madness. For if diversion is the chief end, it must be had at any price. No serviceable expedient must be refused, though never so scandalous. And thus the worst things are said, and the best abused; religion is insulted, and the most serious matters turned into ridicule! As if the blind side of an audience ought to be caressed, and their folly and atheism entertained in the first place. Yes, if the palate is pleased, no matter though the body is poisoned! For can one die of an easier disease than diversion? But raillery apart, certainly mirth and laughing without respect to the cause are not such supreme satisfactions! A man has sometimes pleasure in losing his wits. Frenzy and possession will shake the lungs and brighten the face; and yet I suppose they are not much to be coveted. However, now we know the reason of the profaneness and obscenity of the stage, of their hellish cursing and swearing, and in short of their great industry to make God and Goodness contemptible. 'Tis all to satisfy the company and make people laugh! A most admirable justification. What can be more engaging to an audience than to see a poet thus atheistically brave? To see him charge up to the cannon's mouth and defy the vengeance of Heaven to serve them? Besides, there may be somewhat of convenience in the case. To fetch diversion out of innocence is no such easy matter. There's no succeeding, it may be, in this method, without sweat and drudging. Clean wit, inoffensive humour, and handsome contrivance require time and thought. And who would be at this expense when the purchase is so cheap another way? 'Tis possible a poet may not always have sense enough by him for such an occasion. And since we are upon supposals, it may be the audience is not to be gained without straining a point and giving a loose to conscience. And when people are sick, are they not to be humoured? In fine, we must not make them laugh, right or wrong, for delight is the *chief end of comedy*. Delight! He should have said debauchery. That's the English of the word and the consequence of the practice. But the original design of comedy was otherwise. And granting it was not so, what then? If the ends of things were naught, they must be mended. Mischief is the chief end of malice, would it be then a blemish in ill nature to change temper and relent into goodness? The chief end of a madman, it may be, is to fire a house; must we not therefore bind him in his bed? To conclude. If delight without restraint or distinction, without conscience or shame, is the supreme law of comedy, 'twere well if we had less on't. Arbitrary pleasure is more dangerous than arbitrary power. Nothing is more brutal than to be abandoned to appetite; and nothing more wretched than to serve in such a design. * * *

JOHN DENNIS

The Usefulness of the Stage[†]
(1698)

Part I, Chapter I. That the Stage Is Instrumental to the Happiness of Mankind.

Nothing can more strongly recommend any thing to us than the assuring us that it will improve our happiness. For the chief end and design of man is to make himself happy. 'Tis what he constantly has in his eye, and in order to which he takes every step that he makes. In whatever he does, or he does not, he designs to improve or maintain his happiness. And it is by this universal principle that God maintains the harmony and order and quiet of the reasonable world. It had indeed been an inconsistency in Providence to have made a thinking and reasoning creature that had been indifferent as to misery and happiness; for God had made such a one only to disturb the rest and, consequently, had acted against his own design.

If then I can say enough to convince the reader that the stage is instrumental to the happiness of mankind, and to his own by consequence, it is evident that I need say no more to make him espouse its interest.

I shall proceed then to the proving these two things.

First, that the stage is instrumental to the happiness of mankind in general.

Secondly, that it is more particularly instrumental to the happiness of Englishmen.

The stage is instrumental to the happiness of mankind in general. And here it will be necessary to declare what is meant by happiness, and to proceed upon that.

By happiness, then, I never could understand any thing else but pleasure; for I never could have any notion of happiness that did not agree with pleasure, or any notion of pleasure that did not agree with happiness. I could never possibly conceive how any one can be happy without

---

[†] Published in June 1698, the first large-scale answer to Collier. Dennis's introduction, not included here, argues that Collier's real purpose was not to reform the stage but to abolish it. Reform is necessary, Dennis allows, but for him the theater has a civilizing power, "instrumental to the instruction of mankind," and must be defended as an institution in the face of attacks such as Collier's.

being pleased, or pleased without being happy. 'Tis universally acknowledged by mankind that happiness consists in pleasure, which is evident from this, that whatever a man does, whether in spiritual or temporal affairs, whether in matters of profit or diversion, pleasure is, at least, the chief and the final motive to it, if it is not the immediate one. And Providence seems to have sufficiently declared that pleasure was intended for our spring and fountain of action when it made it the incentive to those very acts by which we propagate our kind and preserve ourselves. As if self-love without pleasure were insufficient for either; for, as I myself have known several who have chosen rather to die than to go through tedious courses of physic, so, I make no doubt, but several would have taken the same resolution rather than have supported life by a perpetual course of eating, which had differed in nothing from a course of physic if eating and pleasure had not been things inseparable. Now as it is pleasure that obliges man to preserve himself, it is the very same that has sometimes the force to prevail upon him to his own destruction. For, as Monsieur Pascal[1] observes, the very men who hang and who drown themselves are instigated by the secret pleasure which they have from the thought that they shall be freed from pain.

Since, therefore, man in every thing that he does proposes pleasure to himself, it follows that in pleasure consists his happiness. But though he always proposes it, he very often falls short of it; for pleasure is not in his own power, since, if it were, it would follow from thence that happiness were in his power. The want of which has been always the complaint of men both sacred and secular, in all ages, in all countries, and in all conditions. "Man that is born of a woman is but of few days, and full of trouble" says Job, ch. xiv, ver. 1. Of the same nature are the two complaints of Horace, which are so fine and so poetical and so becoming of the best antiquity.

> Scandit aeratas vitiosa naves
> Cura; nec turmas equitum relinquit,
> Ocior cervis et agente nimbos
>   Ocior Euro.   Hor., Ode 16, Lib. 2.[2]

And that other, in the first ode of the third book.

> ———Timor et Minae
> Scandunt eodem quo dominus: neque
> Decedit aerata triremi et
> Post equitem sedet atra Cura.[3]

1. Blaise Pascal, seventeenth-century French philosopher.
2. "Morbid care boards even the bronze-beaked ship, nor abandons the troops of horse, swifter than stags, swifter than the east wind driving the storm."
3. "Fear and Threats climb to the place of the master: nor does black Care withdraw from the bronze-beaked galley and even settles behind the horseman."

In short, they who have made the most reflections on it have been the most satisfied of it; and above all, philosophers who, by the voluminous instructions, by the laborious directions, which they have left to posterity, have declared themselves sensible that to be happy is a very difficult thing.

And the reason why they, of all men, have always found it so difficult is because they always propounded to owe their happiness to reason, though one would think that experience might have convinced them of the folly of such a design, because they had seen that the most thinking and the most reasonable had always most complained.

For reason may often afflict us and make us miserable by setting our impotence or our guilt before us; but that which it generally does is the maintaining us in a languishing state of indifference, which, perhaps, is more removed from pleasure than it is from affliction, and which may be said to be the ordinary state of men.

It is plain then that reason, by maintaining us in that state, is an impediment to our pleasure which is our happiness: for to be pleased a man must come out of his ordinary state; now nothing in this life can bring him out of it but passion alone, which reason pretends to combat.

Nothing but passion, in effect, can please us, which every one may know by experience. For when any man is pleased he may find by reflection that at the same time he is moved. The pleasure that any man meets with oftenest is the pleasure of sense. Let anyone examine himself in that and he will find that the pleasure is owing to passion; for the pleasure vanishes with the desire and is succeeded by loathing, which is a sort of grief.

Since nothing but pleasure can make us happy, it follows that to be very happy we must be much pleased; and since nothing but passion can please us, it follows that to be very much pleased, we must be very much moved. This needs no proof, or, if it did, experience would be a very convincing one; since anyone may find, when he has a great deal of pleasure, that he is extremely moved.

And that very height and fullness of pleasure which we are promised in another life must, we are told, proceed from passion or something which resembles passion. At least no man has so much as pretended that it will be the result of reason. For we shall then be delivered from these mortal organs, and reason shall then be no more. We shall then no more have occasion from premises to draw conclusions and a long train of consequences; for, becoming all spirit and all knowledge, we shall see things as they are: we shall lead the glorious life of angels, a life exalted above all reason, a life consisting of ecstasy and intelligence.

Thus is it plain that the happiness, both of this life and the other, is owing to passion and not to reason. But though we can never be happy by the force of reason, yet, while we are in this life, we cannot possibly be happy without it, or against it. For since man is by his nature a reasonable creature, to suppose man happy against reason is to suppose him happy against nature, which is absurd and monstrous. We have shown that a man must be pleased to be happy and must be moved to be pleased; and that to please him to a height, you must move him in proportion. But then the passions must be raised after such a manner as to take reason along with them. If reason is quite overcome, the pleasure is neither long, nor sincere, nor safe. For how many that have been transported beyond their reason have never more recovered it? If reason resists, a man's breast becomes the seat of civil war, and the combat makes him miserable. For the passions, which are in their natures so very troublesome, are only so because their motions are always contrary to the motions of the will; as grief, sorrow, shame and jealousy. And that which makes some passions in their natures pleasant is because they move with the will, as love, joy, pity, hope, terror, and sometimes anger. But this is certain, that no passion can move in a full consent with the will, unless at the same time it be approved of by the understanding. And no passion can be allowed of by the understanding that is not raised by its true springs and augmented by its just degrees. Now in the world it is so very rare to have our passions thus raised, and so improved, that that is the reason why we are so seldom thoroughly and sincerely pleased. But in the drama the passions are false and abominable unless they are moved by their true springs and raised by their just degrees. Thus are they moved, thus are they raised in every well-written tragedy, till they come to as great a height as reason can very well bear. Besides, the very motion has a tendency to the subjecting them to reason, and the very raising purges and moderates them. So that the passions are seldom anywhere so pleasing and nowhere so safe as they are in tragedy. Thus have I shown that to be happy is to be pleased and to be pleased is to be moved in such a manner as is allowed of by reason. I have shown too that tragedy moves us thus, and consequently pleases us, and consequently makes us happy. Which was the thing to be proved.

Part I, Chapter III. The Objections from Reason Answered.

* * * The corruption of manners upon the Restoration appeared with all the fury of libertinism even before the playhouse was reëstablished, and long before it could have any influence on manners; so that another cause of that corruption is to be inquired after than the reestablishment of the drama; and that can be nothing but that beastly Reformation which, in the time of the late civil wars, was begun at the tail instead of the head and the heart; and which oppressed and persecuted men's inclinations instead of correcting and converting them, which afterwards broke out with the same violence that a raging fire does upon its first getting vent. And that which gave it so licentious a vent was not only the permission but the example of the court, which, for the most part, was just arrived from abroad with the king, where it had endeavored by foreign corruption to sweeten, or at least to soften, adversity, and having sojourned for a considerable time both at Paris and in the Low Countries, united the spirit of the French whoring to the fury of the Dutch drinking. So that the poets who wrote immediately after the Restoration were obliged to humour the depraved tastes of their audience. For as an impenitent sinner that should be immediately transported to heaven would be incapable of partaking of the happiness of the place, because his inclinations and affections would not be prepared for it; so if the poets of these times had written in a manner purely instructive, without any mixture of lewdness, the appetites of the audience were so far debauched that they would have judged the entertainment insipid; so that the spirit of libertinism which came in with the court and for which the people were so well prepared by the sham reformation of manners caused the lewdness of their plays, and not the lewdness of the plays the spirit of libertinism. For it is ridiculous to assign a cause of so long a standing to so new, so sudden, and so extraordinary an effect, when we may assign a cause so new, so probable, and unheard of before, as the inclinations of the people, returning with violence to their natural bent upon the encouragement and example of a court that was come home with all the corruptions of a foreign luxury; so that the sham Reformation being, in a great measure, the cause of that spirit of libertinism which with so much fury came in with King Charles the Second, and the putting down the playhouse being part of that Reformation, it is evident that the corruption of the nation is so far from proceeding from the playhouse, that it partly proceeds from having no plays at all.

That the corruption of manners is not to be attributed to the licentiousness of the drama may appear from the consideration of the reigning vices, I mean those moral vices which have more immediate influence upon men's conduct and consequently upon their happiness. And those are chiefly four.

1. The Love of Women.
2. Drinking.
3. Gaming.
4. Unnatural Sins.

For drinking and gaming, their excesses cannot be reasonably charged upon the stage for the following reasons.

First, because it cannot possibly be conceived that so reasonable a diversion as the drama can encourage or incline men to so unreasonable a one as gaming or so brutal a one as drunkenness.

Secondly, because these two vices have been made odious and ridiculous by our plays instead of being shown agreeable. As for drunkenness, to show the sinner is sufficient to discredit the vice; for a drunkard, of necessity, always appears either odious or ridiculous. And for a gamester, I never knew one shown in a play but either as a fool or a rascal.

Thirdly, because those two vices flourish in places that are too remote and in persons that are too abject to be encouraged or influenced by the stage. There is drinking and gaming in the furthest north and the furthest west among peasants as well as among dukes and peers. But here, perhaps, some visionary zealot will urge that these two vices, even in these remote places and these abject persons, proceed from the influence of that irreligion which is caused by the corruptions of the stage and will, with as much reason, and as much modesty, deduce the lewdness which is transacted in the tin-mines in Cornwall and the coal-pits of Newcastle from the daily abominations of the pits of the two play houses as he would derive the brutality of the High-Dutch drinking from the profaneness of our English drama.

But what will they say then to those gentlemen who neither are supposed to go to our theaters, nor to converse much with those who do, nor to be liable to be corrupted by them? What will they say to these gentlemen if they can be proved to have a considerable share in the two afore-mentioned vices? What can they answer? For it would be ridiculously absurd to reply that the clergy are corrupted by the laity, whom it is their business to convert. But here I think myself obliged to declare that I by no means design this as a reflection upon the Church of England, who, I am satisfied, may more justly boast of its clergy than any other church whatsoever; a clergy that are equally illustrious for their piety and for their learning. Yet may I venture to affirm that there are some among them who can never be supposed to have been corrupted by playhouses, who yet turn up a bottle oftener than they do an hour glass; who box about a pair of tables with more fervor than they do their cushions, contemplate a pair of dice more frequently than the Fathers or Councils, and meditate and depend upon hazard more than they do upon Providence.

And as for that unnatural sin which is another growing vice of the age, it would be monstrous to urge that it is, in the least, encouraged by the stage; for it is either never mentioned there or mentioned with the last detestation.

And now, lastly, for the love of women, fomented by the corruption and not by the genuine art of the stage; though the augmenting and nourishing of it cannot be defended, yet it may be in some measure excused.

1. Because it has more of nature, and consequently more temptation and consequently less malice, than the preceding three, which the drama does not encourage.

2. Because it has a check upon the other vices and peculiarly upon that unnatural sin, in the restraining of which the happiness of mankind is, in so evident a manner, concerned.

So that of the four moral reigning vices, the stage encourages but one, which as it has been proved to be the least of them all, so it is the least contagious and the least universal. For in the country fornication and adultery are seldom heard of, whereas drunkenness rages in almost every house there: from all which it appears how very unreasonable it is to charge the lewdness of the times upon the stage when it is evident that of the four reigning moral vices the stage encourages but one, and that the least of the four and the least universal and a vice which has a check upon the other three, and particularly upon that amongst them which is most opposite and most destructive to the happiness of mankind.

Part I, Chapter IV. The Objections from Authority Answered.

* * * While I am pleading in defense of the stage I am defending and supporting poetry, the best and the noblest kind of writing. For all other writers are made by precept and are formed by art; but a poet prevails by the force of nature; is excited by all that's powerful in humanity, and is, sometimes, by a spirit not his own exalted to divinity.

For if poetry in other countries has flourished with the stage and been with that neglected, what must become of it here in England if the stage is ruined; For foreign poets have found their public and their private patrons. They who excelled in Greece were encouraged by the Athenian state, nay and by all Greece, assembled at their Olympian, Istmean, Nemean, Pythian games. Rome had its Scipios, its Caesars, and its Maecenases. France had its magnanimous Richelieu, and its greater Lewis; but the protection that poetry has found in England has been from the stage alone. Some few indeed of our private men have had souls that have been large enough, and wanted only power. But of our princes how few have had any taste of arts! Nay, and of them who had some, have had their heads too full, and some their souls too narrow!

As then in maintaining the cause of the stage, I am defending poetry in general; so in defending that I am pleading for eloquence, for history, and philosophy. I am pleading for the reasonable pleasures of mankind, the only harmless, the only cheap, the only universal pleasures; the nourishments of youth and the delights of age; the ornaments of prosperity and the surest sanctuaries of adversity; now insolently attempted by furious zeal, too wretchedly blind to see their beauties or discern their innocence. For unless the stage be encouraged in England, poetry cannot subsist; for never was any man a great poet who did not make it his business as well as pleasure and solely abandon himself to that. And as poetry would be crushed by the ruins of the stage, so eloquence would be miserably maimed by them; for which, if action be confessed the life of it, the theater is certainly the best of schools; and if action be not the life of it, Demosthenes was much mistaken. * * *

WILLIAM CONGREVE

Amendments of Mr. Collier's False and Imperfect Citations[†]
(1698)

I have been told by some that they should think me very idle if I threw away any time in taking notice even of so much of Mr. Collier's late treatise of the Immorality, *etc.* of the English stage as related to myself, in respect of some plays written by me; for that his malicious and strained interpretations of my words were so gross and palpable that any indifferent and unprejudiced reader would immediately condemn him upon his own evidence and acquit me before I could make any defense.

On the other hand, I have been taxed of laziness, and too much security, in neglecting thus long to do my self a necessary right, which might be effected with so very little pains; since very little more is requisite in my vindication than to represent truly and at length those passages which Mr. Collier has shown imperfectly and for the most part by halves. I would rather be thought idle than lazy; and so the last advice prevailed with me.

I have no intention to examine all the absurdities and falsehoods in Mr. Collier's book; to use the gentleman's own metaphor in his preface, *an inventory of such a warehouse would be a large work.* My detection of his malice and ignorance, of his sophistry and vast assurance, will lie within a narrow compass, and only bear a proportion to so much of his book as concerns myself.

Least of all would I undertake to defend the corruptions of the stage; indeed if I were so inclined, Mr. Collier has given me no occasion, for the greater part of those examples which he has produced are only demonstrations of his own impurity, they only savor of his utterance, and were sweet enough till tainted by his breath.

I will not justify any of my own errors; I am sensible of many, and if Mr. Collier has by any accident stumbled on one or two, I will freely give them up to him, *nullum unquam ingenium placuit sine venia.*[1] But I hope I have done nothing that can deprive me of the benefit of my clergy; and though Mr. Collier himself were the ordinary, I may hope to be acquitted.

[†] Published in July 1698, just after the initial flurry of pamphlets on the subject had reached a peak in June. Congreve's reluctance to enter an argument of this kind is clear; but Collier had reserved his plays (except *The Way of the World*, not yet written) for especially severe treatment, and Congreve, obviously angered, felt it necessary to defend himself. Most of his reply is spent in explaining specific passages by placing them in the context from which Collier had sometimes wrenched them. These portions are omitted here in favor of the more general comments with which Congreve introduced his essay.

1. From Seneca, *Epistles* 114.12: "No man's talent has ever been approved without pardon of something."

My intention, therefore, is to do little else but to restore those passages to their primitive station which have suffered so much in being transplanted by him. I will remove 'em from his dunghill and replant 'em in the field of nature; and when I have washed 'em of that filth which they have contracted in passing through his very dirty hands, let their own innocence protect them.

Mr. Collier, in the high vigor of his obscenity, first commits a rape upon my words, and then arraigns 'em of immodesty; he has barbarity enough to accuse the very virgins that he has deflowered, and to make sure of their condemnation he has himself made 'em guilty. But he forgets that while he publishes their shame he divulges his own.

His artifice to make words guilty of profaneness is of the same nature; for where the expression is unblameable in its own clear and genuine signification, he enters into it himself like the evil spirit; he possesses the innocent phrase and makes it bellow forth his own blasphemies; so *that one would think the muse was legion.*

To reprimand him a little in his own words, if these passages produced by Mr. Collier are obscene and profane, *why were they raked in and disturbed unless it were to conjure up vice and revive impurities? Indeed Mr. Collier has a very untoward way with him; his pen has such a libertine stroke that 'tis a question whether the practice or the reproof be the more licentious.*

He teaches those vices he would correct and writes more like a pimp than a p——. Since the business must be undertaken, why was not the thought blanched, the expression made remote, and the ill features cast into shadows? So far from this, which is his own instruction in his own words, is Mr. Collier's way of proceeding, that he has blackened the thoughts with his own smut; the expression that was remote, he has brought nearer; and lest by being brought near its native innocence might be more invisible, he has frequently varied it, he has new-molded it, and stamped his own image on it; so that it at length is become current deformity and fit to be paid into the devil's exchequer.

I will therefore take the liberty to exorcise this evil spirit and whip him out of my plays wherever I can meet with him. Mr. Collier has reversed the story which he relates from Tertullian; and after his visitation of the playhouse, returns, having left the devil behind him.[2]

If I do not return his civilities in calling him names, it is because I am not very well versed in his nomenclatures; therefore, for his *foot pads,* which he calls us in his preface, and for his *buffoons* and *slaves in the Saturnalia,* which he frequently bestows on us in the rest of his book, I will only call him Mr. Collier, and that I will call him as often as I think he shall deserve it.

---

2. Collier had cited Tertullian's story (*De Spectaculis* 26) about a woman who brought the devil home with her from the theater.

Before I proceed, for method's sake, I must premise some few things to the reader, which if he thinks in his conscience are too much to be granted me, I desire he would proceed no further in his perusal of these animadversions, but return to Mr. Collier's *Short View*, etc.

First, I desire that I may lay down Aristotle's definition of comedy, which has been the compass by which all the comic poets since his time have steered their course. I mean them whom Mr. Collier so very frequently calls *comedians*; for the distinction between *comicus* and *comoedus* and *tragicus* and *tragoedus*[3] is what he has not met with in the long progress of his reading.

Comedy (says Aristotle) is an imitation of the worse sort of people. Μίμησις φαυλοτέρων, *imitatio pejorum*. He does not mean the worse sort of people in respect to their quality, but in respect to their manners. This is plain from his telling you immediately after, that he does not mean κατὰ πᾶσαν κακίαν, relating to all kinds of vice; there are crimes too daring and too horrid for comedy. But the vices most frequent, and which are the common practice of the looser sort of livers, are the subject matter of comedy. He tells us farther, that they must be exposed after a ridiculous manner. For men are to be laughed out of their vices in comedy; the business of comedy is to delight as well as to instruct; and as vicious people are made ashamed of their follies or faults by seeing them exposed in a ridiculous manner, so are good people at once both warned and diverted at their expense.

Thus much I thought necessary to premise, that by showing the nature and end of comedy we may be prepared to expect characters agreeable to it.

Secondly, since comic poets are obliged by the laws of comedy, and to the intent that comedy may answer its true end and purpose above-mentioned, to represent vicious and foolish characters—in consideration of this, I desire that it may not be imputed to the persuasion or private sentiments of the author if at any time one of these vicious characters in any of his plays shall behave himself foolishly or immorally in word or deed. I hope I am not yet unreasonable; it were very hard that a painter should be believed to resemble all the ugly faces that he draws.

Thirdly, I must desire the impartial reader not to consider any expression or passage cited from any play as it appears in Mr. Collier's book, nor to pass any sentence or censure upon it out of its proper scene, or alienated from the character by which it is spoken; for in that place alone, and in his mouth alone, can it have its proper and true signification.

I cannot think it reasonable, because Mr. Collier is pleased to write one chapter of *Immodesty* and another of *Profaneness*, that therefore every expression traduced by him under those heads shall be con-

3. I.e., between tragic actor and tragic poet, etc.

demned as obscene and profane immediately, and without any further inquiry. Perhaps Mr. Collier is acquainted with the *deceptio visus*, and presents objects to the view through a stained glass; things may appear seemingly profane, when in reality they are only seen through a profane medium, and the true color is dissembled by the help of a sophistical varnish. Therefore, I demand the privilege of the *habeas corpus* act, that the prisoners may have liberty to remove and to appear before a just judge in an open and an uncounterfeit light.

Fourthly, because Mr. Collier in his chapter of the profaneness of the stage has founded great part of his accusation upon the liberty which poets take of using some words in their plays which have been sometimes employed by the translators of the Holy Scriptures, I desire that the following distinction may be admitted, *viz.* that when words are applied to sacred things and with a purpose to treat of sacred things, they ought to be understood accordingly; but when they are otherwise applied, the diversity of the subject gives a diversity of signification. And in truth he might as well except against the common use of the alphabet in poetry because the same letters are necessary to the spelling of words which are mentioned in sacred writ.

Though I have thought it requisite and but reasonable to premise these few things, to which, as to so many *postulata*, I may when occasion offers refer myself, yet if the reader should have any objection to the latitude which at first sight they may seem to comprehend, I dare venture to assure him that it shall be removed by the caution which I shall use, and those limits by which I shall restrain myself, when I shall judge it proper for me to refer to them.

It may not be impertinent in this place to remind the reader of a very common expedient which is made use of to recommend the instruction of our plays, which is this. After the action of the play is over and the delight of the representation at an end, there is generally care taken that the moral of the whole shall be summed up and delivered to the audience in the very last and concluding lines of the poem. The intention of this is that the delight of the representation may not so strongly possess the minds of the audience as to make them forget or oversee the instruction. It is the last thing said, that it may make the last impression; and it is always comprehended in a few lines and put into rhyme, that it may be easy and engaging to the memory. * * *

Steele and Dennis:
On *The Man of Mode* and *The Conscious Lovers*

RICHARD STEELE

The Spectator, No. 65[†]
(1711)

After having at large explained what wit is, and described the false appearances of it,[1] all that labor seems but an useless inquiry, without some time be spent in considering the application of it. The seat of wit, when one speaks as a man of the town and the world, is the playhouse; I shall therefore fill this paper with reflections upon the use of it in that place. The application of wit in the theater has as strong an effect upon the manners of our gentlemen as the taste of it has upon the writings of our authors. It may, perhaps, look like a very presumptuous work, though not foreign from the duty of a Spectator, to tax the writings of such as have long had the general applause of a nation. But I shall always make reason, truth, and nature the measures of praise and dispraise; if those are for me, the generality of opinion is of no consequence against me; if they are against me, the general opinion cannot long support me.

Without further preface, I am going to look into some of our most applauded plays, and see whether they deserve the figure they at present bear in the imaginations of men, or not.

In reflecting upon these works, I shall chiefly dwell upon that for which each respective play is most celebrated. The present paper shall

---

[†] Steele's attack in 1711 upon *The Man of Mode*, by then a well-known play of the previous generation, was part of his extensive effort to establish a new mode of comedy which would present virtuous behavior as a pattern for imitation. His earlier plays, such as *The Lying Lover* (1703) and *The Tender Husband* (1705), had already indicated his interest in moral drama, and not long after his essay on *The Man of Mode* he began work on a play intended to serve as the complete formulation of the new comic mode. This was *The Conscious Lovers* (1722), and it was preceded by a sly publicity campaign, largely of Steele's own composition and represented here by the selections from his periodical *The Theatre*.

1. Numbers 58–63 of *The Spectator* concerned the subject of wit.

be employed upon Sir Fopling Flutter. The received character of this play is that it is the pattern of genteel comedy. Dorimant and Harriet are the characters of greatest consequence, and if these are low and mean, the reputation of the play is very unjust.

I will take for granted that a fine gentleman should be honest in his actions and refined in his language. Instead of this, our hero in this piece is a direct knave in his designs and a clown in his language. Bellair is his admirer and friend; in return for which, because he is forsooth a greater wit than his said friend, he thinks it reasonable to persuade him to marry a young lady, whose virtue, he thinks, will last no longer than till she is a wife, and then she cannot but fall to his share, as he is an irresistible fine gentleman. The falsehood to Mrs. Loveit, and the barbarity of triumphing over her anguish for losing him, is another instance of his honesty, as well as his good nature. As to his fine language, he calls the orange-woman, who, it seems, is inclined to grow fat, "an overgrown jade, with a flasket of guts before her;" and salutes her with a pretty phrase of, "How now, double tripe!" Upon the mention of a country gentlewoman, whom he knows nothing of (no one can imagine why), he "will lay his life she is some awkward, ill-fashioned country toad, who not having above four dozen of hairs on her head, has adorned her baldness with a large white fruz, that she may look sparkishly in the forefront of the king's box at an old play." Unnatural mixture of senseless commonplace!

As to the generosity of his temper, he tells his poor footman, "If he did not wait better——" he would turn him away, in the insolent phrase of "I'll uncase you."

Now for Mrs. Harriet: she laughs at obedience to an absent mother, whose tenderness Busy describes to be very exquisite, for "that she is so pleased with finding Harriet again, that she cannot chide her for being out of the way." This witty daughter and fine lady has so little respect for this good woman that she ridicules her air in taking leave, and cries, "In what struggle is my poor mother yonder? See, see! her head tottering, her eyes staring, and her under lip trembling." But all this is atoned for, because "she has more wit than is usual in her sex, and as much malice, though she is as wild as you would wish her, and has a demureness in her looks that makes it so surprising!" Then to recommend her as a fit spouse for his hero, the poet makes her speak her sense of marriage very ingeniously. "I think," says she, "I might be brought to endure him, and that is all a reasonable woman should expect in an husband." It is, methinks, unnatural that we are not made to understand how she that was bred under a silly pious old mother, that would never trust her out of her sight, came to be so polite.

It cannot be denied but that the negligence of everything which engages the attention of the sober and valuable part of mankind appears very well drawn in this piece; but it is denied that it is necessary to the character of a fine gentleman that he should in that manner trample upon all order and decency. As for the character of Dorimant, it is more of a coxcomb than that of Fopling. He says of one of his companions that a good correspondence between them is their mutual interest. Speaking of that friend, he declares their being much together "makes the women think the better of his understanding, and judge more favorably of my reputation. It makes him pass upon some for a man of very good sense, and me upon others for a very civil person."

This whole celebrated piece is a perfect contradiction to good manners, good sense, and common honesty; and as there is nothing in it but what is built upon the ruin of virtue and innocence, according to the notion of merit in this comedy, I take the shoemaker to be, in reality, the fine gentleman of the play; for it seems he is an atheist, if we may depend upon his character as given by the orange-woman, who is herself far from being the lowest in the play. She says of a fine man who is Dorimant's companion, "There is not such another heathen in the town, except the shoemaker." His pretension to be the hero of the drama appears still more in his own description of his way of living with his lady. "There is," says he, "never a man in town lives more like a gentleman with his wife than I do; I never mind her motions; she never inquires into mine. We speak to one another civilly, hate one another heartily; and because it is vulgar to lie and soak together, we have each of us our several settle-bed." That of "soaking together" is as good as if Dorimant had spoken it himself; and I think, since he puts human nature in as ugly a form as the circumstance will bear, and is a staunch unbeliever, he is very much wronged in having no part of the good fortune bestowed in the last act.

To speak plainly of this whole work, I think nothing but being lost to a sense of innocence and virtue can make any one see this comedy without observing more frequent occasion to move sorrow and indignation than mirth and laughter. At the same time I allow it to be nature, but it is nature in its utmost corruption and degeneracy.

The Theatre, No. 1[†]
(1720)

In the beginning of a work which I design to publish twice a week, it is necessary to explain myself to the town and make them understand why I attempt to entertain them under this title. When I have informed my

---

[†] *The Theatre* appeared twice weekly for three months in 1720. The fictional scheme of the early numbers, which included characters from *The Conscious Lovers*, was not consistently carried through; instead, Steele turned the journal to his own purposes in the internal politics of the theater.

reader that I am in the sixty-first year of my age[1] and have been induced to frequent the theater by the persuasion of my son, it will perhaps raise attention and curiosity to know what are the particular circumstances which make the father ductile to his child, instead of the son's governing himself by the example of his father.

I have always abhorred living at distance with him, and ever gave him his freedom in all his words and actions, so that I have seldom expostulated with him concerning them; but of late years, observed him mighty conversant at the theater and living in occasional familiarity with the chief actors. This turn was so particular that I inquired what he could find thus delightful to him among persons singularly remarked to their disadvantage. He begged of me (as I had formerly advised him) to judge for myself in those matters, and prevailed with me to go with him to the play very frequently; where I soon recovered the taste I had had for those entertainments in my youth, and reflected that this, above all other diversions, was proper and pleasing rather to the young or old than to the middle-aged. The middle of our days, thought I, is generally taken up in the hurry and eagerness of business; but the days we pass before we mingle with the world, and after we are retired from it, are the seasons wherein plays well acted give greatest pleasure. Young men learn from the stage the knowledge of that world they are scarce yet acquainted with; old men look back on the road which they have passed through with equal delight and satisfaction.

My son *Harry* is a gentleman of a discernment above his years and affects the company of elder men. He has a vivacity in his manner and a good-natured quickness of spirit that renders him very agreeable to his acquaintance. When he comes into a room, I have observed the company look upon him with the aspect which people usually have when one enters from some place whence they expect news. His manner is uncommon and his thoughts on any subject give that sort of pleasure which we receive by fresh intelligence from some scene of action. His imagination dispenses new reflections on any subject, and he is always a great addition to the entertainment by the pleasant and peculiar relish he has of it.

This boy of mine who brought me back to the play-house is as proud of his good-humoured old man, as the pert thing calls me, as I am of him, and never makes a new acquaintance, though with a young lady, but the first thing he promises is that the party shall be acquainted with his father. He has introduced me to a particular friend of his, a lady of great quality and merit, with whom, and her visitants, I am often very well entertained, and the theater is no small part of our conversation. *Sophronia*, for that shall be her name, is, according to the course of

---

1. Steele is writing in the guise of "Sir John Edgar," a fictional personage who was to become "Sir John Bevil" in *The Conscious Lovers*.

nature, in a stage of this life not far from a better being, but under no manner of decay as to her senses and understanding. From experience added to her great wit and good humour, you would take her, by her discourse, to be only a very wise young woman. She has always encouraged theatrical diversions and admitted the eminent performers (from *Hart* and *Mohun*, to those of our time) to her presence and conversation, and has a very excellent taste both of the composition and performance of a good play.

At this lady's house, elegance and decency, not licentiousness and luxury, are consulted as the most inviting entertainment of the company that meet there. There is a purity in their manners and a kind of chastity in their very dress. Their mirth has no noise, their joy little laughter; but freedom is bounded by respect, and their familiarity rendered more agreeable by good breeding. A romp would there look like a prostitute, and a rake would be as terrible as a ruffian.

There are but very few of either sex who are capable of being well pleased at her assemblies; for as 'tis said, the vicious could not be happy were they to be translated to Heaven; so (with reverence in the comparison) may I aver that the ordinary people of fashion would be there very much at a loss, and those who pass for fine gentlemen and ladies in other conversations would be in the apartment of *Sophronia* uninformed savages.

Deviation from reason and good sense is there the only error, and uninstructed innocence is pitied and assisted, while studied faults and assumed singularities are banished or discountenanced.

* * *

The Theatre, No. 3
(1720)

Upon my producing my second paper[1] at *Sophronia's* tea-table, the ladies had the goodness to express a delight in that they now began to be convinced of my being determined to go on with the work. And in order to it, I had leave to lay before them a new scheme for the government of the public diversions. I told them that it had long been a great cause of distress to the actors to know who were properly the town and who not; they having been often under the nicest perplexities from the very different opinions of people of quality and condition.

There is, they tell me, scarce any play put up in their bills, or that they propose to revive, but has as much the dislike of some as the appro-

---

1. I.e., the second issue of *The Theatre,* here omitted.

bation of others, even before it comes on, and that the same happens in most of their private affairs. Whenever they fall into public company, it is very difficult to preserve that deference due to the opinion of their superiors and at the same time to pursue their own measures, and what their experience convinces them will most probably contribute to the public entertainment. Therefore, that the players may be better justified in what they shall do hereafter, I have proposed:

1. That a select number of persons shall be chosen as real representatives of a *British* audience.

2. These persons so elected shall be styled *Auditors of the Drama.*

3. No persons to have free voices in these elections but such as shall produce certificates from the respective door-keepers of the theater that they never refused to pay for their places.

4. The players shall choose two of their own society, *viz.* one male and one female, to take care of their interest, and for the better information of these *Auditors*, in matters immediately relating to their customs and private economy.

5. One dramatic poet to serve for the liberties of *Parnassus*; to be chosen only by tragic or comic writers.

6. Three of the fair sex shall represent the front-boxes.

7. Two gentlemen of wit and pleasure for the side-boxes.

8. Three substantial citizens for the pit.

9. One lawyer's clerk and one *valet de chambre* for the first gallery. One journeyman-baker for the upper-gallery.

10. And one footman that can write and read shall be *Mercury* to the Board.

11. This body so chosen shall have full power, in the right of the audiences of *Great Britain*, to approve, condemn, or rectify whatever shall be exhibited on the *English* theater.

And the players guiding themselves by their laws shall not be accountable to or controlled by any other opinions or suggestions whatever, nor ever appeal from the judgments of these duly elected *Auditors*. Provided notwithstanding, that any daily spectators shall have reserved to them and their successors for ever their full right of applauding or disliking the performance of any particular actor whenever his care or negligence shall appear to deserve either the one or the other. But in matters merely relating to the conduct of the theater, the said elected *Auditors*, from time to time, shall be deemed able, and to have right, to give laws for ever.

This scheme was approved by the whole assembly at the Lady *Sophronia's*, and they desired me accordingly to appoint the day of the election of *Auditors*. I am therefore to acquaint the town that due notice shall be given of some play to be acted, after which the audience will proceed to choose representatives for the *British* theater by way of ballot;

which every door-keeper is hereby impowered to receive at the same time he takes their money.

This matter has already taken air, and there are candidates who already appear and have desired my interest and recommendation. The first who addressed me with a modest discovery of that ambition is *Lucinda*, who hopes to be chosen for the boxes.

Lucinda is the daughter of Mr. *Sealand*, an eminent merchant; she is a young woman of a most unaffected, easy, and engaging behavior, which has brought her much into fashion among all the great families she visits. She is conversant in books and no stranger to household affairs, of a discerning and quick spirit in conversation, and has a mortal aversion to all coxcombs; she has the modesty, in the account of herself, to pretend only to a judgment in the dresses and habits of the theater. But as I love to be fair in all representations, I must give the electors notice (who may act accordingly) that she is a great favorer of the woollen manufactures; and she intends on the election-day to appear in a white stuff suit, lined with cherry-colored silk, in the second row of the front-boxes. For, besides the consideration of her country's good, she has skill enough to know that no woman is the better dressed for being in rich clothes, and that 'tis the fancy and elegance of an habit, and not the cost, that makes it always becoming to the wearer. She is in hopes too, as I am privately informed, to introduce, even on the stage, dresses of our own growth and labor, which shall be as good, as cheap, and becoming, as any imported from abroad. This method, she imagines, will give the world a very advantageous opportunity of judging of the commodiousness, beauty, and ease of those habits by the appearance they make upon the players in parts proper to them. She concludes that the theater should be made serviceable to all parts of life and all trades and professions, that it may the better deserve the support of the public.

Mr. *Charles Myrtle* stands for the side-box. He is a gentleman of a very plentiful fortune; a student, or rather an inhabitant of the *Temple*; he has a fine taste of letters, and from thence bears some reputation of a scholar, which makes him much more valuable in that of a gentleman. He has many agreeable qualities, besides the distinction of a good understanding and more good nature. But he has little imperfections that frequently indispose his temper; and when jealousy takes hold of him, he becomes untractable and unhappily positive in his opinions and resolutions; but I must not say too much on the less side of his character, because my son *Harry Edgar* offers himself at the same time to the town, and hopes for their votes and interest for the side-box.

We have a candidate for the pit, an eminent *East India* merchant, Mr. *Sealand*, father of *Lucinda*. This gentleman was formerly what is called a man of pleasure about the town; and having, when young, lavished a small estate, retired to *India*, where by marriage, and falling into the knowledge of trade, he laid the foundation of the great fortune of which he is now master. I am in great hopes he will carry his election, for his thoughts and sentiments against the unworthy representations of citizens on the stage may highly contribute to the abolition of such ridiculous images for the future. His knowledge and experience, by living in mixed company as well as in the busy world here, balanced him against approving what is either too frivolous or too abstracted for public entertainments. He is a true pattern of that kind of third gentry which has arose in the world this last century; I mean the great and rich families of merchants and eminent traders, who in their furniture, their equipage, their manner of living, and especially their economy, are so far from being below the gentry that many of them are now the best representatives of the ancient ones and deserve the imitation of the modern nobility. If this gentleman should carry his election (as from his having the whole city-interest of *Jews*, as well as Gentiles, in the pit, it is very likely he will), we shall have great assistance from him with relation both to the real and imaginary world. He is a man that does business with the candor of a gentleman, and performs his engagements with the exactness of a citizen.

The players are in much hurry about the election of their proper representatives, there being but two female candidates, who are both remarkable for their great merit and industry in their profession. My son tells me he finds by their discourse about the playhouse that every one, consulted apart, speaks of them in different modes. I'll vote, says one, for a lady that values her self only as she is eminent in the theater, that never when she is in her part has her hero in the sidebox instead of on the stage, but is acting as well when another is speaking as when she speaks herself; who expresses in her countenance as much what she hears as what she utters. This description could relate to but two of all the house; but it is thought the actors will choose the less handsome out of their complaisance to those ladies who are candidates for the audience, because it is remarkable that people of quality bear to see their inferiors in fortune their equals in wit and knowledge, with patience enough, provided they do not also come up to them in their manners and beauty.

The first gallery has offered to it a representative who is an underling of the law, one who knows a great deal, as the quirks of it may perplex, but not a word as the reason of it may protect and serve mankind. I hope he will not carry it, because such a creature can be in no place where he does not consider rather how he can, as he is situated, disturb his neighbor than enjoy his own. And this kind of creature will show himself as much during his term in a seat at a play as in the possession of an estate for ever and ever.

My man *Humphrey*, who has lived with me for many years, proposes himself for the first gallery. He is a diligent, careful, sensible man and has had a right in all that comes off my person these forty years; for so long has he been my *valet de chambre*, or gentleman, as they call it. I cannot accuse him but of one ungentlemanly thing during our whole time together; and that was, he brought a tailor to see me as I walked in *Lincoln's-Inn* Garden, and sold him the coat I had then on my back, while I was musing concerning the course of human affairs in the upper walk. This I cannot call an injustice, for I had given him the suit, and he put me in it, because it was warm, the day after I gave it him being cold. However, I may call it an unpoliteness and an *indecorum*, because his master had it on while he was making the bargain. After I have said all this, I think I may put up a man for the gallery whose greatest offense he ever committed was only against decency.

I had, when I proposed this scheme, a journeyman-baker in my eye, as well that in case of danger of famine from any outward cause, the house might bake for themselves, as also that he is a robust critic, and can by way of cudgel keep silence about him in the upper-gallery, where the wit and humour of the play will not always command attention.

I have not yet heard of any other candidates; but when I do, shall give timely notice. In the meantime shall rest with great content in the hopes I conceive from the assistance of a well chosen board. The election of a poet for the landed interest of *Parnassus*, as well as the choice of the actors who are to accompany the *Auditors of the Drama*, are matters that deserve to be treated of distinctly; but the qualification of so much *per annum*,[2] in order to be deemed a man of capacity for this service, I cannot allow to be necessary, though I have very good friends of another mind, who will also take upon them to say that for the dignity and safety of *Arcadia* a comic or tragic poet should have three hundred pounds a-year; and an epic poet cannot be truly such, except he have six hundred a-year. From which worthy gentlemen I must beg leave to differ; and I take the liberty to say that there is no such accomplishment mentioned by *Aristotle*, *Horace* or any other Critic, ancient or modern.

JOHN DENNIS

A Defense of *Sir Fopling Flutter*[†]
(1722)

* * * How little do they know of the nature of true comedy, who believe that its proper business is to set us patterns for imitation. For all such

---

2. Steele is joking about the Landed Property Qualifications Act of 1711, which set requirements of landed wealth for candidates to the House of Commons.

† Published as a pamphlet on 2 November 1722, just five days before the opening of Steele's *The Conscious Lovers*.

patterns are serious things, and laughter is the life and the very soul of comedy. 'Tis its proper business to expose persons to our view whose views we may shun and whose follies we may despise; and by showing us what is done upon the comic stage, to show us what ought never to be done upon the stage of the world.

All the characters in *Sir Fopling Flutter*, and especially the principal characters, are admirably drawn, both to please and to instruct. First, they are drawn to please, because they are drawn in the truth of nature; but to be drawn in the truth of nature, they must be drawn with those qualities that are proper to each respective season of life.[1]

✻   ✻   ✻

A comic poet who gives to a young man the qualities that belong to a middle-aged man or to an old man can answer neither of the ends of his art. He cannot please, because he writes out of nature, of which all poetry is an imitation, and without which no poem can possibly please. And as he cannot please, he cannot instruct; because, by showing such a young man as is not to be seen in the world, he shows a monster and not a man, sets before us a particular character instead of an allegorical and universal one, as all his characters, and especially his principal characters, ought to be; and therefore can give no general instruction, having no moral, no fable, and therefore no comedy.

Now if any one is pleased to compare the character of Dorimant, to which the knight[2] has taken so much absurd exception, with the two forementioned descriptions, he will find in his character all the chief distinguishing strokes of them. For such is the force of nature, and so admirable a talent had she given Sir George for comedy, that, though to my certain knowledge he understood neither Greek nor Latin, yet one would swear that in drawing his Dorimant, he copied the foresaid drafts, and especially that of Aristotle. Dorimant is a young courtier, haughty, vain, and prone to anger, amorous, false, and inconstant. He debauches Loveit and betrays her; loves Bellinda, and so soon as he enjoys her is false to her.

But secondly, the characters in *Sir Fopling* are admirably contrived to please, and more particularly the principal ones, because we find in those characters a true resemblance of the persons both in court and town who lived at the time when that comedy was written. For Rapin[3] tells us with a great deal of judgment: "That comedy is as it ought to be when an audience is apt to imagine that instead of being in the pit and boxes they are in some assembly of the neighborhood or in some family meeting and that we see nothing done in it but what is done in the

---

1. Dennis goes on to quote Horace, Aristotle, and the French critic André Dacier to support his argument that each character should possess traits appropriate to his years.
2. "The knight" is Sir Richard Steele.
3. René Rapin, a seventeenth-century French commentator on Aristotle.

world. For it is [says he] not worth one farthing if we do not discover ourselves in it, and do not find in it both our own manners and those of the persons with whom we live and converse."

The reason of this rule is manifest, for as it is the business of a comic poet to cure his spectators of vice and folly by the apprehension of being laughed at, it is plain that his business must be with the reigning follies and vices. The violent passions which are the subjects of tragedy are the same in every age and appear with the same face; but those vices and follies which are the subjects of comedy are seen to vary continually. Some of those that belonged to our ancestors have no relation to us, and can no more come under the cognizance of our present comic poets than the sweating and sneezing sickness can come under the practice of our contemporary physicians. What vices and follies may infect those who are to come after us, we know not; it is the present, the reigning vices and follies, that must be the subjects of our present comedy. The comic poet therefore must take characters from such persons as are his contemporaries and are infected with the foresaid follies and vices. * * *

Now I remember very well that upon the first acting this comedy, it was generally believed to be an agreeable representation of the persons of condition of both sexes, both in court and town; and that all the world was charmed with Dorimant; and that it was unanimously agreed that he had in him several of the qualities of Wilmot Earl of Rochester, as his wit, his spirit, his amorous temper, the charms that he had for the fair sex, his falsehood, and his inconstancy; the agreeable manner of his chiding his servants, which the late Bishop of Salisbury takes notice of in his life; and lastly, his repeating on every occasion the verses of Waller, for whom that noble lord had a very particular esteem; witness his imitation of the Tenth Satire of the First Book of Horace:

> Waller, by nature for the bays design'd,
> With spirit, force, and fancy unconfin'd,
> In panegyric is above mankind.

Now, as several of the qualities in Dorimant's character were taken from the Earl of Rochester, so they who were acquainted with the late Sir Fleetwood Shepherd knew very well that not a little of that gentleman's character is to be found in Medley.

But the characters in this comedy are very well formed to instruct as well as to please, especially those of Dorimant and of Loveit; and they instruct by the same qualities to which the knight has taken so much whimsical exception; as Dorimant instructs by his insulting and his perfidiousness, and Loveit by the violence of her resentment and her anguish. For Loveit has youth, beauty, quality, wit, and spirit. And it was depending upon these that she reposed so dangerous a trust in Dorimant, which is a just caution to the fair sex never to be so conceited of the power of their charms or their other extraordinary qualities as to believe they can engage a man to be true to them to whom they grant the best favor without the only sure engagement, without which they can never be certain that they shall not be hated and despised by that very person whom they have done everything to oblige.

To conclude with one general observation, that comedy may be qualified in a powerful manner both to instruct and to please, the very constitution of its subject ought always to be ridiculous. Comedy, says Rapin, is an image of common life and its end is to expose upon the stage the defects of particular persons in order to cure the defects of the public and to correct and amend the people by the fear of being laughed at. That therefore, says he, which is most essential to comedy is certainly the ridicule.

Every poem is qualified to instruct and to please most powerfully by that very quality which makes the forte and the characteristic of it, and which distinguishes it from all other kinds of poems. As tragedy is qualified to instruct and to please by terror and compassion, which two passions ought always to be predominant in it and to distinguish it from all other poems, epic poetry pleases and instructs chiefly by admiration, which reigns throughout it and distinguishes it from poems of every other kind. Thus comedy instructs and pleases most powerfully by the ridicule, because that is the quality which distinguishes it from every other poem. The subject, therefore, of every comedy ought to be ridiculous by its constitution; the ridicule ought to be of the very nature and essence of it. Where there is none of that, there can be no comedy. It ought to reign both in the incidents and in the characters, and especially in the principal characters, which ought to be ridiculous in themselves, or so contrived as to show and expose the ridicule of others. In all the masterpieces of Ben Jonson, the principal character has the ridicule in himself, as Morose in *The Silent Woman*, Volpone in *The Fox*, and Subtle and Face in *The Alchemist*; and the very ground and foundation of all these comedies is ridiculous. 'Tis the very same thing in the masterpieces of Molière: *The Misanthrope*, *The Imposter*, *The Avare*, and the *Femmes Savantes*. Nay, the reader will find that in most of his other pieces the principal characters are ridiculous; as, *L'Étourdi*, *Les Précieuses Ridicules*, *Le Cocu Imaginaire*, *Les Fâcheux*, *and Monsieur de Pourceaugnac*, *Le Bourgeois Gentilhomme*, *L'École des Maris*, *L'École des Femmes*, *L'Amour Médecin*, *Le Médecin Malgré lui*, *Le Mariage Forcé*, *George Dandin*, *Les Fourberies de Scapin*, *Le Malade Imaginaire*. The reader will not only find upon reflection that in all these pieces the principal characters are ridiculous, but that in most of them there is the ridicule of comedy in the very titles.

'Tis by the ridicule that there is in the character of Sir Fopling, which is one of the principal ones of this comedy, and from which it takes its name, that he is so very well qualified to please and to instruct. What true Englishman is there but must be pleased to see this ridiculous knight made the jest and the scorn of all the other characters for showing, by his foolish aping foreign customs and manners, that he prefers another country to his own? And of what important instruction must it be to all our youth who travel to show them that, if they so far forget the love of their country as to declare by their espousing foreign customs and manners that they prefer France or Italy to Great Britain, at their return they must justly expect to be the jest and the scorn of their own countrymen.

Thus, I hope I have convinced the reader that this comical knight, Sir Fopling, has been justly formed by the knight his father to instruct and please, whatever may be the opinion to the contrary of the knight his brother.

Whenever *The Fine Gentleman*[4] of the latter comes upon the stage, I shall be glad to see that it has all the shining qualities which recommend *Sir Fopling*, that his characters are always drawn in nature, and that he never gives to a young man the qualities of a middle-aged man or an old one; that they are the just images of our contemporaries, and of what we every day see in the world; that instead of setting us patterns for our imitation, which is not the proper business of comedy, he makes those follies and vices ridiculous which we ought to shun and despise; that the subject of his comedy is comical by its constitution; and that the ridicule is particularly in the grand incidents and in the principal characters. For a true comic poet is a philosopher who, like old Democritus, always instructs us laughing.

Remarks on *The Conscious Lovers*[†]
(1723)

* * * When Sir Richard says that anything that has its foundation in happiness and success must be the subject of comedy, he confounds comedy with that species of tragedy which has a happy catastrophe. When he says that 'tis an improvement of comedy to introduce a joy too exquisite for laughter, he takes all the care that he can to show that he knows nothing of the nature of comedy. Does he really believe that Molière, who, in the opinion of all Europe, excepting that small portion of it which is acquainted with Ben Jonson, had borne away the prize of comedy from all nations and from all ages if for the sake of his profit he had not descended sometimes too much to buffoonry? Let Sir Richard or anyone look into that little piece of Molière called *La Critique de*

---

4. I.e., *The Conscious Lovers.*
† Published as a pamphlet on 24 January 1723, about two months after Steele's play had appeared in print.

l'école des femmes, and he shall find there that in Molière's opinion 'tis the business of a comic poet to enter into the ridicule of men and to expose the blind sides of all sorts of people agreeably; that he does nothing at all if he does not draw the pictures of his contemporaries and does not raise the mirth of the sensible part of an audience, which, says he, 'tis no easy matter to do. This is the sense of Molière, though the words are not his exactly.

When Sir Richard talks of a joy too exquisite for laughter, he seems not to know that joy, generally taken, is common, like anger, indignation, love, to all sorts of poetry: to the epic, the dramatic, the lyric; but that that kind of joy which is attended with laughter is the characteristic of comedy, as terror or compassion, according as the one or the other is predominant, makes the characteristic of tragedy, as admiration does of epic poetry.

When Sir Richard says that weeping upon the sight of a deplorable object is not a subject for laughter but that 'tis agreeable to good sense and to humanity, he says nothing but what all the sensible part of the world has always granted; but then all that sensible part of the world have always denied that a deplorable object is fit to be shown in comedy. When Sir George Etherege, in his comedy of *Sir Fopling Flutter,* shows Loveit in all the height and violence of grief and rage, the judicious poet takes care to give those passions a ridiculous turn by the mouth of Dorimant. Besides that, the subject is at the bottom ridiculous; for Loveit is a mistress who has abandoned herself to Dorimant, and by falling into these violent passions only because she fancies that something of which she is very desirous has gone beside her makes herself truly ridiculous. Thus is the famous scene in the second act of *Sir Fopling* by the character of Loveit and the dextrous handling of the subject kept within the bounds of comedy. But the scene of the discovery in the *Conscious Lovers* is truly tragical. Indiana was strictly virtuous. She had indeed conceived a violent passion for Bevil, but all young people in full health are liable to such a passion, and perhaps the most sensible and the most virtuous are more than others liable. But besides that she kept this passion within the bounds of honor, it was the natural effect of her esteem for her benefactor and of her gratitude; that is, of her virtue. These considerations rendered her case deplorable and the catastrophe downright tragical, which of a comedy ought to be the most comical part for the same reason that it ought to be the most tragical part of a tragedy.

*   *   *

The filial obedience of young Bevil is carried a great deal too far. He is said to be one of a great estate and a great understanding; and yet he makes a promise to his father not to marry without his consent, which is a promise that can do his father only a vain imaginary good and may do him real hurt. A young man of a great understanding cannot but know that if he makes such a promise he may be obliged to break it, or perish, or at least be unhappy all the rest of his life. Such a one cannot but know that he may possibly be seized with a passion so resistless and so violent that he must possess or perish; and consequently if the woman who inspires this passion be a woman of strict virtue, he must marry, or perish, or at least be mortally uneasy for the rest of his life. Children, indeed, before they come to years of discretion are obliged to pay a blind obedience to their parents. But after they are come to the full use of their reason they are only bound to obey them in what is reasonable. Indeed, if a son is in expectation of an estate from his father, he is engaged to a good deal of compliance, even after he comes to years of discretion. But that was not Bevil's case: he enjoyed a very good one of his mother's, by virtue of a marriage article; and therefore it was unreasonable in him to make such a promise to his father, as it was unreasonable in his father to urge him of it, especially upon so sordid a motive as the doubling a great estate. This is acting in a manner something arbitrary. And it ill becomes an author who would be thought a patron of liberty to suppose that fathers are absolute when kings themselves are limited. If he had not an understanding of his own to tell him this, he might have learned from Mr. Locke, in his sixth chapter of his admirable *Essay on Government*:

> That every man has a right to his natural freedom, without being subjected to the will or authority of any other man. Children, I confess, are not born in this full state of equality, though they are born to it. Their parents have a sort of rule and jurisdiction over them when they come into the world, and for some time after; but it is but a temporary one. The bonds of this subjection are like the swaddling clothes which they are wrapped up in, and supported by in the weakness of their infancy. Age and reason, as they grow up, lessen them, till at length they drop quite off, and leave a man at his own free disposal.

*   *   *

From what I have quoted from so judicious and so penetrating an author, I think it is pretty plain that young Bevil, who disposed of part of his estate without, nay, and as he might reasonably suppose, against the consent of his father, might *a fortiori* have disposed of his person too if it had not been for his unreasonable promise; and that it is highly improbable that one of the estate and understanding which he is said to have should absurdly make a promise which might possibly endanger the happiness of his whole life. 'Tis said, indeed, in more than one place of the play that the son has uncommon obligations to his father; but we are neither told, nor are we able to guess, what those obligations are. What uncommon obligations can a son who has a great estate in possession have to a father of so sordid a nature as Sir John Bevil shows himself? Act IV. Besides, what obligations can be binding enough to make a man of a great estate part with liberty, with the very liberty of his choice, in the most important action of his life, upon which the happiness of all the rest depends?

But as unreasonable as this promise is, which young Bevil made to his father, by which he gave away his birthright, his liberty, yes, the very liberty of his choice, in an affair upon which his happiness most depended, his behavior to Indiana is still more unaccountable. He loves her and is beloved by her; makes constant visits and profuse presents to her; and yet conceals his passion from her; which may be perhaps a clumsy expedient for the author's preparing the discovery, but is neither agreeable to nature nor reason. For it is impossible that any young man in nature, in health and vigor, and in the height of a violent passion, can so far command himself by the mere force of reason. I am willing, indeed, to allow that he may be able to do it by the assistance of the true religion. But the business of a comic poet is only to teach morality; Grace is not taught, but inspired. The dreadful mysteries of Christianity are but ill compatible with the lightness and mirth of comedy, or with the obscenity and profaneness of a degenerate stage, or with the dispositions of an assembly composed of persons who have some of them no religion and some of them not the true one. Besides that, nothing but a doctrine taken from the moral law can be a just foundation of a fable, which every true comedy is.

Nor is such a behavior any more agreeable to reason than it is to nature. Bevil loves Indiana and is beloved by her; she adores him, she dies for him, and he knows it; he observes it, and observes at the same time that so violent a passion is attended with equal anxiety; and that anxiety is entirely caused by the perplexing doubt she is in, whether she is beloved or not, as appears by what he says himself, Act II. Why then doth he not declare himself and by that declaration compose her mind and qualify her to expect with patience the benefit of time? 'Tis indeed true that he had promised his father never to marry without his consent while his father lived; but he had not promised him never to love without his consent; for that would have been a ridiculous promise; a promise the performance or nonperformance of which was not in his own power and would depend entirely on what the people call chance and what philosophers call providence. What could he mean then by not declaring himself? As the love he had conceived for Indiana was no breach of the promise he had made to his father, so neither could he violate it by any declaration of that passion! What then, once more, can he mean by his silence? His only reasonable way of proceeding had been to acquaint not only his mistress, but his father and all the world, with the passion which he felt for her and with the necessity he was in to marry her, or to be forever miserable. Such a declaration was not at all inconsistent with his duty; and if his father had either reason or compassion, would have caused him to relent and to release his son from a promise, the persevering in which must prove unhappy or fatal to him. If it should be said that such a concealment of his passion was necessary that he might make a retreat with honor in case his father should still be obstinate; to this I answer that there was no retreat for him unless he would at the same time retreat from virtue and honor; that his behavior had fixed and determined him; that by his generosity and constant visits he had raised the passion of Indiana to such a height that his leaving her would in all likelihood be followed by madness, or by self-murder, or by dreadful hysterical symptoms as deplorable as either; of which, what passes between her father and her in the fifth act is a sufficient proof. Beside, that such a retreat would prove as fatal to her honor as to her person. He had for some time made constant visits; he had made very extravagant presents to her; he had made no declaration of the affection he had for her, either to her or to her Aunt Isabella, or acquainted any one with his design to marry her if he could obtain his father's consent. Now can anything be more plain than that such a behavior, if he left her, would ruin the reputation of the poor lady and cause all the world to entertain such thoughts of her as Sealand and Myrtle had already expressed? And thus I have endeavored to show that the behavior of Bevil to Indiana, in his concealing his passion from her, is as ridiculously whimsical as that of Cimberton to her sister Lucinda.

The catastrophe, I must confess, is very moving, but it would be more so if it were rightly and reasonably handled, because it would be much more surprising. For the surprise is, in a good measure, prevented by the behavior of Isabella upon the first appearance of Sealand; which, if it had not been out of all probability and nature, would have prevented it more. It was highly in nature and probability that Isabella, upon the first discovering her brother, should fly into an excessive transport of joy and have run to embrace him; for when she is made to say that her brother must not know her yet, she is made to give no reasons for it, nor can the audience imagine any. 'Tis not Isabella who says that, but the author, who clumsily uses it to serve a turn; for if she had discovered herself to her brother at his first appearance, it had prevented the audience's sorrow and compassion for the imaginary distress of Indiana and, consequently, their return to joy. But as Aristotle and all the great critics after him have taught us, that there is to be no incident in a dramatic poem but what must be founded on reason, it happens, as we observed above, very unluckily here, that there is no incident in the *Conscious Lovers* but what is attended by some great absurdity. For the action of Indiana in throwing away her bracelet is of the same stamp and is entirely the author's and not the dramatic person's; for it was neither necessary nor profitable that Indiana, in the height of her agony, should so much as think of her bracelet, or if she did think of it, should resolve to throw away the greatest token that she had to remember her dead mother, for whose memory her grief and distress ought naturally to renew and redouble her tenderness. But the author is obliged to have recourse to this as an awkward expedient, though the best he could find, to bring on the discovery. But had he known anything of the art of the stage, he would have known that those discoveries are but dully made which are made by tokens; that they ought necessarily or probably to spring from the whole train of the incidents contrary to our expectation. And how easy was it to bring that about here? For such a discovery had been very well prepared by what young Bevil says to Humphrey in the first act and by the hint Indiana gives to Sealand in the fifth act, which hint the old gentleman readily takes; for when she tells him she had been made an infant captive on the seas, he immediately cries out, "An infant captive!" and after some interruption given by Indiana, he says, "Dear lady! O yet one moment's patience, my heart grows full with your affliction, but yet there is something in your story that —— ". She answers as if she were at cross purposes, "My portion here is bitterness and sorrow." To which he replies, "Do not think so. Pray answer me, does Bevil know your name and family?" So that a few questions more, pertinently answered, would have brought on the discovery. Now if the discovery had been made this way and Isabella had not known her brother at her first seeing him, but had come in to Sealand and Indiana just after the discovery had been made, there would have been two surprises, both greater and more agreeable than now they are and both of them without absurdity. * * *

Stages, Actors, and Audiences

EMMET L. AVERY AND
ARTHUR H. SCOUTEN

The Theatrical World, 1660–1700[†]

Rarely does an art form have its professional development interrupted for a generation. In some respects, however, this happened to the public theaters in London from the prohibition against acting passed late in 1642 by the Commonwealth[1] to the restoration of the monarchy in 1660. For twenty years the Commonwealth, opposed in principle and practice to theatrical entertainments, kept the playhouses under relatively tight rein and frequently reduced acting in the public theaters so severely as to make financially unprofitable the operations of a company and the composing of plays for public presentation. Although plays did not wholly disappear from the stage, the eighteen years from 1642 to 1660 represent an unusual hiatus in the public practice of the various forms of dramatic art, a situation especially unusual for a country which in the preceding century had had a glorious dramatic renaissance.

With the restoration of Charles II early in 1660, an opportunity arose for the theatrical world to begin anew and the player, manager, playwright, and spectator to restore the drama to its former position in England's culture. By 1660 the principal actors of the days of James I and Charles I had died or had so drifted out of touch with dramatic enterprise that the continuity of acting had been impaired, though certainly not lost. Furthermore, most of the pre-Commonwealth theaters had been closed, destroyed, or converted to purposes other than theatrical. In addition, the playwrights of the old regime no longer were productive. And a new generation had appeared in London, one which had little intimate knowledge of acting, the drama, or the playhouse. One can note this frame of mind in Samuel Pepys, who in 1660 and for some years later found the reopened theatrical scene a dazzling sight and who

† From *The London Stage: 1600–1800,* Part I, edited by William Van Lennep (Carbondale, Ill.: Southern Illinois University Press, 1965), xxi–xxviii. Reprinted by permission of the publisher.
1. See Leslie Hotson, *The Commonwealth and Restoration Stage* (Cambridge, Mass., 1928), pp. 5–6.

occasionally mentioned, as though it was interesting but not exceptional, taking to the theater a friend who had never before seen a staged
play and was therefore vague concerning the traditions of the drama.
During the Commonwealth the drama had not, of course, been extin-
guished, for old plays had been given (sometimes in public, often in
private) and new ones, such as Sir William Davenant's operatic works,
had been composed and staged. Nevertheless, the professional theater,
experienced actors, and knowledgeable spectators had to be re-created.
In bringing the theater to life again, the managers, playwrights, performers, and the public developed after 1660 many practices, including
some striking innovations, which set the pattern for the London professional theaters for the next hundred and fifty years.

Although it is difficult to determine the relative importance of the
innovations and alterations, it is not difficult to select those which had
important effects upon the English stage to the end of the eighteenth
century: (1) The creation of a monopoly of theatrical enterprises, ordinarily restricted to two patent companies, sometimes compressed into a
single company; (2) the introduction of women to act upon the stage,
altering the old custom of the boy actor in female roles; (3) the altered
design of the playhouses, with the development of the pit as a main
seating area, the stage-boxes, front-boxes, and side-boxes as the more
expensive and, theoretically, more desirable locations, and the first and
second galleries for less expensive tastes; (4) the greatly increased use of
scenes, especially changeable scenery, and machines, with an accompa-
nying emphasis upon spectacle in both dramatic and operatic productions; (5) an increasing enlargement of the day's program by means
of entr'acte entertainments of singing and dancing, accompanied by a
correspondingly greater emphasis in the public concert halls upon vocal
and instrumental music. During the forty years from 1660 and 1700 and
during most of the eighteenth century, these practices, both singly and
in unison, had extremely important effects upon the course of English
drama and stagecraft.

Although the first of these events—the creation of a two-company
monopoly—apparently came about without extended discussion of the
wisdom of a theatrical monopoly, it did not materialize without opposition. Because the continuity of management had been interrupted by
the Commonwealth, a mild scramble for power occurred in 1659 and
1660. The energy and prestige of two men, Sir William Davenant and
Thomas Killigrew, as well as their access to Charles II's ear, gave them
an exceptional opportunity to secure exclusive rights to form companies
and to present plays. At first, however, they were opposed by John
Rhodes, Michael Mohun, and William Beeston, theatrical entrepre-
neurs who wished to form their own companies, and by Sir Henry Herbert, who, as Master of the Revels, opposed the grants to Davenant and
Killigrew not because he objected to a monopoly in principle but

because he desired that all grants be put directly under his control. Within a short time, Davenant and Killigrew won the struggle against other competitors by securing patents to form a monopoly of two companies, and they succeeded in securing considerable, though not complete, independence of the Office of the Revels. Although legal measures had to be taken occasionally to suppress upstart companies and although some leniency was allowed to a series of Nurseries for relatively untrained actors, control by Davenant and Killigrew rapidly became effective. The Duke's Company and the King's Company, the names by which these groups were familiarly known, dominated London's theatrical enterprises; and when they had erected two new theaters, Dorset Garden and the Theatre Royal in Bridges Street, they made it virtually impossible for any other company to achieve equality in London. The patent houses strengthened their control by securing regulations which prevented an actor from exercising easy freedom of movement from one position to another.

Nevertheless, monopoly by two companies did not necessarily guarantee financial success. By 1682 the King's Company, weakened by internal dissensions, misfortunes (including the burning of the Bridges Street playhouse a few years earlier), and poor patronage, made overtures to the Duke's Company to form a united enterprise. This amalgamation, essentially an absorption of the weaker King's by the more powerful Duke's Company, exercised until 1695 a virtually unchallenged control over theatrical offerings. In the season of 1694–95, however, fresh internal dissension caused a secession by the best actors, with the result that from 1695 to the close of the century London again had two companies. This pattern—a two-company structure altering to a single-company monopoly—occurred again in the early years of the next century. In fact, the kinds of monopoly established in 1660 and 1661 set the pattern for limiting the number of legally-operating theatrical companies to two for a great many decades, with the exception of several seasons in the first third of the eighteenth century, when the authorities closed their eyes to violations of this principle. The Licensing Act of 1737 restored a rigorous legalization of a two-company monopoly of dramatic offerings in the regular winter season.

A second innovation, the admission of women to act in the public theaters, also occurred within a year after the reopening of the playhouses in 1660. No doubt, the employment of actresses would have come about in due time as a result of social change, but the interruption in dramatic continuity provided both a stimulus and an occasion. For a very brief time the playhouses retained the employment of boy actors for female roles: for example, Edward Kynaston, William Betterton, and James Nokes. Nevertheless, the dissolution of the repertory companies during the Commonwealth had inhibited the training of boys as female impersonators at the same time that the sojourn of the English court in

France had demonstrated the practicality of having women perform upon the stage. Andrew Newport, writing to Sir Richard Leveson upon the new practices in London, 15 December 1660, reflected the influence of the Continent: "Upon our stages we have women actors, as beyond seas."[2] In fact, by the early autumn of 1660, during the formation of the patent houses, a petition (13 October 1660) indicates that the companies had in prospect the engaging of women.[3] We do not know just when the first actress played a major role or who she was, but a woman certainly acted Desdemona in *Othello* in late 1660.[4] Thereafter, although the stage was not a proper place for proper young gentlewomen, many actresses gained recognition and fame—Nell Gwynn is a shining example—even if, in the words of John Downes, prompter to the Duke's Company, they often "by force of Love were Erept the Stage."[5]

The impact of the introduction of actresses is immeasurable. Early in the 1660's it was argued that their presence in the companies would improve the moral tone of the playhouses and the drama. In the patent issued to Killigrew, 25 April 1662, the argument runs as follows:

> for as much as many plays formerly acted doe conteine severall prophane, obscene, and scurrulous passages, and the women's part therein have byn acted by men in the habit of women, at which some have taken offence, for the preventing of these abuses for the future . . . wee do likewise permit and give leave, that all of the woemen's part . . . may be performed by woemen soe long as their recreacones, which by reason of the abuses aforesaid were scandalous and offensive, may by such reformation be esteemed not onely harmless delight, but useful and instructive.[6]

That this pious hope was not fully realized requires no demonstration, for numerous commentators deplored the private and public lives of the actresses and the fact that the immoral tone of the stage was not genuinely improved by the presence of women. John Evelyn, for example, frequently referred in his diary to the corrupting influences of actresses upon the Court. (See his strongly-worded disapproval in the entry for 18 October 1666.) On the other hand, the delight with which Pepys followed the acting and careers of such actresses as Nell Gwynn and Mary Knepp testifies to the pleasure as well as to the more effective acting which the abilities of women brought to the stage. The actresses, nevertheless, did not fully achieve equality in position, for among the

2. HMC [Historical Manuscript Commission], Fifth Report, Part I (1876), p. 158.
3. Hotson, *Commonwealth and Restoration Stage*, p. 204. See also *The Dramatic Records of Sir Henry Herbert*, ed. J. Q. Adams (New Haven, Conn., 1917), pp. 94–96, where a petition by several actors states that they "had by convenant obliged [themselves] to act with woemen."
4. For a comprehensive account of Restoration actresses, see John Harold Wilson, *All the King's Ladies* (Chicago, 1958).
5. *Roscius Anglicanus*, edited by Montague Summers (London, n.d.), p. 35.
6. See Percy Fitzgerald, *A New History of the English Stage* (London, 1882), I, 80.

early sharing groups there are no women sharers, although in 1695 actresses and actors became equal sharers in a new company. In numbers, also, the proportion of actors to actresses usually was at least two to one, although this inequality reflected primarily the needs of the companies, as the number of male to female roles in most plays was a disproportionate one. On the other hand, by the end of the seventeenth century the London theaters had trained several women of considerable talent and great proficiency: Nell Gwynn, Katherine Corey, Mary Saunderson Betterton, Frances Knight, Elinor Leigh, Anne Bracegirdle, Elizabeth Barry, and Susanna Percival Mountfort Verbruggen. These women established the actress as an integral part of English theatrical enterprises.

Another result of the long closure of the theaters was an alteration in the physical accommodations. When acting resumed, not all of the older theaters were available, although the old Cockpit in Drury Lane sufficed for a while. Temporarily, Gibbons' Tennis Court, constructed much earlier, was converted into a not wholly satisfactory playhouse. In these circumstances, both the Duke's and King's companies early planned to build new theaters, and these new structures set the characteristic features of the playhouses for several generations. First of all, the principal new ones—the two in Drury Lane and the theater in Dorset Garden—were of moderate size, permitting an intimate atmosphere. The stage extended in front of the proscenium arch into the pit, which was fitted with benches (backless), continuing the growing practice of seating nearly all of the spectators and eliminating the large proportion of standees which had been characteristic of some earlier playhouses. Extending from the stage on both sides of the pit were tiers of boxes, commonly referred to as stage-boxes (often a double tier); side boxes (those extending along both sides of the interior); and front-boxes (those facing or fronting the stage, at the rear of the pit). Rising above the front boxes and pit was a gallery or (in some theaters) a lower gallery as well as a smaller upper one. With benches rather than individual seats as the prevailing mode, particularly in the pit, the playhouses had a flexible rather than a fixed capacity. If the performance was sparsely attended, spectators might sit comfortably upon the benches; but if the attendance was very large, the increase was accommodated in part by crowding. At all times, in spite of a tendency for the socially or financially elite to sit apart from those of lesser quality, the spectators talked and listened in an atmosphere of conviviality, as Pepys makes abundantly clear in many entries in his diary. These types of accommodation and the informal, intimate atmosphere essentially prevailed until, in the second half of the eighteenth century, the proprietors embarked upon a steady enlargement of the playhouses, an alteration which affected not only the cohesion of the audience but also its relationship to the actors on stage.

Another change in the technical operations of the playhouses was a vastly increased emphasis upon changeable scenery and devices ("machines") for creating such special effects as flyings of persons and objects. Much of the impetus for this movement came from the imagination and ingenuity of Sir William Davenant, who, some years before the restoration of Charles II, had envisioned public theaters with elaborate embellishments to the action. Although he had experimented in this vein in a few productions during the five years preceding 1660, he lacked a genuine opportunity to develop his theories until he secured a patent and formed a company to act in Lincoln's Inn Fields.[7] John Downes, prompter to Davenant's company, stressed these innovations when he described the opening of that theater (probably on 28 June 1661) with The Siege of Rhodes, an operatic work "having new Scenes and Decorations, being the first that e're were Introduc'd in England."[8] Pepys' first glimpse of this play (2 July 1661) much impressed him, for he found the opening "indeed is very fine and magnificent." By the summer of 1662 Davenant's reliance upon these devices was sufficiently on record that a poem characterizing recent dramatic events referred to the progress of this theater, "Where the Knight with his Scenes doth keep much adoe."[9]

Davenant constantly improved his stock of scenery, and although the King's Company, Davenant's rival, somewhat slowly followed his lead, within ten years both companies had invested large sums in this phase of their operations and had set the London theaters upon a venture leading to more and more elaborate and costly creations. Although Davenant did not live to see the new theater in Dorset Garden which his company constructed, he would have been delighted with the attention given to settings and contrivances in this elegant playhouse. As was true of other innovations, there was no turning back from Davenant's pioneering; thereafter, for many decades, the companies vied with each other in colorful scenes, startling machines, realistic properties and embellishments to the dramas and entr'acte entertainments. In fact, they occasionally praised their own initiative, as did the speaker in the Second Prologue to Shadwell's revision of The Tempest, 1674:

> Had we not for y^r pleasure found new wayes
> You still had rusty Arras had, & thredbare playes;
> Nor Scenes nor Woomen had they had their will,
> But some with grizl'd Beards had acted Woomen still.

Alterations in the daily program accompanied these changes. Possessing increasingly elaborate gear, the management placed greater

7. For a full discussion of the history of scenes in the English theaters, see Richard Southern, Changeable Scenery: Its Origin and Development in the British Theatre (London, 1952).
8. Roscius Anglicanus, p. 20.
9. Hotson, Commonwealth and Restoration Stage, p. 246.

emphasis upon spectacle. Although the play remained the center of the day's offerings, spectacular staging provided a drawing attraction. Shakespeare's *The Tempest*, for example, owed much of its popularity to its transformation into a dramatic opera or musical drama in which flyings, sinkings, and machines augmented the appeal. Each burst of applause for an operatic spectacle, even if sometimes the receipts did not equal the large expenses, caused the rival companies to launch still more expensive productions. In addition, these spectacles stimulated a taste for musical and terpsichorean novelties, and the managements larded many comedies and even some tragedies with songs, dances, and "vocal and instrumental entertainments," some of which, though not all, were thematically related to the action. The fresh faces, engaging talents, and novelty of actresses popularized these augmentations. Pepys, for example, often expressed his delight in the singing and dancing of Nell Gwynn and Mary Knepp, sometimes being so engrossed by them that he failed to mention his response to the play proper; he occasionally found the incidental music so ravishing that he secured a copy of it for his own collection. Further proof of the drawing power of this new trend appears in the Preface to Thomas Shadwell's *The Humorists* (10 December 1670), where he credits the triumph of his play over its enemies to the delightful dancing of Mrs. Johnson, whose talents drew both friends and foes and silenced the loud critics. By the end of the century the newspaper announcements make it evident that song and dance as entr'acte entertainments had begun to assume the dominant position which they were to make secure in the first half of the eighteenth century.

* * *

ELIZABETH HOWE

The Arrival of the Actress[†]

Why Actresses in 1660?

Some time during the last months of 1660, a professional English actress appeared in a play on the English public stage for the first time — a historic moment for English theatre. While Englishwomen may occasionally have performed in public entertainments such as mystery plays as early as the fifteenth century,[1] they were never regularly employed in

[†] From Elizabeth Howe, *The First English Actresses* (Cambridge: Cambridge University Press, 1992), pp. 19–26. Reprinted by permission of the publisher and the author's estate.
1. See T. S. Graves, 'Women on the Pre-Restoration Stage,' *Studies in Philology* 22 (1925), pp. 184–7.

the commercial theatre in any capacity until the Restoration. The exact date of the actress's debut is not known, but is usually assumed to be 8 December 1660, when it is known that a woman played Desdemona in a production of *Othello* by Thomas Killigrew's King's Company. A special prologue was written by the poet Thomas Jordan 'to introduce the first Woman that came to act on the stage in the tragedy called the Moor of Venice': 'The Woman playes today, mistake me not, / No Man in Gown, or Page in Petty-Coat.'[2] A week later one Andrew Newport wrote to Sir Richard Leveson that 'upon our stages we have women actors, as beyond seas'. On 3 January 1661 Pepys recorded his visit to *The Beggar's Bush* by the King's Company that day was 'the first time that ever I saw Women come upon the stage'.[3]

The possible reasons for the advent and public acceptance of actresses at this particular time continue to preoccupy scholars. It was certainly not the case, as some have assumed, of women being automatically superior to boys in the performance of female roles. English theatre finally relinquished a ludicrous convention many years after France, Italy and Spain (women were acting in these countries by the latter half of the sixteenth century).[4] For the twentieth-century theatregoer, accustomed to seeing actresses, it might be easy to agree with Colley Cibber that the removal of boys playing women instantly transformed theatre for the better:

> The other Advantage I was speaking of, is, that before the Restoration, no Actresses had ever been seen upon the English Stage. The Characters of Women, on former Theatres, were perform'd by Boys, or young Men of the most effeminate Aspect. And what Grace, or Master Strokes of Action can we conceive such ungain Hoydens to have been capable of?[5]

One modern commentator quotes Cibber's words approvingly, adding, 'for the first time ever, English playwrights could write women's roles for women, giving them the same weight and complexity in the overall fabric of their plays as the male characters'. Another theatre historian declares that 'the slightest imaginative consideration of the problem [of boys as women] will show that the awakening stage sorely needed a change in this essential factor'.[6] However, the Renaissance transvestite convention was in fact very successful. The parts written for boys by Shakespeare, Middleton, Webster and others suggest that these perform-

2. Thomas Jordan, 'A Prologue to introduce the first Woman that came to Act on the Stage in the Tragedy, call'd the Moor of Venice', in *A Royal Arbor of Loyal Poesie* (1664), p. 21.
3. Andrew Newport to Sir Richard Leveson, 15 December 1660, cited in Wilson, *All the King's Ladies*, p. 3. Pepys, *Diary*, vol. II, p. 5.
4. See Rosamund Gilder, *Enter the Actress: The First Women in the Theatre* (Boston, 1931), pp. 50–99.
5. Cibber, *Apology*, p. 55.
6. *Restoration and Georgian England 1660–1788*, compiled and introduced by David Thomas and Arnold Hare (Cambridge University Press, 1989), p. 138. Henry Wynsham Lanier, *The*

ers were highly skilled and well able to perform a wide range of leading, challenging female roles. For contemporaries, the boys seem to have been as effective in every way as we now find women. For example, a spectator watching *Othello* performed by the King's Men in 1610 was absolutely convinced and overwhelmed by the acting of the boy playing Desdemona:

> They also had their tragedies, well and effectively acted. In these they drew tears not only by their speech, but also by their action. Indeed Desdemona, killed by her husband, in death moved us especially when, as she lay in her bed, her face alone implored the pity of the audience.[7]

The writer here significantly refers always to Desdemona by a feminine pronoun: '*she* lay in *her* bed', '*her* face implored' and so on. Unquestionably, boy or not, she *was* a woman to him.

With an eighteen-year gap in theatre production after the theatres were closed in 1642, there was of course a shortage of boy-actresses when they reopened in 1660. As the *Actor's Remonstrance*, a pamphlet of 1643 put it, 'our boyes, ere we shall have libertie to act againe, will be grown out of use like crackt organ pipes, and have faces as old as our flags'.[8] Nevertheless, while a lack of suitable boys may have precipitated an abrupt change to actresses, this does not explain why the change was considered desirable in the first place. The theatre of 1660 certainly possessed one outstanding female impersonator in Edward Kynaston (Pepys described him as 'the prettiest woman in the whole house'[9]) and there were several others. Had theatre-goers so desired, more could presumably have been trained. The reasons for the shift from boys to women were social and cultural rather than practical.

The acceptance of women players after 1660 has been related to a profound change in contemporary attitudes to women, female sexuality and theatre among the upper and upper-middle classes in the late seventeenth century. Whereas during the late sixteenth and early seventeenth centuries female sexuality and theatrical representation were both subject to vigorous attack, after 1660 they were positively relished: 'the infinite variety of the theater, and the infinite variety of the seductress . . . grew to be celebrated rather than condemned'.[1] This shift in attitude

---

First English Actresses from 1660–1700 (New York, 1930), p. 31. Other critics who have assumed that actresses must automatically be better than boys are Gilder, *Enter the Actress*, pp. 134–5, and Wilson, *All the King's Ladies*, p. 90. A lively discussion of the topic is Stephen Orgel's article 'Nobody's Perfect: Or Why did the English Stage Take Boys for Women?' *South Atlantic Quarterly*, 88 (Winter 1989), no. I, pp. 7–29.

7. Letter translated from the Latin, quoted by Geoffrey Tillotson, '*Othello* and *The Alchemist* at Oxford in 1610', *The Times Literary Supplement* (20 July 1933), p. 494.

8. Quoted by Gilder, *Enter the Actress*, p. 137.

9. Pepys, *Diary*, vol. II, p. 7.

1. Katharine Eisaman Maus, ' "Playhouse Flesh and Blood": Sexual Ideology and the Restoration Actress', *English Literary History*, 46 (1979), p. 609.

can be linked to a wider change in how relationships between the sexes were defined. As the seventeenth century wore on, a new model of sexual relations became increasingly accepted, in which the woman as well as the man was entitled to full and adequate individuality. Rather than being considered merely inferior to man, woman began to be defined as the opposite, yet indispensable sex, excluded from the male spheres of public and professional life but vital in the field of domestic management—her own private sphere of home and children. Although the working actress was an exception to the typical domestic female, she was subject to the same ideological constraints and her gender difference was emphasised (and enjoyed) by constant reference to her sexuality, both on stage and off.

However, while this theory explains the public support for actresses after 1660, it fails to take into account the fact that female actors had actually gained considerable currency and even a token acceptance in court culture during the first half of the seventeenth century. Queen Anne and her ladies took prominent roles in the great Jacobean masques of Jonson and Inigo Jones and such female activity increased after Henrietta Maria married Charles I and took to the stage in 1626. It has recently been discovered that the first time that the word 'actress' was used with the meaning 'female player on the stage' was not, as the OED states, in 1700, but directly after Queen Henrietta Maria's first court performance in a French pastoral on Shrove Tuesday, 1626: in a contemporary account of the performance Sir Benjamin Rudyerd referred to the queen as a 'principal actress'.[2] Women continued to act at court and in some private houses, and with William Prynne's attack on women actors as 'notorious whores' in the Puritan tract Histriomastix (1633), the issue became a subject of debate in a wide range of texts.[3] Prynne's condemnation was taken by the court as a direct criticism of Henrietta Maria when Histriomastix was published, just weeks before the queen acted in William Montague's drama The Shepherd's Paradise. A number of plays of the 1630s refer to the topic, usually making some kind of satiric attack on the would-be female actor, or ridiculing the affected French taste of those who would support her. For example, in James Shirley's The Ball (1632), a satiric comedy of London town life, the buffoon Jack Freshwater complacently shows off his knowledge of Paris and its customs by declaring that there 'women are the best actors, they play their own parts, a thing much desired in England by some ladies, inns o'court gentlemen, and others'. Shirley is clearly mock-

2. See Sophie Tomlinson, 'Theatrical Women: the Emergence of Women as Actors in English Theatre and Drama before the Restoration', Ph.D. dissertation, Cambridge University, in progress.
3. See Alfred Harbage, Cavalier Drama (1936), p. 15.

ing those who favour the idea of actresses and inviting his audience to join him. 'Some ladies' presumably refers to the queen and her followers.[4]

What needs to be explained is why, although women acted during the 1630s in court privacy, they were not generally accepted and, indeed, why there were no actresses on the public stage, whereas in 1660 actresses were both introduced and welcomed in the public theatre. The answer lies in the fact that although both before and after the Civil War support for the actresses came from the court, the relationship between court and public theatre in the two periods is strikingly different.

In the Caroline period theatre at court and other theatres in London, both private and public, were emphatically separate. Although the private Caroline theatres outside the court—Blackfriars, the Phoenix and Salisbury Court—have traditionally been seen as extensions of the court theatre, that is, as a narrow, exclusively royalist milieu, in actual fact this was very far from the case. 'The theatre audiences, while not lacking strong links with the court, were themselves drawn from those same parliamentary classes from which the political challenge to Charles in 1640 would come.'[5] Although spectators at the private theatre were principally gentry, they comprised a much broader social and geographical group than did the Restoration theatre audience: they even included a number of Puritans. The difference between this audience's opinion of female players and that of the Caroline court is vividly illustrated by their very different reactions to the visit of a troupe of French actresses to London in November 1629. When these performers appeared at Blackfriars, they were apparently 'hissed, hooted, and pippin-pelted from the stage'.[6] While the dislike was probably partly due to xenophobia and professional jealousy, the violence of the reaction suggests that for many theatre-goers the sight of women acting and speaking on the public stage represented an outrageous rupture of social as well as theatrical convention. However, in stark contrast immediately after this incident, Henrietta Maria entertained the French troupe at court and then recommended to her husband that they visit Whitehall.

During the Interregnum, when the theatres were closed, Royalist support for actresses must have been strengthened, since the court spent much time in exile on the Continent where actresses had long been an accepted feature of theatre. Charles II and his court (including at various times William Davenant and Thomas Killigrew to whom the

4. James Shirley, *The Dramatic Works and Poems of James Shirley*, now first collected; with notes by the late William Gifford Esq. (New York, 1966), vol. III, p. 79. See also Shirley's *Bird in a Cage* (1633), Richard Brome's *The Court-Beggar* (1640) and William Cartwright's *The Lady-Errant* (1628–43?).
5. Martin Butler, *Theatre and Crisis 1632–42* (Cambridge University Press, 1984), p. 100.
6. See Harbage, *Cavalier Drama*, p. 20.

patents to open theatres were granted in 1660) spent some considerable time in Paris taking part in court masques as well as attending plays. The theatre manager George Jolly, who also went into exile, even had the distinction of introducing female players to Frankfurt, where Charles II apparently saw them when he visited the town in September 1655.[7] When Sir William Davenant eventually returned to London he used a female singer, Mrs Coleman, in a private production of his opera *The Siege of Rhodes*, some time in the late 1650s.

Thus it is not surprising to find women players being introduced as soon as the king returned to power in 1660 and granted permission for two theatres to open. Now, because the Restoration theatre was more exclusively a court milieu than it had been in the Caroline period, actresses were readily accepted by theatre audiences. Although, as we have seen, Restoration spectators were by no means exclusively aristo-cratic, the vast majority of them, even if they were professional men like Pepys, favoured the court and shared its attitudes and interests. Charles II was more closely involved with the public theatre, as opposed to the court theatre, than any other English monarch, and where he went his supporters followed. The Restoration theatre was a coterie theatre, not as small a coterie as was once believed, but a coterie none the less, in contrast to the more mixed theatre before 1642. It was within the select atmosphere of a particular social group that the first English actresses were introduced and flourished.

Some time around 21 August 1660, when the king granted them a London theatre monopoly, Killigrew and Davenant both seem to have recruited and begun to train a handful of actresses. A petition addressed to the king by a group of players on 13 October 1660 mentions that they had been obliged by Killigrew to act under his management 'with women'. Davenant's agreement with the chief players of his company, dated 5 November 1660, included a clause that seven shares were to go to Davenant 'for maintaining the actresses of the company'.[8]

In 1660 Davenant certainly recruited six actresses: Hester Davenport, Mary Saunderson, Jane Long, Anne Gibbs, Mrs Jennings and Mrs Nor-ris. Four of these were boarded at his own premises adjacent to his new theatre. Killigrew probably acquired at least four actresses at the start: Katherine Corey, Anne Marshall, Mrs Eastland and Mrs Weaver.[9] It is presumably one of these four who played Desdemona in the King's Company's historic production of *Othello* on 8 December 1660. Anne Marshall seems to be the most likely candidate. Although Mrs Eastland's

7. See Leslie Hotson, *The Commonwealth and Restoration Stage* (Cambridge, Mass., 1928), pp. 136–7, 171–2.
8. Petition of 13 October 1660, quoted in Thomas (ed.), *Restoration and Georgian England*, p. 13. Davenant's agreement given in Hotson, *Commonwealth and Restoration Stage*, p. 207.
9. See Wilson, *All the King's Ladies*, p. 8. Wilson suggests (pp. 6–7) that Anne Marshall or Mary Saunderson are the most likely candidates for the role of Desdemona—apparently forgetting that Saunderson was always a member of Davenant's company.

name appears on the prompter John Downes' list of Killigrew's original actresses and there is no reason to dispute this, her name appears on no dramatis personae until 1669 and she only ever played minor parts. Mrs Weaver, also known as Elizabeth Farley, played bigger roles than Mrs Eastland later on, but never lead roles, and she usually performed in comedy. Although in 1689 Katherine Corey described herself as 'the first and is last of all the actresses that were constituted by King Charles the Second at His Restoration' in a petition to the Lord Chamberlain,[1] this simply means that she was the first woman sworn in as a servant of the king, or that she was the first actress recruited by Killigrew. Her casting as Desdemona is extremely unlikely: she was large and plain and later specialised in ugly, comic parts. Anne Marshall, on the other hand, was both talented and attractive; from 1661 she played lead roles such as the Lady in Beaumont and Fletcher's *The Scornful Lady* and she soon came to specialise in tragedy.

In his haste to get his actresses on the stage before those of his rival Davenant, Killigrew may have had them perform in public before they were ready. Only four weeks after *Othello*, Pepys complained that a production of Middleton's *The Widow* by the King's Company on 8 January 1661 was 'wronged' by the women not knowing their lines. Four weeks of more rehearsal and the women seem to have improved; when Pepys saw Killigrew's production of *The Scornful Lady* on 12 February 'now done by a woman', this 'makes the play appear much better than ever it did to me'.[2] Progress was rapid so that by the middle of 1661 actresses were an established feature of the English stage.

During the early months of the theatre's reopening, male actors continued to play women as well. On 18 August 1660 Edward Kynaston (who seems at the time to have been the most proficient and experienced performer of female roles in England) played the Duke's sister in *The Loyal Subject*, prompting Pepys to record delightedly that he made the most beautiful woman in the theatre, although his 'voice not very good'. However, Kynaston was already playing male as well as female parts. For instance, on 6 December he played Otto in *The Bloody Brother*, having played the heroine Arthiope in the same play only a few weeks before. On 7 January 1661, three days after he had seen a woman on the stage for the first time, Pepys saw Kynaston play Epicene in Jonson's comedy.

> Kynaston had the good turn to appear in three shapes: I, as a poor woman in ordinary clothes to please Morose; then in fine clothes as a gallant, and in them was clearly the prettiest woman in the whole house—and lastly, as a man; and then likewise did appear the handsomest man in the house.[3]

1. Ibid., p. 7.
2. Pepys, *Diary*, vol. II, p. 35.
3. Ibid., vol. I, p. 224 and vol. II, p. 7.

The casting of Kynaston in this way implies a final effort to extract as much entertainment value as possible from his ability to impersonate women, now that actresses were beginning to supersede him and his kind. The transvestite convention, instead of being the accepted theatrical norm that it had been in the Renaissance, had become a curiosity. In his *Apology* Cibber relates how 'Kynaston, at that time was so beautiful a Youth, that the Ladies of Quality prided themselves in taking him with them in their Coaches, to Hyde-Park, in his Theatrical Habit, after the Play'[4]—Kynaston had become a theatrical freak. On 28 December 1661 he was still playing the eponymous heroine of John Suckling's *Aglaura,* but the 1661–2 season appears to have been the last in which he played female parts, although he remained a successful tragic actor for many years.

At the beginning of 1662 the casting of women in women's roles became not merely the popular choice but law. In a patent dated 25 April 1662 to Thomas Killigrew it was decreed that henceforth women should play women's parts:

> And for as much as many plays formerly acted do contain several profane, obscene and scurrilous passages, and the women's parts therein have been acted by men in the habit of women, at which some have taken offence, for the preventing of these abuses for the future, we do hereby strictly command and enjoin that from henceforth . . . we do . . . permit and give leave that all the women's parts to be acted in either of the said two companies for the time to come may be performed by women, so long as their recreations, which by reason of the abuses aforesaid were scandalous and offensive, may by such reformation be esteemed not only harmless delight, but useful and instructive representations of human life.[5]

The mention of 'some' having 'taken offence' at the wearing of women's clothing by men refers to attacks on the stage by Puritans, like Prynne. Leo Hughes suggests that the Stuarts 'had had enough experience with puritans to insure their taking no chances',[6] and so the weighty language of the patent makes the introduction of women appear as some kind of social reform. In actual fact, of course, the use of female players had the opposite effect to the one specified in the patent—a good deal of the subsequent licentiousness of Restoration drama may be blamed on the sexual exploitation of the actresses. But in any case, whatever its consequences, the change was effected: woman had replaced boys forever in the English public theatre.

* * *

4. Cibber, *Apology*, p. 71.
5. Cited in Thomas (ed.), *Restoration and Georgian England*, pp. 17–18.
6. Leo Hughes, *The Drama's Patrons* (Austin, 1971), p. 140.

EMMET L. AVERY AND
ARTHUR H. SCOUTEN

The Audience[†]

The common assumption is that the Restoration audience was essentially of upper-class composition by contrast with the greater diversity of classes, education, and taste of the Elizabethan era. Nevertheless, the Restoration audience was not of the single complexion which some subsequent theatrical historians have emphasized. The range of social classes, professions, and cultural attainments was fairly great, and the taste of the spectators as well as their motives in attending the playhouses varied considerably. Some, like Pepys, were fascinated by the stage, by the sense of illusion, and by the social structure of the spectators. Others, like James Brydges, in the closing decade, apparently regarded the theater as a port of call on the social round, where Brydges might look in and quickly withdraw if the atmosphere did not attract him. Many men of letters attended frequently, sometimes as arbiters of taste, sometimes because the theater was, except for the Court, the coffeehouses, and private homes, a center where intellectuals met and kept abreast of literary tendencies, the old and new drama, and the climate of acting. To it also came many wits, gentlemen, Persons of Quality, citizens, Templars, and others of varying social and financial status.

In fact, the audience seems to have been of almost unceasing interest to itself, to playwrights, to authors of prologues and epilogues, and to pamphleteers. They tended to categorize the spectators and to define their habitats. Pepys, an observant man, often responded to the composition of the audience, partly because he was delighted when interesting wits and lovely ladies attended, and disappointed when lower social groups dominated. He also enjoyed a play more when there was a full house, for a meager one had a desolate air. In fact, the social atmosphere of the theater was rarely better captured than by Pepys, attending *Heraclius* on 4 February 1666 / 7; he had

> [an] extraordinary content; and the more from the house being very full, and great company; among others, Mrs Steward, very fine, with her locks done up with puffs . . . and several other great ladies, had their hair so. . . . Here I saw my Lord Rochester and his lady, Mrs Mallet, who hath after all this ado married him; and, as I hear some say in the pit, it is a great act of charity; for he hath no estate. But it was pleasant to see how everybody rose up when my Lord

† From *The London Stage: 1660–1800*, Part I, edited by William Van Lennep (Carbondale, Ill.: Southern Illinois University Press, 1965), clxii–clxxi. Reprinted by permission of the publisher.

> John Butler, the Duke of Ormond's son, come into the pit towards the end of the play, who was a servant to Mrs Mallet, and now smiled upon her, and she on him. I had sitting next to me a woman, the likest my Lady Castlemayne that ever I saw anybody like another; but she is a whore, I believe, for she is acquainted with every fine fellow, and called them by their name, Jacke, and Tom, and before the end of the play frisked to another place.

How like a social afternoon, lacking only tea to make the gossipy atmosphere complete. In other vignettes Pepys suggests the informality of the auditors. On 16 September 1667 he recorded that "one of the best parts of our sport was a mighty pretty lady that sat behind us, that did laugh so heartily and constantly, that it did me good to hear her." Or a touchingly sentimental scene, at *The Mad Couple*, 28 December 1667: "It pleased us mightily to see the natural affection of a poor woman, the mother of one of the children brought upon the stage: the child crying, she by force got upon the stage and took up her child and carried it away off of the stage from Hart [the actor]." Or a moment of near tragedy, averted skillfully, on 2 November 1667 at *I Henry IV*: "And it was observable how a gentleman of good habit, sitting just before us, eating of some fruit in the midst of the play, did drop down as dead, being choked; but with much ado Orange Moll did thrust her finger down his throat, and brought him to life again."

Some contemporary writers attempted to understand the composition and alteration in the audiences during the forty years preceding 1700; usually, they made distinctions between the spectators during the reign of Charles II and those from the accession of William and Mary to the end of the century. The author of *Historia Histrionica* (1699) briefly examined conditions before the Civil Wars, during the Commonwealth, and after the Restoration. In his opinion, although London was much more populous after 1660 than before the Commonwealth, the increase in admission charges in the Restoration playhouses (which he blames upon the introduction of costly scenes) narrowed the range of individuals who could afford to attend. As a result, there was "better order kept among the Company that came; which made very good People think a Play an Innocent Diversion for an idle Hour or two." In addition, he believed that the plays after 1660 were, "for the most part, more Instructive and Moral."[1] From a vantage point in the early eighteenth century, John Dennis also looked back upon the reign of Charles II and analyzed the nature of the audience at that time. First of all, he believed that "a considerable Part" of the auditory "had that due application, which is requisite for the judging of Comedy," the leisure to attend to dramatic theory and practice, for "that was an age of Pleasure, and not of Business." Gentlemen had the financial security and leisure to be "serene

1. In Cibber, *Apology*, I, xxvii.

enough to receive its impressions."[2] Later, Dennis returned to this subject and emphasized another factor which he thought made the audiences of the reign of Charles II superior: There "were several extraordinary men at Court who wanted neither Zeal nor Capacity, nor Authority to sett [the audiences] right again." He named, among others, George Villiers Duke of Buckingham, John Wilmot Earl of Rochester, the Earl of Dorset, Sir John Denham, and Edmund Waller. Men of their culture, knowledge, and taste could strongly influence an audience. When "these or the Majority of them Declared themselves upon any new Dramatick performance, the Town fell Immediately in with them."[3]

An examination of the known records of attendance at the theaters between 1660 and 1670 will document some of the analysis which Dennis made. The diaries and correspondence for that period show that a considerable number of literary men attended the theater, some with considerable frequency: Sir Charles Sedley, Sir George Etherege, the Earl of Dorset, George Villiers Duke of Buckingham, Thomas Shadwell, John Dryden, Roger Boyle Earl of Burlington, Sir William Coventry, the Earl of Rochester, William Cavendish Duke of Newcastle, Thomas Killigrew, Sir William Davenant. No doubt, many of the dramatists attended the opening performances of their own plays and, probably, those of rival playwrights. Pepys also gave particular attention to the nobility, gentlemen, and ladies attending the theater. He noted that Charles II attended frequently, sometimes accompanied by the Duke and Duchess of York, often with other nobles and Ladies of Honor; in addition, the Lord Chamberlain's records list many other occasions on which royalty was present. When Elizabeth, Queen of Bohemia visited in London, she also attended the theaters. Other frequenters during this period were Lord Brouncker and Sir William Penn, both close friends to Pepys; he often accompanied other members of the Penn family. Among other upper-class auditors were: Sir Christopher North, Sir Philip Carteret, John Evelyn, Prince Rupert, Lord Lauderdale, the Duke of Ormond, Lord Arlington, the Duke of Norfolk, the Duke of Albemarle, Lord Sandwich, Sir William Batten, Dr. Thomas Sprat, Bishop of Rochester, Lord Fauconberg, Henry Savile.

Pepys also frequently recorded in his Diary the presence of "fine ladies." He was particularly aware of Lady Castlemayne's presence in the playhouse and occasionally, seeing her carriage outside the theater, could hardly resist the temptation to go into the playhouse in spite of a resolve not to do so. He noticed also that the actresses from one company attended the opposition offerings whenever practicable, seeing Mrs. Knepp and Betty Hall of the King's Company at the Duke's The-

2. *Works*, I, 293–94.
3. *Ibid.*, II, 277. At this point he offered as an influence their verdict on *The Plain Dealer*, referred to earlier, which turned the opinion of the town in its favor.

atre on 30 March 1667. Nell Gwynn and Hester Davenport were sometimes conspicuously present, Mrs. Davenport sitting in the box at *The
Villain* on 1 January 1662 / 3 and catching Pepys' eye. Later, as we know
from the Lord Chamberlain's records, Nell Gwynn attended the theaters frequently on the King's bounty. Lady Dorset, Lady Penn, Lady
Elizabeth Bodvile, Mlle Le Blanc, Queen Elizabeth of Bohemia and
other ladies of fashion filled the boxes.

Attending as regularly as his conscience and purse would allow, Pepys
makes it clear that some of his friends were equally attentive playgoers.
Captain Ferrers and John Creed, a Deputy-Treasurer to the Fleet, often
were Pepys' companions on a playgoing afternoon. On other occasions
he attended with the Penn family, sometimes with Lord Brouncker, or
with ladies of the circles in which Pepys moved. He refers occasionally
to the presence of "gallants," sometimes as though they were a dis-
turbing breed but rarely naming them. Much of what Pepys reports
bears out Thomas Killigrew's assertions, 12 February 1666 / 7, concerning the improved atmosphere at the King's Theatre: earlier "the Queen
seldom and the King never would come; now, not the King only for
state, but all civil people do think they may come as well as any." In
addition, Killigrew "tells me plainly that the City audience was as good
as the Court, but now they are most gone."

Nevertheless, Pepys makes us aware that a greater diversity of persons
by class, birth, and occupation attended occasionally and, apparently,
with greater frequency year by year. On 27 December 1662 he was "not
so well pleased with the company at the house to-day, which was full of
citizens, there hardly being a gentleman or woman in the house." On 1
January 1662 / 3 he reported: "The house was full of citizens, and so the
less pleasant." Attending *Tu Quoque*, 12 September 1667, he disliked
the play, adding, "but it will please the citizens." At *I Henry IV*, 2
November 1667, he especially noted that "The house [was] full of Par-
liamentmen," as a result of a holiday for them. In a thoughtful mood on
1 January 1667 / 8 at *The Feigned Innocence*, he reflected on the
changes he had seen in several years of theatergoing: "Here a mighty
company of citizens, 'prentices, and others; and it makes me observe,
that when I begun first to be able to bestow a play on myself, I do not
remember that I saw so many by half of the ordinary 'prentices and
mean people in the pit at 2s. 6d. a-piece as now."

If we turn to the last twenty years of the seventeenth century, the
evidence suggests that changes had occurred in the composition of the
audience. Dennis believed that the quality and taste of the spectators
had seriously declined by 1700. Commenting upon the audiences of
1702, he found there "three sorts of People . . . who have had no education at all; and who were unheard of in the Reign of Charles the Second." These included (a) a "great many younger Brothers, Gentlemen
born, who had been kept at home, by reason of the pressure of the

Taxes"; (b) individuals "who made their Fortunes in the late War" and who had risen "from a state of obscurity" to a "condition of distinction and plenty"; and (c) "that considerable number of Foreigners, which within the last twenty years have been introduc'd among us; some of whom not being acquainted with our Language, and consequently with the sense of our Plays, and others disgusted with our extravagant, exorbitant Rambles, have been Instrumental in introducing Sound and Show." The second group, in his view, "could never attain to any higher entertainment than Tumbling and Vaulting and Ladder Dancing, and the delightful diversions of Jack Pudding . . . and encourage these noble Pastimes still upon the Stage." The third group, furthermore, like "Sound and Show, where the business of the Theatre does not require it, and particularly a sort of soft and wanton Musick, which has used the People to a delight which is independent of Reason, a delight that has gone a very great way towards the enervating and dissolving their minds." Finally, he argued that by 1702 "there are ten times more Gentlemen now in business, than there were in King Charles his Reign." They have been disturbed by war and pressed by taxes, "which make them uneasie." As a result, they "are attentive in the events of affairs, and too full of great and real events, to receive due impressions from the imaginary ones of the Theatre."[4] In a somewhat similar vein the author of *Historia Histrionica* (1699) emphasized that in the late years of the seventeenth century "The Play-houses are so extremely pestered with Vizard-masks and their Trade (occasioning continual Quarrels and Abuses) that many of the more Civilized Part of the Town are uneasy in the Company, and shun the Theatre as they would a House of Scandal."[5]

An associated influence was a change in the management. In the fifteen years following 1660 management lay in the hands of individuals who, frequently, were both proprietors and dramatists (Sir William Davenant is an example), and the actor-sharers had an interest in attracting audiences who responded to the best in dramatic offerings. After 1682, and especially in the last decade, when Rich and Skipwith bought into the United Company, they catered to a diversified audience. In part, they responded to a change; in part, they broadened the range of spectators and tastes.

The writers of Prologues and Epilogues and of pamphlets also show the diversified nature of the audience, especially from 1670 to 1700.

---

4. *Ibid.*, I, 293–94. One cannot help being reminded, at this point, of the way in which Pepys, concerned with the affairs of the navy and the state, nevertheless responded to the illusion of the stage. On 5 October 1667, dropping behind the scenes at Bridges Street, he expressed this sense of illusion: "But, Lord! to see how they [Mrs. Knepp and Nell Gwynn] were both painted would make a man mad, and did make me loath them; and what base company of men comes among them, and how lewdly they talk! and how poor the men are in clothes, and yet what a shew they make on the stage by candle-light, is very observable."
5. In Cibber, *Apology*, I, xxvii.

They tend also to characterize the spectators in each section of the house, from the boxes to the upper gallery. In a Prologue spoken after the King's Company had suffered a fire at Drury Lane in 1672, Dryden presented a panoramic view of the audience.

> Here's good Accommodation in the Pit,
> The Grave demurely in the midst may Sit.
> And so the hot Burgundians on the Side,
> Ply Vizard Masque, and o're the Benches stride:
> Here are convenient upper boxes too,
> For those that make the most triumphant show,
> All that keep Coaches must not Sit below.
> There Gallants, You betwixt the Acts retire,
> And at dull Plays have something to admire.

Examining the habituees of the pit, some writers look at them caustically, some gently. In *The Young Gallant's Academy* (1674) the satirist pictures the young man who attends the play to draw attention to himself.

> Therefore, I say, let our Gallant ... presently advance himself into the middle of the Pit, where having made his Honor to the rest of the Company, but especially to the Vizard-Masks, let him pull out his comb, and manage his flaxen Wig with all the Grace he can. Having so done, the next step is to give a hum to the China-Orange-Wench, and give her her own rate for her Oranges (for 'tis beneath a Gentleman to stand haggling like a Citizens wife) and then to present the fairest to the next Vizard-mask. And that I may incourage our Gallant not like the Tradesman to save a shilling, and so sit but in the Middle-Gallery, let him but consider what large comings-in are pursued up sitting in the Pit.

The Gallant, the satirist continues, can thus gain a "conspicuous Eminence," and, if he is a knight, secure a mistress. In addition, "It shall frown you with rich Commendations, to laugh aloud in the midst of the most serious and sudden Scene of the terriblest Tragedy, and to let the Clapper (your Tongue) be tossed so high, that all the House may ring of it." Further, the Gallant can "publish your tempera ... to the world, in that you seem not to resort thither to taste vain Pleasures with a hungry Appetite; but only as a Gentleman to spend a foolish hour or two, because you can do nothing else."[6]

From 1660 to 1700 the writers of prologues and epilogues emphasize the conspicuous behavior of the young-man-about-town in the pit. According to the Prologue to *The Comical Revenge*, March 1664:

> And Gallants, as for you, talk loud i'th' Pit,
> Divert your selves and Friends with your own Wit.

6. Pp. 56–58.

More caustic is the Prologue to *The Ordinary*, ca. January 1670 / 1.

> Some come with lusty Burgundy half-drunk,
> T'eat China Oranges, make love to Punk;
> And briskly mount a bench when th' Act is done,
> And comb their much-lov'd Periwigs to the tune
> And can sit out a Play of three hours long,
> Minding no part of't but the Dance or Song.

That for *The Rival Queens*, 17 March 1676 / 7, ridicules the gallants who "with loud Nonsense drown the Stages Wit," a point reiterated in the Epilogue to *Sertorius*, ca. March 1679: "[Our Poet] scorns those little Vermin in the Pit, / Who noise and nonsense vent insteat of Wit."[7] They tended to put on a show of their own (Epilogue to Mrs. Behn's *The False Count*):

> You Sparks better Comedians are than we;
> You every day out-fool ev'n Nokes and Lee.
> They're forc'd to stop, and their own Farces quit,
> T'admire the Merry-Andrews of the Pit.

Although many commentators lashed the gallants and fops in the Pit, the boxes commonly held more sedate and, theoretically, more sympathetic spectators. Here frequently sat the Ladies to whom the writers of Epilogues turned with requests that the warm-hearted "Fair Sex" lead the spectators to a favorable verdict. Here, too, sat the upper classes, a fact which attracted Pepys on 1 May 1667: "We sat at the upper bench next the boxes; and I find it do pretty well, and have the advantage of seeing and hearing the great people." Even Robert Gould's caustic satire, *The Play-House* (1685), acknowledged the gentility of the boxes: "And for the Muse a Nobler Scene prepare, / And let Her breathe in Milder air." Even so, the side-boxes irritated commentators by inattentiveness to the play and by devotion to flirtation. As Lord Foppington in *The Relapse*, December 1696, remarked: "But a Man must endeavour to look wholesome, lest he makes so nauseous a Figure in the Sidebox, the Ladies shou'd be compell'd to turn their Eyes upon the Play."

For the Galleries, however, the commentators often saved their sharpest barbs. Just as the fops sometimes turned to the side-boxes for intrigue, so they, as the Prologue to Shadwell's *Woman Captain*, September 1679, states, "Whom mounting from the Pit we use to see / (For dangerous Intrigues) to th'Gallery." In the Epilogue to the opening of the theater, 16 November 1682, Dryden vividly re-created the scene.

> Methinks some Vizard Masque I see,
> Cast but her Lure from the mid Gallery.
> About her all the flutt'ring Sparks are rang'd;

---

7. The Prologue to *Bellamira*, 12 May 1687, also criticized the excessive noise in the Pit: "Tho the shrill Pit be louder than the Stage."

> The Noise continues though the Scene is chang'd:
> Now growling, sputtring, wauling, such a clutter.
>
> . . . .
>
> Then for your Lacqueys, and your Train beside,
> (By what e'er Name or Title dignify'd)
> They roar so loud, you'd think behind the Stairs
> Tom Dove, and all the Brotherhood of Bears:
> They've grown a Nuisance, beyond all Disasters,
> We've none so great but their unpaying Masters.
> We beg you, Sirs, to beg your Men, that they
> Wou'd please to give you leave to hear the Play.[8]

The Prologue to Southerne's *The Disappointment*, 5 April 1684, spoke still more sharply.

> Last, some there are, who take their first Degrees
> Of Lewdness in our Middle Galleries:
> The Doughty Bullies enter Bloody Drunk,
> Invade and grabble one another's Punk:
> They Caterwoul, and make a dismal Rout,
> Call Sons of Whores, and strike, but ne're lugg-out.

The Playhouse (1685), consistently caustic, was most severe in castigating the galleries.

> The Middle Galle'ry first demands our View;
> The filth of Jakes, and stench of ev'ry Stew!
> Here reeking Punks like Ev'ning Insects swarm;
> The Polecat's Perfume much the Happier Charm.
> Their very Scent gives Apoplectick Fits,
> And yet they're thought all Civit by the Cits;
> Nor can we blame 'em; for the Truth to tell,
> The want of Brains may be the Want of Smell.
> Here ev'ry Night they sit three Hours for Sale;
> The Night-rail always cleanlier than the Tayl.

If one believed the exaggeration of the commentators, the theater would appear to be a place wholly inimical to the art of the drama. In fact, a disparaging view was summed up by Jovial, speaking in James Wright's *The Humours and Conversations of the Town* (1693), who replied to a question concerning the value of attending plays:

> What wou'd you go to the Play for? . . . to be dun'd all round with the impertinent Discourse of Beardless Fops to the Orange-Wenches, with Commodes an Ell high; and to the Vizor-Masks: of the Rake-Hells, talking loud to one another; or the perpetual Chat

---

8. The problem of footmen in the galleries was to become a serious one in the eighteenth century.

of the Noisy Coquets, that come there to get Cullies, and to disturb, not mind the Play. Or to what Effect has all the Plays upon you? Are not your Fops in the Pit and Boxes incorrigible to all the Endeavours of your Writers, in their Prologues and Epilogues, or the variety of Characters that have been made to reform them? Tho a Play be an generous Diversion, yet 'tis better to read than see, unless one cou'd see it without these Inconveniences.[9]

Obviously, these views are extremist, an exaggeration of the worst elements in the theaters, for no playhouse could exist if all the audiences at all times were composed of spectators like those described in these vignettes. Nevertheless, the satirists strike at characteristics of audiences lamented by all players and playwrights: their inability to be quiet, to lend full attention to the play, and to subordinate their personal interests to the serious aims of author and actor, who had a good deal of right on their side. After all, quarrels and disturbances sometimes made the pit a noisy place and disrupted the play. The orangewomen bargained for their goods and charms not only in the intervals but sometimes during the action on stage. The intrigues of the gallants almost never ceased. And the gentlemen, wits, and Templars considered it their privilege to be critics, wise or witty but usually vocal. In the long run, however, the best of the drama survived and the worst died away as the judgment of the spectators surmounted temporary confusions of the moment.

CHARLES BEECHER HOGAN

[Scenery and Lighting][†]

* * * Between the audience and the proscenium arch, with its large, green proscenium curtain, was the sunken pit in which the orchestra sat, and beyond which lay the area known, at least in theatrical history, as the forestage. (I am reminded by Professor Allardyce Nicoll that this part of the stage was never referred to as the "apron" until about 1900. Even the term "forestage" was seldom, possibly never, employed in the eighteenth century, i.e. everything from the footlights to the furthest upstage piece of scenery was called, and quite properly, merely "the stage.") In any event, this area was one of the first importance in every production of every evening's entertainment. From it were heard prologues, epilogues, announcements of changes of play; on it took place

9. Pp. 105–6.
† From *The London Stage: 1660–1800,* Part V, Vol. I, edited by C. B. Hogan (Carbondale, Ill.: Southern Illinois University Press, 1968), 1v–1ix, 1xv–1xvii. Reprinted by permission of the publisher.

not only songs, monologues, incidental dances and other forms of inter-
mediary activity, but also a considerable part of the action of the play
proper. At moments of stress or tension in the unfolding of the plot the
actors would want to be in as close proximity as possible to the audience,
and would advance well beyond the proscenium arch to deliver an
important speech, whether a soliloquy or not. On either side of the
forestage stood a door, which generations of stage convention had
accepted as an integral part of the scenery, as, that is, either an exterior
or interior door in or near whatever kind of building the action of the
play—otherwise progressing on the stage proper behind the proscenium
arch—might be located. These doors were even used for entrances and
exits in scenes not connected with a building at all: a scene in a park or
a forest, by the seashore or on a country highway. The forestage was, in
other words, for all purposes completely and intimately associated with
the entire acting area from front to back.

The measurement of the depth of the forestage varied from theater
to theater; an average, however, would be about twelve to fourteen feet.
At the opera house it was somewhat deeper, in order to provide a larger
space for the elaborate ballets produced there. The footlights, or
"lamps," extended along the entire front of the forestage. At either end
of the footlights it was customary to install a curved and ornamented
grille-work of iron, perhaps eighteen inches in height. These grilles were
known as the "spikes," and had been introduced at a much earlier time
when, during serious riots, members of the audience attempted to clam-
ber into the orchestra pit and thence onto the stage. For the same reason
rows of similar spikes, also of an ornamental nature, were affixed upon
all three sides of the inclosure surrounding that pit. Whether these
devices ever effectively deterred a serious-minded rioter may be
questioned. As time went on they became more a matter of accepted
convention in theater architecture than of genuine defense against mischief.

The curtain was, therefore, taking into account the depth of both the
orchestra pit and the forestage, situated at a distance of perhaps twenty-
five feet from the front bench in the pit proper. When, after the playing
of the last "music," it finally rose, it did so by being pulled up in the
form of three or four shallow festoons. It was never pulled all the way
out of sight, but remained at the top of the proscenium arch, and hence
served as a border that helped to conceal the flies and the grid. As it
rose the audience saw a flat scene extending all the way from one wing
to its opposite wing, and standing in a groove about an inch and a half
wide and an inch and three-quarters high. This scene was supported in
like manner by a comparable groove situated upside down underneath
the flies at the top of the stage. These grooves were used in all
eighteenth-century English theaters. They were brought to America,

but, except in a modified form developed in Holland, never found their way into any public Continental theater. The scenes which they held, known as "flats,"[1] consisted of two pieces, divided vertically in the middle. These pieces were drawn on or off the stage, right and left, by scene shifters who were working behind them. No concealment of this operation was ever attempted; it was carried on in full view of the audience.[2]

The grooves were arbitrarily known as the "first groove," being the one nearest the footlights, the second, the one next upstage, the third and so on. For moving the flats two different things therefore happened. The opening scene of an act might be placed in the fourth groove and the next scene in the third. When this opening scene was concluded the flats of the following scene "closed" upon it, and oftentimes upon the actors still remaining in that scene. Or the situation might be reversed. At the end of the first scene, in which the third groove had been elected for use, the actors would make their exits, whereupon the flats would be pulled offstage, revealing the following scene, placed in the fourth groove. But any one of the grooves, no matter how far apart, could of course be used successively. The choosing of them was usually dictated by the exigencies of whatever play was being performed, in particular as regards characters who appear in two consecutive scenes. For this very reason, most eighteenth-century dramatists were careful, as far as possible, to begin each scene with a different set of characters than those on whom the flats of the preceding scene had just closed. In other words, changes were always made, provided the scene shifters were properly alert, with great rapidity.

But oftentimes it was unnecessary, again because of what was demanded by the plot of the play, to move the scenes from upstage to downstage, or vice versa. This was made possible because the grooves were not constructed as individual units. They were assembled into what were called "sets," each set consisting of anywhere from three to five grooves laid side by side. Thus, for two successive scenes that had to be played downstage, their flats would be arranged within the same set, and operated exactly as has been described in the preceding paragraph. An example of how the various grooves were chosen is found in connection with the property plot for *Love in a Village* as acted at Covent Garden on 15 September 1788. It is reproduced by John Williams in his *Poems* in 1789.[3]

---

1. This term first came into use about 1736. Throughout the hundred years previous they were known as "shutters."
2. "The scenes visibly shifted in your sight."—Sir Joshua Reynolds, *Literary Works* (London, 1852), II. 72. For a full discussion of the mechanism of the grooves and of their operation see Richard Southern, *Changeable Scenery* (London, 1953), and the same writer in *The Oxford Companion to the Theatre*, 2nd ed. (London, 1957), pp. 238–42.
3. (London, 1789), II, 264.

ACT I

Scene i.   A Garden — 5th groove.
Scene ii.   A Hall in Woodcock's House — 2nd groove.
Scene iii.   A Field [this scene was in common use in many other plays; it was known as the "Stratford"] — 2nd groove.
Scene iv.   A Village Green — 5th groove.

ACT II

Scene i.   A Parlour in Woodcock's House [this scene, like that in I.iii, was known as the "Beausett"] — 2nd groove.
Scene ii.   As I.i — 5th groove.
Scene iii.   As I.ii — 2nd groove.

ACT III

Scene i.   As II.i — 2nd groove.
Scene ii.   A Greenhouse ["Open Cutt Wood back'd by Garden Cloth"] — 3rd groove.
Scene iii.   Another Hall in Woodcock's House [this scene, like that in I.iii, was known as the "Picture"] — 3rd groove.

It will be observed that the first and fourth grooves were not made use of at all, and that on two occasions (I.ii, iii and III.ii, iii) the flats for two successive scenes were installed in the same set of grooves. For the exterior scenes representing the Garden and the Village Green the stage was open to its fullest extent. In order to give a sharper effect to the scene of the Village Green—that of a busy and well-attended fair—the "Stratford" scene of the Field, which was introductory to it, was played downstage. So were all the interior scenes of the two Halls and the Parlor, in either the second or third groove.

More was called for than merely the flats. The principle underlying, and the necessity for, the use of wings had long been known. The wings were placed in the groove that, in each of the sets, lay furthest downstage. The number of the sets of grooves corresponded to the number of the wings, which, in Drury Lane and Covent Garden, were usually ten, i.e. five to a side. The reconstructed King's of 1791 had six wings to a side.[4] No line drawing of the stage of the Haymarket appears to have survived, but the number was probably also five. The sets containing the wings and grooves at all the theaters were roughly six feet apart. The wings could be called extensions of the flat scenes that ran in and out on the grooves. When pulled off the stage each flat came to rest immediately behind the wing to which it corresponded. The wings themselves were in grooves, and had to be changed to fit the scene as a whole: a "tree" wing for a park or countryside, a "palace" wing for any interior of a building, etc. Being of a more or less generalized design they were frequently, like the "Stratford" and "Beausett" flat scenes, used again and again in different plays, and would in fact be held over for several

4. *Oracle*, 24 Feb. 1791.

successive seasons. When on the playbills the expression, "With New Scenes," appears, the reference is almost invariably to the flats alone. The entire system lay parallel to the footlights. Had the wings been set at an angle the grooves could not then have been placed in a straight line from one side of the stage to the other.

* * *

The stages of all the London theaters received their illumination from three sources: the lighted auditorium, the footlights, and oil lamps and candles fastened at intervals behind the proscenium and behind each of the wings. Concealed lighting from behind the borders at the top of the proscenium may also have been employed, but no positive evidence of this has survived. The stage was therefore given a steady flow of undiminished light, whenever such a light was required. But years of practice and the ingenuity of more than one machinist and scene designer—notably De Loutherbourg[5]—had made possible a good deal of variety in obtaining various effects of light and dark.

The first important change had come at the beginning of the 1765–66 season when at both Drury Lane and Covent Garden the large chandeliers, or "rings," that from the time of the opening of the theaters in 1660 had hung suspended over the stage of every theater in London, were abolished. In his *Personal Sketches of his own Times* Sir Jonah Barrington speaks of the Dublin theaters of the eighteenth century being lit "with tallow candles, stuck into tin circles hanging from the middle of the stage, which were every now and then snuffed by some performer."[6] That London actors were obliged to do likewise was certainly the case. These chandeliers were a deterrent both to the illusion of the scene and to a complete view of the stage on the part of those seated in the upper gallery. Garrick, just returned from a long journey on the Continent, had insisted on doing away with these bothersome objects—in fact, the idea of doing so had come to him while seeing the lighting arrangements on some of the stages in the foreign countries he had visited. In any event, the Covent Garden management took up the idea, too, and in place of the chandeliers long, vertical strips, probably of tin, were installed out of sight of the audience on either side of the stage. On these strips the lights were fastened. Behind each light was a reverberator or reflector, and beside each light was a curved metal shield. These shields could be drawn slowly or rapidly, as the occasion demanded, across the lights, with somewhat the effect achieved by a modern rheostat, and, if entire darkness was desired on the stage, the footlights were so arranged that, at the same moment, they could be lowered until they were entirely out of sight.

5. Philippe Jacques De Loutherbourg, an Alsatian painter and scene designer who came to London in 1771 and became famous as the scenic director at Drury Lane [*Editor*].
6. (London, 1827), II, 197.

These devices continued to be used at Drury Lane and at Covent Garden—they were presently adopted by the Haymarket as well—until the end of the century and for some years thereafter. A more simplified and efficient system was that installed in the opera house. It is described, with a fine flourish, by the *Oracle* on 10 January 1791, as follows: "Upon our theatres are generally affixed to the wings [the stage lights, which can be] darkened by folding blinds; but here the lamps are suspended before the wings upon posts, which by one mechanic power are moved together—gradually receding for the coming on of night—gradually approaching with the increasing blushes of Aurora."

De Loutherbourg went even further. By stretching silk screens of different colors working on pivots in front of bright lights he was able to obtain effects of clouds, storms, etc. that perpetually astonished and delighted the audience. Henry Angelo describes how, by this method, "a sudden transition [was brought about] in a forest scene, where the foliage varies from green to blood colors and . . . so illuminated the stage as to give the effect of enchantment."[7] Transparencies De Loutherbourg brought to a high point of beauty and of accuracy. They had long been in use in theaters everywhere, and consisted usually of a scene placed well upstage made of linen or of calico and painted in transparent dye. The "Cavern of Despair," in the penultimate scene of pantomime, painted on the front side of the transparency, would be visible when light shone on it; on the back side would be painted the "Temple of Virtue," which when lighted from behind in the concluding scene, would burst suddenly into view. Effects of this nature were, as just indicated, much more commonly utilized in the Drury Lane and Covent Garden pantomimes than in anything else, but they were also seen from time to time at the opera house, especially in the elaborate allegorical ballets performed there. Another experiment with lighting at this theater aroused the admiration of a reviewer in the *Gazetteer*, 28 March 1791, who refers to the scene of the Elysian Fields in a ballet based on the legend of Orpheus. There, "by means of lights placed behind gauze, a filmy hue is thrown over the stage, and the figures assume the appearance of aerial beings."

The footlights lay at the front of the forestage, which obviously needed additional illumination, since a good deal of the action of the play took place on it. They were situated in a long metal trough, the "footlight trap," which was filled with oil, on which were floating a series of small rectangular saucers, each holding two candles which were fed by the oil. The entire contrivance could be lowered by means of a system of lines and pulleys attached to a winch in the prompter's corner whenever it was necessary to give to the stage as much darkness as possible. * * *

---

7. *Reminiscences* (London, 1830), II, 326.

Model reconstruction by Richard Southern of Wren's design for a playhouse (probably Drury Lane), c. 1674. The actors are shown on the forestage. Entrances and exits were usually through the proscenium doors, shown stage right. The large area to the rear of the stage was used for movable scenery. *Photograph from Richard Southern, Changeable Scenery (London: Faber, 1952) plate 28. Reproduced by permission of Faber and Faber Ltd.*

The interior of Drury Lane in 1775, showing the pit, boxes, and galleries after gradual enlargement during the eighteenth century. *Photograph from Allardyce Nicoll, The Development of the Theatre, 5th ed. (London: Harrap, 1966) figure 201. (Original from the Art Collection of the Folger Shakespeare Library. Reproduced by permission.)*

CRITICISM

CHARLES LAMB

On the Artificial Comedy of the Last Century[†]

The artificial Comedy, or Comedy of Manners, is quite extinct on our stage. Congreve and Farquhar show their heads once in seven years only, to be exploded and put down instantly. The times cannot bear them. Is it for a few wild speeches, an occasional license of dialogue? I think not altogether. The business of their dramatic characters will not stand the moral test. We screw every thing up to that. Idle gallantry in a fiction, a dream, the passing pageant of an evening, startles us in the same way as the alarming indications of profligacy in a son or ward in real life should startle a parent or guardian. We have no such middle emotions as dramatic interests left. We see a stage libertine playing his loose pranks of two hours' duration, and of no after consequence, with the severe eyes which inspect real vices with their bearings upon two worlds. We are spectators to a plot or intrigue (not reducible in life to the point of strict morality) and take it all for truth. We substitute a real for a dramatic person, and judge him accordingly. We try him in our courts, from which there is no appeal to the *dramatis personæ*, his peers. We have been spoiled with—not sentimental comedy—but a tyrant far more pernicious to our pleasures which has succeeded to it, the exclusive and all devouring drama of common life; where the moral point is every thing; where, instead of the fictitious half-believed personages of the stage (the phantoms of old comedy) we recognize ourselves, our brothers, aunts, kinsfolk, allies, patrons, enemies—the same as in life—with an interest in what is going on so hearty and substantial, that we cannot afford our moral judgment, in its deepest and most vital results, to compromise or slumber for a moment. What is *there* transacting, by no modification is made to affect us in any other manner than the same events or characters would do in our relationships of life. We carry our fire-side concerns to the theater with us. We do not go thither, like our ancestors, to escape from the pressure of reality, so much as to confirm our experience of it; to make assurance double, and take a bond of fate. We must live our toilsome lives twice over, as it was the mournful privilege of Ulysses to descend twice to the shades. All that neutral ground of character, which stood between vice and virtue; or which in fact was indifferent to neither, where neither properly was called in question; that happy breathing-place from the burden of a perpetual moral questioning—the sanctuary and quiet Alsatia of hunted casuistry[1]—is broken up and disfranchised, as injurious to the interests of society. The privi-

---

[†] First published in the *London Magazine* in 1822 and included (in the version followed here) in Lamb's collection of essays called *Elia*, 1823.
1. I.e., a haven or sanctuary for men burdened by logic and morality [*Editor*].

leges of the place are taken away by law. We dare not dally with images, or names, of wrong. We bark like foolish dogs at shadows. We dread infection from the scenic representation of disorder; and fear a painted pustule. In our anxiety that our morality should not take cold, we wrap it up in a great blanket surtout of precaution against the breeze and sunshine.

I confess for myself that (with no great delinquencies to answer for) I am glad for a season to take an airing beyond the diocese of the strict conscience—not to live always in the precincts of the lawcourts—but now and then, for a dream-while or so, to imagine a world with no meddling restrictions—to get into recesses, whither the hunter cannot follow me—

> ————Secret shades
> Of woody Ida's inmost grove,
> While yet there was no fear of Jove—[2]

I come back to my cage and my restraint the fresher and more healthy for it. I wear my shackles more contentedly for having respired the breath of an imaginary freedom. I do not know how it is with others, but I feel the better always for the perusal of one of Congreve's—nay, why should I not add even of Wycherley's—comedies. I am the gayer at least for it; and I could never connect those sports of a witty fancy in any shape with any result to be drawn from them to imitation in real life. They are a world of themselves almost as much as fairy-land. Take one of their characters, male or female (with few exceptions they are alike), and place it in a modern play, and my virtuous indignation shall rise against the profligate wretch as warmly as the Catos[3] of the pit could desire; because in a modern play I am to judge of the right and the wrong. The standard of *police* is the measure of *political justice*. The atmosphere will blight it, it cannot live here. It has got into a moral world, where it has no business, from which it must needs fall headlong; as dizzy, and incapable of making a stand, as a Swedenborgian bad spirit that has wandered unawares into the sphere of one of his Good Men, or Angels. But in its own world do we feel the creature is so very bad?— The Fainalls and the Mirabels, the Dorimants and the Lady Touch-woods, in their own sphere, do not offend my moral sense; in fact they do not appeal to it at all. They seem engaged in their proper elements. They break through no laws, or conscientious restraints. They know of none. They have got out of Christendom into the land—what shall I call it?— of cuckoldry—the Utopia of gallantry, where pleasure is duty, and the manners perfect freedom. It is altogether a speculative scene of things, which has no reference whatever to the world that is. No good person

2. Milton, *Il Penseroso*, lines 28–30 [Editor].
3. Cato was known for condemning luxury and decadence in Rome [Editor].

can be justly offended as a spectator, because no good person suffers on the stage. Judged morally, every character in these plays—the few exceptions only are *mistakes*—is alike essentially vain and worthless. The great art of Congreve is especially shown in this, that he has entirely excluded from his scenes—some little generosities in the part of Angelica perhaps excepted—not only any thing like a faultless character, but any pretensions to goodness or good feelings whatsoever. Whether he did this designedly, or instinctively, the effect is as happy, as the design (if design) was bold. I used to wonder at the strange power which his *Way of the World* in particular possesses of interesting you all along in the pursuits of characters, for whom you absolutely care nothing—for you neither hate nor love his personages—and I think it is owing to this very indifference for any, that you endure the whole. He has spread a privation of moral light, I will call it, rather than by the ugly name of palpable darkness, over his creations; and his shadows flit before you without distinction or preference. Had he introduced a good character, a single gush of moral feeling, a revulsion of the judgment to actual life and actual duties, the impertinent Goshen would have only lighted to the discovery of deformities, which now are none, because we think them none.

Translated into real life, the characters of his, and his friend Wycherley's dramas, are profligates and strumpets—the business of their brief existence, the undivided pursuit of lawless gallantry. No other spring of action, or possible motive of conduct, is recognized; principles which, universally acted upon, must reduce this frame of things to a chaos. But we do them wrong in so translating them. No such effects are produced in *their* world. When we are among them, we are amongst a chaotic people. We are not to judge them by our usages. No reverend institutions are insulted by their proceedings—for they have none among them. No peace of families is violated—for no family ties exist among them. No purity of the marriage bed is stained—for none is supposed to have a being. No deep affections are disquieted—no holy wedlock bands are snapped asunder—for affection's depth and wedded faith are not of the growth of that soil. There is neither right nor wrong—gratitude or its opposite—claim or duty—paternity or sonship. Of what consequence is it to virtue, or how is she at all concerned about it, whether Sir Simon, or Dapperwit, steal away Miss Martha; or who is the father of Lord Froth's, or Sir Paul Pliant's children.

The whole is a passing pageant, where we should sit as unconcerned at the issues, for life or death, as at a battle of the frogs and mice. But, like Don Quixote, we take part against the puppets, and quite as impertinently. We dare not contemplate an Atlantis, a scheme, out of which our coxcombical moral sense is for a little transitory ease excluded. We have not the courage to imagine a state of things for which there is neither reward nor punishment. We cling to the painful necessities of shame and blame. We would indict our very dreams.

Amidst the mortifying circumstances attendant upon growing old, it is something to have seen the *School for Scandal* in its glory. This comedy grew out of Congreve and Wycherley, but gathered some allays of the sentimental comedy, which followed theirs. It is impossible that it should be now *acted*, though it continues, at long intervals, to be announced in the bills. Its hero, when Palmer[4] played it at least, was Joseph Surface. When I remember the gay boldness, the graceful solemn plausibility, the measured step, the insinuating voice—to express it in a word—the downright *acted* villany of the part, so different from the pressure of conscious actual wickedness—the hypocritical assumption of hypocrisy—which made Jack so deservedly a favorite in that character, I must needs conclude the present generation of play-goers more virtuous than myself, or more dense. I freely confess that he divided the palm with me with his better brother; that, in fact, I liked him quite as well. Not but there are passages—like that, for instance, where Joseph is made to refuse a pittance to a poor relation—incongruities which Sheridan was forced upon by the attempt to join the artificial with the sentimental comedy, either of which must destroy the other—but over these obstructions Jack's manner floated him so lightly, that a refusal from him no more shocked you, than the easy compliance of Charles gave you in reality any pleasure; you got over the paltry question as quickly as you could, to get back into the regions of pure comedy, where no cold moral reigns. The highly artificial manner of Palmer in this character counteracted every disagreeable impression which you might have received from the contrast, supposing them real, between the two brothers. You did not believe in Joseph with the same faith with which you believed in Charles. The latter was a pleasant reality, the former a no less pleasant poetical foil to it. The comedy, I have said, is incongruous; a mixture of Congreve with sentimental incompatibilities: the gaiety upon the whole is buoyant; but it required the consummate art of Palmer to reconcile the discordant elements.

A player with Jack's talents, if we had one now, would not dare to do the part in the same manner. He would instinctively avoid every turn which might tend to unrealize, and so to make the character fascinating. He must take his cue from his spectators, who would expect a bad man and a good man as rigidly opposed to each other as the death-beds of those geniuses are contrasted in the prints, which I am sorry to say have disappeared from the windows of my old friend Carrington Bowles,[5] of St. Paul's Church-yard memory—(an exhibition as venerable as the adjacent cathedral, and almost coeval) of the bad and good man at the hour of death; where the ghastly apprehensions of the former—and truly the grim phantom with his reality of a toasting fork is not to be

4. Jack Palmer, who in the late eighteenth century was famous for his performance as Joseph Surface [*Editor*].
5. A publisher of prints whose shop was at St. Paul's [*Editor*].

despised—so finely contrast with the meek complacent kissing of the
rod—taking it in like honey and butter—with which the latter submits
to the scythe of the gentle bleeder, Time, who wields his lancet with
the apprehensive finger of a popular young ladies' surgeon. What flesh,
like loving grass, would not covet to meet half-way the stroke of such a
delicate mower?—John Palmer was twice an actor in this exquisite part.
He was playing to you all the while that he was playing upon Sir Peter
and his lady. You had the first intimation of a sentiment before it was
on his lips. His altered voice was meant to you, and you were to suppose
that his fictitious co-flutterers on the stage perceived nothing at all of it.
What was it to you if that half-reality, the husband, was over-reached by
the puppetry—or the thin thing (Lady Teazle's reputation) was persuaded it was dying of a plethory? The fortunes of Othello and Desdemona were not concerned in it. Poor Jack has passed from the stage in
good time, that he did not live to this our age of seriousness. The pleasant old Teazle *King*,[6] too, is gone in good time. His manner would
scarce have passed current in our day. We must love or hate—acquit or
condemn—censure or pity—exert our detestable coxcombry of moral
judgment upon every thing. Joseph Surface, to go down now, must be a
downright revolting villain—no compromise—his first appearance must
shock and give horror—his specious plausibilities, which the pleasurable faculties of our fathers welcomed with such hearty greetings, knowing that no harm (dramatic harm even) could come, or was meant to
come of them, must inspire a cold and killing aversion. Charles (the
real canting person of the scene—for the hypocrisy of Joseph has its
ulterior legitimate ends, but his brother's professions of good heart center in downright self-satisfaction) must be *loved*, and Joseph *hated*. To
balance one disagreeable reality with another, Sir Peter Teazle must be
no longer the comic idea of a fretful old bachelor bridegroom, whose
teasings (while King acted it) were evidently as much played off at you,
as they were meant to concern anybody on the stage—he must be a real
person, capable in law of sustaining an injury—a person towards whom
duties are to be acknowledged—the genuine crimson antagonist of the
villainous seducer Joseph. To realize him more, his sufferings under his
unfortunate match must have the downright pungency of life—must (or
should) make you not mirthful but uncomfortable, just as the same
predicament would move you in a neighbor or old friend. The delicious
scenes which give the play its name and zest, must affect you in the
same serious manner as if you heard the reputation of a dear female
friend attacked in your real presence. Crabtree and Sir Benjamin—
those poor snakes that live but in the sunshine of your mirth—must be
ripened by this hot-bed process of realization into asps or amphisbaenas;
and Mrs. Candour—O! frightful! become a hooded serpent. Oh who

6. Thomas King, who originally played Sir Peter Teazle [*Editor*].

that remembers Parsons and Dodd—the wasp and butterfly of the *School for Scandal*—in those two characters; and charming natural Miss Pope,[7] the perfect gentlewoman as distinguished from the fine lady of comedy, in this latter part—would forego the true scenic delight—the escape from life—the oblivion of consequences—the holiday barring out of the pedant Reflection—those Saturnalia of two or three brief hours, well won from the world—to sit instead at one of our modern plays—to have his coward conscience (that forsooth must not be left for a moment) stimulated with perpetual appeals—dulled rather, and blunted, as a faculty without repose must be—and his moral vanity pampered with images of notional justice, notional beneficence, lives saved without the spectators' risk, and fortunes given away that cost the author nothing? * * *

L. C. KNIGHTS

Restoration Comedy: The Reality and the Myth[†]

* * * Apart from the presentation of incidental and unrelated "wit" (which soon becomes as tiring as the epigrams of the "good talker"), Restoration comedy has two main interests—the behavior of the polite and of pretenders to politeness, and some aspects of sexual relationships. Critics have made out a case for finding in one or other of these themes a unifying principle and a serious base for the comedy of manners. According to Miss Lynch, the "thoroughly conventionalized social mode" of the courtly circle "was discovered to have manifestly comic aspects, both when awkwardly misinterpreted, and when completely fulfilled through personalities to which, however, it could not give complete expression,"[1] and both these discrepancies were exploited by Etherege and his successors. Bonamy Dobrée, attributing to the comic dramatists "a deep curiosity, and a desire to try new ways of living," finds that "the distinguishing characteristic of Restoration comedy down to Congreve is that it is concerned with the attempt to rationalize sexual relationships. It is this that makes it different from any other comedy that has ever been written. . . . It said in effect, 'Here is life lived upon certain assumptions; see what it becomes.' It also dealt, as no other comedy has ever done, with a subject that arose directly out of this, namely sex-antagonism, a consequence of the experimental freedom

7. Jane Pope, the original Mrs. Candour [*Editor*].
† From *Explorations: Essays in Criticism Mainly on the Literature of the Seventeenth Century* (London: Chatto & Windus, 1946), pp. 135–49. Reprinted by permission of the author and New York University Press.
1. K. M. Lynch, *The Social Mode of Restoration Comedy*, p. 216.

allowed to women, which gave matter for some of its most brilliant scenes."[2]

These accounts, as developed, certainly look impressive, and if Restoration comedy really answered to them—if it had something fresh and penetrating to say on sex and social relations—there would be no need to complain, even if one found the "solutions" distasteful. But Miss Lynch's case, at all events, depends on a vigorous reading into the plays of values which are not there, values which could not possibly be expressed, in fact, in the prose of any of the dramatists. (The candid reader can turn up the passages selected by Miss Lynch in support of her argument, and see if they are not all in the factitious, superficial mode that I have described.)

We may consider, by way of illustration, Etherege's *The Man of Mode*. When the play opens, Dorimant ("the finest of all fine gentlemen in Restoration comedy") is trying to rid himself of an old mistress, Mrs. Loveit, before taking up with a new, Bellinda, whilst Young Bellair, in love with Emilia, is trying to find some way out of marrying Harriet, an heiress whom his father has brought to town for him. The entertainment is made up of these two sets of complications, together with an exhibition of the would-be modishness of Sir Fopling Flutter. Events move fast. After a night spent in various sociabilities Dorimant keeps an appointment with Bellinda at 5 A.M. Letting her out of his lodgings an hour or so later, and swearing to be discreet "By all the Joys I have had, and those you keep in store," he is surprised by his companions, and in the resulting confusion Bellinda finds herself paying an unwilling visit to Mrs. Loveit. Dorimant appears and is rated by the women before he "flings off." Meanwhile Young Bellair and Emilia have secretly married. Dorimant, his equanimity recovered, turns up for the exposure, followed by his mistresses. The lovers are forgiven, the mistresses are huddled off the stage, and it is decided that Dorimant, who, the previous day, had ingratiated himself with Harriet's mother, and whose "soul has quite given up her liberty," shall be allowed to pay court to the heiress.

It seems to me that what the play provides—apart from the briskly handled intrigue—is a demonstration of the physical stamina of Dorimant. But Miss Lynch sees further. For her, Dorimant is "the fine flowering of Restoration culture." Illustrating her theory of the double standard, she remarks: "We laugh at Sir Fopling Flutter because he so clumsily parodies social fashions which Dorimant interprets with unfailing grace and distinction. We laugh at Dorimant because his assumed affectation admits of so poor and incomplete an expression of an attractive and vigorous personality."[3] The "unfailing grace and distinction" are perhaps not much in evidence in Dorimant's spiteful treatment of

2. Bonamy Dobrée, *Restoration Comedy*, pp. 22–23.
3. *The Social Mode of Restoration Comedy*, p. 181.

Mrs. Loveit;[4] but even if we ignore those brutish scenes we are forced to ask, How do we know that there *is* this "attractive and vigorous personality" beneath the conventional forms? Dorimant's intrigues are of no more human significance than those of a barn-yard cock, and as for what Miss Lynch calls "his really serious affair with Harriet" (I feel this deserves a *sic*), it is purely theatrical, and the "pangs of love" are expressed in nothing but the conventional formulae: "She's gone, but she has left a pleasing Image of herself behind that wanders in my Soul." The answer to the question posed is that Miss Lynch's account is a mere assumption. Nothing that Dorimant actually *says* will warrant it—and nothing in the whole of Restoration comedy—in the words actually spoken—allows us a glimpse of those other "personalities" to which the conventional social modes "could not give complete expression." The "real values"[5] simply are not there.

A minor point can be made in passing. It is just possible to claim that Restoration comedy contains "social criticism" in its handling of "the vulgar." "Come Mr. Sharper," says Congreve's Belinda, "you and I will take a turn, and laugh at the vulgar; both the great vulgar and the small," and Etherege's Lady Townley expresses the common attitude of the polite towards the social nuisances: "We should love wit, but for variety be able to divert ourselves with the extravagancies of those who want it." The butts, unfortunately, are only shown as fools by the discrepancy between their ambitions and their achievements, not because their ambitions are puerile. The subject is hardly worth discussing, since it is obviously nothing but an easily satisfied sense of superiority that is diverted by the "variety" of a constant succession of Dapperwits, Froths and Fopling Flutters. "When a humour takes in London," Tom Brown remarked, "they ride it to death ere they leave it. The primitive Christians were not persecuted with half that variety as the poor unthinking beaus are tormented with upon the theater. . . . A huge great muff, and a gaudy ribbon hanging at a bully's backside, is an excellent jest, and new-invented curses, as, Stap my vitals, damn my diaphragm, slit my wind pipe, sink me ten thousand fathom deep, rig up a new beau, though in the main 'tis but the same everlasting coxcomb."[6]

In the matter of sexual relations Restoration comedy is entirely dominated by a narrow set of conventions. The objection that it is only cer-

---

4. See II, ii and V, i, where Dorimant, trying to force a quarrel with Mrs. Loveit, attributes to her a fondness for Sir Fopling. The first of these scenes was too much for Etherege, and he makes Bellinda say: "He's given me the proof which I desired of his love, / But 'tis a proof of his ill nature too. / I wish I had not seen him use her so." But this is soon forgotten, and we are not, of course, called on to register an unfavorable judgment of Dorimant.
5. "The love affairs of Courtal and Ariana, Freeman and Gatty [in *She Wou'd if She Cou'd*] are similarly embarrassed by social convention. . . . The conduct of these polite lovers acquires comic vitality through the continually suggested opposition of artificial and real values."—*Op. cit.*, p. 152.
6. Tom Brown, *Works*, Vol. III, *Amusements Comical and Serious*, "At the Playhouse," p. 39.

tain characters, not the dramatists themselves, who accept them can be more freely encountered when the assumptions that are expressed most frequently have been briefly illustrated.

The first convention is, of course, that constancy in love, especially in marriage, is a bore. Vanbrugh, who was the most uneasy if not the most honest of the comic dramatists (I think that in *The Provok'd Wife* he shows as unusually honest), unambiguously attributes this attitude to Sir John Brute:

> What cloying meat is love—when matrimony's the sauce to it! Two years marriage has debaunch'd my five senses. . . . No boy was ever so weary of his tutor, no girl of her bib, no nun of doing penance, or old maid of being chaste, as I am of being married. Sure there's a secret curse entail'd upon the very name of wife!
>
> The woman's well enough; she has no vice that I know of, but she's a wife, and—damn a wife![7]

What Vanbrugh saw as a fit sentiment for Sir John had by that time (1697) served the Restoration stage—without change—for thirty years. In *She Wou'd if She Cou'd* Etherege had exhibited Sir Oliver Cockwood in an identical vein: "A pox of this tying man and woman together, for better, for worse." "To have a mistress love thee entirely" is "a damn'd trouble." "There are sots that would think themselves happy in such a Lady; but to a true bred Gentleman all lawful solace is abomination."[8] If Sir Oliver is a fool it is only because he is a trifle gross in his expression. "If you did but know, Madam," says the polite Freeman, "what an odious thing it is to be thought to love a Wife in good company."[9] And the convention is constantly turning up in Congreve. "There is no creature perfectly civil but a husband," explains Mrs. Frail, "for in a little time he grows only rude to his wife, and that is the highest good breeding, for it begets his civility to other people."[1] "Marry her! Marry her!" Fainall advises Mirabell, "Be half as well acquainted with her charms, as you are with her defects, and my life on't, you are your own man again."[2] And Witwoud: "A wit should no more be sincere than a woman constant; one argues a decay of parts, as t'other a decay of beauty."[3] Appetite, it seems (and this is the second assumption), needs perpetually fresh stimulus. This is the faith of Rhodophil in *Marriage à la Mode* and of Constant in *The Provok'd Wife*, as well as of Wycherley's old procuress, Mrs. Joyner. "If our wives would suffer us but now and then to make excursions," Rhodophil explains to Palamede, "the benefit of our variety

7. *The Provok'd Wife*, I, i; II, i.
8. *She Wou'd if She Cou'd*, I, i; III, iii.
9. *Ibid.*, III, iii.
1. *Love for Love*, I, ii.
2. *The Way of the World*, I, ii.
3. *Ibid.*

would be theirs; instead of one continued, lazy, tired love, they would, in their turns, have twenty vigorous, fresh, and active lovers."[4] "Would anything but a madman complain of uncertainty?" asks Congreve's Angelica, for "security is an insipid thing, and the overtaking and possessing of a wish, discovers the folly of the chase."[5] And Fainall, in *The Way of the World*, speaks for a large class when he hints at a liking for sauce—a little gentleman's relish—to his seductions: "I'd no more play with a man that slighted his ill fortune than I'd make love to a woman who undervalued the loss of her reputation."[6] Fainall, of course, is what he is, but the attitude that makes sexual pleasure "the bliss," that makes woman "delicious"—something to be savored—as well as "damned" and "destructive," demands, for its support, "the pleasure of a chase."[7]

> Would you long preserve your lover?
> Would you still his goddess reign?
> Never let him all discover,
> Never let him much obtain.[8]

Restoration comedy used to be considered outrageously outspoken, but such stuff as this, far from being "outspoken," hovers on the outskirts of sexual relations, and sees nothing but the titillation of appetite (" 'Tis not the success," Collier observed, "but the manner of gaining it which is all in all").[9] Sex is a hook baited with tempting morsels;[1] it is a thirst quencher;[2] it is a cordial;[3] it is a dish to feed on;[4] it is a bunch of grapes;[5] it is anything but sex. (This, of course, explains why some people can combine a delighted approval of Restoration comedy with an unbalanced repugnance for such modern literature as deals sincerely and realistically with sexual relationships.)

Now the objection referred to above was that sentiments such as these

4. *Marriage à la Mode*, II, i. Cf. *The Provok'd Wife*, III, i: *Constant*, "There's a poor sordid slavery in marriage, that turns the flowing tide of honour, and sinks us to the lowest ebb of infamy. 'Tis a corrupted soil: Ill-nature, sloth, cowardice, and dirt, are all its product."
5. *Love for Love*, IV, iii.
6. *The Way of the World*, I, i.
7. *The Old Bachelor*, I, i; III, ii ("Oh thou delicious, damned, dear destructive woman!"); IV, ii.
8. *Ibid.*, II, ii.
9. A *Short View of the Profaneness and Immorality of the English Stage*, Fifth Edition, 1738, p. 116.
1. " 'Tis true you are so eager in pursuit of the temptation, that you save the devil the trouble of leading you into it: nor is it out of discretion that you don't swallow the very hook yourselves have baited, but . . . what you meant for a whet turns the edge of your puny stomachs."—*The Old Bachelor*, I, i. "Strike Heartwell home, before the bait's worn off the hook. Age will come. He nibbled fairly yesterday, and no doubt will be eager enough to-day to swallow the temptation."—*Ibid.*, III, i.
2. "What was my pleasure is become my duty: and I have as little stomach to her now as if I were her husband. . . . Pox on't that a man can't drink without quenching his thirst."—*The Plain Dealer*, III, i.
3. "You must get you a mistress, Rhodophil. That indeed, is living upon cordials; but as fast as one fails, you must supply it with another." *Marriage à la Mode*, I, i.
4. Because our husbands cannot feed on one dish, therefore we must be starved."—*Ibid.*, III, i.
5. "The only way to keep us new to one another, is never to enjoy, as they keep grapes, by hanging them upon a line; they must touch nothing, if you would preserve them fresh."—*Ibid.*, V, i.

are not offered for straightforward acceptance. Many of them are attributed to characters plainly marked as Wicked (Maskwell, for example, is the black-a-vised villain of melodrama), or, more frequently, as trivial, and the dramatist can therefore dissociate himself. He may even be engaged in showing his audience the explicit, logical consequences of the half-unconscious premises on which they base their own lives, saying, as Mr. Dobrée has it, "Here is life lived upon certain assumptions; see what it becomes." To this there are several answers. The first is that reflections of the kind that I have quoted are indistinguishable in tone and style from the general epigrammatic stock-in-trade (the audience was not altogether to be blamed if, as Congreve complained, they could not at first "distinguish betwixt the character of a Witwoud and a Lovewit"); and they are largely "exhibited," just as all the self-conscious witticisms are exhibited, for the sake of their immediate "comic" effect. One has only to note the laughter of a contemporary audience at a revival, and the places where the splutters occur, to realize how much of the fun provides a rather gross example of tendency wit.[6] The same attitudes, moreover, are manipulated again and again, turning up with the stale monotony of jokes on postcards, and the play that is made with them demands only the easiest, the most superficial, response. But it is, after all, useless to argue about the degree of detachment, the angle at which these attitudes and assumptions are presented. As soon as one selects a particular comedy for that exercise one realizes that all is equally grist to the mill and that the dramatist (there is no need, here, to make distinctions) has no coherent attitude of his own. A consistent artistic purpose would not be content to express itself in a style that allows so limited, so local an effect.

But it is the triviality that one comes back to. In Dryden's *Marriage à la Mode* the characters accept the usual conventions: constancy is dull, and love only thrives on variety.

> PALAMEDE. O, now I have found it! you dislike her for no other reason but because she's your wife.
> RHODOPHIL. And is not that enough? All that I know of her perfections now, is only by memory . . . At last we arrived at that point, that there was nothing left in us to make us new to one another . . .
> PALAMEDE. The truth is, your disease is very desperate; but, though you cannot be cured, you may be patched up a little: you must

6. The Freudian "censor" is at times projected in the form of the stage puritan. The plays written soon after the Commonwealth period appealed to Royalist prejudice by satirizing the "seemingly precise"; and even later, when "the bonfires of devotion," "the bellows of zeal," were forgotten, a good deal of the self-conscious swagger of indecency seems to have been directed against "our protestant husbands," city merchants, aldermen and the like; the "daring" effect was intensified by postulating a shockable audience somewhere—not necessarily in the theater. Not that the really obscene jokes were merely bravado: Collier quite rightly remarked that "the modern poets seem to use smut as the old ones did Machines, to relieve a fainting situation."—*A Short View*, Fifth Edition, p. 4.

get you a mistress, Rhodophil. That, indeed, is living upon cordials; but, as fast as one fails, you must supply it with another.

The mistress that Rhodophil selects is Melantha, whom Palamede is to
marry; Palamede falls in love with Doralice, Rhodophil's wife, and the
ensuing complications provide sufficient entertainment (the grotto
scene, III, ii, is really funny). Mr. Dobrée, however, regards the play as
a witty exposure of the impossibility of rationalizing sex relations, as
Palamede and Rhodophil attempt to rationalize them. Dryden "laughs
morality back into its rightful place, as the scheme which ultimately
makes life most comfortable."[7] But what Dryden actually does is to *use*
the conventions for the amusement they afford, not to examine them.
The level at which the play works is fairly indicated by the opening
song:

> Why should a foolish marriage vow,
>   Which long ago was made,
> Oblige us to each other now,
>   When passion is decayed?
> We loved, and we loved, as long as we could,
>   'Till our love was loved out in us both;
> But our marriage is dead, when the pleasure is fled:
>   'Twas pleasure first made it an oath.
>
> If I have pleasures for a friend,
>   And further love in store,
> What wrong has he, whose joys did end,
>   And who could give no more?
> 'Tis a madness that he should be jealous of me,
>   Or that I should bar him of another:
> For all we can gain, is to give ourselves pain,
>   When neither can hinder the other.

The lovers make no attempt to "rationalize sex" for the simple reason
that genuine sexual feelings no more enter into the play as a whole than
feelings of any kind enter into the song. (The obviously faked emotions
of that heroic plot are, after all, relevant—and betraying.) And according
to Mr. Dobrée, "In one sense the whole idea of Restoration comedy is
summed up in the opening song of *Marriage à la Mode*."[8]
    In a sense, too, Mr. Dobrée is right. Restoration comedy nowhere
provides us with much more of the essential stuff of human experience
than we have here. Even Congreve, by common account the best of the
comic writers, is no exception. I have said that his verbal pattern often
seems to be quite unrelated to an individual mode of perceiving. At best

7. *Restoration Comedy*, p. 133.
8. *Ibid.*, p. 106.

it registers a very limited mode. Restoration prose is all "social" in its tone, implications and general tenor, but Congreve's observation is *merely* of the public surface. And Congreve, too, relies on the conventional assumptions. In *The Way of the World*, it is true, they are mainly given to the bad and the foolish to express: it is Fainall who discourses on the pleasures of disliking one's wife, and Witwoud who maintains that only old age and ugliness ensure constancy. And Mirabell, who is explicitly opposed to some aspects of contemporary manners, goes through the common forms in a tone of rather weary aloofness: "I wonder, Fainall, that you who are married, and of consequence should be discreet, will suffer your wife to be of such a party." But Congreve himself is not above raising a cheap snigger;[9] and, above all, the characters with some life in them have nothing to fall back on—nothing, that is, except the conventional, and conventionally limited, pleasures of sex. Millamant, who says she loathes the country and hates the town, expects to draw vitality from the excitement of incessant solicitation:

> I'll be solicited to the very last, nay, and afterwards . . . I should think I was poor and had nothing to bestow, if I were reduced to an inglorious ease, and freed from the agreeable fatigues of solicitation . . . Oh, I hate a lover that can dare to think he draws a moment's air, independent of the bounty of his mistress. There is not so impudent a thing in nature, as the saucy look of an assured man, confident of success. The pedantic arrogance of a very husband has not so pragmatical an air.

Everyone seems to have found Millamant intelligent and attractive, but her attitude is not far removed from that expressed in

> Would you long preserve your lover?
> Would you still his goddess reign?

and she shares with characters who are decidedly not attractive a disproportionate belief in "the pleasure of a chase." Which is not surprising in view of her other occupations and resources; visiting, writing and receiving letters, tea parties and small talk make up a round that is never for a moment enlivened by the play of genuine intelligence.[1] And although Congreve recognizes, at times, the triviality of his characters,[2] it is to the world whose confines were the Court, the drawing-room, the play-house and the park—a world completely lacking the real sophistication and

9. Ay there's my grief; that's the sad change of life, / To lose my title, and yet keep my wife. / *The Way of the World*, II, ii.
1. As Lady Brute remarks, "After all, a woman's life would be a dull business, if it were not for the men . . . We shou'd never blame Fate for the shortness of our days; our time would hang wretchedly upon our hands."—*The Provok'd Wife*, III, iii.
2. *Mirabell:* You had the leisure to entertain a herd of fools; things who visit you from their excessive idleness; bestowing on your easiness that time which is the encumbrance of their lives. How can you find delight in such society?—*The Way of the World*, II, i.

self-knowledge that might, in some measure, have redeemed it—that he limits his appeal.

It is, indeed, hard to resist the conclusion that "society"—the smart town society that sought entertainment at the theaters—was fundamentally bored.[3] In *The Man of Mode* Emilia remarks of Medley, "I love to hear him talk o' the intrigues, let 'em be never so dull in themselves, he'll make 'em pleasant i' the relation," and the idiotic conversation that follows (II, i), affording us a glimpse of what Miss Lynch calls "the most brilliant society which Restoration comedy has to offer,"[4] suggests in more than one way how badly society *needed* to be entertained. It is the boredom—the constant need for titillation—that helps to explain not only the heroic "heightening" of emotion, but the various scenic effects, the devices of staging and costume that became popular at this period. (Charles II "almost died of laughing" at Nell Gwynn's enormous hat.) The conventions—of sexual pursuit, and so on—were an attempt to make life interesting—an impossible job for those who were aware of so limited a range of human potentialities.

The dominating mood of Restoration comedy is, by common account, a cynical one. But one cannot even say that there is here, in contrast to naïve Romantic fervors, the tough strength of disillusion. If—recognizing that there is a place in the educational process for, say, La Rochefoucauld—one finds the "cynicism" of the plays distasteful, it is because it is easy and superficial; the attitudes that we are presented with are based on so meagre an amount of observation and experience. Thus, "Elle retrouvait dans l'adultère toutes les platitudes du marriage" has, superficially, much the same meaning as, "I find now, by sad experience, that a mistress is much more chargeable than a wife, and after a little time too, grows full as dull and insignificant." But whereas the first sentence has behind it the whole of *Madame Bovary*, the second comes from *Sir Martin Mar-all*, which (although Dryden shares the honors with the Duke of Newcastle) is perhaps the stupidest play I have ever read, and the context is imbecility.

But the superficiality is betrayed at every turn—by the obvious rhythms of the interspersed songs, as well as by the artificial elegance of the prose. And the cynicism is closely allied with—merges into—sentimentality. One thinks of the sentimentally conceived Fidelia in the resolutely "tough" *Plain Dealer*; and there is no doubt that the audience was meant to respond sympathetically when, at the end of *Love for Love*, Angelica declared her love for Valentine: "Had I the world to give you, it could not make me worthy of so generous a passion; here's my hand, my heart was always yours, and struggled very hard to make this utmost

---

3. The constitution, habits and demands of the theater audience are admirably illustrated by Alexandre Beljame in that neglected classic of scholarship, *Le Public et les Hommes de Lettres en Angleterre au Dix-Huitième Siècle*, 1660–1740. See also C. V. Deane, *Dramatic Theory and the Rhymed Heroic Play*, Chapter I, Section 6.
4. *The Social Mode of Restoration Comedy*, p. 177.

trial of your virtue." There is, of course, a good deal of loose emotion in the heroic plays, written—it is useful to remember—for the same audience:

> I'm numbed, and fixed, and scarce my eyeballs move;
> I fear it is the lethargy of love!
> 'Tis he; I feel him now in every part:
> Like a new lord he vaunts about my heart;
> Surveys, in state, each corner of my breast,
> While poor fierce I, that was, am dispossessed.[5]

> A secret pleasure trickles through my veins:
> It works about the inlets of my soul,
> To feel thy touch, and pity tempts the pass:
> But the tough metal of my heart resists;
> 'Tis warmed with the soft fire, not melted down.[6]

"Feeling," in Dryden's serious plays, is fairly represented by such passages as these, and Dryden, we know, was not alone in admiring the Fletcherian "pathos." But it is the lyric verse of the period that provides the strongest confirmatory evidence of the kind of bad taste that is in question. It is not merely that in Etherege, Sedley, and Dorset the feeling comes from much nearer the surface than in the Metaphysicals and the Caroline poets, intellectual "wit" no longer strengthens and controls the feeling. Conventional attitudes are rigged out in a conventional vocabulary and conventional images. (The stock outfit—the "fair eyes" that "wound," the "pleasing pains," the "sighs and tears," the "bleeding hearts" and "flaming darts"—can be studied in any anthology.)[7] There is, in consequence, a pervasive strain of sentimental vulgarity.

> Farewell, ungrateful traitor!
>   Farewell, my perjured swain!
> Let never injured creature
>   Believe a man again.
> The pleasure of possessing
> Surpasses all expressing,
> But 'tis too short a blessing,
>   And love too long a pain.
>
> .   .   .   .
>
> The passion you pretended,
>   Was only to obtain;

---

5. *The Conquest of Granada,* Part I, III, i.
6. *Don Sebastian,* III, i.
7. See, for example, Aphra Behn's "Love in fantastic triumph sate," Buckingham's *To his Mistress* ("Phyllis, though your all powerful charms"), Dryden's "Ask not the cause why sullen spring," and "Ah, how sweet it is to love," and Sedley's *To Chloris*—all in *The Oxford Book of English Verse,* or Ault's *Seventeenth Century Lyrics.*

> But when the charm is ended,
>   The charmer you disdain.
> Your love by ours we measure
> Till we have lost our treasure,
> But dying is a pleasure
>   When living is a pain.

This piece of music-hall sentiment comes from Dryden's *The Spanish Friar*, and it does not stand alone. The mode that was to produce, among other things of equal merit, "When lovely woman stoops to folly," had its origin in the lyrics of the Restoration period. Most of these were written by the group connected with the theaters, and they serve to underline the essential criticism of the plays. The criticism that defenders of Restoration comedy need to answer is not that the comedies are "immoral," but that they are trivial, gross, and dull.

JOCELYN POWELL

[Visual Rhythm in *The Country Wife*][†]

*   *   *

The Country Wife is provided with a distinctive visual rhythm that articulates the whole play through the pictorial structure of its scenes. Act I takes place in Horner's lodging, Act II in Pinchwife's House, the change of scene after the first interval pushing the play forward. These two settings were probably taken from stock, though contrasted in tone as were the characters of their proprietors. Shadwell, in *Bury Fair*, calls for 'the rich lodgings', and such a setting might well do for Horner's wealthy but impotent image—the 'Bury Fair' setting is from a later play, of course, but it indicates the kind of contrast that conventional settings might make. Pinchwife would presumably require a gloomier, shabbier dwelling to match his clothes. The contrast also provides a neat emblem of Horner's sexual prodigality and Pinchwife's sexual meanness. The various elements of the play's design are sharpened in this way by the visual backing, and in Act III a climactic transformation is contrived with a scene that may well have been got up for the occasion. Pinchwife's House rests through the second break, and continues into Act III. Margery demands to be taken to the New Exchange, and the old stock scene slides away as wings and shutters change either to a deep perspective of a covered arcade, or perhaps a view of the open courtyard and lower walks of the favourite shopping centre. This may well have been

†   From *Restoration Theatre Practice* (London: Routledge & Kegan Paul, 1984) 132–35 and 137–
    44. Reprinted by permission of the publisher.

thronged with painted people, emphasising the freedom granted by the move from the closed house to the outside world. The scene was a witty blend of fantasy and reality. The style of the place was preserved, but we learn from the text that the shops' signs are all of horned beasts. Though the New Exchange contained Bull's heads and Ram's heads enough, it makes one wonder if Clasp's bookshop had not the publisher Cademon's sign of the Pope's Head, with horns on. The obvious symbolism makes a nice comment on a popular meeting-place as well as upon Pinchwife's fears.

The visual development through two kinds of private world to the public world has an almost classical precision, despite its use of different locations, and within this simple movement a series of gestic actions are devised whose formality of manner makes for clear articulation against the progression of scenic images and throws the complexity of the dialogue into relief. Wycherley contrives out of the dialectic of stage and forestage, comment and presentation, another dialectic of observation and involvement. This is obviously a function of his own response to life and art; but it creates an emotional texture that is important to a satirist. If the characters or situations are completely objectified or distanced, the audience loses the crucial experience of feeling a part of themselves involved in the action they are criticising. Objectivity of comic style seems simply to ensure that the audience associate the vices and follies they see with others rather than with themselves. Wycherley's technique arouses a deeper level of response. By associating the audience in the feelings underlying the behaviour observed, he makes them not only analysts, but also the subjects of analysis. This sets up a fascinating tension between thought and feeling.

The technical devices employed to create this effect are simple but striking. In the first place, the dramatist gives each of the characters their moments with the audience. Pinchwife and Alithea both comment on the simplicities of Margery, but Alithea also comments on the follies of Pinchwife. When Sparkish or Sir Jaspar are there, Pinchwife gets his turn to comment on the absurdities of their behaviour. In his first-act scene, Sparkish was given a story about a joke he made at the expense of Horner's impotence. He tells his tale in front of Horner, and it becomes a marvellous gesture of thoughtless self-display. He is similarly thoughtless with Alithea, but now Wycherley presents a more complex demonstration. Sparkish is so busy using Alithea to show off his 'parts' that he refuses to see the way in which his friend Harcourt is openly trying to seduce her. Pinchwife stands aside during the scene, exclaiming 'Monstrous!', 'Wonderful!', etc., out to the audience. His presence as commentator here objectifies Sparkish, and also demonstrates Pinchwife as a reasonable being. The real emotion of the scene is thrown into relief. Alithea becomes genuinely distressed at Sparkish's insensitivity. She tries to show him what Harcourt is doing, but he con-

stantly turns its significance in a positive ecstasy of vanity. Finally her
distress turns to anger and malice. 'He said you were . . . a senseless
drivelling Idiot,' she tells him. This is in fact not true. There was no
'drivelling' in the speech she was reporting. It is her own reaction to the
whole event that is expressed in the word, demanding a new timbre in
the voice of the actress. Because of the texture of observers and
observed, this slight but crucial moment catches and grips the imagination.

These moments of feeling are embedded in the rigorous artificiality
and formality of the style. The choric dialogues continue, in repartee
with the audience, not between the characters:

SQUEAMISH: That Men of parts, great acquaintance, and quality
              shou'd take up with, and spend themselves and for-
              tunes in keeping little Play-house Creatures, foh.
LADY FIDGET: Nay that Women of understanding, great acquain-
              tance and good quality shou'd fall a keeping too of
              little Creatures, foh.
SQUEAMISH: Why, 'tis the Men of qualities fault, they never visit
              Women of honour and reputation, as they us'd to do;
              and have not so much common civility, for Ladies of
              our rank, but use us with same indifferency, and ill
              breeding, as if we were all marry'd to 'em.
LADY FIDGET: She says true, 'tis an errant shame Women of quality
              shou'd be so slighted; methinks birth, birth shou'd
              go for something; I have known Men admired,
              courted, and followed for their titles only.
SQUEAMISH: Ay, one wou'd think Men of honour shou'd not love
              no more than marry out of their own rank.
DAINTY: Fye, fye upon 'em, they are come to think cross-
              breeding for themselves best, as well as for their
              Dogs and Horses.
LADY FIDGET: They are Dogs and Horses for't. (II.i)[1]

The ambiguity of such a passage on the Restoration stage is brilliant.
The actresses are playing ladies who despise the relationships men of
their own class have with actresses. They are doing so in front of the
very ladies and gentlemen they describe, and they are able in the light
of the auditorium and fore-stage to address their comments personally
to the pit and boxes. Lady Fidget's 'She says true' is not to the other
ladies on the stage, but to the ladies in the audience, and her comment
on women-keepers rather bold since the audience would know that the
author of her words had himself been kept by Lady Castlemaine. The
real situation in the playhouse forms a piquant dimension to the fictional double-think that is displayed by the 'ladies' as they use moral

1. The references are to the text in *The Plays of William Congreve*, ed. Arthur Friedman.

stricture in order to complain of sexual neglect. The passionate vulgarity of the final image is extremely telling, hurled in insult at the laughing gentlemen in the pit.

Such verbal iconography is complimented with a suitable visual iconography developed out of the changing relationships of the plot. Wycherley continues to provide 'entrance moments' for the actors; but he also follows these up with an even greater precision of physical *gestus* as the play proceeds. He often marks the climax of his scenes with formal pictures significant to the design. In Act II, when Sparkish has loosed Harcourt on Alithea and Pinchwife objects, 'Sparkish *struggles with* Pinchwife *to keep him from* Alithea'. This must be formalised and pictorial. It is directly related in style to such gestic groupings as Abenamar's embrace in *Granada*. Any kind of naturalistic scrap would be clumsy and detract from the main dialogue of Alithea and Harcourt. The struggle must be phrased to move from picture to picture as provoked by the increasing intimacy of Harcourt's gestures to Alithea. In between the picture is held—not frozen, but sustained in a breathing, listening 'attitude'. The actors would phrase their actions to incarnate the designed contrast between the characters of the jealous husband and the complacent lover.

* * *

The whole inter-relationship of actors and audience, words and gestures comes into its own in the famous china scene in Act IV. At its opening we seem to be returned to the very beginning of the play with Horner and Quack discovered: there is an almost musical sense of homecoming created by their appearance and the return to the opening set which has not been seen since Act I. We have arrived, as it were, at the moment promised by the opening of the play. Again, too, Quack is to be a witness to the action, this time concealed behind a screen. This was certainly no practical property in the manner of *The School for Scandal*. Perhaps it was painted on a downstage wing, through which Quack would simply exit, or the upper door of one side of the fore-stage may have been used, and the screen itself merely mentioned. The latter location is certainly most convenient for the progress of the scene, though the directions in the text say 'behind'. He is stowed away on just such a 'framed' entrance as we had in Act I. Quack and Horner are talking on the fore-stage:

> (*Enter* Lady Fidget. *Looking about her*)
>
> HORNER: Now we talk of women of Honour, here comes one, step behind the Screen there, and but observe if I have not particular privileges with the women of reputation already, Doctor, already.
>
> LADY FIDGET: Well, *Horner*, am I not a woman of Honour? You see I'm as good as my word. (IV.iii)

She sees him, reverences, and comes down on to the fore-stage.

Their love-scene proceeds on the fore-stage, and in the full light of the Restoration auditorium takes on a curious ambivalence—all that talk of secrecy and the 'wicked censorious world', when in fact totally exposed to it, and getting it to agree with your points about it!

> LADY FIDGET: A secret is better kept I hope, by a single person than
> a multitude; therefore pray do not trust any body else
> with it, dear, dear Mr. *Horner.*
> (*Embracing him.*
> *Enter Sir Jaspar Fidget*)
> SIR JASPAR: How now!

Sir Jaspar enters behind, and as he speaks the *tableau* freezes. Lady Fidget turns her head to the audience and deliberately, with no sense of hurry communicates her idea of the situation:

> LADY FIDGET: (*aside*): O, my Husband—prevented—and what's
> almost as bad, found with my arms about another
> man—that will appear too much—what shall I say?

The lines have a splendid richness of implication that must not be rushed. Each utterance encapsulates a new aspect of the situation. The 'freeze' is easily sustained by the stage picture, Lady Fidget need not go into her tickling act until she is good and ready. In the brusque improvisation that follows, Wycherley allows both Horner and Sir Jaspar their own moments of direct communication with the audience.

Lady Fidget runs off through one of the lower fore-stage doors, and the scene now builds gradually around the nice baroque wit of the truly locked door, and the fictional action. The locked door itself, in fact, contains a neat cross-reference. Pinchwife uses one of the doors—probably that on the opposite side of the stage, since such an action concludes the preceding scene—to lock Margery away whenever he goes out of his house. The husband who locks up his wife is opposed to the wife locking herself in with her lover. The joke is elaborated again in Act V, when Horner locks Margery behind the door behind which Lady Fidget is here locking herself. If poor Margery is not being locked away on one side, she is on the other! The symmetry of the stage arrangements would make these felicities of design immediately apparent. Horner goes out to Lady Fidget by the upstage door on her side, and Quack rounds off the section by a comment from his hiding-place which emphasises the designed artificiality of the sequence: 'This indeed, I cou'd not have believ'd from him, nor any but my own eyes.'

With Act IV, however, the play seems to get structurally and emotionally out of control. The last two acts are almost as long again as the first three, and packed with action in a way that makes them seem cramped in the reading. As in so many plays of the period, after a classical and ordered start, the author seems to find himself with a great deal too much material to get through in the final acts. This sense of rush is reflected in the scenic rhythm. Instead of the clear gestures of the first acts, there is now a constant changing of location. In Act IV there is Pinchwife's lodgings, a bedroom, Horner's lodgings, then Pinchwife's house again; in the fifth Pinchwife's house, Horner's lodgings, the Piazza at Covent Garden, and Horner's lodgings. The reader becomes very conscious of the propriety of neo-classical tenets in a theatre that uses scenery to indicate place. The constant visual changes required in a scenic theatre seem clumsy and confused, and break up the logic of an act as a unit of action. In fact, however, it is another disproportion, that of feeling, that manages, in the theatre, to hold the unwieldy structure together. This depends, to a very great degree, on the development of the character of Pinchwife.

As has been pointed out, Pinchwife is a man of the same class as Horner and the gallants, and not of very much greater age—Alithea is after all his sister. He is not, therefore, a figure of grotesque comedy. Though his clothes are shabby, his outward manners are correct. This is very important, since the play traces the cracks in this social armour. In Act II we see that the trace of brusqueness in his behaviour in public comes close to cruelty in private. He is not a physically unpleasant person, and his wife could be fond of him. His behaviour to her is brutal:

MRS PINCHWIFE: O my dear, dear Bud, welcome home; why dost thou look so fropish, who has nanger'd thee?
PINCHWIFE: You're a Fool.
(*Mrs Pinchwife goes aside and cryes*)

This is both nasty and very funny, and is also well observed. Her baby-talk is tiresome beyond words, but a neat stroke of character. His bluntness is both sympathetic and harsh, but there is a careless violence implicit that is definitely dangerous. Wycherley emphasises this in his directions. Pinchwife does not simply lock Margery in her room, for example, he *thrusts her in*. The brooding tone of this violence is quite alien to Molière's character, upon whom Pinchwife is based, as is the brutality of behaviour and its physical reality.

The direct consequence of this conception of Pinchwife's character is that the comic conventions by which it is contrived to display this character also serve to push him over the edge of comedy. When Pinchwife takes Mrs Pinchwife to the New Exchange in boy's clothes (Mrs Boutell liked boy's clothes, and even managed to get into them in *The Conquest of Granada*), Horner contrives to actually kiss Mrs Pinchwife in front of her husband. The scene is of course designed as the complement to that in which Sparkish invites Harcourt to kiss Alithea, given a new intensity since it is now in public (there are not only the actors present in the New Exchange, but also shopkeepers and customers painted on the set). He then carries her off into a shop. Pinchwife runs desperately in and out of the wings, searching for her, until eventually she reappears with a hatful of oranges and plums. Pinchwife's rising fury has as usual been communicated in asides; what is unusual is that these asides have an increasingly graphic and emotional tone—'The Devil', 'I am upon a wrack', 'O Heavens! what do I suffer?' His language too, becomes extraordinarily physical, even within the conscious design of the scene:

PINCHWIFE: Come, I cannot, nor will, stay here any longer.
HORNER: Nay, they shall send your Lady a kiss too; here, *Harcourt, Dorilant*, will you not?
(*They kiss her*)
PINCHWIFE: (*aside*): How do I suffer this? Was I not accusing another just now for this rascally patience, in permitting his Wife to be kiss'd before his face? Ten thousand ulcers gnaw their lips. (III.ii)

It is true that we tend to be rather over-squeamish these days about the humiliations heaped so freely by the dramatic poets of the seventeenth century upon their comic characters. Pinchwife is ridiculous, because his exaggerated caution and distrust have brought him to precisely the pass he was trying to avoid. He is hoist with his own petard. The last line, too, is grossly melodramatic and therefore funny. But it is also important to remember that Major Mohun was a great tragic actor, renowned for those sudden outbursts of uncontained emotion Dryden exploited so tellingly.[2] Pinchwife's comments on his own behaviour are similar to Abdelmelech's on his, but here, the strength of his suppressed feeling is played out against the farcical manoeuvres of the wits and the greedy complicity of his wife. This kind of aggressive comedy, the laughter at pain while feeling it, gives backbone to Wycherley's work. It is the laughter of Juvenal in his *Satires* (from the sixth of which the author took a number of hints for this play), and has been called by Baudelaire, in a fine essay, 'le rire de Satan'. There is a very nasty note in it which has nothing intellectual about it. It is a catharsis of personal hate. When Mrs Pinchwife offers her husband one of her oranges, he strikes it out of her hand.

The 'letter' scene in Act IV creates a fascinating tension from this interaction of comedy and drama. In interrogating his wife, and in forcing her to write to Horner, Pinchwife is violent in word and deed. While he makes her write to her supposed lover of his 'nauseous, loath'd Kisses and Embraces' (IV.ii), he threatens her with a penknife, which he offers to stab into her eye unless she does as she is told. Pinchwife's violence

---

2. Refers to Dryden's *Conquest of Granada*, in which Major Mohun played Abdelmelech [*Editor*].

in this scene is obviously based on that of Corvino in *Volpone*, whose threats to his wife not to get within three yards of the window, Pinchwife adopts; but the aggression of Jonson's writing is here modified by its being exercised on a far from passive victim. Pinchwife is both comic and frightening: frightening because of the explicitness and intensity of the threats; comic, because Margery learns to manipulate them. The audience finds itself in a position of constantly changing its side. The balance between the two characters is finely maintained. Pinchwife's violence makes us enjoy his discomfiture; yet Margery's innocent lust is presented equally satirically in her graphic picture of the country girl's heavy persistence at the card-table. Finally, the physical aggression of the penknife is released in the farcical energy of the swapping and sealing of the letters. Comedy and violence are perfectly matched, and Wycherley even manages to point up the psychological undercurrent of this terribly private scene by setting it in their bedroom.

The bedroom scene ends as Pinchwife, having locked Margery in, *holds up the letter* for the attention of the audience and promises to 'deal with the Foe without with false intelligence'. The scene changes to Horner's Lodgings, and the china scene follows, reaching its climax as Pinchwife appears upstage framed by the proscenium arch. He is holding the letter in the very same attitude as that with which he ended the previous scene. His re-entrance binds the first three scenes of the act together, and his ferocity in the previous scene is revoltingly complemented by the smarmy self-satisfaction with which he demonstrates his supposed victory. The threat of his personality has not disappeared, however. Pinchwife himself is ever ready to join challenge with unction, and is constantly on the verge of calling Horner out. One of the most original aspects of Pinchwife's character, and one which must have been emphasised in Major Mohun's performance, is that there is no hint at all of the cowardice conventionally present in comic bluster of this type. Pinchwife becomes yet more aggressive, in the final scene of the act, when he catches Margery writing another letter and actually draws his sword on her. The weakness implicit in this violence against a woman is set off against his readiness for violence against his own sex. Pinchwife is clearly prepared to go through with both, and the absence of the physical impotence which is a cliché of characters of this sort gives the accumulating action a real sense of danger, as well as underlining the spiritual impotence that really lies at the root of Pinchwife's nature.

The emotional and violent presence of Pinchwife forms the unifying factor in the diverse scenes and images of the fourth act, and endows the farce with a kind of passionate seriousness. The fifth is held together by the spread of that violence to other supposedly comic characters. When Sparkish, for instance, learns, quite wrongly, that Alithea is unfaithful to him, he loses his complacency with a vengeance and pours scorn upon her, enabling Wycherley to contrast with the passionate violence of Pinchwife, the spiteful violence of the weak, as nasty as it is feeble: 'I wish you joy, Madam, joy, joy; and to him too, much joy; and to myself more joy for not marrying you' (V.iii). It is a waspish utterance, and Haines almost certainly made it even more unpleasant by that foppish lengthening of the vowels into an 'a' sound which Macaulay mentions as one of the verbal affectations of the upper classes at the time.[3]

Wycherley's satire conflates the moral and the social: he is interested in the way vice degrades its subject, and the growing sense of moral and physical squalor is brought to a striking climax at the beginning of the final scene, which returns at the last to Horner's lodgings. We have been prepared for this moment very cleverly in Act IV.

> HORNER: I tell thee, I am now no more interruption to 'em when they sing, or talk bawdy, than a little squab French Page, who speaks no English.
>
> QUACK: But do civil persons, and women of Honour drink, and sing bawdy Songs?
>
> HORNER: O amongst Friends, amongst Friends; for your Bigots in Honour are just like those in Religion; they fear the eye of the world, more than the eye of Heaven, and think there is no virtue but railing at vice; and no sin, but giving scandal. (IV.iii)

Wycherley now stages a scene of 'good fellowship' for the ladies of quality. They assemble with 'a table, banquet and bottles', and sit down with Horner in a kind of perverse parody of the male drinking-scene. This gets under way with a show-stopping drinking-song for Mrs Knepp as Lady Fidget:

> Why should our damn'd Tyrants oblige us to live
> On the pittance of pleasure which they only give?
>   We must not rejoyce
>   With Wine and with noise;
> In vaine we must wake in a dull bed alone,
> Whilst to our warm Rival, the Bottle, they're gone.
>   Then lay aside charms,
>   And take up these arms. (*The Glasses*) (V.iv)

The words are masculine in tone, and so are the actions. The image of the lady of quality, her foot on a chair, roaring her lungs out to the delight of her female colleagues is a telling one, heightened by the brilliant way the song itself inverts the usual male emphasis on drink and liberty. The ladies maintain the inversion in their conversation:

> DAINTY: Dear Brimmer, well in token of our openness and plain dealing, let us throw our Masques over our heads.

---

3. T. B. Macaulay, *The History of England*, vol. 1, p. 369.

HORNER: So 'twill come to the Glasses anon.
SQUEAMISH: Lovely Brimmer, let me enjoy him first.
LADY FIDGET: No, I never part with a Gallant, till I've try'd him.

The physical images of throwing off the masks in parody of the male custom of toasting and throwing the glass over the shoulder, and of elegant women huddling over their brimmers and cuddling them like lovers is magnificently perverse, and Wycherley develops the scene into a kind choral ode, similar to the choric style of earlier scenes, but here operating very differently:

LADY FIDGET: Dear Brimmer that mak'st our Husbands short
              sighted—
DAINTY: And our bashful gallants bold.
SQUEAMISH: And for want of a Gallant, the Butler lovely in our
              eyes, drink Eunuch.
LADY FIDGET: Drink thou representative of a Husband, damn a
              Husband.
DAINTY: And as it were a Husband, an old keeper.
SQUEAMISH: And an old Grandmother.
HORNER: And an English Bawd, and a French Chirurgeon.

The coarseness of the scene is far more shocking than the earlier *doubles-entendres*, as is the looseness of language and behaviour, characterised by little personal touches such as Mrs Squeamish's venomous 'and an old Grandmother'. The effect is both more naturalistic and more gestic. The table has been set up by the servants just inside the proscenium arch (the fore-stage needs to be clear for the complications of the dénouement). The ladies are seated about it, with Horner in the middle, crowned as it were with wine and roses. We again get a strong sense of a framed picture, of looking in on a private gathering, the squalor of which, both physical and moral, was doubtless brought out by the actresses in the way in which they sprawled about the table. It is like a Hogarth morality—at once intimate, observed and significant—as the eunuch joins the female chorus, adding his grievances to theirs:

HORNER: And an English Bawd, and a French Chirurgeon.
LADY FIDGET: Ay we have all reason to curse 'em.
HORNER: For my sake Ladies.
LADY FIDGET: No, for our own, for the first spoils all young gallants
              industry.
DAINTY: And the others art makes 'em bold only with com-
              mon women.
SQUEAMISH: And rather run the hazard of the vile distemper
              amongst them, than of a denial amongst us.

It is a long scene, and static in narrative terms; but it forms the climax to the play, arising compellingly out of the darkening emotional atmosphere of the last two acts. Emblematically, the ladies throw away their masks and we see their real personalities. The exposure is moving as well as unpleasant, because it comments not only upon the characters, but on the society that makes them what they are. Lady Fidget's song exposes the roots of hypocrisy in contemporary social and sexual relationships. It is shown to grow inevitably from the experiences of the individual life—the tradition of the loveless marriage and the search for alternative excitement, boredom, drunkenness, familiar things, the seeds of which we have seen being sown in the marital relationships of the play, in the essential selfishness of Horner, Sparkish, Pinchwife, Sir Jaspar Fidget. The private sore is literally exposed to the light, and the experience may well have been yet more painful then than now, since the audience could not conceal themselves in the dark comfort of a modern auditorium. As the ladies get drunk and accept Horner in common, the final touches are given to Wycherley's theme—the degradation of contemporary life, and the audience's complicity in it.

※   ※   ※

HARRIETT HAWKINS

[*The Man of Mode*][†]

> I perceive the Laws of Religion and those of the *Stage* differ extreamely.
>
> JEREMY COLLIER

> Lying, Child, is indeed the Art of Love; and Men are generally Masters in it.
>
> CONGREVE

The reader who turns from *Sir Fopling Flutter, or The Man of Mode* to certain recent discussions of this comedy is due for a sobering experience. For instance, any frivolous mirth occasioned by the play would tend to be dampened by Jocelyn Powell's argument that the play shows the emptiness of Dorimant's 'life of isolation', and 'All the devices of comedy, charm, cleverness and wit, encourage one to laugh with Dorimant at his victims, but the sympathy with which those victims are themselves described make us aware that the approval we have been giving through our laughter is of what we hate. We are given a double view of the situation, a view of the pretence, and of the truth, and before

---

† From *Likenesses of Truth in Elizabethan and Restoration Drama* (Oxford: Clarendon Press, 1972) 79–81 and 93–97. Reprinted by permission of the author. Footnotes have been abridged.

it we are helpless, aware that our intellectual and emotional responses form a devastating contradiction.' For James Sutherland, 'Without Sir Fopling ... *The Man of Mode* would be almost a dark comedy', since 'It is Dorimant, a Restoration Don Juan and almost too intense a personality to be the hero of a comedy, who dominates the play ... He never wastes a word, his comments are devastating, and he has a detachment and self-control that put all the other characters, except Harriet, at his mercy. Even Harriet's courage and self-possession occasionally tremble on the verge of defeat, and the duel between the two generates an unusual tension.' For Dale Underwood, the activities of Dorimant are 'explicitly' and 'predominantly' the expression of 'a Hobbesian aggressiveness, competitiveness, and drive for power and "glory"; a Machiavellian dissembling and cunning; a satanic pride, vanity, and malice; and, drawing upon each of these frames of meaning, an egoistic assertion of self through the control of others'.[1] It seems to me that the righteous solemnity of these passages distorts Etherege's comic emphasis on the Ovidian game and art of love—an emphasis which deserves more discussion later. Also, these descriptions of Dorimant sound more suited to a Volpone, an Iago, or even Satan, than to Etherege's 'genteel rake of wit',[2] and the fact that they do so raises some elementary critical questions. Can the recognition of traits that are shared by a whole range of comic and, for that matter, tragic characters—Tamburlaine, Richard III, Volpone, Macbeth, Iago, Satan, Dorimant, Maskwell, the Vicomte de Valmont, Julien Sorel, Sammy Glick, and James Bond, to name just a few—give us very much insight into any single one of these characters? Or do these traits represent *données* of characterization, points of departure from which writers move on to develop their characters into tragic, heroic, comic, sympathetic or villainous individuals? Furthermore, the very vices Underwood names may, on the stage or in the study and even, occasionally, in life, appear embodied in figures so attractive that moral judgement is merged with aesthetic enjoyment, intellectual appreciation, and even emotional admiration of them.

Indeed, audiences have often delighted in characters whose behav-

---

1. See Jocelyn Powell, "George Etherege and the Form of a Comedy," *Restoration Theatre, Stratford-upon-Avon Studies* 6, ed. J. R. Brown and Bernard Harris (London, 1965), pp. 61, 68; James Sutherland, *English Literature of the Late Seventeenth Century* (Oxford, 1969), pp. 110–11; Dale Underwood, *Etherege and the Seventeenth-Century Comedy of Manners* (New Haven, Conn., 1957), p. 73. The same severity appears in Norman Holland's description of the country, which, he says, "as a place highly unpleasant because close observation forces the inner self to conform to visible mores" Is therefore a "suitable House of Holiness for Dorimant's penance" (*The First Modern Comedies* [Cambridge, Mass., 1959], p. 93). Charges of triviality and irrelevance to the best thought of its time, which have been directed at Restoration comedy in general by L. C. Knights, in "Restoration Comedy: The Reality and the Myth," *Explorations* (London, 1946), pp. 131–49, may have influenced modern criticism to discuss and defend Etherege's comedy with undue solemnity. For the sake of argument, I have deliberately selected quotations that illustrate the moralistic tone of modern discussions of this play; but everyone who has read the studies in which they appear knows how valuable they are.
2. Dr. Lockler's description of Dorimant in Joseph Spence, *Observations, Anecdotes, and Characters, of Books and Men*, ed. Edmond Malone (London, 1820), p. 115.

iour and attitudes shock them, in characters who have the pride, energy, intelligence, cunning, or power to overleap moral fences and to invert traditional values. And certainly playwrights have always enjoyed creating such characters, perhaps taking it for granted that what would outrage the moral philosopher might nevertheless please an audience— that, like themselves, their audiences would just as soon imagine an Iago as an Imogen, a Dorimant as an Emilia. It is mainly in judicious retrospect that characters whose vices do become them represent a combined critical and moral dilemma to their audience; for a different order of theatrical salvation and damnation can take place on the stage down here, where, in the course of the action, Falstaff, Richard III, and Cleopatra always steal the show (and the audience) from the Lord Chief Justice, Richmond, and Octavia—characters who have all the moral virtues but none of the theatrical ones.

*   *   *

Granted that we need a modern approach to Restoration comedy, is it really necessary to require an Etherege *moralisé* in order to enjoy *The Man of Mode*? The games people play in Etherege's comedy are timeless (if trivial) ones, and like *The Art of Love*, *The Man of Mode* is still amusing and relevant enough on its own terms. It seems unnecessary to deplore the amorous intrigues of rakes and flirts in such a light comedy unless the comedy itself specifically calls for a harshly moral attitude towards its characters—an attitude which the Ovidian norms and the dramatic emphasis of *The Man of Mode* seem designed to preclude. In a different play moral evaluations of the characters may be quite appropriate. In *The Way of the World* the values of *The Man of Mode* are held up to question and found wanting. But the best way to enjoy Etherege's comedy seems to be to follow the advice given in its prologue, and 'be not too severe'. Recognizing all Dorimant's rakish ways, John Dennis, in his *Defense of Sir Fopling Flutter* declares that 'all the World was charm'd with *Dorimant*', and describes *The Man of Mode*, very accurately, I think, as 'one of the most entertaining Comedies of the last Age, written by a most ingenious Gentleman, who perfectly understood the World, the Court, and the Town'.[3]

Dennis's praise seems to me to be much truer to the spirit of *The Man of Mode* than the moralistic interpretations of modern critics. For the light comic spirit pervading the play allows us to look at the social spectacles that it mirrors and magnifies and see them as—spectacles. The primary purpose of this comedy seems to be neither immoral nor moral, but rather spectacular—to exhibit, rather than to censure, the features of fashionable vice, fashionable virtue, and unfashionable folly,

---

3. See *The Critical Works of John Dennis*, ed. Edward Niles Hooker, vol. II (Baltimore, 1943), pp. 248, 242. Dennis is refuting Steele. [For the argument between Dennis and Steele, see "Contexts" above, pp. 515–32—*Editor.*]

and to show their interaction in a glittering, amusing, and witty dramatic spectacle. And if the play reveals that fashionable vice and fashionable virtue frequently were one and the same when the play was written, just as they are now, this is true to the subject and important to the spectacle. For the more elegantly, spectacularly, rakish the rake (the more foppish the fop, the more dejected the rejected mistress) the better. Since Mrs. Barry (who made the part of Loveit so much her own) could play passionate women with great fire, the more passionate her part, the better. Betterton's own elegance and sex appeal projected across the footlights and so (like its counterpart on the stage) all the world was charmed with Dorimant. Traditional morality has nothing to do with all this. And traditional morality remains outside the imaginative focus of Etherege's comedy precisely because traditional morality is not spectacularly portrayed within it.

Traditional morality is not portrayed spectacularly in *Antony and Cleopatra* either, and a primary concern with the spectacular, as opposed to a primary concern with morality, is not unique to Restoration comedy. Shakespeare, says Coleridge, 'had read nature too heedfully not to know that courage, intellect, and strength of character were the most impressive forms of power, and that to power in itself, without reference to any moral end, an inevitable admiration and complacency appertains, whether it be displayed in the conquests of a Napoleon or Tamerlane, or in the foam and thunder of a cataract'.[4] The drama's inevitable concern with the spectacular, in all its forms and for its own sake, may be the main reason why moralists have attacked the drama throughout its history, and why so many failed efforts to moralize drama clutter up the same history. For the drama mirrors the spectacular in life itself, and the spectacular is not necessarily the moral—not down here in the theatre of the world. It therefore is futile to argue that dramatists do not load their dramatic dice in favour of their most spectacular characters. They may do so obviously or subtly, consciously or unconsciously, but they do it all the time. Etherege's dramatic dice are loaded in favour of Dorimant and there is no point in arguing that Young Bellair *really* represents Etherege's dramatic ideal, since, within the comedy itself, the rake gets all the lines. 'Who gets all the lines?' is not a silly question to ask about a play. The answer may be very obvious but because it is very obvious it is likely that it may also be very revealing. For the success or failure of a play is dependent upon the immediate responses which it commands within the theatre itself, and the over-all emphasis of a play, even a very subtle play, must make itself evident before the final curtain. Thus to argue that some subordinate, easily overlooked, easily forgotten characters can significantly refute, qualify, or obliterate a play's primary emphasis is to turn minor co-ordinates into

4. *Coleridge's Shakespeare Criticism*, ed. T. M. Raysor, vol i (London, 1930), p. 58.

major ones. For while it is true that Young Bellair is a very nice boy, his minor role gives him no real opportunity to challenge our primary response to Dorimant.

Certainly when, where, and if—but only when, where, and if—morality is important to the dramatic purposes of a playwright, the playwrights themselves make morality itself spectacular. A glance at some Shakespearian dissemblers comparable (as such) to Dorimant can illustrate this fact. Shakespeare himself makes Macbeth's moral awareness and suffering just as spectacular and moving as possible. A moral recognition shadows every immoral action of this man, who never for one moment enjoys collecting his wages of sin. On the other hand, Richard III loves collecting his. He is determined to prove a villain and by proving himself such a spectacular villain he releases us from any moral need to prove him one. Where Macbeth's moral nature rebels in horror against his own mutation into a hell-hound, against his own tragic fate, Richard's immoral nature exults in his dramatic destiny:

> March on, join bravely, let us to it pell-mell;
> If not to heaven, then hand in hand to hell.
> (v. iii. 312–13)

Richard gleefully enjoys his own spectacular vices, and so do we. But nobody else on the stage enjoys them. For Richard is placed within a larger frame of reference, a context of nemesis, of history, of guilt and suffering, a context which lends grim irony to his (and our) enjoyment of his spectacular actions. In contrast to Richard, Iago is the arch-enemy of the spectacular. He is diabolically jealous of it. Thus he is frequently the spokesman for ordinariness, for statistical reductions and promotions by grade, and thus he sets out to destroy the spectacular whenever he finds it—to destroy heroic love, heroic virtue, heroic poetry. This is one good reason why he is so much more chilling and despicable than either Richard or Macbeth, who both commit far more murders. They are on the side of the spectacular. Within their dramatic worlds, they are the embodiments of it. Iago, in the world of *Othello*, is its nemesis.

Dorimant's domain is dramatically worlds apart from the realms of any of these dissemblers, but within his own sphere he is the embodiment of the spectacular. Dorimant's sphere itself differs significantly from the spheres of Shakespeare's dissemblers. It differs according to Etherege's subject, which is not the tragic destruction (and tragic renewal) of a great love, nor the anguish of a damned soul, nor the cruelly necessary instruments of history and retribution, but social and amorous intrigues. And this diversity of subject gives diversity of signification to Etherege's specific dissembler, to the play's master of social and amorous intrigues. Dorimant experiences no moral retribution of any kind. He does get his comic come-uppance, but the limits of his power are defined by Harriet, the play's mistress of social and amorous intrigues, his ultimate partner and adversary in the game of love. The irresistible force meets the immovable object (and vice versa) and the game will go on in the country. If we wish it to, a comedy like *The Man of Mode* may instruct us—but not about moral crime and punishment. It may instruct us about its historical social scene, and about the comparable social scene we all know, about the masks people wear, and about the way people play the game of love. And its creator does explicitly instruct us. He instructs us to sit back and relish both the spectacle on the stage and the spectacle round about. For he is a comic poet, and (in the words of Dennis) 'a true Comick Poet is a Philosopher, who, like old *Democritus*, always instructs us laughing'.[5]

* * *

ELIN DIAMOND

Gestus and Signature in Aphra Behn's *The Rover*[†]

> Where the dream is at its most exalted, the commodity is closest to hand.
> —Theodor Adorno, *In Search of Wagner*

Near the end of act 2 of *The Rover*, after the wealthy virgins and hungry gallants have been introduced, and the reader-spectator is made aware that comic symmetry is pressing toward chase and final reward, mention is made of a beautiful courtesan whom the gallants, including the affianced ones, are trying to impress. Angellica Bianca would seem to be a supplement to the intrigue plot—a supplement since one need not intrigue to visit a whore. Yet before the virgins are rewarded with the husbands they desire, they will traverse this whore's marketplace. In "scenes" and "discoveries," they will market themselves as she does, compete for the same male affection, suffer similar abuse. The courtesan herself enters the play not in the way the audience might expect, behind an exotic vizard, or "discovered" in her bedchamber after the parting of the scenes, but as a portrait, as *three* portraits, a large one hung from the balcony and two smaller ones posted on either side of the proscenium door designating her lodging. Willmore, the play's titular rover, arrives at her door, and in the absence of the courtesan he cannot afford, he appropriates her in representation—he reaches up and steals a portrait.

5. Dennis, p. 250.
† From "*Gestus* and Signature in Aphra Behn's *The Rover*," *English Literary History* 56 (1989): 519–20 and 524–37. Reprinted by permission of The Johns Hopkins University Press. Footnotes have been abridged.

Willmore's gesture, I will suggest, contains information beyond the local revelation of one character's behavior. We might read Willmore's gesture as a Brechtian *Gestus* or "gest," a moment in performance that makes visible the contradictory interactions of text, theater apparatus, and contemporary social struggle.[1] In the unraveling of its intrigue plot, Aphra Behn's *The Rover* not only thematizes the marketing of women in marriage and prostitution, it "demonstrates," in its gestic moments, the ideological contradictions of the apparatus Behn inherited and the society for which she wrote. Brecht's account of the *Gestus* is useful for alerting us to the vectors of historical change written into dramatic texts, but he makes no provision for gender—an unavoidable issue in Aphra Behn's own history. Educated but constantly in need of money, with court connections but no supporting family, Aphra Behn wrote plays when female authorship was a monstrous violation of the "woman's sphere." Since the reopening of the theaters in 1660, Frances Boothby and the Duchess of Newcastle each had had a play produced, but no woman had challenged the Restoration theater with Behn's success and consistency.[2] Indeed, that she could earn a living writing for the theater was precisely what condemned her. The muckraking satirist Robert Gould wrote typical slander in a short piece addressed to Behn that concluded with this couplet: "For Punk and Poetess agree so Pat, / You cannot be This and not be That."[3]

In her suggestive "Arachnologies: The Woman, The Text, and the Critic," Nancy Miller implicitly proposes a feminist version of the *Gestus*; texts by women writers, says Miller, encode the signs or "emblems of a female signature" by which the "culture of gender [and] the inscriptions of its political structures" might be read.[4] In a woman-authored text, then, the gestic moment would mark both a convergence of social actions and attitudes, and the gendered history of that convergence.

1. John Willett's translation of *Gestus* as "gest" (with the adjective "gestic") has become standard English usage (see *Brecht on Theatre; The Development of an Aesthetic* (New York: Hill and Wang, 1964, 42). Further references will appear in the text. Like many concepts in Brecht's epic theater theory, *Gestus* is terrifically suggestive and difficult to pin down. Words, gestures, actions, tableaux all qualify as gests if they enable the spectator to draw conclusions about the "social circumstances" (105) shaping a character's attitudes. The gest should be understandable, but also dialectical, incomplete: "[the] expressions of a gest are usually highly complicated and contradictory . . ." (198). In an excellent essay the semiotician Patrice Pavis describes *Gestus* as "the key to the relationship between the play being performed and the public, [as well as] the author's attitude [toward] the public." See *Languages of the Stage* (New York: Performing Arts Journal Publications, 1982), 42.
2. Margaret Cavendish's play was produced under her husband's name. See Maureen Duffy, *The Passionate Shepherdess: Aphra Behn 1640–1689* (London: Jonathan Cape, 1977), 95–104, and Angeline Goreau, *Reconstructing Aphra: A Social Biography of Aphra Behn* (New York: Dial, 1980), 115 ff.
3. Robert Gould, cited in George Woodcock, *The Incomparable Aphra* (London: Oxford Univ. Press, 1977), 103.
4. The full citation from Nancy K. Miller is as follows: "When we tear the web of women's texts, we may discover in the representations of writing itself the marks of the grossly material, the sometimes brutal traces of the culture of gender; the inscriptions of its political structures." See "Arachnologies: The Woman, The Text, and the Critic" in *The Poetics of Gender*, ed. Nancy K. Miller (New York: Columbia Univ. Press, 1986), 275.

Robert Gould's verse, with its violent, unequivocal equation of "poetess" and "punk," provides some evidence of the culture of gender in Restoration London. Like her male colleagues, Behn hawked her intrigue comedies and political satires in the literary and theatrical marketplace, and like them, she suffered the attacks of "fop-corner" and the sometimes paltry remuneration of third-day receipts. In her case, however, the status of professional writer indicated immodesty: the author, like her texts, became a commodity.

Deciphering Behn's authorial "signature" obliges us to read the theatrical, social, and sexual discourses that complicate and obscure its inscription. I am aiming here to open the text to what Brecht calls its "fields of force" (30)—those contradictory relations and ideas that signify in Behn's culture and are, as this reading will indicate, symptomatic of our own. Like Brecht, in his discussion of Shakespeare's *Coriolanus* (252–65), I am interested less in interpretative truth than in exploring a complex textual system in which author, apparatus, history, and reader-spectator each plays a signifying role.

*   *   *

Virgin Commodities

The Rover (1677) and *The Second Part of The Rover* (1681), both drawn from Killigrew's *Thomaso, or The Wanderer* (1663), are Behn's only plays to label a character a courtesan; in her wholly original *The Feigned Curtezans* (1679), witty virgins impersonate famous Roman courtesans and near-debauches occur, but, as befits the romantic intrigue, marriages settle the confusion of plots and the financial stink of prostitution is hastily cleared away.[5] If courtesans figure by name in only three plays, however, the commodification of women in the marriage market is Aphra Behn's first and most persistent theme. Beginning appropriately enough with *The Forced Marriage; or The Jealous Bridegroom* (1670), all of Behn's seventeen known plays deal to some extent with women backed by dowries or portions who are forced by their fathers into marriage in exchange for jointure, an agreed-upon income to be settled on the wife should she be widowed.

There was a lived context for this perspective. The dowry system among propertied classes had been in place since the sixteenth century, but at the end of the seventeenth century there were thirteen women to every ten men, and cash portions had to grow to attract worthy suitors. As the value of women fell by almost fifty percent, marriage for love,

---

5. *The Town Fop* (1676) and *The City Heiress* (1682) contain two practicing bawds, and Behn creates several adulterous wives; the latter, however, all claim a prior love attachment that was cut off by a forced marriage. *The Lucky Chance* (1686) is most concerned with what Eve Kosofsky Sedgwick calls the homosocial bonds between husbands and lovers. See *Between Men: English Literature and Homosocial Desire* (New York: Columbia Univ. Press, 1982).

marriage by choice, became almost unthinkable.[6] Women through marriage had evident exchange value; that is, the virgin became a commodity not only for her use-value as breeder of the legal heir but for her portion, which, through exchange, generated capital. If, as Marx writes, exchange converts commodities into fetishes or "social hieroglyphics," signs whose histories and qualitative differences can no longer be read (161), women in the seventeenth-century marriage market took on the phantasmagoric destiny of fetishized commodities; they seemed no more than objects or things. As Margaret Cavendish observed, sons bear the family name but "Daughters are to be accounted but as Movable Goods or Furnitures that wear out."[7]

Restoration comedy, from the earliest Etherege and Sedley through Wycherley, Dryden, Vanbrugh, D'Urfey, and Congreve, mocked the marketplace values of marriage, promoting the libertine's aesthetic of "natural" love, verbal seduction, and superiority over jealous husbands and fops. But Aphra Behn concentrated on exposing the exploitation of women in the exchange economy, adding vividly to contemporary discourse on the oppressions of marriage. "Wife and servant are the same / But differ only in the name," wrote Lady Mary Chudleigh.[8] "Who would marry," asks Behn's Ariadne (*The Second Part of the Rover*), "who wou'd be chaffer'd thus, and sold to Slavery?"[9] The issue arises repeatedly in plays and verse of the period: not only are marriages loveless, but once married, women lose both independent identity and control of their fortunes. Ariadne again:

> You have a Mistress, Sir, that has your Heart, and all your softer Hours: I know't, and if I were so wretched as to marry thee, must see my Fortune lavisht out on her; her Coaches, Dress, and Equipage exceed mine by far: Possess she all the day thy Hours of Mirth, good Humour and Expence, thy Smiles, thy Kisses, and thy Charms of Wit. (1)

The feminist philosopher Mary Astell would have had no sympathy for the sensuous appetites of Behn's females, but Ariadne's sentiments receive astute articulation in Astell's *Some Reflections Upon Marriage*. The money motive for marriage produces in the man contempt and "Indifferency" which "proceeds to an aversion, and perhaps even the Kindness and Complaisance of the poor abused'd Wife, shall only serve to increase it." Ultimately, the powerless wife ends up "mak[ing] court

6. See Angeline Goreau, *Reconstructing Aphra*, 77–78. See also Lawrence Stone, *The Family, Sex, and Marriage in England, 1500–1800* (New York: Harper and Row, 1979), 77–78.
7. Margaret Cavendish, cited in Hilda Smith, *Reason's Disciples: Seventeenth-Century English Feminists* (Urbana: Univ. of Illinois Press, 1982), 79.
8. Lady Mary Chudleigh, "To the Ladies," from *Poems on Several Occasions*, in *First Feminists: British Women Writers 1578–1799*, ed. Moira Ferguson (Bloomington: Indiana Univ. Press, 1985), 237.
9. Aphra Behn, *The Second Part of the Rover*, in *The Works of Aphra Behn*, ed. Montague Summers, 6 vols. (London: Heinemann, 1915), 1:152.

to [her husband] for a little sorry Alimony out of her own Estate."[1] Two centuries later Engels merely restates these comments in his observation that forced marriages "turn into the crassest prostitution—sometimes of both partners, but far more commonly of the woman, who only differs from the ordinary courtesan in that she does not [hire] out her body on piecework as a wage worker, but sells it once and for all into slavery."[2]

Yet in order to launch *The Rover*'s marriage plot and to provoke sympathy for her high-spirited aristocrats, Behn dissimulates the connection between virgin and prostitute. When Florinda, Hellena, and Valeria don gypsy costumes—assume the guise of marginal and exotic females—to join the carnival masquerade, they do so explicitly to evade the patriarchal arrangement of law and jointure laid down by their father and legislated by their brother Pedro: Florinda shall marry a rich ancient count and Hellena shall go into a convent, thus saving their father a second dowry and simultaneously enriching Florinda. The opening dialogue of *The Rover* is also implicitly "gestic," raising questions about women's material destiny in life as well as in comic representation:

> *Florinda:* What an impertinent thing is a young girl bred in a nunnery! How full of questions! Prithee no more, Hellena; I have told thee more than thou understand'st already.
>
> *Hellena:* The more's my grief. I would fain know as much as you, which makes me so inquisitive.[3]

Hellena dons masquerade because she desires not a particular lover but a wider knowledge. Given the conventions of Restoration comedy, this wish to know "more than" she already understands is troped as a wish for sexual adventure. But if we hear this dialogue dialogically—in its social register—other meanings are accessible.[4] Women's lack of access to institutions of knowledge spurred protest from writers as diverse as Margaret Cavendish, Bathsua Makin, Mary Astell, and Judith Drake. Aphra Behn mocks a university fool in *The City Heiress* and a learned lady in *Sir Patient Fancy*; she criticizes neoclassical aesthetics in "Epistle to the Reader," appended to *The Dutch Lover* (1), for having nothing to do with why people write or attend plays. When she translates Bernard de Fontenelle's *A Discovery of New Worlds*, however, she reveals as passionate a hunger for esoteric knowledge as these early English femi-

1. Mary Astell, cited in Smith (note 16), 133, 135.
2. Frederick Engels, *The Origin of the Family, Private Property and the State* (New York: International Publishers, 1985), 134.
3. Aphra Behn, *The Rover*, ed. Frederick Link (Lincoln: Univ. of Nebraska Press, 1967).
4. "Dialogism," associated with the writings of M. M. Bakhtin and V. N. Vološinov (a cover name for Bakhtin), implies that utterance is always social; any single utterance interacts with meanings in the larger discursive field. As Vološinov puts it: "A word is a bridge thrown between myself and another. . . . A word is a territory shared by both addresser and addressee, by the speaker and his interlocutor." (See *Marxism and the Philosophy of Language*, trans. L. Matejka and I. R. Titunik [Cambridge: Harvard Univ. Press, 1986], 86.)

nists. Unfortunately, the controlling conceit of Fontenelle's work—a mere woman is informally taught the complexities of Copernican theory—produces an untenable and revealing contradiction for Behn: "He [Fontenelle] makes her [the Marchionness] say a great many silly things, tho' sometimes she makes observations so learned, that the greatest Philosophers in Europe could make no better."[5] Insightful yet silly, wise yet a *tabula rasa*, Fontenelle's Marchionness oscillates between intellectual independence and slavish imitation. She is perhaps less a contradictory character than a projection of a male intellectual's ambivalence about female education.

Aphra Behn's Hellena seeks knowledge "more than" or beyond the gender script provided for her. She rejects not only her brother's decision to place her in a nunnery, but also the cultural narrative of portion, jointure, and legal dependency in which she is written not as subject but as object of exchange. Yet Hellena, too, oscillates—both departing from and reinforcing her social script. Her lines following those cited above seem, at first, to complicate and defer the romantic closure of the marriage plot. To have a lover, Hellena conjectures, means to "sigh, and sing, and blush, and wish, and dream and wish, and long and wish to see the man" (7). This thrice-reiterated wishing will result in three changes of costume, three suitors, and three marriages. As with the repetitions of "interest," "credit," and "value"—commodity signifiers that circulate through the play and slip like the vizard from face to hand to face—this repetition invokes the processes underlying all wishing, to desire that will not, like a brother's spousal contract, find its "completion."

If we incorporate insights from feminist psychoanalytic theory, the virgins' masquerade takes on added significance, or rather this discourse helps us decode what is already implied—namely, that in an economy in which women are dependent on male keepers and traders, female desire is always already a masquerade, a play of false representations that covers over and simultaneously expresses the lack the woman exhibits—lack of the male organ and, concomitantly, lack of access to phallic privileges—to material and institutional power. Unlike the theatrical mask, which conceals a truth, the masquerade of female sexuality subverts the "Law-of-the-Father" that stands "behind" any representation.[6] Underneath the gypsy veils and drapes of Behn's virgins, there is nothing, in a phallic sense, to see; thus no coherent female identity that can be coopted into a repressive romantic narrative. Willmore, titillated by Hellena's witty chatter, asks to see her face. Hellena responds that underneath the vizard is a "desperate . . . lying look"—that is, she, like

---

5. Cited in Smith, 63.
6. According to Lacanian psychoanalyst Michele Montrelay, masquerade has always been considered "evil" because, in flaunting the absent-penis, it sidesteps castration anxiety and repression, thus threatening the Father's law (incest taboo) and all systems of representation. See Montrelay, "Inquiry Into Femininity," *m / f* 1 (1978): 83–101.

her vizard, may prevaricate; represented may mingle with representer—for the spectator (Willmore) there will be no validating stake.

Yet, as Behn well knew, there is means of validation, one that guarantees patriarchy's stake in portion, jointure, and the woman's body: the hymen. In Restoration comedy no witty unmarried woman was really witty unless she had property *and* a maidenhead. Behn's virgins may re-"design" their cast of characters but they cannot change their plot. Ultimately their masquerade is dissimulation in the classic representational sense, a veil that hides a truth. Hellena's mask merely replicates the membrane behind which lies the "true nature" of woman: the equipment to make the requisite patrilineal heir. Thus Willmore's masterful response to Hellena's "lying look" is a mock-blazon of her facial features, ending in a fetishistic flourish: "Those soft round melting cherry lips and small even white teeth! Not to be expressed, but silently adored!" (56). The play in Hellena's discourse between knowing and desiring, which extends through the masquerade, completes itself in the marriage game. She exercises her will only by pursuing and winning Willmore, for as it turns out he has the "more" she "would fain know."

Willmore acts not only as the rover but as signifier for the play's phallic logic. His name metaphorizes the trajectory of desire as he roves from bed to bed "willing more," making all satisfactions temporary and unsatisfying. Desire's subject, Willmore never disguises himself (he comes on stage *holding* his mask); until enriched by the courtesan Angellica Bianca, he remains in "buff" or leather military coat. In another sense, though, Willmore is already in disguise, or rather the entity "Willmore" covers a range of linguistic and social signifiers. Behn's model for Willmore (like Etherege's for Dorimont) was reputedly the womanizing courtier, the Earl of Rochester, whose name, John Wilmot, contains, like the rover's, the word ("mot") "will." Rochester was also the lover and mentor of Elizabeth Barry, the actress who first played Behn's Hellena. In Tory mythology Charles II, on the verge of fleeing England, disguised himself in buff—a leather doublet.[7] Indeed, Willmore's first lines refer to the offstage Prince who, in exile during the Commonwealth, was also a rover. Doubled mimetically and semiotically with both Rochester and the Merry Monarch (who attended at least one performance of *The Rover* before the play was restaged at Whitehall), Willmore needs no mask to effect his ends: his libertine desire is guaranteed and upheld by patriarchal law. Hellena's playful rovings, on the other hand, and her numerous disguises, signal both ingenuity and vulnerability.[8] Ironically, the virgins' first costume, the

---

7. See Susan Staves, *Players' Scepters: Fictions of Authority in the Restoration* (Lincoln: Univ. of Nebraska Press, 1979), 2.

8. My view that Hellena is fully recuperated into the economy she rebels against contrasts with, among others, Frederick M. Link's interpretation in his Introduction to *The Rover* and, more

gypsy masquerade, represents their actual standing in the marriage market—exotic retailers of fortunes (or portions). Their masquerade defers
but does not alter the structure of patriarchal exchange.

Painting(s), Person, Body

In contrast to the virgins' "ramble" are the stasis and thralldom that
attend the courtesan Angellica Bianca. While the virgins are learning
artful strategies of concealment, Angellica's entrance is a complicated
process of theatrical unveiling. She arrives first through words, then
through painted representation, then through the body of an actress
who appears on a balcony behind a silk curtain. She is also the site of a
different politics, one that explores desire and gender not only in the
text but in the apparatus itself.

The first references to Angellica situate her beyond the market in
which we expect her to function. According to Behn's gallants, she is the
"adord beauty of all the youth in Naples, who put on all their charms to
appear lovely in her sight; their coaches, liveries and themselves all gay
as on a monarch's birthday." Equated thus with sacred and secular
authority, Angellica gazes on her suitors and "has the pleasure to behold
all languish for her that see her." This text in which desire flows from
and is reflected back to a female subject is immediately followed by the
grouping of the English gallants beneath the courtesan's balcony. They
wait with the impatience of theater spectators for Angellica to appear—
not in person but in representation, as "the shadow of the fair substance."

At this point the problematic connection between shadow and substance preoccupies them. Blunt, the stock country fool, is confused by
the fact that signs of bourgeois and even noble status—velvet beds, fine
plate, handsome attendance, and coaches—are flaunted by courtesans.
Blunt is raising an epistemological issue that Behn and her colleagues
often treat satirically—the neoclassical assumption regarding mimesis
that imitated can be separated from imitator, nature from representation, truth from falsehood, virgin from gypsy. By suggesting that whores
are indistinguishable from moral women, Behn revives the problematic
of the masquerade, casting doubt on the connection/separation of sign
and referent. Significantly, when Hobbes constructed his theory of sovereign authority, he employed theater metaphors to distinguish between

---

recently, to DeRitter Jones's in "The Gypsy, *The Rover*, and the Wanderer: Aphra Behn's
Revision of Thomas Killigrew," *Restoration* 10 (Fall 1986): 82–92. Both Link and Jones argue
that Hellena represents a positive alternative to both the ingenuous Florinda and the rejected
Angellica; her contract with Willmore is "no marriage for 'portion and jointure,' no marriage
arranged to perpetuate a family's name or increase its wealth, but a contract between two free
and like-minded people" (Link, xiv). Even from a humanist perspective, this view is dubious:
Hellena's freedom is inconceivable outside the market economy; from a historical or gestic
perspective, Hellena's "identity" is at the very least divided and ambivalent.

"*natural*" and "*feigned* or *artificial*" persons. But he noted that "person" was itself a slippery referent:

> The word Person [persona] is Latin . . . [and] signifies the *disguise*, or *outward appearance* of a man, counterfeited on the stage; and sometimes more particularly that part of it, which disguiseth the face, as a mask or vizard: and from the stage, hath been translated to any representer of speech and action, as well in tribunals, as theatres. So that a *person* is the same that an *actor* is, both on stage and in common conversation.[9]

Since, as Christopher Pye notes, everyone is already a "self-impersonator, a mediated representation of himself," the difference between "natural" and "feigned" rests on highly unstable assumptions about identity which, both "on stage" and "in common conversation" are capable of shifting.[1] Blunt's confusion about the true status of apparently noble women may also be read as an extratextual reference to the Restoration actress and her female spectators. As kept mistresses, actresses often displayed the fine clothing and jewels of aristocrats like the notorious Duchess of Cleveland, who regularly watched the play in vizard-mask from the king's box. Yet the respectable Mrs. Pepys also owned a vizard-mask, and on her frequent visits to the theater occasionally sat in the pit near the "real" vizards.

Given the theatricality of everyday Restoration life, and the ambiguity of signs representing the status and character of women, Angellica's three portraits allow Aphra Behn to comment on the pleasures and politics of theatrical signification. Though I have ignored the specifics of Behn's adaptation of her source play, it is helpful here to compare her handling of the paintings with that of Killigrew in his ten-act semiautobiographical closet drama, *Thomaso, or The Wanderer.* In both plays, one portrait is prominent and raised, and two smaller versions are posted below, one of which is snatched by the rake—Thomaso in the source play, Willmore in Behn's. But there is an important difference in the disposition of the paintings vis-à-vis the woman they represent. In *Thomaso*, 2.1, anonymous parties of men pass in front of the paintings, react scornfully to the courtesan's high price, and wander on. But in 2.2, with the arrival of Killigrew's main characters, Angellica Bianca is sitting on the balcony in full view of her prospective buyers. Her bawd challenges the men to "compare them [the paintings and the woman] together."[2] With neoclassical correctness, the men agree that the woman exceeds her representation: "That smile, there's a grace and sweetness in it Titian could never have catch'd." By the time the English Thomaso and

9. Thomas Hobbes, *Leviathan*, ed. Michael Oakeshott (New York: Collier, 1962), 125.
1. Christopher Pye, "The Sovereign, the Theater, and the Kingdome of Darknesse: Hobbes and the Spectacle of Power," *Representations*, 8 (Fall 1984): 91.
2. Thomas Killigrew, *Thomaso, or the Wanderer*, parts 1 and 2, in *Comedies and Tragedies* (London: Henry Herringman, 1663).

his friends arrive, the viewing of the paintings and the viewing of Angellica are almost simultaneous:

> *Harrigo:*   That wonder is it I told you of; tis the picture of the famous Italian, the Angellica; See, shee's now at her Window.
>
> *Thomaso:*   I see her, 'tis a lovely Woman.

(Killigrew)

Aphra Behn's Angellica Bianca never invites such explicit comparison. In fact, Behn prolongs the dialogue between titillated suitors and suggestive portraits: Angellica's simulacra, not Angellica, preoccupy her male audience. When the English cavaliers first view the paintings, Belvile, the play's fatuous moral figure, reads them as "the fair sign[s] to the inn where a man may lodge that's fool enough to give her price." That is, the iconicity of the paintings, their likeness to Angellica, which so impresses Killigrew's cavaliers, is in Behn's text suppressed. Gazing on the portraits, the gallants rewrite the courtesan's monarchial description, now figuring her as a thing, a receptacle for depositing one's body. To underscore the point, Behn has Blunt ask the ontological question to which there is a ready answer in commodity discourse: "Gentlemen, what's this?" Belvile: "A famous courtesan, that's to be sold." The infinitive phrase is curious. To be sold by whom? Released by her earlier keeper's death, Angellica and her bawd seem to be in business for themselves. At this point, however, Blunt reminds us again of the object status of the woman, as of her painted signs: "Let's be gone; I'm sure we're no chapmen for this commodity."

Willmore, however, monarchy's representative, succumbs to the lure of the signs, believing not only in their iconicity but in their value as pleasurable objects—for the original one must pay one thousand crowns, but on the portraits one can gaze for nothing. Penury, however, is not the real issue. Willmore seems to understand that the appeal of the paintings is precisely that they are not the original but an effective stand-in. After the two Italian aristocrats draw swords in competition for Angellica, Willmore reaches up and steals one of the small paintings, in effect cuts away a piece of the representation for his own titillation. His intentions, like his actions, are explicitly fetishistic:

> This posture's loose and negligent;
> The sight on't would beget a warm desire
> In souls whom impotence and age had chilled.
> This must along with me.

(38)

This speech and the act of appropriation occur *before* Willmore sees Angellica. Only in Behn's text do the paintings function as fetishes, as substitute objects for the female body. When challenged why he has the right to the small portrait, Willmore claims the right "of possession, which I will maintain."

At the outset of this paper I described Willmore's acquisitive gesture as a Brechtian "gest"—that moment in theatrical performance in which contradictory social attitudes in both text and society are made heuristically visible to spectators. What does this gest show? Willmore removes Angellica's portrait the way a theater manager might lift off a piece of the set—because without buying her, he already owns her. Her paintings are materially and metonymically linked to the painted scenes, which were of course owned, through the theatrical hierarchy, by patentee and king—who, in Behn's fiction, validates and empowers Willmore. This "homosocial" circuit, to use Eve Sedgwick's term, extends into the social realm.[3] As innumerable accounts make clear, Restoration theater participated in the phallic economy that commodified women, not in the marriage market, but in the mistress market: the king and his circle came to the theater to look, covet, and buy. Nell Gwyn is the celebrated example, but Behn's biographer Angeline Goreau cites other cases. An actress in the King's Company, Elizabeth Farley, joined the royal entourage for several months, then became mistress to a Gray's Inn lawyer, then drifted into prostitution and poverty.[4] The answer to the question, "Who is selling Angellica?" is, then, the theater itself, which, like Willmore, operates with the king's patent and authorization. When Angellica sings behind her balcony curtain for her Italian admirers, and draws the curtain to reveal a bit of beautiful flesh, then closes it while monetary arrangements are discussed, she performs the titillating masquerade required by her purchasers *and* by her spectators. This is mastery's masquerade, not to demonstrate freedom, but to flaunt the charms that guarantee and uphold male power.

If Angellica's paintings stand for the theater apparatus and its ideological complicity with a phallic economy, what happens when Angellica appears? Is illusionism betrayed? Interestingly, Aphra Behn chooses this moment to emphasize presence, not only of character but of body; Angellica emerges in the flesh and offers herself, gratis, to Willmore, finding his scornful admiration ample reason for, for the first time, falling in love. In their wooing/bargaining scene it becomes clear that Angellica wants to step out of the exchange economy symbolized by the paintings: "Canst thou believe [these yielding joys] will be entirely thine, / without considering they were mercenary?" The key word here is "entirely"; Angellica dreams of full reciprocal exchange without com-

3. See Sedgwick's *Between Men*, particularly her analysis of Wycherley's *The Country Wife* (49–66). Interestingly, when cuckoldry drives the plots of a Behn play, as in *The False Count*, the wife's passion, trammeled by her forced marriage, is given as much weight as homosocial competitiveness.
4. See Goreau, 174.

merce: "The pay I mean is but thy love for mine. / Can you give that?"
And Willmore responds "entirely."

A commodity, Marx writes, appears as a commodity only when it "possess[es] a double form, i.e. natural form and value form." Angellica's
name contains "angel," a word whose meaning is undecidable since it
refers simultaneously to the celestial figure and to the old English coin
stamped with the device of Michael the archangel, minted for the last
time by Charles I but still in common circulation during the Restoration. By eliminating her value-form, Angellica attempts to return her
body to a state of nature, to take herself out of circulation. While the
virgins of the marriage plot are talking "business" and learning the powers of deferral and unveiling, Angellica is trying to demystify and
authenticate herself. She wants to step out of the paintings, to be known
not by her surface but by her depth. As she "yields" to Willmore
upstairs, the portraits on the balcony are removed—a sign that the courtesan is working. In this case, not only does the (offstage) "natural" body
supplant its painted representation, but the courtesan, who has been in
excess of, now makes up a deficiency in, the marriage plot: Angellica
(with Willmore) labors for love.

Though the paintings disappear in act 3, however, the signs of commodification are still in place, or are metonymically displaced through
properties and scenes to other characters in the marriage plot. We learn
that Hellena's portion derives from her uncle, the old man who kept
Angellica Bianca; thus the gold Willmore receives from the courtesan
has the same source as that which he will earn by marrying the virgin.
Like Angellica, too, the virgin Florinda uses a portrait as a calling card,
and at night in the garden, "in undress," carrying a little box of jewels—
a double metonym for dowry and genitals—she plans to offer herself to
Belvile. Unfortunately Willmore, not Belvile, enters the garden and
nearly rapes her.

Florinda's nocturnal effort at entrepreneurship takes place in the
upstage scenes, where Aphra Behn, like her fellow Restoration dramatists, situated lovers' trysts and discoveries. The thematic link between
commodified "Scenes" and females is particularly crucial, however, in
The Rover. In 4.4, a disguised Florinda flees from Willmore by running
in and out of the scenes until she arrives in Blunt's chamber, where
another near-rape occurs. Blunt has just been cozened by a prostitute
and dumped naked into the city sewer; he emerges vowing to "beat" and
"kiss" and "bang" the next woman he sees, who happens to be Florinda,
but now all women appear to be whores. In fact Willmore, Frederick,
and even Belvile arrive soon after to break open the door and "partake"
of Florinda. If Angellica Bianca makes a spectacle of herself through balcony curtains and paintings, Florinda's "undress" and her proximity to
the painted scenes signify a similar reduction to commodity status.

"I . . . Hang out the sign of Angellica"

Angellica's paintings, I have argued, are the bright links in a metonymic chain joining the text of *The Rover* to the apparatus of representation. Angellica's portraits represent the courtesan in the most radical sense. They produce an image of her and at the same time reduce her to that image. Notwithstanding her passionate address, Angellica cannot exceed her simulacra. In effect she is doubly commodified—first because she puts her body into exchange, and second because this body is equated with, indeed interchangeable with, the art object. When Willmore performs the "gest" of appropriating the painted image of Angellica, he makes visible, on the one hand, the patriarchal and homosocial economy that controls the apparatus and, on the other hand, the commodity status of paintings, of their model, and, by metonymic extension, of the painted actress and the painted scenes.

Flecknoe and Pepys, we noted earlier, testify to the intensity of visual pleasure in Restoration theater. It is a fascinating contradiction of all feminist expectation to discover that Aphra Behn, more than any of her Restoration colleagues, contributed to that visual pleasure by choosing, in play after play, to exploit the fetish/commodity status of the female performer. The stage offered two playing spaces, the forestage used especially for comedy, where actor and audience were in intimate proximity, and the upstage or scenic stage, where wing-and-shutter settings, as much as fifty feet from the first row of spectators, produced the exotic illusionistic discoveries needed for heroic tragedy. Writing mostly comedies, Aphra Behn might be expected to follow comic convention and use the forestage area, but as Peter Holland notes, she was "positively obsessive" about discovery scenes.[5] Holland counts thirty-one discoveries in ten comedies (consider that Sedley's *The Mulberry Garden*, 1668, uses one; Etherege's *The Man of Mode*, 1676, uses two), most of which are bedroom scenes featuring a female character *"in undress."* Holland reasons that such scenes are placed upstage so that familiar Restoration actresses would not be distractingly exposed to the audience. We might interpret Behn's "obsession" differently: the exposed woman's (castrated) body must be obscured in order to activate scopic pleasure. Displayed in "undress" or loosely draped gowns, the actress becomes a fetish object, affording the male spectator the pleasure of being seduced by and, simultaneously, of being protected from the effects of sexual difference.

Is it also possible that this deliberate use of fetishistic display dramatizes and displaces the particular assault Behn herself endured as "Poetess/Punk" in the theater apparatus? The contradictions in her authorial status are clear from the preface to *The Lucky Chance* (1686). Behn

---

5. *The Ornament of Action: Text and Performance in Restoration Comedy* (Cambridge: Cambridge University Press, 1979), p. 41.

argues that "the Woman damns the Poet," that accusations of bawdy and plagiarism are levied at her because she is a woman. On the other hand, the literary fame she desires derives from a creativity that in her mind, or rather in the social ideology she has absorbed, is also gendered: "my Masculine Part the Poet in me."[6] In literary history, the pen, as Gilbert and Gubar have argued, is a metaphorical penis, and the strong woman writer adopts strategies of revision and disguise in order to tell her own story.[7] In Behn's texts, the painful bisexuality of authorship, the conflict between (as she puts it) her "defenceless" woman's body and her "masculine part," is *staged* in her insistence, in play after play, on the equation between female body and fetish, fetish and commodity—the body in the "scenes." Like the actress, the woman dramatist is sexualized, circulated, denied a subject position in the theater hierarchy.

This unstable, contradictory image of authority emerges as early as Behn's first play prologue (to *The Forced Marriage, or The Jealous Bridegroom*, 1670). A male actor cautions the wits that the vizard-masks sitting near them will naturally support a woman's play and attempt to divert them from criticism. He is then interrupted by an actress who, pointing *"to the Ladies"* praises both them and, it would seem, the woman author: "Can any see that glorious sight and say / A woman shall not prove Victor today?"

The "glorious sight" is, once again, the fetishized, commodified representation of the female, standing on the forestage, sitting in the pit, and soon to be inscribed as author of a printed play. If this fascinating moment—in which a woman speaking a woman's lines summons the regard of other women—seems to put a *female* gaze into operation, it also reinforces the misogynist circuitry of the theater apparatus: that which chains actress to vizard-mask to author.

At the outset of this essay we asked how Aphra Behn encodes the literary and theatrical conditions of her production. Behn's "Postscript" to the published text of *The Rover* provides a possible answer. She complains that she has been accused of plagiarizing Killigrew simply because the play was successful and she a woman. Yet while claiming to be "vainly proud of [her] judgment" in adapting *Thomaso*, she "hang[s] out the sign of Angellica (the only stolen object) to give notice where a great part of the wit dwelt." This compliment to Killigrew may also indicate what compelled Behn to embark on this adaptation. The "sign[s] of Angellica" both constitute and represent the theater apparatus, serving as metacritical commentary on its patriarchal economy, its

6. The Prologue to *The Rover*, "Written by a Person of Quality," dramatizes that ambivalence; the lines indirectly addressed to Behn use the pronoun "him": "As for the author of this coming play, I asked him what he thought fit I should say." This is unusual. In Behn's prologues the masculine pronoun is used only as a general referent for poets / wits, as in the last line to the prologue to *Sir Patient Fancy*: "He that writes Wit is the much greater Fool."
7. See Sandra M. Gilbert and Susan Gubar, *The Madwoman in the Attic: The Woman Writer and the Nineteenth-Century Literary Imagination* (New Haven: Yale Univ. Press, 1979), 3–92.

habits of fetishistic consumption. They may also constitute Behn's authorial signature, what Miller calls the "material . . . brutal traces of the culture of gender." As a woman writer in need of money, Behn was vulnerable to accusations of immodesty; to write meant to expose herself, to put herself into circulation; like Angellica, to sell her wares. Is it merely a coincidence that Angellica Bianca shares Aphra Behn's initials, that hers is the only name from *Thomaso* that Behn leaves unchanged?

The "signs of Angellica" not only help us specify the place of this important woman dramatist in Restoration cultural practice, they invite us to historicize the critique of fetishization that has informed so much feminist criticism in the last decade.[8] Certainly the conditions of women writers have changed since the Restoration, but the fetishistic features of the commercial theater have remained remarkably similar. Now as then the theater apparatus is geared to profit and pleasure, and overwhelmingly controlled by males. Now as then the arrangement of audience to stage produces what Brecht calls a "culinary" or ideologically conservative spectator, intellectually passive but scopically hungry, eager for the next turn of the plot, the next scenic effect. Now as then the actor suffers the reduction of Angellica Bianca, having no existence except in the simulations produced by the exchange economy. The practice of illusionism, as Adorno points out above, converts historical performers into commodities which the spectator pays to consume.

If Restoration theater marks the historical beginning of commodity-intensive, dreamlike effects in English staging, Aphra Behn's contribution to contemporary theory may lie in her demonstration that, from the outset, dreamlike effects have depended on the fetish-commodification of the female body. When Willmore, standing in for king and court, steals Angellica's painting, Behn not only reifies the female, she genders the spectatorial economy as, specifically, a male consumption of the female image. Reading that confident gesture of appropriation as a *Gestus*, the contemporary spectator adds another viewpoint. Angellica Bianca's paintings appear to us now as both authorial "signature" and "social hieroglyphic," signs of a buried life whose careful decoding opens up new possibilities for critique and contestation.

---

8. Feminist film theorists have taken the lead, with Laura Mulvey's path-breaking article on the fetishist position produced by Hollywood narrative cinema ("Visual Pleasure and Narrative Cinema," *Screen* 16, no. 3 [1975]: 6–19. For a full elaboration of this and other psychoanalytic concepts in film, see Mary Ann Doane's *The Desire to Desire: The Woman's Film of the 1940s* (Bloomington: Indiana Univ. Press, 1987). In literary study, see Naomi Schor's "Female Fetishism: The Case of George Sand" (in *The Female Body in Western Culture: Contemporary Perspectives*, ed. Susan R. Suleiman [Cambridge: Harvard Univ. Press, 1986], 363–72). For fetishism in theater as well as in film and fiction, Roland Barthes's work is particularly useful; see "Diderot, Brecht, Eisenstein" in *Image, Music, Text*, trans. Stephen Heath (New York: Hill and Wang), 69–78.

MARTIN PRICE

[Form and Wit in *The Way of the World*][†]

* * * Flexibility, the power to accept and adapt to the world without yielding to it, marks the central figures of Congreve's *The Way of the World*. Here once more the lovers are confronted with a tangle of intrigue, but it is their skill in extricating themselves from it that we admire. They show the same skill in extricating themselves from the patterns of conduct the world imposes; their integrity is preserved by a tact that resists both the shallowness of affectation and the cruelty of blind passion. Mirabell and Millamant exist only within the framework of the play; their characters, like those of the lovers in *All for Love*,[1] are defined by the symmetrical disposition of the other figures around them.

The most obvious foils are Witwoud and Petulant, who, like Fielding's Square and Thwackum, represent contrasting patterns of a common false wit. Petulant is the would-be man of candor, who masks no sentiment, however displeasing. He is, in fact, a bad actor even in that undemanding role, and he is soon exposed in all his vanity and hypocrisy as a man pretending to a more wholesome humor than he possesses. Witwoud is more obvious and yet more interesting. Congreve has presented him in greater depth, and he supplies the most brilliant epitome of wit without judgment. To that extent he is a fine embodiment of the way of the world in which he is a prominent parasite: his every gesture is designed to impress, and the bustling energy of the effort consumes all his powers. He is wholly dedicated to erasing his past and winning acceptance in the world of fashion on whatever terms it sets. Witwoud has his ugly traits, but he is so desperately affable, so fatuously self-congratulatory, and so transparently foolish, that he is at once somewhat shabby and altogether disarming. His harmlessness gives him a privileged status in the reader's eyes as it does in the ladies' cabals. He may remind us of the fictitious author of Swift's *Tale of a Tub*, again a desperate hanger-on, too dense to be guileful, too voluble to be subtle, a fool who gives away the game of the knaves he aspires to imitate. The cynicism of other men's epigrams, as Witwoud repeats them with an air of worldliness, becomes curiously abstract and unmotivated. When he says with a smirk, "a wit should be no more sincere, than a woman constant; one argues a decay of parts, as t'other of beauty," the effect is far different from that created by Fainall's more cruel and urgent remarks. The comparative ingenuousness of Witwoud's stylish malice underlines the strength and depth of Fainall's. Witwoud is a kind of industrious but

---

† From Martin Price, *To the Palace of Wisdom* (New York: Doubleday & Company, 1964), pp. 241–245. Reprinted by permission of the author.
1. Dryden's tragedy, which Price has discussed earlier in this chapter [*Editor*].

incompetent apprentice in an inverted world. What Witwoud and Petulant dramatize so well is summed up in Mirabell's couplet at the close of the first act:

> Where modesty's ill-manners, 'tis but fit
> That impudence and malice pass for wit.

Lady Wishfort is, of course, the center of the plot. She is a tyrant, a hypocrite, and a lecherous old fool, but she exists more to be manipulated and hoodwinked than to control the situation. She, too, gives away the game by her overplaying; and there is at least a touch of pathos in the savagery with which she contests the ravage of age:

> FOIBLE: Your ladyship has frowned a little too rashly, indeed madam. There are some cracks discernible in the white varnish.
> LADY WISHFORT: Let me see the glass.—Cracks, sayest thou?—why I am errantly flayed—I look like an old peeled wall. Thou must repair me, Foible, before Sir Rowland comes, or I shall never keep up to my picture (III, i).

Like Witwoud, Lady Wishfort serves as a bathetic reduction of all the stratagems of this world. Foible remarks, "a little art once made your picture like you; and now a little of the same art must make you like your picture." Art rules nature in this world ("tenderness becomes me best—a sort of dyingness—you see that picture has a sort of a—ha, Foible! a swimmingness in the eye"). And Lady Wishfort is the kind of artist who so crushingly overwhelms nature that she somehow reveals it anew in unexpected ways. Her fondness for ratafia, her closet full of Puritan tracts, her avowed esteem for "decorums"—all these make her a torrential force of humor: her affectations and habits are borne on its surface like the debris that attests to the power of the current. In this way, Congreve frames a world in which the malice and polish are, after all, less universal than they seem. The situation anticipates that of the London of *Tom Jones*, where, beside such consummate scoundrels as Lady Bellaston, the would-be rogues like Lord Fellamar and Jack Nightingale seem backward pupils in an exacting school. The full range of human warmth is suggested too, in the nuptials of Waitwell and Foible, the cheerful stolidity of Sir Willful Witwoud, and the generous lack of jealousy in Mrs. Fainall.

The figures who seem the masters of this world are Fainall and Marwood. It is they who have used the world with a hard and joyless egoism. Fainall, at the opening of the play, sets himself off from Mirabell by the quality of his temperament:

> FAINALL: . . . I'd no more play with a man that slighted his ill fortune than I'd make love to a woman who undervalued the loss of her reputation.

> MIRABELL: You have a taste extremely delicate, and are for refining
>   on your pleasures.

The note of corruption that Fainall sounds allows us a glance ahead to
such cold and perverse sensualists as Blifil; it establishes a character
which is consistently presented. He can recall to his mistress the lies she
has used in their behalf: "I meant but to remind you of the slight
account you once could make of strictest ties, when set in competition
with your love to me." And it is with reason that Marwood replies, " 'Tis
false, you urged it with deliberate malice! 'twas spoken in scorn, and I
never will forgive it" (II, iii). The disdain in which Fainall holds the
world is best seen when he confronts Lady Wishfort with his demands,
sparing her no humiliation, and finally—as he is defeated—turning
upon his wife with all the malice of an outwitted Machiavel.

The case of Marwood is not much different; she wins more sympathy
because the passions that possess her are less coldly egocentric. Her
resentment of Mirabell's indifference has become a goad that makes her
put up with a lover she seems half to hate. But, like Fainall, she flourishes in those moments when she can relieve her bitterness in the promise of pain to others; like Fainall, she needs to be revenged, and her
need colors her plotting with a note of extravagant malice. She turns to
an easy victim like Lady Wishfort with strong relish: "Here comes the
good Lady, panting ripe; with a heart full of hope, and a head full of
care, like any chemist upon the day of projection" (III, vii).

Millamant seems to sense this excess of Marwood's temper: in their
scene together, she plays upon Marwood's jealousy with a cruel
lightness that appears to be the only way to meet the other's rage, and
the song she calls for sounds the note of Marwood's and Fainall's ambition:

> Then I alone the conquest prize,
>   When I insult a rival's eyes:
> If there's delight in love, 'tis when I see
> That heart, which others bleed for, bleed for me.

I think that we can set Millamant's powers in this scene; she is constantly unsettled herself by the intensity of Marwood's attitude, and she
improvises until she finds the right level of malice herself to hold Marwood off and keep their relations on a basis of ingenious insult. Even
so, Marwood can scarcely contain herself: "Your merry note may be
changed sooner than you think."

What gives the play its form is the way in which Mirabell and Millamant can, through their own peculiar balance of wit and generosity of
spirit, reduce the bumbling Witwoud and the mordant Fainall to the
same level of false wit. Just as the fools lack any depth of awareness and
power of judgment, so eventually the villains overplay their hands. Fai-

nall and Marwood turn out, after all, to be victims of their own passions. Their cynical manipulation of social convention is too assured; they cannot believe in the wit of others or in the capacity of others to elude their control. The way of the world in which Fainall takes taunting pride is more complex than he can understand, and his frustration, like Marwood's, exposes the savage compulsions driving him. If at one point in the play, Fainall's seems the most knowing view of the world, it is finally revealed in its shallowness, a shallowness arising from his disbelief in the reality of any being other than himself.

Mirabell and Millamant dramatize the true wit that is so carefully and symmetrically defined through opposition. An adequate performance of the play must present their strong hold upon each other throughout and their resistance to the claim that each has on the other's integrity. Unlike Dryden's Antony and Cleopatra they do not glory in their oneness, nor celebrate the world they have in each other. They are wary and difficult, resenting the loss of judgment that love imposes even as they accept it. "As for a discerning man, somewhat too passionate a love," Mirabell describes himself; "for I like her with all her faults: nay, like her for her faults. . . . They are now grown as familiar to me as my own frailties; and in all probability, in a little time longer, I shall like 'em as well." And Millamant's charming declaration: "Well, if Mirabell should not make a good husband, I am a lost thing,—for I find I love him violently." These confidences do not prevent their careful and rational testing of each other and of their own chances for honesty in marriage. Millamant's affectations do not reveal her as artificial. They are clearly defensive maneuvers. She seems at every point to be inviting Mirabell to separate himself from this world and to free her from it.

In the famous proviso scene, they are fighting, humorously and banteringly but still generously, for a vision of marriage free from the cant and hypocrisy that surround them. These speeches, like the characters themselves, cannot exist except within the play that contains the Fainalls, Lady Wishfort, and Witwoud. They represent, like Mirabell's successful counterplot, a rational intelligence playing upon the energies it cannot command but can at least direct. The lovers must find their proper order; it is hardly one of saintly abandon of the world—as in *All for Love*—nor is it simply the old order of the flesh of Fainall and Marwood given more shrewdness and lightened to rococo frivolity.

The triumph of the play is in the emergence of lovers who, through a balance of intense affection and cool self-knowledge, achieve an equilibrium that frees them of the world's power. They can use the world and reject its demands. They have assimilated the rational lucidity of the skeptical rake; they are awake to the world's ways and their own, but they are beyond any pained horror or need to wound those who have betrayed honesty. They accept what, through exploration, they have found in themselves; and they need only be sure that they can be both themselves and each other's. The quality that marks them is a critical acuteness—true wit—that is ready to submit to what, by all the rational tests they can manage, promises to be sincere and is, in any case, irresistible love. * * *

LAURA BROWN

[*The Way of the World*]†

* * *

The Way of the World depends upon a strongly represented social environment, to which the main terms of its characterization and action are attached. The play's subordinate characters are all designed to flesh out "the way of the world" with comic manners and local ridicule, and to provide a context for the protagonists' emblematic relationship and their opponents' schemes. Taken together, characters like Petulant, Witwoud, Sir Wilfull, and Lady Wishfort represent a world very much like that of conventional social satire, but even the simple ridicule directed against them is qualified by the undermining of stereotypes, pervasive in this comedy. Petulant and Witwoud are not simple fools, but impudent and malicious wits. Sir Wilfull is neither devoid of wit (III.i) nor lacking in genuine and effective benevolence (V.i). And Lady Wishfort, unlike Lady Touchwood, is a victim, not an agent, of the hypocritical schemes.

This satiric background also provides the play with the fundamental concerns that are explored in the course of the action. Marriage is consistently ridiculed and denigrated, in the conventional satiric manner, by one witty commentator after another (e.g., II.i).[1] The related issue of honest friendship receives similar harsh treatment. In fact, social exchange is characterized throughout the action as the hypocritical sparring of false friends: Fainall and Mirabell, Mrs. Marwood and Mrs. Fainall, Mrs. Marwood and Millamant, and Mrs. Marwood and Lady Wishfort. In effect, the social context pronounces its conventional cynical judgment upon the possibilities of meaningful human contact, either in marriage or friendship. But once again, that judgment is complicated and qualified, specifically, as we shall see, by the genuine emotional commitment implied in the relationship between Mirabell and Millamant.

† From *English Dramatic Form, 1660–1760* (New Haven: Yale University Press, 1981) 130–35. Reprinted by permission of the publisher.
1. M. E. Novak, "Love Scandal and the Moral Milleu of Congreve's Comedies," in *Congreve Consider'd*, by Aubrey Williams and M. E. Novak (Los Angeles: Clark Memorial Library, 1971). Citations from *The Way of the World* are from *The Complete Plays of William Congreve*, ed. Herbert Davis (Chicago: University of Chicago Press, 1967).

The social world also dictates the terms of the play's main action. Mirabell and Millamant are the most adept and successful members of their society. Both of them are apparently possessed of unrivaled sexual attractiveness, and Mirabell is not only able to win the hearts of all the major female characters in the play, but even the loyal aid of his cast mistress, Mrs. Fainall. This conventional framework is reinforced by the incessant repartee that dominates the comedy. The first two acts open with conventional set pieces that display the prospective antagonists of the plot in witty and probing debate. In Act I, Mirabell and Fainall, just getting up from cards, exchange charged comments upon Mirabell's affairs, each attempting to ascertain the proximity of the other's relationship with Mrs. Marwood. In the parallel scene at the beginning of Act II, Mrs. Marwood and Mrs. Fainall engage in a similar tense verbal parlay in which they trade vituperative condemnations of "those Vipers Men" (II.i), each subtly seeking to discover the extent of the other's interest in Mirabell. By means of these matched manners debates, the central characters are immediately incorporated into the world of Petulant and Witwoud, and their schemes, unlike Maskwell's extraterrestrial plots, appear to emerge directly from "the way of the world."

But once again Congreve deliberately differentiates between the special, problematical world of his comedy and the stereotypical material of dramatic satire. The debates do not in themselves serve to distinguish fool from wit, or even villain from hero.[2] All four characters are socially adept, all appear to have virtually equal control of themselves and the situation, and all conceal their motives behind the equivalent dexterity of their tongues. In effect, the inscrutability which in *The Double-Dealer* is simply the product of hypocritical villainy is in this play the consequence of those very conventions upon which the action is based. We are introduced to a world that proposes a kind of comprehensibility essentially like that of dramatic satire, but simultaneously subverts the simple judgments that it invites the audience to apply.

Congreve's provocative use of the materials of social comedy is symptomatic of the particular form of *The Way of the World*. His qualifications and complications of this conventional social material constitute an attempt to make moral and ethical values genuinely dependent upon the social world with which they are at odds. Whereas *The Double-Dealer* or even *The Relapse* poses its moral dimension in blatant opposition to the typical terms of social evaluation, in his most mature comedy Congreve makes the ethical values of an inner life the product of a deepened exploration of "the way of the world." The result of this merg-

---

2. N. Holland, *The First Modern Comedies* (Cambridge, Mass.: Harvard University Press, 1959), pp. 187–90; I. Donaldson, *The World Upside Down* (Oxford: Clarendon Press, 1973), pp. 125–31; M. E. Novak, *William Congreve* (New York: Twayne, 1971), pp. 148–49; and Harriett Hawkins, *Likenesses of Truth in Elizabethan and Restoration Drama* (Oxford: Clarendon Press, 1972), pp. 119–23.

ing of social and moral judgment is a unity of tone unique among the transitional comedies of this period.

The core of the ethical assessment that emerges from the social context of this comedy is embodied in the formally central relationship between the witty lovers. In keeping with the terms of their environment, they speak the language, strike the poses, and fight the battles of dramatic satire. Mirabell's pragmatic scheming throughout the play is designed to procure him Millamant's fortune. Millamant, in turn, treats her admirer with the wanton cruelty of a social opponent (e.g., II.i). But their relationship reveals depths strangely out of keeping with the superficial manner of their exchanges, and suggestive of an inner life inaccessible to the normal means of social assessment. Mirabell himself voices the surprising contrast in his own character between pragmatism and passion:

> *Fainall.* For a passionate Lover, methinks you are a Man somewhat too discerning in the Failings of your Mistress.
> *Mirabell.* And for a discerning Man, somewhat too passionate a Lover; for I like her with all her Faults; nay, like her for her Faults. [I.i]

He is, in fact, a genuine lover, whose emotion actually gets in the way of his wit (II.i). His final statement flatly contradicts the play's concluding warning against "mutual falsehood" in marriage: "Well, heav'n grant I love you not too well, that's all my fear" (V.i). Similarly, Millamant breaks the surface control of her sharp repartee with the sudden admission:

> Well, If *Mirabell* shou'd not make a good Husband, I am a lost thing;—for I find I love him violently. [IV.i]

All of the implications of these emotional depths, which are shown to coexist with the external constraints of social exchange, are focused and explored in the proviso scene. This scene represents Congreve's most conscious and explicit recourse to comic convention,[3] and simultaneously his most concentrated and subtle revelation of the psychologies of his disputant lovers. Millamant explicitly seeks a relationship fully and elegantly conformable to the manners and "ways of the world," but in addition she requires, within that studied conformity, an assurance of continued affection and the space for a private existence. She seeks to prevent their being "asham'd of one another for ever After" (IV.i), and

---

3. This trope begins its career early in the century with John Palmer's characterization of *The Way of the World* as a "pageant" (John Palmer, *The Comedy of Manners* [London: Bell, 1913], p. 191) and H. T. E. Perry's emphasis on the play's superficiality (*The Comic Spirit in Restoration Drama* [New Haven: Yale University Press], pp. 70–73). More recent critics have elaborated the metaphor, N. Holland (*The First Modern Comedies*, p. 197) and Van Voris (*The Cultivated Stance* [Dublin: Dolmen Press, 1965], pp. 130–31, 146–48, and 151), by describing the self-referentiality of Congreve's dramatic artifice and H. Teyssandier in "Congreve's *Way of the World*: Decorum and Morality," *English Studies* 52 (1971), 124–31, by discovering an aesthetic ideal in the social decorums of the drama.

she demands the specific and limited independence available to her as a married woman (IV.i). Mirabell's provisos reflect similar concerns with the working details of a meaningful private relationship. He forbids the eccentricities and excesses that would endanger the genuine emotional commitment required of sexual partners, urging Millamant, in effect, not to trifle with their love (IV.i). He also covenants for the health and safety of his prospective offspring, for which we can already discern a fatherly affection extraordinary in the conventional rake (IV.i). The lovers negotiate in this scene for a mutual private happiness within the confines of a rigid and demanding social context, and they establish their relationship upon the possibility of such a reconciliation. Thus, Congreve presents the most conventional device of the manners tradition in all its studied satiric elegance, but makes it include a psychological verisimilitude that can suggest a separate inner standard of evaluation.

A common trope of Congreve criticism is the evocation of the graceful and polished social "dance" of the characters. The elegance and artificiality of "the way of the world" depicted in this play certainly lend credence to the dance metaphor, and the manner of Mirabell and Millamant's exchanges is nothing if not polished and controlled. The matter of their relationship, however, completely escapes from the mode of decorous dance, as it does from the social form to which that metaphor refers. Congreve uses the pervasive social context of *The Way of the World* to the same ends as Maskwell's hypocritical inscrutability in *The Double-Dealer*: to suggest the possibility of a different kind of characterization and assessment based upon a sense of the insufficiency of social stereotype.

The perspective provided by this complex relationship between Mirabell and Millamant confers an ethical standard upon the whole social action of the comedy. From the moment of their opening repartee, Mirabell and Fainall are indistinguishable. Both are witty rakes. The contrasting critical interpretations of Mirabell, one finding him to be a representative of the ideal gentleman of Congreve's time[4] and the other claiming that he is an object of satire,[5] testify to this deliberate complexity of characterization. It is only by means of the gradual revelation of their inner natures that we are eventually able to tell villain from hero. Mirabell's genuine love for Millamant and his attempt to establish a meaningful marital relationship are contrasted with Fainall's vicious, manipulative, and unsympathetic attitude toward both his wife and his mistress, Mrs. Marwood. The distinction between Mrs. Marwood and Mrs. Fainall is similarly indirect. The initial apparent inscrutability of their characters is the product of the social context, according to which

4. J. Gagen, "Congreve's Mirabell and the Ideal of the Gentleman," *PMLA* 79 (1964), 422–27.
5. Charles O. McDonald, "Restoration Comedy as a Drama of Satire," *Studies in Philology* 61 (1964), 522–44.

they are shown to be equivalent in wit and vituperation. But they are subsequently separated by the revelation of motives which that initial context obscured.

These characters are finally defined not so much by their social actions and manners as by the inner motives and meanings of those actions, gradually revealed by reference to the values of Mirabell and Millamant's love. In this context, the issues of friendship and marriage, initially introduced as conventional objects of social satire, succumb to an ethical assessment that the earlier convention cannot explicitly supply. We are provided with a means of distinguishing Fainall's reprehensible attitude toward marriage from Mirabell's admirable and ethical one, just as we declare against Mrs. Marwood's denigration of the values of friendship and honesty. Without subverting the social context of "the way of the world," Congreve gives it a moral valence that reconciles the rival forces of transitional form. The unprecedented, and unduplicated, complexity of characterization in *The Way of the World* is a consequence of Congreve's application of other, extrasocial standards of assessment to the characters of a social comedy. The resultant tension between social judgments and ethical commitments creates a vital inner world, defined in other terms than the context to which it must accommodate itself. And this inner world in turn deepens, complicates, and challenges the stereotypical judgments of dramatic satire.

Congreve's last play, then, is the formal culmination of the warring assumptions of transitional comedy. In this respect, like the other transitional dramatic forms of the period, it contains both aristocratic and bourgeois elements. Congreve's complex and original blending of social and moral is a successful attempt to rejuvenate an essentially aristocratic form through the integration of selected aspects of bourgeois ideology.[6] *The Way of the World* represents in effect the fusion of two forms that are simply contrasted in *The Double-Dealer* and *The Relapse,* and incoherently juxtaposed in the mixed drama of Durfey, Southerne, Cibber, Farquhar, Steele, and others. But Congreve's brilliant experiment in formal reconciliation is a casualty as well as a consequence of its particular time and place. His own accurate estimate of *The Double-Dealer* and especially *The Way of the World* was not shared by the theatrical consensus of the period, and these two plays were misunderstood, misevaluated, and surprisingly unsuccessful on the stage, especially in comparison with the great popularity of his formally conservative comedies, *The Old Bachelor* and *Love for Love.* With *The Way of the World,* Congreve ceased original dramatic composition. The brief freedom afforded

6. For discussions of the ideology of Congreve's comedy, see John Loftis, *Comedy and Society from Congreve to Fielding* (Stanford: Stanford University Press), 1959, pp. 43–44; Van Voris, *The Cultivated Stance,* pp. 125–32, 139, and 149–50; Novak, "Love, Scandal, and the Moral Milieu of Congreve's Comedies"; and William Myers, "Plot and Meaning in Congreve's Comedies," in *William Congreve,* ed. Brian Morris (London: Benn, 1972), pp. 73–92.

to the best dramatists of the period by the instability inherent in this formal transition did not extend to a blanket acceptance of the innovations which that freedom produced, and Congreve's comedies are fundamentally at odds with the prevailing conventions of the time. An audience accustomed to the stereotypical characterization of social satire and mixed transitional comedy was vehemently unappreciative of the soliloquies and complexities of *The Double-Dealer* and *The Way of the World*. A drama that was dominated by the constraints of a powerful prior convention could not utilize the experiments of its greatest innovator.

RAYMOND WILLIAMS

[Sentimentalism and Social History][†]

* * * When an art-form changes, as the direct result of changes in society, we meet a very difficult problem in criticism, for it quite often happens that a local judgment will show a form that has been brought to a high level of skill and maturity being replaced by forms that are relatively crude and unsuccessful. With the ending of a Restoration drama based on an aristocratic and fashionable audience, and its replacement by a very mixed middle-class drama based on a wider social group, we see one of the clearest and most famous of these cases. Most critics have been natural Cavaliers, and have represented the change as a disaster for the drama. Yet it is surely necessary to take a longer view. The limited character of Restoration drama, and the disintegration of a general audience which had preceded it, were also damaging. Again, while the early products of eighteenth-century middle-class culture were regarded (often with justice) as vulgar, we must, to tell the whole story, follow the development down, to the points where the "vulgar" novel became a major literary form, and where the despised forms of "bourgeois tragedy" and "sentimental comedy" served, in their maturity, a wide area of our modern drama. The development of middle-class drama is in fact one of the most interesting cases we have of a changing society leading directly to radical innovations in form.

Opposition to the theater, by the commercial middle class, can be traced back to the sixteenth century, and the renewed wave of criticism, from the 1690s, which effectively broke the Restoration dramatic spirit, in one way contains little that is new. Behind the criticism of Collier (*A Short View of the Immorality and Profaneness of the English Stage,*

† From Raymond Williams, *The Long Revolution* (London: Chatto & Windus, 1961), pp. 256–60. Reprinted by permission of the publisher.

1698), with its itemized complaint against the licentiousness of current
comedies, the old hostility to the theater as such can be detected. But
now, with the court changed in character, and no longer actively pro-
tecting the theater, middle-class opposition had to be taken more seriously, and while a Vanbrugh replied in kind, Farquhar and a new school
of dramatists consciously reformed the drama to meet the immediate
objections. The complexity of any adequate judgment of eighteenth-
century drama follows from the fact that in some cases forms were
changed reluctantly or superficially in response to the new moral tone;
in other cases, new forms were made, by extension or discovery, as a
positive expression of the new spirit. This mixed result is understandable
in terms of the actual change in audiences. From the 1680s, merchants
and their wives had begun to attend the theaters, and in the eighteenth
century this element in the audience grew steadily. Yet there was no
sudden changeover from a dissolute court audience to a respectable
middle-class audience; indeed it was not until Victorian times
that the audiences of ordinary theaters became "respectable" in this
way. The real situation, in the eighteenth century, is that of elements
of the rising middle class joining a still fashionable theater public, at a
time when the public tone of the court and aristocracy had itself been
modified. Many authors began to be drawn from the commercial
middle-class public; this is a period in which the "one-play author" is a
characteristic figure. It is fair to say that an important part of eighteenth-
century drama offered a conscious image of the middle class and its
virtues, but the creative possibilities of this new consciousness were very
uneven, and in the drama, particularly, they were further limited. The
uncertainty in dramatic forms combined with the strong fashionable
element in the audience to produce a concentration of interest on actors
as such. Whenever this happens, and plays, in consequence, are valued
primarily as vehicles for particular acting talents, the drama tends to
become mixed and eclectic. Thus one finds, in eighteenth-century
drama, a characteristic interest in theatrical effect for its own sake, and
it is in this context that the new forms had to make their limited way.

Sentimental comedy is the least attractive of the new forms, though
it has continued to hold the stage, as a majority form of English drama,
to our own day. We can trace its conscious development from Cibber's
Love's Last Shift (1696) and *The Careless Husband* (1705), and Steele's
The Lying Lover (1704). Elements of its particular consciousness can
indeed be traced from much earlier in the century, but the direct application to contemporary behavior is now much more obvious. A passage
from Steele's preface to *The Lying Lover* clearly shows the new
emphasis:

> He makes false love, gets drunk, and kills his man, but in the fifth
> act awakens from his debauch with the compunction and remorse

which is suitable to a man's finding himself in a gaol]. . . . The anguish he there expresses, and the mutual sorrow between an only child and a tender father in that distress are, perhaps, an injury to the rules of comedy, but I am sure they are a justice to those of morality: and passages of such a nature being so frequently applauded on the stage, it is high time we should no longer draw occasions of mirth from those images which the religion of our country tells us we ought to tremble at with horror.

The essential point here, as a description of the new form, is the mixture of comedy and pathos, with an explicit moral reference, that led to the alternative descriptions of "weeping comedy" or the "comedy of sentiments" (moral opinions)—the two elements uniting in the complicated history of the word "sentimental." Yet we must note also the curious way in which the "compunction and remorse" are approached, for this element of "fifth-act reform," after all the excitements of customary dramatic intrigue, became the basis of continued charges of hypocrisy and sentimentality: "enjoy it while it lasts, then say you're sorry." Goldsmith had this in mind, when in attacking sentimental comedy he wrote:

> If they happen to have faults or foibles, the spectator is taught, not only to pardon, but to applaud them, in consideration of the goodness of their hearts.

This criticism reaches home, in many such plays, and this aspect of sentimental comedy has been so persistent that Goldsmith's words could be transferred, as they stand, to a considerable part of modern drama. He continues:

> But there is one argument in favour of sentimental comedy, which will keep it on the stage, in spite of all that can be said against it. It is, of all others, the most easily written. Those abilities that can hammer out a novel are fully sufficient for the production of a sentimental comedy. It is only sufficient to raise the characters a little; to deck out the hero with a riband, or give the heroine a title; then to put an insipid dialogue, without character or humour, into their mouths, give them mighty good hearts, very fine clothes, furnish a new set of scenes, make a pathetic scene or two with a sprinkling of tender melancholy conversation through the whole, and there is no doubt but all the ladies will cry, and all the gentlemen applaud.

This again is just, but the casual dismissal of the novel should make us pause. Both novels and sentimental comedies were often, certainly, confections of this kind, and Goldsmith despised them by reference to older standards (his attack on mixing comedy and pathos was in classicist terms, as a confusion of the old distinct kinds). Yet, while the bad

examples multiplied, the feelings which they exhibited were part of the
new consciousness, and could not in fact be summarily dismissed. The
ability to take a judgment right through, as in traditional tragedy and
comedy, showing sin leading to disintegration and disaster, vice and
error to thorough ridicule, rested on a more absolute morality, based
either on religious sanctions or the strict standards of an established
society, than the new middle class actually had. Already in Elizabethan
drama, and certainly in some seventeenth-century developments, we
see the traditional kinds, and their basic attitudes, often confused, and
their modes of judgement muted, for similar reasons. Romantic comedy
had pioneered the way of sentimental comedy, and "fifth-act reform,"
where in spite of everything a happy ending must be contrived, is evident from Shakespeare. Restoration comedy contains these elements,
but gains a measure of unity of feeling by confident judgments with
reference to a very limited social scale: to offend against polite society
was to be driven out of it, and that was that; but equally to offend against
God and man, while respecting the polite code, was forgivable. At different levels, and for some good reasons, the new middle-class drama tried
to go beyond this, to a new kind of judgment. Certainly, like its predecessors, it contrived happy endings, and padded the lash of the old comedy, often on sentimental grounds. But also, in dealing with
contemporary life, it necessarily challenged the temporary certainties of
the Restoration comedy of manners, offering as absolute virtues the
sanctity of marriage, the life of the family, and the care of the weak.
These had been neglected, or made ridiculous, in Restoration comedy,
simply because the class which it served was parasitic: the true consequences of behavior had never to be fully lived out. Narrow as the new
bourgeois morality was, it at least referred to a society in which consequence was actual, and in which there was more to do than keep up
with the modes of an artificially protected class. When we speak of the
"sentimentality" of appeals to these values, and of the "smugness" of
what we think we can dismiss as merely "domestic virtues," we should
be quite sure where we stand ourselves. The identification which some
critics seem to make, in fantasy, between themselves and the insouci-
ance of Cavalier rakes and whores, is usually ridiculous, if one goes on
to ask to what moral tradition they themselves practically belong. Nor is
this the only respect in which, if we are honest, we shall confess ourselves the heirs of the eighteenth-century bourgeois. The wider basis of
sentimental comedy, and of a main tradition in the novel, was that particular kind of humanitarian feeling, the strong if inarticulate appeal to
a fundamental "goodness of heart"; the sense of every individual's close-
ness to vice and folly, so that pity for their exemplars is the most relevant
emotion, and recovery and rehabilitation must be believed in; the sense,
finally, that there are few absolute values, and that tolerance and kind-

ness are major virtues. In rebuking the sentimental comedy, as in both its early examples and its subsequent history it seems necessary to do, we should be prepared to recognize that in the point of moral assumptions, and of a whole consequent feeling about life, most of us are its blood relations. * * *

Selected Bibliography

• marks items included or excerpted in this Norton Critical Edition.

COMEDY AND THEATRE 1660–1800: GENERAL STUDIES

Bateson, F. W. *English Comic Drama: 1700–1750.* Oxford: The Clarendon Press, 1929.
——. "Second Thoughts: L. C. Knights and Restoration Comedy." *Essays in Criticism* 7 (1957): 56–67.
Birdsall, Virginia Ogden. *Wild Civility: The English Comic Spirit on the Restoration Stage.* Bloomington: Indiana UP, 1970.
• Brown, Laura. *English Dramatic Form, 1660–1760.* New Haven, Yale UP, 1981.
Canfield, J. Douglas, and Deborah C. Payne, eds. *Cultural Readings of Restoration and Eighteenth-Century English Theater.* Athens: U of Georgia P, 1995.
Dobree, Bonamy. *English Literature in the Early Eighteenth Century: 1700–1740.* Oxford: The Clarendon Press, 1959. (Chapter VII)
Donaldson, Ian. *The World Upside-Down: Comedy from Jonson to Fielding.* Oxford: The Clarendon Press, 1973.
Fujimura, T. H. *The Restoration Comedy of Wit.* Princeton: Princeton UP, 1952.
Gill, Pat. *Interpreting Ladies: Women, Wit, and Morality in the Restoration Comedy of Manners.* Athens: U of Georgia P, 1994.
Harwood, John T. *Critics, Values, and Restoration Comedy.* Carbondale: Southern Illinois UP, 1982.
• Hawkins, Harriett. *Likenesses of Truth in Elizabethan and Restoration Drama.* Oxford: The Clarendon Press, 1972.
Holland, Norman. *The First Modern Comedies: The Significance of Etherege, Wycherley, and Congreve.* Cambridge: Harvard UP, 1959.
Holland, Peter. *The Ornament of Action: Text and Performance in Restoration Comedy.* Cambridge: Cambridge UP, 1979.
• Howe, Elizabeth. *The First English Actresses.* Cambridge: Cambridge UP, 1992.
Hume, Robert D. *The Development of English Drama in the Late Seventeenth Century.* Oxford: The Clarendon Press, 1976.
Krutch, Joseph Wood. *Comedy and Conscience after the Restoration.* New York: Columbia UP, 1924.
Leacroft, Richard. *The Development of the English Playhouse.* Ithaca: Cornell UP, 1973.
Loftis, John. *Comedy and Society from Congreve to Fielding.* Stanford: Stanford UP, 1959.
——. *The Politics of Drama in Augustan England.* Oxford: The Clarendon Press, 1963.
Lynch, Kathleen M. *The Social Mode of Restoration Comedy.* University of Michigan Publications in Language and Literature, Vol. III. New York: Macmillan, 1926.
Markley, Robert. *Two-Edg'd Weapons: Style and Ideology in the Comedies of Etherege, Wycherley, and Congreve.* Oxford: The Clarendon Press, 1988.
McDonald, Charles O. "Restoration Comedy as Drama of Satire: An Investigation into Seventeenth-Century Aesthetics." *Studies in Philology* 61 (1964): 522–44.
Nicoll, Allardyce. *A History of English Drama, 1660–1900.* 6 vols. Cambridge: Cambridge UP, 1952–59.
Pearson, Jacqueline. *The Prostituted Muse: Images of Women and Women Dramatists, 1642–1737.* New York: St. Martin's Press, 1988.
• Powell, Jocelyn. *Restoration Theatre Practice.* London: Routledge & Kegan Paul, 1984.
• Price, Martin. *To the Palace of Wisdom.* New York: Doubleday, 1964.
Sherbo, Arthur. *English Sentimental Comedy.* East Lansing: Michigan State UP, 1957.
Smith, John Harrington. *The Gay Couple in Restoration Comedy.* Cambridge: Harvard UP, 1948.
Sutherland, James. *English Literature of the Late Seventeenth Century.* Oxford: Oxford UP, 1969. (Chapters II and III)

• Van Lennep, William, et al., *The London Stage: 1600–1800*. 5 Parts. Carbondale: Southern Illinois UP, 1960–68.

Wain, John. "Restoration Comedy and Its Modern Critics." *Essays in Criticism* 6 (1956): 367–85.

Wilson, John Harold. *A Preface to Restoration Drama*. Boston: Houghton Mifflin, 1965.

THE COUNTRY WIFE

Berman, Ronald. "The Ethic of *The Country Wife*." *Texas Studies in Literature and Language* 9 (1967): 47–55.

Chadwick, W. R. *The Four Plays of William Wycherley*. The Hague: Mouton, 1975.

Righter, Anne. "William Wycherley." *Restoration Theatre*. Ed. John Russell Brown and Bernard Harris. London: Edward Arnold, 1965.

Zimbardo, Rose A. *Wycherley's Drama*. New Haven: Yale UP, 1965.

THE MAN OF MODE

Davies, Paul C. "The State of Nature and the State of War: A Reconsideration of *The Man of Mode*." *University of Toronto Quarterly* 39 (1969): 53–62.

Hayman, John G. "Dorimant and the Comedy of a Man of Mode." *Modern Language Quarterly* 30 (1969): 183–97.

Powell, Jocelyn. "George Etherege and the Form of a Comedy." *Restoration Theatre*. Ed. John Russell Brown and Bernard Harris. London: Edward Arnold, 1965.

Underwood, Dale. *Etherege and the Seventeenth-Century Comedy of Manners*. New Haven: Yale UP, 1957.

THE ROVER

• Diamond, Elin. "*Gestus* and Signature in Aphra Behn's *The Rover*." *English Literary History* 56 (1989): 519–37.

Duffy, Maureen. *The Passionate Shepherdess: Aphra Behn*. London: Cape, 1977.

Goreau, Angeline. *Reconstructing Aphra*. Oxford: Oxford UP, 1980.

Jones, DeRitter. "The Gypsy, *The Rover*, and the Wanderer: Aphra Behn's Revision of Thomas Killigrew." *Restoration* 10 (1986): 82–92.

Pearson, Jacqueline. "Women and Feminism in the Plays of Aphra Behn." In Pearson, *The Prostituted Muse: Images of Women and Women Dramatists, 1642–1737*. New York: St. Martin's Press, 1988.

THE WAY OF THE WORLD

Leech, Clifford. "Congreve and the Century's End." *Philological Quarterly* 41 (1962): 275–93.

Mueschke, Paul, and Miriam Mueschke. *A New View of Congreve's Way of the World*. University of Michigan Contributions to Modern Philology, No. 23. Ann Arbor: U of Michigan P, 1958.

Peters, Julie Stone. *Congreve, the Drama, and the Printed Word*. Stanford: Stanford UP, 1990.

Taylor, D. Crane. *William Congreve*. Oxford: Oxford UP, 1931.

Van Voris, W. H. *The Cultivated Stance: The Designs of Congreve's Plays*. Dublin: Dolmen, 1965.

THE CONSCIOUS LOVERS

Kenny, S. S. "Richard Steele and the 'Patterns of Genteel Comedy.'" *Modern Philology* 70 (1972): 22–37.

Loftis, John. *Steele at Drury Lane*. Berkeley: U of California P, 1952.

Parnell, Paul E. "The Sentimental Mask." *PMLA* 78 (1963): 529–35.

THE SCHOOL FOR SCANDAL

Kronenberger, Louis. *The Thread of Laughter*. New York: Knopf, 1952.

Rodway, Allan. "Goldsmith and Sheridan: Satirists of Sentiment." *Renaissance and Modern*

Essays Presented to Vivian de Sola Pinto. Ed. G. R. Hibbard. London: Routledge & Kegan Paul, 1966.

Sprague, Arthur C. "In Defence of a Masterpiece: *The School for Scandal* Re-examined." *English Studies Today*, 3rd Series. Ed. G. I. Duthie. Edinburgh: Edinburgh UP, 1964.

Worth, Katharine. *Sheridan and Goldsmith.* New York: St. Martin's Press, 1992.

Norton Critical Editions